THE DESERT QUEEN OMNIBUS

By

M.L. Bullock

Table of Contents

The Tale of Nefret

By

M.L. Bullock

Dedication

I dedicate this book to Luke Broadhead, my nephew, blacksmith, archaeologist-in-training and professional brainstormer. I have three words for you, "To the swords!"

I am your darling sister.
I am to you like a bit of land,
With each shrub of grateful fragrance.
Lovely is the water-conduit in it,
Which your hand has dug,
While the north wind cooled us.
A beautiful place to wander,
Your hand in my hand,
My soul inspired,
My heart in bliss,
Because we go together.

Egyptian poem, 2000 BC

Prologue

Egypt—18th Dynasty

Farrah stood outside the door of the tent and stared up into the night sky. No matter how heavily time etched cruel marks on her face, the view grabbed her breath as if her dark eyes were seeing it for the first time. The lines on her brown face deepened as she pursed her lips. The air around her was pregnant with the future, but her inner sight was dark and full of mystery. Her limited insight into the other world made her uncomfortable. She made the sign of peace to the Dancing Man that hung above her in purple-blackness as he rose above the tribal camp. The Cushite traders called the Dancing Man a different name—Osiris he was called in the Black Lands and beyond—but here in the Red Lands where the red sands swirled and swam about the desert people like a dead ocean, he was known as the Dancing Man.

How long will we travel this path? An endless caravan moving from one rain oasis to another? Many of the clan no longer know from whence they came or that there had once been a place for them. How many Meshwesh must die in the Red Lands before we see those white walls again?

Once the Meshwesh dwelled in a city of white stone, Zerzura. What a city it had been! Farrah could barely remember the feeling of cool stones under her feet, the tastes of orange fruit sweet on her tongue, and the many pools of clear blue water that her young body had swum in. Had it been just a dream? No, Farrah remembered the day when the cowardly old king, Onesu, had fled the city ahead of the horde of giants who rushed in to claim it. But he had not lived one day after he left Zerzura, for Farrah had cut his throat while he slept. When he awoke to see her face above him, she whispered why she had done it as she watched him bleed. He had lost the city and had abandoned Ze, his queen and Farrah's sister, leaving her to the pleasure of the giants who no doubt raped her to death. Farrah shuddered inwardly thinking of what she had done. Nobody knew, yet it was a spot on her soul. She did not regret it, although the gods had seen fit to take her inner sight from her as punishment for her crime. That had been long, long ago. His face no longer haunted her. Yet often she imagined she heard Ze's screams in the clear night.

Now, with a silent prayer Farrah considered again the stars above her. Regardless of the constellation's name, this sour omen was an inauspicious sign for the birth of a royal child, but there was nothing she could do to prevent it. Even her magic could not stop a child who wanted to enter this realm.

Farrah suddenly felt old. Had she, leader of the Council of Old Ones, become too old to consider the deeper meaning of such things? Was she too old to help bring another baby into this increasingly difficult world? The sounds the mother made, the painful moaning, the calling of her name, let Farrah know that she indeed still had a purpose. She took a deep sigh, breathing in the warm desert air and shaking off the unseen trepidation. She tossed her head cloth to the ground. No heads covered this night. She smiled peacefully as she walked to the birthing bed and looked down into the face of the beautiful Kadeema.

What a beauty the young queen had been when she first arrived here as the bride to Semkah! However, the Red Lands had sapped away her pretty softness like it did to all women who were not of true Red Lands' blood. She had become hard, hard like the clay that lay beneath the rough sand. Kadeema's olive skin was no longer pale but red, and her hair no longer like bright copper but dark and dull. The young queen's eyes still had their sea-green beauty, but the sparkle, the joy of love and living, had faded. A wife of a young tribal king tied to the Red Lands people only by the most tenuous of threads—love. Farrah looked into those eyes, saddened to see that where there had been hope and excitement, there was now fear and regret.

When Kadeema arrived, the people had loved her, celebrating her light skin and unusual eyes with poems and songs. She had been like a child—a treasure to them, for the tribe treasured children above all things. Their young prince needed a bride, and why should he not take a beautiful bride like Kadeema? She was the daughter of a faraway Grecian king who was a friend to the tribe, so it was a good match.

Semkah was not a king like his brother Omel, who was fierce, strong and brave yet crafty and changeable. Semkah was steady and ever obedient to the Council, trusting them in all things that concerned the Meshwesh. Omel never displayed such devotion.

Semkah wore the tribal king's robes early after the death of his father, but he cut a fine figure even as a young man. Farrah remembered that day. She'd watched as his arms were tattooed with the sign of the tribe, the falcon's wings with a swirl of sand wrapped around it. He had worn his hair long, with two long braids at his temples. His chest gleamed with turquoise and gold necklaces from the mines of the Meshwesh, and at his wrist were the slender snake bracelets that only kings wore.

The young king's older brother Omel had an unabashed love for all things Egyptian. He wore linen Egyptian tunics that showed his scrawny, tanned legs. Tall and thin, Omel kept his dark hair shaved and his head shone with oils. Sometimes he wore a folded cloth on his head, but always his eyes were lined with black, as if he were an Egyptian royal. There was no doubt amongst the Council that Omel loved the Black Lands and would abandon his heritage if given a chance. But for that, he needed his brother. Semkah and Omel had received a divided inheritance—a smart and seemingly prophetic move by their wily father, Onesu. Semkah held the turquoise mines and Omel the gold, but they shared a workforce and the resources required to continue the work. Farrah suspected that Omel would seek to correct this. Already he drew men to his side like flies to a sweet fruit. She wondered what he promised them.

The brothers had different ideas about the future of the clan. Omel wanted with much passion to bring them into Egypt's good graces. Farrah spat on the ground at the thought of such nonsense. Semkah's dream was different—he dreamed of reclaiming Zerzura, as was his right, but he had no way of accomplishing that. No more than his father had.

Omel often met with Semkah and other tribal leaders to try to rally them to his point of view. "We need Egypt, brothers! They have wealth beyond measure and green lands that are just waiting for our plows. Come with me to Egypt and meet with Huya. He has given me his oath that Pharaoh wants to honor us with these lands." Semkah had laughed at this idea and made no secret that he wanted no part of Omel's Egyptian ways.

"And what will Pharaoh require, brother?" Semkah had said with a patient smile that only further angered Omel. "The king of

Egypt does not simply give away lands to appease his neighbors. What of our inheritance? Have you given up finding our homeland, all for a bag of beans from Egypt's hand? I know what it will require, and that I cannot do. Pharaoh will take our mines, our cattle—maybe even our wives and children—and for what? Some soggy ground so wet that only mosquitos dwell there? How can you ask this of me? What do I say to my tribe?"

Omel had scowled but said nothing else on the matter at that time. Farrah did not think any of the Council or the other leaders believed they had heard the last of Omel's desires. But Semkah never saw the dark side of his brother; he only recognized the good. He had a heart of gold.

Farrah mumbled to herself remembering the night Semkah was born. What were the words she had said over him as she cradled him on that first night? "He will pursue love from one end of the desert to another. He will give his life for love, and that is the noblest of deaths."

That had been her proclamation then. She wondered what the hidden words would be tonight or if her old ears would even hear them. She shook her head, reminding herself to stay in the present; she had a habit of getting lost in the past so many times lately. With authority, she flipped up the dress of the writhing Kadeema. She prayed and swayed, calling on her ancestors to assist her.

"No! Do not call on them. They must not know…!" Kadeema shouted savagely.

Farrah could not help but shudder. In her madness, Kadeema could offend a wandering spirit or worse. Farrah made a secret sign to ward off evil curses. Before she could protest further, Kadeema's womb burst forth blood and she screamed into the musky night. Farrah nodded and prayed silently as she examined the woman's body.

Something was amiss. Ignoring Kadeema's scream, she probed inside her with expert fingers and felt the baby's head. No! Inside the queen were two babies, two lives struggling to emerge into this world. Without knowing how she knew, she did know—these would be the only children of Semkah and Kadeema. Before they were born, it had been prophesied that from Semkah's tribe would come the mekhma, the leader who would carry them home. Farrah felt an excitement greater than the fear, an urgency like none she had experienced before. These children must be born!

Kadeema screamed again as the children turned, each fighting to emerge first from their mother's womb. The sharp scent of birthing blood filled the tent, and Farrah sniffed. Did she smell death? Ah, yes, it lingered there, just beyond the gathered crowd.

She rubbed her hand with oil and soothed the expectant mother, numbing Kadeema to the pain with expert movements. Quietly Farrah called Mina, her acolyte. "Listen to what I say. Go about the camp and untie all the knots. No one must wear anything that is knotted. It is a bad omen for this birth, for this night. Do as I tell you, Mina!" Mina, who rarely spoke, nodded and touched her forehead as a sign of respect, and then fled from the tent. Farrah heard a hush fall over the camp; even the animals were mute. Farrah went about the tent untying everything she could find as Semkah watched her nervously. Finally, she untied Kadeema's gown and covered her with a blanket. Even the braids in her hair were removed and left untied.

"What are you doing, Old One?" Semkah inquired, a worried look on his handsome face.

"No questions now," Farrah warned. Was it her fault that the king did not understand birthing magic? That by untying the strands near and around the queen she would prevent strangulation of the children on the mother's cord? She clucked at him with her teeth as she attended his wife.

The woman's breathing quickened, her birth pains coming more strongly now.

Ten minutes later, Kadeema's water seeped out of her and the birth began in earnest. Kadeema leaned forward in her sitting position, gripping her knees. Semkah sat behind her, whispering in her ear. Farrah could not hear the words that he spoke, but she was sure they were words of love.

That is a shame. He will not have her long.

She thought these things without ever questioning why or how she knew them. She just knew them. There was no denying that. More often than not, she was correct, but why cause anguish at such a time? A birth is a time of joy—a time to celebrate, not a time to cry and mourn. *"Ah, but mourning there shall be, and much mourning..."*

Farrah spoke the words of life as the first pink head crowned from between the mother's loins. But as quickly as it began to slide out, a tiny hand reached out and grabbed its shoulder, pulling it back inside the mother. Kadeema screamed in great pain as the second child now emerged. In amazement, Farrah watched and faithfully caught the first child to emerge from the womb. Would this be the first or the second? Who came first? She smiled at their luck—two children! She tossed the first birth rag into a nearby container. She would burn it later at a special ceremony; it was a precious and rare item to possess.

Thank you, ancestors!

The second child began to emerge. Farrah helped guide the child into this realm, cooing softly to the emerging soul. "Come out, come out now," Farrah purred to the second child. "No more fighting. You are no longer number one, but now you are number two. Let us see what you are—oh, another girl, Semkah. Two girls for you!"

Semkah's beautiful smile reflected his full heart. He had come to the tent dressed for receiving a new princess or prince, a royal child—he was now doubly blessed. No man had ever loved a woman more than Semkah loved Kadeema. And although it would have benefited him and his tribe a great deal if he had married a daughter of the Red Lands, he would have no one but the princess he met in a faraway land. He kissed his daughters' foreheads, even before Mina and Farrah cleaned them, and then turned his attention to his wife.

"Girls, Kadeema. Fine girls!"

Semkah's wife smiled weakly, shallow grooves appearing briefly at the sides of her mouth. She was too thin, too gaunt, but her vivid green eyes showed her emotion so clearly. Hers was the face of weary happiness.

Until...

As Farrah wrapped the second child in linen and wiped the blood from her skin with a damp cloth, a strange thing happened. Two birds flew into the musky desert tent. The flap had been opened slightly so the well-wishers could pray for and sing to Kadeema as she gave birth to the treasures of the tribe.

The larger bird, a falcon, swooped and screeched as it circled the inside of the tent, chasing the smaller bird with reckless ferocity. The larger bird, a Heret falcon, was a rare sight this far out into the Red Lands but not unheard of. His prey was much rarer—it was the green Bee-Eater, a tiny bird that found bees as tasty as humans did honey. At Zerzura, the Bee-Eater would have been a welcome sight—it was, after all, the Oasis of the Little Birds. No bird was smaller than the Bee-Eater. The falcon screamed in the tent as it crashed into Farrah's collection of ivory idols, unlit candles and various bowls of dried herbs and flowers. A surprised Kadeema protected her daughters from the melee by waving her hands at the birds. Semkah captured the falcon easily with a cloth, but the Bee-Eater escaped out of the tent, ducking the reaching hands and makeshift snares. Semkah took the falcon outside—it was wrapped in the cloth that had become the creature's net.

The king opened the cloth to release the bird, but it did not take to the wind. On closer inspection, it had a bloody wing and seemed unable to fly. Semkah covered it back up, intending to cage it until the injuries healed—then he would set it free. Before he could argue or protest, Farrah reached for the bundle. Her faded dark eyes appraised the animal astutely, and then she gripped it and twisted its neck until it snapped.

"Why? Why did you do this, Farrah? I could have saved it."

"You would try, but you could not. Now it is dead and you are alive. See to your wife, now. She needs you." Farrah felt tired—too tired to explain to the king the hidden meaning of her actions.

Semkah jutted out his square jaw. The two turned to walk back into the tent and were surprised to find Kadeema standing nearly naked and bloody at the tent entrance. The people had pushed back and were standing close to the fire in the center of the camp. They whispered, wondering what the omen of the birds meant.

The Dancing Man above us, the birds in the tent, twins? What did it all mean?

Farrah heard what they said. Feeling their eyes upon her, she waved her hands, easily capturing their attention. With purposeful steps she walked toward the fire and stared into the flames. She saw nothing—nothing but shadows—yet the words formed easily on her tongue. Prophecy began to bubble up from deep within, somewhere beneath her navel. Each utterance was her offspring, birthed from within her, rare seeds planted there issuing from her ancestors, or perhaps from the gods themselves.

"Peace, sons and daughters of Ma. Tonight is a night to be remembered, for we have been doubly blessed..." Farrah wanted to bring hope and encouragement to help the tribe see that the arrival of the two girls was nothing to be feared, but other words burst forth and would not be held back.

"Two destinies have been born tonight, Meshwesh! You have a choice! Follow the Old Ways or fall under the shadow of death and be lost forever!" The crowd gasped and stirred uncomfortably in the sand. Farrah's mind futilely grappled with what to say. The seer inside her would speak unfiltered. *"Evil arises from the sand... who can be saved? Ah, I see it!"* She screamed despite her mind's instruction to remain calm. The images of a great battle spanned before her; many Meshwesh perished before the golden swords of giant beasts of men. *"Two mekhmas—two paths, Meshwesh. One will lead you to safety behind the white walls of Zerzura, and the other to a future unknown. You saw the Heret pursue the Bee-Eater—so shall one child chase the other. What will be your fate, Meshwesh? Will you disappear into the red sand?"* A dry laugh escaped Farrah's lips as she fought for control of her own mind. She spoke words in a language she could not comprehend.

Semkah put out his hands to his wife, intending to hold her and wrap her in his arms, but she let out a bloodcurdling scream—and she didn't stop screaming. There were no words spoken, only an agonizing cry that came from deep within her soul. Her eyes were wide and full of unspoken, unknowable fear. Farrah helped Semkah place her back in the bed. She fought them at first, pointing and staring at something no one else could see. Finally he calmed her and she allowed Farrah to place her in her covers and pat away the blood. Semkah held her shaky hand, wept, and cajoled, but he could not coax her to speak to him.

For days, Kadeema spoke not a word to any living soul. Farrah stayed with her, watching over her, feeding her, but still she never spoke. Farrah knew what this was. Kadeema had had a vision—a vision of the future. Farrah suspected that Kadeema had the gift all along, but the younger woman was obviously untrained and unaware that she could do and see such things. Since her vision had undoubtedly occurred when Farrah and Semkah had been dealing with the birds, it must have been a vision concerning her daughters. For Farrah, this was impossible to bear. She had to know what hovered just beyond the veil in the other realm.

Quietly she called Mina to her and gave her a list of flowers and roots to find. She would need these things if she was to stir Kadeema's memory. A few hours later, her dark-skinned acolyte returned with the things Farrah had requested. Again, Mina made the sign of respect and walked out of the tent backwards. Farrah stoked the fire in one of the firepots. She snatched strands of Kadeema's hair out by the root and tossed them on the fire. The mystified Kadeema hardly flinched. Next, Farrah tossed the items Mina had brought her into the low flame and slowly said the words of power as she did so.

She waved a small branch of shrubby rose over the smoke and waved it again over Kadeema to cleanse the young woman's mind. Using the smoke had some risks, but not to Farrah—only to Kadeema. She had seen that Kadeema would die soon, and perhaps this would hasten her passing, but that was a risk Farrah had to take. The future of the Meshwesh could depend on this! Sometimes, the smoke led a person into the dream world never to return, but Farrah suspected that Kadeema was there already. She was lost in a world of visions. How Farrah envied her! Since she'd taken the life of Onesu, she could not see fully. Now she strained and muttered, sometimes inaccurately, sharing what she saw in the flames or in the water.

Kadeema breathed in the fumes and soon was sitting up on the bed, staring harder at whatever it was she saw in the smoke.

"What do you see, Kadeema? Tell me!"

The queen began talking, low at first, then louder and more clearly. "I see a city far in the desert—hidden away from the eyes of men." Kadeema's voice, small and timid, reflected her wonder at what she saw. "Nothing there now, nothing but shadows…shadows of the fallen ones." She began to shake, and her lip quivered. "Ah…I am so cold."

Farrah ignored her and pushed her to share more. "Tell me, Semkah's wife. What do you see now? Can you see the fountain? What about the tower? Are any fires burning there? I must know!"

To Farrah's surprise, Kadeema laughed at her. "So you wish to go back? You've forgotten the way, haven't you, Old One?"

For a moment, it was as if Farrah could hear a different voice speaking, a familiar voice. She felt her mouth go dry, and her eyes widened.

"There is no path back for you, Far-rah. What is done is done."

"Ze? Sister?" Farrah's hand shook with excitement. "Speak to me, sister!"

Kadeema's face changed. The spirit of Ze had passed by, leaving the slack-faced queen behind. She mumbled, "My daughters! I see them! My beautiful girls! How much they look like me!"

She got up on her knees, staring into the smoke, mesmerized by whatever it was she saw. "One will overtake the other! See? See them? How cruel you are, Farrah—you spoke the words. Now look! Can you see them? My daughters!" Kadeema began to cry softly in the smoky tent. Farrah feared that someone would hear the queen's cries.

"Now, now, my queen. All will be well." Her hands still trembling, she smoothed the queen's tangled hair.

"I cannot stay here, Farrah. I cannot stay and see what shall become of my daughters. You cannot have them both, Old One." Farrah could see Kadeema's awareness returning. The power of the smoke was fading. "You cannot kill them both."

Farrah drew her hand back in shock. "I would never do such a thing! Children are treasures of the tribe!"

Kadeema gripped the older woman's hands and stared at them. "So you say, but you lie! They shall both rule. Ah…but then…" A sigh came from the depths of her heart. "I see blood on your hands, Old One! I have seen what you have done."

Farrah's eyes narrowed. How could she know? Could she have seen Farrah slide the blade across Onesu's neck in the clouds of smoke? Before she knew what to say or do, the queen commanded, "Kill me, with your sharp blade! The one you have hidden there in the box. Slide it under my chin and into my brain, Farrah! Please do not leave me in my misery, for I know you shall kill my daughters." She clutched Farrah's hand desperately, her green eyes rivers of pain and hopelessness.

"How can you ask me to do this? You speak like a madwoman, Kadeema." Farrah stood, pushing away from the grasping queen. She gathered her thoughts as Kadeema wept. She had little patience for talking more with the young woman. The queen's mind was feverish, lost—that's what Farrah would say. No one would believe Kadeema.

"Sit, rest, eat. You will feel better soon. Stay here, and I will fetch your husband for you. Semkah has been caring for your daughters, but I suspect that his heart is truly with you. Let me find him." Farrah had to leave; she had to consult the Council on what to do next. She had pledged never to take another life, and so she would not, despite what the queen might believe.

Kadeema did not look at her but stared off into her dreamland with her own private vision. "Yes, I shall wait—for a little while."

Only a brief time had passed when Farrah and Semkah returned. Semkah's handsome smile quickly disappeared, and his dark looks clouded with concern. "Wife?" When she didn't answer, he turned to Farrah and frowned. "Where is she?"

Farrah couldn't hide her surprise. "She was here in her bed, my king. She had a vision! A vision of your daughters!" Quickly she lied, "She asked me to find you. Could I deny her the presence of the king?"

"Why would you leave her?" He growled at Farrah, careful not to strike her as he might like to. "Kadeema? Kadeema? Are you here?" Semkah called again and again. Soon the entire camp was summoned and the search began in earnest. By the time a search party took to the desert sands, the wise woman knew in her bones that Kadeema was dead or very near it. The herbs had increased Farrah's ability to see, if only for a little while. She knew because she could see Kadeema now, glimpses of her. Farrah didn't bother to seek for her; she would never be able to find her, only see her in her mind's eye. Farrah stared into the darkness and watched the queen.

Kadeema walked as far as she could, lay down in the sand, and allowed it to wash over her. Her beautiful eyes focused on a point in the dark sky; the Dancing Man careened above her. With her last breath she shook herself, realizing with sadness how she'd come to be lying in the perilous sands of the Sahara. The queen did not fight her fate, for she had chosen it—finally, for one instant in her life, she showed courage. *No sense in fighting now, Kadeema. You now die, and that is your fate.*

Farrah tried to remain aloof, unmoved by the picture of the lovely upturned face disappearing beneath the red sands, her thin bloody gown fluttering around her frail body. Yes, she had loved the girl. How could one not love a beautiful face and cheery laugh? Still, Kadeema had saved Farrah the trouble of silencing her.

You have blood on your hands, Old One!

How foolish to think that Farrah would kill the treasures of the tribe, the daughters of Semkah. The queen had been wrong, surely. A small voice inside her whispered, "Yes, you would. You would do even that to go home."

Surprised by her own thoughts, an unexpected wave of sadness washed over Farrah as the queen's soul slipped from the earth's realm.

Suddenly, she yelled at the queen, "Stand! Rise, now—before it is too late!" But the green eyes did not see Farrah; they saw nothing now.

Semkah never found her.

Chapter One

Rivalry—Nefret

Clapping my hands three times, I smiled, amused at the half-dozen pairs of dark eyes that watched me entranced with every word and movement I made. "And then she crept up to the rock door and clapped her hands again…" *Clap, clap, clap.* The children squealed with delight as I weaved my story. This was one of their favorites, The Story of Mahara, about an adventurous queen who constantly fought magical creatures to win back her clan's stolen treasures.

"Mahara crouched down as low as she could." I demonstrated, squatting as low as I could in the tent. "She knew that the serpent could only see her if she stood up tall, for he had very poor eyesight. If she was going to steal back the jewel, she would have to crawl her way into the den, just as the serpent opened the door. She was terrified, but the words of her mother rang in her ears: 'Please, Mahara! Bring back our treasures and restore our honor!'"

I crawled around, pretending to be Mahara. The children giggled. "Now Mahara had to be very quiet. The bones of a hundred warriors lay in the serpent's cave. One wrong move and that old snake would see her and…catch her!" I grabbed at a nearby child, who screamed in surprise. Before I could finish my tale, Pah entered our tent, a look of disgust on her face.

"What is this? Must our tent now become a playground? Out! All of you, out! Today is a special day, and we have to get ready."

The children complained loudly, "We want to hear Nefret's story! Can't we stay a little longer?"

Pah shook her head, and her long, straight hair shimmered. "Out! Now!" she scolded the spokesman for the group.

"Run along. There will be time for stories later," I promised them.

As the heavy curtain fell behind them, I gave Pah an unhappy look. She simply shook her head. "You shouldn't make promises that you may not be able to keep, Nefret. You do not know what the future holds."

"Why must you treat them so? They are only children!" I set about dressing for the day. Today we were to dress simply with an aba—a sleeveless coat and trousers. I chose green as my color, and Pah wore blue. I cinched the aba at the waist with a thick leather belt. I wore my hair in a long braid. My fingers trembled as I cinched it with a small bit of cloth.

"Well, if nothing else, you'll be queen of the children, Nefret."

I smoothed wisps of curly hair with both hands as I stared at my reflection in the brass mirror. "Then it's settled. I'll rule the children and you can have the adults." I smiled at her, hoping one last time to make peace with her. It wasn't to be. With an eye roll she exited the tent, and I stepped out behind her to greet the day.

My stomach growled. I was ready to break my fast. I could smell the bread baking on the flames. Although banished from my tent earlier, "my" children—Ziza, Amon and Paimu—followed me. Ziza and Amon were born Meshwesh, but the tribe had adopted Paimu.

Many seasons ago, a small band of stragglers from the Algat came to trade with us. When they left early in the morning, they left Paimu behind. My father had been convinced that it was an oversight and that the Algat would return to claim their daughter, but they did not. Paimu was now everyone's child, but secretly I pretended that she was mine.

"You will win today, Nefret! You will win and be the mekhma!" She whooped and danced around me, and the other two children, her followers, imitated her. I hissed at her playfully as Pah stomped away.

"Stop that now—you'll jinx me. Have you eaten? Where is your breakfast, Paimu?" I knew she had not. The little girl with the black curls ate like a bird.

"I shall eat with you."

"Not today, little one. I have to eat with Semkah."

"Oh, I see." Her bottom lip protruded, and I tousled her curls.

"But when I am done, I shall look for you. You want to climb that tree today? You think you are strong enough?"

"Strong like a monkey!" Paimu pretended to scratch under her arms and played at being a monkey. We had seen many of the nasty animals in the past few months. The traders loved to bring them to us as if we'd never seen them before, parading them around in golden chains. Despite my aversion, I felt great sympathy for the animals. Nothing deserved to be chained. "Can't we do it now? Before you go eat?"

I paused on the path, and people jostled past us. The camp was full today; I had been so consumed with my own thoughts that I hardly noticed the arrival of my uncle's people. Their green and yellow costumes were everywhere. Many of them greeted me, smiling, and the gold about their necks glinted in the early morning light. I felt my stomach twist, and I gladly accepted Paimu's excuse to put off breakfast. "Only a few minutes, though. I dare not keep the king waiting."

"Okay then!" Paimu and the other two children hopped and skipped around me like happy goats. I laughed at their playfulness. We walked to the edge of the camp, where the palm trees swayed above a pool of clear blue water. Our temporary home, the Timia Oasis, was my favorite of all the oases that our tribes visited. Lush and green, oranges and pomegranates hung everywhere. Clusters of dates, vegetables and fresh herbs grew abundantly. Every time we left Timia, my heart broke a little. To me this was home, not distant Zerzura, although I would never confess that to anyone.

I skipped down the path with the children until we came to the tree that Paimu had been trying unsuccessfully to climb. As we entered the clearing, my heart sank. There under the tallest tree was Pah, her back propped against the curved trunk and Alexio laughing over her, touching her hair. I would have preferred to turn and walk away, but I had promised Paimu. I avoided making eye contact and helped Paimu tie up her skirt so she could climb.

I knelt down beside her, tucking the fabric neatly in the cord at her waist. "You remember what I told you? Don't look down. Take your time but keep moving. If you move too slowly, your arms will tire and you will fall."

"I won't forget, princess."

"No princess. Just Nefret." I tweaked her nose and walked with her to the tree.

"Okay, Nefret. I can do this."

"I know you can, Paimu."

Like many times before, Paimu skimmed easily up the first five feet of the tree. I talked to her patiently and soon, Alexio was climbing the tree next to hers, demonstrating his technique as she watched.

"That trunk is too large for her to grasp." Pah suddenly stood beside me, frowning up at the dark-haired girl above us. "She will hurt herself, Nefret."

"Nonsense. She's just climbing a tree, and she'll never go high enough to hurt herself."

"This isn't about you, Nefret. Get her down."

"Leave her, Pah!"

"Fine! Let her fall, then. It's no matter to me." Pah turned to walk away from the whole scene.

Nervously, I called up to the girl. "That's high enough, Paimu. Come down, brave girl." Alexio scampered down his tree, walked toward the trunk of Paimu's tree and patted it.

"Look how far I've climbed." Paimu climbed higher and higher until I could see only her feet. Ziza and Amon clapped and cheered her on.

"Look at you, Paimu! You did it! Now come down. Slowly now. Use your entire body." I truly had begun to feel frightened for her.

"Okay," Paimu yelled down, her voice unsteady and unsure. I gasped as I watched her tiny body slide down the tree. Ziza screamed, and I raced to the trunk.

"Stop, Paimu! Be still for a moment. Don't look down—stop looking down!"

"Okay," she said, her voice cracking with fear.

"I told you this would happen." Pah hadn't left; she lingered behind me.

Aggravated, I spun on my heel. "Yes, you did. Thank you, Pah." Alexio stripped off his jacket and sandals again and prepared to climb the tree, but I stopped him. "No, she's my responsibility. I will get her down." Alexio smiled patiently, giving me a mock bow. At least he didn't argue with me, and for that I was thankful. I kicked off my shoes and began to climb.

"I am coming up, my monkey girl. Be still. Are you secure?"

"Yes, but my arms are shaky, princess—I mean Nefret. I can't hold on. I am scared." I climbed as quickly as I could in an attempt to reach her; the tree shook beneath me.

"No! Stop!" she screamed, attracting more attention to our situation.

"I cannot leave you there, Paimu. What will the birds say? Now hold on while I come closer."

"What is your plan? To fall out of the tree with her?" Pah mocked us from the ground. I heard Alexio scold her, but I kept my attention on the little girl above me.

"See how clever you are. You climbed very high, but now we have to come down. I am going to move very slowly, okay? Why don't you climb down to me and meet me halfway? Then this poor old tree won't shake so much."

"I can't!"

"Yes, you can. You can do it. I am going to move up now just a tiny bit. Hold still."

I eased up the tree another short space. I did this again and again until I could reach out and touch her dirty foot.

"No, no! Please. I will fall."

"No, Paimu. I will not allow you to fall. I am the princess, remember? What I say has to be, right?"

"I guess so."

"It is so. Now I am going to climb up next to you, and you are going to hang around my shoulders like my little monkey, okay? Together we will climb down."

"I will try."

"No, you can do it."

"Careful, Nefret," someone called up to me, but I didn't answer. I had to stay focused on my task. The sweat crept across my brow, and I felt the muscles in my arms and legs burn.

"Come now. Here I am. See?" I smiled at her, but she didn't return my smile.

"I'm afraid! I am going to fall!"

"Nonsense. Here's what I want you to do. First, I am going to inch a little closer, but I will not touch you. You will put this leg around my waist and then scoop your arm under my armpit. That way, you won't fall."

"Can you hold me?"

"Of course I can. A little monkey like you is easy to carry. Take your time now. Here I come." I inched closer, my hands sweating. What would I do if something happened to Paimu, if she fell out of this tree and it was my fault? "Now first your leg. It's okay, take your time." Paimu held her breath and put her leg around my waist. She was so small that I barely felt the weight of her. "No, not around my neck. You can't choke me. Under my arm, please. Yes, that's it."

In half a minute she was on my back, and I began our descent. As I made my way down, a strand of long copper hair dangled irritatingly in my face. I couldn't help but notice that half the camp had come to witness the rescue but Pah had disappeared. Once we got a few feet from the ground, Paimu threw herself off my back and into Alexio's waiting arms. My tribe clapped at the happy ending before they walked away to attend to their chores and various jobs.

I stood grinning at Paimu. "Good job, little monkey. Next time, though, don't climb so high." I kissed her head, and she went running back down the path to find her friends. "Thank you for your help, Alexio."

"I was happy to provide it. You'll make a monkey out of her yet. Although I don't think your sister appreciated the show. Aren't you expected at your father's table this morning?"

My eyes widened. "Oh no! I have to go! Thank you again!" I ran down the path, his playful laughter in my ears.

Father's colorful tent was at the center of the camp. It was easy to spot—the falcon banner, the symbol of our tribe, flew over the top of it. I walked through the crowded camp, greeting those who greeted me without stopping too long for small talk. A few of my uncle's tribe openly sneered at me; it was no secret that they hoped Pah would become the mekhma. I wasn't sure why, but it was no matter to me. I had no skill at politics and no desire to seek support from anyone. I stepped inside the tent and was immediately greeted by Mina.

Farrah's acolyte greeted me silently with a demure smile and a bowl of fresh water. Quickly, I sloshed water over my hands as was the custom before dining with the king. The tent was full of dignitaries, including our uncle Omel and his sons except Alexio, his youngest. I took my seat to the left of our father; Pah always sat at his right during these official visits. We sat cross-legged around a low round table that was heaped with food. I stared at the tempting wheel of cheese near me, but I didn't dare partake until Father did. The king always took his food first. Father had the bearing of a king, or so I believed. He dressed in his royal blue tunic with the gold hand stitching around the hem. His dark brown hair was oiled and braided, and it hung down his back. He wore no jewelry today; his arm tattoos shone, and I imagined I could see them twist around his arms like living snakes. I shook myself, reminding myself to stay present in the moment.

Looking around the room, I recognized most of the faces. Sitting exactly opposite of our father was his brother Omel, another Meshwesh tribal leader. Omel's tribe and ours migrated from one rain oasis to the next as our people had done since we'd lost Zerzura to the Nephal, the giants who came down from their homeland far to the north. The giants believed this was their land, although Egypt's kings had defeated them a lifetime ago. Occasionally, they still made incursions into the Red Lands to murder, terrorize and rape our women. After they took Zerzura, they disappeared again, but not before hiding the city in the sand first. Or at least that was the story we were told.

I shivered, feeling as if someone were staring at me. I looked around the room and saw that it was Farrah, the Old One, the head of the Council. Her lips were pursed as she seemed to look right through me. I shivered again and crossed my fingers behind my back to prevent her from reading my mind. With those dark piercing eyes, I suspected that she had the power to stare into my soul.

Our father was king, but the Council acted as the spiritual leaders of all the Meshwesh. They heard various matters concerning inheritance and sickness, and they settled property disputes. They were wise and learned and could detect a lie before it was told, or so they told us. Truthfully, kings did not hold much power in our clan. Naturally, they were the leaders of our clan when there was no mekhma, but beyond protecting the people and developing military strategies, their powers were limited.

For a millennium, the Meshwesh were ruled by the mekhmas, wise young women selected by the Council of Old Ones. According to the legends, many had special magical powers bestowed upon them by the gods they served, and the king and clan served the mekhma with their lives—if it was so required. My mother had been no mekhma—she was born in a faraway land called Grecia. She served as the king's consort only—the Meshwesh had not had a mekhma since Ze, the sister of Farrah who died during the flight from Zerzura.

I smiled at Farrah to stop her staring and began doing some studying of my own. There was much to see here today in our camp. Thankfully, there were no monkeys or tigers, no traders telling us fantastic stories. How many hoped that by doing so we would divulge the location of our sacred gold and turquoise mines? No Meshwesh would ever do such a thing.

I watched our uncle; I could see that he did not defer to his people in anything. I suspected he had no desire to have a mekhma to lead him. He wanted nothing but to be king—and to convince his brother to make a lasting peace with Egypt. To this suggestion, our father always laughed. And despite the seriousness of today's gathering, Omel did not miss an opportunity to bemoan what he considered his brother's lack of foresight in regards to Pharaoh's most recent offer.

"Again, brother? I have given my answer." Our father took a handful of grapes, popped a few in his mouth and handed the bowl to Omel, who accepted it. He did not take any grapes but put the bowl back on the low cedar table with an odd thumping sound. Omel wasn't satisfied.

"Hear me out, Semkah. This is what our father would have wanted! Peace and safety for the Meshwesh. I have it on good authority that Egypt is willing to give us lands—lands of our own! No more traveling the sands, brother, searching for a lost city! We can be a nation again with a strong defense—walls to protect us." When Father didn't answer him, Omel continued with his plea. He may have thought he was convincing his brother, who said nothing, but I could have told him not to waste his time. For Father and our entire tribe, Zerzura would be our only home. Meshwesh blood had been shed there, holy blood. It would not be forgotten.

"I have been talking to the traders, brother. They say that families have disappeared, never to be seen or heard from again. Let me call Ohn in here to tell you what he saw. He's just returned from Siya, where he was to trade with the men there. Nobody was there. The oasis was empty, yet the tents remained."

Father raised his hands, his tattoos plainly showing. For the briefest of seconds, again it appeared as if the snakes were alive and writhing. I gasped and blinked as Father said, "Brother, enough of this! I will hear Ohn later, but let us tend to the things that are before us first."

Omel rose to his feet in a shot. I did not know what his intentions were, but he looked dark, very dark indeed. "You sit here in your comfortable tent while people die in the Red Lands! I tell you the Nephal have returned, and they care not for your kingship or the mekhma! We need the help of Egypt if we are going to withstand them!"

Father rose to calm him, but Farrah stood instead. "Omel! Do not disgrace these proceedings! You will have a chance to speak, just as Semkah said, but now is the time to bless your brother's daughters before they begin their trials." Omel unhappily returned to his seat but refused to look at his brother, even when he addressed him. The proceedings were long. Farrah recited the long list of mekhmas that had served the Meshwesh over the centuries. I knew them all by heart, as Pah did. Pah and I were formally introduced at *anni-mekhmas*, or queens-in-training. The leaders politely clapped for us as we stood before them. The tent grew hotter as the day went along, and there seemed to be no end to the formalities. Finally, Farrah and the others were ready to dismiss us, warning us not to discuss with the others anything that was said or done.

"These are sacred proceedings, and even as anni-mekhmas you must take care to preserve our traditions. Go now. Enjoy your final night together."

"What?" Pah and I stared at one another. "What do you mean?" I asked Farrah.

"Tonight is the last night you share a tent. Tomorrow, you begin your new life and your trials begin in earnest—we will present you to the tribe as anni-mekhmas. When you leave this tent you are no longer Nefret and Pah, sisters, daughters of Semkah. Hug one another now." We hugged awkwardly, and then Pah pulled away from me and waited silently to be excused. Farrah nodded while our father and the others clapped respectfully. Pah disappeared out the door flap and I ran after her.

Chapter Two

The Necklace—Nefret

Despite my most ardent attempts at conversation, my sister refused to speak with me beyond a few words. When we left the king's tent she ran to be with her friends and left me behind once again. I spent the rest of the day playing with the children and avoiding adult conversation as much as possible. If this was to be my last day as a child, simply a daughter of Semkah, then I would make the most of it. At the end of the day, I walked back to our tent but Pah was not there. I took my supper alone and crawled into bed, only to fall asleep waiting for her.

I did not hear her return. When I did wake, it was near morning. As usual, I awoke before Pah. I longed to push back the wheels of time so the two of us might become children again. Then I would wake her with tickles or a playful nudge. She would not bark at me or deride me for being childish. How long ago that had been! Now I dared not disturb her in such a way. "Pah, are you awake?" I whispered in the darkness. She did not answer me. I heard her soft snore. Still in the dream world; it would be cruel to wake her now.

Dread washed over me. The unknown challenges yawned before me, and my imagination began to spin fantastic tales about what things I may have to accomplish. I sighed in the darkness.

Sliding out of my pallet, I reached for my robe. Many of the gold thread tassels were missing, but I could not part with it; it had been one of the few items that belonged to my mother. Pah had Mother's braid—her princess lock—I had her robe. I slid into the comfortable garment and stepped outside through the fold in the back of the tent. I did not want to draw attention to myself.

Fingers of red light looked like a hand as the first glints of the sun stretched across the far horizon. Our herdsmen would be long gone to their destination by now. Anyone doing trade with the tribe would soon arrive. Most avoided the midday heat and chose to linger inside the tents of the Meshwesh where the air was cool and sweet.

I walked down the small hill behind our tent, digging my heels into the sand to maintain my balance. I was only a few yards from the oasis but since I could no longer see it, I might as well have been a hundred miles away. I liked the imagined distance. Sometimes I craved adventure. Oh, to be Mahara or one of the other courageous women in my stories!

As children, Pah, Alexio and I whispered long into the night, talking about the places we would go, the things we would see. Alexio had traveled to many places, including south to the gold mine and east to the edge of Thebes. The stories he told us of what he saw were hard to believe, but I could tell by the wonder in his eyes that he told us the truth. Pah and I had known only life in our camp.

Ungracefully, I climbed another sand dune. Satisfied finally that I was completely by myself and far enough away from my tribe to not be found, I pulled my mother's robe tighter around my body and lay back on the sand. The glistening stars above me were beginning to fade, threatened by the nearness of the sun.

I sighed and stared up at the distant moon. I imagined flying up, up and up, like a jinn or one of the gods, then looking down upon the earth. What would I see if I were a bird? What must it be like to see the Red Lands from the sky? I had to admit that I envied the gods and their vantage point—if they existed. I did not pray to them as I should. Or to anything at all, really.

Pah had a heart for faith, but I did not. How could I worship an invisible being that insisted on sacrifice, adoration and perpetual prayers? Some claimed to have seen a god or goddess, but I had seen nothing. According to the traders, the local deities were a jealous lot who would kill mortals on a whim to get what they wanted—which was often a human woman or a special musical instrument. Now the gods commanded that I compete with my sister to lead the tribe and the entire clan. As spokesman for the gods of the Meshwesh, Farrah should be able to tell us who it should be! Why must we go through trials? I felt angry, even rebellious as I lay in the sand.

How many times had Farrah taken me to the fire and commanded me to look? "Look harder, Nefret. Look with your mind's eye!" Despite her encouragement, I never saw a thing besides the flickering of the flames and the burning herbs. No queenly visions for me. My sister had that gift, and to me, Pah's vision was the proof I needed that the gods had made their decision. They had chosen my sister to lead. Although my spirit resisted this thought, my heart was happy. I only wanted my sister to be happy, I reminded myself. Suddenly I sat up. "That's what I'll do. I will tell them my sister should be the mekhma. Then we can end all this!" The idea suited me, and I ignored the small, still voice that said, "No! You must be queen!"

I frowned at the moon above me. "You do not control my life!" I was tempted to raise my fist at the moon, but what good would it do me? *What would you know of Nefret and Pah, moon? Do you even know who we are?* Of course, the moon said nothing to me. I dug my toes into the cool, red sand. I dug first with my big toe, and then I buried all my toes in the sand. Pah would complain later than I had strewn sand in our tent, but wasn't there always sand in the tent? You could not avoid it. I hardly noticed it anymore.

I leaned forward and put my elbows on my knees. This was a special moment, out here alone in the quiet. Today, the camp would be full of visitors come to watch Pah and me compete. My stomach twisted, and I felt another sigh rise from within me. I wiggled my toes deeper and felt something cold and foreign under my foot. I drew my toes back, afraid that a scorpion or snake was hidden there. The sand did not move, so I poked it again with my toe. It wasn't a creature. Now sitting cross-legged, I dug at the spot where my toes had been.

Suddenly a tiny whirlwind in the sand appeared; I fell back and watched as it spun. I shielded my eyes with my fingers to protect them from the spinning sand. When the whirlwind's work was complete, it simply dissolved into nothing; all was calm once more.

There! I could see something, something shiny. I touched it—it was a flat chain with the shine of gold. But it wasn't gold, at least none that I had ever seen. I tugged on the end until the full length of chain was free from the sand. Curious, I examined the necklace. It was beautifully made with exquisite, unfamiliar craftsmanship. Even in the muted darkness I could see this was a rare treasure. Hanging from the chain was an oval-shaped pendant. It was flat with inscribed images like I had never seen. I could see a snake, the sign for water—the rest I could not make out. Still, I knew I had found a precious thing. Perhaps it had fallen off one of the trader's caravans? I had no explanation for the small whirlwind that had unearthed it.

I looked about me nervously. Cupping the necklace in my hand I spun about the top of the dune. I didn't see anyone, and there was no evidence that anyone had been near recently. However, the sand shifted daily. How would I know that anyone had been here? I felt the cool metal in my hand. I would keep it, but I would keep it to myself. I grabbed my robe. My heart beat fast in my chest as I scurried back to my tent. Pah was awake and dressed but still not speaking to me. She stroked her hair with her brush and wrapped it into a neat braid. How I wanted to talk with her! To hear her speak kindly to me, but she did not. I shoved my secret treasure under my blanket and watched her balefully.

My stomach twisted again. Mina told me once—and I had heard her voice only a handful of times in my life—that there were two snakes of destiny fighting inside each of us. These snakes caused the twisting sensation. "The gods place the snakes inside your belly before you are born. As you grow, they grow, and one struggles to dominate the other. When the struggle ends, your destiny is decided." I begged to hear more, but she said nothing else. I understood none of it. The thought of snakes in my belly made me even more nervous and nauseous.

Farrah's acolyte had a soft voice, which always sounded raw and husky—probably because she rarely used it. Mina lived under a vow of silence, a vow to Ma'at. She was a master at nonverbal communication, using her facial expressions and hands to say much more than I could ever express with my storytelling. I admired the woman's quietness and calmness—two qualities I did not possess.

As I brushed the tangles from my own hair with an ivory comb, I watched Pah begin her day. She tossed spoons of fragrant incense into the hanging burner, filling the room with lush scent. She leaned close to the golden lamps and fanned herself with the thick clouds of smoke. How bitter it was to know that she prayed against me! Pah opened her cedar box and examined each of the items. Although I always made a show of not watching her, I knew each item by heart. A braid of light brown hair from our mother, a block of rare fragrant wood, a seashell given by a friendly and handsome servant of a Cushite trader and one more item that she took great pains to hide from me. It was the newest treasure in her collection—a stolen piece of blue fabric from Alexio's shirt. Something she kept after repairing a tear for him.

I felt a sad sigh rise in my chest but said nothing. My hands wove my hair into a braid, and I tied the end with a piece of leather. Pah and Alexio—I could not wrap my mind around it. She loved him, of that I was sure. At least she thought she did. Perhaps she only thought she loved him because she believed I did. Maybe she wanted to hurt me as only another woman could? How could I have predicted that our childhood friend would drive us further apart?

How did I feel about Alexio? My cousin had strong, muscular arms and legs. He ran faster than anyone I knew and was frequently called upon to carry out the wishes of the kings—both his father and mine. His dark hair, which he kept at shoulder length, hung about his face like strands of silk. His warm brown eyes seemed to grow more expressive as he grew older. His face was square, with a straight nose and proud lips, but he was always laughing at someone or something—most of the time at me. He laughed much less now. We all did. How different he was from the boy I once knew! We were no longer children, the three of us.

I pretended that I did not see Pah kiss the cloth and place it back inside the box. Didn't she know that I would gladly see her and Alexio marry, if that was the will of our tribes? Pah did not hide her affection for Alexio—her dark green eyes always sought his face. Still, that was not to be. Omel had made marriage arrangements for his son long ago and made no secret that he expected him to fulfill that obligation. That was the way it was for sons of Meshwesh kings; we women had much more freedom. Alexio's intended, Farafra, the daughter of a minor king named Walida, could refuse him, but she had expressed no intention of doing so. Rather, she was proud of her handsome prize. I thought she was an unpleasant sort of person who tended to laugh at the misfortune of others. She knew nothing about Alexio beyond the fact that he had a handsome face and strong arms.

After Pah's review of the contents of her box, she closed it and then lay on her rug, bowing at the waist. I could hear her whisper a prayer but could not hear the name of the god she entreated. Her fervent whispers filled me with sadness. As quietly as I could, I attended myself and prepared to leave her in peace.

"Why do you pretend you do not hear me? I know you are listening, Nefret." She rose from her rug, never looking in my direction.

I felt ashamed for spying. It had been wrong to do, but how could I not? Not knowing how to answer, I changed the subject. "Who do you pray to, Pah? Hathor or one of our mother's goddesses, Aphrodite or Hera, perhaps?"

She stood before the ivory basin, scooping up the water with a clean linen cloth. I did not think she heard me at first; she washed her face and arms, whispering as she did. I could see her shadow bounce against the tapestries, her movements like that of a lithe dancer. Pah had an elegance that could not be taught. I was awkward, unsure and at times even clumsy. I envied her that natural grace. Finally, she slid on her tunic.

My twin said, "Does that concern you? Does it matter to whom I pray?"

"No," I said with a sigh. "I am sorry I asked."

She slid on her gold bracelets and looked at me. "What do you pray for, Nefret?"

"You know I do not pray. Why should I pray to the gods that want to divide us? Don't you care, Pah?"

Avoiding my question she said sternly, "You *should* pray, Nefret, for today I will beat you—tomorrow I will beat you too. I will best you, and everyone will see that I am the mekhma. You should pray that you do not fall and break your neck."

I made the sign against curses and whispered back, "Why say such things to me, Pah? I am not your enemy. I am your sister!"

"What does that mean, Nefret? Nothing! The prophecy has been spoken, and I will not give up my life for you. I will be the one to bring the Meshwesh back to Zerzura!"

Sudden awareness crept upon me. "Who has poisoned your heart against me, sister? We could rule together! We could! You cannot let Farrah or any of the Council divide us. If we stick together, we will stand. Remember your promise? We would always be together."

"The promises of a child. They mean nothing! How dare you speak so about the Old One, an elder of our tribe? Farrah sees the past and the future—she knows the way back home!"

"If she knows the way, why aren't we there?" To that, Pah said nothing. The silence between us grew, and I felt worried. Perhaps Pah had seen something! Had she seen my death? "Sister, please. Let us stand together and refuse to be divided!"

"You only say that because you know I am better than you, Nefret. I am faster and cleverer. You may have a prettier face and figure, but it takes more than that to be a strong mekhma."

As she spoke, tears slid down my face. "How can you speak to me so? What has happened between us?"

"Destiny has happened, Nefret. It is time to leave childhood behind and be women."

"All I want is your happiness, Pah. And…" My voice lowered, as if someone might hear us. "If that happiness includes Alexio I would not stand in your way."

She laughed sourly. "Ah, my happiness…why do you lie to yourself, Nefret? Do you think you have the power to give him to me? It is you he wants—at least for now. You and I both know that you would do anything to have him! How can you deny it?"

"I do deny it! How can you hate me so? What has changed between us? Tell me and I will fix it! I would gladly resign my right if you would only love me again. Please…sister."

Pah didn't argue with me. Instead she said quietly, "I will earn my right to rule, Nefret. That is why I *should* rule. I do not hate you, but I will win. That is my destiny."

"If it is your destiny, than I will gladly give you my vote."

She laughed—it was a dark, empty sound. "Always the weak one. I will not accept it. We will do things the right way. And when I have won, everyone will know I am the better choice."

I stared at her, refusing to believe what I heard.

"One more thing, Nefret...I have seen the future—I know that Alexio is not *my* fate. He is a dream only, for both of us, I think."

Her words burned a scar into my heart. I felt like one of the goats that the herdsmen branded with their hot prods. I could not remember when it all began, when we drifted apart, but this conversation was proof that Fate had had her way with us.

With a confident smile, she stalked out of our tent. I numbly finished dressing for the day. Although today was not a celebration for me, I obediently wore my silver earrings and bracelets and gold anklets. How I appeared mattered to my father and my tribe. I considered wearing my newfound necklace; it felt cool in my hand as I held it briefly. Deciding against it, I placed it inside my mother's robe, rolled the robe up snugly and tucked it in my bed. I walked outside and went to break my fast before joining the others in Father's tent.

"Morning, Isha," I greeted the older woman who handed me a small round bread from her basket.

"Morning, treasure of the tribe." She kissed my cheek, and I smiled at her. Such had been my greeting every morning for as long as I could remember, as it was for all children of the Meshwesh. Now that today was here, the last day of my childhood, it suddenly occurred to me that I would never hear it again. Staring at the bread in my hands, I was swept up in the emotions of the moment.

"No need to rush, princess. The Council meeting has been postponed for a little while. Surprising news from Siya." Alexio's hand was upon my shoulder. "Are you going to eat that? I'm starving."

"What? Postponed why? What happened in Siya?" With a nod to Isha, we walked away and I tore the bread in half. "Here, greedy one." Relief washed over me. I wouldn't have to face Pah now—at least not for a little while.

"Someone has been raiding the outposts along the Great Oasis of Siya. The messenger from Siya said that warriors have been seen riding there."

"Warriors? Who could it be? Is this messenger reliable?" We strolled through the camp to the pool where Paimu had raced up the tree the day before.

"I think so. He seems level-headed enough. I've spoken to him before but not today. He was ushered into Semkah's tent as soon as he climbed off his camel."

"I see." I chewed on the soft bread and wondered what this could mean. "Have you seen Pah this morning?"

"After she was turned away at the tent? No. She didn't speak to me. I get the feeling that she's angry with me."

"Pah is mad at the world. Especially me," I added. We sat at the side of the pool and finished our bread. For a long while neither of us spoke.

Finally, Alexio said fiercely, "You have to win, Nefret. No matter what! You have to win."

"I don't want to win, Alexio. I want to have my sister back."

He sighed, tossing the last of his crumbs on the water. Hungry fish sucked up the tidbits quickly and lingered near the surface hoping for more. The palm trees beside us creaked in the early morning breeze. He wanted to say something but didn't.

"You think I am stupid for hoping so, don't you?"

"No, I do not think you are stupid, but surely you can see that that time has passed. There is more at stake than your sister's feelings and your own. You think that if you don't try, Pah will love you again; that if you don't fight for your right to lead, Pah will welcome you back with open arms. You are wrong, my friend. With all her heart, Pah wants to be the mekhma. Nothing you say will change that. Even if you were to give up your right to compete—and you cannot—you could not please her."

"She said as much this morning." Feeling sorry for the golden fish, I tossed small pieces of bread in the water. "Why does it have to be like this? Why can't we serve together? Surely that is better for the people!"

In a burst of emotion he said, "Why won't you fight, Nefret? Fight for your people! Fight for your right, for Paimu—and for me? You are not a coward! You are strong with a bow, fast on your feet. And you have wisdom, a deeper wisdom than your sister! You say all you want is to keep your sister, but the truth is you are hiding, Nefret—hiding from your destiny! You are afraid, and your fear brings us no honor."

His outburst shocked me. He had never spoken so frankly with me, at least not concerning Pah. I felt as if I had been slapped. "You're asking me to give up my sister. You can't ask me to do that."

He stood and glared down at me. "I am asking nothing of you except that you try. Pah is already lost to you, Nefret." Frustrated, I called after him, but he walked away and did not look back.

Chapter Three

The Old Ways—Nefret

I observed the fish darting back and forth as they hoped more crumbs would fall into the water. They tapped at one another with their noses, jostling for a better position. I understood them. How perfect life had been just a few minutes ago when there were no crumbs in the water to disturb their peaceful world! Now that they had had a taste of bread, they thought of nothing else. They were like Pah and me in a way. There was no peace left in our world. Why was I fighting this? Maybe Alexio was right—nothing would make Pah happy. Was I simply afraid?

As I sat wondering what to do with myself, a small pair of arms encircled my neck. By the dirty nails and dark brown skin, it was easy to identify my sneaky visitor. "Good morning, Paimu. What have you been doing with yourself this morning?"

"Helping." She kissed my cheek and plunked down beside me. Her light brown dress was soiled and needed changing. I would have to wash it soon.

"Helping who? Tam the goat boy? You smell like a goat."

"Nobody cares what I smell like, Nefret. Why are you sitting here by yourself? Did you make Alexio angry?"

"My meeting has been delayed…have you been spying on me?"

She smiled, crinkling her wide nose. Paimu was a pretty girl, in an Algat sort of way. The Algat were generally friendly people but naturally suspicious and notorious for stealing whatever they wanted. My father said they would sell their children if they could get a good price for them. Algat loved nothing more than gold and silver. From what I remembered, Algat had high foreheads, wide noses and toothy smiles, but it had been six years since any of Paimu's people had visited our tribe. It was a strange thing indeed that some mother or father would leave a child behind.

She ignored my question and scooted up beside me. "Are you worried that Pah will beat you?"

"I don't know, Paimu." Attempting to change the subject, I asked her, "Where are Ziza and Amon?"

"Fighting with one another, as always." She offered me some of her grapes, and I accepted them from her sticky hand. "About you, of course."

I popped a grape in my mouth and frowned. "Me? Why are they fighting about me?"

"It's all foolishness. Who cares what they think?"

I could judge by her grown-up tone that she disapproved of their disagreement, which was more than likely about my sister and me. She tossed her last grape into the pool and laughed as the fish dove after it. Rinsing her hands in the cool water she said, "Can we go for a swim?"

"I cannot now; I am waiting to be summoned. But maybe later, little one."

With a sigh, she sat down beside me again and toyed with my silver earrings. Silver was rare in the desert. She touched them with her tiny fingers. "It's getting hot out. I think we should swim. Maybe if we swim deep enough we'll find some treasure in the water. Yes, we should find treasure!" She stood with a smile and tugged at my hand.

"Paimu, I told you I cannot. Please, come sit." She obeyed, but I could tell something troubled her. Finally she shared what was on her heart.

"Are you going to leave me, Nefret?" Her smile vanished, and distrust and anger flashed in her dark eyes. "I know you are—I had a dream."

"What are you talking about, Pai? I am not leaving." I shivered as a fleeting shadow passed behind her. It surprised me, but it was gone as quickly as it came.

"You will, and you will leave me behind. I will never see you again."

"What are you talking about?" Standing, I hugged her. She felt so frail and tiny, but she had the heart of a warrior.

"I had a dream about you—you and Pah. You left me, Nefret, and I never saw you again." She cried loudly, and the sound filled me with desperation.

"No, it was only a dream...hush now, little one. I will never leave you. I promise. Where I go, Paimu goes too." I cupped her face in my hand and stared her in the eye to show her I meant it.

Her lip quivered and she nodded. "You promise?"

"Yes, I promise."

She threw her arms around me again, hugged me once and then ran down the path that led to a nearby row of tents.

Pondering the meaning of her outburst, I was surprised by the arrival of a messenger. It was time to assemble for the meeting, time to hear what the Council had to say. I caught my breath and followed behind the tall, thin warrior. People gathered along the sides of the sandy path. Their smiling faces encouraged me; some even openly called me *anni-mekhma* as I passed by. I did not answer them or acknowledge the title—it would be inappropriate to do so with the trials having just begun, and I did not wish to court ill luck.

Pah arrived at the same time, also summoned back to the massive tent by a serious-faced messenger. We stood before the tent door, wondering who should enter first. I waved my hand to show deference to her as she stepped in front of me with her head held high. Walking behind her, my eyes widened at the sight of Father in his royal attire. He wore a tunic and pants of blue cloth; the tunic's neck dipped to the center of his chest to show an array of scars, chains and pendants, each representing something meaningful. The Meshwesh often memorialized special events with gifts of jewelry, and Father's display showed how much he was venerated by his tribe. His stone face revealed nothing, and with a wave of his hand, Pah and I obediently knelt before him. His brother Omel was to his left, and the tribal council surrounded them on either side. Farrah, the Old One, the oldest and most powerful member of the Council, sat to the king's right. She wore robes of white and gray, and her long, thick gray hair hung around her like a soft veil. Of all the faces that watched me, hers was the most intimidating. She spoke first, and her commanding voice filled the tent.

"Welcome, daughters of Semkah and Kadeema. You come before the Council today to declare your intentions to compete for the role of mekhma. Is this correct?"

Pah said calmly, "Yes, Farrah."

"Yes, Farrah," I replied less confidently.

"Very well, daughters." She paused and looked at each of us. "Know this…once you cast your incense into the smoke there is no turning back, no changing your mind. The smoke is a covenant with the tribe—you cannot call back smoke once it rises to the heavens. If it is truly your heart's desire to serve as mekhma, take the spoon in front of you and toss the incense into the flame. We will wait while you consider."

My mind ran through multiple scenarios, none of which I had the courage to pursue. Simply fleeing from the tent was not an option. How could I shame our father in such a way? I reached for a spoon, but not before Pah did. With unexpected quickness, she tossed the yellow incense into the fire, and the smell of ground herbs filled the tent. As her cloud faded, I held my breath, dug into the powder and tossed it into the flame. Our actions were met with an unexpected song from Mina.

She who gives her life for the tribes
will always have life to give
Our mekhma is the blood of the clan,
the heart, the life
Yield to her, enemies of the Meshwesh,
for she is mighty!

When her song was complete she nodded to us and made the sign of respect, a raised upright palm. We acknowledged her with a nod, and Farrah continued.

"Today is both a happy day and a troubling one. Happy because we know that our clan will soon welcome a new leader, a woman to lead our people back to Zerzura, just as the prophecy foretold." The Council nodded their agreement and repeated the word "Zerzura" with reverence. "For some time the Council has considered your special circumstances and have sought the gods' help to discern the way forward."

I stared at her, the haze of the incense burning my eyes slightly. I tried to focus, to pay attention to every word as if my life hung upon her words. Truthfully, it did.

"I, Farrah, was there the night you were born, the night the falcon and the Bee-Eater flew into the birthing tent. From that day forward, we knew that you were not ordinary children—you had a special destiny. It has been many years since we had a mekhma to lead us, although your father has been an honorable king and has given his tribe much wealth through his wise dealings. His brother also has led his own tribe with wisdom and strength. We give thanks to them for keeping their tribes safe, but it is the Meshwesh way to serve queens rather than kings." Farrah paused so that the gathered leaders had the opportunity to agree with her. All did except for Omel, who merely stared at us, his face a mask. I was not the only one who noticed this. Father raised his hand to Farrah to prevent her from speaking further. His eyes flashed with anger as he brought the meeting to a halt waiting for Omel's acknowledgement.

Omel's face softened, but his eyes never changed. "That's the way it has always been," our uncle said finally. Satisfied that everyone was in agreement, Father relaxed and waited for Farrah to continue, but Omel had more to say. "But if we are going to adhere to the Old Ways, we must adhere to all of them. One cannot pick and choose which of the customs to follow. These things must be properly administrated or we risk again the wrath of the gods."

Father's deep voice bellowed, "What do you mean?" I watched the scene with wide eyes. I glanced at Pah, who was equally entranced. But like Omel, her face masked her emotions.

"Brother, my king, these are troubling times as you well know. We need a strong leader with undisputed authority. Our clan must not repeat the mistakes of the past."

Father seemed ready to thrash Omel, but Farrah's voice broke the tension. "Omel is correct, Semkah. The Old Ways must be followed."

"You can't ask me to do this."

"I haven't," Farrah said, drawing herself up, her back as rigid as her voice. Even sitting amongst the men who towered above her, she was a forbidding figure. *It was like magic, how she did that.*

"What is happening? What do they mean?" I whispered to Pah, but she ignored me. She sat perfectly still, her hands resting on her knees, palms down. Nobody answered me, although I knew they could hear me. Father's face said it all. Whatever custom our uncle referred to, it was not good. Would they require a life? My life? Would one of us have to die? My stomach twisted into knots. "What are these Old Ways you speak of, uncle?" I blurted out. "Tell us. We have a right to know."

Farrah answered for him, "It is Una and Uma we speak of."

Wracking my brain, I recalled scant portions of their story. It was never a tale I told around the fires at night, nor did anyone. This was only the second time I had heard the names spoken aloud. "What of them? Who were they?"

"Sisters they were, sisters who fought to lead the Meshwesh, and in doing so nearly destroyed the clan. Their hatred for one another was legendary—many families were left with no sons and daughters. From that day to this one, sisters have never ruled together in our clan."

Pah's voice sounded like cold steel. "One shall rule, one shall leave." Her voice sounded firm, deliberate. There was no surprise there.

"Leave?"

"Surely there must be another way," Father said.

"It must be *this* way. Omel is correct, Semkah."

Father's shoulders slumped and I whispered, "Father!" His eyes were tender as he gazed upon us. "Please," I pleaded with him.

"If it is the will of the clan, there is nothing I can do." His words hit my heart like well-placed arrows.

Desperation swelled inside me. Did everyone know this already? Was that what Alexio was trying to tell me? I stared into my twin's face, her green eyes averted, her face still a taut mask. "Pah, we can rule together, can't we? Tell them!" She did not answer me but kept her eyes focused on her hands. I saw nothing, not a tear, not a smile, nothing. Hopelessness swept over me.

Then the truth rose like the sun over the desert. She had known Omel's intentions all along. For Pah and our uncle, it was all or nothing.

Farrah spoke again, her voice softer, more patient but unyielding. "Even if you had the purest of intentions, Nefret, even if Pah did, it would not be enough. Ambitious men would always seek to divide you, and that would further divide the clan."

To Father she said, "Have you forgotten the bird, Semkah?"

"No, I haven't, and I remember that it died at your hands."

Farrah didn't flinch. "If you want them to live, it must be this way."

He did not answer. Wisely, his brother kept his peace while the Council agreed that these trials would follow the Old Ways.

I could do nothing to prevent it. Never had I felt so alone.

Chapter Four

The Trials—Nefret

"Now that you know what is at stake, perhaps you will take these trials more seriously. There will be three tests. You must pass all three, and the mekhma will win at least two. It is now that we ask your blood kin to leave us. No one shall influence the outcome of these trials." Without a question, our father, uncle and cousins left us with the six members of the Council and the two acolytes. I wanted to run after Father, but he offered me no solace; he did not meet my gaze or say a word to us. Even if I withdrew from the trials, it would do me no good. I had cast incense into the fire and released my soul to reach its destiny. Whether it would be here or somewhere else, I did not know.

"The mekhma is more than merely a queen. She is the keeper of the clan's stories—and its secret." It was Orba who spoke to us now. He was the youngest person on the Council and also generally the quietest. Small of frame with very little hair, he rarely appeared in public. "As our leader, you must know our stories, for they are a part of us. The mekhma is the keeper of stories. For this first trial, you will tell us a story. Who will go first?"

Pah spoke before me. "I shall go first. I am the oldest."

Farrah laughed at her. "How do you know this? I was there when you were born. Was it your head or your hand that emerged first from your mother's womb?" Pah looked confused. She had established herself as the oldest early in our childhood. I hadn't thought to argue with her.

Stunned into silence, Pah said nothing else. Orba spoke again, "Very well, Pah. You may go first." For the first time in our trials, Pah glanced at me, her head down, an unsure look upon her face. That was a rare thing to see, but it did not fill me with joy as I was sure it would have if the tables were turned. Was it true? Was I the oldest?

To everyone's surprise I said, "Please. I will go first, Orba."

With wide eyes the man looked at Farrah, who glanced about the tent. Nobody disagreed, and he gave his consent. Pah said nothing as I stood…

My mind raced—what story should I tell? The only one I could think of was the story of Zerzura. I took a deep breath and began.

"Hear me then, wise ones. Hear the story of Ma, the brave young man who, during the Times of Storms, led the people out of the dying desert to the abandoned White City of Zerzura.

"Once, the beautiful city had been home to the fair-skinned giants, the Nephal, but these giants had angered a powerful god. For crimes forgotten by men, the Nephal were cast out of Zerzura by the Unknown God after falling to his victorious arm in a great battle. The offended god cast them into a place beyond seeing. Ages would pass before another living thing walked on the streets of that city.

"For many seasons the Meshwesh endured the vicious sandstorms, the most ferocious the desert people had ever seen. The blasting red sands killed the livestock, destroyed the fruits and trees and stole the lives of many Treasures of the Tribe. Such a heartbreaking time has never since been known by our people.

"Desperate to find a place of refuge for the Meshwesh, Ma did the unthinkable; he stood before the white walls of Zerzura and prayed to the Unknown God. He begged the deity to allow him to take the city, to claim it for his own so his people would have shelter from the blasting sands. After he prayed, Ma looked up to see a Heret falcon watching him from the gate post. It observed Ma for a few minutes and then flew to take its spot atop the tallest tower in the city. All who had been reluctant to follow Ma now changed their minds—this was a sign! Ma led the Meshwesh into Zerzura and claimed it as his own.

I licked my lips and continued with my story.

"The Meshwesh rejoiced! They found refuge from the crushing sands and the relentless heat. Never again, they vowed. Never would they pack up their tents. Zerzura, the city nestled safely in the hills of the wilderness, would always be theirs. The giants who built the city had done so with skill—Ma knew the place would stand for a thousand years. Many fountains, patches of green grass and even orchards were contained within the city walls; there was more than enough to keep everyone happy. Many great houses stood empty, the beautiful artwork still perfectly painted

on the walls. Scattered throughout the city and along the prome-nade were massive marble columns with intricate carvings. It was a rich place—even the bedchambers of the smaller homes were like lavish palaces to the Meshwesh. Ma and his warriors found an arsenal of weapons, some of which no man had ever laid eyes upon. He even found a great library, but many of the scrolls were written in a language he did not know.

"One such scroll had an unusual script that glowed in the moon-light. Ma and his wife, Sela, became obsessed with the scroll—they were convinced it would lead them to an undiscovered treas-ure.

"Some on the Council warned Ma and Sela against pursuing the knowledge of the scroll, but they would not heed this admonition. Ma called together the wisest members of his tribe and consulted the traders who came to visit Zerzura until he found one who could read the words. Finally they had their answer!

"'Beware the Lightning Gate! Moonlight opens the door, but a woman holds the key.'

"These were the words of the scroll. Ma trembled with fear at the warning, but his wife was intrigued. Some say that Sela had been enchanted by the scroll itself, that the words wove a spell around her heart. From that day forward, she no longer loved her hus-band or her tribe. The Council decided that the scroll referred to the western gate, which was flanked by unusual stones cut in the shape of lightning bolts. Every night the door would be shut, and no woman would be able to pass through the gate until sunup for fear of whatever door would be opened.

"For many years, nothing happened. All was well in Zerzura—it had truly become home to the Meshwesh, who thrived in the White City. Traders from around the desert came to see the great place. But in Sela's heart, all was not well. She had spent much of her time learning the language of the scroll. She found other scrolls to read until she spent every day in the library, forgetting her hus-band and children.

"One night, Ma's wife had a dream. A handsome man with pale skin and silver hair appeared to her. He rode the moonlight into her chambers and told her that her beauty had drawn him to her

and that her knowledge of his language impressed him. Eventually, he revealed himself as the true king of Zerzura. He told her a woeful story of his wrongful imprisonment, of an unjust god, and how he deeply longed to walk through the White City, how he ached to hold her in his arms so she could become the true queen of Zerzura.

"Night after night the Moonbeam King, as Sela came to call him, visited her in dreams. He praised her beauty and confessed his love for her, even as Ma slept beside her. One night, the man told Sela how to set him free from his prison. She had to walk through the gate when the moon was full and whisper his name.

"The man told her his name, but he also commanded her to tell no one else. Revealing his secret name would mean death for her. Ecstatically, Sela hatched a plan. One night when the city was full of foreign traders, she would shed her queenly robes and breach the gate dressed as a man. Her handmaiden and confidante, Niri-ka, begged her mistress to change her mind. She reminded her that her husband loved her, but Sela was determined. Obediently, Niri-ka helped Sela slip out of her chambers, out of the palace and down to the courtyard. She passed easily through Zerzura to the Lightning Gate and made her way to the edge of the city. Nobody stopped her. Niri-ka watched in amazement as her mistress walked calmly past the guards. She watched when the queen passed through the gate, unveiled herself and called out the name of the Moonbeam King.

"Suddenly a powerful light shone on the other side of the Lightning Gate! It was so bright that it nearly blinded all the guards who kept the gate. Sela's garments flowed behind her as an evil wind began to blow into Zerzura. The man with the silver hair and pale skin walked toward the gate, and behind him were six giants of angry countenance. The silver man scooped up Sela as easily as he would a child and cut her throat with his sword before the guards could rescue her. She had been warned not to reveal his name, but she had not obeyed. In a panic, Niri-ka ran back to the palace to tell Ma what had happened. Ma and his warriors raced to the arsenal and charged to meet the unearthly foes. Ma fought bravely, but the giants overwhelmed the Meshwesh and killed many of the king's warriors.

"Niri-ka watched in horror. In the melee of swords and arrows, a tiny green Bee-Eater flew down and sat upon the Lightning Gate. It turned his head and stared at her. Despite her fear, she felt compelled to follow the bird. She walked through the scuffle, seemingly unseen. Giants and Meshwesh were all around her, but all she could see was the gate and the bird; it was always watching, coaxing her along. As she walked toward the gate, Niri-ka understood what she had to do. It was a woman who had released the Nephal, and it would be a woman who put them back into their prison. Niri-ka stepped through the gate. Her unfaithful mistress had told her the Moonbeam King's name, and now Niri-ka called to him, commanding him to leave Zerzura forever.

"The Moonbeam King and the giants dropped their weapons. They raged and cursed the Meshwesh but could not fight the invisible force that pulled them to the gate. The light once again blasted from the gate, and suddenly they were gone. Thanks to Niri-ka, the Meshwesh had been saved! Ma married Niri-ka, and the Meshwesh were happy once again."

I paused for a moment to catch my breath before continuing.

"Until many generations later...one night the Nephal poured through the Lightning Gate, and this time there was no woman's voice to send them back. No one knows who would have done such a thing—anyone who knew the name of the Moonbeam King was long dead. That night, giants stampeded through the city, shaking the ground as they ran, killing everyone in their path. They took back Zerzura with a white-hot rage. The Meshwesh fled the city and ran far into the desert. They watched the fires turn the White City black and listened with breaking hearts to the screams of the unlucky ones who had not escaped. The sounds of despair filled the night air. Onesu, their king, tried to comfort his people even though his young wife Ze had not escaped.

"As they wept and watched, one of the wise women rose up amongst them and prophesied that one day a mekhma, a woman of strength and power, would take back the city and exact vengeance on the evil giants and their pale leader. So has been the hope of the clan for all these years." That was the end of the story, but passionately I added, *"One day, we will take back Zerzura, banish*

*the giants and bring the Lightning Gate down so that never again
will we lose our home."*

The Council had kept their silence the entire time, but now I could
see the shimmers of tears in their eyes. They were moved, touched
by the story—even Pah appeared transfixed. Nobody spoke, nobody moved. Only Mina smiled, and I took my seat beside my
sister. The brazier in front of us sputtered, and the flame burned
white.

Pah stood and began her story. She told the Story of the Bee-Eater
and how it came to be the tribe's second symbol. I knew Pah hated storytelling. She would rather sulk than speak, but she told the
story flawlessly, remembering to use her movements and facial
expressions perfectly, as if she had told it a hundred times before.
I listened respectfully and sat quietly even when she struggled to
remember a point here or there.

When her story had ended, Pah returned to her kneeling position.
The gathering did not cry as they had during my turn, but I could
see they were impressed with Pah's retelling. They said as much
as they complimented us on our recitations and our passion for the
tribe's history.

"Now we must decide who won this trial. Let us pray to our ancestors to guide us." Obediently, we bowed our heads as Farrah
entreated our foremothers and forefathers to guide their decision.
When her pleas were completed, she gave instructions. "Pah, Nefret. Go now and stand by the doorway, one on either side. Hold
out your hands, for each of us has a coin to give. Whichever
daughter leaves with the most coins has won this trial. Whether
you win or lose, save those coins. If you lose the trials you will
need the coins for your journey. We will break our fast now but
return this evening before the sun disappears into the sand."

We rose and did as we were told. My throat felt tired, and my
thirst increased by the minute, but I held out my hands obediently.
The Council members walked toward us, each holding a shiny
gold coin in his or her hand. First in line was Farrah, her majestic
gray and white robes hanging elegantly from her tall, thin body.
She paused and looked at both of us before dropping her coin in
my hand. I felt Pah's eyes upon me as all the Council members
but one deposited their coins in my hands. Orba had decided

against me and for Pah; I nodded politely as he left us. We were alone with only Mina and one other acolyte to attend us.

I clutched the coins in one hand. Feeling uncomfortable and hoping to make peace I said, "What if I were to give you these coins, Pah? Would it make a difference? What if I let you win? What would you say to that?"

Without warning, Pah slapped me. My skin radiated heat from the stinging strike, and my coins fell out of my hand. They made a dull sound as they fell on the thick carpet. Instinctively, I stepped back from her in case she struck me again. I had never been hit before, except on the practice field when we were children, learning the ways of the maiden warriors. Those strikes had not been deliberate, but this one was—and it struck right at my heart.

"I want nothing from you, Nefret! Nothing! Everything I have ever received has been at my own hands. I am not Father's favorite, nor do I hold Alexio's heart in my hand—I am not the tribe's treasure or the children's savior. I am Pah! I am the mekhma!" Her voice rang loudly in my ears. "I will *earn* my right to be called such. You cannot give that to me. It is not within your power! Queen's blood is in my veins too. Would you like to see it?"

Pah showed me her wrist and drew a small circular blade from her waist. My eyes widened, and I shook my head quickly.

"Are you sure?"

I shook my head over and over, clutching my face where she'd struck me. The shock of the assault had surprised me enough to stun me silent.

Mina did not speak, but she came to me and took my hand. She shook her head at Pah and defiantly stood between us. Pah snorted at me derisively and said, "I will win this, and you will leave. Save yourself some embarrassment if that is possible. Leave now, Nefret. I am telling you, you should leave now! If you do not, you will always regret it." I felt a slight shift in the air around us. It was as if in the otherworld, the words had been repeated, written down forever in eternity's library. With a wave of her hand she stormed out, leaving me gaping after her.

Mina picked up the coins and placed them in my hands, folding my fingers over them. She leaned forward, and I thought she would break her vow and speak to me. She had done so earlier when she sang for us; perhaps she was allowed to sing for us. I didn't know. Nevertheless, she did not speak to me now. She leaned her forehead against mine and hummed a haunting tune that I didn't remember but certainly felt as if I knew. It comforted me. She swayed to the sound of her song and gathered me into her arms. It reminded me of the mother I had never known. I laid my head on her shoulder. All of the fear, the grief, the uncertainty erupted into sobs. I cried until I could not cry anymore. When I was done, she took me by the hand and led me to the door. With a kind smile she left, and I walked out behind her.

"Nefret, your tent is this way." Alexio waited for me outside. I stumbled, making the coins jingle in my pocket as I walked behind him. I hoped no one stopped me—I wanted no one to see my sister's handprint on my face.

"Wait. Where are we going?"

"I am taking you to your new tent. Pah remains in your old one."

I had forgotten about that. For the first time in my life I would spend the night by myself. Thankfully, my friend did not interrogate me or scold me as he had earlier. The camp was quiet, much quieter than it had been just a short time ago. People moved out of the way as we walked through the short grass to my new home, for however long that might be. No matter what had happened today, I did not believe that I would win. In my heart of hearts, I truly did not. Pah was the better warrior, the bravest, the most determined. I could tell a good story and had some skill with a bow, but that was it. What was I thinking?

I did not linger outside the tent. I was anxious to be alone, away from the curious eyes of my people—and Alexio. "Thank you," I muttered as I slipped inside. My new tent was smaller than the one I had shared with my sister, but it was no less comfortable. Someone, no several someones, had been very busy making everything tidy for me. Suddenly, I remembered my treasure and ran to the neat pile of my personal belongings. Reaching for my mother's robe with shaking fingers, I untied the cord that I had bound it with. The necklace tumbled out of the sumptuous fabric and into my hands. Nobody had found it! I clutched it close; the metal felt cool and then warmed under my touch. So unusual, so rare. I couldn't help but wonder what treasure this was—perhaps it had magical powers. Adding my coins to the robe, I placed the necklace back inside and rolled it up again.

I collapsed on my cool blanket and rolled on my back, closing my eyes. Today seemed like a nightmare. If I tried hard enough, perhaps I would wake up. I rolled over on my side; my eyes felt heavy and soon I fell asleep.

I dreamed that I was in Zerzura. At least I thought it was Zerzura.

I wore white sandals and anklets of gold. I walked through the streets of the city, the walls white and shining bright in the morning sun. I heard the happy chants of my people saying, "Bless our mekhma! She is our treasure!" I felt a cascade of flower petals falling upon me as people tossed basketfuls of scented blooms down from structures high above me. I had never seen such a place! What walls! Surely giants had built these! The flowers tickled my face, and I brushed at them with my hand…I awoke in my own tent. Hanging above me, secreted in the cedar timbers that supported my tent, was a cluster of purple flowers. The petals had fallen onto my face as I slept.

Alexio! He must have hung them there when the tent was constructed. I smiled at the sight—what a thoughtful gift!

Someone must have visited me while I slept because a tray of bread, cheese, fruits and a pitcher of clear water waited for me on a nearby table. I ate hungrily, toying with the flower petals and daydreaming about life as Alexio's wife. It could never be; he was pledged to serve his tribe as husband to Farafra. I would serve my destiny in my own way, whether here or cast out in the sand sea. A lump rose in my throat as I devoured the warm, chewy bread and gulped down the water.

"It's time, Nefret. The trials continue." I looked up to see Alexio at the door of my tent.

"Have you heard? We will follow the Old Ways."

He nodded and strode toward me, his arms outstretched. I stood and fell into them. I didn't cry or make a sound. I clung to him like I was standing in quicksand and he was the only thing that could save me. We were so close; I could feel his heart beating through his tunic.

"You must win, Nefer-nefer." I smiled at hearing him use the name only he called me. "You have to win." Never had he hugged me so. In fact, we rarely touched, much less hugged. It was a bittersweet moment, to be so close to one destiny but commanded to seek another.

Alexio had been right all along. Pah was lost to me. I had to fight, not because I wanted my sister to lose but because I wanted to live. She had made it clear that she did not want any help from me. So be it. The gods would have their way after all, and there was nothing I could do about it.

Chapter Five

The Painted Stones—Nefret

I stepped away from Alexio, straightened my clothing and poured some water in a shallow bowl. I washed my face and patted it with a towel. "Are they all there?"

"Yes, all but you and your sister."

"Very well. Let's go." I ducked out of my tent and held my head high as we walked back through the crowd. Apparently, word that the loser would be banished had traveled around the camp. Even my children had gathered to see me. I smiled at them as they whispered, "Mekhma Nefret." No sense in playing coy now. I had won the first trial, and now I faced the second.

I wondered what the trial would be, but I did not bother to ask Alexio. He would not know, and I was not in the mood to speculate. As we approached the tent, the guards stepped out of the way and pulled back the flap for me. Alexio did not follow me in. Pah sat where she had sat before, her hands resting perfectly in her lap. I quickly sat beside her and faced the Council. I noticed that our father had not returned to the proceedings, which unsettled me.

Orba said, "Welcome back, daughters of Semkah. Let us proceed with our matter. Today you will show us your skills in intuition and strength. Before each of you is a row of stones." Mina removed the linen cloth to reveal the carefully arranged stones. There were seven in each row, each round and smooth. He continued, "There are times when a mekhma must rely upon her intuition alone. She should be strong and confident in her decision-making. She must also be able to speak to the gods to search out a matter and choose wisely. You have the same number of stones in front of you; each set has three stones with painted symbols on the bottoms. Each of you will take a turn uncovering the stones until one of you reveals all three of your symbols. You must prove the strength of your connection to the gods—and your intuition. Since Nefret went first the last time, Pah, you will go first now."

Looking confident, Pah nodded. She had changed her garments and unbound her hair; her long auburn tresses flowed behind her like a shimmering copper waterfall. She bowed down on the carpet, just as I had seen her do each night as she prayed to her many beloved deities. As she did so, I studied the rocks, looking for clues but seeing none. Finally Pah rose and selected a rock. She turned it over to reveal a red painted figure. She cast a sidelong glance at me, and I could see a smile curl on her lips.

How could I win this trial? I never prayed! Not to gods or ancestors; I sometimes talked to my mother, but she never spoke to me. I only worshiped when the tribe did. I had no connection to any god, nor would I pretend now that I did. It appeared as if my rebellious heart would cost me more than I could have imagined. Biting my lip, I stared at the stones and turned one over. Nothing. My heart sank.

My sister bowed herself to the ground again and entreated Hathor to guide her this time. She rose and selected another rock, which showed another red figure. Raising the rock over her head, she laughed. Apparently, the gods and goddesses were aligned against me. All eyes were on me as I stared at the stones. Looking at each one, I listened to my inner voice this time and finally decided on a stone. I guessed correctly, which surprised even me. I tossed the rock over and kept my focus on the remaining rocks.

Pah did not bow or beseech her deity aloud this time. She closed her eyes, and her upper body swayed slightly as if she were under some kind of spell or hearing music that no one else could hear. This continued for at least a full minute, but no one said anything to her. Stone-faced, the Council waited patiently for the annimekhma to make her decision. A cold shiver ran down my spine. Finally, with a dramatic nod of acknowledgement to some unseen voice, she reached for a rock and showed it to the Council. So confident was she that she did not even look—she flashed a joyous smile. When the Council did not applaud she turned the rock over to see for herself. The stone had nothing on it! Pah appeared confused and angry. She tossed the rock to the ground and glared at me as if I had something to do with her results.

My hand flew to my heart as the seriousness of the moment overwhelmed me. Calling upon my intuition, I studied the surfaces of the stones. Again, they gave me no clue. I reached for one but felt an unexpected disquiet rise in my spirit. No. Not that one. I touched the stone directly in front of me. No affirmation came, but no warning arose either. Holding my breath, I picked it up and turned it over to see my results. I did it! The Council politely gave their approval, and then their attention refocused on my sister.

Pah again began to pray and beseech Hathor for guidance. Less confident now, she ran her hands along the row of stones as if she could detect their undersides with just her palm. With a cool smile she touched a stone and flipped it over. Nothing! It was bare! Shocked, I turned my attention back to the stones. I did not pray aloud, but my mind pleaded for help.

I am Nefret, daughter of Kadeema and Semkah. If you ever loved me or cared for me, help me now...

Time seemed to slow as I stared at each stone. I reached for one and heard a small, still voice speak in my head.

No!

I drew my hand back with a gasp.

With shaking fingers I reached toward the next stone.

NO! I heard again, louder this time. I was surprised that no one else could hear the voice. Withdrawing my hand, I reached for the last stone in the row and heard nothing. Not a whisper. I picked it up and stared at the bottom. The sign of the Dancing Man was painted there, and I turned the stone around to show it to the Council. With loud trills and whistles, they celebrated. I won another round of the trials! Pah's face was like glass, hard and unmoving. I knew underneath her mask she fumed. I knew her too well to think otherwise, but the knowledge did not bring me joy.

"Come now." Farrah rose from the carpet and beckoned us to follow her. "Let us see who is the strongest. This trial is not over yet, Pah, Nefret. The tribe is waiting."

Without a word of congratulations or anything else, Pah stepped in front of me and followed Farrah and the Council out of the tent. I heard someone call, "Nefret has won the round!" I tried not to smile at our father, who lined the path with the other members of our tribe. Some shouted Pah's name, and others shouted mine, but our father looked sad. I had not thought much about it before, but Father would lose no matter who won. He was not an affectionate man, not as some fathers were, but at times he spoke kindly to us and often gave us gifts. Some of the older women said that when

Kadeema disappeared, she took all of his love with her. I did not know what to believe. Pah had the idea that Father loved me more, but in that she was wrong. I was sure of it.

Now, Father looked more distressed than I ever remembered. One daughter would be cast out of the tribe—for the first time, I selfishly hoped it wasn't me. I kept my head down and followed behind Pah.

We stopped at the end of the camp. Someone had set up an array of short spears, and two bows with quivers full of arrows lay on the ground. I recognized my bow immediately, and seeing it made me more confident.

"Daughters of the tribe, Pah and Nefret. We thank you for your willingness to prove yourselves worthy to be mekhma. You honor us. Now, show us your strength!" The crowd cheered for us, and the Council clapped respectfully. Without an argument about who would go first, Pah walked to the edge of the prepared field and waved at the viewers. They clapped for her, women trilled and children chanted her name. Aitnu, the tribe's most prominent warrior, walked to her and gave her instructions. Alexio stood near me at the edge of the crowd. Our eyes did not meet, but his presence encouraged me.

Poised and confident, Pah picked up the short spear. Without much effort she adjusted her grip and walked back from the target. Like a dancer, she stepped and spun, sending the spear soundly to its mark. The gathering clapped in admiration, tambourines shook and music played. Pah's beautiful hair shimmered as she reached for another spear from the stand. Her lovely face revealed nothing, but I knew she was pleased with her performance. If I had not been her opponent, I would have cheered for her too.

This time, Pah walked further away from the target. The crowd whispered, and Aitnu appeared unhappy. My sister was obviously not following instructions. Even for Pah, this would be no easy shot. Again, she spun on her strong legs and lunged, sending the spear down the track. I watched the gleaming wood flash in the sun as it pierced the massive sandbag. More cheers for Pah erupted as she removed the last spear from the stand. She walked to the end of the path, which was marked with a bright flag. Playfully, she balanced the spear in her hand and walked back even further.

She was showing off, showing our tribe that she was the stronger sister, the braver one, the more daring of the two of us. I could have told her she need not have worried. Everyone already knew that Pah was stronger than me. The crowd whispered; I could not hear what they said, but I knew they were impressed.

She spun about, stepped twice and threw her body forward, sending the spear toward its intended mark. The spear arced and sailed through the air, falling a few feet in front of the target. She missed! Nobody clapped, but I had no illusions about what happened. I glanced at Alexio. He gave me a resolute stare, and I got the message.

"Nicely done, sister," I said as she passed me.

"Good luck to you, Nefret," she purred proudly. I waited as the son of Aitnu retrieved the thrown spears and returned them to their stand.

My palms were sweaty as soon as I picked up the spear. It was not my weapon of choice, and it felt heavy and clunky in my hand. Nevertheless, I walked to the marker and stood staring at the target, which seemed to rest on the other side of the desert. Gripping the weapon, I ran back and then forward two steps, arched my back and released the spear into the sky. It whizzed to the target and hit it near the bottom. My throwing technique was not as efficient as Pah's, and I had no dancing skills, but I could do this. If I stayed focused and didn't attempt fancy shots as my sister had, I could at least finish without shaming our father.

Tambourines shook, and some of my tribe supported me with cheers and applause. Especially vocal were my children, led by Paimu. With a sigh of relief, I picked up the second spear and walked back to the throwing line. I spoke to that inner voice again: *Help me!* I heard nothing and decided that what I had heard earlier was my own imagination. The setting sun cast vivid colors on the horizon, and time slipped by as I gauged the target again. I stepped back, then forward, arched my back and threw. I gasped as the spear blew past the target and landed with a thud in the sand. The crowd grew quiet, and I did not wait for their applause for none would be coming. With the last spear in my hand, I walked back to the line. I tucked a wayward strand of hair behind my ear, stepped back, then forward using the strength of my whole body to launch the spear this time. This time the spear landed in the center of the sandbag, and my tribe cheered with excitement. I tried not to look but stole another glance at Alexio, who smiled at me. I noticed that Aitnu hung close by my sister and whispered to her as she watched me. She nodded her head and frowned.

Farrah announced, "This round has ended in a tie!" She clapped, her colorful bracelets rattling. She raised her hands, encouraging the crowd to cheer loudly for the anni-mekhmas. "Now we shall watch as the daughters of Semkah show us the power of their bows!" More applause erupted from the gathering as my sister and I took our spots on the line.

"Do you think you have a chance at beating me?" Pah taunted me quietly as we stood side by side strapping on our quivers. I nocked an arrow, released it and watched it zip to the sandbag.

"Yes, I do. You are a show-off, Pah. You make mistakes."

She hissed at me and followed my arrow with one of her own. There were seven arrows in each of our quivers; for each pull of my bow, Pah matched me perfectly. No arrows missed. No arrows fell short. When the first round was spent, Aitnu instructed us to walk back and refire our refreshed arsenal. It would make the trial more challenging, but I felt confident that I could manage the distance. My arms began to burn a little as I took shot after shot at the sandbags. Pah and I did not miss a shot.

"It is clear that the daughters of Semkah are both strong women," Farrah said to the crowd. "But now we shall see another demonstration. Aitnu, prepare to release the birds. Now, Pah and Nefret, show us again your skill with the bow. The first to strike the bird with an arrow will win this round."

Pah's face crumpled. She cared nothing for children and had even less care for adults, but birds she loved with all her being. How many wounded birds had she healed, with help from Father? Even now she had a cage of tiny songbirds in her tent. At times it seemed as if she spoke their language. Aitnu's son handed us a fresh batch of arrows. These were longer, with shorter tufts of feathers that would help the arrow scurry along to its intended victim. My arrows had bright red feathers and Pah's were blue, presumably to help the Council determine who delivered the winning shot if there was any question. I hoped that if I was lucky enough to strike a bird it would die quickly and not suffer.

Two men carried a rattan basket of birds to the sandbags. We nocked our arrows and raised our bows to the sky waiting for the birds' release. Aitnu watched us and gave the signal to the men, who then released the birds. I shot first, and the arrow narrowly missed a darting wren. Darkness encroached on the tournament, so I quickly lined up another shot as Pah took hers. With precision her arrow whizzed through the air and struck a less fortunate wren, which immediately tumbled to the ground. Today's contest had finally ended with Pah as the victor.

The tribe applauded and cheered for Pah, and her sadness quickly disappeared. I stepped out of the way as the people clamored around her. Some were polite enough to congratulate me as well, but it was Pah's performance that most impressed them. I left the crowd behind hoping to find some food and somewhere to think about what had happened and what would come next.

"Nefret! Wait," Father called to me. Tired and sweaty, I did as he asked.

"You did well. You should be proud of your performance—I am." He put his hand on my shoulder and looked me right in the eyes.

"Thank you, Father," I murmured. He hugged me, which was a strange experience. Savoring the moment, I closed my eyes and clutched my quiver and bow. When I opened my eyes, I saw Pah staring at me from the center of the cheering crowd, her green eyes flashing angrily. Before I could say her name she stormed away, a retinue of young men and women clustered around her. I sighed and our father grasped my arms gently.

"We will talk tomorrow. I must go find your sister now. Rest well, for tomorrow's trial will require all your skill and strength. That is all I can tell you."

"Thank you, Father. I will." We parted ways, and I walked back to my tent with Paimu dashing to my side.

"Princess, you almost won. I cheered for you! But it is no matter, for you won the other challenges. Just one more now!"

I smiled down at her. "Yes, just one more." She hugged my leg and raced away. "Where are you off to now?" I called after her.

"I am going to get my things."

"Why? Where are you going?"

"With you! I am moving in to your tent now."

I laughed. "Of course you are. Go get your things." Her beautiful smile spread across her face, showing her missing front tooth and otherwise perfectly white teeth.

This could be my last night with my tribe. I should spend it with someone who loves me.

Chapter Six

Treasures of the Tribe—Nefret

The Council dispatched a guard to stand at the door of my tent. My guard, a young man named Essa, surprised me by calling me outside. With a confident, over-friendly smile, he let me know that he had been sent for my security. I could not discern if there was some unknown threat that warranted such an action or if he was meant to keep me from running away, but I didn't ask him any questions.

Awareness crept over me. Now I clearly knew that I wanted to be mekhma, to serve my people, to protect Paimu, to lead us all back to Zerzura and take back what was ours. I did not discern the exact moment that this occurred, but my heart had indeed changed.

Singing to myself, I removed my tunic and washed my body with the scented water Farrah had so graciously provided for me. It had been a kind gesture, and I half wondered if Pah was being treated so royally. I had a lavish buffet of the tribe's best food on my cedar table, and my pitcher was full of sweet pomegranate wine—a truly thoughtful gift. The servant who had brought them was not a man I recognized, but I accepted them graciously. I was dressing for bed and thinking of pouring some wine when a scream outside my tent startled me out of my song. I ran to the sound, the voice of a young girl—Paimu! Essa had restrained her, holding her by her skinny arms and laughing at her as she struggled against him. I wanted to slap him in his pretty face.

"Let me go! Let me go! Nefret!"

"Stop that! Essa—what do you think you are doing? Turn her loose!"

Essa laughed, and his shoulder-length dark hair half hid his perfect nose and wide, dark eyes. "If I do, she may bite me, anni-mekhma."

"Nonsense. Let her go now. I command it."

He released her and lifted his hands in a gesture of surrender. Paimu kicked his shin, and he laughed again as he hobbled away from her. "She can't be here, anni- mekhma! The Council has given strict orders that both you and your sister are not to be disturbed or have any visitors. You should rest because tomorrow's trial will be grueling."

Paimu pushed past him and into my tent. He reached for her, but I stepped in his way, unaware that my bare shoulder was showing. He stared at it as if he had never seen a bare shoulder before. Maybe he hadn't. Suddenly, I blushed and covered my shoulder with the loose robe.

"Paimu is my guest. I have taken care of her all her life. I am not going to abandon her tonight just because the Council wants to keep me away from everyone. She has no one but me."

"I only want to be obedient to the Council—and to serve you, Nefret." He stepped toward me. He towered over me by at least a foot and a half. Essa had a fine, strong body, as far as I could tell, and I could see his face had softened as he looked into mine. No woman could deny that Essa was the most beautiful man in the Meshwesh or any other Red Lands clan—even Alexio paled in comparison to him for physical beauty. In a whisper he said, "What if I could arrange for us to be alone later? Would that interest you? You are a beautiful woman, Nefret, and I find you…" He lifted a strand of hair from my face and touched my cheek briefly. "I watched you every day and hoped you would see me. Am I not appealing to you?"

"I think the heat has gone to your brain, Essa." I stepped away from his friendly hands and seductive eyes. "Go take a few draughts of water to clear your head." I stepped backward and nearly tripped. It was dangerous being too close to him, under the stars, with my skin perfumed with exotic scents.

Suddenly the truth occurred to me. *This was a test! A test set by Farrah! She seeks to prove my virtue!*

I smiled and stepped back again. "I am going inside my tent now with Paimu. If the Old One wants to speak to me, I will be here. Please do not come in unless I ask you to. Thank you, Essa."

I walked inside and found Paimu still whimpering about her arm. She reached for the wine, but I forbade her to drink it. What if it had a love potion in it? I took the pitcher outside and poured it in the sand right in front of Essa. I wanted him to know that I knew what he was up to. The Council would test me, would they? Well, let them! I would not fail this particular test. I shook out the last drops of the wine and stared at the mess it left behind. It looked like blood poured out on the sand.

"What are you doing?" Essa demanded. His seductive attitude had vanished like smoke in the wind.

Farrah, whose tent was only a few feet away from me, walked outside, her scarf covering her head. It was common knowledge that she spent her evenings wandering the desert looking for signs and portents. I supposed she was headed out for just such a walk now. She stared at the red sand and then at me. Essa walked away, embarrassed, but Farrah smiled as if to say, "Ah, you passed the test." With a nod and a quick scan of the heavens, the old woman walked down the path and out of the camp. If I followed her, what I would see?

I snickered thinking of how Pah might have done with her test, if she'd had a similar one. I wondered who they would send to tempt her. *Oh no! Alexio! Please, my ancestors, do not let it be Alexio! He is not for her!*

I walked back inside and found that Paimu had made her bed right beside mine. I recognized the familiar sapphire silk blanket I had given her, some of my old tunics from when I was a child and the soft white leather sandals a friend of mine had made for Paimu. Reaching for my hairbrush, I cajoled her into letting me brush her hair. She complied and even allowed me to make a small braid and cinch it with a piece of white leather. She looked one hundred percent better, and I told her so. Handing her the dull mirror, she gave herself a gap-toothed smile.

"Eat, Paimu, and then we will go to bed. Have you washed your hands and feet?"

"No, but I am not dirty."

I popped her bottom playfully. "Let us see them. Oh my." I pretended to be shocked. "Those are so dirty, we could plant flowers with them. Let's wash the sand away, if you don't mind."

She giggled and allowed me to help her. She could do it all herself, but what if this was indeed the last time that I would be able to do such a thing? How was I ever going to leave her? My own heart? I loved Paimu—she was the little sister I never had. Perhaps that was why Pah hated her so much. Who knew?

Pah is lost to you, Nefret.

I could hear Alexio's voice ringing in my ear. Alexio! I would have to see him, somehow. Essa had stormed off, but knowing Farrah she would have him back here in a few minutes, if nothing else to save face and demand that he actually "protect" me from whatever dangers she imagined I faced.

After her bird bath, Paimu talked animatedly about the contest and how she could climb a tree now without any help. "When all this is over, you can show me again." She nibbled on the chula bread, dipping it in olive oil and pepper sauce before gobbling it up. Once she finished off the chula, she devoured the olives and the dates. I thought she would be sick if she didn't slow down and told her as much. "Oh, I never get sick. Never. One time I ate an entire pat of goat cheese without anyone to help me. I did not get sick at all."

"Don't you miss staying with Ziza?"

"Ziza has her sister, and I have you."

"Yes, but it's only one night, little one. I don't know what tomorrow may bring. If anything were to happen to me, return to Ziza's family. Her mother loves you."

At long last, Paimu stopped eating. Her wide eyes were full of tears. "You cannot go! Please do not leave me. I will have no one if I do not have you." Her smile disappeared, and her face contorted into a sob.

"Paimu, you must be brave. I have to make myself be brave, believe me, but I am trying. You try too. Be my sister, be my brave sister. No matter what the gods have ordained for us, we will meet it bravely and with kindness to others." I held my arms out to her, and she cried on my shoulder. I scooped her up and carried her to the bed. We lay down together and I held her while she cried herself to sleep.

Silent tears slid down my face too. Some tears were for Pah, my first friend and twin sister. I cried for the sweet girl I knew, the one that was hidden under layers of bitterness and imagined offense. I cried for our childhood that had been far too brief, and then I cried because one of us would leave and we would never see each other again. Then my tears were for Paimu. Eventually the tears subsided and I covered Paimu with the thick quilt, and soon I was sleepy too. I hadn't meant to cry; now I felt empty, tired. As I closed my eyes, within seconds I traveled to the dream world...

My heart pounded and my bare feet stomped on the cool stones as I ran through a narrow entrance inside a series of stone walls. Someone ran behind me, but I dared not look back. Up ahead I saw a flicker of flame; the light pierced the darkness and beckoned me to safety. My image and that of my husband mocked me from the painted walls that surrounded me. My long hair streamed behind me, and I felt naked in the thin white gown I wore. Gold cuffs were at my wrists and a heavy necklace thumped on my chest as I bolted toward the light. The sound of sliding stone came from behind me, and a thunderous shake followed. Trapped! I am trapped! I spun about to see a small child, a boy with red hair and dark eyes, reaching for me. I grabbed his hand and we continued to run with all our might to the light ahead of us.

Almost there...Run, Smenkhkare!

We turned the corner. The light was just a few feet away and moving...

I awoke with a start, immediately aware that someone else was in the tent with Paimu and me. She slept peacefully beside me, unaware of my terror and overwhelming anxiety. I peered into the darkness, wondering if perhaps an assassin had come to take my life. It had been several years since our camp had been raided by cutthroats, but it had happened many times in the past. I slid my hand under my pillow and felt for the small blade I kept there. In a panic, I remembered that I had taken no such preparations in my new tent. I sat up slowly, peering into the black.

A flicker of light appeared in the corner of the room. It bounced and expanded until it was the size of a man's fist. My breath caught in my chest as I froze, mesmerized by the sight. The light flickered again and expanded to the size of my shield, which lay on the other side of the tent along with my arrows and bow. Suddenly, the light blast brightly, so much so that I had to shield my eyes with my hands.

Fear washed over me and I fell to the ground on my face, unable to look at the increasing light. I remained in that position for an unknown length of time.

I heard a warm voice say, *"Do not be afraid."* At his words, the uncontrollable fear lifted, and I cautiously raised my eyes. A man wrapped in white fire hovered in the corner of my tent, his face obscured by the radiance. The light pulsed once and then dimmed, but his face remained hidden in the moving light.

"My lord, who are you? Why are you here?"

"I am known by many names, but none that you would know." The light decreased in brilliance, but I still could not see his face. *"I would make myself known to you."*

"I do not understand."

"Peace, daughter of the Red Lands. You will understand. It is I who leads you. Even now I lead, but will you follow? Even when you cannot see the way? Will you trust me even when you cannot see me? When all others turn against you?"

"Yes, lord. I will."

I had no idea what I had promised this Shining Man, but I knew I must obey. His light swirled about me, filling me with joy like I had never experienced. For one brief moment, love surrounded me and my soul leaped. No words passed between us, but knowledge flowed into me. Knowledge I promptly forgot.

He knew all about me, and somehow I realized that I knew him. He accepted me, welcomed me, called me to him. I caught my breath—how wonderful to be known by such a one! Then in a blast of light the Shining Man vanished, taking all his delightful, unearthly love with him.

With a heart full of peace, I fell into a deep slumber.

Chapter Seven

The Accusation—Nefret

I awoke to the sound of shouting. Paimu was gone, probably off to see her friends Ziza and Amon. I rubbed my eyes. Feeling tired from my night's encounter, I had no time to consider all that had happened. The Council would expect me to appear in my father's tent ready to perform the last trial, but from the sounds of stirring in the camp I needed to move quickly.

"Pah! Pah! Pah!"

I walked to the tent flap and watched as people streamed by me. Forgetting my knotted hair and crumpled clothing, I followed them, curious to see what was happening.

"Powerful with a spear—of great courage and strength! Pah should be our mekhma! Who is with me?"

One of my sister's friends, Ayn, stood beside Pah, holding her hand in the air; it was the sign of victory. Some of the crowd cheered and applauded; others murmured and pointed at the show Ayn was making. One of the children noticed me and shouted my name. This silenced the crowd, and their attention turned to me.

"This is her sister. Isn't she anni-mekhma too? Have the trials ended?" they asked one another. Ayn ignored both their questions and my presence. Paimu found me and clung to my leg fearfully. Ayn walked in a circle, holding Pah's hand high with one hand and one of Pah's spears with the other. She continued with her rant.

"Can anyone compare to Pah? Offer your pledge now and greet our new mekhma!"

"What is this?" Farrah entered the circle and challenged Ayn. "What are you doing?"

The tall young woman dropped Pah's arm and raised a defiant chin to Farrah.

"I am showing my support for Pah—the true choice for mekhma!" A few of the young women cheered at the acclamation until they fell under Farrah's watchful eye. The only sound heard then was the sound of banners flapping in the breeze and the distant sound of a goatherd's lute.

"Foolish girl! Do you think you can sway the Council or the people with this unseemly show? What is the meaning of this?"

Ayn did not back down, although I noticed that Pah had wisely cast her eyes to the ground, avoiding Farrah's piercing gaze. "I meant no disrespect, Old One, to you or the Council. However, is there a rule that says I cannot recommend my friend? That I cannot testify to her commitment and integrity?"

"What are you suggesting, Ayn?" Alexio stepped out of the crowd and stood beside me.

Farrah waved at him, warning him to be silent. "Speak plainly now, girl," she said to Ayn.

Ayn raised her head higher and returned Farrah's bitter stare. "Very well. Isn't it true that an anni-mekhma must be prepared to yield her soul, mind and body for the good of the clan?" Here she paused. "And that her maidenhood must be intact?"

"You know that it is true. What is your point?"

I stiffened—a feeling of dread rose up from within me.

"How can you be sure that Nefret has not yielded her body? I know Pah has always acted virtuously, but how can we vouch for someone whose heart has so obviously been given?"

My face reddened as the whispers circulated around me. "That is a lie!" I yelled. "I have yielded nothing!" Even as I said the words, I knew in my heart that it was not entirely true. I had not given my body to Alexio, nor had he asked me to, but my heart...that was another story.

"Have a care for your words, girl! These are serious charges." She lowered her voice and circled Ayn like a hawk stalking a snake. "Is this a charge you bring too, anni-mekhma Pah, or is this merely camp gossip?"

Pah swayed nervously and shook her head. "I do not accuse my sister." I breathed a sigh of relief but she added, "However, I do not condemn those who have doubts about either of us. I only want what is best for the people."

"Very well." Farrah drew herself tall and straight. "Let us settle this matter now. Follow me to my tent, anni-mekhmas. We will know who is intact and who is not."

Farrah stormed through the camp, and the people shuffled to get out of the way. I walked behind the older woman with my head held high. For once I was not going to let Pah step in front of me. How dare she accuse me of such a thing! She knew perfectly well I had not given away my maidenhood! I had no idea what test I would now be forced to undergo, but I would have to endure it. On this I was in the right. Mostly.

I stepped inside Farrah's tent and explored the contents with my eyes. It had been many years since I entered her abode; I had been small enough to perch on her ebony and enamel stool then. I used to trace its ornamental pictures of cavorting animals with my fingers. How delightful to see those animals there again, but how sad was this moment. My mind was filled with memories of Farrah exhorting me, "Look into the fire. Tell me what you see." I never saw anything, and eventually the Old One stopped inviting me to look or to visit.

Now the same gold medallions hung from the tapestried walls, new birds chirped noisily in their silver cages and the aroma of exotic scents again overwhelmed my senses. It was as if nothing had changed. Except I was no longer that child and the Old One looked truly old now.

"Sit. Both of you. Mina, prepare for the examination." Surprised, I glanced behind me. As quiet as a sand mouse, Mina had slipped in unnoticed, except by Farrah. She scurried away to attend to her task, and I sat facing my sister and the Council's head. "There can be no question about your qualifications. I want you to tell the truth now. Have you, Nefret, lain with a man?"

"No, I have not." I met her gaze squarely.

"Have you made any promises or pledges to anyone?"

"No, I have not. I would have thought you knew this, since you sent Essa to my tent last night."

"I sent no one. What are you talking about?"

Shocked, I said in a rush, "Essa came to my tent and said that the Council had sent him to watch over me. Is this not true?"

"I sent no one and know nothing about this. Perhaps your sister can enlighten me."

"Me? I know nothing, Farrah. Why ask me?" Her eyes flashed in anger, but behind them shifted something. Amusement? Her voice lacked sincerity.

Farrah grunted and pulled something from her pocket and tossed it in the flame of a nearby candle. The flame sparked, turned blue and returned to its low burn. "Your words do not fill me with confidence, Pah."

Pah's dark green eyes were like two steady fires burning back to Farrah. "I know nothing."

"Very well. As your friend has raised doubts about your sister's maidenhood, I am forced to confirm it. Still it would be unfair for her to endure this humiliation alone. You too will be examined, and my findings will be shared with your father, the Council and in fact all the Meshwesh."

I blushed but we both agreed, and Farrah's tone softened. "We must show the people that the mekhma is in control of her heart." She sighed and added, "If your uncle had not insisted in following the Old Ways, this would not have been necessary. Now we must do all things with care. Nefret, follow me."

I did as I was told. Pah turned her back respectfully as Farrah lifted my tunic and I endured her uncomfortable probing. It was quick yet humiliating, just as she predicted. "No, you are intact. Now Pah."

As my sister did for me, I turned my back as Farrah repeated the physical examination and declared her also intact. "All this fuss for nothing! Do you see? A few words can change a life! It can change your destiny. Have a care, anni-mekhmas, for what you allow to be done in your name." Farrah washed her hands and rubbed them with oils. "Now, Nefret, comes your first test of leadership."

"What do you mean?" Pah blurted out, her offense obvious. I imagined her thoughts: *Why does Nefret get chosen for a test and not me?*

"An accusation was made against Nefret. It has been proven a lie. As anni-mekhma, she must address the lie and deal with the offender. Unfortunately, you do not have much time. The final trial begins after breakfast."

Pah gasped in surprise. "What? What do you mean deal with the offender?" Ayn was and had always been her closest friend. I had no doubt that my sister had encouraged Ayn's outburst, but as always, she did not think things through. My sister may have had all the courage, but she had not much in the way of wisdom.

"Yes, it is her right. She may claim the girl's property—she may have her beaten by her mother or she may make a public spectacle of her and parade her about the camp on a rope if she likes. It is no concern of yours, unless you have something to say."

Pah stared at the carpet and shook her head.

"Speaking lies or repeating them about an anni-mekhma is as serious a charge as speaking against the mekhma. It will not be allowed, nor will the people allow it to go unpunished."

"Nefret, you cannot do this," Pah said, rising to her feet. "She has done nothing but repeat what she heard. It is no secret that you desire Alexio! How can you deny it?"

It was my turn to rise now. "You would come to Ayn's defense but would leave me to face an angry crowd? You have no right to ask me anything! It is you who pines for Alexio! It is you who sent Essa to my tent! Go ahead! Deny it!"

"I deny nothing!" she said, her eyes like lightning glass again, her mouth a firm pair of pink lines.

Farrah laughed sourly. "And you wanted to serve together? Now do you see why this is not possible? Make a decision, Nefret. We must go outside now, and I will tell the Meshwesh the truth."

Farrah rose from the carpet with Mina's help. She walked out to face the curious crowd, and again we trailed behind her. I was surprised to see my father standing outside with his king's robes on and ready to pass judgment if called to do so.

Farrah did not stop to speak with him, and neither did we. The gathering moved to the edge of camp, to the site where Ayn had made her accusations against me. My mind ran wildly; what would I say? I had no idea. I stood beside Farrah with my head held high, hoping that inspiration would come quickly.

"Words were spoken here this morning. Serious words." The crowd murmured their agreement and surrounded us in a loose circle. "I have examined our anni-mekhmas and found these words to be false." The people expressed their shock and disapproval with hisses.

All eyes were on me as Farrah continued, "Where is the accuser?" Hands shoved Ayn into the circle. As she stood before me I could tell by her demeanor that she was unrepentant yet a little less confident now. I knew that I should not, but I felt sympathy for her; Ayn was another victim of Pah's incessant scheming.

I wondered what prize she had been promised for perjuring herself. For her sake, I hoped it was worth it. Ayn's family hovered at the edge of the crowd, her mother's face the picture of fear and worry.

Farrah faced the girl. "Ayn, you have brought dishonor upon yourself and your family today with your false accusations. Look at your mother's face! See your father Nari's shame! Now, we shall hear from the one you slandered. It is Nefret's right to demand retribution. What say you, anni-mekhma?"

The morning air felt stagnant; any breeze blowing had disappeared. The eyes of the tribe watched anxiously, and even my father seemed uneasy about my decision. If I condemned Ayn, the tribe would fear me and Farrah would approve, but if I showed her mercy, the family would thank me and my children would approve. I had no way of knowing what Father would recommend. I had seen him sentence a man to die and in the same afternoon, forgive another. What would Pah do if she were in my place? I cast those questions aside. If I was going to rule, I would have to follow my own conscience.

"Daughter of the tribe, I bear you no ill will. I know that until this day you have not been a malcontent, nor have you brought shame on your family. Is this not true, my people?"

The Meshwesh agreed with me. Indeed, until this day, Ayn had done nothing but serve the tribe as an honorable and worthy person. "Therefore, I am inclined to believe that you did not conceive this deception yourself but were under the influence of others." The crowd gasped at my words, and I could see my father shuffling amongst them. Ayn dropped her face to the sand and stared at her sandals. That was all the proof I needed. Tellingly, Pah had not flinched or showed any response to my veiled accusation. I expected nothing less, yet it angered me that she who had begged for her friend's life in private would not lift a hand to save it now. I had no doubt Pah's whispers had ignited this flame.

When Ayn did not answer I pushed her harder. Stepping close to her I said in a loud whisper, "You said yourself that others told you this lie about me. Am I not to know who these others were, Ayn?" Still she offered no answer. Ayn's mother, Namari, began to cry softly; her husband tapped her shoulder to remind her to appear strong.

With a firm resolve, I stepped back and said, "Mother and father of Ayn, come speak to your daughter now before I pass judgment. Remind her that it is better to tell the truth than to spread a lie." Namari ran to Ayn's side and grasped her hand. Her father did not stir but stood firm, glancing ashamedly at his king.

Although Namari spoke in low tones, I heard her plead with her daughter, "Speak the truth and all will be well, Ayn!" Ayn shook her head, staring at the ground and refusing to speak or acknowledge Namari's pleas. Paimu lingered nearby, but I gestured for her to stay back.

"Very well, Ayn. You leave me no choice. As Nefret, I forgive you for your hasty words…" Ayn lifted her surprised face to me. Whatever she had expected, it had not been this. But I wasn't through. "However, as anni-mekhma, I must demand repayment for your offense against me. Do you now confess that you were wrong in accusing me?" I stood in front of her. We were so close, I could hear her breathing.

"I do so confess it. I was wrong." The older girl's voice broke, and she could see that Pah, her dearest friend, had not laid a finger on me to prevent me from punishing her. Her round, brown face crumpled like a flower crushed beneath the weight of a heavy foot. Still, Pah said nothing. She looked bored with the proceedings, unconcerned with the fate of her friend although she had begged for leniency just a few minutes ago. Pah was nothing if not changeable. To some her unwillingness to defend the outspoken Ayn meant very little, but Pah's silence surprised the friends who had prematurely acclaimed her as their mekhma. No one would trust her now.

"I claim all your silver, Ayn hap Nari." Ayn's face fell, but the girl offered no complaint. "And there is one more thing…I command you to care for Paimu if something should happen to me. You will love her and take care of her like she was your own sister, no matter what happens. Do you understand?" Ayn raised her curly head, her dark brown eyes meeting mine.

"You honor us, anni-mekhma," Namari said in a relieved voice. Ignoring the whispers of the people who gathered around us, I completed my judgment with a pronounced nod of my head as I had seen Farrah do a hundred times before. No doubt many would express disappointment that I had not sought greater retribution, as my sister or Farrah would have done.

"Gladly, anni-mekhma Nefret. I will do this."

"NO! I will stay with Nefret! Let me go, Alexio!" I ignored the child and whispered in Ayn's ear. "Be a better sister to her than Pah has been to me. Do you have sisters, Ayn?"

"No," she whispered back.

"Now, you do."

To my utter surprise and shock, she fell to her knee and raised her palms to me in the sign of respect. She was offering me her fealty and friendship! I waved my hands over her to show her I accepted her. She rose with a relieved look on her face. Looking to my left, she stared at Pah, who still seemed unmoved. Suddenly Ayn spat on the ground near Pah's feet and went to speak to Paimu. The little girl was still combative and ready to fight for her chance to stay with me.

I called to her, "Go now, Paimu. I must begin my next trial. I shall come see you in Ayn's tent when I am finished. Be a good girl." She relented and followed after Ayn, who tried to engage her in small talk. Pah drifted off into the crowd, no doubt to reinvigorate her supporters. Or try to.

Farrah smiled at me, showing perfectly white teeth. "Child, you are full of surprises. A reasonable and thoughtful judgment. You will make a great mekhma. But tell me, who provides you with such good counsel? I see that Pah has her supporters. Where are yours? Your father, perhaps?"

"No, I have no supporters. Except Paimu and the other children. It just came to me." Thoughtfully I added, "I guess the Shining Man is leading me."

"Who is this Shining Man you speak of? An Egyptian god, perhaps? Amun?" Farrah's eyes peered into mine, looking for an answer to a question she had not asked yet.

"No. He is not an Egyptian god, at least I do not think so... but I have seen him."

Farrah clucked her tongue and shook her head, mumbling under her breath. "No Isis or shining god for me. I prefer to pray to my ancestors or to Ma'at. They have seen us this far, and they can carry me back to Zerzura."

She spun about in her grey and white robe, her hair a beautiful mass of curls that trailed down her back. Words came to my mind, words I did not speak aloud.

No, you shall not go to Zerzura, Old One. Your time here comes to an end.

I shivered as the words drifted away and Farrah paused on the path still speaking to me. I saw her mouth and focused my mind on understanding what she said.

"Come, come, now. Let us go! Orba and your father will be waiting!"

Chapter Eight

The Final Trial—Nefret

For this trial, the tent was full of people. Pah and I were invited to sit on the tiger furs before our father's seat. We faced the people, who smiled and offered us well wishes. Nobody spoke about what might happen, about how either Pah or I would be banished to the Red Sands if not chosen. How morbid! If only we could have found a way to defy the prophecy and rule together.

Ah, but Pah would never allow such a thing to happen. I knew that now, even if I had not believed it before. Feeling sentimental for a moment, I slid my hand under hers and sighed as she snatched her hand away. She did not look at me or open her mouth, but that was the reminder I needed that she played for keeps.

In front of us were two ebony chests; the lids had been removed and lay next to the chests. One chest was for Pah and one was for me, no doubt, but for what purpose? I didn't have long to wait; musicians began to play a tune on their skin drums and string and wood instruments. How I loved the sound of the wood instruments, so lonely, so forlorn. It sounded like my heart! Tears brimmed in my eyes as I scanned the crowded tent. I loved these brown and olive-skinned faces. I loved the Meshwesh; we were family, tied together by the blood of Ma and the hope of a prosperous future at Zerzura.

Our father spoke now, "Come now, Meshwesh. Bless the anni-mekhmas as they prepare for their next trial. If you have a gift to offer, place your gift inside one of the chests and please bless the anni-mekhma who will receive your gift as you leave." He greeted the people as they approached us. He touched the heads of the children and kissed the cheeks of the older women. Father was always careful to show all due respect to the people, for it was them he served. After the offerings were collected, the chests were closed. Both of us had received quite a few gifts, enough to show that the people truly loved us, but I could tell Pah had received more than I. More evidence that I had no skill at politics. Apparently many still trusted her, despite this morning's controversy.

No matter. I can overcome this!

Farrah stood in the center of the tent and prayed to our ancestors for guidance. When the benediction ended, she invited Orba to address us. "Now, anni-mekhmas, the final test—the final trial has arrived! As mekhma, you must have the respect and trust of our neighbors and fellow tribes. We send you out now with our treasures to procure for us something of value. You can take no adviser, only yourself, your treasure and any supplies you may need. I now cast lots to determine who will go first and where." He shook his bag of ivory pieces and scattered them on the floor. He and Farrah peered at them, and Orba declared, "Nefret! You go to Biyat! Pah travels to Kemel. Go now! Represent your tribe!" The Meshwesh cheered, and the women clucked their tongues to show their approval.

Our father rose and stretched his arms out to us. Hugging us both, he surprised us with a rare show of emotion by kissing the tops of our heads. "Go now, my daughters. Have a care for yourselves and return to me."

"Yes, Father," we murmured and immediately left the tent. Camels had been prepared for us, and the treasures were poured into bags to hide their value from would-be thieves. I felt no fear; I felt nothing at all but grim determination. Feeling the pack and checking the saddle, I rearranged my bow so it would be nearer to me.

"Go now! Return to us, anni-mekhmas!" I petted my camel, who sat obediently waiting for me. Paimu ran to me crying; her small arms flew around my waist. At that moment, it occurred to me that I had not properly dressed for the day. My sister's hair was brushed and gleaming, yet mine was still in my sleeping braid. I sighed. Nothing to be done about that now.

"You promised me, princess! That I would never be without you. You cannot leave me. I will go with you! See—I have sandals and can run very fast. Please!"

Ayn stood behind her, looking exasperated. "I am sorry, anni-mekhma, but she would not listen to me."

I smiled at the child and waved a hand at Ayn to calm her. "Not this time, my monkey. I have to ride very fast to Biyat, too fast for a monkey like you."

"I can ride fast. I know I can! Please, don't leave me, Nefret." She sobbed now, and even Ayn's heart began to melt. She stroked the girl's hair and spoke softly to her.

"I cannot take you, Paimu, because if I do, the tribe at Biyat may want to keep you. I am there to make a trade, am I not? You are my treasure, Paimu. I could not bear to lose you. Now please listen to me. Stay with Ayn and help her. Teach Alexio how to climb the palm if you like."

That answer seemed to satisfy her. "When will you be back?"

Alexio passed by Pah and joined us, answering her, "Three days unless she stays the night." He cast his lovely eyes on me and said, "It's a straight shot, Nefret. Follow the sun and you can't miss it. I packed a knife in your hip bag, just in case. Do not stop for any reason until you get to Biyat. It is a long day's ride, but you can do it easily."

I climbed on the camel, hoping to avoid any further gossip about my relationship with Alexio. Still, I wanted to fling my arms around him one last time. I thanked him politely and walked the camel to the edge of the camp. Pah rode away, a boisterous crowd of young people cheering for her as she disappeared riding hard for the south. Now as I left the tribe behind, I heard cheers for me too; they were not as loud as Pah's, but they still warmed my heart and filled me with purpose. Waving goodbye, I scanned the faces for Father but did not see him. Kicking with my heels and clucking my tongue, I spurred the camel on and rode westward with all my might.

I rode steady for some time before the heat of the day began to burn my skin. Without dismounting, I covered my head with my worn brown cloak and took some refreshment from my goatskin. I drank the cool water and felt refreshed immediately, but my thirst quickly returned. In the distance my hot eyes spotted an unfamiliar small oasis. This would not be Biyat; it was too close to Timia. But if the occupants were friendly, perhaps I could take my rest there to avoid the midday sun.

I had traveled to Biyat when I was just a child, before I had breasts, and I remembered it well. Unlike Timia, which had a diamond shape, the Oasis of Biyat ran long and skinny, the lushness sprouting up around an underground stream. The sheltering land before me was nothing as large as Biyat and appeared as a clump of green grass in the midst of a sea of red sand. As I drew closer, I wrapped my cloth tighter around my face, hoping to avoid drawing unwanted attention with my red hair and green eyes.

"Kitch, kitch!" I clucked at the camel. I sat tall in the saddle despite my sore back and aching bottom. I drew close but not too close. Observing the oasis for a moment, my fears were allayed. The visitors were merely goatherds seeking to do the same thing as I was, find shelter from the heat. Riding closer, I called out in a friendly manner, "Peace to you."

"Peace to you as well!" A young boy called back and ran to find the goatherd, probably his father. Leading the camel to the water's edge, I settled under a palm and unwrapped my head. I splashed my face and hands, then set about searching for my lunch—chula bread and a cluster of dates from Timia. A crooked-backed old goatherd made his way to me, and his young protégé tagged along behind him. A third man hovered near the goats. My bow was on the other side of the camel, but my knife was on my side. I prayed I would not have to use it.

"Peace to you." The goatherd smiled politely and for a few minutes we exchanged pleasantries. But remembering Alexio's words, I did not tell more than I had to. The goatherd offered me some of his wine, but I politely refused. Drinking wine in the heat of the day with strangers seemed a poor choice.

"What brings you to this little spot? There is nothing much here, sister."

Ignoring his attempt at friendliness I said with a smile, "I am only passing through."

"To Biyat, then?" He frowned, his forehead wrinkled with concern. The goatherd's face, like the faces of most who had spent their lives in the Sahara sun, was a map of lines and dark skin. "Oh no, do not go to Biyat. There are strange things happening. Go home. Go back to Timia."

"I did not say I was from Timia." I stopped unpacking my bag and stared at the old man.

"I can see plainly, red-haired one. These eyes have not failed me so far. Those are the colors of the Meshwesh," he said, pointing to my embroidered collar, "and they do love Timia this time of year. Tell me, does Farrah still live?"

"You know Farrah?"

He laughed as if he knew the most wonderful joke but had no intention of telling me. "Of course, of course, sister. And if you are here, that means she has yet to find Zerzura." He laughed even louder, as did his helper.

I had no desire to engage in more conversation with the goatherd, but I felt I had to know what dangers possibly lay ahead of me.

"What strange things do you mean?"

"Tall men, so tall they could touch the sky. A hot wind blows, hotter than any I have ever known. The Dancing Man has risen in the night sky, and a voice—a whispering voice—is carried on the breeze." He froze, his hand cupping his large ear as if he could hear it even now.

"These men, are they Nubians? The Nejd?"

He waved his hand as if I were stupid. "No Nubians—no Nejd." He muttered in a language I did not know and continued his story. "Tall they are, tall and spindly like these trees. And wherever they go, they sow unhappiness behind them. It is not wise to be out here by yourself, red-haired girl. These tall men come from beyond the southlands of Mut where no decent tribe dwells. They are at war with everyone! Go home now."

A chill crept down my spine, but I masked my fear. I nodded my thanks for his warning and offered him some dates; he happily accepted, thanking me profusely before he left.

Nervously, I watched the trio as surreptitiously as possible. If they were a danger to me, there was no need to boost their confidence by appearing afraid and vulnerable. As I sat under the tree and leaned against the trunk, I took out my blade and began to rub it with an oily cloth until it shone. I hoped they would spot the glinting metal and take the warning. It seemed they did, as they did not bother me again. The two older men rested under their makeshift tent while the boy cavorted with the goats until he too sought shelter. The bright day burned on. I ate my food and tried to stay awake, but the heat sapped the strength from my bones. I longed to brush out my hair and retie it, but doing so would not be wise. It would have to wait until I returned home or perhaps this evening if the people at Biyat were thoughtful enough to provide me with a bed.

My camel hunkered down, and I clucked at him playfully. Leaning back against the tree, I closed my eyes, thinking again of my dream. How real it had seemed to me! The coolness of the stone under my bare feet, the pounding of my heart as I turned each sharp curve in the confusing corridor. Would I ever forget seeing that fear reflected in the face of the boy who ran behind me?

Smenkhkare!

I felt my body relax and before I knew it, I had succumbed to sleep. I dreamed but did not remember it.

I awoke with a start, jolted awake by a noise that only my dream-self heard. Breathing hard from the rush of adrenaline, I found myself on my feet with my knife in my hand. I circled around the tree but saw nothing, no one. In fact, the others were gone, all three men and the dozen goats that accompanied them. I shielded my eyes with my hand and peeked at the sun. Hours had passed, but I did not know how many. It would be dark soon, and I did not want to be caught in the desert by the tall men the goatherd spoke of. And regardless, I had a job to do. I hoisted my supplies back in the saddle and climbed aboard the camel. Wrapping the cloth around my head, I continued my trek west, faster now as if giants indeed chased me.

I leaned into the camel, twisting the leather strap. I whispered in his ear, "Kitch, kitch!" Obediently, he ran faster, and I kept my spine straight and in line with his head. He ran as if he knew something I did not. As we hurried toward Biyat, I kept my eyes trained on the horizon, praying that I would see trouble before it approached me. How would I defend myself out here with no shelter and nobody I knew? I found myself missing Alexio again.

Focusing on the task at hand, I urged the animal forward and began to think about my trade. What would benefit my tribe? What was I expected to do? I had no idea, no inspiration, but I hoped that it would come to me when I needed it, just as it had earlier in the judgment of Ayn. My thoughts turned toward the Shining Man.

What if, like the fated "Queen of Zerzura," I was being tricked? What if my dreams were nothing more than dreams? It could not be true! His words were burned in my heart…

Will you trust me even when you cannot see me? When all others turn against you?

Time passed quickly as I rode. The sun hung low in the sky and soon it would be dark in the desert. If I did not arrive at Biyat soon I would be forced to sleep in the sand. As I cleared a tall dune, an acrid smell filled my nose. I gasped and stood amazed at the sight that lay before me. There were fires everywhere, and even from this distance I could see the charred remains of a camp.

My first instinct was to spur the camel toward the disaster, but the animal refused to obey me. Despite my attempts to convince him, he resolutely refused to take another step forward. Sliding off his back, I led him by the reins to get closer to the fiery scene. When I got as close as I dared, I stood still waiting and listening but could detect no sound except the crackling of fire. No one cried for help. I had to get closer. My unhappy camel tolerated my curiosity until we stepped into the camp. Then, with a snort, he pulled away from me and loped away. Clucking at him softly to calm him, I tied the strap to the tree and patted him, assuring him I would return. As he must have known, I needed him far more than he needed me. If he ran into the desert, he would easily find his way home. But without him, I would certainly perish.

I gagged as I walked into the camp. Quickly I balled my tunic's edge and covered my nose with it. The Meshwesh at Biyat did not belong to my tribe, but they were Meshwesh all the same. My stomach lurched as I walked past an avenue of scorched earth and debris that had once been tents. Walking carefully to avoid burning my sandaled feet, I paused every few feet to listen for calls for help or any sign that whoever did this was nearby.

Suddenly a thought occurred to me: what if the old man was right? What if this was proof that the "tall men" had been here? The Meshwesh obviously had not planned on leaving. The fire had consumed much, but many valuable things were left behind, like the clay pots that our women took pride in working. I picked up a broken one from the sand and rubbed the geometric patterns with my fingers.

I walked past one charred pile after another, my heart falling further in my chest with each step. "Hello?" I called. "Is anyone here?" My imagination could not muster a scenario of what must have taken place. Even if an uncontrollable fire had blazed through the camp, the Meshwesh would not have left their cooking pots or anything else. Yes, something evil happened here. The residue lingered.

"Hello?" I called again. Rising desperation forced me to dig deeper. I picked up a stick and used it to probe a smoking pile. I lifted the burned tent canvas and screamed. A tiny burned hand appeared, and I dropped the stick. Yes, this was the work of evil men. Feeling a surge of panic, I ran to the edge of the oasis hoping against hope that I would see a caravan in the distance, that I would see proof that someone had escaped. Leaving the green and brown grass behind me, I scurried up a small dune and climbed up to get a better look. Surely someone had escaped!

As I reached the sandy peak an intensely bitter aroma assaulted my senses. The smell of death rose up from the sand below me like a living thing. In a shallow valley were the bodies of my people. Dead Meshwesh covered the ground, their bodies half hidden in the sand. Mothers and fathers were tossed together with their children's limp bodies. Wicked gashes from unforgiving blades had opened their necks, and there were gaping spear wounds in their bellies. Falling to my knees, I cupped my mouth to prevent a scream from escaping. This was a place of death! Rocking back and forth, I could not turn my eyes from the carnage. Tears filled my eyes, and I let them flow unashamedly.

I don't know how long I stayed there on my knees in the deathly silence of the desert. My camel's long complaint called me back, and the reality that I was in danger came crashing down on me. There was nothing I could do for the Meshwesh before me, but what about my tribe? With one thought—save my people—I carefully slid down the sand to retrieve the evidence I needed. As I approached the first victim, a small boy whose face was hidden in the sand, I removed my knife from my belt. Quickly, I cut a piece of his singed garment away and tucked the cloth in my tunic. Sliding the knife back into place, my weariness vanished. It had been replaced by a surge of purpose and overwhelming fear.

My mission had changed. There would be no deal made here in this valley of death, but I cared not. The faces of the people I loved—Paimu, Alexio, Father and Pah—flashed before me. Could they now be in the path of whoever had mercilessly destroyed this tribe?

My legs ran hard and fast back to the camel. I threw myself in the saddle and, with a slap of my leather strap, spurred the animal toward home.

I prayed I was not too late.

Chapter Nine

The Girl Who Climbs—Paimu

"Paimu! Come down from there. It is well past time to eat!" Ayn called impatiently. I could tell by her expression that she was less than happy with me.

"Go away," I shouted from the top of the palm. I would never admit that I was afraid—too afraid to come down. Besides, the sun had set and Nefret had been gone for two days. I wanted to be the first to see her return with some great prize, for I had no doubt she would. Like Mahara who outsmarted the serpent and the winged lions to retrieve her clan's magic treasure, Nefret would not fail. She could not!

"You know she won't be back today. Be patient and come down. My mother has even made a honey cake just for you."

"No. Go away."

Ayn sighed in exasperation and then called up the tree again. "I suppose I could find Pah and have her come get you down, since I can't climb too well. She is probably rested from her travels."

A surge of panic hit my hungry belly. "I will come down now. The sun has gone away, and I cannot see anything anyway."

Ayn chuckled. "Indeed you cannot. Come now. Mother is waiting."

I crept slowly down the slick trunk, using my thighs and ankles to counterbalance my hands and arms. Somewhere below the tree were my shoes, a present from Nefret, my only true friend. With an impressive leap, I landed on the ground and wiped my dirty hands on my clothes.

Ayn crinkled her nose. "You smell terrible. When was the last time you bathed?"

With my hands on my hip I said, "You don't tell me when to take a bath! You are not my mother, Ayn!"

She grabbed my hand and pulled me with her. I struggled for a moment until her strong hand patted my behind. "Listen! Nefret asked me to take care of you, and that's what I am going to do.

We can do this pleasantly, or you can make it hard on yourself. Which do you want?"

I snatched my hand away and rubbed it. It didn't really hurt, but I wanted her to know that I did not approve of her touching me. I did not care to be touched unless I did the touching. Even Nefret did not touch me. "I know you don't really want me with you, Ayn. Nobody ever does. Why shouldn't I smell like the goats? Even Nefret gave me away! I am just your punishment." I had not intended to vent such emotion, but the words tumbled out of my heart before I could think about them.

She tilted her head and gazed down at me. Ayn was not a pretty girl, not like Nefret with her dark red hair, olive skin and cat's eyes. Even Alexio was prettier than Ayn, but she was strong and brave—and foolish, as she proved the other day.

Ayn stood much taller than me. In fact, she stood much taller than all the girls her age, but she did not seem to mind or notice. In comparison, I felt small, very small indeed. "Maybe you are right, and maybe you are not," she observed. "I do not know. I do know I gave my word to the anni-mekhma, and I will not fail to keep it. I do not mean you any harm, Paimu. I would very much like to be your friend if you have room for one more." I pushed my bangs from my eyes and stared at her, hoping to perceive any ill will she might have held for me. She had never cared to speak to me before, and now she wanted to be my friend?

Ayn's eyes shifted, and I turned to see what she spotted. Was it Nefret? My heart leaped, but only for a moment. It was not Nefret but Pah who walked toward us, now washed and dressed like a mekhma in a blue gown that revealed one perfect shoulder. The gold thread embroidery at the sleeves and neck made me think of Mahara's magical gown.

"Is this one giving you trouble, Ayn?" Pah purred as she reached out and absently stroked my messy hair. "You *can* handle her, can't you?"

Ayn reached for me, snatching me away from Pah. I did not argue with her this time or lecture her on how I did not like being touched. Pah frightened me, and she always had. Maybe it was because I dreamed about her once—she'd run toward me, first with her own face and then with the face of a snarling bear.

"No trouble at all, anni-mekhma." Ayn took my hand protectively and murmured, "Excuse me." We had taken only a few steps toward Ayn's home when Pah called my keeper back.

"I do not excuse you! That is all you have to say to me? You were my biggest supporter, Ayn. Now you turn your back on me when we are so close to reaching our goal."

Ayn stopped and glanced at me. "Go home. I will be there soon."

"No," I said, partly because I wanted to stand with her against Pah and partly because I wanted to hear what Nefret's sister had to say.

"Go now!" the girl commanded, and I walked away but only as far as the nearest tent. I squatted beside it in the shadows, hoping to hear what words they exchanged.

"How dare you accuse me of turning my back on you? You were going to let me die!"

"Nonsense, Ayn. Nefret would never have killed you—she doesn't have the stomach for such things."

Ayn snorted. "Ah, but you do. Don't you?"

"Yes." I saw the smile creep across Pah's face, and I shivered in the shadows. "I do. There is nothing I am not willing to do to be mekhma!"

In a sad voice, Ayn answered her, "I believe you, Pah."

"Do I still have your support, or do you like your new job as babysitter to Nefret's pet monkey?"

"Don't call her that, and I am not a babysitter."

Pah laughed. "Ayn, the great warrior, watching over orphans!" I saw Ayn's hand curl into a fist, but Pah did not seem afraid, not as I would have been. Pah bravely stepped toward the tall girl, and her shiny jeweled necklace glinted in the fading light. "You are called to a higher purpose, Ayn. You could be someone great, a woman-warrior that future generations will sing about. I will win. It is my destiny. I have brought home a great prize, far greater than any Nefret could buy or find. I am now mekhma in all but formality. Pledge your support to me again, while I have no doubts about you." I leaned forward to hear what Ayn would say, but a swatting hand smacked my bottom.

"Hey! You girl! Get away from there. What are you doing? Hoping to steal something? Go now!"

I ran from the woman's cruel hands and toward Namari's tent. I had nowhere else to go, unless I wanted to sleep in Nefret's empty tent. I did not like being alone at night—I was afraid of the dark. Or more truthfully of what waited in it.

What an evil woman! She made me leave my spot just when Ayn would speak and tell her true heart! I wanted to know the truth so I could tell Nefret when she arrived, but now I could not. Namari was waiting for me and presented me with the promised honey cake. Ayn's mother had been kind to me, kinder than most.

She crinkled her nose. "You need a bath."

"I know." I grinned at her as I smacked on the honey cake. My stomach rumbled loudly.

"You will have to take one tonight, little one, or you shall sleep with the goats."

I scowled but did not argue with her. Just once I would like to do what I wanted to do. Why had Nefret left me behind? Treasures of the tribe indeed! That was something the Meshwesh liked to say, but it was rarely true. At least not for an unwanted Algat girl who had nowhere else to go. I savored each morsel of the honey cake and finally licked my fingers clean.

"I will bathe in the pool tomorrow," I told her.

"No, you will bathe here tonight. See? I found a new tunic for you. You can wear it while we clean your other one. It belonged to Ayn when she was a girl." She held the tunic up to my chest and frowned at the ridiculous length. "We can shorten it a bit, and it will be perfect."

I couldn't help but smile. To have two tunics! How rich I would be! I removed my clothing and allowed Namari to wash my body. She complained and compared the skin behind my ears to the desert we lived in. "Have you left any sand in the desert, Paimu?"

I suffered through the scrubbing and endured the cold water. She scrubbed my feet with a camel hair brush, and I tried not to kick her as I laughed.

"Be still, monkey girl!"

"It tickles! I can't help it!"

She wanted to remain serious and focused on her task, but I could see a glimmer of a smile on her face too. It was a rare flash of happiness, and for a moment I pretended that Namari was my true mother. I enjoyed the fiction until her husband walked in. I grabbed the new tunic and clutched it to my naked body.

He did not acknowledge me but spoke tersely to his wife. "The anni-mekhma is back. I must go to see Semkah now. I do not know when I shall return." His strained face reflected worry, as did Namari's. I did not understand the exchange.

"Very well. Peace, husband."

"Peace to you, wife."

Without drying my hair or body, I slid the tunic on and searched for my sandals.

"Where do you think you are going?"

"I must go see Nefret."

She lit the lamp that hung from the center pole and laughed joylessly. "No, you *must* stay here. See, here is Ayn. Tell her that she must stay here—she is like a wild cat. The king's tent is no place for her."

"She is right, Paimu. I am sure Nefret will come when she can."

My fists clenched as I thought about what I should do next. Scream, set the tent on fire, kick Ayn and run? Nothing was clear except that Nefret had returned. "She is my friend. I have to see her." Tears filled my eyes.

"Shh…Paimu. Nefret has other matters to tend to besides you. I am sure she will come see you when she can. Take your rest now. If she comes while you are sleeping, someone will wake you."

Sullenly, I climbed into the pallet where I had slept the night before. I did not feel sleepy at all, but I could see that arguing with

Ayn would get me nowhere. I cuddled up to the soft blanket and twisted the corner worriedly. The harder I strained to hear Ayn and Namari, the sleepier I became. The warm honey cake and cool bath had done their work on my tired body. I would never admit this to Ayn and her mother, but the feeling of being clean and having a new tunic comforted me more than I could have imagined.

Later, I awoke to the sound of Nari and Namari talking in hushed, worried tones. If it had been merely Namari and Ayn in the tent, I would have thrown back the blanket and demanded to know what they were talking about. I did not dare to speak to Nari in such a way. Remaining very still, I did not bother to push back the dark hair that had fallen in my face. I kept my breathing even and did not move. I was good at spying, a practice that made me feel powerful and safe. People always underestimated me.

"All of them?" Namari whispered.

"That's what she says. Run through with spears and their throats cut with a blade."

Nari's wife gasped and turned to look at Ayn and me. "What should we do? Where should we go?"

"Where *can* we go? There is nowhere to go, wife." He hugged her close and whispered in her ear. She nodded and put her arms around his neck. "I think the best thing to do is wait to hear what the scouting party discovers."

"I am surprised you didn't offer to go with them."

"Semkah prefers to keep me close by." He glanced at Ayn and she nodded, understanding the hidden message. Since Ayn's accusation, Nari's reputation as a faithful warrior and friend to Semkah had been tarnished. Even a child could predict that would be the result of such behavior.

"So what does this mean? Will they continue or wait until the scouts return?"

"I feel sure that Farrah will not want to wait, especially in light of this latest development. In her mind, we will need a mekhma to face whatever army may be advancing toward us."

"Yes, I can see that. You don't agree?"

"I think we should wait, but I have no voice on the Council. No influence with the king anymore. Nefret was not able to fulfill her trial. It seems only fair that we should wait. However, I am sure Pah will make a good mekhma. She is a strong leader. Always has been."

"So the Council has decided?"

Nari leaned back on his bed and pulled his wife to him. "Nothing is decided yet, but I can see which way the wind is blowing. Come here. Enough talk for now." They fell silent, and soon they both began to snore. The small oil lamp on the table flickered weakly until it burned away its fuel. I slid back my covers quietly and paused. My young heart beat wildly in my chest. I had to see Nefret. I had to, and no one would stop me!

Slowly I sat up. Nobody stirred and the snoring continued. I put on my shoes and stood. Ayn shifted on her pillow but did not wake. I walked to the tent flap and, as quickly as a Bee-Eater, stepped outside and ran through the dark, down the sandy pathway to find Nefret.

Aitnu strolled past me but did not spot me. He wore his battle gear, a leather tunic, a shield and his sword. Wrapped in his thoughts, he neither acknowledged me nor spoke to me, even when I thought his dark eyes fell upon me. I ducked behind a pile of saddles and heard him speak to two young men. They walked to the edge of the camp, with me following them as secretively as possible. The men selected camels, arranged the saddles and left under the cover of darkness. They headed west, presumably to Biyat.

As Aitnu and the other warriors rode away, I stepped out of my hiding place.

I felt a great sadness wash over me. Things were changing, and I did not like change. It always brought bad things.

It worried me that some of our warriors were leaving. Who would protect Nefret now? I raised my chin defiantly as I watched the men disappear into the thick darkness. I would go find Nefret! Focusing on my task, I stepped back on the path. I *had* to find my friend. Who else would help her if not me?

"Why am I not surprised to find you lurking about? Always in the way, always forgotten, aren't you, Paimu?"

Before my eyes could take in the darkened figure, I felt a pain in my stomach like I had never known. My hands flew to the spot, and with some shock I realized they were now wet.

Wet with blood.

Chapter Ten

A Marriage—Nefret

I squatted in the sand behind the lively fire that burned in the center of the circle. Across the fire, dozens of pairs of young eyes watched my every move with enjoyment. The marriage ceremony had been performed, and now the tribe made merry in honor of my sister and her new husband, Yuni. It seemed sacrilegious to celebrate when Meshwesh lay dead in the sand just a few days' ride away.

However, I was not the mekhma; I did not decide such things.

With her marriage to Yuni, Pah had offered the ultimate sacrifice, her own body on behalf of her people. I had failed my mission. I took comfort in the fact that the outcome had been out of my control. The gods had chosen the mekhma. Nothing could change that. I knew these things, but it left a bitter taste in my mouth. Everything would be different now, and no word came forth about my future.

Sitting in the place of honor were Father, Pah and Yuni. They clapped their hands in polite expectation of my tale. I bowed my head, keeping my eyes on my father—not on my sister whose eyes messaged her hate, and not on her husband, who made no secret of the fact that he lusted after every woman who passed in front of him.

The children clamored for my attention, and I stood, raising my hand to my forehead to my father, the host of the wedding festivities—this would be his last official event and, although no one openly expressed it, it would probably also be mine. He sat bare-chested, wearing only his robes of kingship and a skirt of dark blue. Father's long dark hair had been oiled, and it hung in rows of curls for the special day. He was a handsome man, my father. Pah whispered something to him and he laughed politely. The two shared their joke with Yuni, who laughed too. I did not let it discourage me. I walked toward the fire, my hands behind my back. Such small movements could hold an audience spellbound—at least I had this moment. I had a gift for storytelling, as Farrah told me when she remembered to speak to me at all. Mostly, she just stared at me.

"Daughter, tell us a story," Father said, smiling at me.

Slowly I began to dance as the drummer tapped a happy tune for me. I noticed Alexio's eyes watching as I waved my fingers and pointed my toes. Truthfully my dancing left something to be desired, but I could pose. Suddenly, I gestured with my hand and the drummer, an old, toothless man, stopped. I stood frozen, sneakily digging into my pocket. I grabbed a handful of purple flowers, the kind that spark and flame when tossed into a fire. I spun and tossed the flowers into the fire and stood staring at it. What was this? In the flames I could see again the dead bodies of the people of Biyat, thrown into the sandy valley to be left as food for the animals of the desert. I shook my head and closed my eyes. When I opened them, all eyes were on me.

"Aha!" I said quietly as the story I needed came to me like a living thing that had always been there, hanging in the air, waiting for the telling, as if this were the perfect time and place.

"Hear now, honored guests and treasures, the story of Numa, the woman who had no heart and therefore could not love. Ziza! Come!" I whispered to the little girl, "You must help me. Follow me, okay?" She gave me an embarrassed but willing smile and nodded her consent.

Again my heart broke.

Where could Paimu be? She should be here telling this story with me.

I missed my treasure, my monkey! I had not seen her in two days, and poor Ayn and I had been wracked with worry over her. Ayn swore that she had made every effort to keep her close, but the child had a mind of her own. I knew this to be true, so I did not lay this at Ayn's feet. Neither Namari nor Ziza's mother had seen the girl, and neither had any of her playmates. It was as if she had disappeared into thin air. Perhaps the Algat had returned to claim her? I prayed she had not been lost in the desert but merely was hiding from me to show her disapproval over my leaving her behind. Paimu had a strong will and a stubborn streak as wide as the Sahara.

Ziza scrambled to her feet and made the sign of respect to the king and my sister, just as I had. I patted her head and she knelt quietly beside me, ready to act out the story that I would weave. Ziza was an excellent young actress; in the past she had played the part of a monkey, a parrot, a lost traveler, a warrior princess and even the sun. She could do it all, but she was not my Paimu.

"Buried somewhere in the Red Lands is the body of Numa." I felt a cold chill and suddenly I saw a woman lying in the desert, the sand covering her face.

Who was she? I had never seen her before!

I shook my head and continued on, trying to regain my composure. "She was a beautiful woman, only she was born without a heart. She could not love. She could love neither husband nor children, nor her father or mother although they were honorable people. Numa would go out every day to pray for a heart. As often as she could, she would make a heart of bread and offer it to her tribe's deity, Washtu. She would lay it at the god's feet and return the next day, hoping to discover that the bread had turned into a real heart. Day after day, she rolled the bread, patted the bread and baked it into the shape of a heart. Each day was the same. No heart appeared. This was unfortunate because Numa was to be married in just three days. Her betrothed had great lands and much wealth. Numa desired to be a good wife and mother to the kind king's children.

"Numa had almost given up on receiving a heart. She wanted to love, to be in love, to feel love. She wanted to love others. It was her sole desire." I waved my hands and used my eyes to demonstrate how Numa must have felt. Beside me, Ziza pretended to bake a heart from sand and presented it to the fire.

"See? Day after day it was the same until one day, a jinn from a faraway land heard Numa crying. He dove down from his home in the clouds to see who this was crying in his domain. So surprised to see a woman without a heart, the jinn abandoned the sky and spoke to her.

"'Why do you cry, woman with no heart? If you have no heart, how are you able to cry?'

"'I can cry because tears don't come from the heart but from the soul. Love comes from the heart. I need a heart. Leave me be, jinn!'

"The jinn scowled at her and floated away. This happened for many days. The jinn flew by and came to speak to Numa. Finally, after a week of this, he asked her if she would accept a heart that he had made for her. Numa was suspicious, 'How can I trust a jinn? All jinn are notoriously evil' But even as she said the words, she was uncertain. Her father had always told her never to entertain a jinn, but this one offered her a heart. What should she do? Should she take the heart?

"The jinn flew away in a cloud of blue smoke, and Numa was relieved. But the jinn did not stay away for long. Two days later, on the eve of her wedding, he returned and presented her the heart again. Courageously, she refused to accept it. In this she was wise because it had been the jinn's plan to cause Numa to fall in love with him—the heart had been cast with an enchantment. Aggravated by her lack of trust, the jinn threw the heart at her feet.

"'See, I made this heart for you. If you do not take it, you will never have another one. Take the heart, woman, and experience love—but listen to me! You must swallow the heart before it will work for you. Also, know this, the first living creature you see after you have your heart is who you will love for eternity. Do not open your eyes until you are prepared to be in love. You have until sunset to decide. At that time, the magic of the heart will fail.'

"The woman watched the jinn sail up and up until he finally disappeared into the star-jeweled sky. It seemed like he had flown all the way to the moon. She looked at the heart on the ground, unsure what to do. Carefully she picked it up and dusted it off." Ziza dusted off an imaginary heart and pretended to examine it. "Numa kept her heart in a box, safe from anyone who might steal it. She told no one about the jinn or what she had been given. What should she do? Swallow the heart? Burn it? What if this was a trick to kill her?

"The hours were passing by, and Numa decided it would be better to take a chance on love than to live without it. More than anything, she wanted to love her husband! Numa did not know that the jinn secretly wanted her as his wife, even though marriage was forbidden between humans and jinn-kind. From a distance, the jinn watched her. She began to eat the heart he had made for her. She swallowed it as she stood outside the tent of her betrothed—

the king she wished to marry. She called the name of the king, her future husband, and ran out of the tent to find him.

"When the jealous jinn saw this, he began to blow a wind with his angry lips. He blew so hard on the camp below that he created a storm above the oasis." I made the sound of wind, and Ziza bent and blew about like a palm. The children covered their eyes as the suspense grew.

"Despite her surprise and fear, Numa kept her eyes closed and felt the wind whip around her. She was afraid but did not dare open her eyes to see the destruction, afraid of what or whom she would fall in love with. The jinn traveled back down from the sky but unfortunately, the winds that he had created made this more difficult. He struggled to push through the wind and clouds to reach the human woman he desired but not before a lost donkey, frightened by the storm, ran past Numa and stepped on her bare toes. She screamed in agony and unthinkingly opened her eyes to see the backside of the donkey running away from her.

"All of a sudden, the heart began to speak to her, 'I love this donkey. I love this donkey's behind. I must love the donkey!'" The children began to laugh and howl at the joke. Ziza ran around the fire chasing an imaginary donkey, blowing kisses at it. The children rocked with laughter. I clapped my hands at her performance.

"The jinn, seeing that his trick had not worked, decided to move on to another camp to watch for another pretty woman who needed a heart. Here is the lesson, dear ones. If you happen to meet a jinn who offers you a heart, refuse it. It is merely a trick, and you may end up loving a donkey!"

The kids clapped at the story, and even my father had a good chuckle. The listeners showed their appreciation by tossing coral-colored desert flowers at my feet. I took Ziza's hand and we hugged, plainly pleased with ourselves. We collected our flowers and returned to sit near the bridal couple in a reserved place of honor. Pah made a space for me beside her at the feast, but I could see she had not enjoyed my story. She gripped my wrist and whispered fiercely, "You call Yuni a donkey, sister? Why would you tell such a story at my wedding feast?"

"Such was not my intention, dearest. But he looks much like a donkey, doesn't he?" Suddenly Pah rose and stared down at me fiercely. I thought she would slap me, as she had before, but she raised her hands and invited all the young women present to join her in a dance. I did not join her, and she did not invite me. I was not trying to find a husband, as many of the girls here were. My father looked at me questioningly, but I shook my head. His words from an earlier conversation echoed in my mind: "Please, Nefret. Marry so your sister cannot send you away. If you were betrothed to someone, she would have no power over you." I had given him a weak smile but refused.

Alexio plunked down in Pah's empty spot. "Nefret, you should watch yourself. Don't provoke her," he whispered, pretending to offer me a cup of wine.

"I am not provoking her. I told a story." I handed the cup back to him and clapped for the dancers. Alexio and I had grown apart in recent months, but in the past few days, things had changed. Looks passed between us that I could not readily explain. At times, he looked at me like a hungry man who had returned to the oasis after spending a month lost in the desert. Sometimes I thought he would ask me something, but I did not make that easy.

Somewhere in this crowd was Farafra, his intended. She made no friendly overtures to me, nor I to her. She stared at Alexio constantly but danced with the others, hoping he would notice her. Alexio was tall, with strong arms and legs, a requirement for a young man who wished to be a trader. He could carry sacks of heavy wheat and boxes of goods with little effort. He had smooth, light brown skin and dark eyes with a thick fringe of lashes. He had an easy, friendly manner and a pleasant, deep voice. The dance continued, and we smiled and clapped along.

My beautiful sister appeared to be the happiest woman alive; only I knew her unhappiness. I loved Pah and hoped she would soon forgive me. I had not intended to hurt her. Perhaps it had been a foolish story choice for a wedding, but as far as I could see, she was the only person who had been offended by the telling.

When the dance ended, one of the Council would come and declare good things over the marriage of Pah and Yuni and all would forget about me. It was good to be forgotten.

As if a veil had been lifted from my eyes, I became aware that someone watched me. I searched for Alexio, who had walked away to talk to nearby friends, but it was not him. Now that the dance had ended, he talked and laughed with Farafra. She was pretty, graceful and charmingly breathless after her dance; I felt a momentary stab of jealousy but pushed it away. Why shouldn't Alexio be happy? The girl was his intended, and she certainly appeared smitten with him. He caught me staring and smiled. Embarrassed, I looked away and continued to scan the crowd. The feeling that I was being watched did not fade.

I began to feel more uncomfortable even as I hunkered down into a cushion, tossed my long copper curls behind my back and slapped a smile on my face. Sitting cross-legged, I looked into the darkness beyond the crowd and thought I saw a figure move at the edge of the camp behind my father's massive tent. The height and size of the figure surprised me. And whoever he was, he had unusual eyes; it was like looking into the shiny eyes of a panther. Instinctively, I crossed my fingers to guard against evil magic. Before I could speak or call someone, the eyes faded and the figure disappeared. My heart pounded in my chest like a trapped bird. Everything around me—the smell of burning wood from the fire, the noise of the instruments, the chattering of the people—faded into nothingness. I shot to my feet on wobbly knees. I took a few steps toward the spot where the shiny-eyed being had stood, but I did not step into the darkness. I glanced behind me at my tribe, who continued in their revelry apparently unaware of the visitor. My mouth opened; I thought I should yell to someone, to warn them, but what would I say?

Then another face caught my attention. It was Farrah—perhaps she had seen him too. But she made no gesture and only watched me curiously. Maybe she had not seen anything after all.

I felt the urge to disappear, so I scurried away to my tent. It was time for this night to end. But that was not to be; Pah followed me. I stood on the path and laughed at her. "You are leaving your own wedding party? What will your husband say, Pah?"

"At least I will have a wedding—what will you have, Nefret? You won't have Alexio!" A beautiful smile spread across her face. It doubly stung that a face so like my own should mock me.

"None of us knows what the future holds, Pah. Are you the Old One now? Can you see the future?"

She laughed aloud. "You believe that? She can't see anything. Nothing at all. I don't need the Old One's sight to know you won't have Alexio as a husband. I am the mekhma now! You will marry whom I tell you to marry."

"I shall not marry anyone! What do you want, Pah? You have it all now."

"I want an apology! You had no right to tell such a story at my wedding. Apologize now!"

It was my turn to laugh. "What?"

"You *will* apologize, Nefret. Apologize to your mekhma while you still can." Her voice dropped to a deadly whisper. She inched closer, and the scent of expensive oils wafted around her.

I stared into the face of my first friend and now my greatest enemy. It was as if time stopped for a moment. She stood poised and ready to hear my apology, a proud, victorious look on her face.

"I would rather die." I tilted my chin and matched her stubborn expression.

Her lips set in straight lines, and anger flashed in her dark green eyes. "That can be arranged." She turned on her heel and slung her cloak over her shoulder before marching back to her wedding feast. My hands and body shook as I watched her walk away. There were no tears in my eyes, only emptiness in my heart. I would have to leave. I feared what Pah might do to the people I loved. I quickly returned to my small tent. I needed to pack for my journey.

Paimu! For a second, I imagined the worst. Did Pah have something to do with the girl's disappearance? Could she be that cruel?

I saw a figure waiting for me outside my tent. I froze, thinking it might be the frightening visitor I spotted earlier. But as I drew closer I recognized the tall figure as my father's. "Nefret!" he whispered.

"Come in, Father." We walked inside together, and I decided then and there to tell him nothing. He could not suspect my intentions, for I knew he would try to stop me. If the Meshwesh were to follow the Old Ways, then I would be turned away properly and with the tribe's blessing. That I could not bear. I would rather leave in the night without any type of sendoff. If only I could find Paimu! How could I leave without saying goodbye to her?

"Nefret, I urge you to reconsider your decision. If you marry someone honorable from Omel's tribe, Omel will surely welcome you and you will live with them for the rest of your life or until we return to Zerzura. Please consider this. Much is changing, and I can no longer protect you from your sister."

"I know that you care for me, Father, but I have no desire to marry anyone."

"If you spoke kindly to your sister, I am sure she would make the arrangements if you have your heart set on some young man." I did not answer him. "Please..." For the first time in my life, I saw my father cry. I touched his hand, and he pulled me to his chest and held me close. His hand clutched the back of my head gently as he wept. "I can't bear to lose you. You are so like your mother, did you know? You have her kind heart, and she loved children as you do. What would Kadeema say if I let you wander away into the Red Sands? She saw all this and could not bear it. Now I must bear it alone."

Shocked at his emotional outburst, I did not know what to say; I let his tears soak over me until soon I shed my own. "Father, I think it is too late. Pah is determined to see me gone, and I will not disappoint her."

Breaking our embrace, Father wiped the tears from his eyes with the back of his hand. He paced the small tent. "My brother, damn him! Insisting on the Old Ways! I would challenge him if I thought it would change anything."

"What is done is done. I am not afraid," I lied with false confidence.

His hands on his hips, he paused his pacing and looked at me. "You should be. These are strange times. You have seen it with your own eyes, and it is even more dangerous for a woman traveling the desert by herself."

"What do you mean?"

"In the best of times, the desert is no place for a single traveler, but that is especially true now with these attacks."

"Can't you call all the tribes here? What if we all stood together against these tall men or whoever is behind this?"

"This oasis is not large enough to support all the Meshwesh. I wish there was another way." He squeezed my shoulders and stared me in the eye. "When you leave, go to Petra. It is five days from here, far to the north. Go there and present yourself to the Nabataean king. Take this sigil with you and tell him who you are—he will honor me." I accepted the small painted banner.

"You want me to go to Petra? Isn't that the home of the jinn?"

"Superstition. Myth. There are no jinn, Nefret. If there ever were, they are long dead now. You should fear the living rather than spirits."

"Very well, Father. I will go to Petra."

"When I can, I will send someone to you with supplies. Pack what you can carry, but don't overburden yourself. Remember what you know. You have been taught well. You can make it, Nefret and I promise that I will not leave you alone."

I hugged him. He said, "In the meantime, do not push your sister. Pah holds all the power now, and she has very little love for you, although I cannot understand why."

With a final squeeze of my shoulder, he left me alone. Despite the distant music and the laughter that echoed through the camp, I decided to lie down for a nap. My plan was to rest now and rise early, earlier than even the goatherds. I would leave in the morning and head north to Petra, just as father instructed me. Although fear gripped my heart, I felt some comfort knowing the depth of his love.

I lay down on my pallet and gazed up at the dried flowers that hung from the center pole, Alexio's gift to me. I would miss him. I would miss dear Paimu. I hoped that when she came out of hiding, she would forgive me for leaving. The more I thought about it, the more I suspected that Ziza had hidden her at Paimu's request. As my eyelids drooped, I thought about what I would leave her.

She needed new shoes, but I had none that would fit her. Instead, I would leave her my silver bracelets and a few of my gold coins. To my father, I would send my necklace, the treasure that I had found in the desert.

To Alexio, well, I wasn't sure what to leave him.

I had already given him my heart.

Chapter Eleven

Death—Farrah

My bones hurt, my body and mind felt tired, but I could not refuse the dead girl who stood by my bed.

Her face was gray, her lips were bloodless and her eyes were like bottomless pits of darkness. The girl demanded revenge.

When I first awoke, I thought my spirit-visitor might be Ze, but the dead girl was too small and too young to be my sister. Ze had died as a young woman, not as a child. I lit a candle, and the ghost stepped back, fleeing from the light. She was not ready to leave the shadows until this matter had been settled.

"Paimu!" Realization crept across my face. Without acknowledging what I had said, the dead girl stepped to my tent door and vanished. I followed after her into the darkness. Mina slept at the foot of my bed, but I did not rouse her.

I strained to see into the gloom; an unusual fog had rolled into the camp, making it difficult to see even my own feet. "Where are you, girl?" I whispered into the darkness. Even before the words settled into the air around me, the dead girl reappeared, the fog clearing a bit to reveal her shocking face. "Where are we going? Are you taking me to my death, child?" My heart trembled at the thought.

She raised her finger to her lips. I kept quiet as she led me—a growing feeling of dread cascaded over me. Still I journeyed on behind her. I followed her down the sandy path to the center of the camp. We stood before Pah's tent door. The girl stepped through the canvas, and I followed her by slipping through the tent opening. How ironic that the mekhma's guards were asleep at their post! Surely that was this spirit's doing. Inside were Pah and her stupid husband Yuni, the pair sleeping soundly on a pile of luxurious furs.

I stood over the mekhma and watched as the girl pointed. Ah! Pah had murdered the child, and now Paimu had come for her revenge.

I nudged the sleeping queen with my toe and she awoke with a start, her dark copper hair tangled around her face. "What is it? What are you doing here? Who let you in?"

"They sleep, mekhma…and you have blood on your hands."

Still sleepy, Pah rubbed her face. "What? What are you talking about, Old One? Can't this wait?"

Anger welled up inside me. Was it mine? Was it Paimu's? I did not know. "Standing next to you is the child. The child you murdered and left in the sand. How did you kill her, mekhma? With a dagger? Ah yes, I see her wound." My hand flew to my stomach, matching the child's movements.

Pah flew to her feet and said in a whisper, "Lies! You must have a fever, Old One. Now go back to your tent. Do as I command!" She feigned outrage, but I could see the truth in her eyes. She had done this thing! I laughed at her.

The thin red-haired girl ordered me back to my tent again, and still I laughed but not at her. I laughed because it was I who had created all this misery. I had selected Pah over Nefret. I had chosen poorly.

"Stop that! Leave now, Farrah! Before I have you removed! Guards!"

Had I not held her first when she entered this world, even before her parents? *I* had spoken the words of life over her—*I* had predicted her rise as mekhma, and this was how she spoke to me.

"You do *not* command me, young one! As easily as I raised you, I can bring you down. And…" I said with a dark laugh, "you cannot deny justice to the dead. Believe me, I know. Murder exacts a price, even from mekhmas."

"What is going on here?" Yuni, Pah's big-eared husband, reached for his tunic and rose from his bed.

"Out!" I shouted at him.

"What?" he said, his hands on his hips, unashamed of his nakedness.

"Order him to leave, Pah, or he may hear something he cannot unhear."

Furrowing her brow, Pah told her husband, "Go now, Yuni. All is well, my love." Her eyes never left mine.

He dressed quickly and left us, pausing once at the door. "Should I call someone?"

Pah smiled at him peacefully. "No, call no one. I will come find you." I gave her credit; she had all the skills of a great actress. She reached for her robe, sliding it over her body; her hands had disappeared into the voluminous fabric. With a dainty smile so like her sister's she said, "Now explain yourself, Farrah."

"I wonder how Yuni would feel if it were known that his new wife had come to her marriage bed opened by another man. I care little for these things, but for a mekhma who has pledged to follow the Old Ways, and who came to power under them…"

"You would not dare!" Pah stood so close to my face I could feel her breath on me. The heat of her anger astonished me, but I refused to shudder before one so young.

"Wouldn't I?"

"If you knew, why wait until now to speak of it?"

"As I said, the condition of your maidenhood is of little concern to me. Although it might be interesting to see your father's expression when he hears who plucked the fruit from the vine. However, I care little about this matter, and that is not why I came here."

She eased back a step and drew up her gown with her hands as she stepped back again with narrowed eyes. "Why then have you come, Old One?"

"I awoke with a dead girl standing over me—Paimu, Nefret's treasure. She led me to you."

Her eyes widened again and her lips set in a grim line. She said nothing, so I continued.

"You murdered her, Pah—although your motives for doing so are unclear to me. And fortunately for you, the dead do not speak. Whatever your intentions, you must confess your crime and tell us where you hid her body or else you walk under a curse. You had no authority to do such a thing."

"Lies!" Pah hissed, but I heard the truth in her voice. And the dead girl's pale face testified against her. Although the mekhma could not see her, I could. Awareness crept over me—I could see again!

"This was a shameful act, a poor way to begin your rule, Pah hap Semkah. Perhaps your tribe will forgive you, but you cannot hide from this deed. The dead have come seeking vengeance."

"She wasn't even Meshwesh!"

"Paimu was a treasure of the tribe," I said firmly. Terror flashed in her eyes, but she quickly recovered.

"Now, Farrah. I understand that you think you see things—that you're some type of nabi-prophetess. But the truth is you are getting old. Too old, I am afraid, to lead the Council anymore. How can we trust your judgment when you tell such lies? Now go rest, and I will send someone to attend you. You are weak from the trials, Old One."

The dead child stepped closer to us, staring at Pah's face and then at mine. She shook her head at me furiously, but I could not determine what she wished to convey. Hot anger rose in my gut, and I would not be denied this confrontation. The reality of what I had done, how I had swayed the Council to favor Pah, all my deeds weighed on me now as the truth of her character was revealed to me. I had to make this right!

"How dare you speak to me in such a manner? I am not your foolish husband, nor am I one of your stupid followers, Pah. What could that child have done to you? What crime could she have committed that would have caused you to take her young life—to shed her blood in the sand? I see her! I see the wound in her belly! Confess the truth now!"

"Now you turn your back on me? I only did what you taught me!" Her voice sounded sharp as steel.

"I never taught you to murder, Pah."

"Oh? Didn't you? What do you think the flames showed me, Farrah? I could see very well. I know your secret." Her voice dripped venom. "The flames showed me the day you sat on my grandfather Onesu's chest, spat in his face and slid the knife across his neck! How dare you lecture me! Have you not done the same thing?"

My voice shook with anger. "No! It is not the same thing! I never killed a child! I took vengeance for my sister, something you would know nothing about! How easy was it, Pah, to turn your back on *your* sister? To kill her treasure?"

"Again with Nefret? You were the one who wanted me to win the trials, and so I have! I am the strongest, the fastest, the smartest—but does that matter to you? Nobody ever saw me. Not Alexio, not Semkah, no one! I made a name for myself, and I will never relinquish my power! You have no right to ask me! You are not innocent, Farrah."

Blinking away her accusations, I asked her again, "What did you do, Pah? I must know what happened. You cannot take us to Zerzura with this stain on your soul. The way will be hidden from you unless you confess. You must trust me in this."

"Why should I tell you anything? You don't know what you're talking about, Farrah! Now leave, or I *will* call my guards to haul you out of here." Turning her back on me, she strode to a nearby table and began brushing the tangles from her hair. From the reflection in the brass mirror she held, I could see her pretty face. It appeared calm and fearless, but I knew better. I stepped behind her.

"Do not turn your back on me, girl!"

"I am going to warn you only once more." She stared at me from the mirror. "Leave now, Farrah."

"You cannot send *her* away. You took a life—a debt is owed."

Setting down the brush, she turned to face me. We were inches apart. Out of the corner of my eye I could see Paimu slipping away, her image fading, her mouth open in a silent scream. As she backed away, sadness washed over her face. I reached out my hand to the dead girl to plead with her to remain, but I was unable to express my words.

A shocking pain caused my body to seize all thoughts and feelings. I was consumed by the pain, and my hands clutched at the source of the agony. A blade protruded from my belly. Pah's hand was upon it.

With an anguished gasp, I stared into the mekhma's lovely face. Her lowered lids shielded her eyes, eyes that watched me fall to my knees. A smile crept across her full, apricot-colored lips. As I fell, she twisted the blade once more before she slid it from my body. I wanted to scream but found no voice. This was my end. I kept staring at her face, and she never swayed from my vision.

Mina, if you can hear me. Come now!

I could not speak the words, but my mind called Mina to me. Sometimes she could hear me; perhaps it was not too late.

Mina, please. Come!

Pah knelt beside me. "Now I take *my* vengeance, Farrah. I can see in the flames, remember?" She whispered into my ear, "I saw what you did to my mother. How you led her to the dream world even though you knew it would kill her. You left her there. Then you watched as she walked into the desert and was swallowed by the sand. You have more than one death on your hands, don't you, Old One?"

I tried to explain myself, but the only sound I made was a weak gurgle. I could barely breathe now. Death would arrive any second—excruciating pain radiated from my belly to all parts of my body. I could feel my heart pounding harder and the blood flowed faster.

"You deserve death. How dare you think you could take this from me? I am the mekhma! I *am* the life of the Meshwesh! It is not in your power to stop what the gods have ordained—you who worship dead ancestors. What have they ever done for you, Farrah? I worship the true gods of Kemet—Isis, Hathor and Mut! It is them you have offended with your unholy prayers and deeds. Go now, Old One, and may you never find your ancestors. Reap now what you have sown!"

Mina!

The taste of blood filled my mouth, and the light began to fade from my vision. All that was left for me was the face of Nefret...no, that was Pah's face above me, gloating and victorious.

I curse you, Pah.

From behind her, a sound—a muffled scream. Mina stepped into view and pushed the mekhma aside. She did not speak. I sometimes wondered if she had forgotten how. I missed hearing her voice, so deep and dusky, quite different than what one would expect from such a plain face. I reached for her, but my hands would not obey. She pulled me to her and shook with silent cries as the light dimmed to just a pinhole. My garment felt sticky and wet.

There would be no justice for Paimu now. That thought saddened me.

Even worse than the pain was the knowledge that I would never see Zerzura again. Not in this life or the next.

My misery was complete.

Chapter Twelve

Outcast—Semkah

I was riding the blue waves of the Northern Sea again—I knew this dream. Each time it unfolded differently, but always I would see Kadeema in the distance and rarely did I reach her. This time, the motion of the waves did not leave me retching on the deck like a pregnant woman. No salty waves threatened to drown me as they had when I was a young man and in other dreams. In this dream, things were different. That both worried and excited me.

I stood at the bow of the boat confidently, watching the land of Grecia become larger and larger as I drew near its shores. I had a crew, but their faces were elusive, likely unimportant to the drama that was about to unfold.

I scanned the hills knowing that I would see her. Yes! There she was—high on a hilltop, the highest hilltop. *Kadeema!* Behind her, her long red curls bounced on the breeze and her bare arms were open and welcoming to me. Too far away to see the expression on her face, I imagined it, peaceful and serene. Her coral lips parted as she whispered my name.

"Semkah! Semkah! Hurry, my love!" Her straight, proud nose and wide green eyes set her apart from any of the women I knew.

Suddenly, a mist threatened to cloud my view—I frantically waved my hands and unexpectedly the fog disappeared. I laughed with joy when I discovered that the boat now rested very close to the shore. Soon I would disembark and run up the hill to find her—to be with her again at long last.

"Not long now, Kadeema!" I called up to her.

I waved furiously at her as the boat's anchor fell into the water with a loud splash. The cruel sun rose behind her, and again I could not see her face. Frustration rose within me. To look upon her face again! Her arms were not outstretched anymore; they were at her side, and her hair no longer floated around her. Something was wrong! She was leaving—somehow I knew it!

Desperately I leaped from the boat into the water. With all my might I swam for the shore, knowing that the time grew short. Splashing to the shore desperate for breath, I forced myself to stand. I shed my dagger and heavy wet tunic and climbed the hillside on wobbly legs like a drunken man. "Kadeema!" I called, but no answer came. Higher and higher I climbed, navigating sharp rocks and slick muddy patches. Finally reaching the grassy precipice, I stopped to catch my breath before making the last push to the top of the hill. Too winded to speak, I licked my dry, salty lips and threw myself on the crag.

No one was there. I wept as a man should not, without shame or care for who might witness my weakness. When I had no more tears to shed, I rolled over on my back and stared at the gray sky above me. "Kadeema!" I yelled furiously. "Why have you left me again?"

The clouds lowered, as they could do only in dreams, until they rested right above me. They moved and shook and parted, and I saw her face again. This time I saw it as clearly as I could see anyone's, only it hovered above me from the clouds.

"Why are you here, husband?"

Surprised and troubled by her question, I smiled at her. "My wife! How I have longed to see you, to touch you!" With shaking fingers I reached for her, but she pulled away. "Come to me, Kadeema. I thought I would never find you."

Her face grew sad. "You should not be here, Semkah. This is no place for flesh and blood, my love." Her face began to disappear from my sight.

"No! Why do you flee from me?"

She stared back, her face a mask of solemnity. There was no life there, no desire for me, just sadness and regret. How many times had I traveled here in my dreams and prayed for such a moment? Without moving her lips she whispered, "They're coming...protect my daughters, Semkah. If you love me, protect them." She bowed her head, and disappeared, swallowed into the mist that threatened to take me as well. The fallen cloud was freezing to the touch, and my skin crawled as it threatened to envelop me. I began to run—I did not know where—anywhere but into the mist. As I moved, it rolled behind me like a living thing. I could hear the screams and moans of others trapped in the rolling wall of gray that covered the hill. I ran to the cliff's edge—I had nowhere else to go. As the gray cloud darkened to black and reached for me, I leaped. I screamed and woke up to find Omel standing over me.

"Brother! Wake up! Your daughter calls you!"

"Nefret? I thought you were going home."

"No, not Nefret. It is Pah who has summoned you. I wished to do just that thing, but my son Alexio has ridden out—foolish boy. He has no patience and did not tell me that he was leaving. I cannot leave without him."

"Ridden out where?"

"He is impatient to prove Nefret's story. He rode to Siya for other proof instead of waiting for Aitnu's return from Biyat. Foolish boy! But it is good that I have not left, because Farrah, the Old One, has disappeared along with the other—the Algat girl. That is two disappearances in two days! Something is wrong here at Timia." Omel paused, and his long legs shuffled nervously as if he did not want to tell me something. Ignoring his Egyptian skirt and kohl-lined eyes, I observed him carefully.

"Well, what is it?"

"Nefret left in the night. From the tracks in the sand, it appears as if she traveled to the north. She can easily be found, my brother. Should I go and bring her back? I am sure the mekhma would want to send her off properly, according to the Old Ways."

"Indeed I am sure she would not." I said wearily, Kadeema's condemning eyes still before me. Now was the time for truth, wasn't it? I would never see Kadeema again, and my daughters were now mortal enemies. I had allowed this to happen. "Don't go after her. I will deal with the mekhma. Now that she has been elected by the Council, the mekhma isn't going to follow the Old Ways, I can assure you of that. No way will she want the tribe to shower Nefret with their silver and gold and send her away happily. Nefret did the right thing, Omel."

"I don't think your other daughter agrees…" he said, continuing in a hushed voice, "and you should not say such things to others, even to me. That could be considered treason now that we have a mekhma."

"Then let her send me away too. I am too tired, too old to worry about hurting my daughter's feelings—and I would feel the same way even if she were the Queen of Egypt!" A chill ran up my spine, and I got up and sloshed cold water on my face in an attempt to purge my mind and heart of the dream. "What has happened to Farrah? Another trip into the desert? Some kind of ritual that she has told us nothing about? She has done this before, disappearing for days and then showing up unharmed. What does her acolyte say?"

"Nothing, of course. We cannot question her—she took the oath."

"Yes, I know."

Omel said, "This is not like before. Farrah did not simply walk off the oasis."

"What makes you say that?" I rubbed my face with the linen towel and reached for my belt.

"Because there is blood in the sand, much blood. One of the dogs found the trail but so far not Farrah."

The tribe would be rattled by this news. Too much was happening—it could only mean that our fortunes had turned and not for the better.

"You should hurry, brother, and be warned. I am afraid we have awakened a fierce hawk in Pah."

"Not *we*, brother. This was not my idea. It was you who wanted Pah. It was you who wanted to use the Old Ways when it was advantageous to you. Now I must go and deal with her."

As I slid my dual blades into my leather harness, I glanced at my snake tattoos. Although the purple ink had faded, it was if they were alive today, alive and ready to protect me from my own ambitious child. I hoped they would.

With sadness from the dream lingering in my mind and heart, I walked to Pah's tent and waited to be welcomed in. Pah had chosen blue as her fabric for her royal tent, with a gold top and rich gold cords that streamed from the center pole. Ushered in speedily, I took in my surroundings quickly. My daughter had not wasted any time setting up her tent. A small backless chair sat near the center of the tent, like a throne. So this was how it was to be, then? Not mekhma but queen?

She came into the tent behind me and took her seat in the chair. Spreading her blue gown about her, she sat serenely enough, but I could tell a storm brewed within her. "Father, is it true that you sent Nefret away? Before our tribe could bless her properly?"

"I advised Nefret to marry; that is all. She refused and declared her intentions to leave. I counseled against it, but she was resolute. There was no persuading her."

Pah was not fooling me; I knew perfectly well that she had no intention of blessing her sister before she left. "More is the pity," she said, "because now she stands accused of murdering our beloved Farrah and probably Paimu too."

A laugh flew out of my throat. "I can't believe that! Nefret would never harm any creature—especially Paimu! She loved the girl like a...I mean...like a..."

"Like a sister?"

I turned red. I did not want to stir Pah to jealousy over poor Paimu.

"Now, just now, we have found the body of Paimu, and we have found the body of Farrah. Both were stabbed with a knife, stabbed in their bellies. Nefret is missing. No one has seen her. Isn't that suspicious?"

"It is unfortunate, but I do not think it suspicious. Are you bringing some sort of charges against your own sister, daughter?"

Pah's wide, innocent-looking eyes had deceived me before; I would not fall for it again. She would do what she wanted, but now I had to think of Nefret.

Without answering me, she pressed on. "And Alexio? Am I to believe it is merely a coincidence that he is gone too?"

"Alexio left for Siya because he could not wait for Aitnu's return with the news from Biyat. Your uncle told me this morning. I had no idea he was leaving. Since you seem unsettled by his mission, I assume you did not send him?"

"Of course not." With a nod to her husband, Pah accepted a leather pouch from him and put it in her lap. Unwrapping it with hurried fingers, she revealed what was inside.

"Nefret left this behind in Farrah's tent. I think this may have been the reason she killed her. Perhaps the Old One caught her stealing this—I don't know, but I know my sister never owned such a thing."

The emerald and gold necklace fell into her lap and sparkled like a living thing. She picked it up and held it out to me as if it were a snake.

Blinking like a madman, I stammered, "Where did you get that?"

"I told you, Father. Nefret left this in Farrah's tent. The pouch was wrapped in one of her old tunics. She left some other things too, but this I do not recognize. I am sure it does not belong to her. Do you know where it came from? What is so special about it?"

Accepting the necklace from her, I squeezed it. "This necklace belonged to your mother and her mother before her. The last time I saw it, she was wearing it."

Pah rose from her chair, and her hand flew to her mouth. "How? How did Nefret get this?" Snatching the necklace back from me, she turned it over in her hand as if she would find the clues she was looking for written in the gold. There were letters on the back of the emerald pendant, but in a writing I could not understand. No one in the tribe could, except maybe Farrah. I missed the Old One already.

I had no answers and offered none.

"How do you know my mother had this necklace on when she disappeared? Perhaps she left it with Farrah? Or left it behind and the old woman hid it?"

I shrugged. "I can't know and neither can you, seeing as Farrah is dead now."

Yuni said, "It is the necklace of a queen. You should wear it, mekhma. It is yours by right." He offered to put it around her neck. I watched as she lifted her hair. The young man fastened the necklace, and she spun around so he could appraise her. "Almost as lovely as you, Pah."

She smiled, pleased with his comment. But her smile disappeared when she saw the look on my face. "You don't look pleased, Father. I suppose you are disappointed that I am the one wearing this necklace."

"No, I am remembering a dream I had last night. A warning dream, Pah. Your mother would not be happy—is not happy—that you and your sister have parted ways. She saw this. She saw all this the night you were born. She begged me to stop it, but I could not. I listened to the Council. I should have sent one of you away to Omel. Then I could have prevented this. You are strong together, Pah. You belong together, you and Nefret!"

She swung her thick gown behind her and flew toward me. "Now you say this? Now? What am I to think? It is too late to clear your conscience, Father. You made your choice, and you lost." The surprise must have shown on my face because she added with a smile, "Oh yes, I know all about it. You wanted Nefret as mekhma—this I know, but that is no matter now."

"I never wanted that. I did not want to follow the Old Ways!"

"Perhaps not, but here we are. I have won! I am mekhma! Take your regrets and leave, Father. I am relieving you of your duty." We stood eye to eye for an eternal moment. I raised my hand to plead sense with her, but she would not be swayed.

Yuni stood by her, his hand on her shoulder. "Send for your uncle. Perhaps he will be of better service to you." Pah agreed, and Yuni then left us alone.

My mind roiled with what I should say, what I should do. Kadeema's accusation rang in my ears: "What of our daughters, Semkah?" I would have to answer for my inaction one day. I had buried my heart in my own grief and had failed to protect them from Farrah's prophecy. I had failed.

Feeling an icy stare at my back, I walked out too.

Chapter Thirteen

Loving the Mekhma—Alexio

We heard them before we saw them. So ecstatic, so frenzied were they from their bloody victory that they did not notice us. There were only three of us, not enough to challenge the approaching horde. Phares was barely a man, and his brother Ohn was not much older. Still, they had been the only ones I could persuade to accompany me, and I refused to let Pah win the day. If I was going to sacrifice my life and my happiness for the tribe, it would mean something.

If I could have gone to Biyat to get proof of Nefret's testimony, then surely the Council would have reconsidered its decision. Unfortunately for me, I had not been selected for that mission. So my friends and I went in search of other proof that Nefret's warnings were real. If the threat was real, and I believed it was, our tribe was in danger. We could not afford to wait for Aitnu to return. He was traveling to all the tribes for an assessment. And the longer we waited to know the truth, the firmer the grip that Pah would have on the throne. Pah had stolen the throne from Nefret by refusing to wait for her to complete her task.

I had it on good authority that proof would force the Old Ones to weigh the trials anew. The whole clan needed Nefret—and I did not think that merely because I loved her more than my own heartbeat. I thought it because it was true. Nefret outshone her sister in many ways, especially in kindness, goodness and patience. No doubt Pah had courage, fierceness and strength, but she did not inspire me and would not hesitate in her ruthlessness.

No matter how many sweet words Pah whispered to me, no matter how like her sister she appeared in some ways, I could not give her what she wanted. In the end, I refused her, and it was then that she began her ruthless campaign against Nefret.

Now here I lay in the red sand on the side of a dune watching a black-cloaked band of murderers leaving the tiny oasis of Gemia, north of Timia. Tents burned, children screamed and goats shrieked as the bandits pierced them with spears. I grabbed Ohn's arm to prevent him from reaching for his bow. "There are too many, brother. We need to wait. Wait and watch. Be still, Ohn,

Phares. Be still now." Ohn leaned against the dune and closed his eyes. Tears streamed down his young face.

"Yes, be still now. Our father will not be happy if I do not bring you home," Phares scolded his brother. Ohn obeyed and waited and watched until the raiding party left. They rode off into the distance without ever looking in our direction. They were not jinn or giants but men on a mission. I had seen my share of bloodthirstiness before, but these heinous acts were beyond anything I could have imagined. Children were decapitated, pregnant women had their bellies slit, and their unborn children emerged into the world in an untimely, bloody mess. The old men had their heads removed, but not before their eyes had been gouged out; their mouths gaped open in silent screams. Ohn vomited on his sandals and half the burnt grass of the oasis.

I had seen enough. There was no one alive, no one to testify against the killers. I wondered what I could bring back to the tribes to prove these tall men were indeed real and not a fabrication by a girl who had failed her trial and was desperate to claim the title of mekhma. I had no chance of following Aitnu or making it all the way to Biyat now. Perhaps if I had been by myself, but not with Phares and Ohn. Although brave and keen to serve with me, they did not have the stamina necessary to make such a speedy ride. I needed to go home; it was only a half day's ride back to Timia, too close to stand idly by and wait for the murderers to destroy our tribes. As I scanned the bloody scene, I wondered what proof to bring. Then I saw my answer. Pinned to the chest of a dead young man was a piece of fabric. Someone had taken the trouble to leave this message—it should not be ignored. I removed the sword from the dead boy's chest, saying a silent apology as I did, asking his forgiveness for this one last offense. I removed the cloth and shoved it into my tunic.

"Let us leave this place of death," I told the young men. Anxious to leave the horror behind us, we wasted no time. As swiftly as the animals would allow, we rode pell-mell to the east. I glanced behind me as we rode, trying to shake the feeling that the death god Osiris himself followed us.

I slapped the sides of the camel with my rough leather strap and hugged it, keeping my head down and back straight as I had been taught. Our tribe was known for its desert speed—proper riding technique was something the son of a king or even a half-king such as my father would be expected to know. Now I would put that talent to good use in the hope of saving my tribe and Nefret's. As I raced back toward Timia I prayed that all would be well with my people, although logic suggested that it would not be well at all. These tall men or whoever they were seemed to be specifically targeting Meshwesh. The Algat and other tribes were around, but no reports had come in from their locations. I had witnessed with my own eyes that these people had a bloodlust that knew no bounds.

Whoever they were, their reach was long, for they had traveled to Biyat and to the tiny oasis of Siya without much opposition. It only made sense that they would attack wealthy Timia, and in a way it was fortuitous that my father and his tribe were currently there. Together the tribes made a mighty force, but to withstand such a foe? We were not prepared! I needed the help of the entire clan! The Bee-Eater must be sent and the call made to all the Meshwesh. We would stand together, or we would die!

We crested a dune and suddenly Timia sprawled before us, lush, green and filled to the borders with Meshwesh warriors, their families and their lowing cattle. A heavy plunder waiting to be plucked. To my great relief all appeared safe. The camp was noisier than normal, but that was to be expected; the mekhma trials were historic events to even the lowliest Meshwesh. Representatives from some of the tribes had arrived to hear the decision of the Council; others had not made the trip. But there was not much argument. It had been accepted from their birth night that either Pah or Nefret would be the promised leader who would guide us back to Zerzura. One day we would be safe. Or so everyone assumed.

I pulled the reins of the camel and waved the brothers to me. "Listen to me. We don't have much time. Let me do the talking. I will find Semkah and give a report."

Ohn's eyes widened with surprise. "Yes, but the mekhma…." He appeared unsure. "Should we not speak to her first?"

"Please, you must trust me, brothers. I know what I am doing. Say nothing to anyone. Not yet."

Catching his breath after the furious ride, Phares nodded his consent, and together the three of us rode the rest of the way into camp. They busied themselves with the camels as I went in search of Semkah. From the moment I began to walk through the camp, I could feel the sadness. Something had happened! The faces of the Meshwesh were full of despair. I greeted many by name, but no one offered any explanation. Suddenly, women began to howl—and the hair on the back of my neck stood up. An urgency rose within me, and I ran faster toward the king's tent. What had happened?

Nefret!

I found Semkah in his tent with my father, in the midst of an argument. That was always the way with them, struggling with one another. My father's stubbornness and ambition made it difficult for him to trust anyone. For my uncle's part, he kept his involvement to a minimum, leaving many to believe that he was not confrontational enough to be the clan's warrior-king. I knew firsthand that it was a title that father coveted. Theirs was a difficult relationship to manage, and few tried to interfere.

"What has happened?" I blurted out, trying to catch my breath.

"Foolish boy! What do you mean by leaving without my permission! You know we planned to leave today and now… "

"Farrah is dead," my uncle broke in.

"What? How?" Again the hair on my neck crinkled.

"That is what we must find out, but you must account for yourself." Father's dark brows knitted together.

"I have the proof—Nefret told the truth. Don't you want to know the truth? Look at this! It was found on the body of a dead boy at Gemia. All of them are dead! Just like Biyat and Siya! This is the proof that it was as she says." I pulled the bloody rag out of my tunic and handed it to the king. Without a word, Semkah took it.

"You say you found this at Gemia?" he asked as he spread the crumpled cloth out on the table.

"Yes, uncle."

"The raiders are moving." Semkah's voice shook.

"Yes, my king. The Meshwesh at Gemia were all dead. We saw them—the tall men. One of them pinned this to a man with the man's own blade."

My father made a snorting sound. "We have no king anymore, boy. We have a mekhma, remember? What happens if she finds out you left without permission?"

Defiantly I challenged him. "I am no boy. Uncle, Father, surely this symbol means something. A message, perhaps?"

"More like a warning," Semkah said. He leaned over a lambskin map that rested perpetually on a sturdy table with an onyx top.

Together the three of us stared at the map and then the cloth, but the pattern was not clear to me. After a moment, Semkah turned the cloth and the image became apparent. A lightning bolt clutched in a hand.

"What is this? What does it mean?"

"I have seen this before, Omel. This is Kiffian. The hand symbol—these are the tall men. We thought they were all dead."

"I have seen them, my king. They are indeed tall—taller than any Meshwesh. And they kill without mercy. No one will stand before them if we do not prepare for battle. I have no doubt they will come here next. Why wouldn't they?"

"You should leave the battle planning to us, boy."

"Father, this is…"

Before we could continue, a great commotion filled the camp. The mourning wails were replaced with screams of terror. We raced outside to see with our own eyes what we already knew. The tall men had arrived—they must have followed us here!

"By the gods! We must fight!" I ran behind them toward the racks that held our wicker shields and curved fighting blades, and my father raced before us all.

Semkah reached for me. "Wait! You must find Nefret!"

"Where is she?"

"She left this morning. Look to the north; she headed to Petra."

"But why? Why would she go there?"

"Because I sent her! I let this happen. I have no right to ask, but please help her. Go now—go north. She cannot be that far ahead."

The shrill sounds of swords clashing and screams filled the air. I caught a glimpse of Phares and Ohn, who ran into the fray with their swords drawn and were battling clumsily for their lives. The invaders were tall and muscular—much taller than the slender Meshwesh. Semkah towered over most of his tribe, and even the king was slight in comparison to the red-haired Kiffians. I watched my father run toward a massive beast of a man and with one swing cut the man down. Swords clanged, and the Kiffians pressed into the camp easily, killing all who tried to stand against them.

"But I must fight! You need me!" I screamed at him, still ready to race into battle. "Ohn!"

I saw Ohn fall to the ground not fifty feet away, and blood gurgled from his mouth. A giant laughed above him, ignoring his pleas for mercy. I lurched toward him, but Semkah grasped my arm.

"Please, for the love you bear my daughter! Go! While you still can!" Then the angry king turned on his heel and pulled his curved blade from his belt. With a war cry, Semkah spun and lunged toward the nearest enemy. His blow landed perfectly at the beast's neck.

With a heart torn in two, I ran back toward the nearest camel—I could not linger if I was to obey Semkah. I reasoned with myself that I was merely following the king's commands, not abandoning my brothers or my father. As if he could read my mind, Father called me. His sword banged another and he struggled with his foe. "Alexio! Come now, son! Help us!"

With all my heart I wanted to heed his summons, but I had to find Nefret. Surely he would understand. With the sounds of war in my ears, I rode away as tears streaked my face. Once more I heard someone call my name. I did not look back.

I knew it was a sound that I would never forget.

Chapter Fourteen

For the Tribe—Nefret

The North Star shone bright when I left Timia. I followed it obediently, reminding myself of my father's promise to help me. I was not alone. I followed the star until the sun rose and then kept my path straight toward the north and to Petra.

Farrah had taught us that Petra was haunted, and now here I was racing toward that very place. According to my father it would take five days to reach Petra, but what would I find there if and when I made it? Probably no living soul. I shuddered under my cloak thinking of the story of Numa and the jinn. I had never heard of the Nabataeans until I was sent to their court.

All that we knew—all that we had been told—was a lie. I had seen the Shining Man; he made no claim to be a god, yet I knew he was something other than human. And he was in control of my life. Besides him, there were no gods and goddesses. Isis, Hathor even our dead ancestors—they could not hear the voices of mere mortals. No one cared for man, only men themselves. I struggled with this new realization and thought of my sister, who now ruled our tribe. I had been wise to leave, of that much I was sure. No doubt she would've made an example of me, parading me in front of her friends before she sent me to my death in the desert with no water or food or even the companionship of a donkey or camel.

Poor Paimu! Whenever she came out of hiding, how angry she would be to know that I left without her. *Forgive me, little one.*

How strange it was to see no one. Every morning before, I had been met with friendly Meshwesh faces. Isha, who gave me bread. Paimu and Ziza, who chattered through their breakfast nearly every sunrise. Now I was doomed to a life without the company of my clan. Why had Father sent me here? There were no Meshwesh in Petra. Was I to remain by myself? Surrounded by a sea of sadness, I continued to track north. I spied a few serpents and caught a glimpse of a clever hawk searching for those slithering tasty morsels. They quickly hid themselves in the sand. I was like them now, a lowly snake hiding in the sand. Tears welled up in my eyes but I did not allow myself the luxury of crying. I needed to preserve my water, not shed it over my heartless sister.

Soon the heat of the day was upon me, and I began to worry about where I would find shelter from the blazing hot afternoon. To add to my discomfort, the wind began to blow, kicking up sand all around me. Wrapping the cloak around my face, I made a slit for my eyes and continuously scanned the horizon for a place to camp.

Someone must be looking out for me, I thought, as just a few minutes later I spotted a rocky outcropping nearby. I made for it quickly but cautiously, knowing I may not be the only person looking for shelter. Sweating under my cloak, I dismounted from my camel and led him up the side of the rocky hill. He complained and spat furiously, but I was immune to his disdain. "I am trying to save our lives, stupid," I scolded him. Clucking at him, I snapped the rein a few times, and he unhappily followed me. "Just a little further—come on now. I will call you Ginku, the stubborn one." He snorted his disapproval but obeyed me.

We inched upwards until we came to the flat place. "Here we go. This will do. You sit there." I patted his shoulder and immediately he plunked down, curling his legs under him. In just a few minutes I had a makeshift shelter made of a cloth and two sticks I had carried with me from Timia. Unrolling my bedroll, I sat upon the pallet, happy to be off the swaying camel for a little while. The sun burned above me, but my small patch of shade brought some relief. I took a long drink from my goatskin.

I had been riding for hours—at least six, but it felt longer. Every step away from my tribe was a step toward the unknown. I was too tired to build a fire for food. I looked around nervously, hoping there were no bandits secreted in the caves above me. Even in the land of the Meshwesh it would be foolish to believe that a single woman was safe here among the many peoples of the desert. To the untrained eye, the Red Sands may have seemed like an endless sea. But to the intrepid trader or mercenary, the Sahara was a highway—a rich highway loaded with treasures, including slaves.

For the first time in my life, I whispered a prayer into the surrounding heat. I had no incense, no gifts or food to offer, only my words. "If you can hear me, I beg you. Lead me as you promised you would."

With sleepy eyes but an active mind, I forced my eyes to remain closed.

Suddenly I was flying, soaring above the reddish-brown earth below me. I was no longer Nefret but a falcon—a Heret falcon with massive, curved wings. With just a flick of my wings I rose high, soaring on the gust into the white clouds. With an easy flutter, I sailed downward and began to skim the sands. I screeched and rose higher and higher until again the lands below appeared small and unimportant. From my cloudy hiding place, I watched and waited. But for what I did not know.

Then like a massive snake, a band of tall men on dark-haired camels raced across the desert in perfect formation. The camels were hunkered low as the riders slapped them ruthlessly to run faster and faster. I swooped down to get a closer look at the tall men's faces. Their hands were bloody, evidence of a recent assault. Their black clothing was stained with rust-colored blood. They let out a gleeful shout as they sailed across the sands, happy that they had accomplished their evil deed. I dove even closer to get a look at what bounty they carried away. With my excellent falcon vision, I detected living beings.

Thrown across the saddle of the leader, in a crumpled heap of copper hair and torn clothing, was my sister. An evil gash stretched down her bloody arm, which hung motionless from her side. With her other arm she clutched her ripped gown to cover her naked breasts. I dove down further until I flew beside the giants and was even with Pah. Panicked, I called her name, but all that emerged from my lips was an ear-splitting screech. Pah's fevered eyes opened, and she looked at me with anguish and regret.

"Sister!" she cried out, reaching for me with her good hand.

Suddenly the scene changed—I was no longer a falcon.

I cried out to her again, "Pah!" She was gone, her face disappearing like someone wiped their hand across a pool of water.

I stood in an empty valley. I wore warrior's clothing, a leather vest and armbands, with my quiver on my back. Standing upon a high hill, I watched the horizon and waited for our enemy to approach. Below me were the Meshwesh, few in number but fear-

lessly ready for battle. They gazed up at me and began to sing the song of Zerzura. I raised my arms high and sang it with them.

> *We are the children of the Red Lands*
> *We are the children of Ma'at*
> *Zerzura, Zerzura, let us come home to you*
> *For our blood is your blood, our land is your land*
> *Zerzura, Zerzura, we come home to you...*

On the horizon I saw the tall men approach on their black camels. They were greater in number this time, with a determined look of absolute hatred upon their faces. In that moment, it was as if I could read their hearts and see their thoughts. It was the gold they were after, the gold and the turquoise, and our children and anything of value. There was no mercy in them. In the valley below me I watched an extraordinary sight—a whistle blew, and the Meshwesh retreated into their secret places. They hid under the ground in hollowed-out holes that were covered with grass and branches. In their hands were their curved blades, sharpened savagely and poised for attack. Some had even taken the trouble of wetting the blades' edges with poison so that even the most glancing of cuts would be lethal. My heart swelled with pride. I alone stood on the hill above them, a gold shield in my hand. I turned the shield to catch the sun. It glinted, beckoning the Kiffians toward me and to their fate. Again I could read the minds and the hearts of the approaching horde. "We have them surrounded!" I laughed at them as they ran to their doom. The faces of the dead flashed before me, and I awoke screaming.

Alexio's handsome face hovered over me. "Nefret!"

"Alexio? Am I dreaming still?"

His beautiful smile told me that I was not. I threw my arms around him and held him close. I kissed his cheek and touched his face, hair and arms. "You *are* here. You are not a dream."

"No, I am not," he said gently. "Your father sent me to find you. The camp is under attack, Nefret. The tall men are Kiffians. They are the ones you saw—I am sure of it. They have murdered everyone at Biyat, Siya and Gemia, and I fear for those at Timia. Even with our numbers we are outmatched and were overtaken quickly. I do fear the worst."

He appraised our surroundings. "This is not a safe place. We must go higher."

"What do you mean? We must go back! Our people need us."

"We cannot help them. I have to protect you, princess. The king ordered me to do so."

"Stop calling me that. I am no princess. I am an outcast, remember? I'm nobody."

Walking toward me in angry strides, Alexio said, "And yet you want to go back for them? Stop this foolish talk. We do not have time for it. We cannot go back right now, but we will go back. We must be smart and wait a while. Trust me when I say to you there's nothing you can do for our people now. But they will need you when the battle is over."

"How can you ask me to sit here and wait? They have taken my sister—I have seen it!"

Alexio pushed his hair out of his eyes and stared at me. "What do you mean you have seen it?"

"I saw it in a dream. I know it sounds crazy—I sound like Farrah—but I did see it! They have Pah, and I must get her back."

His face crumpled at the mention of the Old One. "Farrah is dead now. She has died."

"What?"

"And there is more. I don't know how else to tell you this. Paimu—she is dead too. Both were stabbed and buried in the sand. Before you jump to your sister's side, you should know that she implicated you in these crimes. In fact my father and yours were in the midst of an argument over what to do about all this when the enemy rode in."

"She would never—how could she dream that I would do that! Oh gods, not my treasure! Not my heart! Paimu!" I crumpled under the weight of the shocking news. Alexio caught me, and I freely wept for the sweet little girl I had left behind.

Never again would I see her climb a tree or hear her count my silver bracelets.

My heart! I should never have left you, little one! I am so sorry...

After a few minutes of silence, Alexio said softly, "We must go higher; we must find shelter. The Kiffians rode in from the west—I suspect that they will ride south with...their plunder, but we cannot be sure. Who knows? I do know that you and I are no match for the dozens of warriors that fell on Timia. We need to hide. I think I see a cave opening just there. Do you see it?"

I pretended to glance up but saw nothing beyond the wall of red rocks. I nodded.

"Can you make it?"

"Of course," I said woodenly.

With a broken heart I did as Alexio asked. I packed my makeshift tent quickly and followed him up the ragged wall of red. The path to the top was narrow—we left our camels below, but unless someone climbed up, they would not see them.

Alexio scampered ahead of me and thoroughly searched the cave for animals. It would not be unusual to find a desert cat or a nest of snakes hiding in the cool dampness of the cave. Finding shelter from the heat was the priority of every living creature. Fortunately, there were none, only a few dried snakeskins, and we moved in. Alexio made our beds, and I dug through my bag for food. I suspected he had nothing to eat since he left camp so quickly, and I knew he would be hungry. For me, I did not think I would ever eat again. Paimu's trusting face haunted me. I could not fathom who could take her life so callously. No life for Paimu. Her murder took not only her life but also the lives of her children.

Pah! How could you?

If she had done this thing, she would pay for her crime, I vowed.

Alexio prepared his weapons and slid a blade under his blanket. I wondered what he was thinking. That this was my fault? That he should be with his tribe and his father fighting our enemies? I wondered why my father would send him to me.

I shared my bread and water with Alexio, and we hunkered down to wait out the sun. We had a long wait ahead of us; both of us sat in silence wondering what had happened to our loved ones. It was bad enough that Paimu and Farrah were dead, but the truth was that many more would likely die today.

"What do you think we will find when we go back, Alexio? Will there be anyone left? And where shall we go? We cannot go to Biyat or Siya. The only place I can think of is north to Petra. My father told me to go see the Nabataeans. We need help, someone to stand with us. Maybe the Algeans. They're always hungry for our gold. What do you know of our allies?"

"I think we are on our own, Nefret. The Cushites would never stand against the Kiffians—neither would the Algeans. Besides, the Algeans have all moved to the west." His dark eyes appraised me, and he rubbed his hands through his dark curls. "There is only one ally I can think of that would help us; only one that would have the strength to hit these Kiffians with a heavy hand. They could crush them!"

"You mean Egypt?"

"Yes."

"You sound just like your father," I said contemptuously. Just the idea of begging Egypt for help made my blood boil. I had heard this argument many times between my uncle and my father. "You know what will happen if we go to Egypt. They will take our gold—they will take everything. We will be slaves, Alexio."

"Now you sound like *your* father. What choice do we have? Who cares about the gold and the turquoise if we have no blood in our bodies? Who cares about any of this if we have no life? I would not rule anything out at this point."

I leaned against the dry cavern wall and stared at him in the dim light. I sighed and said, "Yes, you're probably right. And we know nothing and will know nothing until we return to Timia." A ragged sigh escaped from deep within my soul. "Now would be a good time for the gods to show us the way back to Zerzura. With Farrah's death, I wonder if we shall ever know."

He lay on his pallet and stared at the cave's ceiling. "She did not know, Nefret. She forgot the way, and you know that. We should rest. If we get up early, we can make our way back and no one will see us—unless we want them to."

"Very well." I lay down too, but my mind would not stop speaking. I agonized over my lost Paimu.

Despite the blazing heat outside, the cave felt cool and comfortable. Eventually I dozed. We would have a long ride back to Timia. Alexio fell asleep quickly, and his light snoring comforted me. It was funny to think that just an hour ago I believed I would live as a hermit, a forgotten one lost in the dead city of Petra. I had not yet made up my mind as to whether I would contact the Nabataean king or not. That was before. Now, I was not alone. How quickly fate changed her mind about me!

I frowned into the dimness. Did I want to return to the people who rejected me? Well, it had been my choice to leave without their blessing. Perhaps if I had stayed, things would have been different.

"Not with Pah," my own voice whispered in my head.

I fell asleep but did not dream. My body was tired, my legs sore. It felt good to sleep without fear. Suddenly I was awake—the cave was freezing, and darkness covered the desert sands. The cold threatened to creep into my bones, and I quickly scampered about the mouth of the cave looking for anything I could burn. A small fire would warm us until it was time to ride.

After I arranged the small pile of debris I found, I cracked my fire stones together to create the sparks. Finally a small blaze began, and I warmed my hands.

"What are you doing?" Alexio tossed handfuls of sand onto my fire.

I gasped in surprise and stared at him with my hand on my hip. "What did you do that for? I am freezing!"

"Do you want to draw attention to us? Then set the cave on fire if you like. I am sure some Kiffian would be happy to take you as his wife."

I gasped at his rudeness, but he did not say more. He quickly surveyed the horizon, returned to his bed and rolled his cover around his body. He was determined to ignore me, but I was still cold. And now I was angry too. I crept to the mouth of the cave to peer outside and saw nothing but darkness. I listened and heard nothing. He was right. How foolish I had been to do such a thing! How would I ever survive on my own? I shivered, wrapping my cloak around me.

"If you are cold, lie next to me. Just don't set me on fire."

I snorted at his comment but made my way to his pallet. My teeth were chattering now, and my sandals offered my toes no warmth. Awkwardly, I dragged my pallet next to his and curled up to his back, my face pressed against him. Still shivering, I enjoyed the warmth. He reached behind his back and offered me his hand. I took it, and he rubbed the back of my hand absently until the warmth returned. Then I wrapped my arm around his. He tossed his blanket around me, and I cuddled closer. Now warm and comfortable, I still could not sleep. Despite the sadness of the day, I was very much aware that I was lying next to the man I loved.

Chapter Fifteen

The Red Sands—Nefret

The ride back to Timia seemed to last a lifetime, but time seemed even slower when we arrived there. Over half of our tribes had either bled out in the sands or perished by Kiffian blades. After a tour of the remains of our camp, it was apparent to Alexio, Orba and me that we had to move quickly. They had not finished their destruction, for some of us yet lived. Our enemies could return at any time, and with our injured we would not survive another assault. Many of our animals had perished, and others had been stolen, including our camels—the only ones that were left were crippled or otherwise harmed. Like most of the Meshwesh, the remaining camels could not endure a long trek across the hot desert. Wherever we went, it had to be close.

My uncle decided to ride home to Fayyum, gather reinforcements and return to us. It would be a day's wait, but if the gods favored us, we would have the time we needed to care for our injured. As I walked through the camp sharing water from my goatskin and distributing any food that we could scrounge, I made a mental list of the fallen. Ayn's parents died in the assault as well as Ziza and her family. We discreetly buried our dead, but I gave strict orders that no warning or lamentation would be offered for our lost ones. We could not risk the sounds attracting the Kiffians or any other traitor who might take advantage of our tragedy. I assured them we would mourn at the appropriate time.

Mina cared for my father night and day. The older woman did not speak, but an endless stream of tears flowed from her eyes. When first she saw me she grasped me as a drowning man would seize the one who came to save him. She collapsed on me, her silent sobs shaking her body violently. At first I thought she herself had been wounded, for she was covered in blood, but after an examination I could see she was not. Undoubtedly, Farrah's acolyte wore the blood of those she had tried to save.

"What happened to Farrah and Paimu, Mina? Can't you tell me?"

She looked at her dirty hands and shook her head slowly. I took her face in my hands and could see the anguish in her eyes.

"What about Pah? Did you see my sister?"

Mina's eyes widened, but she kept her silence. If I was to know what had happened to any of them, I would have to find another source of information. I resisted the urge to express my frustration in a way that would harm Mina. She had been through enough. Forcing her to break her vow of silence would not help heal us.

"It is all right, Mina. Thank you for all you have done."

She made the sign of respect and backed away from me, presumably to return to caring for my father. He had not yet recovered—his right arm had been so viciously sliced that it had to be removed. It had hung by a few pieces of skin and threatened to rot and take his life. I visited him many times a day to check on his progress but always left disappointed. He had not stirred or opened his eyes since he had fallen.

Alexio had been my constant companion. He helped me reorganize the camp, collect any weapons we could scavenge and distribute the food. I honestly did not know how I would have survived without his help. The day of waiting for Omel to return drove me mad. I passed the time wiping away blood and tears and spent any stolen moments I could wondering about my sister's fate. As night fell, I studied the stars, hoping to find a clue, but saw nothing. The people began to openly call me mekhma, and I did not dissuade them. They needed something to believe in, and I would be that rallying point, at least until my sister could be recovered.

Alexio and Orba sat with me, and we discussed our next steps. We would have to move slowly, so the plan was to flee to the rocky outcropping where Alexio and I had spent the night. We believed there were enough caves to keep us safe. From there, we would go north, presumably to Petra. I didn't like the plan, but it was as good as any I could think of.

As difficult as it was to believe, we could very easily disappear into the Sahara and never be seen again, or missed.

When Orba left us, Alexio and I sat quietly with our minds racing. This seemed more and more like an impossible task, yet we never expressed our doubt. We had to live! Although our enemy had stolen our precious treasures, our children, and murdered many of our warriors, they had left us water. Omel would return to the camp in the morning, if all went as planned. I did not even want to think about the possibility that he might abandon us. Surely he would not!

Alexio and I would have only this one last night together. I felt guilty for the thoughts I had about my cousin. All around us were the signs of death. Yet in my heart I thought of nothing but Alexio. I knew he was thinking the same thing, for at every turn I found his eyes upon me, searching me; his desire for me was obvious even to me, an inexperienced young woman.

Late that night, when the camp became quiet, Alexio and I found ourselves at the pool of Timia. We had not planned such a rendezvous, at least neither of us spoke of it, but there we were. Together at last. On my order, the camp was dark except for a few small fires used to cook and offer some light; soon even those would be put out. The moon hid itself behind rare clouds, like the gods themselves hid us from our enemies. It rarely rained in the desert—some people could go a lifetime and not see rain—but I could smell the rain in the air. Farrah once told me that whenever you smelled the rain it was a sign.

Good things always happened when it rained.

As if it were the most natural thing in the world, we removed our clothing just as we had when we were children. Without timidity we slipped quietly into the pool. There was no giggling, no splashing, no children's jokes. We swam close to one another, not talking or smiling. Suddenly, Alexio stood up in the water, and his wet, muscular figure gleamed in the moonlight. He offered his hand to me and I accepted it, rising and slinging water from my hair. There was no space between us. I felt the strength of his body pressed against mine, the shocking hardness of him. I felt soft and small but unafraid. We stood together, our bodies pressed up against one another, and we kissed unashamedly. I felt no guilt that Alexio had once been promised to another, for I knew that girl was gone. I had helped bury her. In all the world, at least in that moment, there was only Alexio and me.

The date palms beside us swayed under the influence of the winds. I half wondered if we were responsible for this storm, our passion suppressed for so long now that it had loosed the elements themselves. We kissed again; neither of us spoke. He took my hand, not bothering to dress. I reached for my tunic and covered my naked body with it, following him into the darkness just beyond the camp.

We were alone at last with no lights in sight. It felt like we were the only people in the world. Rain sprinkled down upon us like an anointing from above. In the rain there was a solemnity, and I was very aware that what we were about to do was not unseen by the gods or our ancestors. I wondered what Farrah would say about our union.

I held Alexio's hands in my own and kissed them. His beautiful dark face radiated a complex blend of desire and seriousness.

"Are you sure you want to do this?" he asked, his voice rough and needy.

"Yes, I am sure." I drew myself up tall and straight as I had seen Farrah do and said, "I am the Queen of the Meshwesh. I take you, Alexio hap Omel, as my consort. From this day forward you are my equal. Hear me, oh gods and ancestors, this is my husband, the one I choose. Bind us together for eternity. Bind us together, body, soul and mind. For we are one."

Alexio's brilliant smile flashed across his face. He repeated my words. "Hear me, oh gods and ancestors, this is my wife, the one I choose. Bind us together for eternity. Bind us together, body, soul and mind. For we are one."

We fell to our knees, and the weightiness of what we had just done surprised me.

With the formalities completed, Alexio and I lost ourselves in one another's arms. He was gentle and kind at first, stroking my skin, touching my hair, kissing my lips. Yet that was not enough for me—I wanted more of him, not to be toyed with. I needed him as a woman needs a man.

With rising urgency, I wrapped my arms around him and pulled him close to me. I knew enough about lovemaking to know that it could be painful, but I welcomed the pain. I who had suffered so little compared to my people deserved to feel pain. I wanted this. I demanded it.

Fiercely I whispered, "Do not be easy, Alexio."

My words made him shudder, and he obeyed me. I kept my eyes trained on his handsome face. I slid my arms under his shoulders and pushed my body against his. He responded, penetrating me quickly as I had asked him to do. I cried out in pain as I felt my maidenhead burn away. It was a sacrifice to the Sahara, a blood covenant between Alexio and me. As the pain subsided, other sensations crept over me; a surprising warmth emanated from all parts of my body. For a moment, we hung there together in our pleasure before he collapsed beside me on the sand.

When it was over, he kissed my neck and stroked my copper hair. I shed no tears. I felt no shame. What we had done was right. It was the beginning of healing for our tribes. According to the Old Ways, our union made us father and mother of Meshwesh. I had been the mekhma, the mother of our clan. Now the clan had a father as well.

We rose from the sand no longer Nefret and Alexio. We were one.

And we would always be together!

Chapter Sixteen

Astora's Eyes—Omel

Astora greeted me with her lovely smile, but the sight saddened my soul. She looked beyond me, expecting to see her son riding behind me, but she would not see him. Never again. Her queen's blue jewel dangled upon her pretty brow and sparkled in the light. Upon closer inspection, the woman whimpered at my appearance.

"Omel? Is that blood? Are you injured? Where is Suri?" Others surrounded me, curious to hear the fate of the young man. "Suri!" she called.

"Cut down. Kiffians overran Biyat, Siya, Gemia and Timia. The tribes at Biyat and Siya have been murdered, but there are a few that remain at Timia. We must go to them. Benada! Omri! Gather supplies and men. We ride for Timia within the hour!"

"Kiffians? How long has it been?" Omri asked, the young man's eyes narrow and angry.

"I will go gather what we need," Benada answered, taking Omri with him.

"Suri?" Astora asked again.

"It is true, Astora. He is gone, but Suri fought bravely," I lied.

The image of the boy pinned to the ground by a Kiffian's blade appeared unsummoned in my mind. It was I who had cut Suri's attacker down, first sliding my blade across the back of his knees. Then, spinning like an angry whirlwind, I had removed his screaming head from his shoulders. In a final act of defiance, the severed head had rolled onto Suri's convulsing body. With a vicious kick I had sent it skittering across the grass and with an anguished cry pulled the weapon from the skinny boy's stomach. His mouth had spewed crimson, and his dark, frightened eyes pleaded for help but only for a moment. I squatted beside him, whispering the words I had never spoken during his life, "My son." He made an inaudible gurgling sound and left this world's realm.

But this I would never tell his mother. Nor would I tell of Alexio's desertion—how he left me and his brother and fled into the desert.

I spat on the ground at the memory. She hated him for reasons I never understood.

Astora buried her face in my chest, and I stroked her hair gingerly. Perhaps I could have delivered the news differently, but there was no time to navigate feelings. I did not cry, although sorrow pierced my heart as well. I could not allow myself the luxury of tears when our lives were hanging in the balance. I would mourn Suri in my own way when the time was right.

"Astora, listen to me. You must gather everything you can—we have to move. It is not safe to stay here. We must gather together all the Meshwesh if we are to stand against these invaders." Her eyes were full of questions, and tears streamed down her dusky face. "No, you must trust me. We will mourn our son, but now we must go. Pack the oils, and we will bury him together. Do you understand?"

She nodded and then examined my face with narrowed eyes. "What of Alexio? Is he dead also?"

"No. Hurry now. You must lead the women. We leave within the hour." Something passed behind her eyes, but I could not fathom it. One day I would get to the bottom of her hatred for my eldest son, but today was not that day.

Chapter Seventeen

The Unseen Hand—Nefret

My uncle had returned—I heard the sounds of jubilation, but I did not join in the welcoming party. Our relationship had always been distant. I had the distinct impression that Omel disapproved of me in some important way. Perhaps because he and Father were always at odds or because Pah went out of her way to endear herself to him. It was not until the trials that I saw clearly how much he favored her. But now she was gone. Grief stabbed in my heart. No, I would not give up on her. Somehow I would find her.

Father stirred beside me. I press the cloth against his feverish forehead. His eyes flickered open, "Kadeema."

"No, Father. It is me—Nefret."

"Nefret." Recognition flickered across his face, and he gave a ragged sigh.

"Do you want some water?" I filled the sponge with water and pressed it against his lips. He pulled the water from the sponge thirstily. I smiled at him. Surely this was a good sign.

"My arm?"

My smile disappeared. I did not want to tell this warrior that he was a warrior no longer, but what else could I do? "It is gone, Father. Orba did all he could to save it." Despite the removal of the nearly severed arm, the chance of infection and death remained. The stitches were red, and Orba had gone in search of the ingredients he needed to cleanse and fuse the wound. Father attempted to move his shoulder but grimaced in pain. His tanned skin was pale—his dark eyes stared at the white canvas that hung above him as he gasped.

"In my tunic pocket—the necklace. Take it."

As I removed the necklace from his bloodstained tunic, my breath caught in my throat. I had forgotten about my found prize. The green stones felt cool in my hand.

"Where did you find this?" he asked me.

"I found it in the sand behind the camp. I know that it is forbidden to leave the oasis unattended, but I needed time to myself. I am sorry, Father."

His head rolled with a halfhearted laugh. "You have no need to apologize. You are the mekhma—you always were. I told those fools! The necklace proves that."

"What does the necklace have to do with the mekhma?"

"It was Kadeema's necklace."

I sat still, trying to comprehend his words. Surely these were the words of a fevered brain. "How can that be?"

He shook his head sadly. "It is not by chance that you found this. Your mother led you to it. Claim it and keep it, Nefret. It is a queen's necklace—it belongs to the queens of Grecia whose blood runs in your veins. Now you are truly the queen of the Meshwesh."

Clutching the necklace tightly, I whispered, "My mother's necklace. I have heard the story of her disappearance, but I know nothing about her. You never speak of her." I did not mean to upbraid him at such a time, but to hear him speak of such things was a rare event. Perhaps it was the fever after all.

"Wear it. Put it on and claim your right."

With shaking fingers I did as he asked me. His warm hand cupped my face, and he gazed into my eyes. "There is much you do not know. I have not been a good father."

"You are the best of fathers!" I held his hand and squeezed it.

"A nice lie. Such love—love that I do not deserve. So like your mother. All these years I believed she left me. I wanted to believe that. In that there was at least some peace." Tears slid down his temples. "I should have known she would never have left me or our daughters." I could hear my uncle and the men of Fayyum, my uncle's tribe, approaching.

"Promise me something."

"Yes. Anything, Father."

"Find your sister. Whatever her crimes, she does not deserve such a fate."

"I will find her—I promise." With a groan of pain, he lay still with his eyes clamped closed.

I mulled over his words, hoping he would sleep. But with sudden ferocity his eyes sprang open and he said, "Omel will say that you are too young to lead—too inexperienced—but do not listen. If you renounce your right to rule, even temporarily, you will never get it back. He is not an evil man, but he is stubborn and ambitious, and these are troubling times."

"Yes, Father."

"Nefret, you must rally the remaining tribes. Go to Saqqara and tell the tribes to meet you there. If Biyat and Siya have fallen, the only place you can go is east."

"But what about the Nabataeans?"

"No, stay away from Petra now. You must go to Saqqara! Have Farrah…no, I forgot. Have Orba send the sigil of the Bee-Eater to all of the remaining tribes. They will answer; they will obey. Go to Saqqara. The Kiffians will not follow you there—it is the City of the Dead. They fear it." Bright red color bled through the bandages that Orba had encircled his stump with.

"Father, your wound! Hold still until Orba returns. We can discuss this later."

"There is no time! Listen to me."

"Yes, Father."

"Egypt is the answer."

"Egypt? What about the Cushites or the Algat? Haven't you said all your life that we cannot trust Egypt?"

"The Kiffians will come again. This time they'll come with fire and they'll burn everything away. There will be nothing left. Go to Egypt, to Pharaoh. He knows the way to Zerzura. You must unite the clan—take us home, Nefret." He groaned in pain, and sweat poured off his forehead.

The snakes of destiny twisted in my stomach. My father had been a wise ruler, and I knew he offered me his best advice.

"Go now. Meet Omel. Do not let him see me like this. Be strong and don't waver. You must build the tribe's confidence—give them something to believe in, Nefret. You can do this."

I kissed his forehead and stood on shaky legs. Thirsty and exhausted, I straightened my clothes and opened my tunic slightly so all would see my necklace clearly. The necklace would be proof to them that I was doubly a queen. I would let no man challenge me. With my head held high, I stepped out from under the canvas. With a purposeful stride, I went to meet my uncle and his tribe.

My uncle and his consort were busy greeting and consoling my people. An old woman wept upon Astora's shoulder, and Astora whispered in her ear. Since my uncle did not greet me as I approached, I called out to him. Without summoning them, Ayn and Alexio took their places beside me; one on my left and the other on my right. I did not look at them, but their presence gave me strength.

"Omel, thank you for returning so swiftly. My people thank you." Omel did not make haste to greet me, but he did not risk ignoring me either. He bowed briefly and summoned his consort to attend me. My father had been right. Omel had a mind to rule. Astora walked toward me with her arms wide open. A look of understanding and sadness was upon her face, but it was merely a mask. Her expressive black eyes revealed something very different. I stepped back from her arms, refusing her embrace, and greeted her with respect.

"Astora, I welcome you to Timia. Your healing hands are welcome here, for there is much to do before we leave in the morning." My words grabbed my uncle's attention, and he faced me now. His expression was angry, even aggravated.

"Go? Where are we going?"

"We leave Timia in the morning before the sun casts its first light over the desert." I looked him steadily in the eyes. He wanted to say something, but I rebuffed him. I turned to face the tribe that was gathering around us. I felt such sympathy for them. Broken, confused and without hope. These were my people!

Once again I felt the unseen hand moving across my heart and mind. In the crowd, I imagined the Shining Man smiling and watching me. It gave me confidence to believe that the words I was about to speak were his words. Indeed, I believed that they were. I raised my voice as I had heard Farrah do a hundred times before. I missed the Old One, but I continued in my speech.

"Sons and daughters of Ma! It is true that Biyat, Siya and Gemia have been overrun! It is true that many of our brothers and sisters here at Timia have vanished from the earth and will never walk in the Land of the Living again. But it is also true that we are alive and that their blood and the blood of our ancestors still flows in our veins. We can no longer be many tribes; we must be one clan! We are Meshwesh!"

Some of the women cried, and I could not help but notice that there were very few children among us. *Oh, Paimu!* Still, many were stirred by my words and shouted, "Hafa-nu, mekhma!" It was a phrase that meant much, both an expression of thanks and an offering of blessing. I raised my hand in acknowledgment and continued.

"These are evil days. Many of us have lost much. Even our mekhma, my own sister, has fallen prey to these evil men. But they shall not prevail. Tomorrow we leave for Saqqara. It is many days' walk to reach the City of the Dead, but we shall be safe there."

Astora scoffed. "Saqqara? What will we do there? There are no oases, and the Egyptians will not welcome us into their territory. Are we to dig graves and become one with those who have been buried in the brick mountains?" She sneered at me. Ayn hissed at her, but I ignored her.

"As mekhma, I will send the sigil of the Bee-Eaters to the remaining tribes, summoning them to Saqqara. I need riders to carry the sigils. Who will ride for me?" Many men volunteered, even my uncle, but I could not risk an insurrection. If my uncle were to rally another tribe against me, it would mean further division and death for the Meshwesh.

"Brave uncle, you honor me with your hand, but I need you here as a valued member of my Council. You men—yes, you four. You must leave with all haste and return to us at Saqqara. Ayn!"

"Yes, mekhma?"

"Take these men to Orba. He will find the sigils. Provide them with everything they need for their journey." With the sign of respect, Ayn backed away and did as I bade her. The men followed close behind her. Alexio and I stood together—I resisted the urge to reach out and take his hand. This was no time to show weakness.

"Tonight there will be no fires. If you must cook, prepare what you need now. When darkness falls upon the Red Lands, let everything be silent. No songs. No mourning. Keep quiet. Mothers, tend to your babies. We will not fall prey to this enemy again. The darkness will protect us. My uncle will assign warriors to watch the camp through the night." Omel stared at me but did not argue. "You will go to the caves and then on to Saqqara. It is a long journey. Pack wisely and leave what you can."

I walked through the crowd, stopping to touch the face of a grief-stricken mother and pat the shoulder of a man who had lost a daughter in the raid. "I know you feel broken—I feel the loss too! Comfort one another!"

"Hafa-nu, mekhma!" someone cried out spontaneously.

"Hafa-nu, my people."

"Tonight, I go before you to Egypt! All will be well. All will be well. I go to Pharaoh, but I promise to return to you. And then, my people, we will return to Zerzura! No more wandering in the desert. It is time to go home." The faces of the people lit up with happiness. They whispered to one another. *Yes, home. We must go home. It is time!*

The shock on my uncle's face silenced his consort. This was what had to be done, and I was prepared to do it. There was nothing Omel could do now to take this away from me. I nodded to him in acknowledgement. With his fist over his heart, in the Egyptian way, he acknowledged me. Astora scowled and turned her back on me.

"Hafa-nu, mekhma! Hafa-nu, mekhma!"

I raised both of my hands again as I had seen Farrah do many times. "Hafa-nu, Meshwesh. All will be well." With tears in my eyes, I walked away.

When I awoke and peeped out of my makeshift tent, the Twin Stars were high in the night sky. I took it as a sign—a sign that my sister still lived.

My sister, my own heart. I pray for you this night.

I whispered her name to the Shining Man and asked for his help. I heard nothing and could only hope that he had heard me. Surely he would help me, for I saw him in a dream. He stood atop a tall mountain and stretched his arms out to me, beckoning me to join him. Suddenly I was high above the mountain and could see the entire land. I opened my mouth to say some word, some magical word, but only a scream emerged. It was the scream of a falcon. With supernatural force, I fell from the sky toward the mountain. Surely the Shining Man would catch me! I would be safe! I screamed again, but again the only sound was the falcon's cry. In a flash, the Shining Man disappeared and I stood alone atop the mountain. Startled, I awoke and reached beside me for Alexio, but he had already risen. He was probably preparing the animals for our journey.

My hand flew to my necklace, as if it would protect me from my troubling dreams. There was no time to waste if we were to leave without notice or fanfare. I dug through my scant possessions and rolled up my green silk tunic with the golden embroidery, stuffing it in my bag. I did not want to appear before Pharaoh looking like a goatherd; even I knew the Egyptians had no love for farmers.

I considered visiting my father before I left, but Orba had found the healing herbs that would allow Father to rest; when I last looked, he slept peacefully. He needed healing rest before the arduous journey, and my course lay before me. I knew what needed to be done. After yesterday's speech, I trusted that the Shining Man would give me the words I needed for my audience with Pharaoh. The more I pondered it, the more I believed that. Somehow, I *would* convince Pharaoh to help us. I did not go to him as a pauper but as the Queen of the Meshwesh and a wealthy queen, despite our current situation. We still held the gold and turquoise mines, dozens of horses in Fayyum and stored wealth in many places along the edges of the desert. The only thing we lacked was a home. For far too long, the Meshwesh had been scattered across the Sahara. Since no one oasis could hold us all, the Old Ones, of which Farrah was the last, had agreed to forgo building homes or cities until we could all be together again at Zerzura. Now no one remembered the way.

But there was hope in Egypt. Father told me something I had never known—Egypt knew the way to the White City!

I did not see my uncle either. All that needed to be said to him had been said. I had no desire to visit him before my journey. I would have to trust Orba and the others to keep things in order during my absence. The people were behind me now—they trusted me to help them. I would not fail them.

I heard a noise behind me and turned to greet Alexio. To my surprise it was not my husband who entered but Astora. She knelt down in our makeshift tent and smiled at me.

"Is there something I can do for you, Astora?"

She smiled wider, and it was an unsettling sight. Astora was not a tall woman, but she was pretty—pretty enough to attract the eye of Omel. However, she rarely smiled. She was not Alexio's mother but had been the wife of some minor warrior who lost his life in a Cushite raid some years ago. She had a son, Suri, but I had not seen him since they returned. "No, but I think I can help you." She spoke in an amusing whisper.

"What do you mean? Is this about Omel?"

She laughed and smoothed her gown over her knees. "Where is Alexio? Has he left your bed already? I had hoped to find him here."

I could not stand in my low tent, but I did rise up on my knees. "Get to it. What do you want?"

"I am surprised to see you sharing a bed with a man who has shared his bed with your sister. However, I suppose it is a rare thing to sleep with two mekhmas in one lifetime."

"You lie!" I blurted out.

"Do I?" Her smirk disappeared, and she said savagely, "You're a fool! How do you think we can trust you to lead us if you make such foolish decisions? It is a serious question that many are asking. I only seek to warn you."

"I do not believe you." My mind raced with the possibility. I knew there had been an attraction, at least on Pah's part, but never had I entertained the idea that he might also care for her.

"Why would I lie? Be careful. If you return from Egypt, you could find there is no place for you anymore. Perhaps the days of the mekhma have died, along with the Old One."

"Get out!" I yelled at her.

With a small bow of her head, she disappeared from my tent. One of my guards poked his head in, but I waved him away. I felt my soul crumple under the insinuation. Surely she was wrong. She must be wrong! Images of Pah and Alexio writhing naked together appeared in my mind. Astora's dagger had struck its target. I believed her.

I knew. I guess I had always known.

I grabbed my bag, bow and quiver and stalked through the forlorn camp to Ayn's bed. I knelt down beside her, nudging her side.

"Nefret? I mean, mekhma. What is it?"

"I changed my mind. I want you to go with me."

"Whatever you say. Is Alexio coming too?"

"No, he stays behind. I have another job for him."

She smiled at me and rose from her bed, stretching her back. "I'll be ready in a few minutes. Thank you, mekhma."

"Don't thank me yet. I don't know what is ahead of us. You may regret this."

Before the camp had settled down for sleep the night before, Ayn had come to me and asked to attend me on my journey to Egypt's capital, Thebes. She had apologized again for allowing Paimu out of her sight and expressed her desire to serve me. I had refused to bring her only because I needed strong allies at camp, but now, things had changed.

Everything had changed.

I made my way through the camp as quietly as I could to find Alexio. With all my heart I wanted to scream at him, tear him down, berate him, but I could not do that without stirring up the troubled hearts of my tribesmen. He was where I expected to find him, with his beloved animals. His dark hair hung loose and fell to his shoulders. He tugged at the complicated leather strapping of the camel's harness. Alexio had designed the harness himself, and many riders had been impressed with his ideas. He was a brilliant horseman and camel rider, quick with a blade and his wit. I had loved him since I was a girl, and so had Pah.

"There has been a change of plans," I said flatly. "Ayn is going with me." I tucked my bag into the leather pocket and patted the camel's side, trying to avoid eye contact with Alexio.

"What?" He laughed incredulously. "I can't let you leave alone. My place is by your side. You said so yourself."

"That was before."

Again he laughed. "Before what? Before you went to bed? I just left you, and I remember no change of plans." He tried to take my hand, but I pushed him to the side.

"I can't help what you remember. The plans *have* changed."

He grabbed me gently by my shoulders and turned me around to face him. "What is this about? Have I done something?"

"Take your hands off me," I growled quietly. A nearby watchman stopped his patrol and stared at us. I wasn't used to all this attention. I waved my hand at him, and he passed us by watchfully. I could see Ayn walking toward us in the darkness. I pointed her to the other camel and finally looked at Alexio. "Astora came to visit me."

With an empty sadness, I watched a range of emotions flit across his face. "Oh?"

"Our lives hang in the balance, and you want to play the fool with me? Fine, have it your way. I know about you and Pah. You should have told me before we…you should have told me!" I saw Ayn pause, but she dared not look at us. I knew she heard us, but there was nothing to be done. Nothing was private anymore. I was foolish to think it would be.

"We were never together! I swear to you, Nefret. I did kiss her, but nothing more. Astora has lied to you!"

"You admit to kissing her, toying with her? Then you come to me? She is my sister!"

"I swear to you, I love you, above anyone else. It has always been you. Astora is not innocent—it was she who pursued me, but I refused her. I did kiss Pah, but only that!"

"Keep your voice down."

He took my hand. "Please, believe me. I am sorry that I did not tell you, but I swear to you I love you and you alone. You know that."

I pulled my hand away, climbed on the camel and turned my face away from him, staring into the dark. "I have made up my mind. I do not want you with me. Not now, not ever."

"Please, Nefret. You cannot mean that. What am I supposed to do? How can I prove my love?"

I clucked at the camel for it to stand. "Keep your love!"

"Please! Don't do this."

I stared at him. "If you love me, find my sister. Bring her home." I hardly believed the words I spoke. Again, I felt the presence of the Shining Man; he was somewhere near, but I could not see him. A shudder ran through me. What I was asking of Alexio could be his death sentence. Despite my anger and brokenness, I loved him still. But I would not let this go.

That was not the task he had hoped for, but he did not shirk it.

"If that is your command, mekhma."

"So it is."

Ayn and I rode east away from the camp and into the darkness. I did not look back for fear that I would change my mind.

Chapter Eighteen

The Queen of Egypt—Tiye

It had been a long time since anyone had requested an audience with me except courtiers who were too old to properly bow to me. They came in with their platitudes, mediocre treasures and endless requests, and then out again they streamed. I held the title of chief wife to Pharaoh, but it was in name only now. All of my carefully cultivated influence had slipped carelessly out of my hands and into the lap of Pharaoh's youngest wife and my nemesis, Tadukhipa. I cursed the day that the Mitanni woman entered our world with her strawberry lips and pale skin. Pharaoh needed to scatter his seed—I would have been a fool to imagine otherwise—but the girl forgot her place.

Unlike Pharaoh's previous wives, Tadukhipa had no intention of dwelling in the shadows behind my throne. She was a fool who cared for nothing except pleasure until she fell prey to the schemes of grasping sycophants who easily used her for their own devices. I tried to warn her, guide her, befriend her, but she had responded to my kindness with distrust. By then her ears were full of lies. Then again, she was a stupid girl.

Absently I slid my small silver knife through a crisp pear. I liked the sound of it and the taste. I stared at the juice as it ran down my hand. When I finished slicing it, I tossed a piece into my mouth. A nervous servant waited nearby. Queens should not cut their own fruit, apparently, but I trusted no one in this court anymore, except Huya. How easy it would have been for an enemy to slide a poisoned knife through my green pears!

I sighed as I reviewed all the honors Pharaoh and I had showered upon Tadukhipa. It was I who had sought to raise her status by nicknaming her "The Favorite" and "The Greatly Beloved." My husband allowed me to do as I wished, but no doubt that had been shortsighted on my part. I chuckled as I ate another piece of pear. For her lack of appreciation and respect, I had taken my revenge. Her new nickname, "Kiya" or "the monkey," was the moniker that had finally stuck. She had been furious when she first heard it. It was an obvious poke at her overly large ears and slightly bowed legs. But she did not dare retaliate. I feigned ignorance, but she knew that the insult had been my handiwork.

Unwisely, I had allowed the Monkey to endear herself to my children. It wasn't until she began openly questioning my orders concerning them, going behind my back with my servants, that I suspected her intentions to supplant me. How many times a day had I watched her walk to the Temple of Arinna, her foreign goddess, dressed as a petitioner? Undoubtedly she prayed for my speedy death so that she might rise to the position of Chief Wife, but every day I woke up and defied her and her incompetent deity. There was room for one only queen here and only one goddess worthy of worship! Had she forgotten that I was Isis incarnate?

And now I was forced to watch her work her machinations on my son, the future King of Egypt! It was too much to bear. I would offer Isis a dozen fine oxen this very day if only she would destroy my enemy! I would cut their necks myself!

Now an unknown queen sought audience with me. I was under no obligation to accept her or receive her, but out of curiosity and boredom, I sent my faithful uncle and confidant Huya to appraise the supplicant. I grew tired of watching Kiya parade about the palace as if I were no longer a queen to be feared. I grew bored of this court. I needed some distraction. Huya entered my chamber and pressed his fist against his heart.

"Gracious One, the Meshwesh queen and her attendant wait for you in the Lower Garden."

I wiped my sticky hands and my tiny blade clean with a damp cloth. I slid it back into the folds of my belt and leaned back in the golden chair, propping my aching back against the green cushion. With a sigh, I changed my mind. "I have had enough of lowly queens today, Huya. Send her away."

"Very well, my Queen." He bowed deeply, but I detected his slowness in leaving my presence.

Sensing his resistance to my command, I asked impatiently, "What is it, Huya?"

"If I may…"

"We're too old for formalities," I snapped. "Speak your mind."

With a demure smile he said, "You should see this girl."

I raised a painted eyebrow and leaned forward, curious now. "You seem near to bursting to tell me something." My mind raced with the possibilities. "Is she an Amazon? It has been many years since I have seen one. So strong—so tall!"

How I would have loved to have been given such a strong, glorious body! The gods had a sense of humor. I—the Queen of Upper and Lower Egypt—was no taller than a child, with ugly flat feet, eyes that drooped and a belly that protruded from childbearing. Yes, the gods enjoyed their little jokes. I had no inclinations toward women, as some in the harem (including the Monkey) did, but I valued strength in women above all other things—even honesty.

"No, my Queen. She is no Amazon but has a wild beauty that is rare outside of Thebes and your own radiance."

I snorted, rose from my chair and pulled a fallen linen strap over my bony shoulder. "Well then, let us go see this wild rare beauty. She is in the Lower Garden, you say?"

"Yes, my Queen. Would you like me to bring her into your court?"

"I shall go, but my knees are not as strong as they once were. I hope she is patient."

"You are as strong as ever, Glorious Queen."

I sighed. His lies did not move me as they once had, but I appreciated the effort. "I will steal a look at this flower of the desert. If I find her to be worthy of my attention, I will enter the garden. If not, then send her away."

With a nod and a mysterious smile he pulled back the curtain partition and allowed me to pass through. I shuffled through my painted apartments, ignoring the dozens of faces that offered me greetings or blessings. Fortunately most of the court had filtered into the younger queen's adjoining apartments, no doubt to play games, tell love stories and coddle their children.

After thirty years I barely noticed the white marble columns lining the courtyard that connected us all. I vaguely remembered being entranced by the crocodiles, storks and lotus blossoms on the tile floors beneath my feet. Grecian—no, Roman—tiles, if memory served. What a mess those artisans had made installing them! The smells of juniper incense, orange peels and perfume wafted through the courtyard. I had a sudden longing to see my husband.

It had been too long since Amenhotep had visited his harem—or me. Now that the flux had struck his bowels, he rarely left his palace. I prayed he would return to me soon and set things in order. Far too many liberties were being taken nowadays.

A cool breeze fluttered through the golden curtains that led into the gardens. Beyond the gardens a blue lake sprawled across the horizon, a lake dedicated to me commanded into existence by my husband. I squinted up at Huya, who had emptied the Upper Garden. Apparently word had gotten out about my unexpected visitors. Life ran very still in Pharaoh's harem; any distraction proved an amusement. Once the upper porch was empty, I stepped quietly to the top of the stairs and observed the women below.

The first woman, a dark-haired spear of a girl, disappointed me. She was dressed in dirty brown clothing, and I could almost smell her unwashed skin and hair. I wrinkled my nose.

And then the second girl appeared. Her glorious copper hair tumbled down her back in sparkling waves. Her skin was paler than any Egyptian's, yet it had a lovely bronze glint to it. She was no Amazon, but the queen or whoever she was had a feminine figure with strong arms and dainty feet. She had no crown but wore an impressive gold and emerald necklace around her slender neck, and her arms shone with silver bracelets. Alas, a tribal queen but nothing more. I could tell at first glance.

The world was filled with lovely faces. She even had good bones, but that hair... A definite sign from the gods! No wonder my household clamored for a peek at her. Red hair had long been a mark of divinity. Yes, a sign! Pausing behind a collection of potted palms, I strained to eavesdrop on their conversation. I felt no shame. This was how one learned things, by listening and watching.

"Ayn, calm yourself! You are not helping," the beautiful queen said.

"I am sorry, but I have never seen such things! Even the walls crawl with creatures—and the colors! Have you ever seen such a blue in all your life? And the red! I wish… I wish…" The dirty girl choked up and wiped her eyes.

"What is it?"

"Paimu. She is never far from my thoughts. She would have loved to see all this."

"She is gone, Ayn, and we cannot bring her back. Now a hundred other Paimus depend on us. We cannot act like wide-eyed fools. Please gather yourself and let me think."

"Yes, of course, mekhma. I am sorry."

The desert queen squeezed the girl's hand, and together they strolled about the garden whispering to one another. The redhead comforted her friend as they walked.

I knew their language; it sounded clunky and odd at first, but it came back to my memory quickly. I would never confess to anyone how I knew it. Of all the people in my court, or in Thebes for that matter, only a few remembered how I got here.

Huya, myself and one other.

My mother's scheming had pushed me to this lofty position, but my own will had secured it. Hearing the desert language again made me feel sentimental—sentimental enough to inspect this "queen" more closely.

Without an attendant I stepped lightly down the limestone steps, entering the garden as stealthily as a cat. The plain-faced girl saw me first and froze. The redheaded queen spun about quickly, but I remained poised on the bottom stair with my hands crossed in front of me as I had been trained to do since I was a child. Neither woman knew what to say, so I let them stew in silence for a moment while I took them in and allowed them to view me. I enjoyed making people feel uncomfortable—it was one of the few benefits of being the Queen of Egypt.

"If you want to speak to me, it will have to be alone." The desert dialect fell easily from my lips; it pleased me to see them so surprised at hearing it spoken by an Egyptian queen. *No, I had not forgotten.* I was no longer a wiry child clinging to her mother's legs. The foreign queen dismissed the girl with a gesture. With a hand gesture of her own, the girl walked backwards out of the courtyard, leaving us alone at last.

"Ah, now we are alone. Tell me Queen of the Desert, why are you here? Why did you choose to speak to me? Wouldn't you rather speak to Pharaoh? He has an eye for beautiful queens. Perhaps my sister-wife, Tadukhipa, could help you. I am merely an old woman with no influence and nothing to offer you."

"But you are the Queen of Egypt! If you cannot help me, no one can. My father, Semkah, sent this to show you. He says you once knew his father, Onesu, and that you would know it."

I felt my hands shake, either from age or from my racing heart. I took the cloth in my hand and sat on the nearby garden bench. Spreading out the rough material with my fingers, I could see the painted symbol—the symbol of the Bee-Eater! A sign of distress, a serious sign to all desert people.

"What is your name?"

To my surprise the girl knelt before me, her hand upraised in the tribal sign of respect. "Great Queen, I am Nefret, daughter of Kadeema of Grecia and Semkah, son of the Red Lands. I am the granddaughter of Onesu, the Warrior-King of Zerzura. I humble myself before you and plead with you for help!" Her passionate speech had her on the brink of tears. I could hear them in her voice. I rose quickly and began to leave.

"Wait! Please!"

I kept my back turned to her. "Have you finished crying?"

"Yes," she sniffled, "I have." I heard the silk of her dress as she hurried to her feet. I returned to my seat and smoothed my dress without making eye contact with her.

"Good. Many years ago, my husband and my pharaoh decreed that tears would never be shed in my presence. He so loves me that he wants me to be happy all the time. May Isis bless him! I cannot stay in the presence of tears. It is the law."

"Great Queen, forgive me. I do not know your laws." She sat on the bench beside me, breaking another law that mandated no one would sit in the presence of the Queen unless invited, but I did not mention it. *She would learn the ways of Egypt. I had almost made up my mind.*

"Tell me about your people, the Meshwesh. Tell me about your home. Tell me what has happened."

She began in a rush, but I calmed her. "No, tell me. Tell me a story. Like the Old Ways." I closed my eyes and leaned back against the wall, waiting. She started slowly, awkwardly, but once she began, her storytelling transported me back in time.

I was again with my own clan, the Algat. Nefret told the *Tale of the Meshwesh*, but it was my own people I thought about. I remembered their faces, so like mine, so foreign to the Egyptian court. The cadence of the girl's gentle voice comforted me as she told me the sad story of the Lightning Gate, the giants and the hidden city. Unlike many of the young people in my court, I believed in the old stories. I remembered them. How simple life had been then! We were too poor to know we were poor, I thought wryly.

As she wove her tale with her sweet, quiet voice, I thought of warm afternoons napping in my tent with my eight sisters. I remembered burrowing under the tent, with my now-dead sister to sneak a peek at the traders who came in daily to see our beautiful women and drink our beer. The Algat brewed the finest beer in the desert, and that was no easy task.

I remembered the nights I spent with my sisters, stealing bits of grilled goat from the spit and scurrying to the tops of trees to see the stars and try to touch them.

How I miss you, Hamrahana, my sister! How I miss you all!

The girl's voice broke my mental wandering: "Another enemy rides against us now and it is time…time to go home to Zerzura where we can defend ourselves." I stared at her face. I noticed that her eye color changed; one minute they were green, in another light they were soft brown—another sign that she had been favored by the gods.

"We lost our way, oh Great Queen. For too long the Meshwesh have been divided, forced to live on oases, never together. Then word came of a wise Queen in the East, the Great Wife of Pharaoh, who once loved and knew the desert people. The Meshwesh, the Algat, the Cushites—all are in danger from the Kiffians, angry men, tall as trees, who ride in secret across the Red Lands—your lands! They steal our women and murder our children. We come to you for justice!"

I grew troubled and considered leaving if only to think. To think and forget again.

"Oh, but more than that, Wise Queen. They want the gold. We have much gold in mines far to the south, more gold than any other clan, and turquoise too." She took a deep breath and said, "As mekhma, I will give you that gold and turquoise, my Queen, if you would only help us. Help us defeat our enemies. Help us find our way home so that we may wander no more. I am only a mekhma—you are the Queen of Lower and Upper Egypt. If you say it will be so, I will believe it. For even more than that, you are also a daughter of the desert."

I sprang out of my seat and walked away, leaving the Desert Queen behind. I had not expected her to identify me so easily. I did not like feeling vulnerable, especially to someone so young and inexperienced.

This morning when the slaves had washed my skin and oiled it with perfumes, I had not thought about my Algat upbringing.

When I broke my fast and dined on the finest eggs, fruits and cold meats, I had not thought of my mother or father. But now all their round faces were before me, and I missed them like I had left them only yesterday.

I missed home. I missed knowing where I belonged.

Amenhotep loved me and I him, but I did not belong here. For thirty years now I had railed against that fact, but it was the truth. Now this Desert Queen had brought those memories back with her storytelling and her shameless pleas for help.

Now, my dear husband, what do I do? It is I who sheds the tears. How can I escape myself?

Chapter Nineteen

The Sun Rises—Nefret

I twisted the corner of my gown nervously and paced the small room I shared with Ayn. The Egyptian court had not been kind to us. We'd been shoved away and told nothing. The Great Wife Tiye had left me in the gardens without so much as a word of warning. I paced the sticky floor and went over the conversation again and again with my friend.

"What will we do now? If they do not let us out of here, I will find a way. We can fight our way out!" Ayn said angrily. She pulled on the door again, but it remained locked as it had all night. Neither of us had slept or eaten. At some point a servant left a tray of unknown meats outside our door, but we refused it. "I should have taken that tray! We would have gotten out then!"

"Keep your voice down, Ayn. We won't get any help here, but we are not beaten yet. Just keep calm. I will see if I can talk to Huya again. He seems a reasonable man."

"Really? What about the Great…"

"Say nothing! Never speak against her! There are many ears here in this palace. We are far from home, Ayn. Very far indeed. Now sit down and rest. We may need it."

As soon as we had a mind to settle down, the door opened and Queen Tiye herself walked in. "Well, Desert Queen, you will have what you asked for. Are you prepared to give me what I want?"

Ayn smiled and stood beside me. I smiled too. "Yes, Great Wife. We give you our gold mines and turquoise. We agree."

"No, that is not what I want. What care I for gold or jewels? I have all I want."

Joy escaped me like the air out of a goat's bladder, a toy we used to play with as a child. "I don't understand. I have nothing else to give."

"For reasons of my own, reasons I do not feel compelled to share with you at this time, I have decided that you can keep your gold and turquoise. Whatever arrangement you have made with my husband, Lord of the Two Lands, is good enough for me. I want something else, Desert Queen."

"What is it you want?"

"I want you. I want you to pledge yourself to me. Pledge that you will stay with me until I die and then when I die, you will stay with my son, Amenhotep."

"What?" I gasped in surprise. I could hardly believe my own ears. Surely I was just tired.

"That is my offer. In exchange for a legion of my soldiers, their provisions and provisions for your people for transport to Zerzura, of which I alone know, I only ask for you."

"Why?" I blurted out.

"As I said, I have my own reasons. What is your answer?"

Ayn looked at me questioningly. I knew what I had to do. I raised my chin defiantly and said, "Yes, I agree. In exchange for all those things, I will stay with you. However, may I ask one thing?"

"You may ask…"

"Give me leave to lead my people to Zerzura. I need to set up my kingdom—I cannot leave it in ruin. My sister, the only other queen, has been abducted by the Kiffians. I need to make sure she is reinstalled as mekhma. Please, I know it is a boon to ask it."

The short queen frowned, but she nodded, closing her heavy eyelids once. "So be it. Huya will make all the arrangements and come for you in three days. In the meantime, you will dine with me at all meals. Leave your servant behind. A room has been prepared for you in my apartments."

I bowed, bending my knees slightly. "I am grateful. Thank you." With a flurry of servants, she left me again. Only this time, the door was left open.

"I want you to go, Ayn. Go back to Saqqara and tell my uncle what has happened. No—wait! Don't tell him that I must return to Egypt. Just tell him that I have made the provisions. Yes, that is all he needs to know for now."

"Wise decision, but I do not like this, Nefret. I can't leave you—not now! What does she want with you? Can she really hold you here?"

"Oh yes, she can. Don't worry for me, Ayn. I will ride back with you. Perhaps the Shining Man will come to me and show me a new path to walk."

"What? Who?"

With a sigh, I sat on the bed with my head in my hands. I wanted to cry, sleep and cry some more.

"Nothing. It's nothing. Go, Ayn. I will meet you at Saqqara when I bring the Egyptians."

"Very well, mekhma." She paused in the doorway and smiled at me, "One day, this will be a story. *The Tale of Nefret*, we will call it. A story of a great mekhma who gave everything for her people. Yes, I will tell that story. I promise."

I nodded and let the tears flow. Ayn stayed with me until I fell asleep.

I awoke with the immediate awareness that I was completely alone and everything had changed.

I would never be the same.

The Falcon Rises

By

M.L. Bullock

Dedication

I dedicate this book to Carolann. You were an oasis of peace in a time of trouble, a sheltering rock for us all. We miss you every day. I love you.

Akhenaten's Poem to Nefertiti

The Hereditary Princess, Great of Favor,
Mistress of happiness,
Gay with the two feathers,
At hearing whose voice one rejoices,
Soothing the heart of the King at home,
Pleased at all that is said,
The great and beloved wife of the King,
Lady of the two lands, Neferneferuaten Nefertiti,
Living forever.

—Akhenaten, 1340 BC

Chapter One

The Bloody Throne—Queen Tiye

I tossed and turned on my golden couch, the sounds of the soothing fountain drowned out by the noise of silly little girls playing a hand-clapping game under my balcony. I huffed, slung back the silken sheets and waved the startled attendant away. There would be no sleep for me this afternoon, and I longed for sleep—just a moment's respite from the sadness that filled my soul. My husband, the great and splendid Amenhotep, languished in Thebes. And if I had any hope of navigating the future successfully, I must remain here in the Grand Harem away from my husband's court. It was difficult, but I was willing to sacrifice whatever time I had with Amenhotep in order to secure our dynasty.

I could not trust these things to men, not even my brother Huya or my husband's most trusted adviser, Ramose. Men were no match for the minds of powerful women, especially women like Kiya and her groping relatives.

I knew what the prophets of Amun had declared: "No child of Tiye's will ever take the throne. She is of common blood." Yet my husband loved me more than he ever feared them. And that love and devotion had cost us everything—it cost us our son, Thutmose. Beautiful, smiling Thutmose, cut down in the desert at the foot of the sphinx, supposedly by some jealous god of the Red Sands. But I knew better. My husband knew better too. It had been the wretched priests who slew my son and left him to die in the sand. His body had never been recovered, but I knew he was dead, his light stolen from this world. What was worse was Thutmose would not be reborn, would never rise from death. His body had not been prepared for the journey, and he would undoubtedly remain in the darkness for all eternity.

It had been a cruel deed and one I would never forget. Neither would Amenhotep. Just last night as I lay beside him, he whispered to me through his dry lips, "Do not forget Thutmose. Do not forget my son."

Obediently I had prevented the tears from falling. The order had been given: no tears would be shed in my presence, not even my own. I agreed and lovingly traced his face with my finger. I held him in my arms until he began to retch the black bile, and then I slipped away as he would want me to. I knew my husband well enough to know he despised appearing weak. To me he would always be Amenhotep, the Strong Bull Rising in Thebes; Amenhotep, Strong of Valor, and he yet lived. But for how long?

Sitting on the edge of the cushion, I listened intently to the girls' song.

Put one date in the basket
Now put two
Put one date in the basket
None for you

Put one date in the basket
Eat it up
Put one date in the basket
Time is up

At the end of their song they would laugh and start again. The sound reminded me of life long ago, living in the Algat tribe with my many sisters. How we had squabbled over the smallest thing, like ribbons and bits of rare glass. What fools we had been to mar our time together with such pettiness. I remembered their names and the sounds of their voices, but their faces were lost to me. I, Tiye, Queen of Upper and Lower Egypt, did not know if they lived or lay dead along with my son. I had been forbidden to communicate with my family, and wisely so. Huya alone could I speak to, but never of the Algat, or of home, or of our siblings. To do so was an offense against Amenhotep. What great favor and benevolence he had shown to me, reaching down from his throne and choosing me, a nobody, to be his Great Wife.

Walking to the balcony, I quietly listened to the girls' song as I daydreamed about the past. I had done this quite a bit recently, ever since the Desert Queen appeared in my court with her Red Lands clothing and her rough desert language. How I envied her the freedom she had enjoyed. I wondered how many sisters she had and if she would miss them as I missed mine. I smiled thinking of my sister Shaffar, the most beautiful and silliest girl ever born. I missed her most of all.

But I had been happy at times since those long-ago days. I had daughters of my own and even two sons, although it pleased Amun to steal one from me. My husband loved me above all women and had showered me with honors throughout our life together. Yet I did envy Nefret. I envied her freedom. The freedom to run with legs bare and arms wide. I envied her, and I would be the one to take that freedom from her as it had been taken from me.

I was the most powerful woman in Egypt, and I was a slave. A slave to a fate I had not sought or ever desired. I thumbed away a rare tear as I listened to the girls sing a new song.

> *Fair of face,*
> *Long of hair,*
> *Isis beauty*
> *Who can compare?*
>
> *Spell her name…*
> *Sacred bowl…clap, clap*
> *Fan of pleasure… clap, clap*
> *Fans of immortal winds… clap, clap*
> *Hawk's fearless stand… clap, clap, clap*

Angry bees rose up inside me. *How dare they sing praises to Kiya—spell her name, no less, and under my window! How dare they mock me so! Don't they know who I am?* In my rage, I grabbed a leather strap from a nearby table, walked out of my rooms and stormed down the marble staircase. Fearful servants and courtiers moved out of my way as I charged toward the group of girls who now stood in surprise. Without a word, I struck at them. They screamed in fear and pain, but I would not withhold their punishment. I swung the strap again, slapping bare legs and round bottoms. As young as they were, they had the good sense not to run but hunkered down obediently, covered their heads uselessly with their small hands and accepted my flurry of blows. They wailed in pain, and a crowd had gathered nearby, but not too near.

I continued to beat them until my wrist hurt and I could barely breathe. In my delivery, I had managed to strike myself a few times. One welt on my lower left arm looked particularly vicious. I was so surprised by the appearance of my own blood that I dropped the strap and glowered at the gaggle of wounded girls. Their skin was well striped with red marks now, but I saw no blood. Nobody raised their faces to me, but they cried all the same.

I turned my gaze to the people around me. They cast their eyes to the ground, except Huya, who stood as always nearly hidden against the wall. I summoned him with a wave and left the courtyard with Huya a few feet behind me. I would not retreat to my chambers or return to the harem; instead I made the long walk across the colonnade to my formal court to sit upon my blue throne. It amused me to do so and today, I needed some amusement. I almost smiled seeing the flurry of activity in the distance. I could hear the servants now: "The Great Queen is coming to her court! Make ready! Make ready!"

Yes, I needed to sit on my throne. It was my latest gift from Amenhotep and likely the last. The huge golden chair was covered with lapis lazuli, and my name was beautifully emblazoned across the back.

A shower of pink petals fell at my feet as I walked into the throne room. Two young slaves rushed before me with their baskets of flowers, careful to toss the flowers where I walked. As I approached the dais, they bowed low and disappeared from my presence, taking their baskets with them. Swinging my robes out of the way, I sat upon the throne and ignored my creaking knees. I held my back straight and kept my dark eyes fierce. The throne was so large and I so small, I had to retain this posture if I wanted to be taken seriously. Otherwise I would appear weak and ineffective, just a tiny woman wearing a crown that was never meant to rest upon her head. As was the tradition when the queen held court, my courtiers rushed into the chambers, still looking fearful and curious about what happened in the harem. Only the women had witnessed my outburst, but they would waste no time in recounting the event. Still, they would do so with respect. Of that I was sure. I smiled with pleasure knowing that I still struck fear into their hard, selfish hearts.

"My Queen, you are bleeding. Allow me to send for an attendant." My face a mask, I raised my right arm and watched the bright blood pour freely. I did not answer Huya, and I didn't need to. He always knew what I needed without my saying a word. Such a good servant was he that I sometimes forgot he was my brother. He shouted for a slave and whispered his request to her. I couldn't take my eyes off the glistening blood that now rolled down to my elbow. It had been so long since I had seen it. It had been many years since my lifeblood had flowed from between my legs. I watched in fascination as a drop of blood splashed onto my throne. I was not the only one to witness it. The gasp of the crowd broke the spell. I wondered at the sound when I heard a hoarse whisper from Heby, the ranking priest of Amun, at least for today. There was always a steady stream of new officials appearing in the courts of Amenhotep.

"Blood has been spilled on the throne. Royal blood! This is not a good omen. No, it is not." Heby's words traveled through the room quickly as my courtiers shared them with the onlookers. As quick as lightning, Huya sopped up the blood with a bit of linen. But before he could dispose of it, Heby stepped forward to collect it.

"The blood of the Great Wife is sacred, steward. You can trust me to dispose of it properly." Heby wisely kept his head down to prevent me from seeing the greed in his piggish eyes. No doubt he would use my own blood to work some obscene magic on me. Anything to raise the status of his pet cow, Kiya. He was the Mitanni woman's courtier, wasn't he? He raised his outstretched hands, expecting to receive the bloody cloth for whatever use he had in mind. How I would have loved to snatch Huya's blade and lop off Heby's grasping fingers! I was sorely offended by this exercise, but I could not refuse him. The priests of Amun held too much power over the people, and their confidence had been bolstered by the unredressed murder of my son not ten years ago. A day of vengeance would come for Heby and his brothers! But today was not that day. It was too soon, and my plans were not yet complete. I gazed at Huya, my eyes telling him what I wanted to say. Huya folded the cloth carefully and placed it in the fat priest's grimy hands.

I glared at Heby as he backed away with his unexpected treasure, his shiny head bobbing and glowing with excessive sweat and expensive oils. Quickly, before anyone else could claim my blood, Huya wrapped my arm himself, first rubbing stinging ointment on the skin. I didn't flinch but kept my eyes trained on the people, who watched curiously. As he tended to his ministrations, I studied the faces. Yes, I still had a few friends here, but only a few. I had been right to add to my retinue. The young, beautiful Nefret would certainly stir the pot. I noticed that Kiya had not bothered to appear before me, but I did spot her companion Inhapi.

"Inhapi, where is your mistress that she cannot attend me?"

"You are my mistress, Great Queen." She smiled pleasantly and nodded as she spoke, as if she were trying to convince herself of her own lies.

"I refer to Queen Tadukhipa." I didn't bother to return her empty smile. And then I added, "Some people call her the Monkey, but I prefer her proper name. Don't you, Inhapi?"

"Yes, Great Queen. I believe Queen Tadukhipa is tending to her daughter, Baketaten."

Beside me Huya whispered, "She is one of the children you punished."

I sneered down at Inhapi and said, "Well, go get her now. Her daughter can wait. Am I not the Queen of Egypt?"

"Yes, Great Queen." She backed away and left the courtyard to fetch the Hittite princess. How dare Kiya avoid waiting upon me?

"I see my daughter Sitamen, wife of Pharaoh, is here today. Tell me, Sitamen, what request have you for me? Have you brought me a present? I can see you have something in your hands."

"Greetings, Greatest of Pharaoh's Wives, Keeper of His Heart. I have indeed brought you a gift." I waved my daughter forward and waited to see what she would bring me. I studied her as she walked the processional to my throne. Taller than me by a head, Sitamen had the slim body of a maiden, a fair face and long, slender fingers. Draped across her arms was a wide silk ribbon in ivory and gold. Sitamen would have made a lovely queen, but alas for her, that would never be. She would never know the love of a kind spouse or feel the hard body of a man next to her, for she was of royal blood. She would die intact just as she had entered the world. My daughter bowed slightly and smiled up at me, offering her gift as she had when she was a child.

I examined it politely and touched the fabric, careful to keep my bloody finger from staining it. The gold stitching was clean and perfect, a simple motif of golden leaves wrapped around a resting snake. It was not a symbol that I recognized, and it likely had no significant meaning. Sitamen lacked the ability or desire to achieve any political goals. Of all the people in Upper and Lower Egypt, she was the least likely to rise up against me. I both loved her and loathed her at the same time. I sometimes wondered how I ever had given birth to such a passive child.

"Who sewed this ribbon, Sitamen? It is well done. It is good to have such a talented slave in your household."

"Oh no, Great Queen. No slave sewed this—this is my work. See the way the stitch is hidden along the seam? Memre says she has rarely seen any work so well made before. I made this for you. Perhaps you can wear it at the Sed festival. I would be honored to see you wear it…Mother," she added in her child's voice.

I withdrew my hand from the ribbon and sat up even stiffer. For the second time that morning anger burst from my belly. "What do you mean by sewing away like a slave? Do you think this is a proper activity for a royal daughter?" I heard snickering in the gallery but did not correct the guilty party. Sitamen needed to remember her place. She should feel ashamed for wasting her time on such menial projects. Sitamen's bright smile vanished, and she stood open-mouthed before me. That too made me angry. "No more of this. Next time bring me something of value, Sitamen." I dismissed her with a wave of my hand and looked for someone else to entertain me. How I longed to see an Amazon again or maybe one of the fair-skinned Pymere from the faraway northern lands.

"Great Queen, Aperel, the Master of Horse, has presented you with six new horses. They are in the courtyard now."

"Come forward, Aperel." I recognized the face. I had seen him many times in my husband's court, but this was the first time I'd had the chance to speak to him. He stood tall and straight and, despite his title, did not appear as if he had just stepped out of the stables. He wore a fine blue tunic with a collar of red stones. He was a handsome man with very few scars and a pleasing voice.

"Thank you for receiving my gifts, Great Queen."

"I thank you for the horses, Aperel. I cannot wait to see them."

"Whenever Your Majesty would like to see them, I will be happy to show them to you."

"Let us go now. I am anxious to see these fine gifts." I stood serenely, surveyed my court again and walked carefully down the dais. There was no one else with the potential to amuse me today. I extended my hand to Aperel, who bowed and blushed as I touched his hand. It was only a light touch, but I was sure that someone would mistake it for something more. Poor Aperel. Did he know what he was doing?

As we walked I encouraged him to tell me about the horses. How fast did they run? Who were their sires? Could they pull a chariot? I felt bored before he answered even the first few questions, but I enjoyed smelling his sandalwood skin and hearing his deep voice. He did nothing inappropriate, yet my mind wandered occasionally.

Oh, Amenhotep! My love! How long has it been since we have lain together as man and wife?

Aperel left me as I climbed the viewing gallery with my court. We watched the horses sprint, walk and parade for thirty minutes. It wasn't until the display was nearly over that Kiya appeared, looking very unhappy. With total disregard for protocol, she neither presented herself to me nor acknowledged me in word or deed. If my husband had witnessed such open abuse, he would have punished her severely. Her gaggle of ladies clustered around her, but they wisely bowed to me and repeated my name. Kiya waved her blue fan furiously as if she were in the midst of a heat stroke. Huya saw her too. I saw his jaw pop angrily at her affront. My brother was a proud man, prouder than even I was.

Poor unaware Aperel continued with his narrative until I finally stood and applauded. I had no idea how long this lecture would have continued without my interruption, but my stomach was rumbling and my mouth was dry.

"Thank you, Aperel. I shall tell Pharaoh of this generous gift. You have pleased me greatly." Aperel bowed low and whispered something to the horses, who also bowed the knee. I applauded again and laughed aloud at the trick. Looking again I could see one horse had failed to follow orders. Instead of bowing her knee she snatched her head away, proudly refusing to participate with the Master of Horse. He scolded and clucked at her, but I laughed again.

"What a wonderful trick, Aperel!" I called down from the galley. "I think you should name that one Tadukhipa—it does not have the intelligence it needs to know when to bow down."

The Master of Horse did not argue with me. He replied loudly, "Yes, my Queen. It shall be done."

I turned to leave the gallery but paused. My court paused with me. "On second thought, do not put such a burden on so beautiful a horse. We shall forgive her this time. I am not without mercy."

"You are ever merciful, Great Queen Tiye." Aperel smiled and bowed again.

With a snort, I fixed amused eyes on Tadukhipa, whose skin turned a deep shade of red—as red as the stones on Aperel's collar. Finally, I felt a small degree of satisfaction. As Huya filed in behind me, he winked but carefully kept the smile from his face. For as much as I hated her, Tadukhipa (or Kiya, the Monkey, as I liked to call her) was also the wife of Pharaoh Amenhotep. At any moment he could withdraw his great favor from me and make Kiya the Great Queen instead. And when my husband died and my son sat upon the throne of Egypt, how long would it be before she convinced him to do just that? He would inherit his father's harem, including the foreign queen who would waste no time in seducing him. Even now I saw her casting those longing looks in his direction.

This I would not allow. Whether she knew it or not, it was too late for Kiya. I had already chosen a wife for my son. A strong wife with the sand of the Red Lands in her veins.

All I had to do now was wait. I was good at that.

Chapter Two

The Stubborn Dead—Orba

Death had blazed through our camp with a mighty sword. A palpable spirit of grief loomed over us, and how cruel was the silence! The absence of the sounds of children playing heightened our sadness as we sheltered in the rocks of Saqqara waiting to hear if we would live or die. The Meshwesh spirit had been broken by the Kiffians, and now our fate hung in the balance. We were at the mercy of Egypt, and all our hopes were pinned on a girl who had never negotiated a trade much less pleaded a case in the courts of Egypt. Still, there was hope. As long as the breath of the divine rested in her, hope remained.

I felt a deep frustration that I could not see the future. I was not a fire-watcher as Farrah had been, although I knew her power had waxed and waned. Sometimes I could see glimpses in the water, like at the pool of Timia, but there was no water here in Saqqara. None that I had found yet, but I planned to continue searching for it, both for drinking and for seeing. Now that most of the Council had been murdered by the red-haired giants, there was only Samza and me left, and Samza had barely spoken a word since the destruction. The kings would ask my counsel, I assumed. And when they did, I would not let them down.

I stepped quietly into Semkah's small cave shelter. I was happy to see that despite his pain and fever, he was finally asleep. He had struggled to recover from his wound; the slice had been clean, but it had been difficult to protect the wound during our journey and now it festered. He had been a good king, much better by all accounts than his father had been. Leela smiled at me as she prepared a pot of food for the wounded king. I nodded and left her to her work. I had other matters to tend to.

I felt good about my decision to enlist the young woman's help. Leela had the potential to become a skilled practitioner in the healing arts but needed my tutelage. There were so few now who knew the Old Ways, I could hardly be choosy. Yet I recalled that Farrah had rejected the young woman for further training for one reason or another. And although we had once been lovers, Farrah did not seek my counsel in the matter or offer an explanation to me or anyone. Her solitary mind had been both her strength and her weakness.

I wrapped a black cloth around my head to protect it from the still blazing sun and walked through the camp. It was near dusk, and I welcomed the darkness and the relief from the heat.

All the tribes had come together. None had refused to rally with us, and that was a good sign, yet I felt unsteady. Whenever you had more than one king in a camp, tensions would rise. Especially now that our elected mekhma had been kidnapped and possibly murdered by the Kiffians and her rejected sister represented us. The camp was quiet; only a few women worked at cooking, and I began to notice that most of the men were nowhere to be found. Omel and his retinue were absent. This did not bode well. I squatted next to Ishna and asked her quietly, "Where are they? Where are the men?"

She tossed dried mushrooms into a brown liquid and pointed to the east without speaking. I reached in my pocket and removed a small pouch that contained a few pinches of herbs. "Here, Ishna. This is a good herb. It will give you strength." With a gap-toothed smile, the older woman accepted the pouch and looked around for something to give me. I dared not refuse her, for this was how we lived. We gave to one another, and there was as much joy in giving as there was in receiving. At least, that was the Old Way, the way both Ishna and I chose to live. She patted her neck and removed a leather necklace with an ivory pendant. She smiled again and handed it to me, and I examined the workmanship with an appreciative smile. "This is very nice. Thank you." Without a word but clearly happy, she stirred her food and sprinkled in some of the herbs.

Happy to have blessed the old woman, I left her to her food and walked purposefully in the direction she had indicated. I did not have far to walk and could hear Omel's booming voice before I saw him. He and the other kings were gathered in a rocky outcropping. Some were sitting and some were standing, but clearly it was Omel who led this meeting.

"Kings of the Meshwesh. From the beginning I have told you that Egypt was our true friend. And now you see that my words are true, although it pains me to say that my brother was wrong. I know our current situation worries many of you, but let me assure you that all will be well. As I have reported on many occasions, we have many friends in Thebes." Many of the men murmured, but nobody openly disagreed with him.

I paused behind the rock to listen to more of Omel's speech. I had always had my doubts about his loyalty to Semkah; now that the king was wounded and possibly dying, Omel no longer bothered to hide his true feelings.

"Even though generous offers were made to us in the past, you and I know that a king's heart, a Pharaoh's heart, can change."

"Get to your point, Omel." The voice belonged to Fraya, a southern king and distant cousin of Semkah and Omel.

"My point is this, brother. If you follow me as king, I will secure the deal we need. *I* can deliver Zerzura and Pharaoh's army. *I* have a powerful ally who will lend his help whenever I ask for it. If we leave this in the hands of the girl, we deserve to die here. Swear your allegiance to me, and I will ride out immediately. We have no time to waste."

"Make you king? We are all kings. Your brother sent the sigil—he summoned us here. We would hear from him on this matter," Fraya said, obviously unhappy with Omel's proposal.

"My brother is not well, King Fraya. In fact, he may not survive the loss of his arm. And even if he did, of what use is a one-armed king?"

"And what will this cost us, Omel? Are you thinking to give away our mines? That is all we have left."

Another man asked, "Will we have to give our daughters and wives to the Egyptians? I heard they prefer boys to girls. Will they demand our sons?"

Fraya calmed the crowd and asked Omel, "What promises will you make on our behalf?" It was clear that this man was not convinced.

"Deal-making is the art of kings, is it not? What makes you think my niece will secure us a better deal than I? She has not gone to Thebes to climb palm trees or shoot an arrow, yet you sent her to represent you. I counseled against this, but nobody listened to me. Now is the time to do something before we are undone!"

The kings sounded as if they were in agreement with Omel, and this was a dangerous thing. I chose that moment to reveal myself to the secret gathering.

"Hafa-nu, kings of the Meshwesh."

"Hafa-nu," they responded, surprised to see me.

"What are you doing here, Orba? I did not summon you."

With a scowl I answered, "You do not summon me, Omel. Nor do you dismiss me. I am a free man, as are all these men."

"Well then, little man, what do you have to say to us? Or have you come to tell us that my brother is dead?"

I was a small man, the smallest present, but I did not hunker down. Nor would I slink away merely because Omel pointed this out. I was no coward. I was no schemer like the man before me.

"Semkah is resting, and I expect him to make a full recovery. As I am sure you are happy to hear."

"My wife, who is a healer, says he will not survive. And even if he does, he will always have one arm. We have never had a one-armed king rule over us. My brother is a good man, but he cannot lead us like this."

"Indeed, we have never had a one-armed king. But then again, we still have a mekhma."

Omel snorted his disgust. "Nefret? She failed the trials, remember? Are you saying now that we should accept her when you yourself previously rejected her?"

"Ah, but she did not fail the last trial—she was unable to complete it. Or have you forgotten that our enemy murdered the tribe at Biyat?" To that he said nothing and only glared at me with his kohl-lined eyes. I continued, "However, I was not referring to Nefret. Pah is the mekhma. And until we know what has happened to her, she is mekhma still. It is acceptable to the Council if her sister held her place until we determine what has happened to her, but even then these things will not be decided like this!"

King Fraya rose to his feet and stood beside me. "I agree with Orba. If this is what the Council wants, then we will wait and see."

"The Council is only Orba and Samza. Are we to let these two men decide our fate?"

"Again you are correct, King Omel. Thanks to the Kiffians, only Samza and I are left, but I have taken steps to correct that. We are seeking new Council members from the Meshwesh, fresh blood to take the place of those we lost. I look forward to speaking with any whom you recommend, for I feel it is important that we keep the Old Ways. All tribes must be represented in our Council. This is what Farrah would want."

"And what does the Council say about Nefret? What is our future, Orba? What do our gods and ancestors say? What have you seen?" Fraya prodded.

The southern king eyed me hopefully. I felt the fate of our people resting on my skinny shoulders, as if Ma'at himself rode me, directing me. Here was a moment to instill hope—a rare moment given by the god. I could not miss this opportunity, yet I was not the kind of man who would lie to impress other men or to manipulate them to do my bidding. I had seen nothing yet, but a vision from many years ago sprang into my mind. As I recalled the details of the vision, I felt the warmth of the god's unction brewing in the pit of my stomach. The words came forth like water from a new spring, slowly at first and then more furiously the deeper I dug into it.

"A day of rejoicing approaches, brothers. A day like no other! We *will* walk the heights of Zerzura and see the sea again. The blue sea will lap our shores, and our children *will* rejoice that they live in a happy city. Oh yes, the sounds of children will echo in the streets! Our sons will grow strong and will wear our clothes, our colors. They will not wear the garments of Egypt, nor shall they be slaves to any man. Our daughters will marry our Meshwesh sons, and many nations will long to see their lovely faces. The bloodlines of our people will once again be sown with great seers and wise kings and leaders who will dispense justice and bring prosperity. In fact, the greatest king our people has ever known has yet to be born—but he will arrive and soon." I could see the face of the young man, a familiar face but one I had not yet seen. "Which of you shall father such a great son? This I do not know, but I do know there is one alive who will." Tears filled my eyes, and unexpected joy bubbled in my heart. I continued, "A mighty army approaches. But do not fear, Meshwesh, because your Deliverer has arrived. A girl with the power of Egypt in her hands! The falcon rises, and we ride upon its wings!"

The men listened wide-eyed at my prophecy, then cheered and hugged one another. All except Omel, whose angry countenance told me he neither believed me nor supported me. He was my enemy, and he would not soon forget that I had defied him. In fact, I had ruined his plan. I did not linger. I left the kings and walked down the trail to explore the caves. More than ever I wanted to find a clear pool of water so that I could seek the future. I knew every word of what I said was true, but now the hunger to see more drove me deep into the cliffs and caves. Like a thirsty wild hare, I scampered through one cave and then another seeking water. I imagined that I could smell it, which seemed improbable; I had seen no clue that there was any to find. It would be pitch black soon, and I didn't dare explore the caves in the darkness. These Egyptians liked their hiding places, even in death.

I looked back down the valley to the camp. I was very high into the cliffs now and could see the fires burning below. The smell of cooking meat made my stomach growl, and I was tempted to turn back when I heard a sound.

It was the sound of a woman singing. It was a pleasant and soothing sound. It came from above me, in a distant cave. I could see the faint light from a fire and was puzzled at the sight. As far as I knew no living person dwelt in Saqqara—this was the City of the Dead, at least if you were an Egyptian prince. I was no such thing. Still, the sound of a woman's song intrigued me. Yes! I knew that verse!

Clumsily and without thought I climbed up the narrow path and then scaled the cliff, desperately hanging on with my cut hands and worn sandals. At last I lay panting on the cave floor. The singing ceased, but I could still see the light. I forced myself to stand. "Who is there?" No one answered, but I heard the sound of laughter. Yes, a woman's laugh. I nearly shouted when some small animal ran by my foot. Clutching my new necklace as if it were a talisman, I walked deeper into the cave until I saw her.

It was Farrah.

"My Orba. I was afraid you would not come."

"Farrah, what are you doing here? You are dead. I saw you with my own eyes. The Kiffians…" I fell to my knees and peered past the flames to see the woman I loved smiling back at me. Her hair was no longer white but brown again, just as it had been when we were young, when she let me touch it and kiss her. A desperate sob escaped my lips, and I said, "I am so happy to see you, even if you are only a dream."

"Tell me, Orba. Why have you come here to this lonely place? Ah…no need to explain. I see now. You want to see, don't you?"

"Yes. So much has happened, and I can't explain it all. I must know how to lead our people. Won't you help me, Farrah?"

With a slight movement of her hand she tossed something into the fire and the flames changed to purple. She invited me to look, but as always I could see nothing. "You know I cannot read the fire. What else can I do?"

"Go to the water then," she said impatiently. Even in dreams I disappointed her. Suddenly Farrah and her fire disappeared.

I gasped, nearly falling backward onto the stone floor. "Wait! Do not leave me, Farrah! I cannot do this by myself."

I sat in the silence of the dark cave, unsure what to do, when I heard a new sound: the sound of water. Using my hands to feel my way, I crawled deeper into the cave. My knee bounced on a sharp edge, and I winced in pain but kept crawling. A purplish light, like the one produced by Farrah's herb fire, appeared in front of me and shone down onto a small fountain that splashed at the back of the cave. So thirsty was I that I drank from the fountain without thinking. When I had drunk my fill, I splashed my face and sat patiently, staring at the water.

The water shone in the purple light, and in just a few seconds I could see images form before my eyes. As always seeing such things delighted and surprised me. I watched the face of Nefret appear; her red hair was gone, and in its place was a wig of dark braided hair. Upon her head was a crown—no, a double crown. Her lovely face vanished, and I saw another face: Omel's wife, Astora. She stood under the moonlight, her body nude and painted with magic symbols. She whispered spells, and as she spoke creatures poured forth from her mouth. Black, writhing creatures that crawled through our camp and wrapped themselves around many different leaders. "What can this mean?" I asked Farrah as if she would answer me. She did not.

Then I saw another scene. Farrah walked through our camp—this must have been around the day of the attack. She followed the child, the dead child, Nefret's treasure. The two walked into Pah's tent, but in my vision I was not permitted to enter. I saw Yuni storm out with an angry look on his ugly face, then Pah emerged, her robes covered in blood, a bloody dagger in her hand. I gasped at the sight. On a surge of foul wind I was carried inside the tent just in time to see Mina enter and issue a silent scream.

As Farrah took her last breaths I cried, "I am sorry, Farrah. We were wrong. It should have been Nefret. Now what do I do?"

Farrah appeared to me, wearing the same bloody robes, her hair white again and streaked with blood. She raised her hand toward me and pointed. "Now you see… You have seen the future, the present and the past. Now you see, Orba hap Senu. You will see in fire and water. Be mindful of your gift. Take no life, or you shall lose it."

In a soft flicker she disappeared, taking with her the purple light. With her she took all warmth from the cave. I had seen troubling visions. I crawled out of the cave as quickly as I could. I had to share all this with Samza.

We had a devious, evil enemy at work in our camp.

And soon we would be without a mekhma.

Chapter Three

The Song of Queens—Ayn

I knew what Omel was up to, and I stalked him nearly night and day. A man like him would never pass up the opportunity to sow discord. Until Nefret returned I would be her eyes and ears. I would not let her down in this. I watched covertly as Omel led his brother-kings out of our camp to the large rock circle to the north. So arrogant was he, so confident in his ability to coerce the other kings to partake in his rebellion, that he did not bother to hide his attempt at creating a coalition. I think he saw me once but paid me no mind. I had been labeled a liar. Who would listen to me now?

Still, I dogged his every step and did my best to avoid a direct confrontation. To her credit, Astora was ever observant and glared at me whenever we met. She knew I hated Omel, but she would probably never dream why.

Living in the Red Lands I had grown accustomed to hiding in plain sight, so even if Omel had bothered to occasionally glance over his shoulder he would have had a difficult time spotting me. My clothes were neither bright nor gay, and I wore no jewelry for I owned none. I could be as elusive as I liked. I frowned as he clapped his friends on the back and spoke in low, serious tones. If only I could hear the words! I heard the shuffling of pebbles behind me and flattened myself against a nearby rock. I slid my sword back into its sheath so the fading sunlight would not glint and reveal my hiding place. Slowly I turned my head to see who approached. I hoped it was Astora. I would love to confront the king's wife with the truth.

It was Orba! The little man was as loud as a blind goat. I considered getting his attention, but he did not look my way. Clumsily he paused as he sheltered behind one of the larger boulders in the Saqqara Valley. He was in the perfect position to overhear Omel's conversation. The rocky hollow in which they gathered created an amplifying effect. What fools men were! I removed my sword, my metal cuffs and anything that would clatter and laid them on the ground. I climbed the rock without detection and lay flat staring up at the sky as Omel began to make his case to the gathering.

He tried to be eloquent, but no words could hide the truth—at least not to me. Omel wanted to be king. It had been his lifelong ambition. I listened as he made insinuations about Nefret and felt hopeful when Fraya questioned him. Ha! This would not be an easy sell for the grasping Omel, Betrayer of Queens!

I warned Pah that her uncle could not be trusted long before she consummated her covenant with him. Even though the closeness of their association sickened me, I loved Pah even in her delusion. I had loved her deeply and even now scarcely let my mind wonder about where she was or what evils had befallen her. I loved her enough to hope she was dead and not suffering.

Pah and I had been childhood friends. I understood her and shared some of her feelings. As the only daughter of a mighty warrior with no sons, I felt the same rejection and witnessed my father's disappointment. Still I trained harder, fought longer and did everything I could to show my father that I had a warrior's heart. I don't think he ever saw it. Now he was dead, and I would never hear the words I so longed for. But Pah had seen it. She had commended me when I bet her at our daily races. She recognized my strength and insisted that I help her take her rightful place as mekhma. At the time, I had felt honored. Now I knew the truth. She had used me for her own ends and abandoned me when I needed her the most. It was the hard, bitter truth.

As I listened to Omel blather on, I thought about the daughters of Semkah. Until this past moon, I had not exchanged more than a few words with Nefret. I had believed Pah, who considered her sister weak and stupid. I related to Pah, who felt lost in the shadow of her radiant sister. The young women were very similar in appearance, but inside they were nothing alike. Pah had an endless need for affirmation—she had to be the best at everything. And when she wasn't, you saw the worst of her. She reminded me of one of the great cats, the black ones with huge marble eyes. Eyes that were wise and dangerous. Nefret was more like the falcon. She stayed aloof, above those around her. Not in an arrogant way, as I once supposed, but as one who must always look at the larger view. Pah was fierce and fast where Nefret was careful, even cautious. But Nefret had a wisdom about her that surprised everyone. What fools they had been—what a fool I had been—to lift up Pah as mekhma. The thought made me want to spit, but the heat of the rock dried my mouth and drained my strength.

When Orba made his appearance, I could hear the surprise in the council of kings. Ha! Such fools men were to let someone like Orba sneak into their midst unseen. And these were our leaders? Omel did not back down at first, but the power of Orba's prophecy disarmed him. I lay upon the rock and listened with tears streaming down my face. When had I last cried? I could not remember. I had not cried when Alexio whacked me with the flat of his sword. I had not cried when my father struck me in a drunken stupor, breaking my tooth and causing me to bleed for hours. I had not cried when I took the warrior's tattoos, although the pain had been almost more than I could bear. Now I heard the promise from the prophet's own mouth.

"A mighty army approaches. But do not fear, Meshwesh, because your Deliverer has arrived. A girl with the power of Egypt in her hands! The falcon rises, and we ride upon its wings!"

The hopelessness that I had carried with me to the top of that rock floated away. I believed Orba's words—I snatched them out of the air like they were living things and wrapped my faith around them. And I knew something else: I would serve Nefret for the rest of my days. That was all I ever wanted. To serve the mekhma, to offer my hands, heart and soul if required on behalf of my people. And even if she never recognized me or thanked me, these words would be enough. As Orba prophesied, Nefret would be our deliverer. She was the promised falcon. She would rise to the heights of power and would need someone she could trust. I had chosen poorly when I chose Pah, and I had failed Nefret once already by losing Paimu, but not again.

Wherever the mekhma went, I would go too—even if that meant traveling the far reaches of the Red Lands or traveling down into death. I would not allow Omel to abuse her as I'd seen him abuse Pah. When Nefret returned I would tell her everything! I heard the men below leaving their rocky fortress with encouragement on their lips. Whatever Omel's intention had been, this surely was not it. I stifled a laugh. I leaned up on my elbow slightly and watched them return to camp. The sun had gone down now, and the first, brightest stars appeared above me. The sky was the color of magic, somewhere between a deep purple and a blazing red. A streak of light slipped across the sky—a messenger of the gods, no doubt. It was an omen, but I did not ponder it. My heart was too full of hope to wonder at what tomorrow would bring. As I lay on the rock, my hands outstretched beside me, a song rose up from within me.

Hear now, Kings and Queens
Warrior and Maid
This is the tale of Nefret.

She is the falcon that rises,
Rises above the earth,
She will lead us home,

The City of White,
The City of Little Birds.

I did not wonder from whence the song came. My mother sang the songs of the gods, or at least she used to, and I heard them many a night when my father would go on long journeys along the trade route with his king. Songs such as these, spontaneous and magical, came unbidden from the gods, she told me. When I was a young girl, before I had breasts and before desire coursed through my veins, I sang too. But when it became clear that I would receive no love from my father Nari's hands, I abandoned the softness of music in favor of the unyielding, unloving metal of the sword.

I let the notes of my song fade on the breeze and then sang it over and over until I had memorized the tune and the words. This was not all...no, this was only the beginning of my gift to the mekhma, for queen she would remain.

As the air turned cool, I slid down from the rock and gathered my items, strapping on my sword and cuffs. I walked back to the camp, wondering who I would stay with tonight. There were only a few tents available; some families were hidden in the caves but even in the camp of the Meshwesh it was not wise for a woman to share a bed with a man. I had a few offers when we arrived but refused them all with a sneer. I needed no man's protection, for I had a sword and knew how to use it.

I decided to see if Semkah had food and wine, but to my surprise another tended to him. She was not from our tribe; perhaps she was from Omel's, but I couldn't be sure. She put her fingers to her lips when I entered, instructing me to be quiet. I stared at the king and watched him breathe for a few seconds before I left. I spotted a boy standing guard outside one tent. I had seen no one enter the shelter in the two days we had dwelt in Saqqara. I wondered to whom it belonged.

"You there. What is your name?" I stalked toward him authoritatively.

The young man, whom I did not recognize, could not have seen more than thirteen winters. He replied, "I am Amaktahef, but people call me Amak. How may I help you?" He was polite with bright eyes and dark brown skin, like the tribes from the west.

"Whose tribe do you belong to, Amak?"

"I am Siti's son. We are from Dahkia."

I saved him the trouble of asking me anything. "I am happy to see such brave young Meshwesh standing guard in our camp. Tell me, whose tent is this?"

He poked out his bony chest and raised his chin, somehow offended that I did not know. "This is the mekhma's tent. We keep it for her until she returns."

I smiled wryly. "And which mekhma are you waiting for, Amak?"

He thought about it for a moment and then answered confidently, "Whichever one comes back first."

I nodded but said nothing. There was no need to correct the boy. Pah was never coming back. She was dead or worse. But Nefret would return—he would see soon enough. "I am Ayn, the mekhma's guard. I will stay here until she returns."

He opened his mouth like a fish out of water. With a sigh I went into the tent and removed my sword, tossing it on the pallet. It was a small tent, but it would do. There were no fine trappings like cedar tables or hanging lanterns, not as when we stayed at Biyat or Timia, but it was better than climbing into bed with a grasping man. To my surprise, the boy followed me inside. I turned to face him and removed my cuffs. "Yes, what is it?"

"I just…are you sure? I don't want to get into trouble with my father. He said no one was to enter until the mekhma arrived."

"Did he now?" Curious and suspicious, I felt the hair creep up on the back of my neck. I picked up my sword and used the blade to shift the blankets around. No snakes slithered out, and no scorpions struck at the metal. After a few seconds, Amak's curiosity got the better of him.

"What are you looking for?"

"It is nothing. I thought I lost something. Tell me, Amak. Is your father a good man?"

"The very best man. He is good to all his children and his people." His grin told me that he believed what he said. This was not propaganda.

"Did he provide all this for the mekhma?"

"Yes, he did. He is a kind man, my father. He says she will return and lead us to Zerzura. It is a wonderful place. My father saw it when he was just a boy, and now he says I will see it. Have you seen it?"

"I have not, but we will. You tell your father that the mekhma's guard stands ready to serve him if he should need me." I put my hand on the boy's shoulder and looked down into his face. I was easily a foot and a half taller than he. "I am grateful for his thoughtfulness. It is good to know that she has friends."

A large smile spread across his wide face. "I will do so. Do you require anything? Perhaps I can serve you? I have been so bored standing here all day."

"Who bakes the best bread, Amak? A warrior needs food."

"Oh! My mother, the wife of Siti! I shall go now and fetch you bread and something to drink."

Amak didn't move but stood at attention.

"What is it?" I asked him, my stomach rumbling at the promise of food.

"Well, don't you have to dismiss me?"

Trying not to smile I said, "Very well, you are dismissed. Return quickly. No dawdling. And bring me an oil cloth for my sword when you return. And do not barge into the tent without announcing yourself first. I have a sword, Amak."

"Yes, Ayn." He scurried out of the tent, and I sat on the disturbed pallet, thankful for this happy turn of fortune. It was dark and getting darker. I opened a small box near the entrance of the tent and found a stub of a candle and a clay candle holder. I quickly stepped outside and lit the candle, returned and placed it in the candle holder. It wasn't much light, but it was more than many people had. By my estimation there were less than two thousand people in the Meshwesh camp; that was significantly less than the estimates had been before the destruction at Biyat. We lost many at Timia, but at least some of us had survived. Biyat's tribe would never walk the earth again. I opened the second box and found it full of Pah's things. I recognized her treasure box, and like a sneak I opened it. I picked up the small block of scented wood and sniffed it.

Oh, Pah. Why did it have to end like this? I pray you are happy in the life after. For some reason I felt compelled to place the items around the candle. I bent in front of them and prayed to my ancestors. I begged them to make Pah welcome, for she had once been mekhma. I prayed to the gods Ma'at and Hathor to forgive her for the evil deeds she had done. I pleaded with them to let her pass into the afterlife or send her back to complete her work. I ended my prayers and heard Amak outside the tent.

"Lady Ayn!" he called to me. "I am here with my father, Siti."

Rising to my feet, I eyed my sword but decided to leave it where it lay. There was a time for swords and there was a time for laying down swords. I could not kill a king, unless it was Omel. Him I could kill.

"Please come in."

Amak's arms were loaded with a basket. He began removing the contents hurriedly to the nearby crate, and I stood with a calm face watching Siti.

"Ayn, you are the daughter of Nari, aren't you?"

"Yes, my father was Nari. He is dead, killed at Timia."

"Sad day for us all." His brown eyes showed sadness as he continued, "The mekhma's guard is welcome to stay with us. We have an extra tent and are inclined to share our hospitality with you."

I couldn't hide my surprise. "I am honored, King Siti, that you would offer your hospitality to me. But my place is here. I will wait for Nefret to return."

"Please, it's just Siti. There are enough kings in this camp already. Speaking of kings, how is Semkah? No one will allow us to see him. As the mekhma's guard, surely you must know."

Ah, so there is a reason…

"I have just seen him. He is resting and has a devoted healer by his side. I am sure he will see you soon."

He breathed a noticeable sigh of relief. "For that I am grateful. Semkah is a good man, a true king. I would hate to discover that he had been mishandled." I could read between the lines: he did not trust Omel. I could not tell him that I felt the same way.

"I can assure you that if that were the case, I would not be standing here."

He had something else to say but before he could share whatever was on his heart, a noise rose in the camp. Shouts and sounds of battle. I reached for my sword and ran out of the tent toward the noise. *Oh, please, ancestors! Don't let it be the Kiffians! We are not ready!*

"Hold! Do not attack! Those are Egyptian flags! That is Nefret! The mekhma has returned!" Jubilation rose from the camp as Nefret galloped toward us, her red hair and green cloak trailing behind her. She rode the largest horse I had ever seen, black with a braided mane and muscled legs. Beside her rode a dark-haired man with a proud face, strong legs and broad shoulders. He was the handsomest and fiercest-looking man I had ever seen. He slid from his horse before it came to a good stop and ran to Nefret, helping her down as easily as if she were a feather. The cheers of happiness diminished as the sound of hundreds of horses' hooves pounded in behind them.

"Greetings, Meshwesh," Nefret called, settling down the retinue.

"Hafa-nu!" a woman called, and others echoed her devotion. "Hafa-nu, mekhma."

Nefret smiled and returned the greeting, "Hafa-nu, Ankanah. All will be well."

The people quieted after a few moments. They eyed the Egyptians suspiciously, but their souls leaped seeing that their brave queen had indeed returned. "This is Ramose, Pharaoh's general, and these men are Pharaoh's soldiers. They will do you no harm. They have brought us food—and weapons and all manner of things. Things we will need to make the journey home." As Nefret spoke I could not help but stare at the black-eyed man. Yes, his physique was stronger than any I had ever seen, but it was his sword that I could not tear my eyes from. It had a double edge and was made of a metal I had never seen before. The hilt shone in the firelight, and I could see a strange script on the glittering scabbard. He stared back, but only for the smallest of seconds.

"All will be well, Meshwesh. Do not be afraid."

"Hafa-nu, mekhma!"

She waved her hand as Farrah used to do. "Ayn!" She reached her hand toward me, and I hugged her as if she were my sister.

"Mekhma, I am glad you returned so soon. I was beginning to worry. Let me show you your tent. King Siti arranged a place for you."

We walked together and she whispered, "Siti? Tell me, what have I missed?"

"Quite a bit," I said sternly. "What did *I* miss? Are you a prisoner, then?"

"Hafa-nu, mekhma," the people greeted her as they passed. Some kissed her cheek, while others hugged her.

"Shh...we will talk more later. First, take me to my father, and then we will see what is what."

"Very well, mekhma."

"Please call me Nefret. I miss hearing my name."

Finally I had something to smile about. "Very well, Nefret. Come, he is just down here."

Chapter Four

The Snakes of Destiny—Nefret

Speaking to my father proved difficult, as many of my people wanted to touch me and speak to their mekhma. Thankfully, the hard-jawed Egyptian general did not follow me but set about his own tasks. I was happy about the absence of his company. During our frantic journey to Saqqara the tension between us did not lessen. Even though I was much younger than he, I could read him quite easily. He did not like me much and thought even less of his errand, but he would never speak against his queen. Still, if I had pulled back my covers at night and invited him in I knew he would have accepted my invitation—his eyes were ever upon my figure, especially my breasts. That was one invitation he would never receive.

Breathing a sigh of relief, I turned my attention to my treasures, my tribe. I didn't mind their reaching hands and greetings; providing them with some comfort and continuity of purpose was the least I could do. A young man with a ragged red wound across his face stepped into my path; his eyes were empty and feverish, and I suspected that his evil-looking cut needed attention. I recognized his face but did not recall speaking to him before this day. "Hafanu, mekhma. Are we going home now?" he asked in a weary voice.

"What is your name? I know you."

"Biel, the son of Jeru."

"Yes, Biel. We are going home to Zerzura." I clasped his hands in mine and looked directly into his eyes. "Very soon. You rest now, Biel, and get your strength back. Find a healer to tend to that wound. We will need your help, and you must be whole and well."

He didn't argue but asked, "What of Alexio? Will he not return with us? I could track him, mekhma. He taught me how. I am sure I could find him."

I gulped at hearing my husband's name, for in my heart he was that still. In an angry moment I had cast him out, sending him on a fool's errand. How would Alexio retrieve my sister from the

Kiffians by himself? I had behaved like a jealous shrew and had likely sent him to his death. I wished that I myself could climb upon a horse and pound the hooves to seek him out, but my place was here. My desire for him was strong, and my heart was breaking, but there was nothing I could do. Sending this boy into the desert would achieve little except kill another innocent. Despite his lion's heart, Biel hap Jeru was in no shape to travel the four corners of the desert. I could not have his death on my conscience. However, perhaps I could ask Ramose to send a squadron of men to find him. That would certainly not be inappropriate, as he was sent to serve me. I did not look forward to asking Ramose for anything beyond his required duties, but for Alexio I would face the giants myself.

"Alexio has gone to find my sister. He will return to us soon, I am sure of it. Rest, Biel, and regain your strength." He did not look happy with my answer. "I have not forgotten Alexio. We will bring him back."

His empty eyes brightened for a moment, and he squeezed my hands and stepped out of my way. Others flooded in, needing my assurances, handshakes and hugs. Ayn remained by my side but did not dissuade them. Finally, I gave her a look that said, "Help me." Without a word, she stepped between my people and me and grasped me by my elbow.

"Come now, mekhma. Semkah awaits." With each touch of their hands, I felt a weightiness and solemnity that I had never experienced before. By the time I had pushed my way into my father's abode, I was emotionally drained and desperate to see his face.

"Greetings, mekhma. Your father is resting now," a tiny young woman said as she stirred a mixture in a bowl.

"Who are you?"

"Leela. Orba asked me to look after the king. As I said, he is resting now. Although I don't see how with all this noise. I have given him a sleeping potion and must apply this poultice to his stump."

I didn't know what to think of Leela, but before I could argue with my father's caregiver, I heard the voice I had so longed for.

"Nefret. Thank the gods. Come. Please, Leela, step out of the way." He was trying to sit up without the use of his right arm. It was a disheartening sight, but I did not try to help him. He would not welcome my assistance or sympathy. When he pulled himself up, his appearance shocked me. He had looked weak and near death's door before I left, but now his skin had taken on an ugly yellow tone, his eyes were red and his frame was gaunt. I masked my surprise and answered him with as much confidence as I could muster.

"Yes, Father. I am back, and Egypt is with us."

"Leave us," he said to the other women.

Without argument they left, although Leela did not hide her disapproval. "I need to apply this poultice while the medicine still has its effectiveness."

"Out," he growled. Once we were alone he reached his hand out to me, and I squeezed it. "I think she is going to poison me with her concoctions," he said sourly.

"I think she is trying to *help* you, and for that I am thankful. Are you feeling well?" I didn't know how to ask what I wanted to know. *Are you going to leave me too?* I could not bear it if after all this I lost him too. Without him, I would have no family left. My treasure, Paimu, was dead. Pah had been stolen from us, and now…

"No tears for me, Nefret. We have no time for that. Tell me everything that has happened. Do not leave anything out. Not even the smallest details."

"I hardly know where to begin. Queen Tiye rules in Egypt. I never laid eyes on Pharaoh or entered the main palace. There is nothing done that she does not know about."

"There have been rumors of this for a long time." With a worried look he added, "Were you presented to any other members of the court? What about the son—the heir?"

"No, Father. I met no one else. Only the queen's steward, Huya. I attended no formal affairs and did not leave the queen's chamber except for bathing and dining. They do much of both, but I was kept mostly to myself unless the queen chose to visit me."

"Tell me about her, daughter."

"I really know nothing at all. She is a small woman but has a great presence. She reminds me of Farrah in that regard. She trusts no one and does not much talk to others except for her steward."

"What did she ask you about? Did she ask about your sister?"

"No, Father. She asked about our people, our festivals, our trade. She was curious to know our stories and songs. I told her many during my stay."

"Curious. Whatever her reasons, it seems you are now the queen's new favorite. You tell your stories too well, Nefret." I didn't know what to say to that, so I said nothing. All I had wanted to do was survive and receive the help we needed. He squeezed my hand and said kindly, "I do not blame you. I will miss you when you leave me, Nefret."

I breathed a sigh of relief. He knew. He must have known all along that I would have to leave him. I would never have imagined that my journey to Egypt would end in such a way. I bent down, kissed his forehead and wiped the tears from his eyes. "Who knows, Father? Perhaps the queen will allow you to come visit me. Maybe she will change her mind. Who knows what the future holds?"

He reached up with his good arm and pulled me close to him. My hair fell around us like a curtain, and we shed tears together. Finally he pulled my forehead to his and whispered, "You will always be mekhma, and you will always be my daughter."

"Semkah!" my uncle called from outside the tent.

"Help me up."

I did as he asked and pulled him to his feet. He wobbled, probably from the effects of the potion Leela had administered. "You must sit, or you will fall down," I said. "Here, sit on the edge of the table."

Father eased himself down on the table, and I quickly threw a cloak over his right shoulder to conceal his wounded arm. He pulled it around him and said, "Come."

"Greetings, brother. It is good to see you well." Dressed in his battle gear, Omel looked quite the king. He wore a leather breastplate with the tribe's sigil carved into the chest. At his arms were Corinthian leather greaves, but the rest of his garments were in the Egyptian style.

"I am hardly well. Nefret was just sharing her report with me. Please continue. You were telling me their terms."

"Yes, I am curious to know that as well. What did we exchange for their help? The gold mines of Abu Simbel? Queen Tiye would be a fool to take less."

Hesitantly, I shook my head.

"The turquoise mines, then? What is it? As you've said many times, brother, Egyptians do not offer their help for nothing."

"The Great Wife, for that is what she is called in Thebes, graciously sent a legion of soldiers, food for our journey and supplies in exchange for my promise."

My father and uncle waited to hear the words. "Promise of what?" Omel asked warily.

"After the conquest of Zerzura, I am to return to Thebes."

"What made you agree to this? Do you know what this means, Nefret? For what purpose? Are you a prisoner? This is an outrage! Call the kings together now, Semkah."

"The deal is done, Uncle. It cannot be undone. General Ramose is here now with orders directly from the queen's own steward. Do you think this is what I want? No, of course not, but as the Egyptians say, it is now written in stone."

"What is Queen Tiye thinking?"

"I do not know the queen's mind, for she keeps her own counsel, but this was the only deal she would make. She would take nothing else. I am to return to Thebes after the conquest, and she says that I can never return home again."

"This can only mean one thing. She intends to give you to her son," Omel said with a sardonic grin.

"What?" I couldn't help but blurt out. "Give like a concubine?"

"Maybe. If you please him, perhaps as a wife. But those kinds of arrangements are usually made more diplomatically with royal daughters who have large dowries. I see no advantage to her in raising you to that exalted position. However, it is possible, for it is Pharaoh who has the last word in those things."

"Uncle? Did you know about this?"

"How could I? This was your idea, mekhma."

Memories of consummating my union with Alexio under the full moon filled my mind. How could I be given to another when I belonged to him? And I had sent him away! What would I do?

My uncle continued, "I would say the Snakes of Destiny have been at work here. I had no hand in this. Would you be surprised to know that Queen Tiye herself was a commoner and had no royal lineage when she came to the throne? Amenhotep did not listen to the priests who had another in mind. He would have no one but the dark queen. They sometimes call her that because of her skin and maybe because of her dark moods. She is a dangerous woman if you cross her. I know for a certainty that Queen Tiye has put whole families to the sword, all in the interest of protecting her lineage. Perhaps she has a softness for desert folk. I would never speak this to another soul, but the Great Wife is rumored to be from the Algat tribe."

"Is this true?" My father sounded amazed by this revelation.

"Yes, but do not repeat that to a living soul—especially an Egyptian, and especially her general. By the way, Ramose has requested to be presented to you, Semkah. Shall I send for him?"

Ignoring his question for the time being, Semkah looked at me and asked, "What of this man? You have spent time in his presence. Is he trustworthy? Has he revealed the route to Zerzura to you?"

"I never learned to read maps, Father, nor was I shown one. But from what I understand, the city lies to the north, very near the sea. It is between Barrani and Matru."

"Do you trust him?"

"He is loyal to the queen. He will do as she has ordered him."

"Very well. It is late, and I am sure the general is tired from his journey. Brother, please send my thanks to the general and tell him the mekhma and the kings of the Meshwesh will meet with him in the morning. We have much to talk about."

Omel made the sign of respect and walked out of the tent. I could not help but notice the smirk on his face.

What will happen to the Meshwesh when I am gone?

Almost as if he could hear my thoughts, Father said, "That is enough worry for one day. Go rest, but come early in the morning. We will break our fast together, and I will summon Orba as well to see what can be done about all this." With a wince he said, "Tell Leela to return to me."

"You don't want me to stay? I can take care of you, Father."

He frowned disapprovingly. "You are the mekhma. I have everything I need."

I didn't argue and remind him that I was also his daughter. This was a matter of pride. I made the sign of respect before leaving.

"When you return in the morning, bring Ayn. Keep her close. She will protect you."

"I will, Father. Good rest." I slipped out into the darkness. Ayn sprang to her feet and walked beside me. I suddenly felt tired, more tired than I had felt in a long time. Even though the tent would not have all the comforts I had grown accustomed to, I would at least be among my people.

"Just this way."

Most of the excited welcomers had gone to their own tents and caves to prepare for rest, but many would sleep with one eye open. They would probably not see the Egyptians as allies, so I would have to be the example to keep the peace. I had no doubt that even now my uncle was thinking about how to use this situation to his advantage.

"Are you hungry, mekhma?"

"Not really, but I am thirsty."

"You rest now. I'll go find something for you to drink."

"Please, no wine. I had enough in Thebes. Water will do nicely." Ayn left me to take care of her task while I undressed. Someone had been kind enough to unpack my bag, and I found my robe and the few other items I managed to salvage from Timia stashed in the tent. I had little else in the way of clothing, but thankfully some thoughtful person had left me a nice soft tunic for sleeping. I tossed off my cloak and slipped out of my sandals and tunic. I noticed the small shrine that had been erected to my sister. Pah's cedar box had been emptied and each item placed around the stub of a yellow candle. I felt a lump rise in my throat. *Sister!* My mouth felt dry, and my feet and hands felt dirty, but I was so tired that I lay down and fell fast asleep.

The next thing I remembered was seeing a spiral appear before me. It reminded me of the whirlpool at Biyat, the one that Pah and I used to toss dried leaves into and then watch them sink away from sight. I watched the spiral with fascination as a bright blue light began to emanate from the center. Although the color resembled hot flame, I felt neither heat nor any other sensation from the spiral. I reached toward it, tempted to poke my finger at the very edge just to see for myself what this thing was before me. I became aware of whispers in the air around me. The closer my hand came to the spiral, the louder the whispering became. It was as if there were a crowd of people excitedly watching my every move. Without moving my head, I glanced to the left and to the right, but I saw no one and nothing.

I surveyed my surroundings. I was in a room—a spacious room with no walls, no doors and no floor or ceiling. It was very dark except for the spiral that spun in front of me. The air crackled, and I felt the hair on my arms rise just as if a thundering storm approached on the horizon. I put my hand toward the moving circle again, and this time I touched it. Nothing happened. I pulled back my hand and examined my finger. I had not been burned or scarred at all. I touched it again, tracing the edge of the spiral, and with some delight watched the light bend underneath it. The more I touched the spiral, the faster it spun. Soon I used my palm to spin the spiral until it was moving so fast that it was only a bright blue blur.

I became aware that someone was standing beside me. I did not feel threatened or afraid, so I spoke to the man. "What is this?"

"Look closer."

I did as the man instructed me. Leaning my head forward a little, I peered hard at the spiral, but the speed at which it turned made it difficult to see anything. As if he heard my thoughts, the man reached out and slowed the spiral to its original speed. In the center I could see figures—people I knew! There was Farrah and Paimu. Then I could see many of the Meshwesh who died in the Kiffian raid on our camp. I gasped at the sight. It was as if I were watching the memories of my past in very great detail, not at all like a dream. The man touched the spiral again, and the picture changed. I no longer saw people I knew but people I would know. I saw children, children with my eyes and dark hair. I saw a man's hands. He placed them on the heads of my children and spoke a blessing over them. I could see a boy's face. He had the look of my father but with eyes like mine.

Smenkhkare! I whispered. How I knew his name I did not know, but my heart reached for him. It claimed him as my own.

The man touched the spiral again, and the movement turned the spiral in the other direction. I saw my face now. I was standing at the top of a stony mountain. I appeared as an old woman with deep lines on my face and white hair. Below me in a valley I could see and hear sheep, many, many sheep. I saw my people, but they weren't my people. In some ways they appeared as Meshwesh, but they were taller and stronger looking. I heard someone shout my name, but it wasn't my name.

I turned to ask the man what this all meant, and for the first time I could clearly see—this was the Shining Man! His face was shrouded in light, but I felt that he was smiling at me.

"What does it mean? Who were those people?" I felt a wave of love, but he did not answer me right away. "Who was the boy?" *Smenkhkare!*

"You will meet him one day, if you choose to follow that path."

My heart pulled toward the boy in a way that I had never experienced before except with my treasure, my Paimu. I loved him purely and completely, yet I did not know him. But I did know I was willing to die for him.

"I must see him. This I know."

He smiled again, and this time the light moved so I could see his features. He had a long, straight nose and dazzling eyes made of every color imaginable. A light shone from his skin, yet he was not frightening.

"Then the path is chosen. Walk in it." He placed his hand on my head just as I had seen the man bless his children in the spiral, and I was filled with warmth.

I fell into a deep, restful sleep.

Chapter Five

An Immortal Name—Ramose

Another day in this stinking camp and I would go mad. These tribe-folk and their incessant drum-banging and off-key singing gave me daily headaches, and my impatience with my current situation was growing. The preparations took days longer than I had originally expected. The Desert Queen insisted that the entire clan make the journey with us as we progressed to the north. Obviously the girl had no idea how to lead an army or a campaign. But contrary to what she might think, her opinion had been of little importance to me. I had my orders.

In the end, I ignored her command and messaged Nebamun of the Third Legion. He would advance on Zerzura, remove the inhabitants and send an immediate report on his progress. Much of the battle would be over by the time we arrived at Zerzura, but I gave him explicit instructions to leave some of the Kiffians alive for appearances' sake. These Meshwesh "kings," as they fancied themselves, would not be denied their glory no matter how false that victory was. And who was I to say otherwise? Only the general of the Egyptian army. I snorted as I rubbed the leather of my greaves with cedar oil.

The Desert Queen would not be pleased, but I did not serve her. Besides, I was anxious to return to Egypt. What was once court gossip had proven to be true, according to my wife, Inhapi, who was Queen Tadukhipa's closest confidante. Amenhotep, Father of Egypt, lay dying. As his general I needed to be by his side, not babysitting a minor queen who struck the fancy of old Queen Tiye. I wondered what the Great Wife had in mind for the girl, but I was not one to worry much about such things. Inhapi did that for me. Once I finished oiling my leather, I polished my blade until it gleamed in the firelight. When I left this stinky hole, I would leave as a son of Egypt, not covered in sand and goat dung. I would make my Pharaoh proud. Like all intelligent men, I feared him, but I loved him too. He had been good to me over the years, granting me whatever I wanted. He had proved a crafty and intuitive leader, but battles had been few during his peaceful reign, and I longed for a decent battle. Perhaps that was why this delay seemed so unfair. I hadn't wet the edge of my blade with the blood of my enemies in some time, except for the necessary executions specifically assigned to me. But what sport was there in lopping off the heads of whining courtiers?

I tried to share these thoughts with Inhapi, but she did not care to hear them. "Why must you question everything? Amenhotep does you great honor by asking you to do these things."

"Yes but I am the general of the Egyptian army—not the chief executioner."

Inhapi's dark eyes flashed at me, and the beads of her expensive wig clicked as she snapped her head around to glare at me. "Then what do you want, Ramose?"

"An immortal name—as any man does," I had answered her, but she waved her hand at me as if I were the stupid slave who had arranged her many silk gowns in the wrong order. My wife would never understand my mind, but I did know hers. She had a lovely face, came to the marriage bed with great wealth and was more ambitious than anyone other than Queen Tadukhipa. I agreed with Nebamun. Men were stronger and more intelligent than women, but in matters of wisdom and ambition, the fairer sex far exceeded their male partners. I was often amused and equally annoyed by the conversations Inhapi had with Tadukhipa. I warned them to keep their schemes to themselves, but they merely laughed.

An intense argument nearby pulled me from my daydreams. I smiled at the sound of the Meshwesh father confronting our soldiers for some conceived wrong. If this continued, I would have to make my suggestion concerning the tribal women an official order. The truth was my men were bored. And when soldiers are bored, they tend to get into mischief. That mischief usually involves drinking excessively or indulging in another sport, women. Because there was not much beer or wine available, the Seventh Legion concentrated on the latter. I warned them to keep their hands to themselves—these desert mongrels would hate to have Egyptian sons-in-law—but these were not boys, and I was not their father. These men had been promised a battle with the Kiffians, a long-hated enemy of the two kingdoms.

"Greetings, General Ramose."

"Horemheb." I eyed the Meshwesh king suspiciously. Here was another one I could do without. "Do you bring an order from your Desert Queen?"

I pretended not to notice his grimace. I could read him well enough to know what he thought about the girl who ruled over him. He was a proud man and had schemed greatly to get the advantage over his brother—all to have the kingdom stolen from him by his own niece. And not the niece he intended either. I found great humor in that and did not bother to hide my amusement.

"I am not a messenger, Ramose. I do not deliver orders."

I grinned and slid my sword into its sheath and set it beside me. "My apologies, then. Why have you come, Horemheb?" The tall man dawdled about as if I could discern his thoughts by merely watching him shift his feet. "Out with it."

Without being invited, the tribal king sat near me close to the fire. I did not care for his proximity but made no mention of it yet. I've always found that you should never refuse information when it is presented to you, and Horemheb looked like someone who might be willing to part with some.

"The kings will meet with you in the morning, in my brother's cave."

"You could have sent a servant to tell me that. Yet you come. What else have you to say?"

I have always dealt fairly with Egypt. You know I have come many times to Pharaoh's court on behalf of my people; I have long desired stronger ties with the Black Lands."

"Yes, you have frequented Pharaoh's court." He appeared to need encouragement to continue, and I hoped my agreeing with him would serve that purpose.

"You know I am a wealthy man, General. The gold mines of Abu Simbel belong to me only. My brother has no claim to them. Of all the men here, I am the wealthiest."

I tossed my last piece of firewood on the waning flames and waited. I could have corrected him by sharing stories of the wealth I had acquired during my service to my Pharaoh, but why bother? His self-importance amused me.

He licked his thin lips and prattled on. "I am not a greedy man. I reward my friends. Help me claim my right, and I will gladly reward you, Ramose. For a man of your skills, what I am asking is a small thing. My people need a strong leader—someone who values Egypt. Not an impetuous young woman who will doubtless embarrass them and worse, lead them into danger. She is too inexperienced, a spoiled princess with a weak father who does not respect Egypt. As king, I would always put Egypt first."

Was he asking me to kill the girl? A smirk spread across my face. "You have asked me nothing as yet, Horemheb, but let me remind you that I am here at the Great Wife's command. I obey her above all others, except for Amenhotep. So unless you have a request from him regarding your 'small thing,' then perhaps you should stop speaking. And if I may be so bold..."

He drew his wiry frame up and glared at me but wisely kept his mouth shut.

"You do not know me so well that you could ask me to do murder for you, if that indeed is what you ask of me. If I were not man enough to kill when I needed to, I would not lower myself to ask another to do the work for me. For that would make me less than a man."

He rose to his feet like a viper had struck his calf. My hand flew to my sword, and a nearby lieutenant set his hand on his khopesh and waited for the man to make the wrong move.

Horemheb stalked off through the sand, and I breathed a sigh of relief. It would do no good to kill one of the tribal kings before I took their mekhma away. The lieutenant laughed mockingly in Horemheb's direction and went about his business. I picked up my sword and strode to my tent. I had had enough of these people for one night. I thought about calling the captains to my tent to review our plan of approach, but we had been over it three nights in a row. It was time to move this bleating, banging tribe to their permanent encampment in Zerzura. And good riddance! From what I heard, it was not the holy land they expected it to be. Then again, what city could compare to Thebes? I had expected to hear something from Nebamun today, but as of yet no messenger had arrived. Perhaps the best thing would be to rest and steer clear of any of these Red Lands dignitaries.

"General," a female voice called from outside the tent. Who could that be? There were no camp women here. Perhaps the Desert Queen had come to her senses after all. I slid back the flap and found myself face to face with the Desert Queen's guard, Ayn. She was as tall as me, but I noticed she had not come dressed in her warrior garb tonight. Rather, she wore a long, soft-looking tunic, and her wavy hair was brushed to a shine. I caught a whiff of her scented skin as I held the flap back to invite her in. I looked about as she ducked inside to make sure none of my men saw my visitor.

"Ayn, isn't it? What can I do for you?"

She didn't answer me right away but instead strolled to my table of weapons. I added the sword I carried to the collection and watched her survey my inventory. "Do you need a lesson in weaponry?"

"Do you think I need a lesson in weaponry?"

I stared at her. I was too tired to play games. "Speak plainly, then. What can I do for you? Are you here in service to your mekhma?"

"No." Her voice sounded rough and serious. "I am here for myself." She stepped toward me, and I studied her. She was not a beautiful woman, but she was attractive. I was a man who admired strength in others, and it was rare to find it in women. Her arms were well made, the muscles sculpted from her warrior's work. Her breasts were small, and she had a slim figure without any woman's curves. I could tell she had never borne children, for her hips were straight and slim. Even in her soft brown tunic I could see that her skin was clear and perfect. She stood quietly and let me appraise her. I noticed with some amusement that she was studying me too. That thrilled me, and I felt my manhood rise.

I stepped closer to her, putting my finger under her chin to stare into her eyes. They were brown and warm like the eyes of a doe. Yet there was no fear in them. Her most attractive feature was her lips, bare, pink and full. I imagined them suckling on various parts of my body but doubted that she had the skill or knowledge to please me in such a way. Perhaps she would allow me to teach her.

"Are you a gift from your queen?"

"I am no man's property. What about you, General? Are you someone's property?"

I gripped her forearms and pulled her close. I saw no fear, only curiosity and desire. My answer was a rough kiss. If she fled from me, I would know she was not worthy of me. But she did not.

Ayn kissed me back, and her frenzied hands ran over my chest. I stripped off my garments and stood before her in my naked glory. With a serious face, she unbound her hair and untied her tunic, letting it hit the floor. Looking at her pleased me, and as we came together I cupped her breasts in my hands. We feverishly kissed again and to my surprise she pushed me down onto my bed. Her dark brown hair fell across my face as she scooted onto my lap. She said nothing, and neither did I. No promises were made, no lies were told. Ayn had come for one reason, and I was obliged to give her what she wanted. I massaged her breasts as she moved in perfect rhythm until I could take no more. I arched up and flipped us, and she struggled with me, perhaps disappointed that she was no longer in control. But after a few minutes she began to shudder beneath me. I rode the crest of the euphoric wave and plunged into her one last time, then fell on her hair and breathed in her scent. She smelled of cedar, some unknown flower and sweat. It was a pleasant combination and a far different one than that of the women of the Egyptian court.

I collapsed beside her. She did not linger long. The dusky-skinned girl collected her tunic and tied her hair. The oil lamp sputtered, and the light flickered.

"Did you get what you came for?" I asked her playfully.

I could feel her observing me in the darkness, but she did not answer me. Ayn ducked out of the tent and left me with my thoughts. So sleepy was I that I did not think of anything much. I drifted off and slept through the night.

Chapter Six

The Gift—Nefret

We rode hard for the walls of Zerzura. After seeing the palatial estates in Thebes and the brightly colored walls of the Egyptian temples that lined the city's roads, Zerzura appeared diminutive in comparison. But to most of my people, it was the reward of a generation of prophecies, and they would not be denied. Smoke billowed from behind the stone walls, and the grand wooden doors were firmly closed against us. Behind Zerzura was a steep line of hills and beyond that the blue waters of Mare Nostrum.

Ramose ignored my request to wait for the Shasu, the most elite warriors of the Meshwesh, and sent another legion of his soldiers to Zerzura to take the city by themselves. In no way did I want Egypt to claim the victory. Everyone knew that what Egypt took, it would not give back. We had not come all this way to be living out of Egypt's hands.

The only reason I did not send Ramose back to Egypt was that he agreed to send scouts to find Alexio. I had told him, "I sent one of my most trusted advisers to track my sister, but that was some time ago. I need someone who knows these lands to bring him back, with or without her."

"Who is this man to you?" he had asked me suspiciously, looking from my face to Ayn's as he munched on one of the last remaining apples.

"Is that important?"

"I think it is, mekhma. My mission, and that of my men, is to provide you with assistance. To take your people back to your homeland. And of course, to keep you protected until we return you to Queen Tiye's protection. I heard nothing about traveling the desert searching for anyone—even a trusted adviser. How is that pertinent to my orders?"

Ramose had peered at me as he squinted into the sun that morning. It rose behind me, and I felt its warmth upon my bare neck. He was wasting my time—I knew he did not want to help me, although Ayn seemed to think differently. I suspected that my guard was smitten with the arrogant general. Regardless of this potential conflict of interest, I knew I could trust her. But I would never trust him.

"It will be difficult to leave my people without Alexio here. He is a voice of reason and knows his father better than anyone. The people need him!"

Ramose had handed the apple core to his white horse and scoffed, "The people need him? I am not so certain. There seem to be a great many kings around this place. Surely the Meshwesh can live without one more leader." He closed the distance between us, but I did not flinch. "Be warned, Desert Queen, I will not allow you to break your promise to the Queen."

My brows knit together, and I dropped my voice menacingly. Ramose wasn't the only one committed to this mission, as he called it. "I have no intention of breaking my promise. Despite what you think, I am a woman of my word."

With a disrespectful glance he murmured, "Hardly a woman at all," as he turned to walk away. I wished I had a knife in my hand.

Ayn shouted, "Do not turn your back on the mekhma! Her request is not unreasonable, General! Unless it was your intention all along to leave the Meshwesh at the mercy of Omel." She leaned on her spear, and her voice was stern—even angry at Ramose's disrespect.

"Omel?" He spun on one foot. "You mean Horemheb?" We had his interest now. "What does he have to do with this?"

I replied, "Alexio is his son and my closest ally, except for Ayn and perhaps one other. His presence here is crucial if we want to keep the people safe."

"Safe from what? Egypt? You will owe her your life before this is over."

I didn't back down. I needed his help, and I felt his resolve weakening. "And how will the Queen view this decision, General? After all the expense? All the time invested? I do not know her well, but I believe the Queen to be a shrewd woman who is accustomed to getting a return on her investment. What will she think when you have to return to this region—to Zerzura—because Omel, or Horemheb, as you call him, has sold the gold mines to the

Greeks? Or better still, the Mycenaeans, who are always hungry for the metal?"

With an angry shout of frustration, Ramose had walked away, but Ayn reported to me that evening that he had indeed sent out a small scouting party to bring Alexio back.

On top of my request, Ramose had not taken kindly to the idea of waiting for the caravan to snake its way through Saqqara and the Red Lands—he had made that plain enough. In the end, the Shasu and the Egyptians led the second attack but did not get very far. The initial attack had done little except alert the Kiffians that we intended to retake the city. The Third Legion had arranged themselves in front of the four towers of the White City, but there was nothing we could do except wait on a better plan.

"This was a mistake!" Amir, the leader of the Shasu, complained to Omel, who stood beside me. "What now?" The canopy was full of tribal kings, including my father, my new ally Siti, Orba, Ramose and two of his men whose Egyptian names escaped me. Ayn and I were the only women present. All eyes were on me.

"Amir, I know you are anxious to avenge our fallen brothers and sisters, and for that I thank you. But now we must work together. We are too close to victory."

General Ramose said, "The fastest way to deal with these savages is to burn them out. A few well-placed fires and they will scream for mercy."

"And destroy our city?" Orba asked him as if Ramose were a child asking to play with a basket of asps. "What happens when you leave and our defenses are down? We will be at the mercy of any who decide to come against us."

"We have used this method before, at the Wall of the Crows and at Kadesh, and those walls were much taller than these. My men can position the flames in a manner that will minimize the damage. Once the city is yours, you will have all the time you need to make repairs. We mean to obliterate these Kiffians quickly."

Some of the Meshwesh agreed with Ramose, while others were not so sure. King Siti said, "We can wait them out. Starvation has a way of humbling a man."

Before we could discuss it further, we heard screams echoing through the tribe. Surely these Kiffians were not so foolish as to attack us with two legions of Egyptian soldiers present. In a rush, I left the tent to see what was happening. Faithful Ayn stood beside me, drew her sword and handed me her spear. Looking around I could see the people pointing in the direction of the city.

"Meshwesh dogs! Look what we have!"

I pushed toward the front of the gathering that faced the gates. A nasty monster of a man with long red hair stood on the parapet between the two center towers. He yelled at us in a language we did not understand. After his tirade had ended, he stood with his hands on his hips, two shield men on either side of him. The doors directly below him opened slowly, and a man rode out on a horse, dragging a half-naked woman with a chain about her neck. My heart melted in my chest. Pah!

"Sister!" I whispered. The Meshwesh gasped, and some even cried at seeing her. Ramose and my father came to my side. I stared in horror as the horseman dragged Pah around, ignoring her screams for help.

"Here is your queen, Meshwesh. See how we have defiled her? Advance any further and we will do more than that. Retreat now, or see her die!" Pah managed to stand, her red hair a matted swirl about her head. One breast was exposed, and she had blood all over her.

Ignoring Ramose's warning, I stepped out of the crowd and onto the sand alone. I waved the rest back. "Hold, men," I heard Ramose warn his archers who undoubtedly had the horseman in their sights. During this show, the parapet had filled with other warriors, including archers with flaming arrows. They wasted no time in shooting their fiery weapons at the ground before us, but I did not move.

I should have been afraid, but I felt no fear. Only anger. Deep, abiding anger. Pah shrieked as the savage jerked the cruel chain again. She began mumbling—no, praying—wildly, pleading with every deity she knew to deliver her. Pah's pleas were met with mocking laughter. "Silence now!" He reeled in her chain to pull her closer to him. She did not resist him and obediently quieted. The monster then turned his attention to me.

"Ah, another queen. Perhaps we should make a trade," he said leeringly. "This one is a bit used."

"What are your demands?" I yelled at him, ignoring my sister's pleading expression. I could not run to her now. We would both die. I had to stall for time, if only for Pah.

"Here is my demand—leave this valley, or we shall kill your queen," he said as he drew his dingy sword, "unless you have one to spare. And take these sons of Egyptian whores with you!"

"No! Do not kill her," I answered him. "We will do as you ask. What else do you want?"

I heard Ramose hiss behind me, but I ignored him. He wasn't in charge here. If I could keep the king talking, perhaps he would not kill my sister. I could tell he was not afraid of the Meshwesh or the Egyptians.

The stupid barbarian didn't seem to know what he wanted, so I prompted him. "Gold? Beer? What do you want? We will give it to you, only do not harm our mekhma."

"Yes, yes. Give us the gold and the beer, and then do not show yourself here again. Or we shall treat you even less hospitably than we did your sister."

"Who are you?" I demanded to know. "What is your name?"

"What does it matter?"

"I want to know who to ask for when I bring you your prizes."

"I am Gilme of the Kiffians. You can ask for me when you come. No tricks, or she dies and we hang her from the tower there." He pointed toward the city gates, but I did not bother to look.

"Very well, Gilme. I am Nefret. We will deliver your prizes to you by tomorrow morning. If you kill my sister or harm her further, we will never stop hunting you."

"Do you think that makes me afraid?" The men on the parapet jeered at me in their rude, rough language. As Gilme turned to grin at them I stole a look at my sister. Her eyes were wide with fear, and she shook her head slightly as if to say, "Please don't leave me." I said nothing and did not move a muscle. I could not appear weak in front of the brutes or my tribe, although there was nothing I wanted more than to cut her captor down. There were too many arrows pointed at us.

Gilme tugged on Pah's leash and dragged her back through the gate. She did not make a sound as she stumbled behind him. She never once turned to glance back.

A hush fell over the camp as they watched me return to them.

Ramose met me first, but he kept his mouth shut. I knew he did not approve of my negotiations, but he also had no idea what I had planned. I had never killed a man before and had no desire to do so until today. But if my ancestors gave me strength, I knew that I would kill Gilme. Slowly and with great pleasure.

The kings followed me and then gathered close, talking wildly about what punishment they wanted to administer to the Kiffian king. The sight of their mekhma in chains had lit a fire in them that no man would be able to extinguish, at least not without the shedding of blood.

"Listen! Start gathering your things. We will move the camp behind those hills there. I know it is farther from the water, but they will have to make do. Tell your people to draw what water they can now and then move quickly. Shasu!"

Amir appeared in front of me. "You must find a way into the city. Go west, behind Zerzura. Orba, you shall go with them. Help them find the Lightning Gate entrance."

Orba's eyes narrowed, and with a toothy grin he said, "I will not let you down, mekhma."

Ramose stepped forward. "Tell me what you have planned, as I am responsible for your safety. If you think I am going to allow you to walk through those gates and surrender yourself to the Kiffians, then you must be addle-brained. You cannot negotiate with these southerners. They know no language except cruelty, and they certainly will not negotiate with a woman—even if she is a queen." The kings murmured against Ramose for the perceived slight. Even my less enthusiastic allies like Walida and Omel made no secret that they did not approve of the Egyptian's tone toward me.

The Shining Man must have been leading me in this because I then knew exactly what I had to do. I asked him in a calm, firm voice, "Have you ever heard the saying, 'The only Greek you can trust is a dead Greek'?"

"Yes, but I am surprised that you have." I ignored his scorn and met his level gaze. "Why do you ask?"

"I am a Greek. I am going to give Gilme a gift he will never forget."

Chapter Seven

Father of Queens—Semkah

As I woke I stifled a scream. Pain sliced through my arm like a hot dagger. I looked down and saw that I had no right arm. How could I experience such pain when the limb was gone, severed by a screaming beast of a man? I remembered the Kiffian who stole it from me and once again vowed that I would find him and repay him. Seeing the other bare arm with the snake twisting about the wrist, I thought wryly, "My destiny has been decided now. No need to struggle anymore."

I wiped the sweat from my face, and almost immediately the woman was by my side. Small and dark, she looked like a shadow in the dimness of my shelter. She barely spoke. I knew her name, but I had forgotten it—my mind felt thick, as if a blanket were wrapped around my memory. I struggled to piece together the most recent events. The tiny woman was constantly stirring pots, crushing roots, whispering over cups before she forced me to drink whatever brew she concocted.

Some days I felt strong, almost as strong as before. Other days I could barely escape the dream world; it was no longer a happy place to dwell. I could not remember the last time I had seen my wife in my dreams, when previously I would see her often even if only from a distance. I still dreamed of the cliffs where I first saw her, but she no longer waited for me there.

"Please, King Semkah. You must sit up and drink. This will clear your mind and ease the pain."

I pushed it away angrily, and the dark fluid sloshed on her hands. "Go away. Where is Farrah?" Then I remembered she was dead too and said, "Send me Orba."

"Orba is too busy to come wait on you. Remember? Your daughter Pah has been found, my King, and the mekhma has ordered us to move. You have to drink this so you can move without too much discomfort."

"I don't want your poisons," I whispered hoarsely. I struggled to sit up, and my tormentor did not help me.

She was not dissuaded. "You must drink this and we must leave. This is what the mekhma has ordered."

"Go away, woman." I leaned on my good arm and pushed myself up.

"You have forgotten my name again, haven't you?" She pursed her lips and without permission leaned toward me, lifted my eyelid and peered into it. "I see I have given you too much lophophora. I will not make that mistake again, but I cannot adjust this healing potion now. There is no time. Please drink. This morning's activities have stolen your strength."

In my sternest voice I said, "I have told you no. Now leave my tent. As far as I know I am still king. Go try your potions on someone else."

She snorted and stood. "Well, King, can you manage to stand up and get dressed? Whether you like it or not, we are short of healers in our camp. I am all you have. As I have said numerous times, we must go."

"I want to see my daughter."

"Then go see her." She stood with her hand on her hip, and her other hand still held the wooden cup. "I am not your prison guard. I am trying to help you, as Orba requested. I am sorry that I have not yet learned everything I need to know, but I shall."

I looked about me to see if there was something to lean on and spied the table not far away, but it wasn't close enough to be of help to me. The truth was I did need her help, or at least someone's help. Without a word, she set the cup down and stooped under my arm. She grabbed my hand and waited for me to stand.

"What is this lophophora you gave me?"

"It is a plant with white flowers. It is rare, but there is an abundance of it near here. The petals are worth more than gold. When you drink their essence, it numbs the mind to painful memories. I also rubbed an ointment made from the palm on your stump, and as you can see it has cleaned the incision beautifully although it stings for a while. The alora and alata herbs have a bitter taste, but they do help with the pain and heal the body."

"I want no more of this white flower. I want to keep my memories—all of them. Do you understand, Leela?"

"Yes," She did not move or offer to help me rise. When I finally got to my feet I thought I would fall, but she walked me the short distance to the table. I leaned against it, happy to depend on something besides her. I felt the blood rush to my head, but despite the discomfort it felt good to be upright again.

"Why am I so weak?" I growled at her. "This morning I was strong."

"Your strength will wane from time to time until the healing is complete. There is nothing I can do about that. Your arm was sliced with a poisonous blade. It did far more damage than you might imagine, and a weaker man would not have recovered. You are fortunate to be alive, my King. I suspect that if the gods did not desire it, you would not be here now. You will get stronger, I promise. You will not die."

"Don't talk to me about gods. I am not afraid to die." I puffed out my chest and grimaced at her. "Leela, that is your name," I remembered suddenly.

"Yes, that is my name."

"Tell my daughter I want to see her."

"I can't do that. She's with Ramose the Egyptian."

"Then tell my brother to attend me now."

She sighed in exasperation.

"What is it, Leela?"

"Drink this. It will give you strength and keep the pain away."

"And it will make me forget."

"Yes, it will."

"Dump it out. I will deal with the pain."

"Very well." She walked out of the tent and left me to tend to myself.

It was a challenge, but I didn't waste time. I stared a minute at my sword but left it behind. I could not use it, so why carry it? I chewed a piece of chula bread and gulped down some water for strength. This morning I had been strong, but now my hand shook and my head felt like a drunkard's, but I managed to get outside. Leela was right. The camp was about to move. Now I remembered Gilme, the Kiffian. And my daughter, chained and bruised by the hands of the savages. As I stepped outside, young women began packing my belongings, and I did not get in their way. "Where is Omel?" I asked one of them.

"There." She pointed to the east. I walked through the camp to find my brother. My daughter was alive. If I could help it, I would keep her that way.

"Omel! Where is Nefret?"

Omel turned in surprise at my voice. "Brother, you should not be here. You nearly fainted this morning. Take your rest."

"Don't talk to me of resting. Tell me about Pah. Who is this Gilme? Where is Nefret?"

Omel nodded to his men and said, "I will follow. Go now." He strapped on his sword and said to me, "Can you ride?"

The thought of having to pull myself up on a horse one-handed discouraged me from trying. "I am not sure."

He did not mock me but said, "Let us walk, then." We walked side by side up a slanted boulder that faced Zerzura. I could hardly believe we were here at the White City after all this time. It was heartbreaking to remember all the people who longed to see this place but never would. Farrah never ceased to believe that this day would come. But she would not be here to lead the triumphant procession into Zerzura; that is, if we did indeed breach the city's gates. Now my daughter was being held prisoner just beyond my reach. Knowing that she was so close but unreachable was torture, more torturous than knowing she would have to pay for her crimes—perhaps with her life. Still she was my daughter. I had to bring her back to us, no matter the consequences.

The city's gates were made of wood, but not any kind of wood I had ever seen. It had a reddish hue that seemed to glow with the fading sunlight. Even from this distance I could see that the planks were taller than any palm tree. The white stone walls flanked the doors neatly with no glimmer of light between them. Great iron rings hung from the front doors as if the giants themselves had bent them and placed them there.

"I don't see the Egyptians. Have they abandoned their task?" It could have been the remaining effects of the herbal brews Leela forced on me, but the back of my neck began to prickle. "Have they taken Nefret with them?"

"No. Why would they? What exactly has the mekhma promised Egypt, brother? Tell me the truth now. The gold or something else? Egypt would be a fool to take less than our mines after all this expense." He eyed me suspiciously as if I knew something he did not. That was Omel's way. He was untrustworthy and thought all other men so too.

"Aren't you always assuring us that Egypt's hands are bountiful? That Pharaoh wished for nothing more than to be a father to the Meshwesh? With my daughter at his court, he shall be. Why would you be so suspicious? And you know that my daughter would never give away our treasures, Omel. Why must you be so distrusting?"

"What about my son? If Pah is there," he said, pointing to the gates, "then where is he?" He spat the question out. "Nefret should never have sent him away."

"We have all lost loved ones, Omel. If Alexio is truly dead, then I am sorry for it. He was a credit to our people, both brave and strong. But you should not bury him just yet. He may still return to us, and my daughter has said he is her most trusted adviser."

"And yet the mekhma chose to send him into the desert. Who advises her now? Ayn? Orba?"

Feeling weak I sat on a nearby rock but did not hesitate to meet his steely gaze. What was he implying? I barely recognized him anymore. The kohl around his eyes had begun to sweat, and he looked more like a demon than my brother.

He continued, "Can't you see this is the time for men to lead? How can we trust a girl to lead us in these difficult times? We need a strong leader, someone with experience."

"And yet you were willing to support Pah. Why is that, brother? Why do you so fear Nefret? Because you cannot control her as you could Pah? I will not make that mistake again."

Omel faced me, and I could see his hand twitch over his khopesh. For the first time, I believed Omel wanted to take my life and leave me dying in the sand. I stood and met his evil gaze with my own unflinching stare. If I was going to die at the hands of my brother, I would die standing, not cowering at his feet.

His hand began to slide the blade from its sheath, but then a strange thing happened. Stars began to shoot across the sky. They were close, so close that I could hear the sound of their powerful wings as they fell to the ground. Omel froze in his tracks and moved no closer to me. The sky lit brilliantly for a moment as one star fell into the desert.

"Semkah! There you are, my King! What a glorious sign! Did you see that? The stars are falling from Osiris' belt! This will certainly frighten our enemies, as they consider the Dancing Man their sigil. The gods are with us!" It was Orba. The small man climbed the rock and stood beside us, panting. "I have been searching for you everywhere. Nefret... excuse me. The mekhma is looking for you."

Omel rushed past him and left us standing alone on the rock. Orba watched him exit, and I sat on the rock again, the world spinning wildly. "I see the bear has a spike in his paw," Orba said quietly.

"If you had not arrived, I think he would have killed me."

"I believe you." He watched as another star flickered above us and sailed toward the mountains that stood behind Zerzura. "You should know that he has approached Ramose."

"What did he say to him?"

"That he should rule because Nefret was too young and inexperienced. He offered him the gold mines of the Meshwesh, but the general did not accept his kind offer."

I grinned at Orba. "You mean bribe. How do you know this, Wise One?"

"I heard them talking. Omel pleaded his case, but the general was unimpressed and assured your brother that he served Egypt only."

"I like this general more and more."

"I agree. Especially since Nefret will be leaving Zerzura soon."

"So you know?"

He bobbed his covered head. "I have seen her wearing the crown of Egypt. And when she does leave, there will be nothing to stop Omel from killing you. Of course if you had not sustained your injury, then none of this would be a question. But as it stands, my King…"

"I am well aware of the restrictions regarding my rule. Maimed kings are not effective."

"I do not believe this, but it is the tradition. However, there may be something we can do."

I sighed. "I am not such a man to believe that only I can rule. I am not my father or my brother. I will be happy to step aside when the time comes. But I am troubled that the Queen of Egypt has taken such an interest in my daughter. If what you say is true, that you have seen Nefret as queen, then that at least is something. I would still like to know how this queen intends to make that happen."

"Who can fathom the heart of a woman? It is unknowable, unfathomable and never predictable." I was surprised by his answer. I had never known Orba to marry or to love anyone. With uncharacteristic intensity he added, "It is not Omel that worries me. I have seen something. Something disturbing and evil."

"What do you mean?"

He shook his head as another star exploded above us. "We will talk more of this later, my King. Time is moving swiftly now, and your daughter needs you. With your brother lurking around with sword in hand, I do not think it is safe for you to be out alone. Let us get through tonight and perhaps tomorrow. Then we can talk about the future."

Slowly I climbed down the steep rock and walked with Orba back into the camp. "What plans have been made to rescue Pah?"

"I had no idea Nefret had learned so much about strategy from her father. Her mind is brilliant, and she shows nothing but confidence. At dawn Nefret is to approach the gate of the city with a wagon full of our treasures. She hopes to make an exchange for her sister. I cannot lie to you—I fear the worst is yet to come for Pah if we do not capture the city and rescue her."

"We have no evidence that the Kiffians will be anything but ruthless with her, and now Nefret will be walking into a trap—they will kill her too!"

Orba smiled grimly and said, "Ah, but it's not that easy to kill her, I think. If it were, she would be dead already. Someone is guiding her, I'm sure of that. No, my King. Her plan is much more complicated. You see, the Shasu are at the Lightning Gate. I have just returned from there. These Kiffians are so arrogant that they did not even bother to secure it! When the signal is given, the Egyptians will appear to breach the main gate. At the same time, the Shasu will approach from the south."

I looked around the camp as we walked. I saw no Egyptians. "Where is Ramose? Where are the Egyptians?"

"Hidden in a place where Gilme would never think to look." Excitedly he began to share with me the details of the plan. I too was impressed with Nefret's ingenuity.

"And this was my daughter's idea?"

"Yes, it was."

"Then let us go see how I can serve her. I will not be left behind in this."

"No one doubts your courage, Semkah. But there is something the mekhma would ask of you."

"Whatever it is, you know I will help."

"This isn't an easy thing she is asking, but I encourage you to trust her."

Before I could question him further, another star, bright blue and burning, sailed across the sky. It was larger than the previous ones, and the size and nearness of it caused some alarm even in me. The people pointed and shouted at the sight. "What does this mean?"

Orba stared upwards and shouted, "It is a king's star! See how it falls?" The people murmured in wonder. "A king will fall soon. See where the star lands?" The crowd watched as the star plummeted behind Zerzura as the smaller one had earlier. "There is nothing to fear, Meshwesh, for the gods are on our side!"

The people clapped and hugged one another, and then went about their tasks. Everyone, from the youngest to the oldest, knew that our fate hung in the balance. But at least now the stars were aligned with us.

Maybe we would have a fighting chance.

Chapter Eight

The Unyielding Spiral—Nefret

It was good to see my father walking and talking. The fact that he was still in the land of the living was nothing less than a miracle. I wanted to run into his arms and wrap my own around his neck, but my people were watching my every move. We were facing the greatest challenge in our clan's history—I could do nothing that would hinder their courage. Most had no idea what I had planned, and the ones who did were not sure it would work. I heard rumors, thanks to Ayn and Orba, that my uncle and Astora were sowing seeds of discord as quickly as they could. Omel made no secret that he did not approve of my plan. The truth was, neither did I. But this was the only plan that presented itself to me, and I intended to execute it.

I helped load another bag onto the wagon. Traditionally we had no wagons in our camps, for we carried most things either on our camels or on our backs, but for this tactic we needed a wagon. The Egyptians had helped us assemble one quickly, and I hoped it would meet our needs. Or at least not fall apart before I made it to the gate. Ramose had left to put the finishing touches on the cart, and I could hardly wait to see it.

I faced my father and welcomed him with a smile. Now was the moment Orba and I had been waiting for.

"Father, won't you come and bless me?"

The people grew silent and waited to see what Semkah would do. Surprise crossed his face, but he did not deny me. Omel's eyes were riveted to us as my father began to bestow the tribe's blessing upon me. This was an ancient ritual, one that Pah had not enjoyed and one that I had not heard of until Orba described it to me. It was an old ritual that resonated with the elders of our tribe. They were the ones who needed to be convinced I could lead them.

Of course I wanted my father's blessing, especially on the eve of what might be my death, but this was for more than just me. Soon I would leave my Meshwesh people and return to Egypt. Someone would need to lead. Someone would need to guide. That had to be my father. At least until Pah recovered. I had seen her in the sand in front of Zerzura and knew that her mind had crumbled like a crushed flower. Who could blame her? What would I have done in that situation? I shivered at the thought. In fact, if it had not been for Pah's ruthlessness, it could have very well been me.

"Yes, I will bless you. Kneel now, daughter." I did as he asked, and he continued, "I bless you, Nefret hap Semkah, Meshwesh mekhma. I bless you with long life and good health. I bless you with all the blessings a father can bestow upon his daughter. Go with our prayers and good wishes." A tear slid down my face as my father's hand rested upon my head. I looked up into his handsome face, and he nodded down at me. "All will be well."

"I receive your blessing. Thank you, Father. Orba, Chief of the Council. Won't you come and bless me?" My father stepped back and allowed Orba to stand before me now. Although I knelt in the sand before the wise man, he barely stood taller than me.

"Nefret hap Semkah, I, Orba, Chief of the Council, bless you. We wrap you in protection and pray that our ancestors watch over you as you face our enemies. May the Unyielding Spiral of Life flow from your belly, renewing you mind, body and soul. May your bow arm be strong, and may you enjoy many days on this earth." His hands rested upon my head briefly, and then he stepped away from me. The gathering was quiet now, and the solemnity of this rare moment echoed through the tribe's consciousness.

"Omel, brother of my father. Won't you come and bless me?"

I kept my head down, but I heard surprised gasps echo through the crowd. Someone hissed quietly, but I did not turn to see who it was. I suspected Astora, and I knew Ayn would tell me later.

"Yes, I will bless you, niece." Omel stood before me and slid his shiny khopesh from its sheath. The sound of the metal rubbing against metal made my heart flutter, but still I did not look at him. I lowered my hands and placed them palms up in front of me.

Now was the moment. Now was the time. I could almost feel Omel's internal struggle. He would either surrender his sword or slice off my hands. I wondered which it would be. He paused for a moment, but I did not waver. I remained perfectly unmoving, my hands upraised, waiting to accept his sword—and his official submission to my reign. If he was to challenge me officially, now would be the moment.

"Nefret hap Semkah, I, Omel, Second King of the Meshwesh, bless you." His deep voice sounded like a growl, but he said the words, "As you accept this sword, may it strengthen you for tomorrow's fight and for all the battles you will face in the future. May victory never cease to be upon your reign as mekhma." He stepped back, and I clutched the sword by the hilt. I stood and raised it above my head, turning in circles so all could see it.

Then I cried out, "My people, my treasure, won't you bless me?"

With rapt faces, my tribe answered me with one voice. "Hafa-nu, mekhma! Hafa-nu!"

"I too bless you, Meshwesh! Hafa-nu! Pray for me this night, for tomorrow victory shall be ours. Finally we will walk into our city. We will take back our mekhma. Tomorrow, everything changes." They cheered, and I lowered my new sword as they rushed in to hug me and greet me. It was a moment I would never forget.

Once the crowd dissipated, only Father, Orba, Omel and Astora stayed behind. I could not help but notice that my uncle's wife had newly painted symbols on her face. Her fierce, painted eyes flashed at me, but she kept her thin lips clamped shut. My uncle did not speak. My accepting his sword had been a symbolic gesture; there was no reason to keep it, but I wanted to see if he would ask for it back. It was his father's sword, and I knew how he valued it. He stood waiting, but when I did not hand it back he stomped away with his wife in tow. I did not stop them or call them back.

With the hint of a smile on his face, my father said, "Orba says you have a task for me? How can I serve you, mekhma?"

"Father, never call me that. To you, let me always be daughter." He smiled broadly at this. It was good to see him smile. For the first time I noticed the strands of gray amongst his dark brown hair. "Yes, I do have a request. It is an unusual one, but please hear me out."

"Of course."

"We cannot talk here. Too many ears to hear." I cast an eye toward Astora, who constantly dogged my steps. Orba saw her too, and I could tell he was uncomfortable with her lingering. Stepping away from the crowd, I spoke to my father in a whisper. "After we have secured our victory, I cannot imagine it will be long before Ramose will want to return to Egypt. If that's the case, we may not have much time to decide on how to proceed. I cannot in good conscience leave you, Father, to fight Omel for the job. Tonight's ritual has bought us a little time, but it is only a temporary fix. My uncle will not stop until he has placed himself above all the Meshwesh. I have it on good authority that he approached the Egyptian general to ask for his help."

"Yes, I have heard that too. What did you have in mind?"

"Pah. She is still mekhma. But Father, she is not the same—she can't be the same as she was when she left."

"What do you mean?"

"You saw her in the sand at the end of the chain. She is out of her head. And even if she survives this, I cannot imagine she would be able to serve as mekhma. It would only be a matter of time before Omel seized control for himself."

Semkah ran his hands through his dirty hair and nodded. Looking at me with his sad eyes he said, "If she is as you say, then yes, we need to do something to protect her and our people."

Orba interrupted, "I mean no disrespect to either of you, but Pah has committed some serious crimes. She murdered twice, including Farrah, the Old One—these crimes cannot go unaddressed. The dead want their justice, and as the Chief of the Council, it is within my rights to demand it on their behalf. However, for the good of the people, for the benefit of the tribe, I am willing to forgo seeking justice until she is well."

Semkah shook his head. "How can you talk of justice now after all she's been through? Hasn't she suffered enough? We don't even know if she will live through this."

"I felt it only right to tell you the truth. What kind of counselor would I be to withhold this from you? I have seen Farrah and the child, and they demand justice."

I knew Orba was telling the truth, and I believed Pah was indeed guilty of the crimes she had been accused of, but my father was right. There must be some consideration for what punishment she had already suffered. Our ancestors had made sure Pah paid a price for her evil deeds. Yet, there were other things to consider besides revenge and justice. We weren't even sure that we could accomplish our plan.

I raised a hand. "Please, let us speak of something else at the moment. Farrah and my treasure, Paimu, will receive their justice, but we need to think about the more immediate danger, which is my uncle. He is maneuvering for something. Even though he has not received the blessing of Egypt yet, I am sure that will not be his last attempt. Here is my request, Father. I have asked Ramose to find Alexio and bring him back." I swallowed and felt the lump in my throat even as I said the words, "Pah needs a husband. A strong husband, a good husband, one who will not be influenced by Omel. I cannot think of anyone better than Alexio. I want you, Father, to bless his marriage to Pah. As her consort, he can lead our people until she is well again. At that time, these other matters can be determined. I fear if we do not take these drastic measures, if we do not find a strong consort for Pah, all will be lost. All of this will have been for nothing. I cannot say I am sad that Yuni died in the raid at Timia. He was a weak, lustful man. Pah was a fool to have married him, but now we must act."

My father lowered his voice. "I cannot tell you how surprised I am to hear this. You would ask Alexio to marry Pah? Do you know what you're asking?" He took my hand and looked into my eyes with concern.

"Yes, Father, I know what I'm asking. It hurts to even say the words, but this is the only way. As king, and you are king still, you can see it done. Alexio might resist you at first, but when he knows that this is my desire I'm sure he will obey. He would never betray me."

Then my father said what I did not think. "Aren't you betraying him? There is no doubt that he loves you, Nefret."

"I am mekhma. I will do what I have to do to make sure the Meshwesh are safe."

"Then if that is your will, let it be so."

"Yes, let it be so." Abruptly, I left them to their own counsel. The tears streamed down my face. Whatever Alexio and I had meant to one another, whatever promises and covenants we had made, I had now broken them. No—severed them with a cruel sword and chopped our love to pieces.

Things would never be the same. He was mine no more.

The camp was settling down now, and I found the makeshift tent that Ayn had installed for us. I had only a few hours to rest before we were to go to the doors of the city. Our camp had quieted, and so had the Kiffians'. Before the star shower there were sickening sounds coming from behind the walls of Zerzura. I could only imagine what kind of beastly things were happening. The sounds of screaming pierced the silence of the desert. Occasionally they would parade across the balcony, tormenting us in their crude language until the stars fell. Even though I served no god, I was grateful the sign had made them stop.

Ayn lay beside me. She smelled like sweat, but I could not complain. So did I. It seemed like forever since any of us had dived into the sweet waters of Timia. I know I should be excited to be so near Zerzura, our ancestral home, but I was not. I wanted to be anywhere but here.

"What are you thinking, Ayn?"

"I am thinking about how I will miss our people when we've gone."

Pushing my dirty hair from my face, I asked, "When we've gone?"

"You did not think I would let you leave by yourself, did you?"

I smiled at her but then pursed my lips. "Does this decision have anything to do with a certain Egyptian general?"

Even in the dark, I could tell that Ayn was uncomfortable with my question. She was not the kind of person who talked openly about her feelings—or her needs. I wondered which one he appealed to the most.

"If you are referring to Ramose, then no. It doesn't. I have no expectations of him. He has a wife, and he is an Egyptian. It would never work."

"I see."

"And what about you, Nefret? Although I think your plan is brilliant, I cannot believe you would willingly give Alexio to your sister. You have to know how she feels about him."

"I know, but we have no choice. It is Alexio or Omel. Omel's people will stir up Walida and others to make him king. He is a dangerous man."

She grunted and said, "You have no idea. Did you know the Egyptians call him Horemheb?"

"What does that mean?"

"Something to do with Horus. I don't know. These Egyptian ways are foreign to me. Apparently he is quite a regular figure at the Egyptian court."

"Is that what Ramose tells you?"

"No, I did not hear that from him."

With a sigh and a surge of concern I said, "Be careful, Ayn. Love is a treacherous mistress."

"I do not know that I love him, Nefret."

I smiled at her in the dark. "Yes, you do. Just be careful. And when we get to Egypt, trust no one." That was the advice I received from Queen Tiye herself. "We go to a dangerous place, Ayn. I fear that we will be at a disadvantage in many ways, and we will have no allies to guide us—unless you count my uncle. I am sure he will waste no time coming to the court, if for nothing else than to gloat over my situation."

It was her turn to laugh now. "That is what you are thinking about? In just a few hours you will drive to the gates of Zerzura and face the Kiffians, and you are worried about going to Egypt? Let us try to live through the morning. Then we will plan a strategy for survival at court," she said with a raw laugh as she tapped my arm playfully.

"I don't suppose there is a chance Ramose will change his mind and leave me here?" I asked hopefully.

"No, there is no chance. And if he heard you say that, he would lock you in chains now just to keep you from escaping." She whispered a warning, "So please do not speak those words in public. If Ramose does not return with you—safe and alive, I might add—he might as well fall on his own sword. He cannot disobey his queen. It would mean death for him, even if he does not truly care for her."

"He does not care for the Great Wife?"

"No, but he loves Pharaoh to no end. He is like a father to him."

"It sounds to me like Ramose trusts you a great deal, Ayn." I leaned on one arm and moved my messy hair behind my shoulder to better see her darkened face.

"I think he likes talking to me."

"And other things…" I said with a smile.

"I admit that I have never met a man like him before." We were silent for a moment after her confession.

"Be careful, Ayn. He is from another world, and we do not know how things will go."

"It is too late for that, Nefret."

Dread filled my stomach. "You said yourself you did not know if you loved him or not. What do you mean it is too late?"

Ayn's voice shook as she whispered, "I have his child in my belly. In our short time together I have given him something his wife never could—a child to carry his name. He will have his heart's desire—Ramose will finally have an immortal name. One that will last forever."

My skin crawled as she spoke. I did not know what to say to her, so I said nothing at all.

"Have I disappointed you, my mekhma?"

"No." I touched her arm and squeezed it. "Who am I to judge you, Ayn? Our tribe needs treasure. You know children are our greatest treasure." I tried to sound supportive, but I knew it would be much more complicated than that. How could I in good conscience take her to Egypt with me knowing she was with child? My eyes were sticky and my brain tired. I would not speak of this to her now. There would be other times to discuss her situation, and she seemed pleased with my answer.

"We had better rest if we can. Morning will be here soon. Hafa-nu, Nefret."

"Hafa-nu, my friend." In a few minutes, Ayn was snoring, probably dreaming about her Egyptian. My mind took me back to Alexio and our one night in the desert. It had not been that long ago, but it felt like a hundred seasons. His sweet smile filled my mind with sadness, and I imagined for a second that I could smell his warm and spicy scent. I could feel his strong arms around me as we lay together under the stars. It was a pleasant indulgence to dream about him now. However, if I was to survive, I would have to change the way I thought about him. I would have to put him out of my mind forever, for he would never be mine.

I suddenly hoped that I would die at the hands of the Kiffians. How much easier it would be if I did die! I would be gone, Pah could rule, and I would never have to miss Alexio again.

Because I could not immediately fall asleep, I let my mind wander like a wild thing. Eventually sleep did come, but it was fitful and full of faces I did not know.

Too soon, Ayn shook me until I was awake. A name fell off my lips, "Smenkhkare!"

Chapter Nine

Flames of Freedom—Ramose

The wagon lurched across the sand as I clung to the undercarriage. Beside me grinned Kafta—the crazy man loved schemes like this. He had not shaved since we left Thebes, and his beard and the sparse tufts growing around his head made him look like even more of a madman. As I clung to the pole with my arms and legs, I wondered if he was in fact mad. I could hardly believe that I, the great Ramose, General of Egypt, hung from a pole hidden at the bottom of a wagon driven by the Desert Queen. The Fates had a strange sense of humor.

When the girl shared her scheme, Kafta could hardly wait to mention using the barrels. He had done a tour with the Fourth Legion far to the north of Egypt when he first saw this battle technique employed. I could not comprehend the power he described until I saw it myself. When the liquid in the barrel ignited, it burst into flames. The explosion flung the dangerous liquid to great distances. It delivered a much more impressive display than an overheated kiln or a few fiery arrows. The barrels we would be using clunked near our heads, and I prayed silently to Amun that they would not explode and kill us all before we made it to the gate.

"Stick to the plan!" I reminded our driver.

"Shut up!" she yelled back as the wagon drove a few more feet before coming to a full stop.

"I like her," Kafta said, grinning at me through his gapped teeth. I rolled my eyes and listened carefully. Through the slit in the front of the wagon I could see that the gates were beginning to open. I could hear the sounds of metal, probably chains used to open and close the wooden doors. I heard the voices of the Kiffians as they jeered at the girl in the wagon. They were completely unaware that hundreds of Egyptians had been hiding in the sands most of the night, unmoving under their sand-covered wicker shields. I could not wait for the moment when this fact became apparent.

"Welcome, my queen!" A familiar voice, the voice of Gilme, called from above. I could see his position on the balcony through the slit in the boards. If only I had a bow and arrow I could kill the man now. But then hundreds of Kiffians would fall upon us and I would bring Egypt to war with these wild southerners. I was not sure what Queen Tiye had in mind for my charge, but I was certain it was not this.

"Please come in. We have been waiting for your promised gifts. My men are parched from a night of sporting." Gilme's rowdy men cheered loudly and laughed at their king's crude statement. "We want to taste this beer. You should pray that it does not taste like camel water. My men have particular tastes."

To her credit the girl did not hesitate. "I want to see my sister, Gilme! Bring her out now."

Without answering Gilme ordered the girl brought forward. I could hardly believe it, but she looked far worse than when we last saw her. Someone had cut off her hair, and she had fresh bruises on her face and naked torso. She was no longer in chains, but she had the look of someone who had been utterly defeated. I knew this look. I had caused it many times in the foreign leaders I conquered. It was common practice to humiliate a defeated king in front of his family, especially his wife. But the sight of this half-naked, broken girl stirred a rare sympathy in me. She did not look at us, nor did she appear to know where she was at all.

"Pah, come to me," Nefret called to her sister.

"She is not sticking to the plan," I complained to Kafta, who frowned back.

Gilme spat into the sand below him. "Nobody leaves here. You bring the wagon through the gate if you want to see your sister. She belongs to me now."

"That was not our deal, Gilme," Nefret growled back at him. Her words brought raucous laughter from the onlookers both on the balcony and in the open doors. I counted nearly thirty, but I was sure there were many more inside.

"I do not make deals with women. I do other things with them." That started another round of laughter from the Kiffians. "You need to learn your place."

The air crackled with tension. Gilme had done exactly as we expected, behaved shamefully and without honor. All the girl had to do was stand and raise her hand—that was the signal. What was she waiting for? I could hear the anger in her voice. She should have known there was no reasoning with a madman.

"This is your last chance, Kiffian king! Release my sister and leave the city! Do as I ask, and no one will get hurt! You have been warned!"

Sweat poured from my brow, and my arms and legs cramped as I held in place, clinging to the wooden pole. I did not take my gaze off of Kafta. Both of us realized that things were not going as planned and we needed to be prepared for anything now. I pulled my dagger from my tunic, ready to release the barrel at any moment.

"Do not refuse my hospitality, queen. Come now—you are wearing my patience thin." To someone below he ordered, "Bring the wench back into the city and close the gates until her sister decides to obey my commands."

I swore under my breath and whispered to her again, "Stick to the plan. Give the signal now!"

"Pah! Hafa yem taffa! Hafa yem taffa!" The Desert Queen yelled at her sister, and I felt the weight of the wagon shift as she rose to her feet. She let out a scream of anger as Kafta and I released the barrels and rolled out from under the wagon. In two seconds we were in the sand, rolling the barrels toward the gate as my warriors raised their sand-covered shields and stood screaming an intimidating war cry that startled the Kiffians. Arrows began to fly around us, and I dove for the half-nude girl standing before the gates. In a matter of moments, I had her in my arms and was running toward the wagon as the Kiffians began to return fire arrows wildly and yell in confusion. A flaming arrow whizzed past me.

"Get down now!" I screamed at Nefret as I ran to the back of the wagon with her sister. The explosion blew the barrels into oblivion and the flames burst up. Kafta's tactic had worked. The Kiffians, frightened and confused, could see my Egyptians now pouring into the gate. I glanced behind me and could see the Meshwesh approaching with unearthly speed on their horses as they streamed in across the desert. Nefret was suddenly beside me, reaching for her sister.

"Stay here!" I yelled at her, happy to deliver Pah into her hands. Releasing my sword from its sheath, I ran toward the gate. Bodies were already on the ground, and I was happy to see none of them were Egyptian.

My sword sliced flesh as I stormed through the gate. A great blond giant tried to withstand me, but he lasted only a moment. He wore no armor and succumbed to a single stab to his abdomen. I did not waste a stab to finish the job; he would die soon enough. I continued to fight my way toward the red-haired giant Gilme. He was my target—the only worthy opponent for Pharaoh's Great General. The Kiffians had no grace, no light hand with their weapons. It was sad, really, how easily they could be bested despite their size and tenacity. They carried evil-looking swords that they thrust at anything that moved.

Minutes later the Meshwesh made it through the gates, and I could see the Shasu running toward the melee from the other side of the city. Kiffians were fleeing before them. I ran up the stone stairs that I suspected would lead me to the tower and the balcony where Gilme had defied the Desert Queen. Despite the Kiffians' stupidity, it was not easy going—the balcony was full of warriors, both mine and the foreign king's. A bloody Kiffian cursed me in his guttural language, and I spun and swung at him. My opponent moved with surprising deftness, apparently more skilled than many of his comrades, but I did not relent. I swung the sword again, this time slicing his cheek and hand. With another howl he drove toward me recklessly. I mocked him with a laugh and moved easily out of his way as he fell on the stairs. In the blink of a hawk's eye, I slid my sword into his throat and grinned down at him as his miserable life left him.

I heard a woman's voice yelling threats beside me, and I turned to see Nefret engaged in single combat. She was in a deadly embrace with a young Kiffian who towered above her. I could see that he meant to overcome her with his reach and brute force. He had her hands clasped above her head and wore a lustful leer. As quick as lightning she brought her knee up into his groin and slammed her elbow into his face. He succumbed to the assault by doubling over, and the girl shoved her sword into his shoulder. The young man thumped to the ground like a bag of sand, and she stepped on his back as she ran up the stairs behind me.

"What are you doing here?" I demanded.

Her mouth was set in a grim smile. "You know why I am here." Ayn bounded up the stairs beside her. With a quick appraisal I could see Ayn did not have a scratch on her. Her long hair was plastered to her face with sweat, and her strong arms and legs were bare. Her sword gleamed red—proof that she had not idled the time away today.

"I am here, my mekhma."

Nefret glanced at her but did not turn her attention away from me. I growled in frustration. "I ordered you to stay with your sister. Why did you disobey my order?"

"Get out of my way, Egyptian." In reaction to her defiance, I reached toward her, but Ayn waved her blade at me threateningly. I could not hide my surprise.

"Do not get in my way, Ramose," Nefret warned me. I knew in an instant what the foolish girl had planned. She was going to challenge Gilme, and that meant she was going to die. I could not allow this—her death meant my death. If that had not been so, I would have happily allowed her to surrender her life to the Kiffian's sword.

In angry assent I nodded once and waved my hand as if to say, "Lead the way." Together the three of us cut into the now weakened line and drove toward our mutual target. Between administering blows I watched the women fight with surprising expertise. Nefret danced around her victims. She chose her offensive movements well and did not fail to deliver damage. To the untrained eye, Ayn's flurry of strikes might have seemed wild and frantic, but not to me. She planned her kills but enjoyed showing off. In that she was not wise. I watched as one of the Kiffians unleashed a fury of swings on her. Almost overwhelmed, she fell to one knee, her sword above her head as she pushed against his. In a burst of rage and a scream, the wild man pinned her to the ground, and a second Kiffian appeared tempted to join the fight or whatever they planned to do to Ayn. I flicked my dagger at him and pierced his right eye. He fell upon the other Kiffian, and Ayn quickly scrambled to her feet, stumbling away from them. Then with a showy swing, Ayn killed the man, grinned at me and ran after Nefret.

Many of the Kiffians were dead, but the few who were still fighting showed they were never going to surrender. Not in this life at least. At the center of the dwindling group was Gilme. He towered above his men, his beard wet with blood, and one of his ears had been nearly severed. The smells of war, blood, broken bone and burning fires filled the city of Zerzura.

"Kafta! Leave him!" I shouted to my second-in-command, who had every intention of claiming the giant for himself. In a few seconds, the six Kiffians remaining on the balcony surrounded the wounded leader. Breathing hard and savagely wounded, they looked at one another unsure what to do.

Finally, they fell to their knees, and two Kiffians immediately tossed down their swords in front of them. With a scream of anger, Gilme swung his sword, killing his own men.

He spat a vicious curse at them in his foreign language as the second man gagged and gurgled to his death. "You are not my son!" he declared to his writhing victim. Panting and weak, he faced us. He waved his sword with a blood-soaked hand and stared at me with burning hatred. "I will deal with you."

"I offer you no deals," Nefret answered him.

"I will never submit to you, girl."

"Yes, you will," she said confidently as she stepped toward him. Kafta looked to me for permission. In just a few steps, he could kill the defeated king or at the very least disarm him. I shook my head and watched Nefret. Gilme had lost much blood and wavered on his feet. She had enough skill to kill the man. Many in her tribe had gathered on the balcony to see their mekhma administer justice. If this helped her finish our mission, then who was I to stop her? Despite the queen's command, I would take matters into my own hands if she did not kill him quickly. I had my own life to consider.

Ayn stood beside me, her sword still drawn too. There was not much room to maneuver on the balcony, which was to Nefret's advantage. She was small, quick and largely undamaged by the battle.

Gilme glanced around him. All of his people, at least those on the balcony, had been mowed down. There was no one to help him. Looking past Nefret he called to me again, "You! I will yield to you!"

Nefret advanced toward him. She took two steps, and Gilme poked at her with his blade, but she ducked, stabbed at his chest and then swung out of the way. Surprised by her boldness, he yelled in anger but did not submit. I sensed someone else standing beside me and turned to see Semkah, Nefret's father, holding a dagger in his hand. Bloody from the fight, he yelled something to his daughter in their tribal language.

"Mey tanakha fama, mekhma Nefret!" In moments, the other Meshwesh—and there were now many on the steps, in the courtyard and outside the gate—repeated the phrase. I could see Horemheb bounding up the steps, and to my surprise he also had the cry on his lips.

"What are they saying, Ayn?"

Without taking her eyes off her queen she whispered to me, "My life for yours, Queen Nefret."

"What does that mean?"

Ayn's dark eyes watched me now. "These are covenant words, Ramose. It is a sacred promise to avenge the mekhma if she should perish. As she has offered her life for theirs, they do the same for her. These are sacred words you hear today."

The swords crashed, and Gilme used his hulking body to shove the Desert Queen away. But she rebounded and swung at him furiously with both hands on her sword. Gilme grunted as he fought her, and I could see his strength was waning now. As his arms fell back she had the opportunity to kill him but instead jabbed at his thigh, which began to bleed profusely. Gilme collapsed to the ground, and Nefret kicked his sword out of the way.

"Bring me my sister!" Nefret yelled at Ayn. The dark-haired warrior sped down the stairs, and the rest of us watched as the fallen king swore at the conquering queen. What was she doing?

Soon Ayn returned with Pah. Someone had tossed an ill-fitting tunic over the girl, but her eyes were empty except for the terror in them. She mumbled to herself, stopping only to scream if some-one besides Ayn touched her or bumped into her. As the two cleared the stairs and stood on the balcony, I thought Pah would run or do something ridiculous like throw herself over the edge. But she froze, her attention on her sister, who stood over the dying giant of a man.

"Pah! Come now! Take your revenge, sister!" The crowd cleared a path for the girl. She did not move at first but soon began to walk and then run toward Gilme. Her father handed her his dagger as a scream of rage filled her lungs. Plunging her body forward, she buried the dagger into the man's heart. He did not fight his fate. We watched as the mad girl drove the dagger over and over into the corpse until, exhausted, she let the blade drop. She rose to her feet, her tunic now covered in blood. She backed away from Gilme and stared at her bloody hands. She took another step back and finally another until she neared the ledge. Yes! She was going to launch herself from the balcony gate.

"Ayn!" I shouted, as she was closer to the girl. Before Pah could finish her deed, Ayn and Semkah had grasped the girl away from the danger. She clung to her father and did not cause any more disruption. Soon the Meshwesh began to cheer for them both, though the cries for Nefret were greater, and the people began to celebrate their victory. Sliding my stained sword back into the sheath, I grasped Kafta's shoulder and congratulated him on his successful plan. Already my mind was moving toward the next phase. We would clean up the bodies and repair any damage to Zerzura, and then we would return to Thebes.

As if she read my mind Ayn caught my attention. She was a charred, bloody sight, but never before had I wanted a woman so much.

Surely she would be the death of me.

Chapter Ten

The Way Home—Nefret

The sun hung low like a dying ember in the sky when we dragged the last body from our city the following day. Such was the swiftness of the attack that none of our allied forces were killed and only a few Meshwesh were injured. Ramose congratulated me privately and informed me that the Egyptian army planned to leave tomorrow—then he and I would leave in the company of a small escort. I had only two days before I had to leave my people.

"So soon?"

His hands on his hips, Ramose replied, "It will not get any easier with the waiting, and the Queen grows impatient."

"You have heard from the Queen?" I asked apprehensively.

He waved his hand dismissively and replied, "I am familiar with the Queen's general disposition, and she is not likely to change her mind or tolerate excuses."

I understood his hidden message. *Do not ask for more time. It will not be given.* Desperation rose within me, but I fought back that wild beast with as much dignity as I could muster. It would do no good to ask Ramose to allow me to remain in Zerzura, and I would not demean myself to do so. The irony was, for all his Egyptian pride, Ramose was as helpless as I was. To the Great Wife, the general was a tool that served her just as any slave or servant did. Just as I did.

"Before I leave, I have a request."

"*Another* request?"

I pressed on, unabashed by his attitude, "It is customary for queens traveling to courts to have attendants, I am told. Is this true?" He nodded, and I continued, "This will be my second trip to Thebes, and I am anxious to proceed in a manner that will please Queen Tiye, my generous benefactor." I could see that my careful answer pleased him.

He flashed a white smile and looked relieved. "You may have attendants. Who did you have in mind? Besides Ayn."

"I wish to bring only two attendants, as we can hardly spare more than that. I will take Ayn and also my uncle." I tried not to smile at his surprise. And I silently prayed that he would acquiesce to my request without argument. I should have known better than to waste a good prayer on General Ramose.

"Now why would you want to do that?" Ramose sat on the edge of the heavy wooden table in my private chambers. Whoever had dwelt here while we were away had been generous enough to leave behind beautifully carved wooden and marble furniture. Surely that had not been the Kiffians.

Ayn lingered nearby, pretending she did not hear our discussion. She busied herself tidying my room, when in truth I owned hardly anything. I had noticed earlier that her things were in here as well, but I did not object. She had proved a faithful friend, even if I questioned her choice of lover. And I had to admit I was no expert on that. I could not make up my mind if I loved Alexio or hated him. I believed Astora less and less, and Ayn told me that she had never seen Pah and Alexio do more than flirt.

"I have never met your master, but I hear he is a shrewd man. He must be, to rule Egypt so well." I offered the flattery nervously, hoping it sounded natural. That got his attention, and he smiled again.

"Yes, he is the epitome of shrewdness." Suspicion grew in his voice, and he looked from me to Ayn, who did not meet his eyes.

"I can only imagine the cost of this campaign. I'm grateful for the Great Wife's attention, but I cannot imagine Queen Tiye would want to repeat this process. For whatever she thinks I am worth, I cannot imagine she would want to pay the price twice. Maybe you are not familiar with our agreement?"

"Enlighten me, please."

I kept my composure and proceeded with my lie. Another skill I had to learn, apparently. My soul cringed at the idea, but I had to think about my father, the children and all my people. I hoped the general did not know the truth about my conversation with the Queen. I was counting on it. "The Queen generously agreed to help me recapture my homeland and bring my people into a peaceful existence. With my uncle left behind, I am afraid the latter will not be true. Omel would surely sell my kinfolk, maybe even my father, as slaves to work in his mines. He is rich and growing richer by the day, but that is not enough for him. My uncle will not rest until he is the King of all the Meshwesh." At least part of what I said was true.

"Well, if you are not here, it seems to me that he would be the obvious choice as leader. If not him, who do you have in mind? For I can see you have thought about this. You are cleverer than I thought, Desert Queen."

Ignoring his last comment, I confessed, "I do have someone in mind. It is Alexio, Omel's son, who should rule." Ramose enjoyed a hearty laugh as he slapped his knee and then rose to pace the room as he rubbed his smooth chin with his tanned hand.

At least he has not said no outright. He is thinking about it, anyway.

Ayn was very near to him, and I could see he wanted to reach out and touch her, but he refrained. How could she bear this man? Yes, he had a handsome face and a strong body, but his condescending nature and rude manners would never suit me.

"How will that be any different? You said yourself he is Omel's son."

"Yes, but Alexio is loyal to me. And he is loyal to the tribe—all the tribes. As my sister's consort, he would keep the Meshwesh safe."

Ramose looked out the arched window of my chambers and watched the people below. The Meshwesh were tired but celebrating. Music rose from the streets, and the sounds of excitement filled the nearly empty city. Many families were camping in the streets instead of taking ownership of the empty houses. It would take some time for my people to become acclimated to this new way of living. I wished more than anything I could help them with this process. Now I knew they needed Alexio more than ever.

"I am sure your uncle would have some opposition to this. And if I allowed him to express his thoughts, he might even convince me to let him stay behind. I am not sure the throne would object."

Ayn finally spoke. "Mekhma, I have pledged to go with you, but if you find it better that I stay, as your father's or sister's protector, I shall. I know your heart is here." That got Ramose's attention.

Leaning his back against the window he quickly added, "In the interest of speeding up this process—I am anxious to be rid of this place—I will grant you your request. Horemheb, I mean Omel, shall return with us to Thebes."

"Thank you, General. Ayn? Will you please ask my uncle to come now? The sooner I give him the news, the better."

"Yes, mekhma. It will be done." She padded away quietly, Ramose looking after her as she departed. He made no secret of his desire for her. I wondered how that would change when we arrived in Thebes. I knew he was married, and so did Ayn. But perhaps in Egypt such things did not matter.

"Mekhma! Alexio has returned. He is on his way to see you," Biel stood panting in my doorway. The concepts of pausing at doorways and courteous knocks were a foreign thing to my people. Living in tents takes away the need for such things as privacy and courtesy. I did not scold him. He would learn the new ways soon enough from Alexio and my father.

"Thank the Shining Man for his protection!" I smiled and hugged the surprised Biel. I could not hide my happiness and had not thought to until I saw Ramose's face.

Biel did not notice the general's dark mood, or if he did, he did not seem to care. "Alexio is tired but anxious to see his mekhma. Did you know there were guards outside?" Finally sensing the tension in the room he added, "I am surprised to see the Egyptian here, mekhma. Is anything wrong?" Now Biel was scolding me for the perceived offense to Alexio. Did everyone know of our previous arrangement? Ramose looked like a tiger ready to pounce on the boy.

"All is well, Biel. Please wait outside. Let me speak to the general in private."

He shuffled his sandals momentarily but stepped outside as I asked, "Why are there guards outside my quarters? Am I to be kept a prisoner now? Couldn't I have escaped a hundred times already?"

"Yes, but now your lover has returned, Desert Queen."

I felt my face burn but did not rise to the general's bait. "I see you have been listening to camp gossip."

"Is it gossip?" He raised his hands to stop me from speaking. "I have no interest in knowing the secrets of a queen's heart, but I represent another interest: the interest of Egypt." He stepped toward me and was only a few inches from my face. He reached his tanned hand up and stroked my hair thoughtfully. When I did not melt under his seductive gaze or flinch away like an offended maid he said, "I cannot deliver you to Pharaoh's harem sullied, Nefret. He is not a man who likes to share anything."

"I am about to leave my home forever, General. Am I not allowed to say goodbye to the people I care about?"

"You may bid farewell to your father, sister...whomever you like."

"Just not Alexio? You know my intention is for him to marry my sister. Why is seeing him a restriction?"

"Do you think me a fool, Nefret? Marry your lover off to your addle-brained sister so that you can hope to one day return home to take her place? I assure you that if you were to do so, the full weight of Egypt would fall upon you and the Meshwesh. You belong to Queen Tiye now—Thebes is your home." As I stood open-mouthed, Ayn returned with my uncle. I was surprised to see Astora with them.

"Uncle," I greeted him, deliberately not acknowledging Astora. She was a snake—of that I was sure—and I would never again acknowledge her presence. "The general and I were just discussing my return to Thebes." Omel looked more of an Egyptian than Ramose did, with his wide gold collar and linen garments. I could see he had completely shed all signs of his Meshwesh heritage. And to think, he wanted to be the king of the clan!

He smiled broadly. "What a great honor this is for you and all of the Meshwesh! If only we had known the details of your new role at court...." He turned to Ramose, who did not deign to answer him. Neither did I. Even if I had known what I would be doing in Thebes, I would not have shared the information with him.

I smiled at him pleasantly. "Yes, an invitation to court is a high honor, as you have often told me yourself, Uncle. In fact, until recently I had no idea how popular you were with the Egyptians. I hear they have even given you an Egyptian name—Horemheb. Isn't that what we heard, Ayn?"

Ayn smiled at me. "Yes, mekhma. That is correct."

"Well, I have been privileged enough to receive a few kindnesses from Pharaoh's hand." He eyed Ramose with suspicion but asked him nothing. "I take pride in my name and in my Meshwesh heritage. I am doubly favored."

"In some ways, I have *you* to thank for this great privilege, Uncle. Without your connections and encouragement I would never have considered asking Egypt for help. Now, in the spirit of gratitude, I have decided that when I return to Egypt, you shall go with me. As my attendant, of course. We must represent our people with all proper decorum. Let me begin my career at court with the proper introductions. Who better to introduce me to the court than the great Horemheb?"

He began to stammer his refusal, but Ramose finally spoke up. "Surely your queen can rely on you, Horemheb?"

"I would never... that is to say...what about the tribe? I cannot just leave without..."

I touched his arm and said, "Leave the tribe to me, Uncle. I assure you I will not leave our people in disarray. Our absence will hardly be missed."

Smothering his surprise he replied, "Then I will do as you ask, mekhma." Astora stepped closer to him and he asked, "What about my wife? She is anxious to return to Thebes—she has family there. I assume she is to accompany her husband."

Still ignoring her, I spoke to Omel, "I have no need for another attendant, Uncle. I am afraid she will not return with us at this time. Perhaps later."

I saw Ayn smile behind Astora, but I kept my face blank. "Please prepare for the journey. We leave in two days."

He raised his hands in the sign of respect, then spun out on his oiled and sandaled feet, leaving only the smell of his cedar cologne. His wife lingered for a few seconds, long enough to cast a dangerous look in my direction, but she did not dare say a word in disagreement. I was still mekhma.

Feeling emboldened I said, "General, I expect you to remove those guards from my chamber doors. I am not planning an escape and have never given you reason to think I would. Whatever camp gossip you have heard, I assure you it is not true."

To my shock he did not argue with me. "Of course, Queen Nefret. I am at your service if you require anything." With a pleased smile he left Ayn and me alone. She reached out, took my hand and squeezed it.

"You handled him in fine fashion," she said, the admiration in her voice apparent.

"I don't think Ramose trusts me at all."

She laughed. "I was talking about your uncle. But no, Ramose trusts no one. Not even me."

I wanted to ask her if she had whispered to the general about Alexio and me. But if I was wrong, the slight would be unforgivable. She had never given me any reason not to trust her. Instead, I simply asked, "Ayn, I can trust you, can I not?"

"You know you can. Why do you ask me this?"

"I do not know. I am tired, Ayn. It is nothing. Please ask Biel to come see me. I am so hungry. Is there anything to eat? Maybe some bread? I can smell it, and it is making my stomach rumble."

With an uncertain smile she said, "I will bring you something. And I will get Biel for you."

The boy entered almost immediately, as if he had been listening at the open door. In a whisper I said, "Tell Alexio to meet me at the Lightning Gate. It will be well past dark, and I do not know how long it will take me to arrive. Please ask him to wait."

Biel nodded grimly and left me to myself. I sank down on a nearby chair, my hands shaking and my heart heavy. Whatever my fate, surely I could have this one night—one last meeting with

Alexio? How unfair it would be to keep me from him for all eternity. No! It could not be! I would see him. I had to. And I would tell no one my plans. That way I would know for sure that no one had followed me.

As I waited for Ayn, I strolled around the massive room. I had not chosen this place; Ayn chose it for me. She said it was fit for a queen. The walls were white stone, smooth with joints so close together that you could not fit a hair between them. It was a magic place, Orba had whispered to me earlier before he left to search for a divine spring or pool for scrying. The doorways and windows were topped with arches, and there were interesting symbols and shapes carved into the surface of the stones above the doorways. I wondered what they might mean, but I did not have long to think about it. Ayn returned with a tray of food, and we ate in silence together.

Orba visited me that night and told me about my father's progress. I had thought to go see him, but the Wise One advised against it. "Semkah has exerted himself beyond what was necessary today, and I fear he needs even more time and care to fully recover. I asked Leela to give him a sleeping potion to help him rest. Naturally he constantly objects to her care, but in the end, he saw reason and is now resting. On the other matter," Orba said cautiously, mindful that Ayn was present, "I think that may prove more difficult than we first imagined. Your sister is not well, mekhma. I have had to move her from your father's room into her own just to keep him rested. Leela assures me that she can care for them both, but I fear Pah is beyond caring for." I swallowed the last piece of my bread and dusted the crumbs from my hands.

"What are you suggesting, Orba? That I put her down like a lame horse or camel?"

"Of course not. I wanted to make sure that you are aware of how sick she really is. She is out of her head and cannot carry on a conversation with another person, much less lead our people. The people will know that her spirit is struggling to keep her mind in one piece. Do you think they will stand by and welcome her once they see her walking around naked talking to herself?"

I no longer cared that Ayn heard our conversation. "This is why I want Alexio to become her consort. She will need his strength in these coming months. I have no doubt she will recover. Pah is strong—as she always has been. Besides, what alternatives do we have? Omel leaves for Thebes. And since my father is disqualified from reigning, there is no other choice. Surely you can see this. Unless the Council or its chief have decided another way around these rules?"

He patted my hand like I was a child and shook his head. "No, mekhma. There is no other way. You are right, of course, but I felt it my duty to share with you my concerns."

I squeezed his small, gnarled hand and returned a smile to him. "I am depending upon you, Orba. There is no one else. Do what you must to help, but do not kill Pah or harm her further. Please, I beg the Council for mercy."

He promised me nothing but said, "Perhaps you should see her. Maybe your presence will help her know she is safe. Also, I hear that Alexio has returned. When will you inform him of your request?"

"We will talk more about that later. I will see Pah soon. Go rest now, my friend, and leave these things to worry over tomorrow. That is when the real work begins. I'm counting on you."

The little man left, and Ayn and I finished tidying the room. This would be the first night we slept in a bed that was not on the ground. As we set about our task, I thought about Pah. With all my heart I wanted to see her, hold her, assure her that all would be well, but I could not forget Paimu. My treasure! How I missed her! I would see my sister, but not today. I was not ready to feel pity for her.

Instead, Ayn and I explored the many empty rooms around us and were amazed at the hawk carvings that stood outside the door of one large room, obviously a feasting area. Feeling tired but anxious to use every minute available to me, I walked the narrow streets beside my home and visited with my people. Many hugged me and reached their hands toward me. Many cried, "Hafa-nu, mekhma!" and I returned their greetings. Tears filled my eyes at the sight of the tired yet relieved faces of the Meshwesh. Tired we were, and many fewer than before, but we were home—back in Zerzura. To my surprise, many Egyptians patrolled the area, although most of them had camped outside the gate and I could hear the sounds of construction. Obviously they were attempting to repair the damage that had been done to the front gates. I had never seen such things as exploding barrels and fire bursting into the air. It was a powerful weapon, and now I could see why Egypt ruled the world. The things they knew far exceeded our own knowledge.

The sun had finally set as we made our way back to my chambers. Ayn hesitated outside the door, and I smiled at her knowingly. "I am sure I will be safe, Ayn. Go. See your general."

"This is our last night before we return to Thebes and to his wife. I do not know what the future holds. I want to treasure every moment."

"I understand that. Go. I'm going to bed." Ayn hugged me. It was a rare thing to receive a hug from the warrior. I accepted it, patting her on the back as she walked quickly down the street. As she turned the corner I took my chance. Now was the time to see Alexio! Ramose would be busy with Ayn and would never know. I turned the corner, deciding to take the long narrow backstreet that led to the Lightning Gate. I had no cloak, but the streets were almost empty. Most of the people had already settled in for the night and were unconcerned with one woman walking through the city. Still I stayed in the shadows as much as I could, silently cursing the bright moon that rose above me. I did not know the city well, but I headed north to where the Lightning Gate once stood. As I had promised, we had destroyed that gate today. There would be no entrance through that gate anymore. The stones had crumbled, and we would forever be safe and protected from the Nephal—and the Kiffians. I was panting as I scurried through the streets. I cleared the corner and nearly gasped when I saw an Egyptian soldier standing just a few feet away. He had not spotted me, so I quickly turned back and stood flush against the wall. I waited for him to walk by or walk away before I continued on my path.

After a short time, I poked my head around the corner to see that the soldier was now gone and the gate was in the distance. I did not see Alexio, but I hoped he had received my message and had found a place to wait until I could come to him. There were no buildings to hide beside now; there was nothing but open space from here on to the gate. I would have to run quickly to make it unspotted. I tossed my hair behind my shoulders, wishing again that I had a cloak to hide it. But there was no time for that now. I raced toward the gate only to hear a loud whistle echo through the courtyard.

"You! What are you doing here?" It was Ramose! Before I could answer him, he gripped my elbow and pulled me back to the edge of the courtyard. "You heard me. What are you doing here, Desert Queen?" I could not get free from his grip and stood frozen, unable to think or speak. Suddenly he shoved me against the wall and pressed his body against mine.

"Let me go!"

He stifled my cries by placing his mouth over mine and kissing me long and hard. I punched at his chest and pushed him as hard as I could, but he was like granite. I could not move him.

"You think to make a fool of me? I knew this was what you would do. Imagine, the great mekhma strolling through the streets like a common street—"

"Get off of me! I will scream, General, and you will have the Shasu upon you before you can think."

With a rough hand he grabbed my breasts and kissed my neck. "Scream all you like. Is this not what you wanted? Leave the boy alone, Desert Queen, or you will get him killed. I am a man, and I will keep your secret. I can please you."

Ramose kicked open the door beside us, and I could see his intentions. He would take me whether I said yea or nay. This was my last chance to reason with him. "And what about Ayn? What about your child? Do you care for no one?"

He froze just a few inches from my face. "What are you talking about?"

"Ayn carries your child. Finally, you will have your immortal name, General. But when I tell her what you've done to me…"

He pushed himself away and blinked at me in the dim light. "You lie."

"I do not. Ask her yourself. She has gone to see you." I straightened my clothing and wiped his kisses from my face.

His mouth opened and closed, but he said nothing for a long minute. He stared at me with his hawk eyes and then said, "Go home then, mekhma. But do not step outside your chamber door again. For if you do, I will not listen to your pleas for mercy."

Feeling numb I walked back to my temporary home, which was now my prison. I did not look over my shoulder or turn around for fear that Ramose was on my heels. I had no doubt he followed me at some length, and I believed his threat. For whatever reason, he would not allow me to see Alexio.

My heart felt like a brick in my chest as I walked up the steps and into my bed. Ayn did not return. After crying for hours and staring at the bright moon from my window I finally fell asleep.

Chapter Eleven

The New Daughter—Queen Tiye

I had no intention of letting the dust settle on her sandals before I made my purpose known to all. As I had learned from my husband, there was nothing like the element of surprise, especially when it came to outmaneuvering your enemies. Today was the day I presented my new daughter to the world. With only a moment's notice, my faithful steward summoned all the queens, the court and even my son to greet my new daughter. For a moment, I considered Sitamen and what this would mean for her, but only for a moment. I was sure she would misunderstand everything, such a sensitive child was she, but what choice did I have? My enemy, Tadukhipa, left me no choice! With my husband hovering between life and death, nothing could be left to chance. We had been foolish to invite Tadukhipa into our home—into our marriage—into our kingdom, and I refused to allow that mistake to continue through my son's reign. Hopefully, the steps I took today would knock that smug smile off her face.

I pushed the door open and walked into the Desert Queen's room unannounced. She stood in the midst of the room; a half dozen women, my cleverest servants, attended her. Immediately they all turned to face me, bowing their heads and shoulders in obedience. Even the girl had the sense to show respect to the Queen of Egypt. She was lovely, lovelier than I remembered. I had not seen her last night when she arrived, but my general made sure I was aware of her presence. Memre would serve her as her steward, hopefully to guide her in subjects like proper etiquette and basic traditions, things expected of her from the court of Thebes. This was such a complicated place, yet she was intelligent and I trusted that Memre would help her assimilate quickly. I had my eye on other candidates, but in beauty, intelligence and bravery, the Meshwesh girl had exceeded them all. I quietly congratulated myself as I walked around her, examining her hair and clothing.

My servants had obeyed me and had not shaved her gorgeous hair, nor had they yet put on her the dark wigs she would soon be expected to wear. Perhaps this was a mistake, but I thought not. Why not let the courts see she had been touched by the gods with her flaming red hair? Why not let them look upon her natural beauty before I took her into my household officially? Her hair was in two braids at her temples, which had been swept up and gathered at the back of her head in an elegant bow. Her startling green eyes were lined with kohl, making them even more intense, and on her lips was a touch of pink. My servants had dressed her in a blue gown that fit her youthful body perfectly, and the material... Ah, the material. It had been sent a week ago to the palace as a gift for Kiya from my husband, who remembered she had admired it during a recent trip with him. My servants had wrangled the delivery from hers and upon seeing it, I could think of no one better to wear it than Nefret. She appeared calm now, but I could only imagine what she was thinking.

"You," I commanded one of the servants whose name escaped me, "bring me those gold cuffs." The young woman quickly retrieved the jewelry and stood before me holding them neatly on a pillow. I removed the cuffs and placed them on Nefret's wrists. "That will do. Leave us."

As I stood close to the girl I could see that she was not quite as confident as I had imagined. She shivered visibly, but I did not ask her about her health. *She had better not get sick, not after the investment I made in her.* Fixing my gaze upon Huya, I said calmly, "You may also go. Wait outside." He did as he was asked, leaving me alone with the Desert Queen.

"How do you like your surroundings? Are your rooms pleasing? You may look at me."

She raised her head, and her eyes were like two pools of a green sea. I felt as if eternity were staring back at me. Yes, she was the one. The priestess had been right.

"Yes, Great Queen. My rooms are pleasing. Thank you for your generosity." I walked around her, examining her slender frame. She was taller than I, which was no surprise, but also taller than many women.

"My general tells me that you left behind some family. Tell me about them."

"My father is Semkah, the King of the Meshwesh. Or he was king until his injury."

"And your mother?"

She looked puzzled at my line of questioning but had enough sense not to ask me questions. "My mother was Kadeema, the Princess of Grecia."

"And where is she now?"

"No one knows, Great Queen. She disappeared into the desert, and no one has seen her since."

"Ah, so it is true. I have come to tell you the truth today, Nefret."

"The truth?"

"Yes. You were not the daughter of Kadeema but of Isis. It was she who gave birth to you and she who placed you in the desert." The look of surprise upon her face amused me, but only for a second. She needed to take my words to heart, remember them and say them.

"I do not understand, Great Queen. I do not know Isis or any other god or goddess. Once I thought I knew one, but now I am not sure."

I grabbed her by the elbows and pulled her close. We were only a breath away from one another. I could almost feel her heart pounding like a frightened rabbit in a trapper's net. I relished these moments far too much. Moments when I held absolute power over another life. But this power was also a grave responsibility.

"Do not say such things. I am the Queen of Egypt, the Great Wife of Amenhotep. I am Queen of the World and Priestess of Isis. I speak the truth, and you need to heed and obey. From this day forward, you are the daughter of Isis. Say it now!"

"I am the daughter of Isis."

Gripping her arms tighter I said again, "Say it louder!"

"I am the daughter of Isis!"

I dropped her arms and stepped back. I captured the dancer's pose—holding my left arm high and my right arm pointed behind me below my waist, I curved my hands in the shape of the holy symbol.

"Do as I do and say it again." I made the girl repeat the sentence over and over again until I was satisfied. "Do not think for yourself. Do not imagine you have permission to think for yourself. You do not. I do the thinking in this court. Still, you have a choice, a choice I did not have. You can live as a prisoner, or you can become a true Queen. Those are your choices. There is nothing else."

I left the Desert Queen alone to consider my words. It would not go well for her if she failed to follow my instructions. I was surprised to see my daughter Sitamen waiting for me outside the doors of the Desert Queen's room.

"Sitamen, why are you here?" I asked in a flat voice. She looked me up and down, examining the garb I wore as Priestess of Isis. She knew the importance of this event, yet I had told her nothing. Why should I? I was the Queen of Egypt and not beholden to any man or woman, even if that woman happened to be my own child. I looked up at her, remembering to soften my voice a bit. She had always been a tenderhearted child, and the condition had gotten worse as she got older. I blamed the Monkey for her latest flares for the dramatic. Before the arrival of the Hittite woman, Sitamen had obeyed every word and followed my instructions perfectly; now she had sold herself to Kiya in exchange for a few pleasant words and false compliments. The girl was a fool.

"So it is true, then. You are bringing this foreign queen into our court, into our family. Why?"

"And you have been putting your nose in places it does not belong, have you not, daughter? I do what pleases me. Why should I explain anything to you?" Fat tears hung in the girl's dark eyes. Sitamen had her father's heavy brows and few of her younger sisters' good looks, but she loved her brother as she loved no one else. While they were young, they were inseparable, but unfortunately for Sitamen, she would not be Amenhotep's true wife. He did not want her, or at least that was what he said now. Men were nothing if not changeable.

Before her emotions overtook her capacity for thinking, I had considered Sitamen intelligent. With a gasp of frustration, I walked past her, and she did the unthinkable—she touched the sovereign without being asked. She grabbed my arm just as I had held Nefret's. I froze and cast a look back, reminding her who was mistress of this kingdom. "How dare you place your hands upon me?"

"Mother, Great Wife of my father, it is I. Have you no care for me? Have you lost your mother's love for me? What have I done—why are you doing this? I am your daughter! You have daughters—why have another?" The servants backed away from us respectfully and silenced their whispering. Sitamen jutted out her angular chin and said, "Am I not a queen too? I should know what it is you are doing."

In a flash, I reached under her wig and grabbed a handful of her thick, coarse hair. I pulled her face to me as she yelped in pain. "I know well what kind of queen you are, daughter. Do you think I do not know where you spend your evenings? How dare you place yourself upon *my* level? How dare you think you are *my* equal! There is no one here who is my equal, not even you—fruit of my womb!" With a savage twist of my hand, I released her, taking with me a handful of her hair. The tears flowed freely down her face now, and she screamed in anger. She reached for the silver knife on the table, my knife, the one I used daily to slice into my pears.

Suddenly Huya appeared in the antechamber, but I raised a hand to him and stopped him in his tracks. Whether she knew it or not, having a blade this close to the Queen of Egypt was a capital offense. Thankfully she was not foolish enough to raise the blade against me. Instead, my daughter held the knife to her own throat.

I laughed. I knew and she knew that she would never have the courage to take her own life. Sitamen pushed the blade into her skin, and a stream of blood flowed down her pale neck. I stopped laughing, but my eyes never left hers. "Go ahead. Drain your life's blood and be done with it. At least then I will be free of your tears." I walked away from her, unwilling to give her one more moment of attention. I heard her weeping behind me, but I did not turn from my purpose. Huya was beside me, and I said to him, "Make sure she is in the court and in her proper place. I do not care if she is dead—I want her there."

"As you wish, my Queen." He scurried away to take care of his duties, and I stepped out on the dais to face the crowd. There were hundreds of faces perfectly painted and observantly staring back at me. In unison, they bowed, raising their hands in respect to me. Once, twice, three times. I held my head high in my fine silver gown, a snake crown upon my brow, a blue scarf wrapped around my shoulders. I accepted their greetings and cheers with dignity as I stood on the dais. I did not sit, for no one sat before the arrival of the Pharaoh or his son. I could hear the crowd whispering—the excitement was growing. If what Sitamen said was true, the gossip had already spread through the courts. I wondered how many knew what I intended to do. There was a stir outside the court doors. My son had arrived, and the other queens were in their places in the lower court. I would not have to punish any of them today. The heavy doors opened, and I saw the face of my son, Amenhotep. He had been a friendly boy, sometimes friendlier than I preferred, but the people loved and respected their Pharaoh's son. Everyone, even the queens and I, bowed at his approach. As I rose, I studied him, remembering the boy I used to know. My mind was also filled with thoughts of another boy, my own precious Thutmose, victim of the schemes of the priest of Amun. They took one son, but they would not have another. Out of the corner of my eye I observed Kiya. She cast a lustful eye on Amenhotep, but she would never have him. In name only would she be his wife.

I turned my attention to Amenhotep. He towered above all those in his kingdom, even his father. He was built like a god. Today, he wore the double crown, reminding the people that he represented all, both Upper and Lower Egypt. In celebration of the special event, which he and only a few others knew about, his eyes were painted and he wore a fine necklace of turquoise and gold. A thoughtful gesture meant to please the Desert Queen. I wondered if she would notice.

Amenhotep climbed the steps of the dais and took his seat upon the throne of his father. It was an inspiring moment, even for me. As Great Wife to the current Pharaoh, it was my privilege to sit beside my son the Regent. He waved his hand respectfully to me, inviting me to take my place. I thanked him with a courteous nod and took my seat beside him. How thankful I was that he trusted me in this matter, and I would never forget it! I would have given my life for my son, just as I had been willing to give my life for Thutmose…if only I had known the danger he was in.

Huya waved his hand, and the court musicians began to play. The gathering whispered to one another, jostling to get a good position along the processional. Then a hush fell over the proceedings. The place was filled to capacity with curious onlookers. It seemed that even the paintings were peering down from the ceiling to see my new daughter. For the first time in a long time, my throne room seemed too small.

Horemheb and Nefret entered the outer court. Even from this distance I could see she made a striking figure. Slowly the pair walked down the aisle, and thankfully the girl did not gawk about her as if she were some farmhand. The people whispered, and she pretended not to hear them; as they approached, I sensed my son tensing. Yes, even he had an eye for beauty despite all of his religious ideas. Huya stood and performed a new song.

"In the name of Pharaoh Amenhotep, may he live forever, we welcome you, Horemheb, friend of Egypt."

As a dutiful and regular attendee of this court, Horemheb answered, matching Huya's cadence and tone. "It is with gratitude and a humble heart that I come here today into the court of my sovereign, Pharaoh Amenhotep, may he live forever."

"Friend of Egypt, what is your business here today?" Huya asked plainly with no song.

"Today I bring to court my niece the mekhma of the Meshwesh, Queen Nefret."

Amenhotep accepted her into his court by saying, "You are welcome in my court and in the court of my father, Queen Nefret." Respectfully the girl bowed her head slowly and showed deference to the greater monarch. I was pleased that she knew her place and did not need to be reminded to bow to her betters.

"Queen Nefret is the daughter of my brother Semkah and the Princess of Grecia, Kadeema."

"Stop!" I said firmly, shocking the crowd into silence. It was not customary for queens, even Great Queens, to interrupt a formal occasion. Still, this was why we were here today. "Is it not true that Kadeema, Princess of Grecia, the mother of Nefret, walked into the desert and disappeared?"

Surprised by my question, Horemheb stuttered and said, "Yes, Great Queen, that is true."

"There is no need to pretend any longer, no need to hide her identity, Horemheb, for I know the truth. She is safe now. I know who this Queen truly is." Horemheb wisely kept his mouth shut.

"Ever since I heard of this Queen, I knew the truth. And my historians have been hard at work to prove what I suspected." I leaned forward on my throne and looked down at the two of them. "This Kadeema, the beauty who disappeared in the desert, was not human. She was Isis, the goddess. For a time, she made herself wife to Semkah, the King of the Meshwesh."

I enjoyed hearing the gasps in the gallery. Even the wide-eyed girl looked surprised by my words. With a small smile I asked Horemheb, "Do you know who I am?" Without waiting for an answer I continued, "I am Isis incarnate, her representative in this realm. And this girl is my daughter." Despite my warning, I heard Sitamen gasp. I would deal with her later. I turned my attention to the waiting crowd. "Do you believe me? Huya, come now. Read the lineage! Let all hear the truth and welcome my daughter! Finally I can reveal what has been hidden all these years."

"Tell us, Great Queen, what have you found?" Amenhotep's deep voice boomed across the gallery. "Let us hear this lineage so that we may also welcome the daughter of Isis."

As Huya began to read the lineage, the court became more excited. At the end of the reading they clapped their hands respectfully, accepting the lineage that had been written.

Amenhotep spoke again, "Today I welcome you, Neferneferuaten Nefertiti. And as the Great Queen gladly receives you into her family as her daughter, so I receive you as my sister. From this day forward you shall be treated with respect and shall be loved by all of Egypt." Huya walked toward Nefret, dismissing Horemheb with a wave of his hand. He led her to Amenhotep, who then took her hand and turned her to face the crowd. She smiled and nodded gracefully to the gathering.

"I shall call you Nefertiti, for truly a beautiful woman has come. Welcome, sister." Then Amenhotep did the unthinkable. He led her up the steps and invited her to stand beside him.

"My sister. You are most welcome here."

The crowd erupted in loud applause again, and many people shouted her new name joyfully. While Nefertiti enjoyed the waves of applause and admiration, I caught my enemy's eye. She did not nod in respect as was the tradition when the Great Wife looked at you or acknowledged you in any way. Queen Tadukhipa's face was a mask. A hard, dangerous mask. Amenhotep invited Nefertiti to stand beside him as he sat again upon his throne.

Just as directed, the court dancers and musicians entered and the celebration continued. All the while Nefertiti kept her composure just as if she had always been there. Music played loudly as the artists twirled and bent their lithe bodies to the tune in homage to the newly revealed daughter of Isis. When the dance was over I stood next to her and said, "Nefertiti, I recognize you as my daughter." In response Nefertiti made the sign of Isis, acknowledging publicly that she accepted the lineage that was read and accepted her place in the court of Thebes. I stared into her beautiful green eyes and gave her a small smile as we enjoyed the adulation pouring in from the court and beyond. The crowd had grown beyond the courts. Word had gotten out that the daughter of Isis had returned home to her mother and her court. It was a day of celebration.

I spotted a scarlet-robed courier pushing his way through the crowd, and my heart pounded. He traveled quickly to the throne and waited to be recognized by Huya. In our court, the wearing of scarlet indicated a very select order of trusted messengers. I held my breath as the courier came closer. Amenhotep waved the crowd quiet. "And what message do you bring?" The courier hesitated, but only for a moment.

"Alas, son of the great King Amenhotep. I bring the saddest news. Your father, King of Upper and Lower Egypt, heir of Ra, son of Ra, Amenhotep, ruler of deeds, beloved of Amun-Re, King of the gods and Lord of the Cataract, Giver of Life, has passed from this world's realm." The servant fell to his knees with his head bowed and waited on word from his sovereign. I gasped at the news. My husband and beloved was gone from me, never to be held in my arms again. I felt the weight of grief fall upon me, threatening to crush me before all who were gathered in this place. In a moment, what should have been the first day of a long celebration turned into an endless agony. Wailing and weeping broke out in the court. My son walked quickly through the silent court out of my chambers, probably to return to his father's palace. The court emptied in a matter of minutes. As the people left, I stared after them. Memre, my faithful servant, the one assigned to care for my new daughter, whisked the girl away. The once full court was empty now except for Kiya. She stood at the other end of the lower dais, and our eyes were fixed upon one another for the longest of moments. Both our hearts were broken, but I made no gesture of comfort to her. I'd had to share Amenhotep while he lived, but I would not do so in death. She offered none to me either. I spun on my heel and left her alone. At this very second, my beloved was preparing for his trip to the land of Osiris.

With wisdom, my servants moved out of my way, and I walked as quickly as I could into my chambers. I felt the warmth rising in my eyes—I had to find a place to let the tears flow. It was Amenhotep's last gift to me—to grieve all alone. What a cruel gift! No one could see my tears. No one could witness my heartbreak. This was the will of Pharaoh.

I remembered the day he said the words to me. The days and weeks after our son Thutmose disappeared into the sands never to be seen again, the palace had wept as one. Tears were flowing constantly, and as mine flowed my heart broke continually. Amenhotep, powerless to help me manage my grief and powerless to save our son, gave the command that no tears should ever be shed in my presence again so great was his love for me.

Oh, Amenhotep! Do not forget me, my love!

Chapter Twelve

The Garden of Life—Nefret

The court had grown quiet during the long mourning for Amenhotep. I was still a stranger in this strange place. Despite the warm welcome offered to me by Queen Tiye and some of her family, I knew this was not where I belonged. Every night I still dreamed of the desert. I dreamed of the ever shifting sand, the brown, smiling faces of the people I loved. I dreamed of my sister, laughing and confident and happy just to be with me. And of course, I dreamed of Alexio, and every morning I woke to find my eyes damp with tears. If it had not been for my constant companion, Ayn, I could not imagine how I would have survived these long weeks. Tomorrow would be the fortieth day—the end of the official time of mourning for the late Pharaoh. And from what Memre told me, what would follow would be a sustained period of celebration in honor of the new Pharaoh and son of the deceased king, also named Amenhotep. Since that first day here at the court following my return from Zerzura, I had seen neither Queen Tiye nor her son. On many occasions, however, I did see Sitamen and Kiya, neither of whom deigned to speak to me.

The court of Amenhotep was a lonely place, but I was used to loneliness. I was used to being counted out. If only I knew what game I was playing—or being forced to play. All I knew was what the Queen had told me. Memre was close-mouthed in regards to what the Great Wife had in mind for me, but I was beginning to see which way the wind blew.

During the quietness, I had the freedom to explore the Queen's palace complex. At the centermost part was Pharaoh's harem. A fine building with colorfully painted columns, many fountains and an abundance of children and women. Some women never left the small palace, but thankfully I was not one of these. They waited on the pleasure of the new pharaoh, and I imagined they thought of ways they could please him and bring themselves into his favor. I had ventured into that inner court only twice but found no friendly faces there. How lonely an existence that must be to wait day after day, week after week in hopes that your husband—or in this case, your royal lover—would visit you and show you some attention? How sad it would be to be one of those women. I prayed that this was not my fate.

Today, Ayn was gone on one of her many errands, and I suspected it involved her lover, Ramose. I never told Ayn of my confrontation with him or his threats to me. I could have pleaded my case to her and perhaps even convinced her to help me see Alexio one last time, but I could not bring myself to do that. Ayn was my friend, my only friend now, and I would do nothing to jeopardize that. For without her I would be truly alone. Horemheb, as I now called him, came to visit me once a week, sometimes bringing small trinkets and gifts and always asking for permission to return to Zerzura. I never granted it and never intended to. I supposed one day I would have to let him return and care for his family and see his wife but at the moment it was not in my heart to do so.

I strolled along an open portico lined with pretty pink and red flowers and enjoyed the sound of droning bees and the smell of citrus fruit. Yesterday, this place had been full of scribes and we had been forbidden to enter. Now the outside wall was painted colorfully and appeared as bright as anything I had ever seen. I had a genuine appreciation for the language of Egypt, much of which involved pictures of strange creatures and bold warriors. They were stories, I was told, and the Egyptians displayed them on almost every wall—even the ceilings of many rooms in the palace.

Over the past weeks, Memre had done her best to teach me some of the words and meanings of these strange symbols. Although I could speak the language as well as any, the writing was a challenge for me. However, I kept at it. I was a storyteller at heart and enjoyed the idea of telling stories with pictures. I stood along the end of the wall and stared up at the figures before me at the center of the action. I could see a tall, thin woman with an elaborate headdress. She wore a blue gown and golden sandals. She was surrounded by rays from the sun, and under her feet was a cartouche. Looking around I saw no one in the immediate area and set about trying to decipher what I saw for myself.

Nf...ger...

I heard the sound of tools working in the soil nearby. There were frequently gardeners in this area, but I had not seen any earlier. I was surprised to spot one now. Thinking to leave without getting him or myself into trouble, I turned to walk away, but the gardener called after me.

"You there." I turned and saw him wave at me. I waved back politely, not thinking to linger, but he said again, "You there. Do you need help?"

"No help. I was just looking."

Taking no refusals, the gardener ambled toward me, leaving his tool in the rich soil of the garden. He was tall and muscular, quite different looking than the eunuchs. "It is no bother. Do you like it?" He pointed to the wall.

So surprised was I that he would speak with me, I stammered a yes. "I do like it," I said, adding with a smile, "but I do not understand its meaning."

"I did not mean to eavesdrop, but I could tell you were struggling with some of the phrases here." He pointed to the cartouche and gave me a friendly smile, and for some reason I felt completely comfortable with him. How strange.

"I was that bad?"

"No, not at all. You see this phrase—the very first one? This is the sound." He pronounced the letters, and we pieced them together. I was surprised to hear that the name was Nefertiti.

"That is me!"

With a delighted smile he said, "Yes, Majesty."

I gazed up at the wall. "What does it say?"

"It says: Beloved sister of Amenhotep, Neferneferuaten, Beautiful of the Beauties of the Aten. This wall is a tribute to you—to your beauty. It is a declaration from Pharaoh to the world. He placed it here because he wanted all who visit this garden to see the beauty of his new sister, the loveliest of blooms."

I could not believe my ears. Why would Pharaoh care to do this? "I do not deserve such a gift. I hardly know what to say. Although I'm grateful, I do not understand Pharaoh's generosity."

The gardener nodded. "It must be difficult to be in a new place, to know very few people. The answer, however, is very simple. Pharaoh wanted to honor his mother's daughter. Just appreciate his gift. That is all that is required."

"I do. We do not have such beautiful art as this where I am from. I am sure my tribe would be astonished to see it." My comment elicited a laugh from the gardener.

"Is this place so different?"

"Oh, yes. Yes, it is. For example, if I were home I would not be spending my days walking gardens or learning this language."

"What would you be doing?"

"I would teach my treasures to climb trees, swim in the pool with my friends, listen to the traders tell their stories." I had not meant to sound so sad. "Forgive me for speaking so. I did not mean—"

"No apologies are necessary." Then he added, "Did you have a large family? Many brothers?"

"No, I had no brothers. I had a sister once." Strangely enough it, was not Pah I thought of but Paimu, the little girl who loved me and trusted me. Until I left her behind. How I missed her. How I wished she could be here with me. She would have loved to see this place. I turned my attention back to the colorful painting.

"Tell me, sir, what do these mean, what is this? It is a strange sign to me, so forgive my ignorance."

"That is the symbol of the Aten. It illuminates all who see it and appreciate it. As you can see here, the Aten has surrounded Pharaoh's new sister, enveloping her in its warmth and light."

I studied it, not knowing what to think or say. Impulsively I touched the stone, tracing the ray that streamed from my hand to the symbols beneath it. "Do your people worship the Aten, then?"

"All should, but only some do. What about your people?"

"There may be some who do. Like Egyptians, the Meshwesh are free to worship whomever they choose. Some worship their ancestors, others worship the gods of Egypt and others worship tribal deities like Ma'at. Here it seems kings and queens are gods. That is very strange to me."

"And whom do you worship, Nefertiti?"

I chewed my lip as I looked up into his bare face. It was strange to see someone who did not wear kohl or wear his skin oiled. "No one in particular. I once dreamed of someone I thought was a god. He was a Shining Man, and he came to me in my dream speaking very kindly. And when he left me, I felt at peace. I've never seen him with my eyes awake, and his visits in my dreams are very few. Sometimes I wonder if perhaps I did not imagine him."

"Tell me more about the Shining Man." I told him a few things that I saw in my dreams, and I was comforted to know I had someone to talk to besides Ayn. Ayn did not enjoy talking about spiritual things. Once she had worshiped our ancestors but no more. Now here I was talking to a strange man in the garden about things I had not spoken to another living soul.

"I think you may be surprised with our new Pharaoh. He does not agree with many of the old ways and does not consider himself to be a god, although many around him want to bestow that honor upon him." In a soft, deep voice he added, "He worships the Aten—the Giver of Life."

"I must learn more about the Aten so I may speak to Pharaoh about the things he loves. If I ever see him again."

In a whisper he asked, "Would you like to see him again?"

"Yes, I would."

Someone was calling my name, and I turned to see who it was. I did not recognize the person but could see that he would not go away. I turned to say goodbye to the friendly gardener, but he was gone. I spun about and saw that even the gardener's tool had disappeared. I walked back to the steps to see what the man wanted.

"Yes, may I help you?"

"The Queen wishes to see you. Please follow me." I walked a long distance to a part of the palace I had never visited before. The eunuch opened the door, and to my surprise Queen Tiye was not in the room. Instead I saw the beautiful face of Tadukhipa, the one some people called Kiya. As we had not been formally introduced, I did not address her but merely stood in the doorway waiting for her instructions.

"Do not dawdle in the doorway, Desert Queen. Come in and take this bowl. Make sure my guests have been offered something to eat."

I did as she asked against my better judgment. The few times we had crossed paths in the past few weeks, I got the distinct impression that this woman did not like me and that her dislike was equal to my indifference. I could not understand why I had earned such a determined enemy, but I was often surprised by the women around me. Even my own sister.

Kiya's party was small. I saw Queen Tiye's daughter Sitamen lurking in the inner room, but she did not come out to greet me or speak to me. I carried the shallow bowl around the room dutifully and offered the selection of fruits to the women who attended Kiya's party. None accepted my offerings; in fact, none of them spoke to me. When I passed through the room with the bowl I dawdled around. Unsure what to do, I stood holding the bowl of fruit waiting for further instructions. Why in the world had she called me all the way here to serve her guests?

I had never been treated as a servant before, but she was a queen of Egypt. I looked at the steward, who pretended not to see me. I walked around the room again with the bowl, trying to stay out of the way. I had just decided to leave the unhappy company when Kiya made a strange sniffling sound.

"Well," Kiya said, sniffing the air as if she detected something foul, "what is this terrific smell? Camel dung? Is that the new scent from the exotic desert?"

Her game partner, Meritamon, shook the amber dice and studied the board before moving a marble game piece. Absently she answered, "Too earthy for me. What about you, Inhapi?"

The third woman did not speak but pretended to gag as she held her fingers over her nose and shook her head. The trio broke out into giggles. Anger whipped up within me like a desert wind. I let the silver bowl full of citrus fruits crash to the ground. It made a terrible clatter, and bright oranges bounced across the courtyard. Kiya sprang to her feet. "You pick that up, stupid!"

I stared at her with all the hatred I could muster. It was time to end this. I'd had enough of her snide comments. Very easily I could beat her to death with the bowl that lay at my feet.

"Never," I whispered ferociously. "I am not your slave!"

"Then I shall have you whipped like the goat that you are! How dare you defy me—I am the wife of Amenhotep! Pick up that tray, now!"

Before she could speak another word, Huya stepped out of the shadows from his hiding place along the outer wall. He was always lurking about. I had not noticed him before. He said nothing but merely stared at us. *Do not do what you are thinking*, his eyes warned me. I do not know what warning Kiya saw in his stare, but it held her anger at bay—at least for the moment.

The reality of my situation struck me as soundly as I imagined striking Kiya.

I was never leaving Egypt.

I had achieved the dream of all mekhmas. I had led the Meshwesh back to Zerzura, but there my story ended. With my sister now ruling in my stead and Alexio at her side, there was nothing left for me to return to. I knew the truth of the matter—my star had fallen, my destiny had changed. I would never see Zerzura or any of my tribe again.

Yet despite it all, I lived. I remembered Queen Tiye's words to me before she left for Thebes, "You can live as a prisoner, or you can become a true Queen. Those are your choices. There is nothing else."

I would not live as a prisoner, nor would I be Kiya's fool. I made my decision.

I took a deep breath and picked up the tray from the floor. As I picked up each piece of fruit I made a resolution. I would condition my mind—I would never think of Alexio, Pah or my father or any of the other Meshwesh again. I would not cry over them or burn incense to any foreign gods for direction and favor.

I knew what I wanted—what I must do.

I would become queen of all Egypt. I would truly become Nefertiti.

Chapter Thirteen

Sisters—Nefret

Another week passed without a summons from Queen Tiye. Although I could feel the positioning of characters around the court, I had no way of determining the politics behind the various moves. Perhaps if I had taken more time to cultivate a relationship with my uncle, I might have consulted him or at least asked him for advice. But as he was not eager to be forthcoming with information, I was less eager to ask him for it.

One afternoon Ayn and I accepted an invitation to hear the musicians play at the Peacock Courtyard. It was so named for the abundance of peacock paintings on the floor and walls and for the wild birds that roamed there. I enjoyed staring at these bold blue animals. They were not friendly but were lovely to look upon. Sometimes they shed their feathers, and I had taken to collecting them for decorations in my stark rooms.

Ayn and I took a seat on one of the empty benches and listened to the tambourines and lutes play fine tunes. The music was different from that of the Meshwesh. It was more melodic, more organized. One man stood before the gathering of seven musicians and raised his hands as if he were magically summoning the notes from the instruments. It was an amazing sight. To my surprise, Queen Tadukhipa joined the gathering and took a seat beside me on a nearby bench. We clapped politely between songs, and during one interim she whispered to me, "They play beautifully, do they not?"

"Yes, they do." This was a complete turnaround from the woman who had mocked me just a few days before. Once the music had ended and the musicians were leaving the court, Kiya turned to me with a sad smile. "Nefertiti. Sister. Please forgive my behavior the other day. Since the death of my husband it has been very difficult to be kind to anyone. You did not deserve such ill treatment."

"I do forgive you." I said the words as I was expected to, but my heart warned me that something was amiss. A shadow passed behind me, and I shivered. Sitamen had entered the courtyard. Upon seeing me, she gave a sound of disgust. Without a word, the girl exited as quickly as she had entered. Kiya laughed and called after her, but she did not answer.

Kiya said, "You must understand Sitamen's position. The poor girl wants to please her mother. To learn that the Queen has a new daughter...well, that was quite a shock to her."

"I deeply regret causing Sitamen any heartache, as she is the Queen's true daughter."

"Perhaps you two can be sisters," she said in a whisper.

"I have a sister," I answered defensively. Ayn poked me in the side, and I immediately regretted giving Kiya any information about myself.

"Yes, I heard. Pah-shep-sut, that is your sister's name?"

"No, just Pah."

"My mistake. I want to show my sincere apologies for my behavior by holding a banquet in your honor and perhaps introduce you, if I may, to my circle of friends. It has been my belief that it is always good to have more friends than enemies. I know a great many people would like to get to know you better. Would you be my guest this evening?"

"Unless the Great Wife needs me, yes, I will be your guest. Thank you, Queen Tadukhipa." In a rush, she rose from the bench and smoothed her gown. With a perfectly lovely smile she looked down upon me and gave me a courteous nod.

"Very well, my steward will come to collect you at dusk. Of course, you should come alone. There will be plenty of people willing to serve you, Nefertiti."

She left me staring after her, and Ayn poked me in the side. "Do not trust her, Nefret."

"Ayn!" I whispered to her viciously. "Be careful what you call me. You know the law here. My name is Nefertiti."

She stared at me suspiciously. "Have you forgotten who you are, mekhma? Who you truly are?"

Frustrated, I snapped, "What can I do but survive, Ayn? What can either of us do?"

"So you have given up, then?"

"What are you talking about? There is no rescue party. I am never going home, and as long as you serve me, neither are you." I hated the sad look that crossed her face, and I immediately apologized. "You must regret accompanying me. Egypt has not been a happy place for either of us, but at least you have your Egyptian."

She seemed offended by my comment, although I had meant nothing by it. "What does that mean, Nefret?"

"I told you to call me Nefertiti."

"I will call you whatever I like." Her hand rubbed her belly protectively. She did that more often lately as her belly had begun to swell. I secretly wondered what the protocol would be when the steward discovered that Ayn was pregnant. I had seen a few women swollen with child during my stay at the Queen's palace, but it was not an everyday occasion. Would they send her away? I prayed not, but I could not imagine that I would be allowed to keep a baby in my chambers. We had never spoken of it, but perhaps we needed to.

"Ayn, please. I did not mean to upset you." I reached toward her, and she squeezed my hand.

"Forgive me. I do not know why I feel so… so… so much of everything right now."

"Come walk with me," I whispered as we strolled along one of the private walkways in the Peacock Courtyard. I shooed one of the territorial birds away. I slid my arm through hers and leaned my head on her shoulder for a moment. "What does Ramose say?"

"I know he is pleased to have a child. I do not see him as often as I once did, but as you know he is not a man to share his thoughts with me or with any woman. Sometimes I think he loves me, and other times I do not. I do not know what I will do, Nefret—I mean, Nefertiti."

"You can go home, Ayn. Home to Zerzura. I release you from your vow to me. Go home and raise your child in peace in our city."

"Where he will be hated because of his father? I would rather stay here, if that is possible. I do not know how much longer I can hide the child, though. Memre watches me like a hawk."

"Memre watches us both like a hawk. In fact, she looks like one." At that we both had a good laugh.

"Yes, indeed." Ayn smiled at me, and we walked some more in silence. "What has become of us, mekhma? Did you ever imagine you would be here? I never did."

"No, I cannot say that I ever imagined this. I wish I could hear something from home. Some word about what is happening. Horemheb is punishing me, I think. He refuses to tell me anything, and yet I know he knows exactly what is going on."

"Did you know that he seduced your sister?"

I froze on the path and released her arm. "What? Omel and Pah? Why would she let him touch her? He is a repulsive snake—not to mention our uncle."

"He filled her head with promises. He promised to make her mekhma, and he was not alone in his choice."

I gulped. "Father?"

"Oh no. Your father was not involved in any of that. He was willing to let the Council choose, but he had no idea Omel was involved in the process. Omel even convinced Farrah that you were too weak to lead. I think she never trusted him."

"Yet she went along with the decision to make Pah the mekhma."

"Yes, but that was mostly because Pah had the sight. She could see in the fire *and* the water. Above all things, except for returning to Zerzura, Farrah wanted to see into that realm again."

"Why have you never told me this?" The sun blazed above us, and Ayn was visibly sweating. I saw my friend the gardener working in a corner and nodded to him as we passed. I hoped he would be around later so we could talk more. I took Ayn by the arm again and led her into the coolness of the palace toward our chambers.

"Why would I have told you? They were wrong. You were—no you *are* the mekhma by right. If not for the Kiffians, I think you would still be at home."

I considered her words for a moment and said, "No. Without the Egyptians we would never have found our home again. To think they knew the way and we did not! Fate is a cruel mistress."

Later that evening, Kiya's steward came to retrieve me. I had no idea what to wear for the evening meal, but at Memre's suggestion, I wore a plain white gown with a jade green necklace. I think Ayn was relieved to be freed from the prospect of an evening with Kiya. I wished I had been in her position, but if I was going to manage to survive in this court I needed to find an ally or two. At the very least I needed to know what my enemy was thinking. And Kiya was my enemy. I had no illusions about that.

I followed the pudgy man down the lighted hallways until I stood once again outside Queen Tadukhipa's chambers.

"Here she is. Our guest of honor. Welcome, Nefertiti." The queen clapped her hands politely and urged her dinner guests to do so as well. There were many more people than I had expected, but I smiled politely and thanked her for her invitation. In a great show of friendliness she kissed my cheeks and complimented me on my dress. She herself was dressed in a pink gown embellished along the hem with gold coins that tinkled as she moved. Her feet were bare, but she wore anklets and her arms were full of gold bracelets. Upon her head was a slender circlet in the appearance of a rising snake. As always, she wore a long black wig. The queen led me to a seat at her table, and I sat beside her. "Sitamen, our guest has arrived. Please, come and greet her."

The smallish woman approached me with her eyes downcast and her hands clasped before her. For some reason the motion reminded me of Pah. "Nefertiti, I am Sitamen. I'm very happy to meet you. Would you like some wine?" The crowd applauded at the kind words and gesture. Kiya thrust an empty cup into my hand, and Sitamen poured the wine with a demure smile.

"Everyone, please raise your glasses in honor of our new sister, Nefertiti. Let us welcome her to Thebes. Please introduce yourselves." The gathering obediently lifted their glasses to me. One by one they visited my seat and told me their names, and I quickly gave up trying to remember them all. I sipped the wine until it was gone and placed the empty golden cup before me on the table. After the formalities were complete, musicians began to play immediately, and I recognized the tunes from the concert earlier.

Sitamen sat beside me on a pink cushion. "Here come the dancers!" She clapped her hands ecstatically. "How I love these new dancers. Wherever did you find such talent, Tadukhipa?"

"My steward, of course. He has a keen eye for talent." Kiya raised her glass again and prompted me to do the same. Still trying to navigate these strange social events, I felt compelled to comply. I picked up the now full cup and took another sip. Yes, I could taste the herbs in this wine—some type of spices. It would be easy to lose yourself in these cups.

"Tell me, sister," Sitamen whispered in my ear, "do you dance? What do Meshwesh dances look like? Are they anything as fine as these?" With her knees pulled up to her chest and her arms wrapped around them, she studied me as she plucked some grapes from a bowl.

"We dance on special occasions, like at weddings."

"Oh, are you naked when you dance?"

I could not hide my shock at her question and laughed nervously. "No, we do not dance naked. I never have."

"That is a shame. I hear it is remarkably freeing. My mother—I mean, our mother—often tells me about her experiences with the Amazon women. She says they dance naked around a big fire before they go to war."

"That must be very difficult during the heat of the summer."

"Are you mocking me?" Sitamen's voice rose as her heavy-browed eyes narrowed.

"No, I am not. I am sorry you would think so."

She pursed her lips and said, "Who are you, Nefertiti? Really?"

"I am as you see me. There is no mystery here." Sitamen took another sip of her wine and raised her glass to me. As it seemed to be the custom, I took another sip myself but silently pledged to drink no more. I had abstained from eating anything before I arrived, as I had believed there would be food served at this banquet. And already my head felt light.

"If that is the case, then I want to hear all about you. Tell me about your sister, your true sister. Was she very much like you? And if so, why did my mother claim you and not her? If I am to believe that you are truly the daughter of Isis, would not your sister also be?"

I blinked at her. My head felt as if it were in a fog. How could a few sips of wine make me feel so woozy? "Why ask me these questions? Why not ask your mother?"

Someone at the other end of the table called to Sitamen, and with a final indignant look she left my company to visit her friend.

Kiya said, "She is very bitter, but she is also a sweet girl. Give her time to acclimate herself to the idea of having a sister."

"She already has two sisters, from what I understand."

"Yes, but they are very young and do not share her interests." She sipped her wine again and poured more in my cup, but I did not pick mine up this time. When a platter of bread arrived, I snatched a piece of it off and wolfed it down without a care for what I looked like. She laughed, and the sound was pretty but empty. "I had no idea you were so hungry. Here, have some of these." She passed me a bowl of dates, but my stomach was not cooperating with me. I felt sick. I rose to my feet quickly, which caused me to feel faint. My stomach did somersaults, and I had a growing suspicion that someone might have poisoned me. At the very least, my stomach was rebelling against the flavor of this Egyptian wine.

"Excuse me," I muttered as I walked out of the dining room and onto the balcony. Perhaps some air would do me good. I stood clinging to the side, hoping the world would stop spinning around me.

As I held onto the balcony railing and waited for the reeling to stop, I saw a man walking up the steps. He was simply dressed in a white skirt and a neatly folded headdress. His hands were behind his back as if he were in deep conversation with himself. His body shone with oils, and around his neck rested a wide gold necklace. As he walked toward me I recognized him. This was my friend the gardener. He did not see me at first until I hissed to get his attention. I did not want him to get into trouble. Men were not supposed to be here, especially after dark, unless they were eunuchs. Although I had no firsthand knowledge of my friend's status, I assumed he was not.

"You cannot be here. Queen Tadukhipa is just inside. Go now."

He paused and laughed as he stood on the top step. "What?"

"You cannot be here. There are no men here, especially gardeners. Now go away before someone sees you."

He laughed again. The curtain separating the dining room and the balcony opened, and the queen stepped out with the evil gold cup in her hand.

"Nefertiti. Drink this. It will clear your head." Seeing my visitor, she froze and bowed to him immediately.

"I can explain," I said quickly, trying not to vomit in the queen's presence.

She did not wait for my explanation. "Pharaoh! I did not know you were here. You honor me with your presence."

My heart thundered. "Pharaoh? What are you talking about?" I pushed my hair out of my face to get a better look. *This could not be true, could it?* As a wave of dizziness struck me, I clutched the low stone wall tighter.

"Tadukhipa. Is my new sister drunk? I will take that," he said, still amused. He reached for the cup, but the queen drew her hand back, sloshing the wine on the clean white stone beneath her.

"No, Majesty. Let me get you a fresh cup. You need not drink after us." Her eyes were wide, and I could see she had caught her breath. It was as I suspected!

Not used to being refused, he said, "Give me the cup, Kiya." With faux confidence, and trying not to react to the insult, she passed him the drink. I watched as he sniffed the contents and looked at her suspiciously. He held it to his lips, and she stiffened. "Is that juniper I smell? No, I cannot drink juniper. Here, you drink it." He passed it back to the queen, and she did as he commanded. Her face became unreadable as she stood holding the empty cup. He waited for a few seconds and then said to me, "Come, Nefertiti. Walk with me." My head and stomach were still revolting against me, but I managed to place my hand upon his and together we left the wretched party.

"I think she poisoned me."

"No. If she had, you would be dead already. However, I would not put it past her to make you sick. Most people do get sick on juniper wine when they first drink it. I suppose if you were to believe my mother, Tadukhipa might do that. Just to embarrass you before her court."

I nodded, thankful that I would not die, no matter how miserable I felt. "I feel sick, Majesty. I am sorry."

"The best way to reverse the effects of juniper wine is to walk."

After a brief pause I accepted his hand again and did my best to keep up with him. "You are Amenhotep. I thought you were a gardener."

"And that is what I wanted you to think. I had to know you for myself, Nefertiti. A man cannot always rely solely upon his mother's word. However, she was not wrong. And it is true that I enjoy the act of planting and bringing forth a harvest from the ground, but I do not share that knowledge with many people."

"Wait. Your mother was not wrong about what?"

"Wrong about you. You are both brave and lovely."

I did not understand completely what he was talking about, for my head was still foggy and my mind screamed that I was walking with the Pharaoh of Egypt. I had expected him to be completely different. Pharaohs were cruel—they were distant kings, untouchable by their people or by anyone—but Amenhotep was not so. He was real and available and a friend. On his arm I glided down the last of the steps, and we walked out into an area of the palace I had not yet explored. My stomach still swirled in turmoil, but I did not slow my pace.

"What is this place? I have never been here before."

"I would imagine not. It is the Great Wife's private gardens. She rarely comes here anymore since my father left for the life beyond."

The dark trees gave off a fragrance I had never smelled before. I breathed it in and found it helped clear my mind somewhat.

"That is frankincense you smell. It is the scent of kings. Did you know that?"

I shook my head and smiled as best I could.

There were white stones under our feet, and birds chirped at us as they settled down for the night. The sun had set, but there was still much light in the walled gardens. "Why did you let me believe you were a gardener?"

"As I said, I wanted to know who you were." Finally, we sat together on a bench under a cluster of palms. He removed his headdress, and I could see close-cropped black hair. And although he did not wear as much kohl as some, he was very much an Egyptian. "I have not stopped thinking about our conversation, about this Shining Man you saw. I have to tell you the truth. I have seen him too."

I could not hide my surprise. "Truly? When? What did he say?"

"He told me that he was the Giver of Life, that he was in everything, that he was the breath we breathe, the life within us. He promised me that he would help me rule my kingdom and that he would guide me throughout my life."

"If you trusted him," I added, remembering what the Shining Man had told me.

"Yes," he said with a surprised laugh. He rose to his feet and took me by the hands. Looking into my face tenderly, more tenderly than any man ever had, he asked, "Will you come with me?"

"Where are you going?"

"I am going on a spiritual journey. I want to find the home of the Shining Man, as you call him. I call him the Aten. I want to find his home and then build him a temple worthy of him. There are no temples to the Aten here; the gods of Amun and Ra own this city. I dream of a new home, a new Egypt. I want all my people, even my slaves, to experience the love and peace that the Shining Man brings. The great Aten deserves the praise of all Egypt. Come with me..." and then he added in a low voice, "and be my queen."

Perhaps it was the wine or his words. Maybe it was the Shining Man. I do not know. I do know that was the night I fell in love with Amenhotep. That was the night everything changed.

In my mind's eye I remembered my dream, the dream of running through a darkened city of stone, a child running behind me.

Smenkhkare!

I would never forget the child's eyes—the eyes of my son. And I was seeing them now. They were the eyes of Amenhotep.

Still under the influence of the juniper wine I whispered, "I have seen my future, and it is you." With a happy smile he put his hands under my chin and tilted my face to him. He kissed me, and the kiss was a promise. A promise of a friend who would walk beside me on this unusual path, the path determined by the Shining Man.

A few hours ago he had been the gardener. Now I would spend my life with him. For him I would abandon all others.

I was now the Queen of Egypt.

Chapter Fourteen

Blue Scarab—Ayn

Nefret had departed the city with Pharaoh, leaving me behind without an explanation. No matter to me—I was burning for Ramose. When I was not crying. Motherhood had weakened my emotions to the point I could not trust myself to speak to anyone for fear that I would snarl at them like a beast or weep at the friendliest word.

I would be lying if I did not acknowledge that I was hurt by Nefret's slight, but then again I was only a servant now. Perhaps I should go home. At least there I would be free.

When Nefret returned to her chambers after Kiya's banquet she was quiet—quieter than usual, and she spent a lot of time staring out the window at the stars. There were no longing looks toward home. Normally she would have told me everything, but that night she remained mute.

The following day, before she departed, I went to the kitchens to find food for the two of us. The palace was abuzz with the news—Nefertiti would be queen. I returned with a bowl of food, some fresh fruit, bread and cheese and barely got through the door before I asked her if the rumors were true. I need not have bothered. Servants began pouring into her chambers, sent by Pharaoh himself. Some carried fine clothing, others jeweled chests containing more jewels. This was all the proof I needed. With excitement Nefret—no, Nefertiti—welcomed them and opened all her treasures.

Sullenly I watched it all. Naturally my mind went to Ramose. It had become more difficult to see him. When I visited the training grounds now he was never there, or if he was, he was too busy to come to the gate to let me in. Yesterday I went to the practice field but was turned away.

Today I was determined to see him—my situation was becoming more desperate, and if Ramose did not agree to help me, then I would have to find somewhere else to take my seclusion. The last thing I wanted to do was return to my tribe with an Egyptian child. I knew I would not be welcome there despite Nefret's recommendations or influence. Children were cruel, even Meshwesh children. No, my son, for I was sure it would be a son, needed to be with his father, the General of Egypt. I had to make Ramose understand—I had to show him how important it was. In the flurry of activity in Nefertiti's chamber, I left easily enough. I wandered around until she left and then I turned toward Ramose's barrack house where I worked during the day training young soldiers and developing plans for Pharaoh's campaigns, which Ramose complained were too few of late.

As I turned into the brick building, a familiar soldier spotted me and disappeared into the inner offices. *So much for surprising Ramose.* I waited patiently outside the barracks—it was not wise for a woman to walk in unattended even though the men there knew who I was. I was pregnant, but I was still strong and could handle myself if necessary. At least that is what I told myself. As I hoped, Ramose walked out to greet me. Before he could send me away I said, "I must see you. If I don't, I will have to leave."

He took me by the elbow, led me into his office and ordered his men to leave. They followed his orders, and only a few cast me sidelong looks. A few months ago they would have been beaten for even looking in my direction. That was not so anymore. I kept my head held high and did not show them the shame they hoped to see on my face. I was a Meshwesh warrior, not some camp follower. I loved Ramose—yes, this was love. I had given myself to him freely, and I felt no shame in it.

Was he going to help me, or should I leave? That was the question. I was not afraid of him, for I knew he would never harm me, but he could be cruel with his words. And as my heart had been quite tender of late, I did not want to engage in a painful discourse. I need not have worried because his lips were upon mine. His right hand kneaded my tender breast, and his left hand went around my waist. I kissed him back, welcoming the warmth and taste of his lips. My desire for him rose as it always did, but my mind would not allow me to surrender without knowing first what he intended.

"Listen to me first." I resisted his embrace, and my lover did not hold me. "What about my son? From what I am told, I cannot stay in the palace in this condition. I will have to leave, Ramose—leave with your child—unless you help me."

"What are you asking me?"

"Do you want me to stay?"

Ramose was never a man who enjoyed talking about his feelings. That I knew. Yet I had to know. I was not so good a lover that I could read his mind. He would have to talk to me.

"I think I have a solution if you will hear me out."

"Very well."

"You know that my wife and I cannot have children. That is plain to me now, but perhaps the gods found another way to bring my son to me."

"Yes, they have," I said with a smile. Feeling a surge of love for him, I reached for his hand and placed it on my belly. "See? There he is, moving and kicking already. A strong boy—just like his father."

Ramose's dark eyes displayed his emotions perfectly. He did want this child—more than I had first thought. I began to feel hopeful again. He had not cast me off—not yet!

Gently he rubbed my shoulders and said to me in a serious tone, "Ayn, you must give the child to me. My wife and I can raise him as our own. She is willing to do this—I have spoken to her already, although it was difficult to do so. Inhapi understands the ways of the world, and she is willing to accept my son, but…"

I could hardly believe my ears. "But what?"

"After today, I cannot see you again. What was between us is no more. That is the price. I am sure you agree it will be worth it."

I stepped back, nearly falling over a pile of empty beer pots. "What? Give up my son? To Inhapi?"

"Stop before you harm yourself," he said gently as he reached for me. "I am not asking you anything unreasonable. It is done all the time here. The gods chose you to be the mother of my son, but surely you knew that I would never put away Inhapi. Nor can I deny her this request. She has been a good and patient wife to me."

"Good and patient? I would not use those words to describe her. Nor would you, until this day. How can you ask this of me? Do you not know that I love you? I have given you my body and been your lover these many months. Why tell me this now?"

"Calm yourself. We never spoke of love, you and I. We were two warriors who battered against each other and found some comfort in one another's arms. I admit that I care for you—care for our son—but this can never be anything more than that."

Never would I have imagined such words would fall from his lips!

I felt as if I were being smothered. I had to get away—out of his presence. I walked toward the door, but Ramose blocked me. "I have to know your answer, Ayn. If you do not agree to this, you will have nowhere to go. Inhapi will see to it that you are turned out of the palace. She has powerful friends, my wife."

"And you? The mighty General of Egypt? You are powerless to stop her? That is what you want me to believe? Curious turn of events, Ramose. I wish I had known from the beginning how weak you truly are." To my utter surprise, the man I had loved so fully slapped me savagely. I fell to the ground immediately, and blood filled my mouth.

I did not stay down for long. "You hit me again—touch me again—and I will kill you." He did not try to stop me again, nor did he strike me. I left the barracks and practically ran back to the palace. The many faces I encountered were a blur to me. They were strangers, and as I ran realization dawned on me. I needed to go home. I could not stay here; there was nothing for me in Egypt. I must leave, even if it meant losing myself in the desert.

I did not enter the front gates of the palace. I chose the side entrance, showing my face only to the palace guard stationed there. He let me pass, although he did look curious at my appearance. I clamped my mouth with my hand to prevent the blood from leaking out. By the time I made it to Nefret's chambers I had a mouthful of blood, which I promptly spit into a nearby bowl. Then the tears came freely. I had no worries about snooping servants; since the new queen was absent, there was no one to spy on me. I could hardly believe my sad situation. I had always prided myself on being wiser than most women, stronger, more independent, and here I was in the same situation that stupid farm girls found themselves in every day.

When I pledged myself to Nefret I had intended it to be for my whole life, but now I had to put my son first. I had to leave Thebes. For where, I did not know. All I had to do now was wait until she returned. I could not in good conscience leave her without speaking to her. I must thank her for all the things she had done for me. She trusted me when no one else would—indeed, I did not deserve such favor. I had been a fool for Pah, and now I was Ramose's fool as well. I refused to be Inhapi's fool too!

I decided I would stay in Nefret's chambers and steer clear of everyone until she returned. It could not be forever, could it? If she did tarry too long, I would simply have to leave. Ramose had made it clear that Inhapi would seek revenge if I did not agree to her terms.

I lay on my bed, the tears gone. My mind swam with possibilities. I dreamed of my mother's arms holding me, swinging me up into the air as she told me to fly, cradling me when I burned with fever. *Oh, Mother...I miss you. How I miss your arms!* In my dreams, I buried deep in them and lay my head upon her chest. I could hear her heart beating, feel the warmth of her skin, smell the scent of the garlic and onions from her kitchen.

It was as if I felt her arms now. I shook myself and found a face hovering over me. Inhapi!

She shook me awake, and I snatched myself from her grip.

"Get up, whore! Get up now!"

"What? What are you doing here? Who let you in?"

Without hesitation she climbed over my bed and came after me with something evil and shiny flashing in her hands.

"I gave you a chance. I gave you a chance. If you do not willingly give me my child, I will cut it out of you."

"You are a madwoman, Inhapi! Leave now!" I threw the bowl of blood at her. It stained her dress and clattered on the floor.

"Go ahead and scream. I hope someone does come. You are to be turned out, Meshwesh whore. Your Desert Queen will not help you now. And the true queen here, Tadukhipa, agrees with me. You and your red-haired friend have to go."

I surveyed the area. My weapons were in the closet, and I could easily kill Inhapi, even though she did not know it. If she did not cease her attack, she would find out. "I warn you, Inhapi. Do not test me. I have been fighting much longer than you, and I will hurt you."

"You can try, Ayn, but you may not find me so easy to hurt. I am Ramose's wife, remember? I know about hurt." She circled around the room. There was a small table nearby with a flat platter on it.

Grabbing the platter with both hands, I warned her again. "Leave now or you will regret it."

"I could say the same to you. If you manage to make it out of this room alive, you had better run as fast as you can because you will never be free. Do you think you are the first, girl? No, you are not. And you will not be the last."

"Then why are you here? Should you not be talking with your husband?"

She waved the knife at me stupidly, and I smoothly ducked her. I felt less worry now about the immediate danger, having seen firsthand her amateur style. She had no fighting skills, except those involving poison and gossip. I put the platter down and waited for her to swing again. She did, and I grabbed her wrist easily, shook it and watched the knife clatter to the ground. "Let go of me! Keep your filthy hands off me."

Feeling tired and frustrated, I whispered to her as I held her close to me. "Why? Your husband did not mind my filthy hands at all." With a vicious scream she slammed her head into mine and punched me in the throat. Crumpling to the ground, gasping for air, I stared up at her in complete surprise. Then she fell on me, and the knife appeared again. She raised her hand above her head and brought it down as if I were an animal sacrifice and she an evil priestess. Grabbing her hands desperately as I wheezed for breath, I twisted the knife and in a clumsy move, she fell on the blade. It slid into her easily, and she collapsed beside me.

"Oh gods! Inhapi!" I stood over her as her mouth moved like a fish needing water, just as mine had a moment ago. I watched in horror as the woman stopped breathing and her blood seeped out on to the floor. Now I had to go. I could not wait for Nefret. There was no time to pack or plan. I grabbed Nefret's cloak and the blue scarab that Ramose had given me some time ago. I looked back sorrowfully at what I had done. It had been an accident, but who would believe that? The general's lover—a foreigner—killed his wife.

Death would be coming for me, with all of Egypt.

Oh, Ramose! How could you do this to me? How could you betray me? Now you will hate me, and we will forever be separated. If not for our child I would have thrown myself off the balcony, but I could not. I had to live. If only for him.

Chapter Fifteen

The Aten—Nefret

When the litter stopped at the dock, I could scarcely believe my eyes as I peeked out from behind the sheer curtain. I had heard of boats and had seen men fish from small flat ones at the Biyat Oasis once, but this was altogether different. This boat was larger than any I could have imagined, and already the sounds of celebration had begun even though Amenhotep and I had only just arrived. A billowing white canvas was staked into the ground, and we were invited to embark under it. Unsure how to behave, I followed Amenhotep's example. I kept the smile from my lips and trained my face to remain unaffected by it all. It was a difficult task.

As soon as I stepped on board my stomach lurched, but I hoped the unsettled feeling would subside soon. If I could survive juniper wine, I could survive anything.

The boat seemed more like a floating palace than anything else. The flat, wide bottom must have helped keep the thing afloat, and for the first few minutes I had a secret fear that we would all sink. More billowing fabric hung from the sides, protecting the occupants from the bright Egyptian sun. It floated and popped in the breeze that blew in from the river. The cedar floors were sturdy, and I could see carpeted floors just inside the doorway. Stepping inside after my attendant, I marveled at the blue walls bursting with images of crocodiles, birds and a myriad of other fascinating animals that were unknown to me. We walked through the open room and through another door. Inside was a bedroom with sumptuous carpets, flickering gold decorations and the faint smoke of incense. I swallowed nervously and looked about the room.

It appeared I would share my chambers with Amenhotep, but that did not surprise me. I was to be his queen now.

"Your bed is made, lady. Food is here too. Would you like me to pour you a bath?"

"Maybe later. What is your name?"

"Menmet, lady." She cast her eyes down, but I could see a small smile on her face. Menmet had an interesting accent, one I had never heard before. She was small, not as petite as Queen Tiye but much shorter than I. And she wore very few clothes. Her gown was sheer, so sheer that I could see her dark nipples through the fabric. Egypt was a strange place. I hoped I would not be expected to walk around so. I blushed and turned my attention to my surroundings.

I walked to an open window and watched the crowd that had gathered at the dock. A few well-wishers had followed us, but now there were many, including a large number of priests. I knew these were the priests of Amun because they wore leopard skins. No others, besides Pharaoh, could wear those. They stared at us, whispering amongst themselves.

"Menmet. What are they doing here?" I might as well ask someone who might know the reason for this gathering. I counted two dozen priests now, and the numbers were growing.

"Lady, those are the priests of Amun. They come to protest this journey."

I was shocked. "Why? Because of me?"

"Oh no, lady," Menmet's narrow eyes widened that I would ask such a thing. "Not because of you, Beautiful One." She whispered, "The priests of Amun do not like the Aten, and they think the Pharaoh is wrong for taking this journey to honor the god. They say to us that there is no real god but Amun, and the priests of the Aten say the opposite." She stared back at them and stuck out her tongue.

"What about you, Menmet? Whom do you worship?"

She sighed as if it were the most difficult question in the world. "Whoever I am with, I worship their god. It is much more peaceful that way. How do I know who is right? I leave those things to the priests."

"Oh, do not say that, Menmet. You can worship whomever you like. Do not let someone else dictate to you who to worship. I do not think Pharaoh would wish that."

She shyly pretended to examine her feet but said nothing.

"What is it?"

"You can say this, lady. You are the daughter of Isis. I am the daughter of Heb and Shupset." Her tone was not disrespectful; it was matter-of-fact. She believed every word. I knew I was no such thing, except to please Queen Tiye.

"Nefertiti!" Amenhotep came into my chambers and surveyed the arrangements. "Do you like your room?"

"Yes, Majesty. I do."

"Good. Very good." He stood with his hands on his hips, his smile brimming with confidence. "Rest now, and I will come to you before sunset. Together we will watch the Aten leave the sky."

I bowed my head in agreement, and he left. I had guessed wrong. He did not plan to share my room. This boat was very big indeed to house us all. "I am not sleepy, Menmet. Let us arrange the things." I could feel the boat move and said, "Ooh…" I sat down quickly.

"Poor lady. Have you never ridden on a boat before?"

"No, I am afraid not."

"It will pass soon. Let me get you some wine."

I made a face and asked, "It is not juniper wine, is it?"

She crinkled her nose, and for a moment she reminded me of Paimu. "I would never serve you that, lady. No, this is good wine from a land far to the north. They call it…what is it? I cannot remember, but I will be right back."

I sat in the chair and clutched the sides as I waited for Menmet to return. I drank what she brought me, and she was right. There was nothing as sweet and delicious as this northern wine. After Menmet led the other women in arranging the room, they lay down in various places. I lay on my cool bed, the wine helping me to sleep soundly. I woke with Menmet talking in a low voice.

"Lady, Pharaoh has come. Rise now, lady."

I climbed out of the bed, sipped some water and exited the chambers under the watchful eyes of my twelve ladies. Amenhotep waited for me along with another man I had never met before. I did not get an introduction before the man departed, and together Amenhotep and I walked to the edge of the boat. The sun was very near the water. It seemed as if it would disappear completely in just a moment. We dared not turn away or we would miss its departure. I did not know if this was the Shining Man, but Amenhotep seemed convinced that what I saw was what he saw. I prayed silently that the Shining Man would visit me again, although I did not pray to anyone directly or in particular.

"Now, Nefertiti. I will show you how to worship the Aten. These are sacred moves that only the initiated can offer the god. Are you ready to learn?" I remembered the greeting of Isis—the one Queen Tiye demanded I learn. I hoped this one was as simple. I nodded and he said, "Watch me."

Amenhotep stretched out his arms and raised them above his shoulders, creating an arc with his hands. Then he pushed his hands outward and bowed low toward the sun. He said, "Aten, Giver of Life, your light shines upon us all." Repeating the gestures, he invited me to follow him. We practiced, and I picked it up easily. Or so I thought.

"Almost. Turn your hands like this." Amenhotep stepped behind me and gently closed his hands around my wrists. "Up, then turn them like this." I followed his movements, out, up, and then I leaned forward, pushing my hands in front of me. His nearness felt comforting and not awkward at all.

"Let us say goodbye to the Aten now." Standing a few feet behind him and off to his right, I mimicked his steps, which he had not shown me previously. They were not difficult to master. We did this three times and then watched the Aten disappear. "Let us do this every day together, as long as the Aten rises and sets."

I smiled up at my future husband. I hoped he would always be as kind to me as he was this day.

"Tomorrow we will go to the Grand Temple and I will show you the monuments of my father."

"Very well," I said pleasantly as I watched the last of the light disappear. "I look forward to that."

"Shall we go dine?" That sounded like a wonderful idea and I told him so. My stomach sickness was long gone, and I could not wait to break my fast.

Like most meals, music played, happy people chatted and every-one hung on Pharaoh's every word. For this meal, he did not say much but we did bump hands once as we both reached for a slice of fruit. He kindly offered it to me and then sliced himself another one. I studied him as discreetly as I could. He was tall, taller than me, thankfully. His father must have been a tall man. Queen Tiye was remarkably petite. He had full lips, not feminine but well-sculpted. Amenhotep had large hands, but they were not clumsy or awkward. He was not the most handsome man I had ever seen, but he had a confidence and an inner joy that made him more at-tractive and interesting than most men I had known. Although I had to admit that I had little experience with men, except for Alexio.

I blushed at the thought of him. No! I swore I would not think of him. I suddenly worried that I would be forced to undergo another excruciatingly embarrassing examination. Surely not. I had heard that Egyptians did not care about those kinds of things, but the rules were often different for kings—and queens.

Leaning toward me, Amenhotep whispered in my ear, "I would very much like to kiss you right now. You are truly a beautiful woman, Nefertiti."

I wished I had worn my hair down or worn a wig because I could feel my ears warming as I blushed. I said nothing but smiled into the wine. Menmet was beside me suddenly, asking me if I needed more wine or food. I nodded and listened to the music. Most of the songs were happy tunes, often without deep meaning, but this one was different. This was about a man who waited on the shore of the river for his true love, who had sailed away on a boat. He pined for her to return, hating himself for some mistake he made. I could not help but feel sorry for him.

> *Sail back to me, glorious face*
> *Return to me, my own heart*
> *For you have taken mine with you*

Without warning I thought of Alexio and how I had sent him away. How I would regret that forever! What if I had taken him with me that day, as I had intended, instead of Ayn? It was too late now, too late to go back and change things. He had taken my heart when he left—just as the song said—and I had sent him away.

I felt my lashes dampen. Amenhotep leaned close to me again, and the smell of his cedar cologne was comforting. "No more of that. Play something lively," he said to the musicians. "This is a celebration, Nefertiti. Why are you crying?"

"Forgive me, Majesty. The song reminded me of home."

"Someone you miss from home?" he asked warily. I knew better than to confess to him my heart.

"No, Majesty. The song told a story, and we are a people who loves storytelling. It may surprise you to know that I myself was a storyteller." I attempted a weak smile.

He sat up and turned to his small court. "Would you like your future queen to tell you a story?"

I should never have told him that. Now what?

As the people began to exclaim excitedly, "Yes, tell us a story!" I began to ponder what to say. Thankfully inspiration came quickly. I slid out of the chair and stood in the storyteller's position.

"Menmet, you shall help me."

"Yes, my lady," she said obediently as she took her place at my feet.

"Hear now the story of Acma, the King Who Captured the Stars."

Still smiling, Amenhotep leaned back in his chair and clapped politely, as did all who attended. I took a deep breath and began my story.

"Acma was the oldest of five brothers. His father was a good king but indecisive and sometimes weak with his counselors. As the father got older, he thought more and more about who he should choose to lead his kingdom after his departure into the next world. Naturally, his first thought was for his oldest son, Acma. Acma was tall and brave and a natural leader. Once he had killed a lion with his bare hands—a feat that greatly impressed the entire tribe. Other voices, members of the king's council, encouraged the king to consider one of his other sons. For you see, Acma had very few friends amongst the council. He was not like his father. He was not swayed by popular opinion, but he was a principled man. So in that way, he was a better man than his father. Acma was so brave and so strong that many were jealous of him. These evil counselors wanted nothing more than to see Acma lose his right to rule.

"The king's heart was torn. He believed Acma truly deserved to inherit his throne, but he felt he had to listen to his counselors. So the king concocted a competition. He would task his sons with a difficult challenge—bring a lost magical item back to the king and demonstrate how it worked. Whoever brought back the most wonderful and unusual item would immediately be made king. When the queen heard about this challenge, she pleaded with her husband, but the king was immovable on this point.

"The following day, the king called his sons to the court and issued the challenge. 'My sons, my days on this earth are limited. I hear the voices of the other world clearly, and my time here will soon end. One of you will be the next king. But as you all are so honorable, so brave, it is hard for me to decide.'

"This statement disturbed the youngest son, Axymaha, who said, 'Father! Acma should be our king. Of that there is no question. Why must there be this challenge?'

"Before the father could answer, the other sons mocked the youngest boy, declaring him a coward and unwilling to take up the challenge. The following day the brothers left to pursue their quest. The middle three sons rode in three different directions, hoping to find the elusive item that their father tasked them with. But Acma had another idea. He was not going to pursue some ancient relic in a faraway land. He knew who he must turn to for help.

"He went to Axymaha and said, 'Come, let us weave a net.' They gathered the supplies and began to weave the net.

"The counselors were amazed at this. They visited the two sons and mocked them. 'What is this? Are you going fishing? You misunderstood the challenge, Acma. This is why you will never be king. You are too stupid to rule.'

"Their words angered Axymaha, who was eager to defend his brother's honor, but Acma told him to keep his peace and continue weaving. Soon the counselors wearied of their fun and left to report to the father what his bravest son was doing. Hearing that Axymaha and Acma were disobeying his challenge, the king summoned them to question them. Surely Acma would not do such a thing! Acma obeyed his father, and he and Axymaha returned to the court, bringing the net with them.

"Just as they returned, the other sons did too. One son brought the king a gold-lined cloak that when worn would make the king young again for as long as he wore it. The king tried it on, and indeed he did appear younger. But soon the cloak grew too heavy to wear and he removed it." I waved at Menmet, and she pretended to put on a cloak. The crowd laughed at her antics. She was quite a good actress.

"The second son gave the king a vial of blue liquid. When the king drank the blue drink, he could see clearly into the Otherworld." Menmet pretended to drink an invisible drink, and her eyes grew large as she "saw" into the Otherworld. "Seeing the kings who had gone before him seated at a feasting table made him long to go there. The liquid's power soon faded, and the king could no longer see that wonderful place.

"Another son gave the king a beautiful necklace made of gold, silver and pendants of red stones." Menmet pretended to tie on a necklace and touched the stones with her hand. "The stones glowed when a lie was spoken in their presence. To test the truth of this, the king asked everyone to speak to him, one at a time. While his sons were found to be honest with their words, the counselors were not. Once the stones began to glow, the angry old king ordered the liars executed. As they were hauled away, begging shamefully for their lives, the king called Acma and his youngest son forward.

"'You see the things your brothers have brought me. What can this net do? Haven't you made it with your own hands? What magic can be in that?'"

I paused in the story here. In the Meshwesh version, Acma gives the answer, "Magic is within us," but for my future husband I decided to change that phrase.

"'Father, with every twist and loop of this rope, we prayed to the Aten,' Acma said." I heard the gathering whisper, but with one look from Pharaoh they became silent again. I continued, "'We pleaded with him to grant us our wish, and he has done so. Watch now, Father!' Together, Axymaha and Acma cast the net high into the sky." Menmet did the same, and I helped her give the illusion that we were the sons casting the net. The crowd laughed again. "So high was the toss and so magical was the net that they captured many bright stars with it. Then they carefully pulled the stars down to earth and held the net in place as their father watched in amazement.

"'This is truly wonderful, Acma! You and Axymaha have captured the stars! But why, my son? What magic is in this?'

"'You may walk upon them, Father, and they will carry you safely to the Otherworld. You see? The Aten has granted us our request.'

"'Yes, I see!' Very excited about traveling to the Otherworld now, the old king kissed his wife and hugged his sons. He stepped on the stars and stood with his hands on his hips. He said a few words of thanks to Acma and Axymaha and declared Acma king. On his command, the two sons released the net and the stars returned to the sky, taking the old king with them. From that day forward, Acma ruled as king, and his brother Axymaha served in an honorable place all his life. The net was burned as an offering to the Aten as it rose the following day. And from that day forward, everyone in Acma's kingdom worshiped the Aten, for it was he who so graciously gave them a true king."

I waved my thanks to Menmet, who smiled back at me and then cast her eyes to the ground. Now I could see why. Amenhotep was leaning on one arm watching me. The look in his eyes told me he was thinking intensely about my story. I remembered myself after a moment and so too cast my eyes to the ground. A hush fell over the hall as we waited for word from Pharaoh. Had I made the wrong choice? Said the wrong thing?

Then he began to clap loudly. I felt relief wash over me as the people joined their Pharaoh in applauding. He stood and called one of his servants to him. "Bring me the gift." So startled was I that I looked him full in the face without permission.

"Nefertiti, I had no idea you were such a skilled storyteller. There was much truth in the words you spoke. It is indeed the Aten that is worthy of our worship, and you do me a great honor by including the god in your story." I blushed and said nothing despite my relief. "This gift is for you. Open it now," he directed his servant. The old man eased the lid of the wooden box up, and inside was the most wonderful necklace I had ever seen. It was a falcon, its wings spread open, the wingtips held by a gold chain. Encrusted with colorful, shimmering jewels, it almost seemed alive.

I reached out to touch it. "It is beautiful, Amenhotep. Thank you."

He smiled, and deep grooves appeared on either side of his full lips. "You are truly pleased?" he asked in a deep voice.

"Beyond description. It is the most beautiful thing I have ever seen."

He removed the necklace and stepped behind me. It felt cool on my skin and heavy, much heavier than my green necklace had been. "It is fit for a queen, I think. My queen."

He stood in front of me now and surveyed me. Pleased with what he saw, he took my hand and led me around the room so the gathered guests could greet me. Without fail, each applauded loudly and said, "Well done, Queen Nefertiti." When we finished our walk we left the gathering and walked into my chambers. My servants immediately disappeared, leaving us alone. I could see that someone had scattered silky, fragrant flower petals all over my floor. I followed the path and saw where it ended. In my bed.

I looked up at Amenhotep, and he said tenderly, "There is no sense in delaying the inevitable, is there? I want to be yours, and you must be mine. Tomorrow, my priests will meet us at the Blue Stone on the way to the temple. There we will be joined in marriage, and from that day forward you will be Queen Nefertiti. Later, we will have a large wedding with many formalities. But tonight, let it be just Nefertiti and Amenhotep, children of the Aten and the Shining Man."

I swallowed nervously, suddenly wishing I had drunk more wine. "Very well, Majesty."

"No, remember. Tonight I am only Amenhotep." He leaned against a nearby cabinet. He was tall, so tall that I felt small standing next to him. He removed his crown and set it to the side, running his hands through his short hair. Following his example I released my long hair from the ebony pins that Menmet had poked in my hair.

As I reached for the necklace he said, "Let me help you." I turned and lifted my auburn curls. He removed the heavy necklace easily, and I could hear it clink as he set it next to the crown. He kissed the bare skin of my neck, and I froze as warmth filled my body. Amenhotep rubbed the arch of my neck and let his hands wander over my shoulders. I faced him and kissed him freely. His hands were in my hair, and his kisses became more urgent. Images of Alexio tried to stir in my mind, but I refused to think about him. I enjoyed the moment, Amenhotep's fragrance and the expert touch of his hands. I could see he was no inexperienced boy but a man who knew how to please a woman.

Breaking away from his embrace for a moment, I untied the gown and stepped out of it. He watched me with an appreciative, serious smile, and we walked to the bed. He stripped his tunic off quickly, and I let my eyes drift over his athletic body. As I stood naked in the cool chamber I felt a moment of doubt. What was I doing? Then reality set in. What choice did I have? I remembered Queen Tiye's words again. Yes, I would be a queen and not a prisoner. Who was to say that this was not what the Shining Man wanted? We fell into the soft bed together; our hands were hungry for one another and our kisses increased our passion.

"Amenhotep," I said in a whisper. He shuddered slightly, so I said his name again as a small smile curved on my lips. I refused to let my mind race. I would be present in this moment. So what if I did not love him with the white-hot fervor of my first love? He was worthy of love, and I had been chosen to love him. I could not deny that I wanted him.

"Nefertiti," he said, "You are mine now. All mine."

"Yes," I said as he entered me. "I am yours."

Despite the building passion between us, Amenhotep did not hurry. He moved slowly at first, kissing my breasts and face. He was playful and patient. I got to know his body and felt as if he completely enjoyed mine. I had not expected that. It was a happy surprise.

Sometime later, we lay in the tangled sheets of my bed. His fingertips traced my face, and I kissed them.

"Do you think you will ever love me?" he asked me quietly.

"What do you mean?"

"Love is not easily produced, and sometimes it never comes. I am no fool in these matters."

"I am sure you are not, Amenhotep. I think there are seeds of love here in this very bed and in our hearts. Let us water the seeds."

He smiled, showing his beautiful teeth. His eyes were now lined with kohl, but I remembered how he looked as the gardener. Those were kind eyes, the eyes of a good man. Yes, I could love a good man. "You are very wise. From whence comes such wisdom?"

I thought of Farrah, Mina and my father. "My tribe. They are a wise people." He kissed my hand, and we looked at one another as the moonlight fell in on us from the open window.

"We are your tribe now. We are your people," he corrected me.

"I know this. Forgive me." I kissed his hand back. "I perceive that you are a good leader—one who cares about his people. For that, I am grateful."

"I have so much to do. It weighs on me sometimes," he admitted. "I am glad to have a partner in this dream of mine. A city—no, a kingdom—that serves the true god. The Aten."

"You have to know that not everyone will be happy about such an idea," I warned him.

"I know this full well. One day I will tell you about my brother; then you will know how aware I am of the price that has been paid. But no talk of kingdoms tonight. We are just two people, not kings or queens. Remember?"

Feeling bold, I slid out from under the sheet and laid my head upon his chest. I wrapped my leg around him and held him close. If this was all I had, I would make the most of it. I heard his heart beating evenly and loudly. I refused to close my eyes, for I did not want to dream about Alexio. Amenhotep caressed my arm, and soon we were kissing. After a few moments, I could feel the urgency rise in him and he was covering me again.

"What are you doing?" I said with a playful laugh.

"I am watering those seeds you were talking about."

I laughed again and kissed him wildly. Sometime close to morning, we fell asleep. I did not dream about anyone or anything. I woke feeling tired but peaceful. Amenhotep was gone, but Menmet drew my bath and prepared me for morning worship. This would be my life now. I was at peace with that. If I could help Amenhotep lead his people to peace and protect my own, so much the better. At least my life would have been worth it.

"Someone did not sleep long enough, I see. Our Pharaoh is an amorous man." As Menmet's statement was not a question, I did not feel compelled to answer.

"My hair is a mess. Perhaps today is a good day to don one of those beautiful wigs."

"Oh yes, my lady. You will look like a proper Egyptian then." She knew by my look that I was offended but quickly apologized. "Please, lady queen. I did not mean that."

"I am too tired to worry about it. Help me get ready."

"The water is hot. Enjoy the bath, and I will go find you something beautiful to wear. Is that acceptable?"

I nodded and stepped into the water, the sore parts of my body thankful for Menmet's thoughtfulness. I called to her, "Nothing that shows my breasts, Menmet." She obeyed me, and somehow at the appointed time I was ready to stand with Amenhotep to welcome the sun. This was the first time I had worn an Egyptian headdress, and I felt nervous about it. When I saw Amenhotep's face I knew I had made the right choice.

"My queen," he greeted me with a look of appreciation.

"My Pharaoh." I nodded at him, trying not to picture him as I had seen him last night. We took our places aboard the deck and, as the attendees watched, made our morning oblations to the Aten as it rose. When it was done, we disembarked with plans to make our way to the Blue Stone. I had never been, but I was anxious to see Amenhotep's kingdom—and my new kingdom.

As we stepped off the boat I saw we had a visitor waiting for us. Ramose. Immediately I thought the worst. Something was wrong at home. Zerzura had fallen. *Oh no!* Dutifully the rugged-looking general slid off his horse, wisely remembering that no one should be higher than the Pharaoh.

"General, I am surprised to see you here. What has happened?"

"Forgive me, my Pharaoh. I have disturbing news to share with you. If we could speak." He indicated that he wished to speak in private, but Amenhotep did not grant him an audience.

"You may speak before my queen, General. What has happened? Out with it." I could see Amenhotep was not a man who was accustomed to asking anyone anything twice. I warned myself to remember this. Ramose's face demonstrated his surprise at the announcement that I was now queen.

"My wife has been murdered by the queen's servant. I seek permission to pursue this girl. I believe she has gone back to her Meshwesh home."

"And you had to come out here to ask me this?" Ramose had something else to say, but he refrained when Amenhotep raised his hand. "What is this servant's name?" Amenhotep asked.

"Ayn," Ramose replied.

"Do you know anything of this?" Amenhotep asked me.

"Ayn came with me, yes, but I know of no plan to kill Inhapi. As far as I knew, Ayn and Ramose were…friendly." I added, "Ayn would not kill unless she were threatened."

"We have no time for a trial now. You may search for the girl, but if she is in Zerzura, do not pursue her. My wife will make sure she is returned in that case. I do not want to send the army of Egypt to steal back one girl. Is that all?"

Ramose wisely held his tongue. Amenhotep continued, "Then that is my command. You may retrieve the girl, but do not harm her. If she has gone home, you will wait. My wife will arrange her return when we return to Thebes."

We climbed aboard the litter prepared for us, and I watched as Ramose and his man returned to Thebes. He had not gotten the audience he wanted, and now I had the Pharaoh's ear. How could Ayn have done such a thing? Why? There would be time to discover that truth, but now was not such a time. This was my wedding day.

I felt Amenhotep's hand in mine and squeezed it. He had been correct. A crown was a heavy thing to wear. Perhaps that was why the mekhma never wore crowns. Serving our people had been a joyful thing. But now I was more than the mekhma of the Meshwesh.

I was truly the Queen of Egypt.

Epilogue

The Falcon Rises—Pah

The woman's eyes glistened as she rubbed my skin with mint oil. The cool sensation soothed my red skin, which had been burned during my trip to Thebes. My head itched still, even after the round-hipped priest had shaved my head and rid me of the ragged haircut left by the Kiffians.

Why was I here? I could not remember clearly. I took the cup of clear water that the priestess, Magg, handed me. Magg, that was her name. As I drank, I felt refreshed for a moment. It was in these moments of clarity that I remembered who I was—or at least who I had been.

And what I had done.

Now here was Magg again covering me with a comfortable, loose robe and leading me to the balcony that overlooked the center of the city. We were up high—higher than any hill I had climbed. I caught my breath as I wrapped my arms around a green painted column. The wind whipped my robe, tossing it in the air and showing my bare legs. Magg pointed and clapped and said something to me in her unintelligible, toothless language.

I looked down in the direction of her pudgy finger and saw her. A woman on her knees before a massive gold throne. Musicians were playing a frantic tune, and the people cheered the woman's name.

Nefertiti! Nefertiti!

The woman beside me repeated it, "Nefertiti! Nefertiti!" She nudged me with her arm, coaxing me to say it too.

It was my sister. I released the column and slowly walked to the edge of the balcony to get a closer look. I could not stand without feeling dizzy, so I knelt and leaned over the edge. My sister raised her hands and said some words that I did not hear. The crowd roared in response, and the man who sat before her rose, reaching out his hands to her. She slowly ascended the steps and took the seat beside him. The meaning was clear. My sister Nefret had her own crown now. She would rule as the Queen of Egypt, and I…

Why was I here? Alexio! I turned to Magg. "Where is Alexio? Where is my husband?"

"No man here. No man at all. This is the home of Isis, and you are her priestess. No man."

"I have to go home. Why am I here?"

She said something else I did not understand and waved around her. "Home of Isis. You home."

"No!" I said as I ran back into the temple and toward the dark green doors with the long golden handles. As I ran I could see the doors were closing. "No!" I screamed as I ran faster. The doors closed in silence, and I beat my fists against them until I fell to the ground in a heap.

Now I remembered how I got here. I had been walking. Walking with Astora. We were looking for the white flowers for my father's tea. He was better now but needed the flowers to get stronger. I had kissed Alexio goodbye and promised him I would return soon. The night before I had slept the entire night without any nightmares, although I did see Farrah and Paimu hovering outside my window. Sometimes I forgot my name and the names of the people around me, but he was always there. My Alexio.

See, Nefret? It is me he loves. You left, and now it is me. Just me.

Alexio, help me!

That is what I shouted when Astora led me outside. She struck me, and I fell to the ground. When I woke up, I was heaped across the back of a camel and my shoulders were burning in the sun. I screamed and screamed, but in the desert, there is no one to help you. I thought my captors were Kiffians, but I soon learned they were not. Just slavers and mercenaries. They were sent to find me, and they had.

Then I passed out. I woke up again and was staring into the eyes of the bright-eyed priestess. Who had done this? Nefret? Astora? I could not imagine, but I was tired, too tired to cry or struggle anymore. I walked back to the balcony, unafraid of any punishment the priestess might give me. She grunted at me and waved at a small table of food. I grabbed a piece of bread and shoved it in my mouth. It was stale and hard to swallow. This was not chula bread at all.

No more bread from home for me. Would I ever see home again?

The sound of her name echoed throughout the city: *Nefertiti! Nefertiti!* I looked up in the sky expecting to see a bird, and I was not disappointed. Others would not see him, but I could see his silvery outline there, just above the courtyard where my sister now sat.

Farrah had been right. The falcon would rise—and it had. Now nothing would stop it from soaring above us all.

I had been wrong. I was not the falcon.

I had always been the Bee-Eater.

The Kingdom of Nefertiti

By

M.L. Bullock

Dedication

To Nicole, my cousin and fan of my first story, "Eyes in the Fire."
We scared ourselves silly!

All my love, Mimi

Chapter One

Sacred Markings—Astora

My Meshwesh husband's tribesman raised his bushy eyebrows at me when he saw my new sacred markings. The scrolling stars were now emblazoned across my forehead, and I refused to wear a head cloth to hide them while they healed. I was not ashamed! Let the people know that I had power! In fact, let them fear me. Orba left my presence as quickly as he came, forgetting what he wanted to say to me. I laughed at his back. Weak man.

Good, I thought, *I was in no mood for his petty complaints today.*

I had bigger things to think about. I let my mind wander as I sewed the last stitches on the robe's hem. How fortunate that I had saved this fine fabric; it would prove useful since no one had seen it. Except my husband, Omel, who had given it to me. I could trust him. I rubbed the soft silk and touched it absently to my cheek.

I missed Omel. It had been a long time since we had lain together, shared bread or even spoken to one another. Our relationship was not a romance like the one I had dreamed of as a young girl, but it was practical and comfortable. When I married him, I had been sure we were destined for greatness. This painful separation was all thanks to the half-breed girl who called herself both mekhma and Queen of Egypt. I snorted at the idea. The world had far too many queens these days. How could it be that she, a commoner from an obscure bloodline, could be queen? I hissed at the thought of my husband's niece wielding power—power she would un-doubtedly use against us. How could she deny him rulership of the Meshwesh? Pah was of no use to anyone, and with Alexio's inter-ference I could neither visit her nor speak with her.

Omel and I had given so much for these people to have received so little in recognition and honor. Did my husband not deserve honor? It was his tribe that saved the Meshwesh. They were the bravest and fastest warriors in the Red Lands, and yet the one-armed king still reigned, thanks to his daughter's influence, no doubt.

And I? I had lost Suri—my only son—my heart and breath. My reason for living. Everything I had done until that day had been for him. He had only begun to ride with his father, to learn how to rule. Now he was no more.

When I agreed to marry Omel, long before Suri entered this world, I had prepared the way for my dear son. Omel had promised to put all his sons aside for mine, for I had been sure I would have a son. He had easily agreed, for he had not loved his other sons' mothers as he loved me. He had been handfasted twice before me; one woman died in childbirth, another of a mysterious fever.

How easy that had been!

No one brought me Suri's body to bury or even presented me a clipping of his hair. I begged Omel to retrieve him, but he refused, saying it would do no good. I assumed that there was not much left of my son's young body. My husband's refusal made me hate the Meshwesh even more.

To this day no one recognized Suri's sacrifice—he was a king's son, after all. No one missed him. None of his brothers or cousins mentioned his name; it was no secret that they did not love my child. Even my husband did not mention his name except on the occasion that I presented him with a votive dedicated to Suri. I could then see the emotion in his eyes and feel his brokenness. We held one another for a long while, but then he was gone again. Now I had empty arms, and the pain of the loss was so deep that it had stolen even my tears. I would no longer touch my son's warm brown skin or shove his dark, silky hair out of his eyes as he swatted my hands away. I would no longer need to make honey cakes every day for his hungry stomach or wash his feet at night.

I accidentally stabbed myself with the needle and quickly shoved the finger in my mouth to stop the bleeding. I could not stain this garment. The spilled blood could reverse the magic or present a result I did not expect. What I was doing was dangerous enough. I snatched up the robe and walked inside my home. The light had faded, and I had much to do. It was usually about this time of day when my son would burst into our tent and ply me with kisses for food.

No, I would never forget Suri. In fact, I would avenge him if it was with the last breath I took.

I had taken my blood vengeance on the Kiffians for their part in his death. I had simply stolen a cloak from one of their dead and snuck into their city once the gate had been breached. Very few women and children were in their camp, and I suspected many were merely prisoners, but I found a boy-child who had the look of one of the Kiffian giants. I found him and quickly killed him. When his screaming mother charged at me, I killed her too. By then the chaos of the battle had crept into their small encampment in the west of Zerzura, and no one thought anything else about me. In fact, no one even knew I had left the wagons. Except perhaps Orba, who had dogged my every step. Or so he thought. I smiled as I smoothed the robe.

What pretty fabric! Rose gold silk with a shimmer of metallic thread. The perfect outfit for a seductive dancer. It had been a thoughtful gift, but it hardly made up for the loss of my son. My husband had showered me with Kiffian plunder before he left for Thebes.

Poor Omel. I had no illusions when it came to him. He married me because the blood of Neferue, the daughter of Hatshepsut, the long-dead Queen of Egypt, flowed through my veins. She had been a true queen! My Egyptian family had long since fallen out of power, but unlike them, I would not deny the blood that coursed through my veins. And I planned to be a queen of another sort.

I had not told Omel my plans beyond a few whispers on our pillow. As always he warned me about my scheming, but I knew he appreciated my work. Besides, he would know soon enough, for he would see me. The less he knew at this crucial juncture, the better.

He had seen my painted skin bring the power he desired time and time again, yet this power frightened him. Men had frail souls. What a joke of the gods! They gave men the physical strength and women the mind of leopards; intelligent, fast and able to make a decision—even a deadly one when needed.

If only I'd had the power to kill Orba! That would have solved many problems. But his magic always overwhelmed me. Sometimes it blinded my second sight, and other times it came at me in waves and made me physically sick. Once I thought he had poisoned me, so sick was I, but it was only magic. Gnarly, old Meshwesh magic. But it was no true match for one who had the power of Egypt coursing through her body!

I needed to leave, at least for a little while. If Omel could not come to me, I would go to him. He needed me—of that I was sure. And my Suri needed his blood vengeance, or he would dwell in darkness for all eternity. The debt must be paid, and it must be paid with the blood of Semkah's children! Pah had the mind of an idiot now; killing her would be doing her a favor. She had been useful in the past, but not anymore. It was Nefret, the upstart, who must pay the price for Suri. Her father's stubbornness had caused this! How long had Omel warned him to accept Egypt's hand of protection? If it had not been for Semkah we would not have been in Timia when the Kiffians stormed across that oasis. If it had not been for Semkah, Suri would be alive—my son would have breath in his body. Now he was no more.

And that was why I called the little boy to me from my window.

I spotted him after I finished folding the robe. I smiled at him in an attempt to allay his fears. My tattoos frightened children, but I had a friendly smile and wide, dark eyes—eyes that children seemed to trust if I wanted them to. Ah...I knew what to do. I picked up Suri's old toy and walked to the doorway. I tapped on the toy goat skin drum and offered the cautious boy a chance to play with it. As I did, I surreptitiously glanced around me to make sure no one saw me. It was dusk now, and the approaching darkness cast purple shadows on the white stone buildings and walls of Zerzura. A lute played tumbling notes a few doors down. I could smell chula bread cooking somewhere. The boy stepped closer— he was only a few feet away now.

"Sumer! Come to me, son!" the boy's stupid mother called to him from a nearby doorway. The boy smiled at me once and then turned and ran home through the white stone arch.

"Curse you, child," I muttered under my breath, scowling at his shadow. I stormed inside my home and flopped in a chair until opportunity brought me another warm body. Another child, a girl-child, came into my home unbidden and unwelcome. Intrigued by her boldness I did not beat her or turn her out.

"Astora? I am Ziza. My mother has sent me to find you. She says my sister Amon is not well. Will you come see her?"

Cautiously I asked, "Why doesn't she call Leela? I am no camp healer. Leela will be happy to heal your wretched sister." I felt sullen and petulant, not realizing the gift the goddess had sent me.

"She does not trust Leela, Astora. She says she trusts only you."

Curious now, I asked, "Does she indeed? Who is your mother?"

"Mareta. You know her. She brings you doves sometimes and the purple flowers that make ink. She says you know how to make the water flow, but I am not sure what she means."

Finally, I recognized the hand of the goddess at work! The girl's mention of the flow of water was a secret phrase that only another acolyte of Ahurani would know. I had thought to take the boy's blood, but it was the girl's blood that the goddess wanted—and she had sent another servant to convey that message to me. "Go now, Ziza. Tell your mother to come to me at once. There can be no delay. If she wants her child healed, she must pay the price. And you must return with her." Thoughtfully I added, "Tell your mother that the flowing water needs a rock to wash over." A true follower would understand my meaning.

Confused but not stupid enough to ask more questions, the girl sprinted from the tent to tell her mother the good news. While I waited, for I was convinced she would return, I prepared the things I would need. A small, gold-handled knife, two leather straps with the sacred knots tied into it and a small offering bowl with a lid. The bowl was made of green jade, something not often seen in the Red Lands or even in the White City of Zerzura for all its hidden treasures. No, this gift came from my father's home-land, and its beauty and craftsmanship rivaled any Egyptian ex-ample. It was Persian-made, by the hand of someone who under-stood and respected the dying magic. I had dwelt there for a time as a girl. It was a good place to live—until I was cast out. One day, I would return in victory, taking my Meshwesh husband with me. Then he would see true power!

"Step inside, please," I called to the woman without looking up from my table. She lingered outside my door, and I heard her gasp in surprise. I did not bother to explain to her that I had heard her sandals on the stones outside and needed no magic to perceive her approach. I could tell she was easily impressed. That both pleased and saddened me.

I welcomed her inside and pointed to the table. I recognized Mareta but had not spoken to her much before this day. She had a square face, small, pale brown eyes and a sleeping, plainly sick child in her arms.

I wondered how she would react when I demanded the due price for my healing magic. Fortunately for her, I did not need to kill the girl—not today. All I needed was her blood—at least a small bowl full.

Rather than alarm the sick child or her sister, I spoke to Mareta in the old language. "I need your daughter's blood. The goddess requires it."

"Which daughter? This one is sick."

"I need good blood, so this one. Ziza is her name?" The girl looked from her mother to me; hearing her name mentioned must have surprised her. With a nod, Mareta laid the sick child on the table and without hesitation clapped her hands once in agreement and bowed her head.

"As the goddess wishes," she said respectfully.

"Good. I will heal your child, but first we must tend to this other matter. The stars that guide me are traveling this way, and this spell is at its most potent under the sign of the bear."

"What is this spell, Astora?"

Although she had the courage to ask me, I did not feel compelled to tell her. I merely smiled. I could feel the woman's excitement at being included in Ahurani's work. We were sisters even though I barely knew her, sisters serving our goddess. Ahurani was a goddess of water and healing, but we kept her name quiet here for many feared her and her husband, Ahurani Mazda. I am glad they feared her, for that meant they would fear me too.

"We will have to tie her down, I am sure of it. She is a fighter. I can tell by the look of her. Does she know nothing of our goddess?" I scolded her.

"Yes, she is a fighter. I have not trained her in our ways, priestess," Mareta replied in the secret language. I could hear her thoughts...*for I barely know them myself.* If I survived this and returned to Zerzura, I would have to remedy that.

I could see the curious girl cast a fearful eye over my knife and bowl. In a flash, Mareta clapped the girl's mouth shut with her hand as I lifted the child's small body up and placed it on the pallet. Vainly she kicked and twisted.

"If you were wise," I said in a low whisper, "you would not fight this, Ziza. Today, you serve the goddess of your mother. This is an honor only a few get to enjoy." But Ziza did not stop screaming, and Mareta continued to muffle her cries. She whispered to her, trying to calm her, but her daughter saw the knife and feared it.

"I am going to take your blood, Ziza, but not all of it. The goddess does not require your life today. Your blood is precious to her; it is sweet and innocent, a fitting offering for this work." Expertly, I tied her feet and hands together with the straps. She struggled as her mother clamped her hand harder over her mouth.

I could have been kind and numbed the area before I sliced it, but I did not. I took my curved blade and slid it into the plump flesh of the child's left palm, right where it curved to make the mound of Ahurani. Many did not know it, but this was the seat of power for the soul. I made a clean slice, and the girl screamed in panic. If I had cared to look, I would have seen her eyes full of tears. I did not. Did she think she was the first child to feel pain?

I pressed the wound with expert fingers and drained the blood into the bowl. Feeling victorious, I covered the jade bowl and slid it with its precious contents back into place in my cabinet. I would use it when I was done with this current task. "See? You are not dead." Mareta untied her daughter while I wrapped her hand with a clean bandage. As soon as she was free, the girl ran out of the house like a fool. Mareta called after her, but she did not answer or return. What did it matter? I did not care who she told now. I had what I wanted, the blood of an innocent. What could be more powerful for what I had in mind?

I quickly examined Mareta's sick child and sent the goddess-sister home, promising to send for her soon. The child had a climbing fever, but I assured her mother it was nothing serious. The child would not die. Once Mareta left me, I quickly forgot about the sick girl. I took the blood-filled bowl and searched for a quiet place where I could be alone under the stars. I remembered the abandoned courtyard that no one visited. I had half claimed it as my own, and it would be perfect for what I needed to do. I drew the sacred symbols in the sand and tossed the holy items into the center of the circle. Still holding the bowl, I fell on my knees and beseeched the goddess to send me to Egypt. "Send me," I pleaded with her. "My son needs his vengeance. Please do not doom him to dwell in darkness."

I raised the bowl above my head and removed the lid. In the holy language, I spoke the words of power and drank the bowl of blood. It was bitter and metallic, so I swallowed it quickly. I had not eaten in many days, and I thought I would vomit it up, but I did not. I lay on the ground in the circle and waited for the change to happen. I waited for Ahurani's response.

Again I pleaded with her, "Take your revenge through me, goddess. I will defeat Egypt's queen for you! Let all fear you!" I whispered into the darkness. Even though my stomach felt sick and my head swam with grief I waited, hoping to see the evidence of Ahurani's approval. I began to wonder if she refused me, but then I felt the change begin. My skin crackled and my bones hurt. In the darkness I stared at my hands and could see the skin smoothen. I now had smaller, younger-looking hands. The tattoos had disappeared! I lay still for a little longer, allowing the goddess to shape me how she wanted. I knew this had been her will! I had indeed heard her voice! She accepted me and approved my plans. Ah, but this was deep magic. What price would this cost me? In my excitement I pushed the fleeting worry away. This was a grand honor!

My body began to convulse, and pain shot through me like a dozen flaming arrows. I flailed under the weight of Ahurani's invisible hand until I passed out. Sometime later, I woke to see that the stars had moved in their courses significantly. I had slept for many hours, but now the process was complete. I scrambled to my feet and walked back to my white stone abode. I was so ready to see my new self in the mirror that I practically ran to my table. I stared into the gold-framed mirror. Moonlight bounced off the white stone outside my window and illuminated the room enough for me to see that I had truly changed. I was younger, fairer. I appeared a strange blend of Ziza and Astora, with no tattoos and extremely long hair. If I had to guess, I would say that I appeared to have seen a mere fifteen seasons. I was very pleasing to look upon. Yes, this incarnation would do quite well for the Egyptian court. Even Pharaoh would not be able to refuse me.

I immediately began to pack my bag. This illusion was a gift that would last only until the next full moon. Then I would be exposed for who I was—the wife of Omel, the true and rightful king of the Meshwesh. There was also another danger. Any person who truly knew me would not be fooled by this magic. I had to be careful to keep myself hidden until I was ready to reveal my true identity. Excited, I stuffed the rest of the items I needed in my bag, including the lovely robe with the enchantments woven into the stitches. Yes, time was my enemy, but I was determined to take vengeance for Suri. Even if it cost me my life, this was all that mattered.

I had forgotten the sick child who was still lying on my table. Setting my bag down for a moment, I retrieved the pouch of medicine I would use for the healing magic from my nearby cabinet. As I began to burn the herbs in the small silver brazier near the child's head, I noticed that she was not breathing. The breath of life had escaped her lips while I had waited on Ahurani, and she no longer dwelt in this realm. Perhaps the goddess had required more than I had imagined? Perhaps the bowl of blood had not been enough? This was unfortunate, yet I could not call her back. I touched her tentatively. Her body was cold and no longer a suitable host for her soul. I blew out the flame and walked out of the house. I had no time to tend to a dead body. Her mother would find her soon enough. At least she could claim her and send her to the Otherworld with the proper ceremonies. My son dwelled in darkness.

The girl had served her purpose, and now I must serve mine.

Chapter Two

Bright Horizon—Nefertiti

Amenhotep and I spent another day exploring one another's bodies, stopping our mutual appreciation long enough to worship the Aten, eat a light meal and perhaps soak in one of the refreshing pools in the palace. How easy it had been to lose myself in that discovery! I felt love, a deep, surprising love—one that I never expected. My husband declared that I would accompany him always and had even moved my belongings to his personal quarters. According to Menmet, my maidservant and confidante, this was never done.

"Even the Great Queen Tiye had not been so honored," she told me with wide eyes. "Pharaoh loves you; there can be no doubt," she whispered in my ear when I saw her briefly earlier that day. "I am sure he intends to make you his Great Wife. I am sure of it!"

"Do not say such things, Menmet. Not here."

She looked around suspiciously and then, seeing no one about, smiled confidently at me. "There are none of Tadukhipa's spies here. Only me." She bowed her head, and the tiny silver bells woven into her wig tinkled lightly. She was a petite young woman with a pretty face and a childlike voice. "However, I hear that those new dancers, the lovely ones with the yellow skin, are from her court."

"Yes, that is what I hear too, but I cannot refuse them. Help me find something to wear, please." Although it was foolish to think it, I felt by avoiding speaking of Tadukhipa or hearing her name, I might prolong my time with my husband a little longer. Amenhotep was not husband to just one woman, but for now he was only mine.

This evening had been one of the few times I had left Amenhotep's side in the past few weeks. With Menmet's words ringing in my ears, we walked back to Pharaoh's apartments. He greeted me as if he had not seen me in a week, although we had been parted only less than a few hours ago.

He wrapped his strong arms around me and showed his broad smile. He now wore a robe of green with a gold scarab on the back. It had a wide golden ribbon stitched along the hem. I had never seen one so finely made. His head was bare, as it always was when we worshiped the Aten, yet even without his double crown he looked every inch a king. He kissed my forehead and led me out into the courtyard, and side by side we walked up the stairs to view the Aten as it set on the far horizon, completing the day's journey. With a nod he directed me to take my position, and I did as he instructed. As the Aten began to drop away, we worshiped with our hands and with our words until the Aten disappeared, leaving only the musky night and a few bright stars behind.

I slid my arm under his, and together we stood on the balcony overlooking Thebes. We were high above the city, which sprawled like a tangled cluster of fireflies below us. Life did not slow in Pharaoh's city after dark; this was not like living in the Red Lands. I laid my head upon his shoulder and closed my eyes. I must have been dreaming. Was this all a pleasant dream? We stood there in silence for a long while.

"Neferneferuaten. Do you know what that means?"

I smiled up at him proudly because I did know. "Perfect are the perfections of the Aten."

"It has a double meaning, my love. What else does it mean?"

I chewed my lip and searched my memory for an answer. My answer seemed important to him, and I did not want to disappoint. After a moment I had to confess. "I do not know, husband. Please tell me."

He touched my lips with his finger and said, "Beautiful are the beauties of the Aten. That is why I named you such. You are a gift to me, from the Aten. A beautiful, perfect gift."

"Then I am happy indeed. Happy to be Neferneferuaten."

"Let us dine. I have invited the court to come and help us celebrate." I swallowed nervously at the thought of interacting with Amenhotep's court. I had few friends here, although since my official marriage no one (including Tadukhipa) had openly spoken against me. He must have spotted my reticence for he said, "As much as I would like it to be true, we cannot hide in our rooms forever."

"Yes, I know." I stood on my tiptoes and kissed him one last time before walking downstairs to the feasting rooms. "I am ready."

We walked down together in the formal way, my hand resting on top of his, our heads held high with a serious gaze, our eyes fixed on what was in front of us at all times. What had once felt unnatural and statuesque was natural to me now. Menmet had helped me practice my posture and movements, and I was thankful for her help.

Immediately the people below us began to bow and praise their Pharaoh. I followed Amenhotep's example, remaining aloof as we walked into the dining room. As this was an informal dinner, or as informal as a dinner could be at Pharaoh's court, we did not wait to be announced but sailed to our seats. Amenhotep and I took our place at the head of the table and immediately cheerful music began to play. There were fewer than a hundred people in the long decorated room, and many faces I had never seen before.

Some I had.

I recognized Ramose immediately. The rugged-looking general was the first to greet us. He kept his eyes trained on Pharaoh but showed me respect as well with a polite half-bow and a murmur of greeting. I was perfectly aware that Ramose was angry with me. Angry that I had not yet produced Ayn—and his long-awaited, highly desired child. Angry that his wife, Inhapi, had not yet been avenged. I sighed inwardly. This was a matter I could not avoid forever. Ayn would have to return and face her crime, if that was indeed what it was. I missed her and had hoped that Ramose would have changed his mind in this matter. My hope appeared to be in vain. I stood awkwardly, waiting for Ramose and Amenhotep to end their conversation. Instead, the two men walked away from the crowd for a few moments, probably to discuss some important matters regarding Pharaoh's recent foray into the southernmost areas of Temehu. Although he did not consult me in his military plans, I hoped his soldiers destroyed what remained of the Kiffians. I could easily conjure Gilme's face again. I would never forget his dying expression, so full of rage and lust was he. Then I remembered he was dead and would always be dead. That gave me a modicum of satisfaction. If only my sister and I could have killed him a hundred more times.

I greeted the string of well-wishers who walked past me with nods and waited patiently for the return of my husband. It took longer than I expected. After the general's departure, Amenhotep returned to my side and many more courtiers came to stand before us. The seemingly endless crowd spoke kind words and bestowed their happy wishes on us. Behind us on the dais, scribes swiftly recorded the visitors and made sundry other notes with their blackened quills and stacks of papyrus. I had learned quickly that nearly everything having to do with Pharaoh and his family got memorialized in some kind of record. It was an odd thing to get used to. I leaned back against my cushion and waited for the formalities to end.

All, including Ramose, offered us gifts of food, oils, silken fabrics or gold. Nobody came before us empty-handed. I nodded when appropriate, but most of the courtiers seemed happy to speak only to Pharaoh, not to me. I felt no slight—that was a great relief. In some cases, Amenhotep would leave his seat and embrace the courtier or whisper something in his ear.

One young man, Karebi, came proudly before us and laid two boxes of incense on the low table that we reclined behind. I recognized him because he had visited the Court of the Royal Harem to wait upon Queen Tiye on several occasions. I thought we had spoken once, maybe twice, but I did not know him. Karebi had wisely waited until the majority of the attendees had completed their speeches before taking his place before our table. Better to be last and remembered, I could almost hear him thinking. I scolded myself for thinking such things, but that was the way it was here in Egypt. Someone was always clamoring for something. I now understood better why the Great Wife had become so sour on court life.

Karebi bowed low and waited for Pharaoh to acknowledge him. My stomach was growling, but I had to wait until everyone had a chance to speak before I could eat. In this, I would follow my husband.

"Karebi. Welcome back to my palace. You have words to speak?" I noticed Amenhotep's tone sounded slightly different with this young man than with the others. But as Karebi seemed not to notice, I thought not much of it either. Perhaps I was just hungry.

Why hadn't I eaten while I was in my rooms earlier? Poor Menmet. I should have taken the fruit she offered me.

"My Pharaoh and my Queen. I have a poem to share with you, my lady, a poem of admiration and love." As this was the first courtier to speak to me directly I purposefully kept my attention on his face and listened with great expectation.

"*She is one girl, but there is not another like her*," Karebi began with a smile. He glanced at his young wife, who sat at one of the lower tables. I recognized her, although her name escaped me now, but I kept my respectful attention on the young man.

She is more beautiful than any other.

Look, she is a star goddess arising in Egypt
Just like the light that rises at the beginning of a happy new year.

Brilliantly white and bright skinned is she;
with beautiful eyes for looking into my soul.

My cheeks turned red under my makeup, and I tried to ignore the giggling of Menmet and the others who thought Karebi's praise was a bit excessive. Neither he nor his wife seemed to notice, and he continued on.

"*Oh, her lips, with sweet lips for speaking; she has not one phrase too many—*"

Suddenly Amenhotep leaped from his chair, knocking it over backwards as he stalked around the table. I too leaped to my feet, wondering what had happened. My husband's body language demonstrated that he was anything but relaxed. Karebi did not expect this reaction—and neither did I. I sat up rigidly and caught my breath. Everything went quiet, including the festive music and the laughter of my silly servants. My husband grabbed the startled Karebi by the arm and led the short man outside the banquet hall. So violent was Amenhotep's manner that I could not hide my look of surprise even though Memre had trained me extensively on concealing emotions. What had happened?

Confused, I searched for Menmet's face in the crowd. She did not look at me; her attention was on the courtyard beyond, and her hand flew to her mouth. I could not see for myself, but I heard someone scream in pain. Soon two of Pharaoh's guards jogged to the courtyard. Now everyone was gasping and whispering except the young man's wife; she was as white as the marble columns that lined the room. I was very near to calling Menmet to me when Amenhotep returned to the banquet hall. As he took his seat, one of his manservants stooped next to him, holding a bowl of water and a linen towel. Without a word, Amenhotep washed his hands, and I watched in shock as the water turned red with blood. Karebi did not return to the hall. In fact, his wife was now being escorted out by the two guards who had assisted Amenhotep in the courtyard.

As Pharaoh wiped his hands with the towel, he called out, "Food!" I could see that his hand was bleeding; that was not just Karebi's blood. I picked up a linen napkin, thinking to pat his wound, but Menmet touched my hand and shook her head discreetly.

As she pretended to adjust my wig, she whispered in my ear, "The blood of Pharaoh is sacred. Do not touch it, for it is a god's blood."

I stared at Amenhotep, wondering what to do. All of the court watched us and tried to determine for themselves what was amiss with the happy young couple.

My husband leaned toward me and whispered in my ear, "I will not share you, Nefertiti. Do not give me a reason to doubt you."

I took his hand and whispered back, "Never! What has happened? Tell me." Suddenly I worried. Had someone spoken to him about Alexio? It had been only infatuation—that I could see now. It had been only the hopeful dreams of a girl. Amenhotep was the one I loved. I could not explain the workings of my own heart. I had not expected these feelings or known the depth of them with Alexio, but it was the truth. "Please," I said, reaching for him as he pulled away. He left the banquet hall again, sending the court to whispering and pointing. I followed him, uncaring about protocol or anything else. I sensed that more hung in the balance than just my feelings. This was not a lovers' spat but an accusation. And one Amenhotep believed.

"Wait!" I called out to him. "My husband, what is the matter? I do not know this Karebi. I swear it!"

He raised a long finger in warning. "I will not share you! Not with anyone!" The intensity of his words and the fierceness of his eyes stunned me, but I felt compelled to soothe his suspicions. My mouth moved, but the words did not form. Amenhotep stood with his hands on his hips and stared at me as if I were a stranger. "Think carefully what you say to me, Nefertiti." He was warning me about something, but what? Everything had been fine between us until we came to dinner.

Until he spoke with Ramose.

As fearful as I was—as desperate as I felt—I could not let the general's accusation go unchallenged. It was true I would never have dreamed that I, Nefret hap Semkah, would ever love an Egyptian, much less Pharaoh. But that was before.

Suddenly, Tiye's words rang in my ear: *"You can live a prisoner, or you can become a true Queen."*

More than anything, I wanted to become Queen Nefertiti—Neferneferuaten, wife of Amenhotep, beloved of my husband and Pharaoh. With every fiber of my being I wanted this. Egypt—no, Amenhotep—had woven a spell around me, but apparently it was a spell that seemingly could be easily broken.

"I have given you no reason to doubt my commitment to you. Although I am not an Egyptian, the Aten brought me to you, Amenhotep. I have been truthful with you in all things. I swear it on my life! There is no one but you, nor shall there ever be. You have no need to worry despite what others may say. I have not been unfaithful in word or deed." I felt a chill, and gooseflesh rose on my arms, but I did not move a muscle. I met his dark eyes with assurance and trust. He appeared to soften a little, but his manner was still guarded. I could not back down! "And I challenge anyone to say otherwise!" To show him how serious I was, I took his hand and kissed his bleeding wound fearlessly. Now he could kill me, if he so chose, for I had touched the sacred blood. This was a test of his love. One that could cost me everything. "I swear it on your blood, my husband and Pharaoh. Let it testify against me if I speak a lie."

Ignoring the rising whispers in the banquet hall—the crowd nosily peered through the opening in the gauzy curtains—I continued to meet his gaze fearlessly. To think all my happiness, all our happiness, could be undone so quickly by a few words. Accepting my gesture at last, he kissed me and breathed a sigh of relief. "I should not have doubted you. I will not do it again."

"You will never have a reason to doubt me, Amenhotep. I am yours. Always." I gave him a confident smile and walked with him back to our dining table. As we settled back down to eat, I cast a warning glance in Ramose's direction. He smiled amusedly and lifted his cup to me, but I kept my face a mask—just as I had seen Pah do during the mekhma trials. Better to let him wonder what I was thinking than give him the satisfaction of seeing his handiwork achieve its goal. Although my husband's fears had been abated for the moment, it wounded me to think he would believe that I would betray him. My mind immediately began to dissect the situation. Inhapi had been Tadukhipa's great friend—and more, if you believed the rumors. Perhaps Ramose had scattered those seeds of distrust on her behalf? I would probably never know. All I could do was prepare for whatever came next.

I forced myself to put on a distant smile and pretend that I wanted to be in attendance. Thankfully there were no more formalities, and immediately the music picked up the notes of a happier song. Neatly dressed servants appeared with trays of decadent food offerings. Each came and stood before us with their temptations. They kept their eyes cast down and waited for Amenhotep's steward to dismiss them.

I had little appetite now, but Amenhotep poured wine into my cup. "Drink, this is not juniper wine," he said teasingly. Obediently I reached for the large silver cup, happy to hide my face behind it if only for a few seconds. I did not want him to see the sudden rush of tears pushing against my eyelids. As if she could read my mind, Menmet came to sit beside me again, and as the platters appeared before us, she dutifully filled my plate with the foods I normally liked to eat. She selected two duck eggs along with fresh berries, dates, a half-pat of cheese and the soft honey bread that the Egyptians loved from the highest to the lowest. I too had begun to love the baked treats, but I longed for chula bread and the sweet waters of Timia. Those to me were the greatest food and drink one could ever have!

I ate timidly at first, and then as I saw no one watched me or stared, I ate to my heart's content. This was the first meal Amenhotep and I had enjoyed outside our rooms in weeks. Now those days seemed like a dream. Tomorrow our honeymoon would officially end and we would begin our life together in earnest. I suspected that I would see him less, but as long as we had some time together I would be content. As he had many matters to attend to, I did as well. I could turn my attention once again to my people. I needed an ally beyond my servants, but the idea of forgiving Omel filled me with revulsion. I worried over the fate of the Meshwesh. How did they fare in their new city? How was my father? Would he marry again? In my last message from Orba, I had heard that he might. I had not disapproved. A king needed a good wife, and I had no doubt that Leela loved my father. I wondered about Pah and Alexio but did not dare put any questions concerning them in writing. Surely if something were amiss, I would know it. And what could I do if there were problems?

I smiled at Amenhotep, who was sharing a joke with another of his closest confidantes, Saho the Prophet. Although Saho did not speak to me, even in greeting, at least he was not Ramose.

Menmet poured me another glass of wine and pointed to the new dancers who had arrived in the hall. These were the gifts sent to us from Tadukhipa. They wore splendid purple ribbons that covered their lithe bodies perfectly. They swayed and wound about the room, and their skin glistened as they paced through their synchronous movements. With upraised palms they surprised us by adding subtle movements that were reminiscent of our Aten worship. I could see by his delighted smile that Amenhotep did not miss the intricate movements either. As the twelve dancers traveled the wide circle they came together in perfect timing, clapping their hands to accentuate the effect of their synchronized steps. The girls appeared remarkably alike; in fact, it was easy to believe they were related. As Menmet noted earlier, they had unusual yellow skin, probably made more unusual with paint, round bottoms and tiny feet. Unlike the servants who brought us food and drink, the dancers met our eyes boldly and constantly wore smiles. I could see one in particular cast a lustful eye on Amenhotep as she waved her fingers in rhythm. He did not bother to hide his appreciation.

How amusing! He all but accuses me of unfaithfulness but does not mind staring at Tadukhipa's dancers. Farrah was right! Men's hearts are attached to their male parts and are easily handled—and stolen.

I took another sip of my wine. I could hardly believe it, but Karebi returned to the festivities. His smooth brown skin was marred by an ugly black bruise that encircled his eye. He appeared a humbled man. At least he was wise enough not to look at me or speak to anyone. He merely ate his food and sat staring at his plate. His wife did not return. Ashamed of her husband, no doubt. Well, at least he was alive. I knew it was not wise, but I felt some sympathy for the little man who reminded me of Orba. However, Karebi was not as wise as Orba. When the song ended, Karebi rose and the dining hall hushed. He walked to the foot of the table again, but I pretended I did not see him. Menmet and I were admiring the golden fish that swam in a large blue glass bowl on the table. It was a beautiful gift from one of Pharaoh's courtiers.

"Watch this, Menmet. Give me some bread." I was tired, and the wine was making me lightheaded. I giggled with Menmet as we dropped the bread in the water and watched the greedy little fish come eat it and stare at us hoping for more. She smiled and looked at me with surprise. "How wonderful! Look how hungry he is! You have hidden talents, my Queen. How did you learn this trick?"

"By accident. I was sitting under the palm tree with…with a friend, and we happened to toss our bread in the water. The fish came to the top and begged for more. After that, we could not make them go away. They love chula bread—and honey bread too, it seems."

"How smart you are!"

Karebi cleared his throat, and I turned my attention to him. My husband watched me as I acknowledged the wary courtier. "Karebi." I did not know what to say; I hardly knew what his original offense had been.

"My Queen, I beg your forgiveness for my inappropriate words."

He had not offended me. I had thought him only a silly man, but I would not go against my husband. I glanced at him, but Amenhotep offered me no guidance in this matter, and I did not seek his counsel. "You are forgiven, Karebi. Please enjoy your meal and send my regards to your wife."

With a sad expression, Karebi backed away from the table and slowly exited the building. Not many people paid much attention to him now. After seeing Pharaoh's wrath break out against him so savagely, I doubted if anyone wanted to offer their friendship to the foolish little man.

Suddenly Amenhotep rose from the table. "Good night to all of you. In the morning Queen Nefertiti and I will rise to greet the Aten. You are all welcome to join us."

The courtiers applauded loudly and cheered. They seemed excited and even honored to be invited to worship the Aten with Pharaoh Amenhotep and his new wife. I rose and placed my hand on top of his. I smiled up at him, but his look was serious and reserved. My heart fell in my chest. I had done nothing to cause him to doubt me. Then it occurred to me that it must be very difficult to be the Pharaoh, to wonder all the time who loved him and who was merely using him. I would never be that—I would never do that! No matter what! Amenhotep was an honorable man who wanted to bring his people into a new age, an age of enlightenment and religious freedom for Egypt.

He frequently said, "The people should be free to worship whom they choose! How can we dictate a man's conscience?" He was so passionate about this it frightened me at times.

He knew the oppression the House of Amun laid on the people. There were times in the past when they demanded up to half of the income of the worshipers. Even Pharaoh was not immune from this taxation—for what else could you call it? I felt honored that he chose me to be his Queen and partner in this great quest. Who was I that fate would snatch me up from my obscure tribe in the Red Lands and bring me here to be a Queen of Egypt?

As our courtiers applauded, Amenhotep and I walked out of the banquet hall. I thought my husband would invite me into his chambers, but he stopped outside the massive golden door.

"Will we not be together tonight?"

"No, I cannot. There are pressing matters that I cannot avoid any longer." He must have noticed my worried expression, for he touched my cheek with his hand and said, "All is well, Nefertiti."

"Very well." I blushed, embarrassed at his refusal. Would the yellow-skinned dancer be visiting my husband's room later? What was I doing? I could not become a jealous shrew! Amenhotep loved me—that I was sure of! I added, "My door is always open to you, my love. If I am asleep, wake me, but come to me if you can." Amenhotep softened his expression and held me against his warm body. I could not help myself and kissed him quickly but did not prevent his departure. With a return kiss on my forehead he left me, and I watched him walk away.

Menmet scampered beside me. "Do not be sad, my Queen. It is good to be apart, for when you come together again there will be much passion. Much passion to be shared and soon many, many babies. Pharaoh will want to have many, many children. Many sons and many daughters."

I laughed and said, "Please, Menmet. I have not had the first child yet, much less many sons or many daughters."

"Don't you want many sons and many daughters?"

"I want as many daughters and sons as the Shining Man will give me, but not all at once. I would like to spend some time getting to know my husband first."

"What is to know, my Queen? He is handsome and virile, and he loves you. How jealous he is of you!" She picked up the clothing I let fall to the ground and helped me remove the wig and the thick, heavy jewelry. Handing them to another servant, she began to brush out my long red hair with her clever fingers and helped me remove my makeup with scented cream.

I watched her as she worked on her tasks. She looked nothing like her father, Heby. I had a chance to see the man up close when he visited her a few days ago. She had not asked me to greet him, and I must admit I was relieved. The more I heard about him and the other priests, the less I liked him. They did not approve of me, I knew this much, just as they had not approved of Queen Tiye's marriage to my Amenhotep's father. Heby had left Menmet in tears, but she had refused to confide in me or reveal the reason for her misery. I could have commanded her, but I would not. Menmet was more of a friend than a servant. How much of a friend would I be to compel her to share her heart with me?

As I bathed, Menmet filled me in on the palace gossip. Aperel, the handsome Master of Horses, finally took a new wife. In her cheerful manner, she explained how many in Thebes thought he loved only his horses. But he had surprised everyone with his marriage to a young girl from the east. It was said she had blue eyes, the color of the sky. I pretended to listen as I bathed and as she dressed me. When I finally climbed into bed I was exhausted. I thought I would stay up and listen to the musicians who played for me in the courtyard below, but I did not. Their seductive soft tunes put me to sleep quickly, and I entered the dream world where I found the Shining Man waiting. I ran toward him with my arms extended, and then suddenly…

I was standing at the Blue Altar again where Amenhotep and I married. Perched above us atop the altar was the Shining Man. The wedding went just as I remembered, but in my dream I could see silver cords—no, silver snakes—wrapping around the two of us as we held hands. Suddenly, the three of us were no longer at the Blue Altar but standing in a high place on a cliff that overlooked a large body of water. It was greater than any pool of water or even the sea. Amenhotep and I knelt before the Shining Man, and he placed shining crowns upon our heads. The crowns were illuminated—they shone like stars. These were crowns unlike any I had ever seen before. Suddenly, the gods of Egypt stood at the edges of the water. I could see Isis, Amun, Set, Hathor and a host of others. As we rose to stand with our crowns atop our heads, they fell on their faces before us. I gasped at the sight. The Shining Man said some words that warmed my heart, but when I woke up, I immediately forgot them.

And when I did wake, Amenhotep was there, smiling down at me in the dark.

"Who were you dreaming of, my love?"

Hearing his voice thrilled me to no end. "The Shining Man, husband. I saw him in all his glory. He gave us crowns and said words of power over us."

"Tell me the words. What were the words of power?" He lay beside me, moving the wild strands of hair from my face.

I hesitated. "I do not know. I can't remember, but I shall try harder next time."

"It is no matter. I am here now. I am not a dream." He slid into the silky sheets with me, and my wandering hands let me know that he had already shed his clothing. "Let us make an offering to the Shining Man and see if we can both have a dream," he said before he kissed me.

"I am in a dream now, surely. Kiss me, Amenhotep. Kiss me, my love."

We made love and then settled down to sleep. I did indeed dream about the Shining Man again, but when Amenhotep asked me the next day I lied to him.

I could not tell him what I saw. It would break his heart.

It surely broke mine.

Chapter Three

Life of Trials—Nefertiti

The priests of Amun, adorned with leopard skin capes, filled the court with the strong scent of their incense. If they thought that their surprise assemblage or their numbers would deter my husband from his not-so-secret plans to uproot their oppression, then they highly underestimated him. Amenhotep was not a man to be swayed by popular opinion. I was neither invited nor forbidden to sit with my husband for this meeting, which I had learned in the past few months of my queenship meant I could come or go at my pleasure.

Today, I chose to stand unseen behind the thick blue curtains that hung behind my husband's throne. He knew I was there and never betrayed my secret attendance. I was curious to hear how he ruled his kingdom. Perhaps one day I would have to do the same. It was better to learn the ways of court from one who understood its deep workings, someone who knew the traditions and expectations of the people who came before him. Menmet stood anxiously beside me and giggled as she peeked through the tiny hole in the veil. Fortunately, the processional was so loud nobody could hear her. Not yet, anyway.

"I will send you away. Now quiet, Menmet!" I threatened her in a whisper.

"As you say, my Queen."

I dropped my voice now as the room began to settle. "Shush…and don't say another word, not even, 'as you say, my Queen.'" She frowned at me. For the fifth time today I missed Ayn. At least with the warrior I did not have to worry about her speaking out of turn.

Ayn, where did you disappear to?

I had sent numerous couriers to Zerzura to ask about her, but nobody knew where she was hiding. I wondered if perhaps Ramose had murdered my friend himself, hidden her body and only pretended not to know her whereabouts. It would be an easy thing to do. Surely her child had been born by now! I had no news to pass on to the general or to the officials who demanded her arrest and conviction. I wondered how long they would tolerate my evasion.

Peeking through the veil, I could see the face of the rugged-looking general in the audience. Many Egyptian women dreamed of a marriage with such a man, but they did not know him as I did. He was cold, callous—more beast than man. He stood to the left of the throne and watched the proceedings with a clenched jaw. I studied him, remembering the bruises he left on my arms when he thought to take me at Zerzura.

Oh yes, Ramose. My mortal enemy.

My husband's voice rang out in the court, "My brother priests of Amun and Re, I greet you as a brother, for have I not worshiped in the temples alongside each of you? Is this why you have come to me today? Are you here unbidden to upbraid me for my worship of the Aten? Surely you can see that Amun has nothing to fear from the Aten or from me."

"No, Pharaoh. You are as a god to us. You may do what pleases you; however, the people have stopped worshiping Amun. Our storehouses are empty, and the priests are starving."

Starving? Not a man appeared as if he had missed a meal. Even the youngest priests were rich men, or so I had heard, and enjoyed every lavish benefit accorded to them.

"A god, you say?" Amenhotep boomed. I knew he did not appreciate the comparison. Unlike his father, he did not think himself a god and in fact considered the thought blasphemous. "Where is your leader today? Maya, step forward."

"Here I am, Pharaoh."

"Tell me more about this problem that has driven so many leopard coats into my court today. It must be a serious matter to see so many faces assembled here before their Pharaoh."

I tried to count them all but gave up. There must have been several hundred all crowded into the court with stern expressions. It would not matter. They could assemble a thousand dissenters—it would not sway Pharaoh. Amenhotep's guard shuffled anxiously at the tone of his speech. Obviously none of these men had witnessed Karebi's thrashing or heard the rumor that Karebi's wife had disappeared into the workhouses. I shivered at the idea that my husband had ordered such a punishment. I had heard of these workhouses but knew little about them except that they were not places to visit or to ask about.

Some of the priests could see that Pharaoh was not pleased with their unannounced visit to his court. Maya quickly continued with his calm reasoning, "Oh Majestic One, I mean no disrespect. We come to you because only you can help us. The people are not bringing offerings to the temples—they are tempting the wrath of Amun!" I could hear the onlookers, the courtiers who regularly attended Amenhotep, whisper fearfully. The priest's words gripped their hearts with fear. Feeling empowered, I supposed, Maya continued on, "Just today we received less than half the normal weight in gold and food. And the people...they see their Pharaoh worshiping before the Aten—he no longer visits the temples. The people do as they see the Lord of the Two Lands do. Whatever your intention, it is clear that the support for the Aten has been to the detriment of those who serve Amun. Please tell the people to return to the temples! It is not wise to anger Amun in this way, Majesty."

Amenhotep stood, jumping up quickly as he had the night Karebi offended him. He paced the dais like a lion, a proud lion about to be sheared before his pride. Finally, he stopped and faced the crowd of men with their painted faces and their arms glittering with gold bracelets. "Who am I to tell Egyptians whom to worship? Some worship this one, some that one; it has always been this way. You want me to command the consciences of free men and women? In Egypt, even the slaves worship whomever they like. If your god has fallen out of favor, perhaps you should ask him why instead of coming to me to command the worshippers' obedience."

Maya stood blinking in surprise. "You are Pharaoh! We cannot command them, but you can. Is it not the place of kings to keep order in the kingdom? To instruct the people? We fear your silence in this matter will be misinterpreted as liberty to abandon our gods. Pharaoh must speak and remind the people of their duty to Amun!"

"You dare?" His voice rose sharply. "I well know my duty, Maya, as my father did before me. Blood has already flowed on behalf of Amun. Is he not yet satisfied?" The gathered men did not answer. That was wise. I held my breath as I watched. Menmet took my hand; I felt her shaking beside me. Poor girl. Yes, I could see He-by in the crowd. How shameful to have such a father!

"What do you mean, my lord?"

"You know very well what I mean, Maya." I was sure the blood he spoke of belonged to his brother. It was an unspoken truth that the priests of Amun had no love for the sons of Tiye. I felt a chill as I wondered what they would think of my children. The children of Amenhotep and the Desert Queen.

In a sudden reversal of mood, Amenhotep waved his hand dismissively and said, "Nevertheless, I see that I have been short-sighted in this. It is not *my* desire to see blood spilled. Where is my scribe? Anai! Come!"

The tall, silent man shuffled forward and sat on the floor at Amenhotep's feet. He stretched out a papyrus and held a feathered pen.

"Send a letter to all of Thebes. Tell the people…tell them that we cannot forget our traditions. We must honor Amun with offerings. On behalf of Maya, I command the people to bring a fifth of this month's earnings to the temples of Amun."

"A fifth? That is too much, Pharaoh. We come only for what is due—no more."

Amenhotep smiled at Maya and said, "I am sure you will get what is due to you, High Priest. Leave now…with my blessing, of course."

I chewed my lip nervously as the priests began to exit the court in complete silence. I did not know what they hoped to achieve, but I was certain this was not it. The anger of the people would rise against them, I hoped. I prayed it did not turn against Amenhotep. As the court emptied, new petitioners entered, foreigners by the look of them. I wondered if these were the Hittites, Tadukhipa's people. I decided I had seen enough. I did not envy my husband.

Menmet whispered, "You saw my father? I am so ashamed. He thinks of nothing but those offerings. The priests are angry because the people support their Pharaoh! If he says the Aten is the supreme deity, then they listen. There is nothing these priests can do to stop that. Not even my father."

"I pray it does not go against our Pharaoh."

"The people will know that the priests of Amun requested this special offering." She pursed her thin lips in a thoughtful expression. Menmet had been snooping for me—there were problems in the kingdom. But weren't there always?

The late Amenhotep had made many promises and pledges to his old enemies; a few foreign kings had sealed their deals with the Hawk of Egypt, as my father-in-law was known, with marriages. Many marriages. Some were official, and others were superficial unions arranged to bring special recognition to whatever dignitaries were in favor at that moment. Recently, I learned from my very knowledgeable Menmet that my Amenhotep was required to keep those wives in a place of honor even after his father traveled to the Otherworld. Amenhotep had inherited all the concubines of the Royal Harem, as was tradition, but the matter of queens and their management was handled quite differently in Egypt.

To make matters tenser, the Hittites were keen to establish their prized princess as the new superior queen and consort. They wanted to see firsthand how well their daughter, Tadukhipa, was being treated by this new dignitary. In fact, Menmet told me in a whisper late last night, they wanted Tadukhipa to be the Great Wife above everyone. I quietly vowed to myself that if she were to achieve that I would run myself through with a sword. I would never live under her leadership. From the few times we had interacted, I knew for sure that she would kill me with a thousand slow deaths before she ever did the actual killing. Still, it was treasonous for me to bring accusations against any of the queens, as they were the wives of Pharaoh, so we did not speak about it any further.

When we returned to my chambers I was surprised to see Memre waiting for me. "Lady, what are you doing here? Is everything well with Queen Tiye?" Memre licked her dry lips and I added, "Forgive me; you must be thirsty." The old lady had a healthy appreciation for wine, so I poured her a goblet full and handed it to her and waved Menmet away.

"Lady queen, Amenhotep's mother, the Great Wife of the late Pharaoh, has sent me to you. She wanted you to know that your sister is in the Green Temple of Isis, just near here."

Puzzled, I tilted my head and asked, "Sitamen, you mean?"

"No, Queen Nefertiti. I mean your true Meshwesh sister."

"You must be mistaken. She is not in Thebes."

"Ah, she is in the Green Temple. I have just come from there, and I saw her with my own two eyes just as my queen bade me."

My hands flew to my chest, and I couldn't hide my shock. "Who would do this? I cannot imagine that she brought herself here."

Memre drained the cup and set it down on the table. I filled it again, hoping she would quickly tell me everything she knew. This was not likely. Memre was a careful woman, much like her mistress, and she would weigh her words before she spoke them. With a grim smile of thanks she continued, "This was not done by the Great Queen's order, if that is what you are thinking. Forgive me, this was not Queen Tiye's order. She just heard this herself."

"What did Pah say? Did you speak with her?"

"The priestess who cares for your sister would not let me interview her. The girl is in seclusion until the new moon rises next week. The priestess, Margg is her name, says she is there to serve the goddess Isis. We will have to wait until then." Her eyes narrowed, and she stared into the cup thoughtfully. "But we know who ordered her installment in the Green Temple."

"Tadukhipa! But why?"

"We can only wait and see, but you can be assured that you have a stone enemy with the Monkey. She will never forgive you for stealing Amenhotep's heart or for the death of her friend."

"I had nothing to do with either of those things. I cannot command a man's heart. Would she harm my sister just to spite me?"

She nodded slowly, her eyes angry and her mouth a red slit. "She will be much more careful than that. Outright kill her? No. But if she can bring you embarrassment with your sister's presence, why wouldn't she?"

With Pah out of her head, wounded to the soul by the Kiffians, there was no doubt that would be quite easy to accomplish. Memre continued, "Whatever Kiya's designs, it can only be for your sister's harm—and yours. Do not think that Tadukhipa is going to lie down without a fight while you are made the Great Queen of Upper and Lower Egypt. She already endured that with Tiye. She does not like being second and has no desire to land in that spot again. She has determined to fight you for that right, and with the Hittites arriving soon she will have the political persuasion she needs to accomplish her goal."

"My husband will never raise her above me. He would never do that."

Memre laughed, "Ah, but he's her husband too, isn't he? And he is Pharaoh and a man—and his father's son. His heart will not rule his head in this matter."

"In name only is he her husband!" I said defensively. "He does not love her, Memre."

"Love?" She snorted derisively. "We are not talking about love, Queen Nefertiti. We are talking about kingdoms and alliances and matters of state beyond your feelings, girl. I thought a Desert Queen would know this already. Love is a luxury reserved for bakers, brewers and farmers—not for kings. Which brings me to the Queen's instructions…"

I knew what she said was true. I was no fool. Deep down I had always known but had allowed myself to be swept up in the magic of Egypt and, in doing so, had lost control of my own heart. I had forgotten the reality of my situation. I sank into my chair, feeling deflated. The truth was I was here only because Queen Tiye put me here. With the old queen losing influence with her son as other advisers moved in, advisers like Ramose, it would fall upon me to secure my position as queen at his side. I could take nothing for granted. Especially a man's heart.

"What does Queen Tiye instruct, Memre?"

In a low whisper she said, "You know my queen hates Tadukhipa above all others. She reminds you of what she has done for you.

You were an insignificant Desert Queen with no home and no army when she met you. Because of her favor, you are where you are now. It is time to get your head out of the clouds and think like a queen—a queen who wants to remain a queen. Queen Tiye orders you to make peace with your uncle. You need an ally. Lift him up with accolades, gifts and whatever honors are necessary. Send him home to rule for a time. Have him return with something of significance, and offer this to the king on behalf of your people. In matters of wealth you likely cannot match the Hittites, but your people can win by proving their loyalty to a greater degree. Prove to your husband and all Egypt that you are more than a peasant queen—more than a pretty face! Begin honoring Isis in public; claim her as your mother often and loudly. I hear that you have never been to the temple. The Queen knows her son worships the Aten, but you must be careful to honor Isis and be seen doing so."

I clamped my mouth shut at the veiled insults and accepted the scolding. This was Tiye's way, and these were her words. "What else?" I asked.

"In a few weeks a group of ambassadors from Grecia will arrive in Pharaoh's court. Although you are Isis' daughter now, it is appropriate for you to greet the Grecian delegates as kinfolk. Queen Tiye says you should do whatever it takes to make an alliance with Grecia. Whatever it takes, Desert Queen! Now is the time to build a following and make some alliances of your own. Fill your personal court with royalty, daughters who will be indebted to you and serve you. If you do not act now, you might as well pack your bags and move into the Royal Harem. Even now it might be too late."

"I see," I said as I tried to process the tasks presented to me. Could she be right? Was I in danger of being supplanted? Why must there always be competition in my life? I had not asked for this life of trials, and I had no idea how to change it.

"It would also benefit you to have an ally among the queens. Tiye is Pharaoh's mother, and Tadukhipa is your enemy, so it must be someone else. In her day, Tiye chose Tadukhipa as second wife not because she loved her but because she was wise."

I snorted in disgust. "Are you suggesting that I endorse Tadukhipa as second wife and hope that she returns the favor?"

"No, that is not the way. Look to the other queens or someone else." She gave me a knowing smile.

"You obviously have someone in mind, Memre. Please tell me."

"I am speaking of Ipy."

I waited for her to explain, but she pursed her lips and stared at me as if I were stupid. "You never heard of Ipy?"

"No, should I have?"

"Yes, I would think so. It is her crown you are wearing, lady queen. Ipy held Amenhotep's heart in her hands once, but her father stole her chances when he betrayed the old king. Forbidden to marry her, Amenhotep moved her to the Royal Harem, and that is where she has been ever since. He visits her from time to time, but not like he used to. Still, she might make a good ally against Tadukhipa; she hates her also."

"Why has he never mentioned her to me?"

"Should he? Have you told the king about your lovers? Anyway, it is old news now. She has never given him any children, and I think he's grown tired of her. If you were to invite her to court from time to time, she would no doubt be in your debt. Remember how lonely it is there? She is young and has no chance at life beyond the harem."

"That seems counterproductive, Memre. Why should I invite another rival to join me?"

"She isn't your rival. Ipy is a concubine with no hope of ever becoming queen. It is the law. A small kindness from you occasionally, like an invitation to dinner, would go a long way in increasing your status at the harem. Go see her when you can."

"Very well, I will do that."

"Oh yes, there is one more thing."

"Another thing?"

"Yes, and this is more important than all the others..." she began slowly, "but I think you may have already accomplished this task." She grabbed my hands and stared at my palms for a few moments, and then cupped my chin with her right hand as she peered into my eyes. The speed of her movements surprised me, and I did not fight her. I stared back into her piercing eyes; the kohl rings around them were messy, and I could easily see a collection of fine lines. Memre was old—older than even Queen Tiye. A light breeze began to blow through the room; it moved through the gauzy curtains and caused the green leaves of the potted palms to flutter. She chuckled and said, "You are pregnant, Queen Nefertiti. Pharaoh has planted his seed in your belly." She pointed her finger at me approvingly. "That is good. That will work in your favor. This is a thing that Tadukhipa has not yet achieved. Yes, the queen will be pleased."

"How do you know I am with child?" I could not hide my surprise.

She fell back in the chair and smiled at me. "You have much to learn about the ways of women, my Queen. Perhaps it is not your fault since you had no mother—no mother except Isis, that is. Call the physician if you like and have him examine you. You will see I speak the truth."

"I do not doubt you, Memre," I said with an embarrassed smile. Eager to come out from under her scrutinizing gaze, I rose from my chair and walked to the window to catch my breath and get some air. I watched the activity in the courtyard below. Many people, Egyptians and foreigners, streamed in and out of the court. The place seemed livelier than normal. I could feel the excitement in the air. Queen Tiye was right. I could not sit idly by and hope that Amenhotep chose me as his Great Royal Wife. I had my child to think about.

"Please tell Queen Tiye I will do as she commands. I have no intention of bowing down to Tadukhipa."

Memre walked to the window and stood beside me. Patting my shoulder kindly she said quietly, "Queen Tiye says to give you this greeting. She says you will know what it means." I pulled my attention from the window and watched in surprise as Memre made the Meshwesh sign of respect and said, "Hafa-nu, Queen Nefertiti." Tears flooded my eyes and a sob escaped my lips. This was a sign that all would be well. I was not alone.

I returned the gesture and hugged Memre, "Hafa-nu, Queen Tiye. And Hafa-nu, Memre."

I turned my attention back to the window as the older woman left to return to her mistress. I watched Amenhotep as he climbed upon one of his new horses. It was taller than any horse I had ever seen, with a long, curved neck and strong, stocky legs. Amenhotep laughed as the animal pitched once and Aperel reached for the reins. I smiled at the sight. Leaning against the cold marble, I twisted a strand of my wig and enjoyed the moment. If Memre was correct, I would give my husband a greater gift than any horse or treasure.

I would give him a son. The breeze returned, and I heard a whisper. A familiar whisper. I had heard it before in my dreams.

Smenkhkare!

Chapter Four

The Heart of a Beast—Ramose

"Brother! What are you doing sitting alone in the dark?" Kafta asked me. His voice always sounded like a man who had been hanged but had escaped seconds before death. He waved the oil lamp at the darkness and lit the larger lamp on the table beside me.

"Who says I am alone?" I replied, tilting the jug upside down and draining the remnants of the sour liquid. It was meru, a stale workman's beer that I usually only drank when traveling with my men. I threw the jug down, sending shards of clay scattering around the room. The chained cat screamed in anger, and Kafta nearly dropped the lamp as he dashed out of its way.

"Gods! Why is that animal in here?" The cat's scream had sent the muscled man to the top of the table.

Any other time I would have laughed at the sight, but this was no laughing matter. "Come down from there. She cannot reach you. She is on a chain."

"I see that, but I do not trust chains."

At that, I did laugh. "But you trust exploding barrels of fire? You are a strange man, Kafta."

"I am strange? I am not sitting in the dark getting drunk with a panther. Or is that a leopard? I do not care for cats."

"This is a panther. She belonged to Inhapi."

Kafta eased down from the table but stood no closer. "Come, brother. Let us go out to get some air. I see you drank all the meru. I have wine with me in my things. Come."

I stared bleary-eyed at the cat and then at Kafta. My eyes had grown used to the darkness. How long had I been sitting here? I could not remember, but it had been bright and sunny when I entered the animal's prison. The cat screamed again, and I yelled back at her as if I were a beast. She began to pace her side of the room, and her cold eyes never left me. They were dark and shiny—like the eyes of my dead wife. I had seen hundreds of dead men, but the sight of Inhapi's lifeless body lying on the priest's table filled me with unexpected dread. Now that I had lost her, it was easy to recall the few happy times we shared. How proud I had been to claim her as my own. She had been beautiful and welcoming, at least when we first married. As I traveled, she became less welcoming, but how could I blame her?

Inhapi had been shallow and silly at times, but she had put my name and my needs above everything else, mostly, and she worked tirelessly to see me elevated. She had not excited me as Ayn had, but she had been my partner in all things. I had betrayed her with the Meshwesh woman, and now Inhapi and my son were gone. It was true that Inhapi loved Tadukhipa, in ways I did not understand, but I knew that she had loved me too. Together we would see our names immortalized and find a place of prominence in this world and the next.

"Inhapi," I said, reaching my hand out to the cat's head.

"Stop that, fool! That cat is not your wife. You are indeed drunk, Ramose. Come, General of Egypt, before that animal tears into your hand. I can see she has not fed in a day or two. What are you trying to do? Feed yourself to the panther?"

With a grunt, he snatched me up, a thing he would never have done if I had been sober. I followed him outside, cursing him under my breath, but the cool evening air did feel good on my skin. "I have a message to deliver, but I will not do so while you are out of your head—and smelling like a beast." He led me to a trough of water. I didn't remember ordering a bath, but before I knew it, I was falling into it. I sputtered and cursed as Kafta laughed. I was too drunk to climb out; all I could do was sit in the trough and yell at him.

"Now, now, General. Why make such a fuss? Wash yourself, and I'll set you a meal. I see there are no servants here now. Did you send them all away?" He spotted my houseboy, Axteris, and yelled for him. As he gave instructions to the boy, I managed to climb out of the trough and struggled to remove my clothing. The cold water had sobered me up some, but not as much as I would have liked. Soon Axteris had my bath prepared, and I followed him to clean myself properly. Kafta followed me, chewing on bread and some kind of roasted meat. I reached for the soap and a sponge and went to work. I rubbed my face with my wet hand, feeling the stubble on my chin. How long had it been since I shaved? Or bathed? Or eaten? Lost in my grief for Inhapi, I had lost all sense of time. I had been in a place of forgetting. Now my friend, likely my only friend, Kafta was calling me back to life. I knew I should be grateful, but at the moment I felt anything but gratitude.

The more I washed, the more I felt myself. What had I been thinking climbing into that animal's hovel? Was Kafta right? Did I have a death wish? I was a man of strategy and reason, but I had no understanding or reasoning for what I had been experiencing. It was as if someone had cast a spell on me. As if I were walking under a shadow of doom.

"How long has Inhapi been dead, Kafta?" I asked him as he poured another pail of hot water into the tub.

With a surprised expression he answered, "Almost two months, General."

"Two months…" I scrubbed my head with the soapy sponge and thought about the months that had traveled so quickly. "The last thing I clearly remember is the night of Amenhotep's wedding party. Is it possible that Queen Nefertiti poisoned me?"

He made a dismissive sound and tossed the bone he'd been gnawing onto a nearby platter. "You know the Desert Queen is not cunning enough to do something like that. I think there is a much simpler explanation for what has happened to you."

"What is it? Sorcery? Magic?"

"No, my friend." He sat on the edge of the tub and said, "It is grief. Grief can bring a man low, low enough even to wish for death. Low enough to make him play dangerous games with wild animals. The loss of Inhapi brought you low, but now you have a second chance at life. And you have the greatest reason of all to live."

"Really? What would that be? Some new battle? I have not heard anything from Pharaoh." I tried not to sneer. I remembered what it was like to be a new husband. Without waiting for an answer I slid under the water. I held my breath and closed my eyes, pretending for a moment that I was dead. I would allow no air to pass through my body. My chest would not rise or fall. I could stay under this water and die. Inhapi would welcome me! In death, there would be no Tadukhipa or Ayn to come between us. She would be mine completely. As much as my mind commanded it, my body struggled; my heart would not stop pumping! My ka refused to leave. I rose up from the water with a scream of anger on my lips.

"Curse you, Osiris!" I shouted at the top of my lungs. Kafta jumped back and made the sign against curses. He was a superstitious man. "I cannot even die! The gods hate me, brother!"

"No, do not say that, Ramose. You are the General of Egypt and the servant of Pharaoh Amenhotep, although I must admit that seeing you taking a bath does not make for such an amazing impression. Get dressed now. We have much to talk about, preferably with your clothing on."

"I do not wish to talk."

"You will," he said. "The queen wants to speak to you. She has something that belongs to you." Kafta grinned, exposing the grand gap in his teeth.

I rubbed the water out of my eyes and blinked the rest away. "Who are you talking about? Nefertiti?"

"No, not the Desert Queen. Queen Sitamen wishes to speak to you."

Accepting the razor from Kafta, I began to scrape the hair off my face. My hands were so shaky I could imagine cutting my own throat without even trying. That might be the remedy to all my problems. I sneered at the idea of meeting with the spoiled, sulking princess. Although I had loved her father as my own, I barely spoke to the girl over the years. I had been present during her "marriage" ceremony to her father, but so had most of the court. She was not overtly attractive, and I never gave her a second look. She was Pharaoh's daughter, not just any noble's daughter. When I was a younger man, I believed perhaps she admired me. Women often admire strength in men, and I had been a strong man—once. "What could the girl have to say to me?"

"She is hardly a girl, in case you haven't noticed," he said somewhat lewdly. "She has a gift for you."

"Well, what is it, Kafta since you seem to know more than I? You seem bursting to tell me something."

In a deep, steady voice he said, "She has your son, Ramose."

I stood naked in the tub, dropping the blade into the water. "What? Do not toy with me!"

"She has your son."

Stepping out of the tub, I yelled for Axteris. The young man returned with fresh linen towels. He immediately began drying my body. I could hardly believe my ears. "How do you know this is true? Did you see him?"

"Yes; it is the truth. I made her show me the boy herself. He is good-looking but small. Then again, I hear babies are generally small. They can't all be coming out of their mothers walking and talking like you and I." Kafta poured me a glass of wine mixed with water. "Here, you look like you need this."

I drank it and sat down in a padded chair as Axteris rubbed oil on my feet and wrapped a linen towel around my waist. "Tell me everything. I want to know everything."

"Sitamen did not confide in me about the details, General. I do not know how she managed it, but it is true. She has your son. Rescued him, I think. She wants you to come in the morning. 'Tell him to come and see his son,' she said to me in that voice of hers. You know it drives me mad."

Again I ignored his insinuations. Sitamen was very childlike in many ways, including her voice. That was a trait that Kafta often enjoyed in women. "What of Ayn? Was she there too? Did you see her?"

"No, I did not."

"I see. Where is Sitamen, then?"

"At her new palace. She has left the Royal Harem for good, apparently. Some falling out with her mother. That is where we will meet her. If you are up to it?"

"Let us go now. I want to see my son."

"It is only a short ride. If we arrive before the appointed time, they may not let us in. You know how these royals are, Ramose. Best stick to the plan."

"Then we will sleep in our saddles, but I am going to see my son."

"Have it your way, Stubborn One. If you want to see the queen and your son looking like one of Osiris' dead army, be my guest."

A chill crawled up my spine. I scowled and said, "I don't look that bad."

"Yes, you do. But at least you smell better than you did." He grinned, showing his missing teeth. "Have patience and wait. Tomorrow will come. It always does! Unless you are dead."

"I was never any good at waiting."

He laughed again and nodded. "That is true. What will you name your son?"

I thought about Inhapi again. She had chosen the boy's name, so sure was she that Ayn would agree to our offer. "Kames will be his name." Weariness washed over me like an invisible force. I could not remember feeling more tired, even after a long campaign.

"A good name, General. Child of the bull, eh? Yes, that is a good name."

Suddenly, the black cat roared from her confinement. I had forgotten her. Maybe Kafta was right. I should stay at home one more night. I had some things to tend to anyway. "We will stay tonight and leave at first light."

"In that case, may I claim an empty bed?"

"Yes, the boy will show you where you can sleep. I will eat some food and sleep a few hours myself."

"Very well, General." He left me alone to dress and sent Axteris away. I could not help but think about my sudden change in fortune. The gods were not through with me after all. My son, he who would carry my name, was alive! As I shaved the last of the unwanted hair from my face, I thought about the cat. I walked to my rooms and retrieved my short sword. The cat screamed again as if she knew what I had planned.

When I entered her dank room, she met me with a low, menacing growl and swiped her wide paw at me. Silently I reached for the chain. Her dark fur was almost blue; her eyes grew larger and brimmed with hatred as if she too blamed me for Inhapi's death.

"I promised you that either you or I would die, Evil One. You accuse me with your eyes, but I have done nothing. I did not know what Inhapi intended, nor did I bid her to do what she did. Now, I intend on keeping my promise. My son is alive, and my purpose continues. Yours, however, has come to an end."

Snarling deeply, she seemed to understand my meaning. I tugged the chain, pulling the cat closer to me as I wrapped the metal around my hand. She was close now, so close that she could assault me easily, just as I could assault her. I raised my knife above my head, gripping the handle expertly in my right hand as I prepared to make my move. We paced around the smelly room until she paused and I knew she was ready to take action. I snatched the chain as the cat pounced, sending her to the ground in a heavy thud. I had only a fraction of a second to deliver my blow, and I did it as if the gods themselves directed my hand. The panther's right paw came toward me again, and the claws gleamed as she extended them fully. Her aim landed, and she scratched me across my chest. I drove the knife into her chest as she screamed once and collapsed on the ground in a lifeless heap of fur and blood. After a few seconds, she stopped breathing and surrendered to her fate.

With one strike I had killed the animal. I drove the blade into the heart of the beast.

I prayed this was a sign of things to come.

Chapter Five

The Aten—Nefertiti

The Aten dove under the far horizon, and Amenhotep and I shed our clothing and slid into the Crescent Pool. I swam deep into the cool darkness and bobbed to the top, kicking my feet as I rose to the surface with a smooth splash. He laughed in delight as I turned to dive again, unashamedly displaying my nude body for him. He dove after me and we swam down together, hiding from the world for a few seconds.

Here in the depths of the blue water we were just Nefertiti and Amenhotep, two people who shared an unbreakable bond of love and purpose. Together we would build a new Egypt, a shining place full of love and peace. With a kiss we rose back to the surface, and soon we were frantically kissing and touching one another. I did not care that Pharaoh's guard, the Mazoi, lingered nearby.

Ever since the priests' unscheduled meeting in my husband's courts, tensions had grown in the Egyptian capital. Amenhotep had done as he promised and encouraged his citizens to give to Amun, but the order had the expected effect. The people took offense to the demand, but no one brought accusations against Amenhotep. As a result, more and more of the people, especially young men and women, abandoned the dark temples of Amun and joined us in worship under the open pavilions of the Aten. After each such ritual, whether it was the welcoming or sending away of the Aten, Amenhotep often talked with them, listening to their ideas and getting to know them. He was young—the crowds he drew were young. Together they were a force to be reckoned with. There was much excitement about this new time—the new age of the Aten.

And the priests were watching.

There had been rumors that some of the other temple priests and priestesses were unhappy too, but none were as vocal as those who represented Amun.

Amenhotep guided me to the side of the pool, and we made love under the stars. I whispered his name, as I knew he liked me to do, and wrapped my legs tighter around his waist. When we were through with our lovemaking, I floated on the water as he held my hands. I gazed at the stars above us. I never tired of looking at them, even though I saw them less often now. For a happy moment, I thought about Pah and how she used to point out each one with such excitement and how she would draw pictures with her fingers to show me the hidden shapes in the night sky. She had been so wise and kind when we were young girls. I had yet to go see her in the temple, but I had plans to do so tomorrow. I did not know what to expect.

"Come, Nefertiti. I cannot let you distract me any longer," he said with a soft smile. "I need to speak with you."

I swam toward him and climbed on his back, kissing him once more. "Is that what I am to you, a distraction?"

He smiled his wide, sexy smile but did not answer with a flirtatious comment as he normally would. As we stepped out of the water, servants ran toward us with clean linen sheets. They dried us, but I took the comb from Menmet's hand. She always seemed to snag my hair, I supposed because she had no hair of her own to contend with. I had yet to shave my head like most Egyptian women of my status, and I had no plans to do so even though Menmet continued to advise me that I should. My husband loved my hair, and so far, I had not succumbed to the scourge of Thebes, brown lice. I had to admit there were times when the combination of my hair, a wig and a crown made it unbearably hot, but my pride would not allow me to take the razor to my head. Not just yet.

I dressed quickly, and we sat at the small table. After combing the tangles from my hair, I handed the comb back to Menmet. She sensed Pharaoh's mood and disappeared with the others. With a nervous glance I could see them exiting the chambers all together, something they rarely did.

"I have something to tell you."

"I too have something to share. But you go first, please." My heart was awash with excitement. The physician had left only a few hours ago, and he had confirmed Memre's expert appraisal. I was carrying Amenhotep's child. I could not believe I had waited this long to tell him my secret. "On second thought," I said quickly, "if

I don't tell you now I will burst! I have to tell you my good news."

Leaning on his elbow, his chin in his hand, Amenhotep gave me a permissive smile. I rose from my chair and stood before him, then suddenly knelt as a supplicant would. He said nothing, but I could tell by his stillness that my movement surprised him. I didn't know what he expected me to say, but I blurted out the words in a rush, "I am carrying your child, Pharaoh Amenhotep. It is confirmed by the physician this day."

When he didn't react the way I expected, I looked up cautiously. He walked away from me and began to pace the room, as he did when in deep thought or worry. I remained on my knees, worried about what he would say or do next. Without standing, I sat on the floor before his chair, my hand protectively over my still flat stomach. Amenhotep paced and said, "This *is* a surprise, a complete surprise."

"A happy surprise?"

"What?" He paused his pacing and rubbing his chin.

I stood swiftly, angry and hurt. "You act as if I told you I stole some figs from the table. Didn't you hear me? I am pregnant, husband!"

"Of course I heard you!" Amenhotep walked toward me in three strides and put his hands gently on my shoulders. "This is the best gift anyone has ever given me, and I love you for it."

I hugged him impetuously, but I could sense that something was still wrong. "Then why is there no smile on my Pharaoh's face?"

"I am happy, but there is more to think about than just my happiness. Please sit, and I will tell you all." I eased into the chair and tossed my wet hair behind my shoulders. The silence was excruciating, but I waited to see what Amenhotep would say.

"Years ago, my father entered into negotiations with several of our enemies. He was a man of peace, my father, despite what you might hear. He was not afraid of war, but he valued the blood of his people. He often said he would fight a thousand wars if the only blood that would spill would be that of our enemies." He took a swig of wine from his cup and continued pacing. "At first the Babylonians and the Hittites refused his attempts at negotiations. But like so many others, they were too tempted by the gold of Kemet to resist. Eventually they came to us, ready to parlay their way into an alliance. It was easy enough to do. Everyone wants Egyptian gold, but we laid heavy restrictions on our neighbors. By restricting the distribution of the gold to approved nations only, Pharaoh very easily brought the Hittites and Babylonians to Thebes."

Like a bolt of lightning striking a Benben stone, the full impact of his words began to reveal to me what this lesson in history was truly about. "This is about Tadukhipa, isn't it?" I swallowed, feeling miserable.

He didn't answer me directly, not at first. "It took work to bring them to their knees, but they eventually came to Thebes to submit themselves to Pharaoh. When they did, they were not humiliated. They were welcomed. Remember, the Hittites had been warring with us at that time for over twenty years. It was time to end the bloodshed. And yes, Tadukhipa's father was very eager to make peace, but one of the stipulations was that Pharaoh would take her into his household."

"I know this story," I said glumly.

"From whom? My mother? It is no secret that she hates Tadukhipa, and I suppose I would feel the same way if I were her. But Tadukhipa is not to blame. I am sure she did not ask to be traded for peace. However, that is only half the story. The Hittites expected to receive a bride in return, and the Hittite king wanted Sitamen. He was disappointed to learn that Egyptian kings do not simply give their daughters away. To make up for the perceived slight, Pharaoh promised to elevate Tadukhipa to the position of wife."

"Please just tell me what you want to say, husband."

"I cannot continue to ignore the wife I inherited, Nefertiti. The Hittites have come to see what I will do with Tadukhipa. I cannot send her back home in shame and risk a war between our nations."

"A war over one woman?"

He laughed bitterly. "Yes, and wars have occurred over much less. My advisers tell me this is no light matter. Can we risk such offense now when we are on the verge of a new kingdom—a new Egypt? I have the plans for our new city, a city dedicated to the Aten. Surely you see this."

"This has nothing to do with cities or the Aten! This has everything to do with us—Amenhotep and Nefertiti!" I was standing now, arms stiff and fists clenched.

"You think I want to do this? I already sent my sister Sitamen away because I know she hates you. That was easy enough, but I cannot do that with Tadukhipa! She is a foreign king's daughter and she was—is—the wife of Pharaoh! How now can she be anything less?"

I could not believe the words I was hearing. After all his talk of love and fidelity Amenhotep was considering taking Tadukhipa as wife—in the truest sense of that word. With all the privileges and experiences that came with that union. "I never asked you to send Sitamen away. We are not talking about your sister!"

"Tell me, my Queen. Have you never had to make a hard decision? Have you never had to go against your own heart? Is it so different in the Red Lands?"

I wanted to scream, "Yes, I have!" but I said nothing. I was afraid that if I opened my mouth, unintended words like, "I never wanted to come here!" would slip off my tongue. Or I might tell him the truth—he had not been my first love.

"This is nothing more than a formality. It will have no meaning at all, Nefertiti."

"A formality? When is lovemaking ever just a formality? Am I supposed to believe that will satisfy Tadukhipa? You and I both know what this is about!" This was about who would be his chief queen, the Great Wife of Egypt. Tadukhipa would do everything she could to convince him to raise her to that position.

"Yes, we do, and I must think about Egypt! I am, after all, Pharaoh!"

"Then think about Egypt!" If I could have stormed out, I would have, but doing so would have broken one of the rules of court. Never turn your back on Pharaoh unless dismissed. I could not deny it—Amenhotep had the upper hand. He always did. He always would. I could not afford to put myself in jeopardy right now. No more than I was at this very moment, arguing with the man who could order the killing of my entire tribe.

Amenhotep was furious at my lack of understanding. "When I first met you, I knew that I would love you, that you would be mine. I wanted you more than any woman I have ever met because you were strong, kind and intelligent. Not just for your beauty. Use that intelligence now, Nefertiti. Do you think I don't know how you must feel? I do know. I have spent my whole life doing things I did not want to do. This is just one more of those things." My jealous heart resisted his reasoning. I did not want to forgive him or believe him. I did not want to accept what I must.

"The truth is, she is already my wife. I cannot now abandon her. Her uncle and cousins are here to observe my care for her. I do not need their approval, but I do not need war either. Not when half the priests are against me! Is that what you want? Will that make you happy?"

"No," I said sullenly. "I do not want that."

Quietly he said, "I do not think the arrival of the Hittites is a coincidence. Tadukhipa has complained to them, and now I must make a show of caring for her. It is only for a short time. Then it will be you and me again, my queen and my love."

I couldn't help myself. I had to ask. "And you will lie with her?"

"You know the answer to that." After a minute of silence he added, "Tomorrow there will be a formal dinner to welcome the ambassadors. Then I will travel north with Tadukhipa for a few weeks."

I stepped back. "You are leaving me for a few weeks? What am I supposed to do while you are gone?"

"It is my desire that the people see you as an extension of me. You will learn to rule, Nefertiti. You need to see the people, and they need to see you. I will instruct my steward on what to do. Follow his advice, and you will be fine."

"I cannot believe you are leaving me," I said in a flat voice, the weight and importance of his request not registering in my understanding yet.

"It is only for a little while. Please, Nefertiti. Now is the time to be queen. Now is the moment that counts. Think of the future."

I stared at him wide-eyed. "What are you asking me to do?"

He reached his hand out and stroked my wet hair, toying with the ends where it was beginning to curl. "Care for the people, Nefertiti. Just as you cared for the treasures of your tribe. Show my people that you are not just my wife but the true and rightful queen of Egypt. Find some reasonable causes to defend without angering the Amun priests. I trust you in this. I know you will not fail."

I raised my chin in acknowledgment, but I could not hide the hurt in my eyes. I refused to say anything else. What else could I say? I would never change his mind.

With a sigh he said, "It will be this way whether you like it or not." With those words, my husband left me alone in his chambers, and I had no idea where he went.

I did not wait for him to return. I wiped the tears from my face and returned to my own rooms. The stares I received from some of the servants told me that our argument had not gone unnoticed. Everyone in the palace would know by now. What did I care? Tadukhipa could have her little victory over me—I had Pharaoh's child in my belly! Menmet shuffled behind me and scampered in front of me to open the door.

"Do not worry, Queen Nefertiti. Menmet will help you." She closed the curtains behind us and took my hand, leading me deeper into my chamber. In a whisper she said, "Tadukhipa will not win."

"Were you listening to our conversation, Menmet?" I frowned at her suspiciously.

"It is no secret, my Queen. This was inevitable. Now is the time to fight and win! You must be our Great Queen. Our Pharaoh needs a good queen to care for his people. I see that you care. Menmet sees. I will help you. Do not cry, beautiful lady." She reached out her open arms, and I fell into them. I cried on to her tiny shoulder as she crooned and stroked my hair. When my heart had wrung out all its tears, I sat on a nearby couch and stared out the window. She offered me a cup, but I refused it. I could not dwell on this any longer. I had to think about something else. I wiped at my nose with a handkerchief. It had tiny blue flowers embroidered around the edges. I wondered where I got these from. Some gift from a courtier, I supposed.

"Tell me about your home, Menmet. Where are you from? Have you always served here in Thebes? I can tell by your language that like myself you were not born here."

"No indeed, my Queen, I am not from here. I have been here only for one year, but my older sisters have been here for many years. My father is an Egyptian, yes, but my mother comes from a land in the East. Priests of Amun cannot marry, did you know?" I turned to look at her and shook my head. "But apparently they can make children." She laughed, but it was not a happy sound. "Well, the highest priests cannot. Still, Heby comes many times to see my mother, and he brings her gifts. He has many daughters but no sons, and he is kind enough to place his many daughters in the courts of Pharaoh."

"Are you the youngest, Menmet?"

"Yes, except one. I have one more sister, Salama, but she is lame and will not walk, no matter how much we plead with the gods on her behalf. Although she is lame, she is clever and can sew beautiful things, like those."

I smiled at her. "She made these for me?"

"Yes." She looked down, embarrassed. "I could not refuse her."

"I love them. The flowers are perfect, and there are no crooked stitches. She is very talented."

"I will tell her. You will make her smile for the rest of her life."

Spontaneously I patted her hand and smiled at her. "Your mother must bring your sister here so that I may meet them both."

Menmet shook her head, her bobbed wig swinging gently as she looked down again. "Oh no, that can never be. I could not offend you in that way."

"In what way, Menmet? I would never be offended by meeting your sister or your mother."

"Yes, but Salama is not perfect. As I said, she is lame. I cannot bring such imperfection into the presence of the Great Wife of Pharaoh."

"I am not that, and even if I were, I would not enforce such foolish rules. I cannot speak for those who came before me, but I assure you, Menmet, I do not feel that way. All children are treasures and should be treated as such. Where I am from..." I knew I should not speak of the past. I had been reminded on more than one occasion to speak only of the present, to speak only of Egypt not of my Meshwesh upbringing. But I felt I had to correct Menmet. "Where I am from, children are our treasures. All children, even the imperfect ones, are loved and cared for. I do not think otherwise, and neither shall those in my court."

Menmet's round face brightened and she said, "Thank you for saying so, my Queen. If everyone thought as you, maybe there would be no more sadness—no child offerings. I suppose we are lucky that Salama has not been offered to the fires. Now, let Menmet help you. We must find the best gowns, the best wigs and the most glorious jewels in all of Egypt. We will show these Hittite savages how we dress in Egypt. They will see who is truly the Greatest Queen!"

"Child offerings? What are you talking about?"

She froze on the spot and answered me as if I were stupid, "The sacrifices. Where the children go, the ones who are imperfect or unwanted for some reason."

I felt sick at the idea. I insisted that she tell me everything she knew. "I want to know about these child offerings. Tell me, Menmet."

"Very well, my Queen." The girl sat down on the painted floor at my feet and sighed. "Sometimes, when a child is born not perfect, maybe she is missing some toes or her legs are crooked, she is given to the gods. They will receive her, reshape her and send her again. Most of these memfre children, for that is what the priests call them, go to the temples of Amun. Not all temples accept children, but many do. The priests give the parents money for the children and then cast the children into the fire. I think Heby wanted to offer my sister to his god. He did not win the argument."

"Fires? What?" I rose to my feet, my hands flying to my stomach again. I felt the nausea rising. How could this happen in my husband's kingdom? "Does Amenhotep—I mean, Pharaoh—know about this?"

"I am sure he knows. Everyone does. It is no secret, my Queen, although it is not spoken of…much."

"This is astonishing. How do they justify such cruelties? Who would do such a thing to a child?"

She shook her head and stared down at her hands.

"Does your father do this, Menmet? Is that why you fear him so? Does he threaten you with your sister?"

She nodded without looking up. "She is still young, and my mother grows too feeble to care for her properly. I do not think she will change her mind, but what if she does? What if she were to die?"

"You have no reason to fear, Menmet. Not anymore!" I sprang from my couch and walked to my cedar closets.

"What do you intend to do?" She scrambled to help me. Her voice sounded fearful and uncertain.

"I am not sure yet, but I can tell you what I don't intend to do. I do not intend to sit around and do nothing. We must be careful, Menmet, but I will put a stop to this. My husband told me to find a just cause. I have." I snatched a few robes from the closet and tossed them on my bed. Like my husband did when he planned something, I began to pace my chambers. "Tell a messenger to send for my uncle. I will receive him this evening. Also, have my chef arrange a meal for us. We will eat together in the outer chamber."

She started to leave, but I called after her. "And send a scribe, Menmet. I have letters to write. Better make that a scribe who knows the language of Grecia. I want to speak to them in their native tongue."

She bowed quickly and said, "It will be done."

I sighed as I sifted through the colorful robes and gowns. So Tadukhipa had won this round. She used her connections to best me, but it would be an empty victory; I had Amenhotep's heart. If only we had stayed in the Crescent Pool. If only I could dive deep into the waters and swim away from all this. But I couldn't. I had someone else to think about now besides myself. I had a child in my belly and children dying right here in Thebes. In just a few minutes my mind had shifted completely. I had a purpose now, something to think about other than myself and my husband's petty wife, Tadukhipa.

I might have won Pharaoh's heart, but now I had to win the hearts of his people. I would begin by dealing with this injustice. I prayed for wisdom as I began to think about how I would challenge this foul tradition and bring down these evil priests. Now I had a reason to destroy them. I rejected all the robes I had selected and walked back to the closet. I found a forgotten robe in the back. It had been a gift from Omel, one that I had never expected to wear, but tonight I would. With renewed appreciation, I examined the back. A falcon soared across it, and tiny jewels dropped from its feathers.

If it was my destiny to be the falcon, then I might as well wear the garment.

Chapter Six

After Life—Tiye

The clumsy servant wrapped my head with the cloth, thinking that I would not see through the flimsy blindfold. What a foolish man! The idea of keeping my husband's grave hidden, even from his wife...as if I would corrupt the body of the only man I had ever loved. These priests took too much upon themselves. What a fool! I did not protest, however, and took the idiot's offered hand while I disembarked from the litter. If he had any intelligence at all, he might have asked himself how I could see his hand. But he did not appear to notice. He led me into the narrow passageway and removed my bandage with a flourish as if I would gasp and swoon over the priests' handiwork. If he thought I would do so, he was doubly a fool.

"Leave me now," I said as I blinked my eyes to adjust them to the light. It was very dim, but there were torches along the walls and I could see the farthest wall in the distance. It was painted with my husband's name and an image of the two of us together holding a lotus flower. I had seen this before. A dozen or so years ago, the builder brought us the model to look at before work ever began. From what I could tell, he had done an excellent job of copying the images and had not missed the details.

The servant left me without protest, and I strolled along the cool tunnel that would lead me to my husband's final resting place. All things had been accomplished; his body would be interred, and soon the tomb would be sealed for all eternity, never to be opened again even for Amenhotep's queen.

They might as well bury my heart here too!

One day, I would rest just on the other side of the thick stone wall that would separate us. The priests said that we would be reunited in death, and until the passing of my husband I had also believed this. But now I was not so sure. Who truly knew the journey of the soul? No one could explain it to me, not to my satisfaction, and I had searched for assurances for months. In our many years together, Amenhotep and I had whispered promises to one another concerning our deaths. He would come to me—I would come to him.

I walked alongside the painted walls and examined the paintings. As I drew closer I could plainly see Amenhotep's broad shoulders and strong arms. The massive painting became even more breathtaking as I entered the room. "My love," I whispered. I stood before the cold stone wall and touched it lovingly with my fingers. I traced the cartouche, reading it a hundred times. I cared not if anyone saw me. I laid my head against the wall and whispered his name, but he did not answer.

Oh, how I wished I had taken the knife and cut my own throat when I heard the news! Oh, how I wished I had thrown myself off the top of my palace! But here I stood, coward that I was, alive, even though many days I felt dead and empty.

I leaned against the wall with the cartouche at my back and took in the view of the room. It had a low ceiling, but there was no shortage of furniture fit for a king. The firelight sparkled off the tips of the golden spears. Here was Amenhotep's chariot and everything he would need to go to war in the Otherworld. It was surreal to think of him at war with someone in the Land of the Dead. Would he see Thutmose, our dear son? I sighed into the silence. No answers came. I traveled about the room touching all my husband's things one last time. As I did, my mind wandered.

Once, when I was young, I drank from the Navel of Isis. The strange pink concoction had overcome me for many days after I consumed it. Unlike some priestesses I never took another drink of that ghastly brew again. I did not enjoy the experience, the feeling that I had no control, the blurriness of my memories. And I wanted to remember. Indeed, the older I got, the more difficult it was to remember recent events. But the past—oh, it was so near. I felt again as if I were drunk from the sacred drink, but somehow I had fallen into the depths of sorrow unable to recover. How long had it been since I'd seen my son?

I found another portrait of Amenhotep. I kissed the wall and rubbed my hands along it again as I explored a nearby corridor. These rooms were also filled with Amenhotep's things. Some new, some old. I could see his collection of jewelry, all pieces polished and shining in open boxes, just waiting for the Pharaoh to claim them again.

I kept walking.

In the next room, there were sealed jars of wine, baskets of bread and garlic and all sorts of foods—all made of stone. It must last for all eternity. What better ingredient than stone? I walked down the corridor and found another room full of the discarded items from Amenhotep's life. These were more personal, more revealing of the man Amenhotep truly was. There were rows of sandals, piles of folded laundry including linen gowns, sumptuous silk robes and many crowns. I opened the nearby chest and saw that it was full of arm bands, all in different colors. I picked them up and then let them fall back to the chest. I closed the chest and stood in the hallway. There were many more rooms to explore, but I did not need to look any further. I could see that all things had been given the appropriate attention and that all things had been done for Pharaoh just as he commanded. The only thing that was not here was his body. It would be delivered tonight; his priests alone would attend the actual burial.

I walked out of his tomb feeling as if I had left my own soul behind. The bumbling servant greeted me, asking if all was well. I mumbled my approval to him and was lifted into the litter. I didn't struggle when he covered my eyes again. A few minutes later we made another stop—this time at my own tomb. Finally my resting place was ready to receive my body. I found the timing ironic. Perhaps it was wishful thinking on their part that after all this time my grave was ready. I could almost hear their thoughts: *As soon as the old king's tomb was readied, he died—maybe this is a portent! The old queen will die too!*

The truth was, I had insisted that this be done immediately, believing the whole time that soon I would join Amenhotep. But each day the sun rose and I was still alive.

Without waiting for the stupid attendant to remove the bandage I snatched it from my own head, ignoring his look of disapproval. *Kill me, then, brave one!* I thought, scowling back at him.

I walked with my head held high into my newly finished tomb. The walls were gaily colored with bright blue peacocks, a palm-lined river flowed along the expanse of it, and a collection of birds fluttered above it all. If by chance I was not permitted into the Otherworld and had to dwell here for eternity, I would at least have something pleasant to look at. Along the entrance wall were portraits of my family. I smiled at seeing the image of my brown-skinned Thutmose and my own parents. How small they appeared to me now! I could also see the list of the names that my beloved had given me over the years. I did not take the time to read them, for I knew them all by heart.

Hereditary Princess, Lady of the Two Lands, Great King's Wife, Mistress of Upper and Lower Egypt, Keeper of Pharaoh's Heart.

What did any of these titles mean now? What wouldn't I have given to spend one more day sailing across the lake with my husband by my side? What wouldn't I have given to lay my head in his lap and feel his hands stroke my hair? I walked to the back of the tomb and into the inner chamber that would hold my sarcophagus. I lay on the golden bier and stared at the ceiling. It had been lovingly painted with stars and heavenly sights. I closed my eyes and crossed my arms over my chest pretending to be dead. What if I could die? I was strong. I could just will myself to die, couldn't I?

Oh, Amenhotep! Let me come to you now! Summon me, my love!

My words echoed through the chamber, trembling in the air. I waited, hoping to hear my husband's voice ring through the emptiness, but alas, I heard nothing. Only the beating of my heart, the pulsing of my blood, my shallow breathing. Determined, I remained still, my arms across my chest in the figure of one who was dead. These actions availed me nothing. I lived still. I sighed into the darkness and whispered once again, "Amenhotep, call me to you. Call me to you, and I will run like a gazelle. Call me to you, and I will crush my own heart to obey. Call me to you, and I will seal myself into these rooms and wait for death to take me. Tell Osiris that I long to join you, I, your rightful wife and Queen of Egypt."

I heard nothing for a long while and then the rustling of something. Quiet at first, then louder, clearer. It was something dry, something unseen. "Amenhotep, is that you?" I whispered, my faithless heart pounding like a tightly bound drum. I heard the sound again and did not move.

Then I heard his voice. Not in the air and not in my ears, but I heard it in my heart. His words came to me: *Remember our sons.*

The one alive, the one who is dead. Remember your promise to me. Do what I failed to do. With a gasp I sat up, swinging my short legs over the side of the cold metal stand. I slid off the box and spun about the room, hoping to see the tall figure of my husband. For a second, I did see a shadow looming in the corner. Then it faded. It was nothing. I knew it was a foolish thing to hope for. He was dead—I had seen him dead. I had visited the embalmers. I knew Amenhotep was gone. Whether by his own choice or by the gods, he was gone. But my promise to him lived on, and I must obey it. I must keep it. For him and for my sons.

"Yes, husband. I remember my promise to you. I will do as you ask, and then I will join you, my love. Prepare a place for me!"

I heard nothing but the soft rustling again and walked out of my tomb with a new resolve. As much as I longed for death, even embraced it, my work here was not yet done. I had heard his voice, and that was proof to me that he was not yet at rest. I would not fail him. I stepped out of the dark tomb rubbing my hands along the cool wall. I did not hesitate in the doorway but stepped into the sun, embracing its warmth by turning my face to it. I breathed in the dusty air and climbed into my litter, waving away the servant who would attempt to blindfold me once again.

"Don't be a fool! This is my own tomb. Do you think that I would rob myself? Do you think that I would tell someone where I shall lie? Move out of my way." Surprised at my abruptness, the man stepped back with his gold cloth in his hand. Memre, my faithful servant, waited in the litter for me. I said to her, "We must go see the new Queen. There are things that I must do—that we must do." With a grim nod, Memre gave the order and the litter began to move. We had barely exited the valley before she and I had worked up our plan. Nefertiti must be queen, and I must have my revenge.

The Desert Queen had not been the quick study I had hoped for, but in truth I had abandoned her to wallow selfishly in my grief. The time for that was ended. I was sure the Monkey had not spent her time mourning my husband.

"Have they arrived yet?" She did not ask me who. Besides Huya, Memre knew my thoughts better than anyone. It was the Hittites I spoke of, the grasping, deceitful Hittites.

"Yes, and their mission is clear. Even now your son is entertaining them, listening to them, hoping to follow in his father's footsteps and keep peace between the kingdoms. I wonder what lies the Hittite woman is pouring into his ear."

"He will entertain her for a time because he is Pharaoh, but it would take much more than some sweet words to lure him away from Nefertiti. Of that I am sure. The boy is smitten with her—I had to do little more than introduce the two of them. Nothing less than Fate brought them together."

She snorted. "Are you Fate now, my Queen? Is that one of the titles of Isis? If I remember correctly the same could be said for you and your husband, but you still had to fight to keep him."

"Do not mock me!" I barked at her. As usual she shrugged it off and I continued, "What can these Hittites offer my son besides a spoiled princess? What would lure him away from his Desert Queen? What threat is there?"

"Perhaps there is none. Like you say, these are merely formalities."

I tapped my lip with my finger and looked at her through slitted eyes. "What are you not telling me?"

"Would I keep anything from you, my Queen? In regards to Tadukhipa, I know nothing beyond what you already know. However, when I visited Nefertiti I saw she had the daughter of Heby in her retinue."

"Heby's daughter? When did this happen? Why was I not consulted?"

"You would not allow me in your room, my Queen. I do not know who made the arrangements for Nefertiti's court, but I can tell you that there are a great many questionable characters in her circle."

I sat up stiffer and gave her a wrinkled frown. "Well, we shall see about that. I'm anxious to meet Heby's daughter and see what other snakes are slithering in the grass."

We rode the rest of the way in silence except for the flickering of my fan and the footsteps of my attendants. I could hear the boisterous sounds of the city as we approached. Thebes was not a quiet place—and it had taken on quite a frenzied feeling of late. With so many new visitors to court, if you could count the Hittites as new, and the arrival of the surprisingly exciting Desert Queen, there was much to be done. Courtiers from around Egypt had arrived hoping to catch a glimpse of the beautiful young monarch and her handsome Pharaoh. Of course there were also other factions present including those representing Kiya and other families, great families, noble families who hoped Pharaoh would look with kindness upon their households and bring their daughters into such elevated states of grace. It was the dream of all noble families to marry into Amenhotep's bloodline. And since there was no limit to the number of wives an Egyptian king could have, all things were possible. Even now Amenhotep's neglected harem was ridiculously large. I would never wish my daughter to fill a spot in the harem, as it was a lonely life, but many fathers did just that.

"What of Sitamen? How does she fare in her new palace? She has not been to see me since her father passed to the Otherworld."

"Perhaps we should go see her first, my Queen. A visit from her mother would do her good."

It was my turn to snort in derision. I remembered that Memre had a particular softness for my daughters, especially Sitamen. Detecting my attitude, she wisely said nothing else. How could I explain to her the complexity of my feelings for my daughter? Finally the swaying slowed. I could tell the attendants were tired, for their feet shuffled clumsily after walking for hours in the heat. I happily got shuffled out of the litter, resisting the urge to rub my tired back and behind. How queenly would that have been? Instead I walked straight up the steps to one of the cool patios. This was my son's palace, and I would not rush into his courts during his negotiations, no matter how much I hated Tadukhipa's people. He had enough to think about now. I quietly vowed to visit him in a day or two before I returned home. It had been too long since I had seen his handsome face, a face so much like his father's.

Immediately a flurry of activity surrounded me. I took a seat and allowed the various attendants to meet my needs. I whispered to Memre, and she left me to do my bidding. I did not have to wait long.

"Great Queen," the young Queen called to me. She bowed and to my surprise greeted me with the sacred Isis gesture. With a delighted smile I returned the gesture and invited her to sit with me.

"Queen Nefertiti, how well you look. I trust my son is treating you well."

She could not hold back her smile. "He is the best of husbands, my Queen. Does he know you are here? I am sure he would want to see you." I took her hand and squeezed it. Yes, she was a beautiful girl. But still too kind, too trusting. I could see that in her eyes. *We will have to drive that out of her.* I also saw something else. What was that? Fear? Loneliness? Ah, she would have to get used to that. Fear and loneliness were a queen's constant companions.

"I will see him soon. It is you I came to see, Queen Nefertiti." I looked at Memre, and without saying a word she collected the servants and shooed them away so that my daughter-in-law and I could speak alone. She appeared to breathe a sigh of relief. "How are things between you two? Memre tells me you are with child. Is it true?"

"Yes, it is true."

"Then why are there no banners? No celebration? Egypt should know that a new Prince or Princess is soon to arrive. Surely your steward has instructed you in these things. The arrival of a child into your household is a holy, wonderful event, and it must be respected. Who do you have advising you?"

"I did as you asked me to. I made peace with my uncle. We have visited, and I have given him some tasks, but I have not planned on doing anything special yet in regards to the announcement of my child—our child. As you know, Amenhotep is in the middle of negotiating with the Hittites over their daughter and other things. I did not wish to complicate matters."

"Nonsense! Your child is the child of Pharaoh. I can promise you that Tadukhipa would offer you no such relief. She would insist on every advantage being bestowed upon her. You must do nothing less. It is a good thing that I have come, for your advisers, whoever they may be, are seriously derelict in their duties." Nefertiti appeared troubled, and I immediately felt sympathy for her.

It was hard being a new queen—especially an outsider, someone with no allies or influential friends. I had been away for too long. Why had Amenhotep not spoken to her about these things? Perhaps I had neglected them both. I chewed on the inside of my lip and peered at her.

"No matter. I'm here now, and I will help you. I can see you have something on your mind. What is it?"

"Amenhotep is leaving. He is taking a trip with Tadukhipa. He says it is to please the Hittites only, that his heart is not hers, but I know how things are. For all his strength he is but a man, and Tadukhipa a very cunning woman."

"There is nothing you can tell me about Tadukhipa that would surprise me. She was my sister-wife long before she was yours, but I know my son. She can throw whatever she likes at him. Flirtatious looks, succulent dishes, extravagant gifts, even decadent pleasures. Amenhotep is a man of character. A thinking man and not one to be won with a few back rubs or guilty pleasures. You are thinking like a commoner. And Tadukhipa is no common street whore. She is royalty, even if it is barbarian royalty. She was raised at a large court, which gives her an advantage over you, but I have no doubt that my son loves you and will put you above all his other wives, including his sister."

"He says that he cannot think only of himself but of all Egypt. He has made no promises to me, and I am to be left here to sit upon his throne. I'm glad you are here, for I do not know what to do." Suddenly she grasped my hands. "Promise me you will stay with me, Great Queen."

I had to remind myself not to flinch or slap her. I was not used to being handled. I took a deep breath and said, "If he has asked you to sit on his throne, he has afforded you a great privilege. He has never asked Tadukhipa to do such a thing. He is giving you the opportunity to show the people of Egypt that you are indeed truly worthy of the title of Great Wife. Do not disappoint him. I will spend a few days with you, but beyond that these things are up to you. I have my own destiny to fulfill, Nefertiti." Then she asked me a surprising question.

"Why did you pick me, Queen Tiye? Of all the women in the Red Lands and the Black Lands, why did you pick me? For I know it was you who orchestrated all this."

I looked deeply into her green eyes. She deserved an answer, but the truth was I did not know what led me to compel her to stay with me. Perhaps it was the desert blood that ran in our veins, calling us to one another. Perhaps it was the sight of her glorious red hair trailing down her narrow back—a true sign of the gods. Perhaps it was her willingness to give everything for her tribe. If she had refused my conditions, would I have helped her?

"I compelled you to stay because you were always meant to be here. This is your place. Not because I said so, and not because my son loves you, but because you were meant to be here. This is your destiny, Nefertiti." She nodded, acknowledging my words, And I added, "I have found it is better to spend less time questioning why and more time thinking about serving your Pharaoh. It helps to keep things in perspective. There is nothing outside of him. No god or goddess. Not even your children can you love as much as you love him." Suddenly my stomach rumbled and hunger struck me just as if it were a tangible thing.

The young queen must have heard my stomach's complaints, for she quickly said, "It would be my honor if you would join me for the evening meal. We can dine in my room where it is cool and quiet. I value your opinion, Great Wife."

I was sure that my presence was known all over the palace by now, so it would do us little good to hide out in the queen's chambers. However, this would serve as the perfect opportunity to meet her servants in an informal atmosphere. I agreed, and together we strolled to her rooms. We walked in silence and as I passed by the familiar painted columns and marble statues I remembered happier days. The echo of Thutmose's laughter. The playful giggles of my daughters. Amenhotep's booming voice as he called his many dogs to his side. To Egypt the palace was a grand place, a thing of beauty, a copy of the mansion of heaven. But to me it had been home. It felt good to be home again.

Chapter Seven

Choices—Sitamen

I rubbed the sandalwood oil all over my hands and arms as I enjoyed the peaceful quiet of my solitary bath house. I stared down into the palms of my small hands. I could hardly believe the things they had done just a few days ago. The blood—oh, so much blood—and the squirming, wriggling life they held.

I would never forget how the smell of the blood filled my nostrils, how it offended me. Warriors like Ramose must have smelled it all the time since they hacked, murdered and maimed as part of their careers. The general waited for me now, and my anticipation of the meeting surprised me. Rubbing the oil furiously into my cuticles, I thought about the few times we had exchanged words. If I were not Pharaoh's daughter, I was sure he would not know my name.

For someone with so much courage, at least that was the talk, Ramose knew very little about women. Like most men he took them at face and figure value. To men like him, women were merely convenient receptacles for their seed. Not equal at all. But that was his mistake.

I stared into the mirror and made an honest assessment of the face that stared back at me. Small like my mother with longer arms and legs, I had an angular face like my father. I also had his full lips and clear, smooth olive skin. Unlike the rest of the court, I had grown my hair back over the past few years, and it was a decision I did not regret. Doing so gave me a power and confidence I had not expected. I brushed my hair and let the dark brown cascades fall around my face. I no longer wore a crown except during those rare matters of state when anyone remembered to summon or include me. I preferred to leave my head bare, but as that was not acceptable for royalty, I did as the Persian women did; I wore jewels on my forehead and always had a wide necklace about my neck. These were my only adornments today. My brows were naturally heavy, but I'd recently had my servant shape them with wax and was pleased with the results.

My ears were too large, but there was nothing I could do about that except keep them hidden. Tadukhipa often said that my mother frowned when she saw me because I reminded her of the small brown bats she so feared, so large were my ears. I sniffed at the thought.

I had large brown eyes that were expressive, too expressive at times, but I had spent the past few months learning to wear the same mask that my mother wore so well. I became a master at controlling my emotions—I had been a child too long. Today would be my first audience with someone outside of my immediate circle of friends, and it would be a test of my abilities.

When my brother gave me this palace I felt such dismay because I knew that he had sealed my fate. He would not take me as a true wife, as some brothers did their sisters. I would not be so honored and would remain a forgotten minor queen until the day I died. I would never love or be loved by a man. I would never have children. The realization was more than I could bear. I would never forget Tadukhipa's expression of pity as I told her the news. How quickly she forgot me when I was no longer of use to her.

It did not take long to reconsider my thoughts about leaving the Royal Harem. I was glad to be free from the constant pulling and pushing between my mother and Tadukhipa. I was glad to be away from the turmoil caused by the redheaded Desert Queen. What a fool I had been to think that Inhapi and Tadukhipa were my friends! I tossed the brush down in anger thinking of the latter. Was I not Pharaoh's daughter? Didn't Amenhotep's blood run in my veins? Let them think me a "mouse" as they sometimes called me. Even a mouse had power. I practiced my smile in the mirror while I doused my skin with perfume. This perfume had been Inhapi's favorite. Whether he wanted to or not, Ramose would find the scent seductive—at least I hoped he would.

"My lady, the general is here."

"Good," I said as I continued to rub my skin until it shone. I had lovely skin, and I intended on showing it off. The servant lingered in the doorway as if to hear further instructions from me. I waved my hand dismissively and said, "You can go now. Make the general comfortable, and make sure he has plenty to drink. The good wine, Mariway."

"Yes lady." The girl scurried away to do my bidding.

I searched my closet for the garment I had in mind. I would wear nothing too grand today. I wanted General Ramose to see me as a woman, not a princess or a cast-off queen. I had to be patient—careful. Men like Ramose did not like to be forced into things; I would have to lead him into my plan.

Not for the first time, I thought about Ramose and the Meshwesh woman. What he ever saw in her I did not know. I did not understand the attraction. She was neither pretty nor intelligent, but apparently she had been skilled enough to produce Ramose a son.

I chose a plain tan-colored gown of ethereal fabric. It would float when I walked. The garment had no sleeves and a low neckline that plunged to my navel. I stepped into it and adjusted the straps as I studied myself in the mirror. Yes, this would do quite nicely. Even I could see how much I had changed!

Although I was dressed and ready to meet my guest, I was in no hurry. I wanted to remind Ramose of his rank and standing. Whether he considered me so or not, I was a queen.

I tore pieces from this morning's bread and tossed it to my birds. I loved my birds. I ran my fingers across the bars of the new cages. They were made of gold and were embellished with sapphires. My father and I shared a love for the blue stones. I had many gifts from him. Why should they not adorn the cages of my children? The dozen or so birds chirped with delight as I tossed the pieces into the cages. I poked my hand inside, and one of my favorites hopped onto my finger. As always I handled them with loving care. My mother had been right. I cared more for these birds than I did for the people around me. Birds were simple, gentle and loving creatures. They were happy to eat whatever came from my hand, and they provided me with endless songs without requiring coins or some benefit for themselves. I loved them, and when one died I always mourned. I prayed that one day I might become one, in either this life or the next. This was probably a fool's dream—a child's dream—but it was mine.

Nobody could steal dreams, could they?

After I finished chattering with my pets, I returned the tiny brown finch to his home. I dusted the crumbs from my hands and strolled along the columned porch outside my chambers. The sun had been up for quite some time, and the purple irises had fully opened to welcome the sunlight. I poked my nose into one and enjoyed the sweet aroma. The supple petals would not last very long in this heat, but luckily this kind produced blooms often. It never lacked flowers.

This bed of irises had been a thoughtful touch from my brother, who knew how much I loved living things. It was hard to hate him, and indeed I did not. I loved him. He and I had both been lost in the shadow of our dead brother Thutmose, forever hidden from our mother's heart. For a time, we had one another. We were as close as the twin stars, forever together, or so I had believed. I remembered the kind boy he had been. How he used to love bringing me birds and small kittens. He never shamed me or mocked me. But that was so long ago, before my mother twisted his mind against me. Before she stole his affection from me! Then she convinced my father to make me his wife and by doing so moved me from our home to the Royal Harem. My father had never claimed his rights as a husband, thankfully, but I had no doubt that my mother had wanted him to do so. "It will be the only way you have children, Sitamen. It is an honor to carry the seed of Amenhotep and your duty to keep our dynasty alive." The idea revolted me, and I suspected it also offended my father for he never engaged in such behavior. Queen Tiye had tidily removed me from my brother's and father's lives. Like most women she was a deceiver, a betrayer.

I heard shouts coming from below me and peered over the edge of the balcony. I heard Ramose's voice demanding to see me. I smiled to myself. Yes, I knew what I was doing.

A few minutes later, I heard the sound of Mariway's heavy feet padding into my room. "Lady, your guests are waiting in the portico. They've refused food and drink. And…"

"And?" I said, walking toward her calmly, my face a trained mask of control.

"The general demands to see you now. He says it is urgent and that he cannot wait any longer."

I could not help but laugh. To think such a Mouse as I could have such power over a man like Ramose. I was enjoying this more than I had imagined I would.

"Tell the general that I will come when it pleases me. Offer him food and drink again, and make him and his friend comfortable."

The girl looked unhappy to hear those words, but that was not my concern. Fortunately for her she did not express her unhappiness to me. She padded away again, and I stood on the balcony, hoping to hear the conversation. At that moment my birds decided to break into loud and boisterous songs. It was probably for the best. I waited another half an hour and then slowly descended the stairs to greet my guests.

Kafta saw me first. He tapped Ramose on the arm to draw his attention. The general had a dark, disapproving scowl on his face, but only for a moment. I could see my improvements had not escaped his notice. That pleased me and warmed my skin. I reminded myself not to look away or appear to notice. I stood at a distance. I welcomed them to my palace and gestured for them to follow me. It was another moment, another opportunity to demonstrate my power to the general. I was in charge here. This was not my brother's palace or the Royal Harem. I traveled the long hallway with the general and his man behind me. I did not engage them in conversation or turn my attention away from my destination. As I had instructed, my servants had gathered in the hallway and bowed obediently as we passed by them. I led my guests out of the palace, down the steps and to the grotto. Until I came to this place I had never seen such a grotto. I lived in an exquisite prison full of hidden delights.

Before we entered the tunnel that would lead us to the child, I paused. "Please wait here," I said to Kafta even as I waved Ramose ahead. Kafta shot Ramose a raised eyebrow, and the general nodded.

"As you wish," the bowlegged warrior grumbled before leaving us to walk through the grotto alone. At this point I did not make him walk behind me. I could tell my change in position made him uncomfortable, but he did not question it.

"I am sorry about your wife, General Ramose. I know she was a great favorite at court."

"Yes, she will be missed. Forgive me, Princess, if I do not feel talkative. I had given up hope on seeing my son, but to hear that he's here with you…I have to admit I am curious to know how he ended up in your care. And…"

We stepped out of the shady grotto and into the sunlit courtyard. Young servants milled about performing their tasks for the child. I had not left out a thing, and I wanted Ramose to see what good care his child had been in. There were small animals, a child's pool and many other amenities to enjoy. "I will answer all your questions, but first…" I waved Naomi toward me. In her arms was the precious, active bundle, the son of Ramose. I pushed my hair behind my shoulder and accepted the squirming child. He was quite handsome, despite the fact that he was only a few days old.

"General, meet your son."

I held the bundle up slightly and watched the man's face soften. I had known the soldier all my life and like many ladies in the court had admired his handsome face. I was pleased to see him immediately reach for the baby. Many men, including my own father, did not care to handle their offspring. I could see Ramose was not that kind of man. And that made me want him even more.

Yes! He is the one for me!

Funny that I should want him at all. He had been unfaithful to Inhapi, but she knew all about his dalliances and did not seem to mind. I would have been wroth with jealousy had he been my husband. The past few weeks I had tended to his lover, at least until the child was born.

I wasn't sure what I would do about Ramose until just now. I would never have children, not in the way most women had them. I would have to adopt mine, and what better child to adopt than the noble child of a decorated general? It was not an easy thing to want, but I wanted this baby and I wanted Ramose!

"Like this," I said with a soft laugh as he fumbled with his grip on the child. I led him by the arm to the shade and invited him to sit as he held his son. The soft white cloth of the child's blanket appeared even whiter next to the general's sun-bronzed skin. For the first time that I remembered, Ramose smiled a smile from the heart. It was a big smile that spread across his face, making him even more handsome, and I saw the fringes of his lashes wet with unexpected tears. My heart leapt at the sight of it. Oh yes, things were going nicely.

"He is well? Not sick or weak?"

"He is the strongest child I have ever seen. You should be proud of him. He will grow to be a strong warrior."

His deep voice rumbled, "I am proud of him." He finally looked me fully in the eyes, and I caught my breath. "Thank you, Princess."

"The pleasure is mine," I said, touching the child's soft hair with my finger.

"Is he always so quiet?"

I laughed. "No, indeed he is not. He can cry quite loudly when he is hungry, but we do not let him cry long. I have a wet nurse here who loves to dandle him at her breast."

He smiled at that and stared again into the sleeping child's face. "I do not want him spoiled. He is a soldier's son and will be a soldier himself one day." I nodded and sat in silence watching him count toes and fingers. "I wish he would open his eyes so I might see them."

"He has two," I said playfully. "Look in any mirror, General, and you will see them, for he has the eyes of his father."

"Please, call me Ramose."

I felt my face flush and said, "Very well, Ramose." Just at that moment the child began to squirm and fuss, as if he knew we were speaking of him. Ramose appeared nervous, and I smiled gently. "Let me take him. It is time to feed. See? He is a strong boy." I scooped up the child and handed him to Naomi, who sped away with him to find the baby's nurse.

I returned to my seat, leaning back on the cushion, I swung my feet up beside me. It seemed odd being so casual with a man, especially Ramose, but I wanted to enjoy every second.

"His name is Kames."

"Kames is a good name, and I am sure it will be on the lips of many throughout his life."

My answer pleased him, but he appeared unsure of me. "Forgive me for not telling you that Ayn was with me. I know that by doing so I extended your grief and worry, but you have to understand, I had only your son's welfare in mind."

"What do you mean? Is she still alive?"

I sipped from the cup of water that sat between us and met his eyes fully. "I was returning from visiting the Green Temple when my servant ran to tell me the news. It was then that I saw Ayn running from the palace and heard the commotion. She had a bruised face and blood on her hands. I hid her in the wine cellars under the Blue Gate for a few days and then moved her out of the city. When my brother gave me this palace as a gift, I brought her here. She was barely able to stand by then, so pregnant was she. I was convinced that she would have the baby immediately, but her pregnancy lasted longer than I expected. She stayed in those rooms there until she…"

He said nothing so I continued, "I don't know what made me hide her. I just did. I cannot explain my actions, Ramose. I wanted to bring her out many times, but I was afraid for the child. After the horrible thing happened with Inhapi, Tadukhipa was so angry that I was sure she would kill both the mother and the child. She said that she would, and I knew she did not care about rousing the wrath of my brother, his wife or anyone else. She had fallen out of his favor by that time. And you know how much she cared for Inhapi."

I blushed at my memories of the two women together. I had seen them often but had never participated in their activities. I did not know how much Ramose knew about his wife's practices, so I spoke cautiously. "I spoke with Kafta one afternoon and asked for his help. He advised me on how to move forward. I apologize for holding the truth back from you."

"She is dead?"

I met his gaze with steely resolve. "I wish I could tell you better news, but perhaps it is for the best. She has met her fate."

He swallowed but said nothing else for a long time. Small birds sailed into the courtyard and skittered about searching for treats. I had similar birds in my menagerie but none as lovely as these, with bold purple and blue feathers. I chided myself for wanting to capture them and put them in one of my pretty cages—I had plenty of birds. Why did I want the ones I could not possess? I should have had more pity, more appreciation for their freedom. But even more, I wanted to possess Ramose. He needed me, I would show him how much, but I had to move slowly. I had some skill in these matters. I had been observing the women in the harem all my life.

"What can I give you to thank you, Princess?" Ramose always addressed me as princess despite the fact that I had been a queen for many years. It used to irritate me, but now I liked hearing him call me by that title. I liked thinking that he still saw me as a princess of Egypt, not a forgotten queen doomed to dwell in this lavish prison except on the rare occasions when I was allowed to venture out. Hearing it made it easier to believe that I had a choice—that I still had a future.

"No thanks are necessary, Ramose. It was a joy to help bring Kames into the world—he is a beautiful child."

"I have taxed your hospitality long enough. I will take my son home now."

"Wait!" I stood swiftly. "Please stay a little while. You asked me what you could give me."

Shielding his eyes from the sun that rose above us, he looked into my face. It stung my heart to see the distrust, but I smiled at him pleasantly. "Stay with me. At least for today. I do not receive many guests, and I would like to hear news about my brother." I knew he wanted to refuse me. "Please," I added. I couldn't give him my proposal yet. I needed more time because I knew he would refuse me if I told him now. He needed to trust me, to listen to reason. The dark circles under his eyes and the haggard look he wore told me that Ramose had not been cared for in a while. He needed me, even if he did not yet know it.

"If it pleases you, then I am happy to stay for a little while," he added. "Once again you show me honor that I do not deserve. I find you very much grown, Princess. Very different from the girl who used to hang on her father's neck. Tell me, do you still keep birds?"

"Please, call me Sitamen. It has been a long time since I have heard anyone call me that name. It is music to my ears and makes me feel young."

He laughed, and it was a pleasant but unpracticed sound. I doubted he had done much laughing lately. "You are very young still. If it pleases you, I will call you Sitamen, at least when we are alone." I suppressed a beaming smile into a demure one. In spite of himself, Ramose was flirting with me. That at least was something.

"That pleases me greatly. Thank you for the indulgence."

As he stood he looked tired, even more tired than earlier. "Princess, one more thing and this may sound strange. I would like to see Ayn. Is her body here?"

I clasped my hands in front of me as casually as I could. "Oh dear. The woman's body is no longer here. I asked the priestesses from the Green Temple to retrieve her. She should be…she is likely no more now." I had to think quickly. No man could enter the Green Temple, but Ramose was a resourceful man. He would find a way if he could. I added, "I know you cared for her; I ordered her consigned with all honors."

"Consigned?" he asked. The suggestion appeared repulsive to him, and if I had thought about it, I would have answered him differently. I honestly had not expected him to care. That was an oversight. He was disappointed, but I could not allow him to probe deeper into my lie.

I frowned at him in mock surprise. "Was I wrong to do so? I am afraid I do not know what gods she served. Have I offended you?"

"No, you have not. Thank you for your thoughtfulness."

With a nod of dismissal I left him in the courtyard. He wasted no time in going to find Kames. I could hear his sandals slapping on the stones as he walked into the child's rooms. Now I had to focus on my task. He had to see that leaving the boy with me was the best option. A child needed a mother.

And Ramose needed me.

Chapter Eight

Fire and Water—Pah

My head itched like a hundred angry ants were biting me. I rubbed at it and felt nothing but fuzz. The itching was inside my head, not on my skin. It was a strange sensation. Surprised at feeling something besides smooth skin, I could not stop touching my head. At last my hair was returning, and along with it, my memory. That I wished I could forget.

My memories came at me in a tangled ball, and the unhappy ones always arose together like an unwelcome group of friends. With those memories came the emotions in a dark mass of ugliness— ugliness all of my own making. My captor Margg slept beside me, and I sighed at the sound of her snoring. It was difficult enough falling asleep without the older woman's night sounds ringing in my ears. Sleeping with someone did not bother me. I had spent most of my nights with my sister. She did not snore but often talked in her sleep. I suddenly wished I could reach out to her and touch her hair or skin. How that used to comfort me, and I longed for comfort before I fell asleep again and slipped into another nightmare.

Sometimes in my dreams the Kiffians came with their pawing hands and biting mouths and…other things to violate me. I would awaken in smothered screams with Margg leaning over me, seemingly immune to the power of my blows. She never struck me back but chided me, I assumed in her own language. Margg's lack of teeth did not help me discern what she was saying. I soon gave up, and so did she. Now we communicated mostly with looks and gestures, but she never failed to wake me from the nightmares. For that I was grateful.

In the past few weeks, or at least I thought it had been that long, I had seen more faces than Margg's. A bevy of priestesses questioned me daily about my home, where I was from and what I knew about their goddess. Their endless questions tired me, and I felt no obligation to answer them, not at first.

"We know you can see in the fire and water," they would say to me. "Tell us what you see. Can you see our Pharaoh?" I refused to look in the flames or lean over the pools at first, but my hunger and thirst got the better of me. Sometimes it was easy to go without food, but there were times when my body screamed louder than my mind. They knew. The priestesses knew I could not hold out forever. So they watched and waited. Daily I demanded that they release me and allow me to go home, but daily they did not. A pot of tea was always by my bedside when I woke for the morning ministrations. One day Margg mumbled at me, trying to compel me to drink. I would not. Believing that I refused because I feared poison, she poured herself a cup, drank it, called me "stupid" (I think) and then walked out. After that I drank the tea without fear, but sometimes I took only a sip or two. Farrah had taught me that sometimes poisons worked slowly, so slowly that you did not know they were working at all. I sipped and waited for death. It never came.

Instead, something else happened. Margg's occasional attempts at language seemed easier to understand. Other things I did not expect began to manifest. Each morning after a dose of the tea I would feel more peaceful than ever before, and I had a greater awareness of my own soul. As awareness rose within me, the burning fires of ambition diminished. I had nothing to prove, and for the first time in a long time I felt fear ebb and release its cruel grip on my heart. During the trials, I would have said I feared nothing, but now I knew that was not true. I feared everything.

Nakmaa, the priestess—the high priestess, as near as I could tell— helped me discern the layers of fear within me. She told me that by doing so I would be free. Free to live without fear. I quickly identified the fear of being bested by my sister; the fear of losing. I also feared the madness that had claimed my mother and caused her to lie down in the sand and leave me behind.

The drink was such an effective medicine that I began to ask for it, and the priestesses happily gave it to me. Of course, their ministrations came with a price, and they were still tight-lipped about how I came to be in the Green Temple. They either did not know or did not think it necessary for me to know. I suspected it was the former. We were in our own world inside the temple. It was like being in a harem, I supposed, without the hope of seeing the man you loved. Some priestesses did entertain guests, male guests, but the men were carefully kept out of sight. I stopped asking about the guests and how I managed to find my way here. Despite my mind renewal, I had no recollection of those events, but I figured eventually it would come. I began to feel more confident that I *would* remember.

When the priestesses were satisfied that I knew nothing that would help them politically, they took advantage of my other gifts. "Look! Look in the fire, bright-eyed sister. Tell us what you see." I would drink, stare into the flames and pass on what I saw. Much of those visions seemed nothing but nonsense, but the priestesses all seemed impressed.

In one vision I saw a cow standing by a great pool. The animal's udders were so full that the cow tipped over from the weight and many of the fish from the nearby waters came to drink from the teats. I giggled at the sight of the brightly colored fish pulling on the cow, but the women hung on my every word. After spending many hours in front of the brazier, they would send me away. I could hear them chattering to one another as I walked down the long, empty hallway. Truthfully it was less a hallway and more a courtyard. Located in the center of the temple, it was the most impressive feature of the building and reminded me of the Timia Oasis. The columns rose like massive palm trees high into the sky above, each one decorated with ornate patterns and colorful pictures that I assumed declared the might of the temple's deity, Isis. There was a row of statues said to be her many faces, but I had given up believing in deities. I, who had been the most faithful of my family, had been betrayed by them.

I sighed on my bed and licked my dry lips. My face and arms were still hot from the flames over which I had hovered for hours earlier, and my eyes felt as if someone had poured great measures of sand into them. Though I was tired beyond belief, peaceful sleep felt like an impossibility.

Instead, I quietly rose from the room I shared with Margg and wandered by the Pool of Isis, hoping that nobody would be there. I went to bed earlier than most, but that had been an hour ago. Many times the pools were empty, except for a few old women who believed the waters washed away their aches and pains. They would strip off their clothing, uncaring that their bodies were wrinkled and flabby. They would slip carefully into the warm waters and swim about as if they were girls. I longed to swim with them, but that would mean I must speak to them. I chose the quieter route, pretending I did not see them even when they greeted me kindly.

At the end of the largest pool was a narrow sandy walkway that led to a series of smaller pools and finally a well. I rarely saw anyone come this far. The Green Temple was actually a massive complex, the main temple being the most popular building. There were other buildings to which I had not gained entrance. Perhaps I did not want to know what occurred behind those closed doors.

I first found this place on one of my many forays to find a way out of the temple grounds. The walls of the Green Temple were higher than any I had seen, even higher than Zerzura's, and they often cast long shadows on the walkways and courtyards. A pair of guards stood at each of the three gates. They wore red tunics and had plumes of purple feathers on their helmets. I assumed the men were eunuchs, as they did not look my way (or any woman's way as far as I could tell).

As I walked past the first three pools, I nodded to one young acolyte who lingered mournfully by the water. She had unusually big eyes that were constantly red from crying. I had seen her many times before. I felt sympathy for her but did not approach her or befriend her. There was no escaping this place, and it was better for her to realize that now. If you were here, you would stay here for all the days of your life. She stared at me as if entreating me to linger and talk, but I did not. I dared not. I had conquered my fears, hadn't I? She must conquer hers.

Leaving her sad countenance behind, I came to the smallest of the pools. The water was still and cooler than the large pools. It was fed by an underground spring that kept it fresh and sweet. Heavy ferns grew around it, and the buzz of a few mosquitoes played annoying music in my ear. I sat beside the water and scooped it up in my hands, splashing it on my face and neck. After a few minutes, I felt refreshed and let my toes dangle in the water as I leaned back on my hands. The stars were appearing now. I knew them by heart, as I had known them since childhood, but they did not comfort me as they once did.

I suddenly longed for Alexio. He would not know where to find me. "The world is a large place with endless spots for hiding," he told me when we were small. How I wished then to be a boy, able to leave my family behind to see the world! Once I almost convinced him to take me with him, to dress me as a boy and stuff me in his caravan so that I too could see the land of the jinn in Petra. He would laugh indulgently and pretend that he would do so, but he never did.

Over time, I did not wish to be a boy anymore. I was glad I was a girl because Alexio began to notice me in new and exciting ways. He noticed my dark eyelashes and the playful tip of my nose, the curve of my face. He did not tell me, but a woman knows these things, even a young one. I was even gladder when he began to play with my hair, brush his hands against mine; smile at me in the way a man would smile at a woman he loved. He toyed with me—I knew it even as a girl—but how thrilling it had been when he kissed me! For him, it had been meaningless, but for me, it had been everything. I loved him, utterly and completely. Until I knew that to him, I was only a means to an end—a way to get to my sister. And then other feelings began to rise to the surface…

I cast a handful of silky white petals into the pool and watched them slowly sink out of sight. A strange bird and other animals made night noises, but I was not afraid of them. This was not the desert. I knew nothing could harm me here.

Except those that lingered outside, hovering between this world and the next.

So far, the spirits had not crossed the temple threshold. But if I stepped outside, I could only imagine what they would do to me. Who said the dead couldn't harm the living? I saw many things in the fire and in the water. Sometimes Farrah's face passed before mine, her eyes full of hatred, her white hair bloody and her skin black. Other times it was Paimu's grasping hands and silent scream that demanded justice. Of the two, it was her murder that I most regretted, for it had been done in my madness. My jealousy had killed her as much as my blade had. Farrah's death was different. She had brought my blood to a boil, not because of her accusations but because she dared accuse me when she herself had done murder. And I knew the truth. She had allowed my mother to die. She did that! I saw it in the fire! She sat back and watched and did not lift a finger to help her. She thought no one would ever know. She was wrong.

Paimu, though…she was another story. She did not deserve what happened to her. The truth was I was a woman possessed that night. Enraged that Alexio had rejected me once again. Enraged that I must lie with Yuni…I hated the man. Enraged that my uncle came to me once again, reminding me of our secret. Driving the knife into her was like killing myself, only it wasn't me who died. I buried her when it was over, and for a little while, she remained hidden. Until she came back.

I shivered in the moonlight and sat still. I could hear someone walking toward me. The crunching of fallen flowers sent the shivers running down my spine. Could my thoughts have summoned the girl here? I didn't know whether to stand up or try to hide. I decided to do neither. I might as well face whatever justice was coming for me. What would it matter if someone found me dead by a pool? Nobody cared. Nobody who mattered. Most here thought I was mad anyway.

"Hafa-nu, queen's sister," said the small figure who had paused on the path. As the clouds above shifted, the moonlight fell on us and I could see her more clearly. It was not Paimu.

The woman before me was small. She wore a simple white gown, but everything else about her declared she was someone of importance, including her twin snake bracelets that wrapped around her arms. They reminded me of my father's. I wondered sometimes if he missed me. My visitor had intelligent dark eyes, and I could see that her heart was heavy. She reminded me of someone, but I could not place her. I stood, but only to show her I was much taller than she. "I am the Great Wife of the Pharaoh Amenhotep, although he is now in the Eternal City."

"How is it you greet me so? Do you know the words you speak, or do you just say them because you have heard others speak them?"

"The desert is in my blood. I was born to the Algat, although I claim no mother but Isis now. I remember the Old Ways and the Old Words."

"I have seen your face in the water. They killed your son, didn't they? Left him lying in the paws of the Sphinx, a bloody tribute to their god. Is it justice you seek?"

My question clearly surprised her, and she stumbled toward me. Her dark eyes grew wide as she moved closer to see my face. "So it is true. You do see!"

I did not feel compelled to prove that I could see anything at all, but it appeared that the priestesses had been talking. I said nothing.

"I could command you to look, for it is in my power to do so. Any priestess here would be glad to serve me, and many do. There are things I need to know, and you have the ability to tell me. Are you willing to help me or not?"

If she wanted me to rebel, to bristle at her importance, I did not give her that satisfaction. Death did not frighten me, only the half-dead. Those who lingered. If she killed me, I would be dead and free from seeing them waiting for me. Perhaps I deserved to die. No, there was no guessing. I did deserve it. I wanted to ask, *Why don't these many priestesses help you, then?* But I did not. "Help you how, Queen Tiye? Whatever you might think, I cannot command what I see. I just see. Seeing the past or the future is not for any of us to command, I think."

With a great sigh of weariness she waved her hand and said, "I did not mean to offend you. It is just my way. People like wasting my time, and I am not a woman who tolerates fools. But I see you aren't either."

"My name is Pah. I am the sister of Nefret, the one you call Nefertiti. I do see in the fire and the water. And I have seen you before, in the flames. The goddess here shows me your face often. She watches you, I think."

The older woman's face softened. I could see that my answer pleased her, but it did not matter to me one way or the other. Without waiting for an invitation she sat beside the pool and patted the ground, bidding me to do the same. It did not take a seer to know that she cared nothing about me; the queen only wanted to know what I saw about her and her family.

I sat back down, determined to feel unimpressed by my unexpected guest. No one had visited me before. Not even Nefret. I put my feet back in the water, enjoying the sensation of the fish nibbling at my toes. Somewhere behind me I thought I heard a strange sound, as if someone were scratching on metal. I was not certain if this was real or something else, so I said nothing about it.

"What about the water? Do you ever see my face there?" Her voice sounded whispery and young. Much younger than she was, for I guessed she was as old as Farrah was when she died. I wondered if the queen knew I had killed the Old One. But how could she?

"Only in the flames. I see you only in the flames." I let the weight of my words fall on her. If she knew anything about such things, she would know what that meant. If she did not, who was I to burden her with such knowledge?

"Are you happy here?"

I kept my eyes averted and my voice even. Over the years I had taught myself to hide my true feelings; this talent came in handy now, for I did not trust the tiny queen. How could I believe that the Great Queen of Egypt did not know about my plight? I banished Alexio's face from my mind and tried not to allow the desperation and longing for him to rise up and betray me. It would not do for a priestess of the Green Temple to have a husband. That information might put me in danger.

I moved my feet in the water to confuse the fish, and they scattered for a moment. "It is safe here, and I am not mistreated."

"Do you want to stay here and serve Isis? You have no memory of how you got here?" Again I heard the sound—not scraping, but scratching, coming from the other side of the wall. I tried not to stare over her shoulder, but I did quickly look just in case it was Paimu. There was no one there, but I could not see too well in the dark.

Maybe she was there. Waiting. I shivered as if somewhere someone had cursed me.

"No, I cannot remember," I told her honestly. "I never knew of this place until I woke up here."

"I see."

"I am not important enough to receive a visit from a queen. Why have you come?"

Her eyes widened at my directness. She had lovely eyes. Her other features were plain, but her eyes were like the dark eyes of a bird, ever attentive yet untrusting. As if everyone she met had a net in their hands and was ready to capture and consume her. Perhaps they were.

Poor Queen Tiye.

"I am told that there is no one greater at seeing than you. Nakmaa reports that you have extraordinary natural skills and can see great details in your visions. You have been very helpful to the priest-esses here, but now I need something from you. I have many enemies, and my enemies are also your sister's enemies. Even if you do not care about me, I am sure you want to help her."

"My sister and I have different destinies." I said, giving her a sharp look. How surprising! I thought I had shed my old resentments toward Nefret. Perhaps a germ of hatred still remained. A subtle wind shifted in the garden, and the palm leaves clicked as they slapped into one another, confused by the change in the air.

"I do not speak of destinies but of loyalty and sisterhood."

"I see."

"Do you hate your sister?" she asked. "Do you believe she brought you here?"

Once I would have immediately answered, "Yes!" but that was before I murdered her treasure. Before I stole the queenship of our tribe from her. Before I betrayed her, first with Alexio and then with Farrah.

"Do you have sisters, Queen Tiye? Have you never hated them?"

"I cannot remember their faces, but no, I never hated them."

Lying to herself. She hates everyone except for the son she lost.

Anxious to talk of something else and ready to be rid of her, I said, "Very well. I will help you. Let us look together. You are here, and the water is here. Let us try." I swept my hand across the surface, making ripples. I had never seen her in the water before, but it was worth a look. The idea of leaning over the hot flames for another moment made me sick to my stomach. The moon rose high above us now, and I could see its light bouncing back in the water. I smelled the white flowers, the kind that appeared only at night. Wide blooms waved around us, and thankfully the mosquitoes had found somewhere else to congregate.

To my surprise, I immediately saw Queen Tiye. She was walking down a corridor with a baby in her arms; she crooned to him quietly. *Was that a desert song? Ah, a lady of the Red Lands.* Then the scene changed, and she stood in a somber audience of people who surrounded a massive golden brazier. A man lay bound in the center of the altar—a sacrifice to some demanding god. I could see fear and regret in his dark eyes, but he did not cry out like a coward. I could feel his struggle. He wanted to cry out her name and tell her he loved her. Tell her that he would love her until the last flame licked away his flesh and bones. But he did not. He could see her on the edge of the brazier, weeping and crying over him. How strange he felt; he regretted drinking the water they gave him. It made him weak and compliant. Then he saw the face of the man he had considered his friend—a man who was like a brother. It was Amenhotep!

I spoke nonstop, describing every detail revealed to me. As Queen Tiye had asked me, I held nothing back. I heard her gasp beside me. Without waiting for permission she grabbed my hand, and I felt the vision transfer to her. I had never done this before, but I had heard it was possible.

"I see! I see!"

She laughed for joy, but soon her face twisted. "No! This cannot be! Sitamen!" I strained to see but could not. "My daughter! Sitamen! No!" the tiny queen cried. To my surprise she leaped to her feet and ran down the narrow path to wherever she intended to go. I did not have a chance to tell her that sometimes the seeing was in the past and at other times it was the future. Or a possible future. One could never be sure.

I sighed and stood, dusting myself off. I felt extremely tired. Empty. I was sure I could sleep now. I had had enough excitement for one day. Just as I turned to walk back to my quarters, I heard the scratching again. Feeling brave for only a second, I called in the direction of the noise.

"Now, spirit. Let us end this!"

I stared into the darkness toward the wall. I waited for a long while but saw nothing. I blinked against the blackness until I could see an arm, a pale, shining arm. It reached toward me from the wall. The small, grasping hand flexed its fingers as if to show me she was trying with all her might to reach me. To take her revenge. I walked toward the hand, closer and closer. My heart pounded and my skin crawled at the sight of the phantom struggling to reach me.

All my being hated every second of this experience, but I could not help but wonder what would happen if I reached out and touched the hand. Would she pull me away and take me to the Otherworld? What would happen to me? As I reached my hand toward hers, my fingers shook. How easy it would be to die now! I had nothing to live for anymore! I had cast off my child—lost my love—and was stolen from my tribe. There was nothing for me now.

Our fingers almost touched. As I got closer still, I heard whispers, whispers coaxing me to reach further, try harder, to come now…

"You, girl! Come away from there!" The guard's voice startled me out of my trance. I blinked at him and then at the wall. There was nothing there. The hand had disappeared, and the strange whispering had ceased. I stood before the wall alone, the only movement the short scrubby brush that swayed slightly in the breeze.

I had almost done it. I had almost surrendered myself to her. I owed her a debt, and she demanded payment, but I realized one of the goddess' servants had saved me.

"Yes," I said, smiling at him as the relief washed over me, "I will come away." The man stood holding his black spear and staring at me as if I were stupid. I did not care. I laughed at his expression. I had escaped death. The goddess had a plan for me—my work here in this world's realm was not done. I ran ahead of the guard and down the narrow corridor that led to my sleeping chambers.

Silently I climbed into my bed and lay there trying to control my breathing. She had come for me, to take me, but I had been saved! At least for now. I had another chance at life. Another chance to hope and dream that I would see the one I loved. Someday.

Before I fell asleep, I whispered in the dark, not to Isis but to my mother. "Watch over him, Mother. He is my husband and my love. Stay close to him, please."

With the sound of Margg snoring beside me, I fell asleep at last.

Chapter Nine

The New Sister—Nefertiti

I clapped and smiled at the sight of the collection of small animals led about on dainty silver chains by the children of the man who bowed before me. One animal, with a long neck and soft-looking fur, chattered away as he took his place on the small platform. A boy much younger than Paimu had been when she died led a similar animal to the opposite end of the toy. He made a whistling sound, and the two furry creatures—mongooses, they were called—began to bob up and down, making the tiny fulcrum move. I smiled at the children as they led the animals through their paces. When they had completed their performances, I tossed the animals the treats that the children provided me and gave the children handfuls of silver coins. Their dark eyes sparkled with excitement, and their father thanked me profusely.

"Thank you, lady queen," the children said, amazed at their collection of coins.

"You are quite welcome. That was a wonderful show. Seeing these animals reminds me of a story I once heard about a white elephant who stole a rare fruit but had to stand on his tiptoes to reach it." The children's eyes widened with delight, and big smiles appeared in anticipation of the story. I straightened my gown and was prepared to invite them to sit—it had been so long since I had told a story—but our meeting was interrupted by Menmet. I sighed sadly, knowing I could not spend more time with the children. I had other tasks to attend to, and the day had just begun.

For the first time in a long time, I would see Pah. My trusted spies (friends of Menmet) informed me that Pah had built quite a reputation for herself in the temple. She was recognized as a gifted seer now, and people from all over Thebes came to the Green Temple to hear her words. If that was true, then it would seem Tadukhipa's plan had not produced the desired effect. At least not for her. Perhaps Pah's experience had been real and her goddess had saved her.

As the litter swung back and forth, I pulled the curtains back occasionally and waved at the gathering crowds who walked along beside us. Looking past their faces, I gazed up at the Green Temple of Isis in utter amazement. The glittering green columns shimmered in the sunshine. The columns and the building's façade were made of an unusual stone that had a streak of gold throughout it. I could see why people from around the world came to see this temple. Although I rarely came here, the sight of it still took my breath away. And to think Pah lived here now.

As a courtesy to me, and to erase any doubts about my heritage, Tiye had quietly recognized Pah as a daughter of Isis. Technically she was a royal and entitled to all the benefits of her status. I sent her gifts and messages, hoping to measure her feelings for me before I arrived, but she had not responded.

A green-robed priestess greeted me on the steps and politely took me to an empty hall that led to an area where Pah and I could visit privately. Without a word the priestess left me standing in the open room, and I waited nervously for my sister.

I heard her bare feet slapping on the stones as she approached. Pah's face was so pale it glowed, and she appeared gaunter than I had ever seen her. She looked so much older than her true seasons. Before all this, before Fate had had her way with us, looking upon her was like looking in a mirror. Even now our eyes remained the same, only mine were lined with kohl applied by Menmet's deft hand. It was an ironic twist considering how much I had hated Egypt and she had wanted to embrace it. Yet now I represented the Two Lands in the most supreme way possible.

Pah's short red hair gleamed in the light—the gown she wore was too large for her thin figure, as if it were not made for her at all but a giant. The sleeves were far too large, and it lacked any adornment. She did not wear the clothing I sent her or anything fine.

When last I saw my sister, she spoke to the invisible world and screamed and cried at random. Now here she was, quiet and composed, without a trace of her former confidence or haughtiness. Before I left Zerzura, Leela seemed convinced that Pah carried a child, but if she were pregnant she should be showing by now—as I was. I had long decided I would offer to care for her child since she could not do so here at the temple, but now that point was moot.

"I cast it out after I arrived here," she answered my unspoken question. "It was my choice, sister. No one forced me."

"Why would you do that? Children are our treasures!" The words fell from my lips before I could stop them. What a foolish thing to say to someone who had endured what Pah had. How could I pass judgment on her?

She did not rebuke me or defend herself. "I am sorry about the child," she said in a low voice, her tired eyes never leaving mine. I could hear the heartbreak in her voice.

"I understand. Truly, I do. I have no right to tell you what to do."

She shook her head sadly. "No, sister. You misunderstand me. It is your treasure I speak of. The girl—Paimu. What I did to her. I robbed you of her love and took her life when it was not mine to take. The deed weighs on me, and I am sorry for it."

I never thought to hear such a confession. A sob of surprise and pain escaped me as Paimu's face came unbidden to my mind's eye. I had put her away in my mind, unwilling to conjure up her sweet face, her cheerful laughter and playful spirit. I felt guilty for leaving her memory behind so easily. She had brought joy to my lonely life, as I hoped I had brought to hers.

"Why, Pah? Why did you do it? She was just a child and no threat to you." My voice rose and echoed through the initiates' hall, surprising the temple guards and my companions who waited for me in the hallway. Menmet could not enter this place. Only the servants or the daughters of Isis could enter here. Whatever happened here, we were by ourselves except for the onlookers' watchful eyes.

Pah's expression lacked her typical disdain and contempt. That had vanished like her haughty looks. Regret took its place. "Nothing I can say will satisfy your need to understand, for I myself do not understand why I did it." Her pretty voice sounded empty of hope. "For a long time I could not think clearly—my mind was a hateful playground. It was as if a wrathful spirit lived inside me and would not go away. No matter how my heart broke, how much I wanted to reach out to someone, I could not. I did not seek Paimu, but when she crossed my path that morning I killed her. I do not even know why I carried the knife with me. I am sorry for this. With all my heart and soul, I am sorry."

"I did not want to believe it. But now that I hear it from your lips, I know that it is true."

"Why have you come here, Nefret?"

"I wanted to… I had to see you. I had to tell you that it was not my idea to bring you here." I dropped my voice to a whisper and said quickly, "I believe my adversary, Tadukhipa, organized your abduction, but I do not know why. Can you identify your captors so that I can question them? I need to know what she has planned."

"Ah, I see."

"What is it you see?" I asked her.

"I see the fires of ambition burning in you, Nefret. I know those fires. They will burn you up if you allow them to."

"You are wrong, sister. I am trying to help you. How did you get here?"

"I cannot remember. I have tried." Suddenly she stepped toward me and said, "Please, Nefret. Let me go home. Home to Alexio. You have your husband. You are queen now. Please let me go."

"I did not bring you here, Pah. The Great Queen's steward, Huya, has been investigating your case. He says that you must have a special dispensation from the priestess here before you can go and that she is loath to release you."

"Why? Why won't they let me go? I want to go home."

"You have been looking in the fire and water. You have seen what they cannot. As it always is, the one who can't see wants to see more. Since you have proved you have skills and can see visions, they do not want to release you."

"What must I do, Nefret? I want to go home. I had thought I would never leave. You did not come to me when I asked for you, but now I feel hope that I will escape. You will let me go, won't you? You are queen now! You can do this!"

"I am trying, Pah. You must make it easier, though. Stop sharing the visions. When people ask you to see, tell them you cannot. Maybe then Nakmaa will release you."

"You want me to lie?"

I took her hands. They were cool to the touch and almost lifeless. "If you want to go home, you are going to have to stop looking into the fire and water. When Pharaoh returns to Thebes, I will ask him to intercede for you. Until then, no more visions, Pah."

She sighed—it was a hopeless sound. "It is Alexio, isn't it? You still love him."

In a whisper, I tried to reassure her, "I regret how I left things with him, but I love my husband. I love Amenhotep like I have never loved anyone. I swear to you, Pah. I did not bring you here, nor am I keeping you from Alexio. I will try to help you, but do as I ask."

"Paimu. The girl," she whispered back. With fearful eyes she scanned the room. Seeing no one she whispered again, "She dogs my steps, sister. I see her lingering outside the gate when the sun comes up and when it goes down. She has not breached the walls yet, but sometimes when I dive deep into the water she is there, waiting for me. I think she will drown me if she can. Sometimes when I look into the fire, her face appears, her eyes like flames of hatred. She wants her life back, and I cannot give it to her." She stepped back quickly and withdrew her hand as if mine were two snakes. "Did you bring her here? Is that why you came? You and Farrah?"

"Paimu is dead, Pah. And in death or life she would never harm you. What you see is your own guilt."

"So you say, but you do not see like I can. I see them both."

"Farrah? Why would she come to Egypt?" I tried to tease her to keep her mind from dwelling on her evil deeds. She pulled away from me and gave me a wide-eyed stare. Her figure appeared so small as she stood in the middle of the sparse room, the looming stone statue of Isis behind her, a basin of water to the left of it, a brazier of fire on the right. She did not belong here, but I did not know what to do to help her. I needed more information—proof that Tadukhipa had arranged her appointment here, against her will. What did my enemy have planned for my sister and me?

With raw fierceness she said, "I killed Farrah, and I will not deny it. Nor do I regret it. She deserved to die. She betrayed Mother and left her to die in the desert. She betrayed you too, Nefret, whether you believe me or not. If she were standing before me now, I would kill her again. A hundred times over!"

"Pah, calm down! Farrah would harm no one! All she ever wanted to do was lead us home to Zerzura."

"Well then, why didn't she lead us home? I will tell you why—because she could not. Farrah did not remember the way, and she could not rely on the sight to lead her. She murdered an innocent, our mother, and her crime cost her. The gods saw fit to take her visions from her. The Old One lied to us when she said she could see. She saw nothing but shadows. It was I who saw!"

"But you have taken two lives, Pah, and you see."

Her lovely eyes narrowed as she considered my words. She stepped toward me out, of the shadow of the hovering Isis. She did not lash out at me or show frustration with what she used to call my stupidity. Her eyes swept me up and down as if she were seeing me in a new light. It made me uncomfortable, but I did not shrink from her gaze. Let her look on me if she wanted to! I was the Queen of Egypt—Queen Nefertiti! All our lives my sister had done only what was beneficial for her, but I had chosen another route and had done what was right for the tribe. Who was she to judge me?

Somewhere in another room I heard bells tinkling and hands clapping. These were likely signs that worship was about to begin, but still Pah made no move to leave me. She continued her silent appraisal and then spoke with renewed clarity.

"I believed their lies—they told me that I was the better mekhma, the better leader. They knew how jealous I was, how unreasonable were my thoughts! You were right. We should have reigned together and dared anyone to stand against us. I cannot go back and change what I have done, but I can help you now. Help me leave here, and I will look for you—only you. I swear it."

My insides melted like wax. I never imagined hearing these words from my sister, and now that I heard them I barely trusted myself to believe them. If only we could go back and change things. If only we could go back and rule together and defeat the Kiffians without making deals with Egypt. But things had changed. I loved Amenhotep, and even if I could change my position in life, I would never leave him; I never wanted to be away from him.

"My husband and I worship the Aten. We do not seek visions of the future. We will build a new Egypt, one free from the oppression of the priests and priestesses. I cannot imagine Isis would like me too well for it."

"When I look at you, I see the shining one—yes, a Shining Man. He is near you now. I can see his image behind you, sister."

I gasped in surprise. I had never shared with her my experiences with the Shining Man. How could she know of him? I was tempted to look behind me, so steady and powerful was her gaze, but I did not.

She wrapped her arms around me, but I stiffened. She whispered in my ear, "Forgive me, Nefret." Try as I might I could not resist her embrace for long, and I hugged her back. Being the Queen of Egypt I had learned a few things from Queen Tiye, such as not letting emotions compromise you in any situation, but at this moment I did not care about those lessons. I heard the tinkling of the bells again and saw a priestess waiting in the opposite doorway. She whispered a word in a language I did not understand but evidently Pah did; my sister stepped back, squeezing my hands reassuringly.

"I must go now. The goddess calls me. Do not forget my promise."

"I will come to see you again soon. Remember what I told you." I smiled at her, thankful for this happy moment. These had been too few. She smiled back, but her expression quickly changed. A frown crept upon her brow, and her lips pursed in serious thought.

"Sister! You have more than one enemy. Trust no one."

Before I could inquire of her further, Pah took the hand of the priestess beside her, and together the two disappeared down the corridor. I stood staring after her, wondering about her words, but

I did not have too much time to linger in the Green Temple. My court—Amenhotep's court—waited for my attention. Menmet shuffled her feet impatiently, and I went to her. We rode back to the Palace in silence. I was thankful that she did not ply me with questions, for I knew she was curious. Menmet was always curious. Queen Tiye's recent warnings rang in my ears: *She is Heby's daughter and a spy. Do not be a fool, Nefertiti!*

I focused on my next task, administering justice in Thebes. I had to focus on the people who came before me. I remembered Amenhotep's admonition. "Make the people love you, my queen. Let them see you as a good queen. Win their hearts!"

Oh, Amenhotep! When will you come home to me?

As I prepared for attendance at court, I was delighted to see a stack of new gifts waiting for me in my chambers. Amenhotep and I had had barely any correspondence in the past few weeks, but he had faithfully sent me gift after gift. Each one I was sure had some special meaning that he wished to convey to me. I spent many a night pondering them, touching them. Menmet clapped her hands joyfully at the sight. I loved her enthusiasm. She celebrated when I celebrated, cried when I cried. Wasn't that the definition of a friend? A sister? She handed me a box from the top of the stack. It was wrapped in blue cloth and had an exquisite silver ribbon tying it together. I pulled the ribbon and released the lid from the top. Inside was an elegant golden brooch in the shape of the sun with a crown that rested on the top. I reached out to pick it up, but Menmet stopped me.

"My queen! Do not touch that!" She swatted at my hands as if I were a child.

"What is the matter with you?" I shouted. If the Great Queen Tiye had seen her do such a thing, she would have put her in irons. I could not blame her. If she was too familiar, it was my own fault.

"That is the crowned sun! A Hittite symbol. This must be from Tadukhipa, not Amenhotep. Knowing her, the thing is dipped in poison or covered in curses. At the very least she is trying to send you a message."

"Perhaps," I said absently as I examined the item without touching it. I knew what the message was, but I did not share my observations. Pah had warned me that I had more than one enemy. I did not want to believe it could be Menmet, but as I had learned of late, anything was possible in Egypt's courts.

I called Harwa to me for answers. "Who brought these gifts in here? Where did this one come from?"

The old eunuch examined the stack of boxes and crates and said, "All these came from our Pharaoh. But this one, I do not know. It was not here before, my queen."

"That means someone brought it here without anyone's notice?"

Harwa frowned at the thought and began to call together those who had been nearby to see what they had observed. I did not wait for the results of his investigation.

I stared at the brooch as I chewed on my lip. We had heard quite a bit lately about Tadukhipa's growing power. People whispered that her sun rose as mine faded. I had even heard she was pregnant and that Amenhotep had made his final decision. He would make Tadukhipa the Great Queen at last, they said. Even my court had become emptier during his absence. Each day it was the same. In the mornings I took reports from our kenbet, a class of leaders who led specific districts on our behalf. These were mostly men from the noble class, but there were also common men amongst this esteemed group. I listened as patiently as I could to their concerns about slaves, water and grain. Sometimes I offered advice, but most of the time I simply listened as the scribes wrote down the complaints. In the afternoons, I heard cases selected from the domestic courts by my advisers. This was not typical behavior for a queen or any royal, but I had taken Amenhotep's instructions seriously.

"Let the people see that you love them! Lead them, Nefertiti."

What if none of that mattered now? What if Amenhotep had truly made his decision? According to whispers, I should go ahead and pack my belongings now and move into the Royal Harem. But I refused to leave the palace.

"Harwa, listen to me. Do not worry with that now. If it is indeed a gift from my sister, Queen Tadukhipa, I must wear it. Although I do not think anyone wears brooches at the moment. They have gone out of fashion, I am afraid. Take this brooch and have it hammered into a crown. Leave its shape—I want her to be able to recognize it when she sees me so she knows how much I appreciate her gift. I want it ready for her return, to demonstrate my gratitude."

Harwa grinned, showing his even smile. He had the perfect teeth of a child and pleasant brown eyes. I instantly trusted him when I met him, but I was also glad that he was on my side. He could be as devious as Queen Tiye and her steward, Huya. Nobody outsmarted those two. "Should we add your falcon crest to the center spire?"

"Harwa, you read my mind."

Amenhotep had invited me here, and here I planned to stay.

Chapter Ten

The Visitors—Nefertiti

The official court was located at the front of the palace. I had to walk downstairs and down the length of the main corridor to access it. As I made the trip I remembered to keep my face a serene mask, just as Tiye taught me. Her tutelage had been invaluable these past few weeks. Although she was impatient with me and sometimes unkind, she had a shrewdness that I envied. She saw problems long before I did, and during those first days in the court she had helped me navigate the formalities without failure. Today I entered the court without her and heard the hush fall upon the waiting crowd. I walked steadily up the back of the dais and stood before the throne.

Trusted members of my court brought me a few cases each day, and lately I began noticing a pattern. More and more of these cases involved children and the priests of Amun. What they were doing was wrong—taking them from their parents, sacrificing them, burning them—and I secretly vowed to stop their horrific rituals and practices. Menmet had been my partner in this.

The throne attendants lifted my heavy robes; I glanced over to see that scribes were waiting with ink and papyrus, ready to make my words the law of the land. I took my seat upon my husband's throne, and the people rose from their bowed positions in expectation. Even after all these weeks, almost months, it was still a humbling sight to me. I refused to take the privilege for granted. The gold fabric draped over the back and across the dais smoothly under the experienced hands of the attendants. I held the heavy brass crook and flail in my hands; the weight seemed easier to manage now. At least, I thought, the regular courtiers appeared less shocked when I sat in Amenhotep's place. I hoped that the news of my work here had reached his ears.

"The people need to see you as Queen of Upper and Lower Egypt. Lead them, my wife."

His confidence in me gave me strength, but it did little to put my heart at ease. He was, after all, in the arms of Queen Tadukhipa even now. I had hotly contested this arrangement, but after a visit from the Hittite-Mitanni king, I could hardly stand in my husband's way. If we wanted peace with the Hittites, Amenhotep would have to honor the marriage put in place by his father.

How strange these Egyptians were! Sons inheriting wives, concubines and harems. It was a strange thing indeed, but my husband assured me his heart remained with me. Like so many things in my life, this matter was out of my control. I would make the best of it. And as Tiye often reminded me, the true prize had not yet been won. My rule these many weeks was very likely a test, Tiye whispered to me during our evening meal last night.

Another test in a life of testing.

I thought about her other words, warnings to me. "Do not trust her. Even at this distance. She has her monsters here. There is one of them." She had pointed at Menmet, who was busy preparing a tray of fresh fruit for us.

I had not argued with her, for it would have done no good. Of course, Queen Tiye refused to eat anything taken from Menmet's hand. Menmet noticed the slight, I could see, but she kept her place.

Queen Tiye hated Tadukhipa beyond reason, almost as much as she hated the priests of Amun. In truth, she seemed to have little love for anyone except her dead husband and her son Thutmose and, of course, Pharaoh Amenhotep. Poor Sitamen was ever lost in the shadows.

Menmet informed me that more royal visitors had come to the Theban court that morning, ready to pay homage to Pharaoh and Queen Nefertiti. I sat up stiffly as Harwa bowed toward me. With a clap of his hands, the outer doors opened and I blinked against the sunlight that poured in through the throne room. My wig itched and my stomach rumbled, but I kept my face like stone as the small contingent approached me.

From the moment he stepped into the inner court I recognized him. Alexio! With shaggy dark hair that hung about his shoulders, he wore a clean blue tunic, leather leggings and sandals. Beside Alexio were a few others: Biel, the young man I had met at Zerzura, had now grown even taller, and I could see that Horemheb had returned to Egypt. I anxiously awaited his report from home.

I felt the eyes of the court upon me, and I forced myself to breathe normally as the group approached. I wondered if any of them knew who this man was who came before my throne. Who he used to be to me? *My husband.* Alexio had not changed—he looked a little older, a little unhappier. He showed no excitement at seeing me, nor did I expect any. I had betrayed him at the highest level. I had taken an oath under the stars, swearing to love him with my mind, body and soul always and call him mine forever. Then I sent him away in a moment of anger. I did not deserve him.

I listened respectfully as Harwa announced the leaders of the Meshwesh. "Horemheb, friend of Egypt, brings gifts of turquoise to Pharaoh and his queen, Nefertiti. May he present them?" I nodded my permission, careful to keep my movements smooth and easy so as not to disturb the scented wig and crown that rested uneasily on my head.

Horemheb stepped forward stiffly. I could see that age was beginning to take its toll on him. I wondered about my father, but I would question my uncle later. For now I focused on the formalities. He knelt on one knee as he held open a round cedar chest full of bits of turquoise jewelry. It was not a fine prize—Horemheb knew that it was not so fine as the gifts the Hittites and Cushites offered—but I knew it was the tribe's best. The Meshwesh were not a stingy people. I thanked them for their kind gifts to Pharaoh.

"Welcome, my father's people," I said warmly. There could be only one reason why they were here—to see their mekhma and, if possible, bring her home. Sadly, I understood that although I was the mekhma who had saved them, brought them back to Zerzura, raised them to a seat of respect in Egypt, I was not the one they came to rescue.

I would never be rescued. My fate was sealed. I was no longer a Desert Queen but the Queen of all Egypt.

"It would please me greatly if you would dine with me this evening. I would like very much to hear the latest news from the White City."

"Thank you, Queen Nefertiti. You do us great honor." Before they could say anything else I gave a long nod of dismissal. Alexio lingered, likely ready to make his feelings known, but Horemheb led him away by his elbow. Harwa watched with some concern. I had promised him that I would dine with the Greeks this evening, and perhaps I would. It was not unheard of to host two banquets at one time. But as Tiye told me, I need not explain myself to the servants. Neither the high ones nor the low ones. "And they are all your servants," she added with authority.

After the whispers settled, we welcomed the next assembly as they approached my throne. There would be no reports today, thankfully. No endless complaints from leaders. Receiving guests to court was much easier, or so I first believed. I quickly learned that each nation had its own greetings and expectations. Harwa sometimes spent hours preparing me for the occasion. "Do not stare at his eye patch," he told me when Cervantes came to court. Another time he instructed me, "Speak to the women first. They take great offense if they are not recognized, and they are the true power in Persia. Also do not mention any other nations when speaking to them. We are in negotiations for access to some of their harbors this winter. They are very jealous for Egypt's attention."

Tiye had been correct. Harwa had become invaluable to me. He knew everyone and everything. What he did not know, Menmet knew. I felt much more confident than I had just a few weeks ago having them by my side. I watched respectfully as an assembly of Greeks walked toward me. I felt a great curiosity about these people, as they were my relatives. The Egyptians had great love for them, but I had seen only a few Grecians during my years in the Red Lands. I had my mother's red hair, but most of my mother's people had blond or light brown hair with bronze skin and light-colored eyes, all features that Egyptians regarded as unusual and attractive. The approaching assembly paused at a respectful distance and waited for Harwa to recognize them.

"Queen Nefertiti, may I present to you Ianos, Kallias and Sophos, ambassadors from King Orestes. I think they have gifts for you, lady queen." I studied them as they approached. They were attractive, but most ambassadors were since they were supposedly representative of their monarchs. Each was tall, much taller than I, but not as tall as Amenhotep. They wore short-sleeved tunics that were cinched at the waist with beautifully worked leather belts. As was the tradition for court, they did not carry weapons, but I could see an empty scabbard on the hip of the man in the middle. He seemed the most striking to me. None wore beards, and they kept their hair short in the soldier's fashion. They had muscular arms and legs, although Ianos, who appeared to be the oldest, had skinny legs like my uncle.

"They are welcome here, Harwa. Welcome to the court of Amenhotep, ambassadors. I am sure Pharaoh will be saddened to know that he missed your visit, but perhaps you will come again when he returns."

My answer pleased them, and they bowed graciously. One of them said to me, "Greetings, Queen Nefertiti. I am Kallias, the son of Alistair, the brother of Princess Kadeema. I am happy to finally meet you. It is a meeting that is long overdue, I think."

I could not help but flash a smile at the man. He had a handsome face, but unlike many handsome faces, he did not have a haughty look or way about him. Kallias wore no jewelry but had an elegant demeanor that proved his noble birth. "Yes, I agree. Welcome to Thebes, Kallias. Have you been here before?"

"No, this is my first visit to Pharaoh's city."

"Then perhaps you and the other ambassadors will join me for a tour of my husband's gardens after I greet all my guests. I would like to hear about Grecia and Kadeema's homeland."

Kallias appeared enormously pleased by my offer. "Nothing would give us more pleasure, Queen Nefertiti. We are at your service. We have a gift for you. May I present it?" I ignored Harwa's questioning look and waved Kallias forward. He walked up the first three steps of the dais, until he heard the throne room guards come to attention. Stopping immediately, he knelt on the marble step and opened a small box that was no bigger than my hand. Inside was the largest, shiniest pearl I had ever seen, and I had seen many since my arrival in Thebes. It was strung on a thin golden chain.

In a soft voice Kallias said, "This pearl comes from the harbor of Illeas, the home of Kadeema. It is a rare jewel. Our king sends the gift with his warmest greetings."

"I can see that it is remarkable," I said with honest admiration. "May I touch it?"

"It is yours, Queen Nefertiti."

I rose from my throne, ignoring the gasps of the people. It was a rare thing to see Pharaoh rise from his throne, except during special occasions. But then again I was not Pharaoh. I had forgotten the rules, but I made no apologies to anyone. The gift moved me.

I reached out and took the pearl in my hand. I slid it up and down the chain, examining the workmanship. "Rise, Kallias. Tell King Orestes that I gladly accept his gift and welcome his friendship. You are all welcome at court. Please remain as my esteemed guests." He stepped down off the dais, and together the three of them bowed again. I heard a noise from the waiting gallery. Feeling a little irritated at the interruption, I kept my voice cool. "Ah, I see more guests have arrived. You may stay if you like." They stepped to the side, and I clutched the pearl in my hand as I took my seat. At least a dozen dark-headed men wearing rich leather armor over brightly colored tunics had gathered. My guards were busy unburdening the visitors of their weapons. It was common knowledge that visitors to court did not bring their weapons with them, so I wondered at the meaning of this. Then they walked toward me, almost marching in time. They stomped across the floor in heavy boots; their long hair flowed behind them as they came toward me. Their fierce, narrow eyes never shifted from me, nor my own eyes from them.

Hittites! Kinsmen of Tadukhipa, no doubt. Let us see how this goes.

Before Harwa could scramble to the front of the dais, the men presented themselves to me. They held their heads high and appraised me unashamedly as they waited impatiently for the formalities to end. Harwa did not name all the Hittites, only one. His name was Tishratta, and I knew it was a name I would always remember.

He was very dark but not black like the men from the south. His skin was almost a strange green color, then I realized it was painted; what wasn't painted was covered with tattoos. I made myself focus on his face and not his painted arms. His black eyes were lined with kohl, which made them look even darker. His hair was so long that the top of it was pulled back from his face with a sturdy-looking leather thong. Like Tadukhipa, he had few smiles for the people around him; he likely assumed that everyone knew who he was, and he commanded their respect. As Harwa began to recite the many titles of King Tishratta, I stood for the second time today.

"King Tishratta, I am surprised to see you here. As you know, Queen Tadukhipa is touring the Nile with my husband and having a memorable time, from what I am told. Did you know she sent me a lovely gift today? Can you guess what it is?"

He did not answer at first, but as the court began to whisper I supposed he felt compelled to do so. "I am not good at guessing games, Queen Nefertiti. Speak what is on your mind."

Looking down at him with a smile I said, "A lovely brooch. In the shape of the sun but with the crown atop it. Can you interpret it for me? Why would she give me such a gift? As lovely as it is, I cannot wear it, not unless I want to offend my husband. For surely the crowned sun is the symbol of the Hittite empire. Was she suggesting that you take me to wife, King Tishratta?" The crowd whispered and pointed at the king and his retinue. They were as surprised as he was to hear my words. "No. That must be wrong because I am the wife of the Egyptian Pharaoh, a great and generous king who has chosen both Tadukhipa and me as wife. I have abandoned my people and claimed Egypt as my own. Hasn't my sister-wife done the same?"

"She has. What are you accusing her of, Queen Nefertiti?" I could see his jaw clench and his fist curl.

Without moving my head I glanced at Harwa, whose eyes reminded me to tread lightly.

"Merely bad judgment. I have no specific accusation against her. I am merely asking about the nature of her curious gift. I do not understand it. I am sure sweet Tadukhipa had some kind gesture in mind, but since I cannot fathom it, I have decided to accept her gift anyway. My steward Harwa has delivered the brooch into my jeweler's hands. He will make sure it is fit for a queen of Egypt. Please stay for my banquet this evening so you can see the gift she gave me. Thank you for attending me today." I rose from the dais, leaving him standing stupidly before the throne. I walked out of the court, smiling generously at my people, stopping to accept their bows of devotion and blessings.

Once we left the long court processional, with the Hittites staring open-mouthed at our backs, Harwa found me and whispered, "My queen, what will Pharaoh say about this? I am sure he will hear about it. You have only given them reason to hate you more."

"Do you think it will come back to bite me?"

Harwa sighed but smiled. "Of course it will, but we'll be ready for them. It sounds to me like tonight's banquet will be interesting indeed. Hittites, Grecians and Meshwesh together?"

"Why not? We are Egypt—the most civilized nation in the world. And if any of our guests have a problem with one another, then it is their problem to have. Make sure the gift is ready for me to wear by tonight, Harwa."

"It shall be done, my queen."

"Tell Menmet to come to me."

I walked back up the staircase with my minor servants a safe distance behind me. I did not invite them to talk with me, though I knew that for many it would have been the dream of a lifetime. I was not feeling so generous at the moment. I had to think. If Queen Tiye had been there, what would she have said? Would she have even received them? She would have scolded me for letting my feelings get the better of me, but I think she would have agreed with my decision. Since Tadukhipa was openly challenging me for the title of Great Wife, I must return the favor. I pushed the door open to my chambers and was surprised to see a young girl waiting for me. She was on her knees, folding scarves. She wore a worn purple gown and a robe of blue. I could see right away that she was Meshwesh.

"Who are you? How did you get in here?"

"I am Sunami. I am sent here by your uncle Horemheb, the man we call Omel. I am to be in your court, Mekhma Nefret. Oh, excuse me, Queen Nefertiti!" Hearing a voice from home delighted my soul, especially at this moment when my hands and confidence were shaking.

"Welcome then, Sunami. Stand. Let me look at you." She stood and raised her face slowly. As she did, I could see she was beautiful. She had an angular face, large luminous eyes the color of mist and short dark bangs with long black hair. Ah, she had been one of Farrah's acolytes. Only those women left their tresses to grow to such lengths. "You look familiar to me. Have we met?" I saw something flash in those expressive eyes, but I did not know her well enough to decipher it. Fear, perhaps? Fear that I would reject her? "You do not have to be afraid of me. I do not eat children or young women, Sunami."

"We have never met, Mekhma, I mean, Queen Nefertiti, but I have seen you many times at Timia and at Zerzura."

"Ziza! That is who you favor! Is everything alright with the girl?"

"Oh yes, Ziza is my little cousin. All is well. She is growing and sends her love to you."

I clapped my hands in delight and hugged her as if she were an old friend. About that time, Menmet bounced into the room ready to serve me. "Never mind, Menmet. Meet Sunami, my new maid-servant. You must show her how to dress. Perhaps we can save her hair and not cut it, but I am not sure it can be avoided, Sunami."

"I will be happy to cut my hair to serve you, Queen Nefertiti."

"We will worry about that later. Right now I need your help choosing clothing for tonight. Menmet is always wanting to show my body with these sheer robes, but as you can see, I have a big belly now. I cannot walk around with my breasts exposed." Menmet pouted at my teasing words.

"No indeed. You are Queen of Egypt. You cannot do such things. Let Sunami help you, sweet queen."

Menmet whispered in my ear, "There is a man who says he must meet with you privately." Even more quietly she said, "It is Alexio, lady queen."

I drew back as if she had bitten me. "What?" She did not speak again but nodded her affirmation.

"Very well. Sunami, you stay here and find something blue for me to wear. The Grecians were wearing blue. I think it is important to show where my allegiance lies, at least today. I will return soon."

She smiled, but there was no warmth in it. In fact, my skin felt clammy at the sight of it. I waved my hand dismissively and left her standing in my rooms alone.

I followed Menmet down to my private gardens and could see Alexio pacing there. "Please, Menmet. Stay with me. He and I cannot be alone together. Also, help me take off my robe. This heat is unbearable."

"Should I ask why?"

"You should not." I knew she loved me. How could I think of replacing her? Tiye had been wrong about her. *Stop thinking about this right now, Nefret. You have bigger things to think about.* There was danger afoot throughout my palace.

I walked out into the sunlight and stood patiently, waiting for Alexio to notice me. I learned this trick from Queen Tiye who loved to surprise people. She moved like Lady Silence herself. And, she bragged once, she learned a great deal just by standing like a statue.

"Oh, Nefret. You came."

"This is Queen Nefertiti, sir. Please call her by her proper name, as it is illegal to do otherwise."

"Forgive me, madam. May we speak in private, Queen Nefertiti? I have a boon to ask of you."

"You can speak freely in front of Menmet. She is my most trusted adviser."

"Sit, lady. I will attend you. Do you want water or wine?"

"Water, please, Menmet."

We waited as she poured us a drink. I sat at the table and invited Alexio to sit with me. He took a drink and looked around him nervously. "It is I, Alexio. Your friend and countryman. Please do not feel afraid here."

He looked at me, and I felt the familiar tug at my heart. He continued, "It's just that there are things I would say to you that I…"

"Speak your mind, Alexio hap Omel." I said the words pleasantly but rubbed my stomach protectively. He swallowed and got the message. I no longer belonged to him. I was Pharaoh's wife.

"I came to plead for the release of my wife, Pah hap Semkah, your sister. I know you do not believe me, or maybe you will understand this now, now that you are so happy with your Pharaoh. I love her. I think I always did. I do not know why it took me so long to realize that, but she needs me and I need her, Nefret. I mean, please, Queen Nefertiti, let her go. I do not know why she is being held in the temple, but you of all people should know that Pah is not well. Please set her free and send her home where she will be cared for by people who know and love her." He spoke so passionately and suddenly that it surprised me. He added in a low voice, "If you ever loved me or cared for me, please, send her back to me." I could see the tears in his eyes, and it was a strange thing to see. I wanted to slap him. Scream at him. Beg him to at least want me, but I did none of those things. I did not love him, not like I loved Amenhotep. Why was I so resistant to his request?

"*I* have not arrested her. *I* did not bring her here. In fact, Pah cannot remember who brought her, nor can she tell us why. But you may visit her. There is an investigation into this matter, but I do not know who arranged this. And I cannot fathom why someone would have sent her to the Green Temple. However, it is more complicated now. She is a proven seer, and her skills have made her a valuable asset to the priestesses there. And, of course, to Isis. I have a suspicion that they might release Pah at a price. They will lose money if she leaves. And more than anything, these temple priests and priestesses here value money. It is something my husband and I hope to change during our reign."

He looked at me with a questioning expression. "So you are happy? You want to be with—I mean, in Thebes?"

Without thinking I leaned forward and took his hand in mine. I whispered to him, uncaring who saw me, "Fate led me away, and I cannot resist my destiny. I am sorry, Alexio."

"I hated you when you left."

"I know."

"Those were lies, Nefr—Nefertiti. And you believed them. You should have believed *me*. You should have let me stay by your side."

"And if I had? How could I have ever released you? But now I know you love Pah. That is good."

He had something else to say, but he did not say it and I did not prompt him to speak his mind. Some things did not need to be and should not be said.

"Go to the temple tomorrow, Alexio. I will arrange for you to visit your wife. There is a small area where sometimes priestesses are afforded visits from family members, but do not tell them you are her husband. I am sure they would not welcome you if they knew. The priestesses of Isis are all unmarried. Talk to her. Find out what you can. Did she take an oath? If she did, it will be more difficult to remove her from the temple, but I would not say it is impossible. I will pay for her release since she did not willingly enter the temple herself. Help her remember, Alexio. Send Horemheb to me tomorrow, and we will meet with Nakmaa, the High Priestess at the Isis temple. Horemheb has charm with women, and she seems like one who enjoys being charmed."

Alexio wiped sudden tears from his eyes. "And you don't hate me?"

"How could I? I should be asking you that question."

"I wish you a house full of children, my friend," he said, gesturing toward my belly.

"And you, Alexio." As we rose from the table, he was all smiles. He hugged me impetuously, and I did not stop him even though Menmet frowned disapprovingly. Soon he was gone, and I watched him leave knowing that would likely be the last time I saw him. I sighed, but it was not a regretful sigh. More an appreciation that a part of my life was officially over. No more days swimming aimlessly in the pool at Timia. No more climbing trees with my treasures or eating grapes from Alexio's hand. Everything was different, and it always would be.

I heard the bells chime, sounding the time throughout the palace. "Oh no! I need to bathe and dress. Let's go, Menmet."

She took my hand, and we ran up the stairs together. I felt free. Freer than I had in a long time. Laughing at myself trying to race with my ball of a belly, I swung open the doors and froze in my tracks. Hanging from the golden rail that led to the top level of my apartment was a body. The body of Sunami! She was obviously dead, having been stabbed multiple times. I felt nausea rise in my belly, and I heard a strange sound. It was a woman's voice, extremely loud, and the enunciations were all wrong.

"Please, mekhma. I only help." In my surprise I had not noticed the second body on the floor. It was Mina! Farrah's acolyte!

"Murderer!" Menmet screamed at her.

"No! Stop, Menmet!" Before I could get a hold of her, the guards were in the rooms. They immediately cut down the body and tried to assess the danger. "No, leave the woman alone. There is no danger here. Please. Just give me a minute." I sat on the floor next to Mina. I could see that she too had slash marks along her arms and chest, and some were very vicious and deep. "What happened, my friend? Who did this to you?"

"I help," she yelled.

"Mina, speak softly now. You do not have to yell. Save your air."

"Astora!" she yelled again, and then I saw her jaw go slack and her eyes roll up to something I could not see.

"Astora? Mina! Come back to me! Where is Astora?"

Menmet screamed in surprise as she knelt by the body of my new servant. "Queen Nefertiti! This is not Sunami! Who is this?"

"What do you mean? She is in Sunami's clothing. Who else could it be?"

The guards had removed the body and laid it on the floor. I pushed back the long hair and could plainly see that it was much shorter now. The face became clearer, and the last of the illusion faded. There was the face of Astora, the wife of Horemheb. She had fresh tattoos on her face, and her eyes were dead. Wondering who else was dead here, I ran up the last flight of stairs and looked around my bedchambers. There were no other bodies, but all my gowns had been slashed to pieces with the same knife that appeared to have been used on Astora. Who had done this? Astora/Sunami? Or maybe Mina? I could not fathom it. I sat on the bed and cried as my servants began cleaning my chambers.

Oh, Amenhotep! Come home soon! Death is all around me!

Chapter Eleven

Twisting Snakes—Pah

Never do I dream. Except last night. Then she came to me—like an angry tiger, growling with snarling teeth and reaching, evil claws. She wanted to take from me what I took from her. She said nothing, just slashed at me. I felt the cuts, one after the other. I felt the blood pouring from my wounds. I fell to my knees, unable to fend off her cruel slices. I raised my outstretched hand to protect my face. I waited for the death strike, perhaps at my throat, but it did not come. The awful tearing, the painful slices ceased.

Crying and begging for my miserable life, I slowly lifted my head.

The tiger with Paimu's face had disappeared. Now it was the girl, her hair disheveled and dirty with desert sand, her tunic stained with dark blood and her eyes…black and lifeless. They peered into my soul.

Her mouth did not move, but her words filled my mind.

Murderess. Murderess. Do you think you can hide from me, murderess? A life for a life.

Her words were like a sword stabbing into my heart.

Suddenly my mind was flooded with memories, unhappy memories of Paimu's hopeful face and my cruel last words to her. I could see and know how she felt. And even more than that, I felt her need for love, her awareness of her abandonment by the Algat. The utter rejection and hopelessness. And all that time I had the power to love, help and comfort her.

But I had not done that. My sister had. I saw Nefret smiling down at her brown face and felt Paimu's joyful heart. The future became hopeful again. I then saw flashes of Paimu's memories—climbing the palm trees, plunging into the cool waters of the pool at Timia, playing with the baby goats, laughing with Alexio, stealing chula bread with Ziza. In the memories she shared I could see Paimu's gap-toothed smile and feel the warmth within her. She who had been cast off had found love.

Then another memory.

I saw my own face in the darkness, rich robes around me, a queen's necklace hanging from my neck. Then the blade, and then the pain. I gasped at what I saw, yet I knew it was all true. I was the one who had done it.

I fell on my face and wept. The girl did not move. She did not offer comfort, nor did I expect it.

"What do you want? I cannot change what I have done. What do you want, Paimu? I am sorry I did this to you. I am sorry."

She moved closer. Still crying, I sat up on my knees and turned my face toward her. When I had the courage to open my eyes, I could see she was as she used to be. Her eyes were no longer black, her clothing was fresh and her hair was brushed and clean. "What do you want?" I asked again. "I deserve to die. Take my life, Paimu. I surrender it to you." I meant what I said, but she did not accept my offer.

Then the dream changed. Paimu was not alone now. Farrah stood beside her, and together the three of us stood outside my tent at Timia. Farrah's hair fluttered up occasionally, lifted by a mysterious wind that blew around us. She did not rage at me, not as I had seen her do before on the other side of the temple walls, with eyes of hatred.

"Why have you come? To kill me?" I asked her. I was no longer kneeling but standing and wearing the robes of the mekhma. The cuts had disappeared from my flesh, although I could still feel the pain of them. Terror flooded me, and I wavered on my feet. A nearby fire lit up the darkness, and just beyond it I could hear voices. Voices of many shadowy beings that watched my every move. There was nowhere to run. Nothing I could do.

"The price must be paid, Pah. The girl deserves justice."

"Are you asking me to take my own life? Is that what she wants?"

Farrah's expression was dark, unhappy, and she shook her head slowly.

"What is it, then? Tell me!"

"Kneel," she said.

Without question I did as she told me. The girl stepped forward—she was mere inches from my face now. Tears slid down my face.

Let me die! I deserve this! This is justice!

I knew Paimu could hear my thoughts just as I had heard hers earlier. I thought about my sister, my father and Alexio…

Ah, Alexio! I will miss you most of all!

Even as I thought those words, Paimu's hand reached out, and I felt an excruciating pain in my heart. I woke with a scream.

Margg shook me, babbling away in an attempt to silence me. I was sure if she'd had her way she would have turned me out of her room, but I did not give her a choice. I fell into her arms, sobbing.

I knew what the girl wanted.

I knew I would have to give it to her.

Chapter Twelve

Golden Crown—Tadukhipa

"Come away, my love, and let me show you something," I leaned against the back of Amenhotep's neck, hoping he noticed and appreciated the feeling of my young breasts pressed against his flesh. He was hardly attentive, and as the weeks dragged by it became more difficult to keep him entertained. He constantly pored over scrolls of reports, explored artifacts and spent much of his time with the priests of the Aten. I frowned over his shoulder as he tinkered with the building model, moving pylons, obelisks and other architectural elements. I knew I had thus far failed in my mission—both of them.

When my father came to me, the tasks had seemed simple enough: seduce Amenhotep and show him the foolishness of abandoning the worship of Amun. How shortsighted of my husband to consider such a thing—the leopard coats had their hands in the workings of many nations. Their presence was growing in Mitanni, and with that growing presence came much wealth and prestige. There were other reasons, much more complex, but I had not paid much attention to these unimportant details. It was the challenge of seduction that delighted me. For the past two years I could only observe Amenhotep, the son, from afar. But now that the old pharaoh was dead, I could finally turn my attentions to more exciting things. Who wanted to make love to an old man? Thankfully, and many thanks to my concoctions, the father had not been able to raise his tent for me.

But I might as well have stayed in the Royal Harem for all the attention my new husband had given me. We had made love less than a handful of times during our time together. Although I made a great show to the servants of how tired I was each morning, these were pleasant lies. Even when he did come to me, he never stayed to sleep with me, nor did he linger long on my pillow after the deed was done.

I had secretly sent my dutiful little birds back to Thebes with messages that I prayed had gotten back to Nefertiti with all haste. I spread the "news" to the court that Amenhotep and I were closer than ever. Perhaps he had put his seed in my belly; love and affection were not required for this.

Privately my magicians had told me that I *would* have a son, but I had yet to hold a baby in my arms.

So impatient, Tadukhipa, I could almost hear Inhapi scold me from the Otherworld.

I wondered how Nefertiti liked the gift I had sent her, if she was intelligent enough to understand it. With a smile I imagined her expression when she realized that the brooch pin had been dipped in poison. I could see her skin grow paler as death claimed her. It had been a foolish thing to do, I knew, but I grew more desperate by the day. While I was here being ignored by my husband, she was ruling Egypt as his regent! It was more than I could bear, although I kept my thoughts to myself.

I rubbed his neck impatiently, but he did not turn from his models. "Soon," he said, reaching for his cup. With a sigh of exasperation I left him alone and walked along the patio. This was a small palace, nothing as grand as the one in Thebes or the Royal Harem, and we had been here for a whole week. I grew bored with the scenery and his indifference. So far I had not given voice to my disappointment. Better to smile and pretend how much I loved him. It was getting harder to do.

Aggravated, I reached for my robe and slid it over my nude body. I did not wish to show myself to the guards below, not that Amenhotep would mind. Still, I could not give up. I would not give up! To do so meant that the Desert Queen would win my place and I would lose the love and support of the Hittite throne.

Hadn't I paid enough? Hadn't I patiently endured the pawing of Amenhotep's father? I shivered thinking of his dry, rough hands all over my body. Although he had not been man enough to take me, he had enjoyed pinching me and feeling my young flesh. I came to my new husband's bed a maid, technically. I did not think he even noticed when he pushed through the veil and made me bleed that first night. With a sigh, I pulled a flower off the vine that grew over the railing and toyed with it for a few minutes before I crushed it in my hand. I missed Inhapi. Her quick smile, her soft lips, her gentle fingers. What advice would she have given me right now?

"Amenhotep, come away now. It is getting late."

Eventually he left his table and came to me. He wore no headdress today, no crown, but his height alone reminded me that he was still Pharaoh. Kings were always taller than other men. My uncle, King of the Hittites, towered over his court, and Amenhotep was taller still. "What did you want to show me?"

"I have a surprise for you. It is in here," I said with my most flirtatious smile. He allowed me to lead him to the door of the inner chamber. The heady aroma of flowers filled the hallway, and just as I had instructed, baskets of blooms were everywhere. Somehow my servants had found night-blooming jasmine; the scent was said to stoke a man's desires. I turned my back to the door and stood between him and the handle. "Now, my king, on this last night here together, I have something special for you. Something you have never seen before."

He smiled patiently. "Something I have never seen before? My mind cannot fathom what it could be."

With a smile of satisfaction I pushed the door open and ushered him into the chamber. The candlelight caught the golden mirrors on the walls and bounced around the room, making it seem like an enchanted place. Sitting on their knees in the middle of the bed were two young women with long golden hair. They wore nothing except shimmering belly chains and scented oils that gave their tanned skin a hint of gold. They looked like two delightful, magical creatures with their round curved hips and shapely arms and thighs. I sent them a stern look, reminding them to please my husband, and then turned to Amenhotep with a seductive smile on my face.

"Have you ever seen such beauty before? And there are two of them. They are just for you, my king." Leaving him alone with his prizes, I walked out of the room and closed the door behind me. I waited a moment, listening to the sounds of the young women giggling, and walked away happy that he did not refuse them.

So he is not as pious and faithful as Nefertiti believes. That is something, at least.

I sauntered to my room. It was smaller than our shared chambers but elegantly decorated. I called my attendants and climbed into a bath to rest before tomorrow's journey. I did not see Amenhotep for the rest of the night, but it was no bother to me. I wanted to be alone so I could think of Inhapi without interruption. In a perfect world, we would still be together plotting our happy future. How I missed her!

I thought of Ramose and wondered if his bed was empty tonight. I once considered seducing the General of Egypt but decided against it. I could not trust that he would be discreet. Ramose was a braggart, and he had loved Amenhotep the father. I wanted to feel close to my lost Inhapi, and what better way to do that than to lie with her husband? But I could not take that chance. Sitamen had disappointed me too. She pretended not to understand my invitations to experience the joys I could offer her. The girl spent all her time plucking away at threads, playing with her birds and singing mournful songs. It was no matter. I had another distraction, for I would have a son—a son to rule—even if Amenhotep failed to give me one. I had to work quickly, for I feared that when I returned to Egypt he would not call for me again. How would I explain away a child if too much time passed?

When I woke the following morning, I felt my stomach cramp. At first I thought it was merely hunger, but the cramping got worse and soon I felt blood trickling from between my legs. I reached down and looked at my hand. Yes, there it was—bright red blood. I was not pregnant. *Lying priests!* I turned into the pillow and screamed in frustration.

I was going to return to Thebes without a child in my womb. Nefertiti's belly would be swollen like a fat pear while I had nothing to show for my troubles. I heard my servants approaching my room and yelled at them. "Stay out. I will come out soon."

I could not let anyone know this. Not yet. How long before Amenhotep abandoned my bed forever? How that would please my enemy, Queen Tiye! How she would rock with laughter to hear that. Her son hated my bed and would never take me as his Great Wife! How delighted she would be when she learned the truth! I decided I must kill her. I thought the old witch would go down into the ground with her husband, but she did not. Too afraid to leave her son in my clutches.

Oh, Amenhotep! You infuriate me!

I knew that he pined for the Desert Queen—that he wanted to make her the Great Wife. I knew he wanted her more than he had ever wanted me. The only thing stopping him from announcing it from the top of the palace were the Hittites, my family. The same family who abandoned me to the whims of Egypt's kings long ago. Amenhotep already believed I carried his child. I had been two months without a flow, I all but declared it. I could not face his disappointment now.

No. I would have to find another way. I would have a child, and I knew who could help me. As I cleaned up the blood and rinsed my stained nightgown, I quickly fomented a plan.

I was not defeated yet.

Chapter Thirteen

The Burning Bull—Ramose

I desired Sitamen like I had never desired another woman. At the beginning of my marriage, Inhapi had stirred my sense of dignity and duty with her cool seductive looks. With her I was the General of Egypt, an unappreciated noble waiting to be recognized for my brilliance and strength. With Ayn I was the rescuer, the strange and distant man who brought pleasure without any demands. There had been others, but they had been meaningless meetings. The grappling of flesh. Needed release. Like eating a meal or drinking a tasty wine. These had been nothing more than wasted moments.

But with Sitamen, I could be Ramose. She neither showered me with flowery speech nor treated me like a stud horse. I did not take her as some women liked a man to do. We embraced one another like people, and for the first time I knew what the poets were talking about with their verses of stars and fate. How was it that a few weeks could seem like a happy eternity? How could it feel as if this had been the only true reality for me?

I felt loved, and I knew I did not deserve it.

I nodded stupidly as Aperel told me about the training for the new horses. I thought of Sitamen's silky hair falling in her eyes as she smiled at me, one shoulder bare and vulnerable. Kafta and I drilled with swords as I oversaw the training of my neglected soldiers. He struck me with the wooden blade and laughed at me. "Head in the clouds, General?" Kafta knew my secret, but I trusted him. I did not answer him—how could I deny it? Even as I bobbed my head to avoid his strike, deep beneath the arc of his practice blade I could see her, walking peacefully among her caged birds like a strange bird goddess. Seeing her with Kames made me love her more. It was as if she were the boy's mother. It was a happy fantasy. A fantasy that would surely change now that Pharaoh was returning to Thebes. Too many people already knew of our meetings. No matter how carefully we arranged our time together, we could not avoid the gossiping tongues forever. Every day I told myself that I must end this, but every evening I fell asleep in Sitamen's arms happy and satisfied.

Tonight, out of an abundance of caution, I waited until dark and walked into the palace using the commoners' entrance near the cooking houses. My stomach rumbled at the smells of baking bread, roasted meat and garlic. A familiar guard acknowledged me but wisely kept his mouth shut. I walked quickly to Sitamen's private chambers, avoiding as many people as I could. It was difficult to do in a palace where hundreds were employed tending to a member of the royal family.

"Look, Kames! Here is your father!" I smiled at Sitamen, who held my son as I laid my sword and belt on a nearby table. She liked me to remove them before I held the child. "See how strong he is, little one? You will be just like your father one day." She kissed the baby's cheek and then stood on her tiptoes and kissed mine.

My arms slid around her waist, and I hugged her to me. With a quick kiss, I accepted the peaceful bundle she offered me and rubbed the child's chin with my rough finger. He opened his eyes and stared at me as if he had something to say. "Fine boy. He grows heavier every day." I never knew what to say to him, but I liked holding him in my arms. "Have you kept the princess busy today?"

She laughed, and it was a pleasant sound. "Indeed he did not. He slept all day, but he watched the birds in between naps." She poured wine into two cups, and we talked for a while before one of her servants took the child away to do whatever it was that small children did. I watched him disappear.

Sitamen's servant raced into the room unannounced and wide-eyed. "Lady! Your mother is here! I could not stop her." Just then the Queen walked into our chambers, her pink robes swinging about her tiny frame. I had forgotten how small she was, how absolutely frail she had become since Amenhotep's journey to the Otherworld.

"So it is true. I never thought you to be a fool, General."

"Queen Tiye!" I rose to my feet but quickly remembered this was my late Pharaoh's wife. I did not think it wise to answer her beyond that, so I kept my peace. Sitamen's eyes were riveted on her mother as the older woman turned her attention to her. "And you.

Your brother will undoubtedly know about this. If I know, he knows! Do you know what this means for you? You will *never* be the wife of Pharaoh now. Any chance you had is gone, along with your reputation. You have broken the law, Sitamen, and you have condemned this man to death." Tiye's pale hand waved toward me, and her voice had an honest edge of fear to it. "Have you learned nothing from me, foolish girl?"

Sitamen threw her cup on the floor, and the wine splashed up and stained the hem of her mother's garments. "Oh, I would say that I have learned plenty from you, Queen Tiye! I have learned that if I do not find my happiness, I will never have it."

"Happiness? Who told you happiness was afforded to you? You are Pharaoh's daughter—and wife! No one cares about your happiness."

"I know this lesson. I learned it at an early age." Sitamen slid her arm through mine and held me tightly. I cupped her hand with my other hand. I had to do something, say something.

"Queen Tiye, I love Sitamen. I never meant for this to happen, but I am willing to pay whatever price I must."

Sitamen said softly, "Ramose! I will talk to my brother. He will understand."

The old queen made a snorting sound. "Even if he does, there is nothing he can do to help you, Sitamen. If he finds you together like this, if someone brings him ample evidence, you might as well cut your own throat. He will obey the law, I promise you. How could you betray us like this, General? My husband loved you like a son. He trusted you with his kingdom, and now you bring his daughter to ruin."

"How dare you speak to him like that—as if he betrayed my father? All he has done is love me. Is that a crime?"

"In fact, it is a crime, Sitamen!"

"How dare you speak so sanctimoniously when everyone knows that you and my uncle…" Tiye crossed the short distance between us in a flash and struck Sitamen's face with her open hand. Sitamen pulled her hand away from me and gasped in surprise.

"You have been listening to Tadukhipa, haven't you, evil girl? How can you believe such lies?"

"Why are you here, Mother? To gloat? To condemn me or better still throw me into the fire yourself?" Sitamen did not cry or hunker down. She touched the red handprint on her face briefly and then with clenched fists stood still.

Queen Tiye's hawkish eyes were on me now. "If I were you, I would think of your son."

"What do you mean?"

"Don't listen to her, Ramose. My brother would never harm Kames. And I have claimed him as my own. Remember?" I wanted to believe Sitamen's words, but I had seen firsthand the ruthlessness of kings. On Pharaoh's command I had executed men for much less than my own crimes.

"What do you advise?" I asked Queen Tiye.

"Ramose?" Sitamen stood between us, facing me now. The look on her face was a turbulent mixture of disappointment and disbelief.

"I love you, Sitamen. I have never said that to another woman, not even Inhapi, but we must think of Kames. I know you love him as I do."

"Do not listen to her. Nobody knows about us. If you listen, she will destroy us."

I could see there would be no reasoning with her. Tiye was right. If she knew about Sitamen and me, then Amenhotep would surely know too. Seeking her help might be the only way my son could survive. "What would you have me do, Queen Tiye?"

"Throw yourself at my son's feet and tell him that Sitamen seduced you. That she compelled you—no, commanded you—to stay with her."

"That is not true!" Sitamen shouted.

"Do you want to save this man or not? If you do not shoulder some of the blame, he is doomed. Do you know the punishment for this? They will cast him into the flames to purify him, Sitamen. He will burn as the law demands."

"I do not believe you! Amenhotep—"

"Will do what the priests tell him." In a softer voice she said, "You should listen to me, Ramose. It is the only way. There will be nowhere to hide for you."

"I cannot allow Sitamen to take the blame. She is an innocent."

Queen Tiye drew herself up and sighed. "I leave that to you. At least in this you are an honorable man."

Sitamen wailed. "I cannot allow you to do this. I won't, Ramose. All will be well. I know it!" She laid her head on my chest, and I held her, uncaring that Tiye witnessed the demonstration of my affection. I kissed the top of her head, and we said nothing for a long minute.

"You have to go. Leave Kames with me. I promise you no harm will come to him. Amenhotep would never injure a child. Go now and let me reason with him."

"I cannot run away. All Egypt knows who I am, and I will not let the weight of this fall on you. Let me go to him. I will do as your mother suggests, and let us see how things go."

"No. Don't leave, Ramose." She sobbed and clung to me with all her might.

"Take care of Kames, Sitamen. Promise me." Through moist eyes and wet cheeks, she agreed begrudgingly. I grasped her arms and pushed her away.

"No! Ramose!"

Her sobs rang in my ears as I walked down the corridor, my heart pounding with fear. Not for myself but for Kames and Sitamen. I knew what my punishment would be.

Queen Tiye spoke the truth.

There would be no mercy. I would burn.

Chapter Fourteen

Moment of Forgetting—Tiye

Sitamen screamed at me, "How can you do this? Why did you come here?"

"I did not create this disastrous situation. You did. And by doing so you left us open to attack from the Hittite woman and all our enemies! Don't you know that even now the kingdom hangs in the balance? Your brother is new to his throne and weak in the eyes of the world."

She wiped her nose with her hand. Her hair came unbound and hung around her face in tangles, catching the excess moisture on her cheeks. It clung to her most unattractively. She tucked the hair behind her large ears and continued to yell at me. "What enemies? Which ones? Do you think I don't know what this is about? This is about you and Kiya! Will this feud never end? Now you have taken everything from me, Mother. Everything!"

No matter how hard I tried to keep my heart a stone, I could not help but feel sympathy for her. She was like a leaf in a bowl of water on a windy day. She always had been. Turning this way and that with no focus, no dream that was real. Sitamen had suffered the disease many spoiled princesses suffered. Daydreaming. I had warned her to turn her attentions to real life, but she had not heeded my words. "No matter what you think, Sitamen, I never wanted to come here. I saw this in the water. I did not come right away because I wanted you to have more time. I hoped it was a false vision. But when even Huya heard the gossip, I had to come and see for myself. It was either me or your brother. Which do you prefer?" When she did not answer me, I continued, "Why do you think I always kept you at arm's length, daughter?"

"Now you call me daughter?"

Ignoring her disrespect, I continued, "Because I knew you would have this life—a life with no husband, no lover, no children—and I could not stand to watch it unfold. I should have known you would do something like this!"

"Like what? Love a man? Love Ramose? Want a child of my own? Desire the things all women have?"

"Women never choose their own destinies."

"But you did, didn't you, *Mother*? You were not the daughter of Pharaoh, yet here you stand. The Great Wife of my father, Amenhotep. You have always done as you chose, and you always chose what was best for you."

"What do you mean?"

"You did not mishear me. As always, you think of yourself above anyone. I wish to the gods you were not my mother. I wish anyone were my mother but you!"

I grabbed her arms and held her tight, even though she twisted and tried to pull away from me.

"Let me go! I want to die!"

Many young women said foolish things when love disappointed them, but something in Sitamen's voice told me I should believe her. I had seen her in the water, her face the picture of anguish. She reached toward the flames and screamed, "Ramose!" I saw my son with a cold look in his eyes, watching as the man burned for his crimes against Pharaoh. And I saw one more thing. I could not let it happen! I could not! I would stay with her whether she said yea or nay. Until there was officially a new Great Queen, I held that role.

"I will not let you go, Sitamen. You cannot leave me, and I will not leave you. Perhaps I have not been the best mother to you, but I am here now. And I swear to you, I will not leave you." Sitamen fell onto her bed of blue silk and curled into a ball. I sat in an uncomfortable chair and watched her cry. I did not touch her or disturb her in her grief. She loved Ramose, I had no doubt. Perhaps he loved her too, but it was of little matter now. Huya would have found him and led him to Pharaoh's palace to await Pharaoh's decision. It would be out of our hands. Better that I tell him than Tadukhipa or some other. When I could, I would plead for the man, but I knew how it would go for him. The law could not be undone. It had never been undone. To lie with the daughter or wife of Pharaoh meant death. Doubly so if she was both. There would be nothing for Ramose but fire in the belly of the bull. I shuddered thinking about the massive golden bull. The priests of Amun would prepare it, making it shine like the sun before they stuffed Ramose inside it and lit the flames. It was a horrible thing to witness. Once, a wife and half-sister of my husband had done the same thing, slept with another man. Amenhotep was fond of her, but it did not matter. The law remained the law. She burned in the belly of the bull along with her lover. It had been so long ago that I could not remember either of their names. But it had been a cruel thing indeed. "Why not give them poison to drink or remove their heads?" I had asked my husband.

His words were, "The law is the law."

And that was the way it was. No amount of tears or love would change that. Not for anyone, even young Sitamen.

Time passed. I grew hungry, but I remained in the chair even when the servants came into the room to raise the curtains and light the torches. One young servant brought in a tray of food to tempt Sitamen to eat. She stared at the girl as if she did not hear her, but I knew she did. Instead she rolled over and gazed up at the moon. It rose perfectly round in the purple sky, and the stars shone happily, completely unaware of the evil that would soon befall the great General of Egypt and possibly his young lover. What would her father say? What would he do if he were here?

Someone brought the baby into the room. He cried a little, but Sitamen did not show any interest in him. "What is his name again? I forgot." I asked the wet nurse.

"Kames, Great Queen. He is the son of…"

"I know whose son he is. He is my grandson and the son of my daughter, Sitamen. She has adopted him as her own." Sitamen sat up in her bed, and for the first time today I saw a glimmer of happiness on her face. She reached for Kames, and I gave him to her.

"Thank you, Great Queen," she whispered sadly. I nodded and stepped back. My words made it law. Let any man—even my son—say differently. He could not! I stared down at the baby. He was a handsome child with dark-fringed lashes, warm, light brown skin and a nose like his father's. I saw nothing of the foreign girl in him. He would be the image of his father, of that I had no doubt. Well, if Sitamen could not have the father, at least she would have the son as her own. This I could do for her. If she lived.

"Excuse me, Great Queen, your son is here to see you and the Princess Sitamen." Huya's eyes told me everything I needed to know. He avoided making eye contact. His bow was stiff and formal. This was not a random visit. Pharaoh had indeed heard the rumors, or perhaps had heard it from the General's own lips.

Now we would see where the fates fell. I made the sign against curses behind my back in case Tadukhipa was behind this. I would not put it past her to curse us all.

I did not mock Amenhotep by pretending I did not know the reason for his sudden visit. He stormed into the room, his fists clenched. He paused at the foot of Sitamen's bed and stared down at her and the child.

"Is this your child, Sitamen? Is this Ramose's child? Confess what you have done! He has already told me from his own lips that he has lain with you. He believes he is in love with you. I had him beaten!" Amenhotep tore off the cover, and I took the baby from Sitamen, afraid that my son would strike her. I had never seen him so angry.

"I adopted Ramose's child. Kames is not my blood, but he has my name. Mother spoke it."

He turned his head to me, his blue and gold striped headpiece swinging sharply, and his eyes flashed with anger. "You did this?"

"The father will die, won't he? Allow the son to live; he is only a baby, not guilty of anything except being born to Ramose. I declared it so already. And..." I continued cautiously, "I am still Great Queen unless you have chosen a wife to take my place. If you have not, it is my right."

"Your right? You approve of this? Did you know the whole time? My own General! Lying with my sister under my very nose! Sitamen! Why?"

"Because you would never have me, and you cannot give me to anyone else. I had no choice. I love him, Amenhotep! I love Ramose! He has my heart, and I have his! Please have mercy! He has been a faithful servant to you. Please, brother! You have always been so kind and good to me. Please. I will never ask you for another thing!"

"Indeed you will not. Ramose is going to burn as soon as the Aten rises. I cannot stop it, for the priests of Amun are even now polishing their bull and readying it for the sacrifice. And as for you, I command you to be in attendance. You will watch what you have done to the man you say you love."

"No, please, Amenhotep. Do not do this! I cannot believe you would kill your friend and the man I love! Look upon the son I have adopted—Ramose's son! Please!"

"You make it worse each time you say his name! Speak no more to me, Sitamen. I am Pharaoh Amenhotep, and I command that Sitamen my wife and sister shall no more speak to me. If she does, she will also die in the fire!"

"Son! You cannot do this! You cannot condemn your sister like this! Have mercy on her! She is your blood and flesh; you are both the fruit of my womb! Amenhotep, listen to me!"

"No more, Great Queen! No more words on this subject." I could see that he was crying, nearly sobbing himself. "Why? Why did they do this? We could have found another way, but now I cannot change it. Ramose will burn in the bull, and Sitamen will witness it. Where is the child?"

I took the baby in my arms and refused to hand him over. So angry was my son that I could not trust him. I would never have imagined this day would ever come.

"I command you as your Pharaoh to give me the child, Mother." Hesitatingly, I did as he asked. I prayed to the Aten to protect Kames, and I made sure Amenhotep heard me doing so.

He held him as Sitamen wrestled pitifully in her bed, sobbing from the depths of her soul. One of the physicians had arrived during our discourse and was now forcing the girl to drink a dose of calming medicine. In just a few seconds I could see it take effect. She became very still, her voice quiet and calm. She had that dreamy look in her eyes as she watched everything. Pharaoh walked around the room with the baby in his arms. Possibly sensing the danger and the anger of the king, the baby began to wail and cry. Amenhotep walked to the balcony and then stopped. For one terror-filled moment I imagined the worst.

"No, Amenhotep. Imagine your own son, protected and safe in his mother's belly. What has this child had? No mother, now no father. Please do not harm him. Give him to me, and you will never have to see him again. I will care for him. I swear you will never see or hear from him again."

Considering my words for a moment, he extended his arms to me and gave me the baby. "As if I would have harmed him," he said in a rough voice. "See to it that you keep your word, Mother." As quickly as I could, I left the room with the child, but I was gone only long enough to return him to his wet nurse. I raced back to Sitamen's room. Sitting on the edge of her bed staring down at her was Amenhotep. She stared back with a blank expression.

"If she had come to me, we might have found a way. I can do nothing now."

"Sitamen loves Ramose. I am sure of it."

"And unfortunately for her, her love comes with a death sentence. I mourn for him. In a different world I would have welcomed him as a brother-in-law, but it cannot be. We have the Phares blood, and it cannot be mingled with any other kind."

I wanted to say, *What about your father? He married me, didn't he?* However, I kept my peace.

"So death is the only option?" I sat on the other side of the bed. I knew Sitamen could hear us, but she would not remember our words or understand them.

"You know this."

"I do."

"I saw her in the water, my son. I saw her dying. I cannot let her die. I have been a poor mother to her, but I refuse to let her die! I will stay with her every moment of the day to prevent it."

"Yes, stay with her, Mother. Keep her safe. I must go now."

"Go see your queen, Amenhotep, and forget this for the night. I will see you tomorrow." With a nod of agreement, he left me; he cast one last sad look at his sister, who stared off into the sky and drooled, the medicine taking full effect. I would have to talk to the physician and ask for more, or she would never survive the burning of Ramose in the morning.

How could this have happened? My poor, sweet daughter.

Then I remembered something I heard a long time ago. Amenhotep and I had visited the Three Oracles at Majayat on our honeymoon. Those old witches were ancient then, and surely they were dead now. We had entered their cave, our hands full of the pearls they loved. We left our gifts at their feet, and they told us what we wanted to know. We would have many children, but many would die. All those who died could have lived, but because of our stars, we had doomed them all to live unfulfilled lives. First Thutmose died, then his little brother, so small and unformed was he that I did not name him. Now the prophecy of the Oracles reached out across time to claim Sitamen too. I would not allow this!

As she began to fall asleep, I slid in the bed beside her. The baby was gone now with the nervous nursemaid, who promised to never leave Kames alone. I lay beside Sitamen and pulled her slack body to mine. It was easy to do, for she was small too. I stroked her hair and touched her face just as I used to do when she was a child.

My daughter! Amenhotep's daughter! How cruel I have been to you! How I love you, daughter!

I fell asleep with tears on my skin. I thought I had lost the ability to cry, but I was wrong. Tears had been there all along.

I needed them tonight. As the servants snuffed out the lights, I began to pray quietly to Isis. If she did not intervene and prevent this disaster, I would worship her no more. I told her so, but I heard nothing in return.

With a last sigh, I fell asleep and did not dream.

Chapter Fifteen

Children of the Aten—Nefertiti

I stormed through the gates of the temple, passing the first pylon without much notice. A row of gigantic statues faced me. The statue of Queen Tiye wore a short, round wig, and her stone husband sat stiffly beside her. Frozen in a moment of time, the couple appeared happy to receive guests at Amun's temple. I was sure she felt differently about it now. After all, these priests had murdered my husband's brother and plundered the fortunes of Egypt without fear. Nobody protested much, but everyone knew the truth. By killing the older brother, they had unintentionally driven my husband to worship the Aten. In doing so, he abandoned centuries of tradition, and that was not an easy thing for the leopard coats to stomach.

Later today, I would see my husband for the first time in months. I knew he was back in Thebes, although he had not come to me last night. I had a growing sense of fear that he had chosen Tadukhipa over me, but I had one last task to do. One more thing to accomplish before I relinquished my role as regent.

Today I wore a long, flowing red robe to show my anger. Let them interpret that as anger for Ramose—the news of that scandal had rocked the capital—but it was truly the priests of Amun who stirred my rage. I pulled my red hair back tightly to hide it and wore a dark wig with no adornment. I was going to see this golden beast, the place where they often burned children to their god. It was an abomination to my eyes and to the parents of those who were sacrificed. What kind of god would allow such things to be done in his or her name? It would stop today!

Menmet had told me about the sacrifice that was scheduled for this morning. Heby had whispered the secret in her ear, and she told me swiftly, loyal servant that she was. I forbade her from coming with me. I did not want Heby to be angry with her, but I was sure he would eventually find out the truth.

I had never been to the temple of Amun. Never had I laid a sacrifice at the feet of the god there, and never would I. Not since I learned of their despicable practices, practices that Amenhotep would learn about. I passed the second pylon and barely glanced at the four statues that faced me. I did not know their names, but I made the sign of respect to them. My servants looked puzzled, but I did not need to explain anything to them. I kept walking. An unfamiliar leopard coat came toward me. He looked amused at my approach.

"Queen Nefertiti," he called as if he were calling an old friend. I did not pause but kept walking. "Wait, my queen! We are not accustomed to royal guests entering the temple without prior notice. What can we help you with?" Still not speaking to the leopard-coated evil one, I gave my guard, Kemaza, a hard stare. The guard stepped between the priest and me, forbidding him to speak to me again.

"Come now, Harwa. Let us see the truth of the matter."

"Down here, Queen Nefertiti." Harwa pointed to a low staircase. I paused at the top of the stairs, seeing only darkness. I was angry, but my mind also suspected treachery. Treachery abounded in Egypt. That much was true. The place drew evil into it like a spider summoned flies and insects. Just like Astora. She had been evil, but I would never know now what had compelled her to come here. Omel had done his best to show me he knew nothing of her intentions, but I did not believe him. Harwa, though? He had given me no reason not to trust him, and he had been recommended by the old queen. I trusted her above everyone else here.

"I will go first, my queen."

"No, I will go." I glided down the stairs quickly and heard the shocked voices of the priests. I walked amongst them, looking each in the eye. Maya stood watching, a blade in his hand. A child cowered at his feet. It was as I had heard, then. They were sacrificing children here.

"You will put down that knife and leave that child alone, Maya!"

He was so angry at my intrusion that he appeared ready to spit on me or stab me, perhaps both. I did not cower. "You think to interrupt the god's worship? You do not command me, Desert Queen! You have no authority here! Get out now and leave with your life, if you value it!"

"You have distorted the worship of Amun! This is not the true worship! No god of Egypt has ever asked for the life of a child, yet you kill them with your own hands."

"These children were given to the god, and we use them as we see fit. Now leave, or I won't tell you again."

I reached for the half-naked little boy. He had a fearful look on his dirty, pinched face.

"Come to me, little one!" I said as the priest approached me. The other priests stepped toward me too, but my guards were ready to shove their spears into anyone who withstood me. The boy clung to my leg, and the other children ran to me. There must have been at least thirty here in this dank, dirty cellar. The massive stone bowl in the center was on fire, but I could see that none had been burned yet today. Such hopelessness in the faces of the children. I wanted to pick them all up. Instead, I clapped my left hand over my own stomach and took the child by the hand with my right.

The priest grinned at me threateningly and stared at my belly. "Try it," I said to him in a venomous whisper.

"Please, if my queen fancies a few children, take them. There will be more tomorrow. You cannot stop the worship, my queen."

"Hear me now, priests." I spun in a circle. "I claim all these children for the Aten. They belong to him now! These and those that come after them!" The priests hissed at me, but I continued, "These are the Children of the Aten! You will cease your unholy worship this day. No more will you spill the blood of a child here. My guards will be here every day to make sure that you obey my command."

"You cannot do this," Maya screamed at me, his anger reaching a dangerous level.

"I can, and I have."

"I curse you, Queen Nefertiti. You will never carry that child to term. He will die in his mother's womb, drowning in his own blood!" I gasped and raised my arm, as if I could protect myself from his curse with it.

I heard a shout from behind me. "Not before I kill you!"

Amenhotep!

His words echoed through the smelly room like a saving wind. I turned to him as a smile spread across my face. "My husband and Pharaoh, I have claimed these children for the Aten. Let them come serve the true god of light and love. I cannot sit idly by while these innocents give their lives for these greedy priests."

"And so it shall be done. All children given to Amun are now property of the Aten. They are indeed Children of the Aten. Is there anyone who would argue with me?"

No one spoke a word against him, although it seemed like he hoped they would. Only Maya continued to look unafraid; he challenged him still.

"And for what you have said to my wife, the Great Wife of Amenhotep, you shall surely pay. Seize him now!" The guards rushed to do my husband's bidding, and together we went up the stairs with the children. Many were lame and had to have help walking. A few priests, those who were intelligent enough to know which way the wind was blowing, decided to help us in our task. In fact, at least five removed their leopard skins right away, happy that someone had stopped the evil practice. They bowed low before us and begged us to allow them to help.

The children were hungry, confused and convinced they were going to die. I held on to the boy and let him cling to my leg without refusing him. Amenhotep gathered me in his arms. "How did you know I was here?" I asked him.

"I am Pharaoh. Do you think I do not know what you do, my love?"

"My love. How I love to hear you say that! Let us take the children to the Aten temple. I have already spoken to the priests there. They have a place prepared for the children. They will treat them with respect and teach them the ways of the Aten. Soon, your whole kingdom will worship him."

"You never cease to amaze me, my wife."

The children were carried away, and we walked outdoors to make the journey to our palace. Many people had gathered to clap and cheer for us. They heard what we were doing and were grateful for our help. Parents who had lost their children as debts to the temple received them back. Children who were unwanted or had nowhere to go were invited to stay at the Aten's temple. It was a truly revolutionary day.

"You did not hear me, did you?"

"What do you mean?"

"You are now the Great Wife. My only wife and my love."

I could hardly believe what I was hearing. "I thought the Hittites, the trials, what about…"

"You let me worry about those things. You just keep doing what you are doing. All will be well. Harwa and my mother have told me everything. You have done well, Nefertiti. You are Egypt's true queen, but the time for celebration must wait." His face changed completely.

I could see the subject pained him, but I asked anyway. "What has happened, my love? What worries you so?"

"You have heard, I am sure. Ramose has been found with my sister. He will be burned this morning in the Golden Bull—the one in the temple courtyard here—and there is nothing I can do. It is the law. In fact, I go there now. I do not expect that you should have to see this. Go home, and I will meet you there."

"No," I said. "My place is at your side. I must be there for Sitamen too."

"You should know that I have forbidden her to speak to me. And when the burning is complete, she will be banished from here."

"No, Amenhotep! Say it is not true. She is your sister!"

"It is the law, Nefertiti. There is nothing I can do."

"Yes, there is. Just like we stopped the sacrifice, we can do this too."

Then I saw the truth. Amenhotep did not want to save Ramose or Sitamen. It surprised me, and for the first time I saw my husband in a new light. He was not perfect as I imagined but flawed, jealous and easy to provoke in areas of loyalty and respect.

"But she has adopted his son. I had hoped to send him away too, but my mother interceded on his behalf. That should please you since you love children so," he said, looking at me steadily. We stepped out of the dark rooms and climbed up yet another level to the auditorium that overlooked the Golden Bull. The fire under it had been built. Occasionally, a priest would toss a living thing, like a rabbit or a snake, into the fire to test the heat. Whatever they consigned to the flames died quickly. I hoped it would be the same for Ramose. He had not been my friend, but he had brought the Meshwesh home to Zerzura. And Ayn had loved him. *Ayn! I am so glad you cannot see this!* The place began to fill up with witnesses called to see justice done.

Queen Tiye stood by her daughter, Sitamen. The girl looked sick, as if at any minute she would throw up on her mother, but Tiye did not leave her side. I could see the worry in the old queen's face.

Others came too. I saw members of the court, including the scribes, Memre, Huya, and so many familiar faces. Even Tadukhipa made an appearance. She wore all her elegance, which seemed out of place since she was about to witness the death of her friend Inhapi's husband. It did not appear to matter to her.

Surprisingly there was not much pomp in the proceedings. Ramose was brought out, and Sitamen's cries grew louder and more pitiful. She called his name. He looked up at her and smiled as if to say, "All is well."

Standing so close to Pharaoh I could see the tears in his eyes as he said, "Ramose, General of Egypt. You have been found guilty of adultery with Sitamen, my sister and wife. Therefore you are consigned to the flames to burn. But since you have been my friend and a friend to my father, I do not deny you access to the Otherworld. You will be buried in a grave that is befitting your station, and all manner of things will be done to facilitate your journey to my father's side. While you leave in shame, you will arrive in peace. Serve him in the Otherworld as you served him here."

"What of my son, Pharaoh? Please. What of my son?"

Suddenly I spoke up. I had not planned to speak, but I did. "I, Nefertiti, am now the Great Wife of Amenhotep. As my first act, I claim your son as my own, as our own. He will be raised in our household and eat at our table." Tiye and Amenhotep shot me a look of surprise, but neither said anything. Tadukhipa's face crumpled, and she steadied herself by putting her hand out to the servant who stood next to her.

"Thank you, Great Queen, Nefertiti. It is more than I deserve." I nodded at Ramose and ignored Amenhotep's shocked expression. I watched sadly as the handsome, brave general of Egypt was bound with ropes and stripped of his clothing. He would leave this world as he entered it.

"No! No, Ramose! Please, let me go, Mother! Ramose!" Sitamen pulled and tugged, but Tiye would not let her go. Four large priests stood beside the golden bull. They whispered something to the doomed man and held out a cup, probably offering him a drug to help him cope with the flames. He obediently took a few sips.

"I love you, Sitamen. Forgive me, Pharaoh, but I do, although this is a great sin. I pray that this fire will purge me."

"Amenhotep," I whispered in desperation. Even as I said it, I knew I could not stop this—and neither could he. The priests came and picked up Ramose. Without much warning they pitched him into the fire, and he began to writhe and scream. Suddenly, a flock of birds flew over the fiery bowl, circling it as if they were there to witness the death of the brave man. Ramose screamed as the priests stoked up the fire higher. He would die soon, but the agony he would suffer no one would ever forget.

Sitamen quit her struggling. She seemed transfixed on the birds that swirled above Ramose. They were unusual birds, blue birds, and not the kind that normally liked to scavenge a burning body— or any body for that matter. As her attendants pointed at the unusual sight, one of them let loose of her hand. I saw her face. I knew what she would do, but before I could speak, Sitamen ran with all her might and leaped over the side of the railing, her arms outstretched as if she too could fly. Instead she tumbled into the fiery pit below. She joined Ramose in the fire, and together they screamed until they were dead. The guards ran to rescue her, but the heat was so great that no one could have gotten near the pit without losing their own lives.

Then Tiye let out a cry of agony, summoning it up from the depths of her soul. "Sit-a-men! My daughter!" Amenhotep was on his feet reaching for her, but it did not matter.

He raced down the stairs to stop the proceedings but it was too late, they were dead, bound together for all eternity.

Amenhotep cried out and cursed Amun. "I will never serve you, murdering god! Do you hear me? Never!" He stormed out of the temple, and I walked behind him. We would never set foot in another temple of Amun as long as we lived.

The news of the death of Ramose and Sitamen had not yet reached the populace, for they greeted us with joyful cries. Amenhotep pulled the litter closed and wept with all his heart. I sat beside him and held him close. What could I say? Nothing. His misery was complete.

Too soon the litter stopped. We stepped out knowing that we would face the crowd again. While they did not yet know that Ramose was dead, that Sitamen had sacrificed herself for love, they did know that I was now the Queen of Egypt, the Great Wife of Amenhotep.

"Hail, Great Wife!" they cheered to me. Amenhotep put on a smile. He was not happy or in the mood to celebrate, but we could not deny the people their happy moment. Sadness would come soon enough.

"Hail to you, people of Egypt." One of my servants appeared with bags of coins. Amenhotep directed me to cast the coins to the people, and so I did. I showered gold down upon them, and they cheered me as if I were Isis herself.

As I did, I spotted a face in the crowd, a face I had not expected to see. It was the face of my sister, Pah. I looked again, and she was gone.

Then I heard some words, her words, as if they were whispered in my ear, "Hafa-nu, Mekhma Nefret. Hafa-nu!"

"Hafa-nu!" I cried loudly to the people. They did not hesitate to call back using the Meshwesh blessing. Soon all of the people gathered, most of the people of Thebes, were speaking the words of the Red Lands, "Hafa-nu!"

Amenhotep stood beside me and whispered in my ear, "You have done what I asked. The people love you, Nefertiti. This is truly your kingdom—and I am your slave."

I kissed him. I probably should not have done so, not after all we had seen that morning, all the heartache that was still to come, but I kissed him. The crowd cheered again, and I reveled in the moment. Even then I knew there would be few moments like this one.

As baskets of flowers were poured out upon us, we stood together for that glorious moment and let the people celebrate. Whether they realized it or not, we were in a new age, an age of peace and love. Let this morning's sacrifice be the last. I was more determined than ever to let love reign in Thebes and in all the Red and Black Lands.

I could do it. I could make it happen.

This was my kingdom, and I was finally Nefertiti.

The Song of the Bee-Eater

By

M.L. Bullock

Dedication

I dedicate this book to sisters everywhere.

To make peace with your sister is to make peace
with your own soul.

Chapter One

Destiny's Daughter—Pah

I walked through the Oasis of Timia last night. A heavy purple sky draped over the encampment. No moon rose, but clear, bright stars pierced the veil above, allowing the glory of the Otherworld to shower down upon the camp below. The light of the heavens filtered through the tiny pinpricks left by the warring constellations of Sah and Sepdet. It bothered me that I could no longer recall the names I once called those constellations; those Meshwesh names now escaped me—and I once had known all their names and could track their movements better than even the Old One, Farrah.

The soft slapping of the palm fronds grew louder on the evening desert breeze, and the chirping of night birds hungry for tasty moths broke the stillness of the early evening. The fluttering gray insects were always attracted to the amber lights of the camp lanterns, and there were many here along the main pathway that led to the tents of the king and the Council.

I smelled pleasant spices, cinnamon and cardamom, lingering evidence of a celebratory meal. Happy memories stirred within me, memories from a more innocent time. As always with the Meshwesh, these feasts would last through much of the night, yet I dared not intrude. For although Timia had been home to me, I felt I was an intruder.

But why?

The memory of something seething and dark, complicated and soul-shattering escaped me even though I reached for it, mentally clawed at it like one of the moths seeking the light that would burn its life away.

Forget, sister. Lest it kill you.

"Nefret?" I whispered into the night air. Her voice was in my ears, but I could not discern her tall, slender frame anywhere. I heard nothing else from her, and I poised hesitantly on the empty camp pathway, hoping no one would find me and cast me out. Now that I had returned home, I never wanted to leave again. Could it be possible that somehow I had returned? Perhaps so! I had never recovered the memory of my journey from Zerzura to Thebes. Couldn't I just as well have traveled home the same way?

The gods will have their way, won't they? They do as they please with us, I thought wryly.

I could see that I wore no royal robes this evening. Only a simple linen tunic of pale yellow fabric. The soft grass beneath my bare feet was softer than any carpet I had ever trod upon. Tiny curls prickled on the back of my neck, rising in acknowledgement of the mystical realm that worked its magic here. Yes, indeed! As a worker of magic myself, I recognized the stickiness of the air, the shimmering movement of the invisible. Instinctively I touched the air around me, as I always did when I looked into the fire and the water. Then I noticed my hands. They were young again—the scars, and I had many, had been washed away by the magic and starlight, and I felt lighter than I had in many years.

Oh, how I have long staggered under the weight of my priestess' robes and the ornate jewels of Isis! Have I truly been set free?

Freedom overwhelmed me, and like a child I spun about in a joyful dance and laughed aloud. The sound was music to my own ears. How long had it been since I laughed or felt peace like this?

The whistling songs of my people, the Meshwesh, floated toward me and tugged at my heartstrings. Yes, I had been correct! A celebration was underway, and I could hear the excitement rising in their voices. From the pitch and tune, I knew what this was—a birth waiting, a holy night for us. I heard the clapping of hands as the expectant mother settled into her tent. How happy they were! Yes, a child would come! A child for the tribe—a treasure.

Treasure? What have I forgotten?

The wind rose again, and the bright blue pennants above my father's tent beckoned to me. Yes, that was where I should go. He would welcome me; he would make them understand that I was a true Meshwesh daughter. I was also a treasure, and I belonged to them. He would put his robes on me and grant me whatever I wished. *Father! I come to you!*

"Hold now, daughter of Isis. What are you doing here?"

Blinking into the dim light I whispered, "Who is there?" A figure hovered at the corner of the tent. It was a woman. She was not tall as Farrah yet carried herself like one with authority. At my question she stepped onto the lighted path, and I caught my breath.

It was Mina! Mina, who was not dead but young again, her raven's wing hair hanging freely down her back. And she spoke! Instinctively I made the sign of respect, but she did not return the gesture. This troubled me.

"What of your vow, Mina?" I felt compelled to ask. While yet a girl, the acolyte had taken a vow of silence. I had heard her speak only a handful of times in my life, and then only in ritual service to the tribe. By her speaking so plainly, I knew that deep magic indeed worked here in this place this night. She said nothing for a long moment; her hair fluttered like the pennants of Father's tent, covering her dark eyes from my view. I felt the power of those eyes as they searched my soul. I did not fight her or argue my case. I could not remember my offenses, so why should she? I only wanted to belong to my people again. To be their treasure once more.

"I ask you again, why have you come, daughter of Isis?"

"I am a daughter of the Red Lands!" I protested at the repeated accusation. "You know me, Mina. It is I—Pah hap Semkah!"

My answer did not move her, and finally the wind lifted her hair away from her tanned face. I could see her liquid brown eyes, and I relaxed under their sympathetic consideration. Her eyes did not condemn me; I saw only sadness there. "Look above you, then, and tell me what you see," she commanded, raising her right hand. Gazing upward I immediately recognized the constellation—it was Osiris with his bow. It was a dark omen indeed.

"I see Osiris, Mina. He faces the west now." Hoping to impress her I added, "And look! A star falls like an arrow from his bow!"

"He is known as the Dancing Man to the Meshwesh. Or have you forgotten all our ways, Pah hap Semkah?"

"I—I know what is important. I know I should be here." Desperation rose in my voice.

Mina inched toward me, her eyes like fire, her voice like steel. "Remember, Pah. Remember your promise to her."

I stepped away from her. "No! I don't want to remember." I raised my hand upward as if she would strike me. "I want to stay here with my father and my people!"

"You want what you cannot have, but that has always been your way. You will keep your promise to her." Though her words stung my heart, I knew she spoke the truth.

I begrudgingly nodded and pleaded, "Let me pass, Mina. Let me go to my father just once more." Like a wraith, she vanished into smoke and I was alone again. The distance to Father's tent was only a few feet, but it might as well have been a mile. I could not will my feet to make that journey. I desperately hoped Mina was wrong. But I knew she wasn't.

I have left something undone. Something important.

A shadow passed beside me, and I spun to catch sight of who came near me. There was no one there. Only whispers in the dark.

"Mina?" I whispered back to the empty air. The shadow whirred by me again, and this time it pinched me. I gasped and felt increasingly alarmed. This was not Mina but some other being that did not want me here.

With a quick, wistful glance toward Father's tent, I began to run toward the pool. Yes. I would find peace there. Maybe a place to hide from this shadow and whatever promise I had made that might prevent me from coming home! A gray moth flapped in front of me, leading me down the now sandy path, and I took it as a sign. Quietly and quickly I closed the distance between myself and the water. I could smell the water now. At last I would taste the waters of Timia one more time!

As I cleared the last of the tents I glanced around me but saw no one lingering. There were no more tents, no place for shadows to hide. All the Meshwesh were at the celebration on the other side of the expansive camp.

All except Alexio, who stood waiting, his back against the tallest palm tree. My mind whispered, "This must be a dream." My heart replied, "No! This is real. Let it be real!"

His arms were crossed lazily in front of him, and his dark hair hung around his shoulders. His expressive almond-shaped eyes watched me approach, and that thrilled my soul. He watched me as a man would watch a woman he desired. And that was all I had ever wanted. To have his love, to own his heart and to share my own with him.

"Alexio? Can it be you? What are you doing here?"

"I came to see you, little dove."

"I have not heard you call me that in such a long time. You came for *me*? Truly?" I dared not hope that his words were true. Alexio often toyed with my heart, and I always let him. It was exquisite torture.

Again the memory of a great wrong threatened to encroach upon this happy moment, and again I willed it away. The mental struggle made me feel weak, and I had the growing sense that I would not be able to prevent its reappearance for long. "How long have you waited, Alexio?" I wanted to hear his warm, melodious voice a little longer. In the distance a lone musician plucked skillfully at the strings of his rebab, and the notes plucked at my heart. Alexio was only a few feet away now. I could see the angled curve of his high cheekbones and smell the cedar oil on his skin. His dark eyes were almost the deepest purple, so brown were they. He did not mock me as he used to do. He did not tease with his eyes. This was the culmination of all my life's desire, to be loved by Alexio and to show him love. I had cast everything aside—yes, even my own sister, Nefret—in an attempt to capture his heart. I loved him with a ferocity few could understand.

"I want to stay here, Alexio. Promise me I can stay with you. Now and forever." I reached for him. My hand shook as it approached his face. He gazed down at me, his eyes half-closed, a sad smile on his face. Just one touch. To know I was real and he was real and we were alive and home.

"Pah!" Mina's voice called from behind me, the warning tone freezing me in mid-motion. My hand was so close to Alexio's face that I could feel the warmth of his skin. "Would you leave with a promise broken? You cannot return here if you do."

I did not want to turn around and see her there. I wanted to forget the horrible things, the promise, the shadow. Alexio's sorrowful eyes were fixed upon mine and mine upon his.

"Alexio?"

"Do what you must, little dove. I will be here." His look was serious, and he cast his gaze at Mina behind me. Still I would not look away.

"Tell me just once," I whispered to him as I lowered my hand.

"Pah! Come away!" Mina's rough voice warned me. I dared not ignore her for much longer.

Only a second more. This is life. This is my everything.

He bent his head down as if to kiss me, but as our lips came together the shadow that dogged my steps earlier zipped between us and he vanished.

"No! Alexio!" I screamed and clung to the trunk of the tree, sobbing in despair.

Mina's hand rested on my shoulder now. I bent under the weight of it; although her touch was light, it brought the heaviness of the memories I had hoped to avoid. "Daughter of Isis, Daughter of the Red Lands, Daughter of Destiny. Do what you must do—keep your promise. Now is the time. A life for a life."

Her words launched me through the grass of the oasis; I passed unseen by my clan as they waited upon the arrival of another treasure. Helplessly I shot through the Red Lands nearly as quickly as the star that had fallen from Osiris' bow. With another breath I flew through the pylons of the outer gate and the massive green-gold doors of the Green Temple of Isis. I flew up and up until once again I was in my room. My acolyte Shepshet did not so much as stir or blink an eyelash, but I bolted upright in my bed in time to see the supernatural wind that had carried me there extinguish all the lights in my room.

That had been no dream. I had been in the Otherworld! Like Mina, who died many years ago, Alexio was dead too. I could not join them because I still had life in my body. But it was a doomed life and would soon end.

The growing perception that there was another presence here with us rose within me. "I know you are here. Come out and show yourself," I said bravely, but all my courage rose from the bitterness that threatened once again to overwhelm me.

"High One? Do you call me? What has happened to the light?"

"Silent, Shepshet. The dead are here. Close your eyes and do not open them until I tell you, lest they take you with them when they leave."

"Yes, lady," she whimpered, burying her face in her covers. I could hear the rustling of cloth, and I examined the darkness, waiting for her to appear. Cold crept into my bones, but I did not move a muscle.

"You have what you want. I have given him up, Paimu. Again! I have given him up. Take my life if you must, but do it now! Do not torment me forever!"

Then she stepped out of the shadows of the open window near my balcony. Paimu, the girl I'd murdered fifteen seasons ago. In the moonlight of this world, I could see her clearly. Thankfully she did not have bloodless skin, black eyes and bloodstained clothing, as she often had when she appeared to me over the years. It was as if I were looking at a true human girl. The vision broke my heart.

"Paimu! Is it time now? Do you demand my life this night? I am ready to go. Ready to return to Timia."

She refused to answer but walked to the balcony, I noticed that she wore the white sandals my sister had given her before her death. Surely that meant something. She gazed toward the west, toward the sprawling desert beyond Pharaoh's massive city Akhetetan, or Amarna as some had begun to call it. To my eyes it was a golden prison. Nothing more.

I remained in the doorway for fear that she would push me over the side of the balcony. From this great height at the top of the Green Temple of Isis, there would be no doubt I would die instantly in such a fall. In fact, Nakmaa, the old priestess before me, had left this realm in such a manner. There had been talk of murder, but no one could prove it.

Paimu's fixed gaze compelled me to overcome my fear. I stepped out behind her, and in that instant a big blue ball of flame passed overhead. Like the star that fell in my dream—or was it a vision?—this star also fell from Osiris' bow. "What now?"

Paimu pointed west, where the star fell. West to Zerzura.

"Zerzura! I must warn the queen!"

Paimu turned slowly, and now her back was against the railing. She was so close that, if she had been alive, I could have pushed her over.

No! Do not think such evil thoughts, Pah! She is but a child, and you have killed her once already!

My face flushed and I asked her, "Why have you come, child? I know I owe you a life. Do you want me to cut my wrists? Am I to jump from here?" Paimu stared at me and gave me no answer. "What is it?" I screamed at her. Shepshet muffled a scream from her pallet next to my bed.

A loud boom reverberated through the temple, and another fallen star illuminated the city below. I wasn't the only one to have seen it. I could hear the people below scream in confusion and fear.

Gliding toward me quickly, Paimu stood a few inches from my face. I could see luminous tears in her eyes, as if she lived!

"What? What is it, Paimu?"

"Nefff—rettt…" she whispered fearfully and then vanished into wisps of smoke. Soon her presence was gone and the room began to warm. Awareness and understanding came over me like a great wave. Oh yes, it was time.

"Shepshet! Get up! We must prepare to see Pharaoh! He will send for us soon!"

"What? How do you know, lady?" She pulled the cloth off her head and ran to me on the balcony. "Who is Paimu?"

"Please! No questions, for we haven't much time."

She screamed as another star fell on Amarna, and I prepared for what was to come. Pharaoh would want to hear from his many advisers, including the High Priestess of the Green Temple of Isis.

As I allowed Shepshet and the others to dress my hair and my body, I wondered exactly what I would tell him.

Whatever it would be, my true mission was clear. Protect my sister. The debt would be collected.

A life for a life.

Chapter Two

Priestess of Isis—Pah

As I rose from the chair, the stiff robe hung heavily from my shoulders. My eyes were lined with gold, and Shepshet had pressed shiny powder all over my face and hands. Staring at myself in the ornate mirror, a gift from Nefret, I thought I looked very much like a being from another realm. *Good. This will play nicely.* Just as I had anticipated, Pharaoh's steward came to collect me. I was ready to leave the solace of my rooms and temple for his court. It was a strange thing for a high priestess to leave the temple for any occasion, except for the birth blessing of Pharaoh's new children or some other royal ceremony.

I walked down the long stairway. Dozens of my acolytes were sitting on the steps watching my every move. I did not rush myself, and I did not miss a step. I did not look at any of their faces, but I could sense their fear. Even the most ignorant priestess would know these falling stars were not omens of prosperity for the kingdom. As I arrived at the final step, I stopped and spoke to one of the acolytes. "I see fear on your face, priestess. What is your name?"

"Yuyu, lady."

"When I return, Yuyu, I hope to see calm and serenity reflected in those eyes. Go now to the water and stay there until you have defeated your fear. Ask the goddess to send you a vision to make you whole again." It might have been wrong to single her out, but sometimes making an example of one gave benefits to many. It was for the greater good.

Shamefaced, she bent her head and bowed before me.

The heavy doors were opened now, the ones I'd flown through earlier. I stepped outside, and the steward led me to the litter that waited for me. "No, I will not travel that way. I want to walk."

"What is that, High One? Pharaoh insists that you come quickly. With the streets so congested now, it would take an hour or more to reach him on foot. I cannot allow that. Please come with me."

I gave him a surly look but obeyed. Whatever he might say, I would walk back. I longed to see the city streets for myself at least once more. It had been so long since I had walked anywhere out-side the complex. I had not previously had the courage to walk through the doors except for on official duties. Tonight's display of falling skies had broken that fear. Paimu would not murder me herself. I would soon lay myself on the altar. For many years I feared her ghost would kill me as soon as I stepped outside the protection of the goddess. I was about to die anyway, and my death would be for a purpose.

And then we will be even, Paimu.

The steward did not speak to me about the celestial event or any-thing else as we rode double time to the Golden Palace. It was once called the Palace of the Happy Sovereigns, in the first years after its building, but that name was not used anymore. Now the palace was an unhappy place with too many wives, too much in-trigue and a spirit of greed and opulence that touched all who en-tered it. As the litter came to a stop and the brightly painted box I sat on touched the ground, the steward slipped out and drew back the curtains to make room for my exit. To my surprise, I had been led not to the entrance of the throne room where these meetings typically took place but to the lower gardens, a private place that I knew my sister used. It was her sanctuary.

"High One, the Great Queen would have audience with you before you join the other mage in the Sky Room."

"Oh, I see," I said, acting as bored as I could. "I hope this doesn't take too long. I am sure Pharaoh is anxious to see me," I lied as I smoothed my gowns neatly. I had no love for Amenhotep. I had admired him long ago, but I'd long since lost respect for him. Too much had happened between him and my sister. He shamed her by bringing his harem into the palace. He was no honorable man.

"Yes, but the Great Queen insists. Please." The steward, a new royal whose name I could not remember, bowed as he opened the small blue door that led to the garden. At least Nefret still held her title. That was something to be thankful for.

"Very well, but do not leave here. I will be inside only a few minutes. I cannot tarry," I told him.

"Yes, lady," he answered none the wiser. Over the years, many rumors had circulated about Nefret and me. That we hated one another, that we weren't truly sisters. And even more notorious rumors that I wouldn't entertain. None of them were true. We did not hate one another. Although I rarely saw her or heard from her, we were not enemies as we once had been. That she would want to see me privately, especially on such an evening, was a rare thing.

I walked silently down the path, my eyes adjusting quickly to the darkness. Vines and shrubs were carefully sculpted into twisted works of art in my sister's garden. They looked like living things, mystical creatures in the low light of the moonless night sky. I'd been here a few years ago at the coming home of Nefret's first daughter, Meritaten. I had not been invited back, although I could not recall the reason why.

In the daylight hours the cheerfully painted walls told the story of a happy family. The white stone walls were painted with images of the royal couple and their family worshiping the Aten, sailing across the lake, offering the lotus and fruits to their favorite deity. One especially touching portrait showed Amenhotep and Nefret playing with their children, but now the images stayed in the shadows. I shivered at the thought. These were sweet pictures of the way things had once been. They were not that way now.

Even though I did not dwell in the palace, I had heard the gossip about my sister and Aperel. Lies. All of them. No one loved Amenhotep more than Nefret, and she would never put her children at risk by flitting about with Pharaoh's horse master. I knew this because I knew what she'd already sacrificed.

The Great Queen was threatened constantly on all sides. She would be cast down from her lofty position, replaced by Tadukhipa or the concubine, Ipy. I did not believe it, but I did not envy my sister. Managing such a tangled web took talent—a talent I did not have.

As I approached the inner garden, trepidation crept up my spine. I heard nothing, not even her voice. Then I saw her. Nefret squatted on the ground looking at something, and I stood quietly in the archway of the garden waiting for her to notice me. Even though I was her sister, I could not barge into her presence without being welcomed. Protocol was everything, and we had to keep up all appearances. Especially now when it mattered the most.

Finally she stood, with whatever it was she examined in her shaking hands. Nefret's red hair hung unbrushed down her back in clumps. She wore a lavender gown that showed the rounded shape of her body and an unbound belt of gold rope. Her clothing was in the Grecian style, a style my sister favored lately, I'd been told.

"Sister, look! Look what they have done!" She held the bundle out toward me.

"What is that? A bird?" Forgetting formality after seeing no one joined us, I did as she asked. I took the bird and examined it. It was no ordinary bird—this was a falcon. Nothing was amiss except its head lolled pitifully as if someone had snapped its neck.

"Who would make such an open threat?"

"I do not know. It was left here where I could find it. I cannot think who would commit such a heinous act."

Who indeed? I thought. The list was endless. The priests of Amun hated Nefret and her husband. Dozens of concubines and a handful of sister-wives also rose up my mental list of potential evildoers. "For now, let's put that question aside and ask another one. Why would they do such a thing? I think the answer is clear, my queen."

"Tell me, then, Pah. I must know. The sight of this fills me with dread. I've seen dead animals before, but this…"

How much to tell her? I couldn't gauge her mind. I sized her up carefully, trying to determine what to share with her. Her makeup was streaked as if she'd been crying. And not over a dead falcon. Nefret's waist was thicker than it used to be, but that was to be expected after producing six children in fast succession. I hated that Amenhotep treated her as a brood mare.

"You came to the throne as the Desert Queen, the Falcon of the Red Lands. Someone is warning you that your time is coming to an end." Nefret gasped and put her hand to her chest. "Surely that hasn't escaped you, sister."

"Can you look for me? Look in the fire and the water, Pah. Tell me who it is! Who will kill me, sister?"

I put the bird into a nest of heart-shaped leaves and pulled Nefret next to me on a nearby bench. My heart broke for her, and I also felt dread rising in me. How strange that my twin and I would still be tied together even after all that had passed between us. I said in a low, stern whisper, "Listen and don't speak." I glanced around me before proceeding. "You must leave, Nefret. I will grant you asylum in the Green Temple of Isis. You cannot stay in Amarna. Disaster is coming here...and to Zerzura. Neither place will be safe. The stars have fallen from the bow of Osiris, the Dancing Man himself! It is a sure sign of disaster to this kingdom and all those living in its shadow."

"What? I cannot leave my husband and my kingdom, Pah! I can't run away because of a dead bird and a few falling stars. Surely you make too much of this. Is this some kind of trick?" She was on her feet now, anger flashing in her eyes.

"Sister, my sister." I rose, taking her hand. "We are beyond this distrust, aren't we? Haven't I faithfully served you all these years?" For a long moment we stared at one another. When she didn't argue, I continued, "You know that I love you above all others, but the time to complete things has come. Paimu came to me again. It is my time, a life for a life, and she will have it no other way. I will die. But you must live, sister. You must live for your children. Smenkhkare, Tasherit and Meritaten, they must live! They are our treasures." I clasped her hands. Tears threatened to flood my eyes, but I held them back. I needed to keep a calm demeanor if I was to face Pharaoh with any degree of authority.

"But Seritaten...all my babies."

"I know you mourn for them, but those children are dead and you cannot take them with you. You must think reasonably. Think of the ones who live still." I could hear the gate opening behind me, and I stepped back from her. "I have to go to Pharaoh now, Great Queen." In a whisper I added, "I will make him believe that all is well, but I tell him this only for your benefit. Listen to me now. We don't have much time."

"Are you sure, Pah? I can't bear to hear you speak like this. Surely you are wrong. And what about Father?"

I glanced over her shoulder, thinking that I saw someone move in the darkness, but there was no one. "What Farrah said about him, that he will die for love, will come true. In this she was right. But you cannot think about him right now. You must do the practical things to prepare. When you receive the sign from me, you must leave with all haste. No dallying, or all will be for naught. And you must cut your hair. Shave it."

"What?" She reached for her tangled hair, her eyes wide with surprise.

"Do you want to live? Or am I wasting my time?"

"I care nothing for my life anymore—but I want my children to live, Pah," she said, swallowing hard.

"No questions, then, and let no one see you do this. You cannot have your servants help you. Burn the hair so no one finds it. Keep your head covered so no one sees."

Nefret was crying softly now, but she didn't argue with me. Time was growing short, and Pharaoh's servants lingered inside the door of the garden. As if his servants and hers worked together, her servants also appeared and hung near her now. She yelled at them, "Go away, Menmet. I am fine." To me she said, "What do you have planned? Can you not tell Akhenaten the truth? Is he in danger?"

"We are all in danger, sister! It is not human hands at work here. Listen and obey, please. I have never asked anything from you since I've been here, but I ask now—do as I ask so I can help you. All will be made clear. Look for a sign, Nefret, if you do not believe me." I felt the magic prickle in my throat. "Yes, a sign you will know. And when that happens, do not question me but obey."

Nefret wrapped her arms around me. "I will do as you ask, only don't leave me, Pah. My own sister, my heart and my treasure!"

She sobbed now, and my heart was not a stone. I wanted to take her hand and run away with her, back to our home at Timia, but there were others to consider. Smenkhkare, Meritaten, Tasherit and yes, even Kames.

"One last thing. Trust no one. You must look to the Greeks, our mother's people, for help. There is one who will help you. His name is Adijah. He will know what to do."

"I have done this to us, haven't I? My ambition. My love for Akhenaten."

"Nonsense. If there is anyone to blame, it is me. It was you who should have been mekhma. You would have led us to Zerzura. But we cannot think about those long-ago things now. Even our home is in danger. Enough with the past! Think of the future! Don't forget—look for the sign. I will make sure Adijah comes to you soon."

"Will I see you again?"

There was no fire and water to peer into, but somehow I knew the answer to that question. "Yes, you will see me once more. I must go, sister. Pharaoh waits." Without waiting for her to stop crying, I walked out of the garden and followed the waiting steward.

Time for lies. And soon it would be time to die.

Chapter Three

Mines of Blood—Semkah

From the rocks above I could see the rebels murder my messenger. They slid a sword down his throat as he screamed and left him pinned to the ground with their blades. I swallowed the bile that rose up within me. I felt Zubal's breath draw quickly beside me and then release angrily, yet he did not put words to what he witnessed. For that I was thankful.

Now that the rebels had claimed the mine, it appeared they had no intention of quickly robbing and relinquishing the property as I had hoped. The mine's secret location had been found, and the nearby tribes—even faraway tribes like the Algat and Kuni—would come in search of it now without fear. I prayed that Omel's hand was not upon this. I could not believe that it was. It was a miracle that the location had been kept secret this long, but no more. I had no doubt that whoever these men claimed to be, they were here by consent of Egypt's greedy pharaoh, my son-in-law. In the past few months, he'd demanded more gold than ever before, much more than we could supply him without killing those who dug for the treasures. I feared that our mines' resources would soon be exhausted as the turquoise mine had been. He had seen to that. He would not seize it for himself directly, the two-faced bastard. Not out in the open. That would break my treaty with him. Instead, he sent robbers to steal from me and pretended he knew nothing about it, all the time demanding more gold. His gold! I spat at the idea. It was Meshwesh gold!

I had not wanted to draw my daughter into our negotiations, if you could call them that, but her husband's gold lust made her involvement a necessity. If I did not succeed here today, I had no other choice. She must help us. Omel had not been successful in shielding us from Egyptian greed. I had warned him of this all those years ago.

"Are those truly Meshwesh, king? Why would they betray us? How could they do such evil?"

"Egypt corrupts everything. That blade is not ours. These odious men were bought with a price, Zubal. We are not safe. Not even behind the walls of Zerzura. These men," I said as I pointed toward the mine, "are no longer Meshwesh but traitors. To kill my messenger, their own brother, is to defy our ancestors and the gods—and me! Now they will pay the price for such blasphemy. Are you ready, Zubal? We will burn the entrance. Seal it up and seal them to their doom."

"Yes, Semkah! We stand ready with the carts and all that you have ordered."

"Call the archers. Line them here, and here." I squatted and drew in the sand, unwilling to reveal my hand to the criminals below. I wanted them to be surprised. "At my command, begin firing. They'll retreat, cowards that they are, at least for a few minutes. During that time, you and the others fill the entrance with everything you can find, anything that burns. We will show them how we treat robbers and murderers."

Zubal nodded grimly, and I gave the shrill whistle that signaled our advance. We couldn't take the mine back without destroying some part of it. They had food and water enough to last for weeks, but time wasn't on our side. Pharaoh expected his gold, and if I could not deliver, he would rain down fire upon us. But I would show him I was no small king, no weak man.

"Run! Now!" When Zubal's men were in place, I whistled again and began making my way down the steep wall myself. It was no easy task with only one arm to steady me, but I did not dare slow down. The blue and green arrows of my archers began to fly through the air toward the front of the mine. As expected, the cowards sought refuge inside, but a few made attempts to return fire. Luckily for us, they were better thieves than warriors. In just a few minutes, Zubal and his men had covered half the front of the mine with the carts and every bit of rubbish they could find. They placed the small keg in the center at the base. The trapped men jeered at Zubal and his men but then sensed that something was seriously wrong and began to plead for their lives.

I considered the plea for as long as it took me to see Alora's body dragged back to my camp. He had been a faithful servant of Leela's. She'd insisted he come to protect me, but now the old man was dead. Now I had to tell my wife the bad news, that her cousin gave his life obeying my command.

Zubal nocked an arrow, a red one signifying my royal vengeance. We stood side by side now, fifty feet from the entrance. I yelled at the rebels, "You have done evil here. You have taken what was not yours. You have killed your brother. You will die."

To my surprise I saw one round face appear. He wore a mocking grin, but his voice was not as confident as he pretended to be. "What? You're going to kill ten of us with one arrow? Come any closer and we'll do more than hurl sticks at you, one-armed king. Go away, old man. Leave this work to the younger men. We have swords, and these rickety carts won't stop us from finishing you off."

"What is your name?" Zubal shouted. He relaxed his grip for a moment and waited.

"You don't remember me? I am Hadja, the son of Garimer. He died in these mines, gave his life to them. Your bastard king sent him here. Now this place belongs to me—I paid for it with my father's blood, as did all these men here with me."

I ignored his accusation. I did not use slaves in my mines. Free men who were freely paid worked here. If he supposed something else, I had no obligation to tell him differently. I had no sympathy for Hadja and his father.

I signaled to Zubal to raise the bow and arrow once more and said, "You are so like your father, Hadja, but at least he accepted his punishment like a man although he was a coward through and through. Why do you think he came here? He abandoned his people when the Kiffians rode through Timia. He begged to earn back his honor, and thus he was given the chance to work in the mine. And he would still be working this day if he had not stolen from us. But enough talk. You are not worth even the cost of a few words." Hadja railed at me, but I did not entertain him further. Zubal and I walked back a few steps, and then I gave the order.

"Now, Zubal." The young man released the arrow, and it shot fiercely from his white bow and landed in the keg we'd placed at the center of the mine. The men behind the carts began to laugh at and mock us. They didn't appear to see the green liquid seep from the wooden casket, not until Zubal nocked the fiery arrow.

Zubal shot the second arrow, and as expected it landed in the casket. We saw the flash of light and began to run to the mouth of the canyon opening. We had only a few seconds. Diving for cover, Zubal threw himself on top of me as the ground shook and the mine's entrance collapsed in a pile of rubble, dust and sand. No sound issued from the rocky chamber, and there were no further pleas for mercy. There was nothing at all.

My men gathered our supplies, and we somberly trekked back to the camp. None of us wanted to discuss what had happened. Our brothers had betrayed us, as Egypt had betrayed us, and we had destroyed our only remaining source of income. I wasn't sure they realized the danger of what we'd done. We would have to abandon the White City. Egypt would come for us. There was no doubting that. Still, for the moment at least, we had victory. I slapped Zubal's shoulder and nodded respectfully at him. "Hironus himself never shot a truer arrow. Thank you, my friend."

"I am grateful for the accuracy, but it is an evil thing to kill another brother. There are so few of us now."

I understood that feeling and respected him for it. "Well, at least there is one fewer coward. You were not wrong to have killed him. Alora deserves vengeance."

He nodded and made the sign of respect. There were only twenty-four in our party; thankfully it had been enough to do the job. Now it was done. Zerzura was two days' ride to the north, but we'd stay one night at Farya, the small oasis just north of the mine. We crested a dune and immediately my heart sagged into my stomach. Our camp burned—the tents were gone, and there was nothing left but a few burned poles and dead cattle. With a shout of anger I spurred the camel on, with my men assembled behind me. Leela and a few other women had traveled with us, and now they were gone, taken by an unknown enemy. I screamed, and the other men wailed as they too saw the camp's destruction. Zubal and I immediately began looking for tracks. We didn't have to search far; the raiders hadn't bothered to hide them. Whoever had taken our women were headed north to Zerzura.

"Why would they leave the cattle behind? This is not a raiding party." Zubal spat on the ground and stood eyeballing the vast stretch of sand that lay between us and home.

"No, it is not," I agreed glumly. "This is an act of war. We must ride! They can't be too far ahead of us; there are still flames from the fire."

My back ached, and a recent sore on my arm had flared. I could feel it bleeding but said nothing. My wife was at the mercy of bandits, likely Meshwesh bandits who betrayed us on Egypt's behalf. I had no doubt the "Heretic King," as he was called, was behind this. A strange wind blew across the sand, and we covered our faces with our head scarves for protection.

We rode hard for a few hours, following the tracks easily until we saw the first body. A blond woman, the foreign wife of Zubal's son, lay nude and bloody in the sand. The sight sickened me but Thiel, Zubal's son, behaved honorably. He and his father wrapped the girl in Thiel's cloak and rolled her lifeless body down the dune, forever out of sight from the eyes of men. Thiel didn't hide his tears but wept silently. Zubal patted his shoulder, assuring him that she would have vengeance, and we returned to the trail. Not long after the first bloody find, we came across two more bodies, a man we did not know and Kay, a Meshwesh wife. We assumed that the man was one of the bandits and killed by Kay, judging by her heartbreaking wounds. Kay was wife to Amadaxes and a dear friend of my own wife.

"They think to slow us down with this murderous parade," Zubal replied quietly.

"And they have succeeded, but I will not deny these men the opportunity to bury their wives. Look at this man. See?" I pointed to his wrist tattoo. "I thought him to be a tribesman, but this proves he is no tribal thief. That is Egyptian script."

"Whether freeman or slave, he is no doubt Egyptian. And look there!"

Smoke billowed in the distance, and we raced back to our animals, eager to make for the scene. With each dune we crested I pressed my dry lips together and prayed that I would not find Leela lying dead in the sand. Then we saw the camp sprawled before us. "Stop! Back and down!" I said to the men behind me. Sliding off the brute camel, I scrambled to the top of the dune on my belly. It had grown dark now; only a few stars had appeared above us. The raiders didn't seem to notice or mind that we'd followed them. They were acting as if they had nothing to worry about. They were either brave or stupid—or this was a trap. I suspected the latter.

"What now?" Thiel said angrily. "I am eager for blood, my king. We should take them while it is dark."

"No. They will expect that."

"But what they've done! We may not have another chance!" Thiel did not approve of my answer, but he was smart enough not to reproach me.

"Thiel, can I trust you?"

"Always, my king. Always."

"Take one other man and ride to Zerzura. Tell Orba what has happened and bring back men. At dawn we will ride down and take back what is ours, and you will have your blood cost. I promise you."

"But what they will endure tonight!" Thiel burst into angry tears. I did not chide him.

I gripped his shoulder. "My own wife is there, Thiel. I know you worry for your mother, but we do not have the men to save our women. We must keep watch tonight. It is the only way."

"It will be done," Zubal said for his son. Thiel's face was a contortion of agony, but he offered no further objections. He walked backwards and made the sign of respect. I signed back and told Zubal, "It will be a long night. No fires, and tell the men to spread out. We must keep watch until our brothers join us."

"It will be done, Semkah." My friend paused and pointed at my tunic. "But do tend to your wound or you'll bleed to death before the sun rises. Your wife will kill me if you die." I grinned at him, thinking of Leela's anger rising upon the brave Zubal. My wife was a fiery woman, not like Kadeema, who'd been all dreams and love and softness. When Kadeema disappeared, I thought she had taken all my love with her. But Leela brought love back to me, and her love was far greater than I deserved.

Now I had to show her how much I loved her. I lay with my back to the sand, staring up at the sky. I recounted the many times we'd lain together. The tender moments when she'd bathed me and cared for me after the loss of my arm. But she'd shown her love in greater ways than that. She cared for Pah in her madness and helped me lead my people into a time of peace, although it was short-lived.

Suddenly, a shrill scream ripped through the night. I could not tell who it was I heard, but I feared the worst.

Stay strong, my wife! Stay strong for me! Endure until the morning!

I refused to allow my mind to wander, to consider what might be done to her even this moment. No doubt her strength and beauty would draw the attention of some evil man. And when they learned who she was, how much more would she suffer? Agony washed over me. I leaned back even harder into the sand, my short sword resting on my chest, when I heard another sound. A dull thud burst above us. I opened my eyes and sat up anxiously as the sky filled with bright blue light. A star fell and then another. They didn't stop falling.

"Look!" Zubal said, pointing below. The camp of men below us, at least seventy-five of them, had rushed out of their tents to watch the celestial display. Their confusion was obvious, and more than a dozen camels fled from the camp. "Perhaps the gods are on our side! We should go down, Semkah, and take them back now! This is a sign." The others gathered around him. There were fewer than twenty men now. Thiel and a few other warriors had left us to do my bidding. Another star fell, this one with a thunderous sound.

I couldn't deny this was a sign from above. Even the simplest among us would know that. Another star passed overhead, and it fell toward Egypt in a burst of white light. My heart sank for my daughters. I could not help them now. They had been beyond my reach for a very long time, but I had one daughter left. *Sumaway!* She was my daughter and Leela's, and she was at home in Zerzura. How could I face her if I let her mother die this night when I could have prevented it? This I had to do for her—and for me.

"Live or die, let us go down. What do you have in mind, Zubal?" I grinned at him, ready to give my life for Leela and the other Meshwesh women. Even if it meant my life, I would see her face one more time.

Chapter Four

The Third Mekhma—Orba

"Time to rise up, Orba. Come now. Don't make it difficult for me; you know I am not as strong as you. Sit up and drink, please." Blinking into the brightness, I tried to obey Sumaway's request, but I felt feeble. My bones ached, and my muscles felt like taut skins pulled over a drum. With so much pain I had to die soon, surely. I welcomed such release. I did not know how much more pain I could bear without behaving like a lunatic. At first the pain came and went, but not anymore. The pain appeared one morning and never departed. It was like a fog that rolled in and tried to smother the life out of me. It had succeeded.

"Very well, you may use the straw. But you must at least lift your head or you'll choke." She poked the straw into the drink and tapped the end of it, capturing the liquid. I opened my dry mouth and allowed her to drip the pain-killing potion in. She did this several times until I had enough of the liquid to affect me. The potion would not heal me, but I would not hurt as much. I felt the warmth of the juice filter through my body; the pain began to sub-side almost immediately, but in a limited way. The truth was if the disease did not kill me, the painkiller eventually would. Either way, death wasn't far from me.

"I know you want to lie there and die, but you can't. My father needs you. He sent a messenger for you. The trouble at the mines has escalated, and my mother and the other women have been tak-en. Semkah needs you! Thiel is just outside the door, Orba. You have to see him." Her pleading voice and her faith in me touched me, but my body had a difficult time obeying her command.

After a few moments of struggle, Sumaway showed her natural impatience. "Are you even trying?"

I did not care for her tone, but I was in no position to school her on manners. Sumaway was not a patient young woman, not like her mother. She reminded me of her sisters in so many ways, but in the area of patience she followed Pah's path, always ready to move forward without question or worry about the destruction it might create. I wished she had known them. I loved the girl like she was my own, but I could not do as she asked. My body would not allow my obedience. I let out a sad sigh.

"Now is the time for you to lead, Sumaway. You must guide the people in your father's stead. At least until he returns. I cannot." I could barely put the sentences together, but I knew she did not believe me. It was as if she believed I lay here on my sickbed because I wanted to, as if I wanted to die.

"You must try," she said as she fussed with my tunic and tried to force me up.

I gasped in pain. It shot through my bones like fire. "Stop fighting me. You cause me even more pain. Send in the messenger, girl."

I was tempted to close my eyes as she left me. I was on the edge now. The line between life and death blurred quickly. Yes, I could close my eyes and drift away from this world, but I did not. I had to stay here a little longer for Sumaway.

Thiel rushed in and bowed on his knee in the traditional manner of a messenger. "Old One, Semkah sends me to tell you what has happened." In a rush the young man told the horrible story. The worst had happened. Egypt had all but seized the mine, and many of our brothers had betrayed us. To make matters worse, Leela and the women who had insisted on traveling with her were now at the mercy of those betrayers. Why had she gone with them? If anyone had bothered to ask me, I would have advised against it. I knew I must do something immediately, but my mind could not gather the proper thoughts. What should I say?

Sumaway stood by my side and dabbed my forehead with a linen cloth. She waited for me to speak. Thiel rose from his knees and towered above me. Sumaway spoke in low tones, "Orba is not well, but I promise you that he hears you. Of course he will obey my father's wishes. Semkah is king of the Meshwesh. Gather the men you need, Thiel, and rest yourself for a few minutes. We will leave within the hour."

"We? You cannot go with us, princess. Not with the Old One in such a state. It is too far a distance, and you are needed here."

I realized he spoke of me, but I had no strength to lie to them. I was waning quickly.

"I *will* go with you. That is not a question—it is my wish. I will not leave my parents stranded in the desert. Is there anything else, Thiel?"

"No, just the stars. They have been falling tonight. We've seen them fall upon the land of Egypt. This does not bode well for our people, I think."

Tears filled my eyes and slid down my wrinkled cheeks. Sumaway dabbed them away before Thiel saw them. "Go now, Thiel," she said quietly. "I will talk to you more soon."

He left us alone, and I grabbed her hand. "When you leave tonight, you will not be coming back. You will go away from here, Sumaway."

She fell down beside me and lay across my chest. "What? How can you know this? This is the sickness talking."

One thing I loved about the princess was that she generally never questioned me. Except for tonight, when she was unsure of everything. She knew I could see in the water, and she believed me. Tonight there was no water, and I had not seen this, but I felt it. Yes, I felt it in my poisoned bones.

"What about my father and mother? Will I find them?"

"I do not know, but I know you must try. Now is the time for the third mekhma. It is your time." Then the fire was upon me, the fire of prophecy. "Ah yes, you will meet a bull in the desert, Sumaway. You will meet a bull in the desert. Do not leave his side. Where he goes, you go. He will lead you to safety. Go now and do not look back."

"What about the people, Orba? I cannot leave them to Egypt's hands. What do I do?"

"They must go north, leave the White City. Tell them to go to the sea. But you, you must find the bull."

With a tender kiss on my forehead, she wiped my face once more. "How can I leave you, old friend?"

I tried to laugh, but it came out of my body as a series of coughs. She patted my mouth and tried not to appear shocked at the sight of the dark red blood. I could feel it in my throat and lungs. I was drowning. Drowning in blood. If the potion did not steal my life's breath, the disease would take me soon. For that I was grateful.

"Easily. I do not want you to see me die. I want to be alone. Go and make your preparations. Send the Council to me. I will tell them my wishes. Go now, Sumaway, last mekhma of the Meshwesh." She squeezed me, and I gasped at the pain but suffered through it for her sake.

She paused in the doorway, and I looked at her one last time. Sumaway was tall, taller than I remembered Nefret or Pah being. She had dark brown hair that sprouted curls around her face. When she was young she enjoyed parading around with no tunic; now she had a woman's body, but she was always one to show modesty. She had soft brown eyes like her mother's but a voice like her father's. She had a natural authority and the grace of a seasoned shieldmaiden. She was not as skilled as her sisters with spear and arrow, but she could toss a dagger better than any man. She would be one to be reckoned with if anyone crossed her path. With one last nod and a wave of her hand, she made the sign of respect and vanished from my sight.

I waited for someone else to come. As time passed I vaguely remembered that the Council was supposed to attend me, but they had not yet appeared. A burst of light filled the room, and from my vantage point I gathered I'd missed a star shower. Yes, this was a good night to die, with stars heralding my passing. As I struggled to breathe, I thought of Farrah. Why hadn't she come to lead me away? Surely she knew I was close to the Otherworld now. Didn't she care? Had she ever loved me?

I was too tired now to care. I would take one more breath and then let my blood drown me. I wheezed in the darkness and heard the sound of a child's laughter. The room began to brighten as the pain in my chest increased. I struggled to breathe and then forgot all about it when I heard the child laughing again. He was somewhere near. I turned my head to look and there he was. My child! Farrah's child! The son who died so long ago that I could barely remember his name. Had we named him? He had been a fine child too. Strong with a lusty voice. He'd died one night not long after his entrance into this world, and his abrupt leaving had broken my heart. And now he was here to see his father.

What had I called him? What name had I given him when I buried him in the sand? I could not remember, and that brought me great agony. He touched me; he was not a baby anymore but a boy, ready to play with his father. And it did not matter that I could not remember his name, for we were together now. Now he took my hand. How young he was. But this could not be, could it? He had died so long ago, even before Nefret and Pah had been born to Kadeema and Semkah. With his help, I could sit up now. Oh yes, I could even stand.

And where was Farrah? She should be here to see him. Yes, I always wanted a son.

And now he was here.

Chapter Five

Son of the Aten—Smenkhkare

I found my father in the usual place—in Ipy's lap. The concubine practically set up court in the grape arbor, but I reminded myself again not to become entangled in my parents' ongoing feud over my father's dalliances. Despite my pledge, I found it hard to hide my surprise at seeing the concubine wearing my mother's golden headdress on her head, a prize I was told first belonged to my late aunt Sitamen. Wisely I said nothing about it. I had come with a purpose, and I would not be denied.

I stood before my father's couch and waited for him to stop toying with Ipy's hair like a lovestruck teenager. She wore it in the latest fashion, long dark braids cinched at the ends with gold bands. Gold heaped off her arms and ankles. She looked a royal, or a grotesque caricature of one. My mother never wore such ridiculous amounts of gold. When he finally deigned to notice me, Pharaoh Akhenaten said absently, "Ah, Smenkhkare...where have you been, my son?"

Stymied at his question since he'd been the one to send me away, I evenly answered, "I went to the School of Agility as you instructed, Father. I have come with the token you requested." I held out my wrist and proudly showed him my latest band of achievement. It was proof of my bravery and skill at arms.

"I see you wear another scripted band. This pleases me. Tell me, what does it say?" He sat up now and waited for my answer.

With flushed cheeks, I read the script to him, "Strength is the Soul of Re," I said proudly. "But it is only one of many that I have earned, my father. You have seen the others. This band completes my courses."

"Well done." He rose to his feet, sweeping his blue and white robes to the side as he stretched his back. He waved at me, inviting me to walk with him. My heart cautiously skipped a beat. If I'd pleased him, I could ask him what I wanted. If I was patient and not too overtly clever. He surely couldn't refuse me now.

To my dismay, Ipy walked with us, fanning herself absently with her white plumed fan. She smiled at her ladies, who appeared enthralled by our every move. Some even cast their eyes flirtatiously at me. Despite her attempt at seemingly neutral femininity, Ipy's wearing of my mother's golden headdress made her my foe, whether she understood that or not. I pretended not to notice her attendance in my private conversation with my father. "What do you hope to accomplish next, Smenkhkare? You have done all I ask, and I am pleased with your achievements. How can I reward you?"

"Father, I ask nothing of you. I need nothing, for you have given me everything already."

Ipy nodded her head in approval at my answer, but Father pressed on. "I insist you speak your heart, Smenkhkare. Surely there is something I can give you. Some reward suitable for a prince of Egypt."

"Yes, speak your heart, son of Pharaoh," Ipy said in her simpering voice, "for you know your father to be a good, giving ruler to all his subjects. How much more to his own son? He speaks often of your courage and cleverness with the sword. I am sure he would refuse you nothing."

I found her comments disingenuous, for I did not believe any of their conversations were serious at all. Ipy was notoriously dull-witted, and if it weren't for her pretty face she would never have caught my father's eye as a young man. Now it seemed their old relationship had been rekindled. I hated that Ipy had inserted herself into our conversation, but as she was my father's concubine, I could only show her honor. "Thank you, Ipy. You are kind to say this, but I know full well what a good and giving man he is. Pharaoh Akhenaten is the best of fathers."

My father walked with his hands behind his back. He was a tall man, taller than I, but in recent months his stomach had taken on a paunch. Still, it seemed the women found him attractive. I knew that my mother loved him a great deal and always smiled in his presence. I wasn't as like him as some of his children were, but I had often been told I had a similar bearing. Taller than most, I spent much of my time stooping down to listen to those around me, but with my father I tried to stand taller than I was. He smiled as if he read my mind. "You have made a fine son, Smenkhkare. I have always been proud of you." He slapped my back once, and we walked a while without speaking. The ladies trailed us, giggling at whatever it was that amused vapid women. Ipy turned to look at them occasionally to remind them to behave.

"What of Kames? How is your brother?"

"I am afraid I do not know, Father. I have not spoken to him these many months. He did not join me at the School of Agility." I too was anxious to hear news of Kames, but Father did not offer more information. There had always been tension between them, a tension that had grown as Father had gotten older. I knew he was not my true brother, but we'd been raised together, schooled together and taught to treat one another kindly. At times, Father raised Kames up as a shining example of strength and virility. It was hinted that I should strive to be more like him, but not so much now. I could not fathom Father's ever-changing feelings toward him. Mother was always tight-lipped when it came to Kames, but my grandmother Queen Tiye thought of no one else. If the whole world burned and nobody lived but Kames, it would be enough for her.

There were three brothers in our household. I had another brother, Tutankhamen, but he was Tadukhipa's son and not with us much, except when my Father summoned him to his court. That seemed strange to me since I'd always heard that Tadukhipa had ambition like no other. Surely she would want her fair-faced, pampered son raised near his father? But no, it had not been so. Not until recently. Yes, much had changed recently. Tutankhamen began visiting our sister Meritaten and with a demeanor not acceptable for a brother. I could not allow such a thing to happen. Father could not give my sister to the petulant, spoiled Tutankhamen. That would be the ultimate betrayal. I kept these thoughts buried as my father posed question after question regarding my training. I explained the school's daily regimen of exercise and strength training. He smiled appropriately and nodded at certain points in my description, but I could tell his mind was elsewhere. As mine was.

"I see," he said. We'd left the grape arbor now and took seats in a small pavilion to seek shelter from the afternoon sun. Ipy quickly sat beside him and smiled graciously at me. He waved me to sit at the lower seat. I quietly resented being placed lower than Ipy. If Mother were here, she'd insist that I sit beside Father. "Now that we've walked this way and heard so much about your recent adventures, tell me. What can I give you, son? Your birth celebration approaches and I want to show all of Egypt how much Pharaoh favors his oldest son."

"Father, there is one thing, if you would consider it. It is such a request that I am loath to ask it, but only you can grant me this." He smiled at me, his dark eyes pleased at my comment. I felt my pulse quicken as I continued. I had to be careful to say the right thing. Diplomacy had never been my strong suit. "You are the sun, and I the son of the sun," I began clumsily. "I think it is time, if you allow it…" I dithered around the subject, but Father patiently waited. Servants approached with wine and a plate of food, but he waved them away as Ipy pouted.

"Please speak your mind, Smenkhkare. I've already said I would not deny you."

With breathless words I spoke what I'd been longing to say. "I want to marry, Father."

He chuckled knowingly and nodded. "Love strikes us all, doesn't it?" Ipy giggled at his comment. With a grin he waved the waiting servants forward. They quickly poured and tasted the wine before handing it to him. "I see you are not immune either. For that, I am both delighted and saddened. For in matters of the heart all men are equal. Even the son of Pharaoh cannot deny love's power."

He drank half a cup of wine before he put it down for the servant to refill it. He appraised me expectantly, looking deep into my eyes as if he'd find the answer to a mystery there. I felt nervous under his scrutiny but didn't flinch. He loved me, of that I was sure. I prayed silently to anyone who would listen: *Please let this happen.* I was suddenly glad that I'd come to Pharaoh first with my request. I knew Mother would not approve of my proposal. No matter how many bands I earned, she wanted me to remain a child at her feet. I was no child but a man.

The older servant handed me a cup and then offered another to Ipy. She batted her eyes at him disapprovingly.

"I envy you, my son. First loves have a heat and power unlike any other." He reached for Ipy, who took his hand and kissed it. Was my Father trying to tell me he loved the concubine? Were the rumors true, then? Why would he now do this? Surely there was a reason. I would never have believed my mother to have been capable of being unfaithful, but the news of her affair with Aperel had spread like wildfire throughout the court. I would never say such a thing to Pharaoh, for what if he'd not heard the latest rumor? I could not put my mother in danger. No, I did not believe it. I would not believe it.

I sipped the wine and placed the cup beside me. I did not enjoy wine as some men did. It made me feel reckless and less in control of my tongue. My father drank it day and night, and I'd never heard him misspeak once. "So, who is it that has stolen my son's heart so completely? A daughter of Salilah, perhaps? I hear her daughters are exquisite and all skilled musicians. Perhaps one of Ipy's daughters?"

"No, Father. Although your daughters are fair, lady. And I do not know these daughters of Salilah, though I have heard of their beauty. It is Meritaten that I speak of, Pharaoh. I love her and want to marry her."

In a sudden rush Pharaoh rumbled to his feet, slamming his half-empty cup on the marble-topped table. Ipy froze, ignoring the wine that splashed across her chest.

"You dare ask me this? Was this the queen's idea?"

"No! It is my own heart that asks, Father. I love Meritaten. I have not told my mother of my intentions. How have I offended you?" I did not know how to move, what to say. Fear fell on me as I winced under Pharaoh's anger.

"You think to take your sister, my daughter, to wife? Do you intend to also ask for my kingdom? For that is what it sounds like!"

At the implication Ipy also stood, and her hand flew to her mouth. "No!" she shouted in surprise. She rushed to Pharaoh's side and steadied him with her hand.

"Never! Never would I dream such a thing, my father and Pharaoh! Please, have mercy! I withdraw my request."

He walked away from me, his fists clenched. Ipy dogged his heels and glanced back at me nervously. She waved at me to stay where I was. I could not hear her words, but she touched his arm and leaned into his ear. He ducked away from her at first, but she persisted until eventually he returned to me. His handsome face was lined with anger, his dark eyes two hard rivets showing no recognition that I was his own flesh and blood. With one word he could kill me. And he might. Many who loved Pharaoh also died by his hand.

He stood with his hands on his hips, staring me down. I thought for one second he would strike me down with the back of his hand. I'd heard of my father's hot temper but until recently it had never been directed at me. Not like this. To think it would turn on me so was more than I could bear. I cast my eyes down ashamedly. I lost all hope that I would have Meritaten. She would never be mine. I'd failed her.

"Lady Ipy has spoken on your behalf, Smenkhkare. She is right, of course. You are a man now and have a man's needs. It is not right that Pharaoh's son should satisfy himself with the flesh of whores and commoners. You deserve a royal wife."

I could hardly believe my ears. Was he saying he would grant me my wish? I lifted my head slowly but did not rise to my feet. I would remain on my knees until told otherwise.

"Thank you, Father! It is all I ever wanted," I whispered nervously, staring at his sandals.

He stared at me again and said evenly, "I will not give you Meritaten. I have already made plans for her. I will, however, give you someone with patience who can teach you how to be a husband. Someone with a lovely face and a pleasing voice."

Again Ipy appeared, this time whispering in Father's ear. He nodded with a smile. "You may have your sister, Ipy's daughter, Ankhesenamun. She is not promised to anyone and will make an excellent wife."

I stood swaying under the weight of his words. How could he do this? This was not fair! I could not help but speak my heart. "As you say, Father, love has no master. I love Ankhesenamun as my sister, but not as a wife. How can I marry her?"

My father stepped toward me. He was so close now I could reach out and touch him. "You will not have my kingdom yet, Smenkhkare. You will take Ankhesenamun as your wife. That is the end of it. That is my word. Go now."

I rose awkwardly and stepped back, bringing my fist to my heart in a show of obedience and spun around, leaving him behind.

As I stepped away, the fear of Pharaoh abated and I began to feel desperation rise. And then anger. So desperate was I that I began to weigh my options. How could I refuse Ankhesenamun and risk my father's wrath? How would I live without Meritaten?

With every step I felt my resolution growing. Yes, I would go to my mother, the Great Queen! She would have to help me. I was her son! I could never marry a daughter of Ipy!

I would take my case to her and pray she still had enough influence to change his mind. I would not tell Meritaten of my failure, not yet. But I could not wait long. Court gossip, especially news of an impending marriage, would travel quickly.

If I could not have Meritaten, I would not marry. I would risk my father's wrath, but I would die if I had to. My cause was just.

Yes, I would go to Mother and plead for her help. I would do anything she asked, even rid her of Ipy.

I had to do this rather than break my own Meritaten's heart. And hers was the only heart that mattered.

Chapter Six

Queen of Despair—Nefertiti

Queen Tiye dawdled into my chamber this morning before my bath, her face askew with worry. "Where have you hidden the baby, Desert Queen? Where is Kames? Give me Kames." I pulled the robe back on and came to her. I held her bony hand in mine and patted it.

"He is a baby no longer, Great Queen. He is a man now and in Pharaoh's service. He has gone on a diplomatic trip to the west. You will see him soon." I led her to a nearby padded couch. I couldn't believe she'd arrived unattended and in the shape she was in. She wore no wig, and her natural hair, thin and curly, sprung up around her face like an unruly cloud. She'd slept in her makeup—slick streaks of kohl slid down the side of her face, and her lips were ringed with stiff red paint.

"Oh yes, I remember now. What of Thutmose? Has he come home yet?" She spoke now of her own son, dead at least twenty-five years. I could not break her heart again this morning, so I told her a pleasant lie instead. I knew the pain of losing a child. I had lost three myself, and the grief never left me.

"No, Great Queen. He is still away, but he too will return soon. For now it is just you and me." I squeezed her hand and poured her a cup of water, which she accepted. Her hands shook, but she drank the water until the cup was empty. Setting it on the table, she took in the view of the room.

"I like this room. I always liked this room. It feels very cool in here. And there are no bats. I dislike bats."

"Yes, it is very cool here. And I never see bats. Are you hungry, Queen Tiye?"

"No, I am not." She rubbed at her nose with her finger and eyed me. "My son is very lucky to have you, Nefertiti."

What to say to that? If she were whole and hale, I'd beg her for help. I'd throw myself at her feet and plead with her to speak to her son for me. But she was not. This was only a fragile shell of the intelligent, quick-witted, sometimes cruel woman I knew. And as far as I knew, Akhenaten no longer allowed her in his court.

We were like two cast-off queens. Forgotten and wished dead. Such a sad ending, but it wasn't really the end, was it? Pah's words from last night rang in my mind, and I had tried all morning to pretend none of it had happened. How could I leave the people I loved behind? Tiye needed me. It was she who had brought me here. She'd been the very Hand of Destiny that led the Falcon of the Red Lands to the throne of Egypt. Now she was losing her mind and had no one to care for her. When Huya was living he took great pains to hide her condition, but now that the old man was gone, there was no one else. No one she would trust. Except me.

"I hear the Hittite witch returns with her son today. I wonder what misery she will bring with her."

I smiled at her. Not because of her insult toward Tadukhipa but because it was evidence that at least some part of her mind worked well enough to recall her hatred for Kiya, the Monkey, as she liked to call our sister-queen to her face.

"Oh? I had not heard that," I lied prettily and bit a piece of fruit.

"Then you are in trouble. You should know every soul who passes through the gate and when they leave again. It is not enough to hide here in your comfortable room, Nefertiti. You must rule your kingdom. Knowledge is everything. When I was your age, I knew daily who came into the kitchens, who slept with my servants—and my husband. And who approached my husband's throne for favors. You must have eyes everywhere if you hope to see the enemy come toward you. If you fail to do so, you will no longer be Great Queen but only the Queen of Despair."

"I know this, Mother. I am just tired this morning." Unexpectedly she pinched me under my arm and stood to her feet. "Ow!" I gasped at the pain.

"Good! I am glad that hurt you. That will be nothing compared to what Tadukhipa will do. She'll no doubt insist that her puny son be married to one of your daughters. I have heard this." Her superior knowledge must have stirred her hunger because she reached for a piece of fruit too. "What will you do?"

Desperately I whined, "What can I do? Your son has taken Ipy to his bed and refuses to speak to me for more than a few seconds. I think he's never forgiven me for Kames." Queen Tiye snorted at that comment. It was refreshing to talk to her like this. I wasn't sure how long it would last, so I took advantage of her keen mind while it was still available to me. "I should have kept silent that day, the day when he announced that I was Great Queen. It was enough that you'd claimed the boy. I thought that with time, Akhenaten would change his mind about Kames. Instead he's come to resent me, but I can't think why. He loved his sister, and I think he also loved Ramose."

"Not enough to save them," she said, tossing the apple core onto the silver platter.

"No, not enough to save them," I agreed, glancing at Menmet as she entered to tidy up my room. Queen Tiye growled at her like a dog, something she'd never done before, and I waved Menmet away.

"I do not like that girl. She has the look of her father, Heby. She has his spirit too. You are wrong to trust her."

"Great Queen, she has been my friend for fifteen years and never once has betrayed me. And she hates her father. Why would you growl at her?" I said with a laugh.

She did not answer my question but just snorted. "Then you are stupid and I cannot help you." I did not argue with her further. I pretended not to worry about the time. Adijah would visit me today in the Queen's Court. Unfortunately, he might be waiting a while. I couldn't hurry the queen.

I hunkered down in the chair, unsure what to do now. *Oh, Akhenaten, how could you abandon us so? We are the women who love you!*

"I saw the stars fall last night, Nefertiti. I know that evil has fallen upon us and that it comes on the bottom of Tadukhipa's sandals. If you have any sense about you, you will refuse her entrance into the palace this morning. Keep her away, for she will be the death of me, Nefertiti! And you too! She hates us all. She hates Akhenaten too!" Her eyes widened with strong emotion, and she began wringing her hands and rocking back and forth.

"Calm yourself, Great Queen. All will be well."

"How can you say that? Nothing will be well again. And where is Kames, Nefertiti? I do not hear the baby. Give him to me."

I bit my lip. Queen Tiye was becoming agitated now. "Why don't you go prepare to greet him, Great Queen? Ask your servants to prepare your finest clothes and dress your hair. I will send him to you when he returns, but we must be ready."

"Yes." She smiled weakly and stood. She gathered the ends of her dingy gown in her hand and walked toward the arched entrance doors of my chambers. "And you will send him to me?"

"Of course," I said, smiling at her comfortingly.

"Very well, but do not forget what I told you." I could see by her expression that she herself had already forgotten her own words.

"Yes, Great Queen." I rose as she left me and watched her disappear into the corridor. "Menmet! Help me dress. I will have to skip the bath this morning. My guests will be waiting for me."

"I don't see why you can't make them wait. They are just Greeks, and you are the Great Queen," she said testily. She was obviously still angry that Tiye had growled at her, but she'd have to keep her opinions to herself. More than once lately I'd had to remind Menmet that she was not to speak her mind so freely. What if someone heard her disparage Tiye or another member of the royal family? It would cost her her life, and I was in no position to help her.

"Hush now. I'll do the brushing. Find me something blue to wear."

"Yes, lady." She scurried off while I tugged at my nest of tangles. Tonight I would do as Pah asked—I would cut my hair. I would shave it away. Could I really do that? It was the one thing that Akhenaten still loved about me. *Are you going to let your vanity keep you in danger, Nefret?* I heard my sister's question ringing in my ears. No, I would not. I would do whatever it took to protect my children.

"Lady, your son is outside and wants to see you."

I put the brush down and couldn't hide my surprise. "Smenkhkare has returned? Since when? Yes, of course. Let him in." I stood and tidied my gown. I gathered my loose hair and wrapped it around my hand before I tossed it over one shoulder. Smenkhkare hurried into the room, so anxious was he to see me. He was the spitting image of his father as a younger man, and in a strange way, he reminded me of someone else too. *Alexio!* My mind whispered the answer. It made sense. He had some of the Red Lands blood in his veins too. Why wouldn't he have the look of our people?

With a polite bow of his head he smiled at me and for a moment, all was right with the world. Until I looked into his eyes. He was hurting, deeply. "Have you eaten, son? You look well. I see you wear a new band. Let me see it." I showered him with smiles and invited him to sit with me.

"Is there anyone else here, Mother? I need to speak with you most urgently."

"No one is here, except Menmet. What is it?" My skin crawled for a moment. I hoped he was not here to confront me about the rumors. I knew what they were saying about Aperel and me, but it simply wasn't true. And Tiye was right—I saw Tadukhipa's hand in that evil gossip.

"I need your help, Mother."

I leaned forward and grasped his hands. They felt rough and strong, like a warrior's hands. When he didn't soften under my touch I released them. He wasn't a child anymore, and I couldn't treat him like one. "What is it, son? What has happened? Is it your father?"

"Yes and no." Smenkhkare's face tensed as he spoke. The grooves around his mouth deepened, and his young brow furrowed slightly. "Must you always think of him? He's not worthy of you, Mother."

"Hush now, Smenkhkare. Do not speak so meanly of your father. He is Pharaoh. And," I whispered, "we are never alone."

He nodded, "I am sorry, but the worst thing has happened. I finished the School of Agility. I did all that he asked of me. He offered me a prize, but he will not give me what I want. Instead he has done the unthinkable! I cannot do what he asks!"

"My son! Why are you so upset? It cannot be as bad as all that. Can it?"

"He was with Ipy, of course. He is like her lap dog, I think." He paced the room now, uncaring that my servant was nearby. "He offered me a prize, said he wanted to honor me before all Egypt. The only prize I wanted was, well, I asked him for Meritaten's hand, and he refused me. I am to marry Ipy's daughter instead. He accused me of trying to steal his kingdom! Can you imagine that? I am his son! Why would I steal what is rightfully mine? Please, Mother. I do not know what has passed between you and my father, but can't you help me now? Surely you see that Meritaten and I should be together."

In my tribe, brothers did not marry their sisters, but I had long ago abandoned my revulsion for these unions. This was the Egyptian way, at least for royals, and my disapproval would not change that. And if Meritaten did not marry a brother or her father, there would be no one for her. She might even end up like Sitamen. I shivered at the thought.

"She loves me and I her. We know that we are meant to be together. Now that will not happen. Please, go to Father and plead my case. He will listen to you."

"No he will not, son. You should have come to me first, Smenkhkare. Now that Pharaoh has spoken, there is nothing to be done. You will have Ipy's daughter as a wife, but do not lose hope. Pharaoh's sons have many wives. It may be that you will have Meritaten in time. Prove to him that he can trust you. No doubt others have whispered suspicions in his ears."

"What could they possibly whisper? I have done *everything*!" He slammed his fist down on the table and glared at me. "And this is your answer? Can't you see what misery your passiveness has brought us already? His concubine struts about wearing one of your crowns, and you do nothing. She's bending his ear to her demands, and he's obeying her. As if she were the master and he the slave!"

"Careful!" I said vehemently. "Do not take that tone with me. You don't know what I have said or done. Do you think I command

Akhenaten? Have I ever been able to do so? You are foolish to believe it."

"Yet he does as *she* commands. It was she who commanded me to take Ankhesenamun. Don't you care?"

I felt great sadness to hear such a report, and even greater sadness to see my son's disappointment, but there was no solution. "As I said, there is nothing I can do now. You must be patient."

"I guess the rumors are true, then. You have fallen out of favor—and why? Because you couldn't keep your hands off Aperel?"

I shot to my feet at hearing such words coming out of my son's mouth. How could he believe such lies about me?

"Will you bring us all to ruin now, Mother?"

I slapped my son across the face. How dare he repeat evil palace gossip in my hearing! Wounded, he towered over me as if he were tempted to strike me back. Tears burned my eyes, but I would not release them over such lies. And to hear them from my own son's mouth! Without another word, Smenkhkare stormed out of my room. I heard a clattering of trays in the outer chamber, evidence of his anger.

"Lady? Are you all right? Has he harmed you?"

"Leave me, Menmet. Tell my guests I will not see them now. I have to…I have matters of state to attend to. See that they are entertained and assure them that I will see them this evening."

With a bow she said, "Yes, lady. I will go now."

As she left me alone, I slid out of my clothing and into the bath. There was a razor nearby. It shone brilliantly in the bright sunshine that filtered through the many windows. All it would take would be one swipe—no, two swipes—and the life would seep out of me. As quickly as I entertained the idea, I dismissed it. I would never do such a thing. I wanted to see my children again, my mother, others who had passed. If I took a life, even my own, that would weigh against me. No, this was not an option.

I sank into the water and let it cover my head. The tears wouldn't come, but my heart was broken. As I emerged from the water, my hair sticking to my body, I heard a sweet sound. I had not heard it in many years: short, chirpy trills and a long one. It was the song of the Bee-Eater! Then I spotted him. He bounced on my windowsill, witnessing my nakedness with no fear or timidity.

This was the sign I'd been promised! There was no denying it! After a few moments, he burst into song again and suddenly flew away. I eased out of the bath and dried my body, patting it with a fresh linen towel.

Yes, it was time. I retrieved the razor and began hacking at my hair. I did not have much time. Menmet would be gone for a while, making the arrangements for Adijah and his company. I did as Pah instructed. As I sliced, I dumped the hair into a basket, one that I would burn on my own. No one must know what I was doing. No one could know. Finally, as I clumsily shaved my head, I wept. My image in the polished bronze mirror was more than I could bear. I wept harder.

Now I was truly the Queen of Despair.

Chapter Seven

A New God—Akhenaten

"Horemheb has left the palace at the queen's command, and he was not alone." I leaned toward Saho and kept one eye on my wife as she approached my throne. It was a formal entrance, but this had been my wish for today. It was a special day, as she would soon discover.

"And?"

"Kames accompanied him. They left this morning."

I waved Saho back and watched Nefertiti now. My skin burned with the heat of my anger. I felt Ipy's eyes upon me, but I was riveted on my wife's cool exterior. She might make these others believe all was well, but I knew her. I knew inside she was twisting, like a battle banner caught in a strong wind. And I was the storm bringer! How could I have been so foolish to trust her? Against all my father taught me, I allowed my heart to lead my mind. My counselors had been correct from the beginning—she would betray me. She was not an Egyptian and not of royal blood. I believed now that she couldn't help but lie, she was of the corrupt Red Lands blood. They were all crooks and worse. And there was no truth in her. It was lucky for her that I did not drag Aperel's dead body through the court, since I heard she loved him so well.

To make matters stickier and far more threatening, her sister—whom she called Pah but whom all Egypt knew as Nephthys, the high priestess of the Green Temple of Isis—now assisted her in her schemes. Nephthys had lied to me before the court, and whether she knew it or not, she'd placed herself in grave danger.

If I believed the priestess, the recent celestial display meant nothing more significant than that my kingdom would soon be awash with the glory of the heavens. That heaven would soon come to earth and my "Golden Kingdom," as she called it, would be established forever. Anyone with sense knew that the falling stars signified something important—something evil—but she had acted as if nothing was amiss. She'd cast those solemn green eyes upon me, and I wanted to believe her, so like my wife was she, only she appeared untouched by time. As far as I knew, she'd never been a mother, and her thin waist attested to this observation. The differences between the sisters were slight, and only someone with a gift for observation would be able to identify them correctly. But I'd been studying people all my life. Discerning their true identities was a talent I prided myself in.

With hooded eyes I studied Nefertiti as she bowed before me. As everyone in attendance expected I waved my hand and invited her to sit beside me. With some hesitation she walked up the dais and took her seat on her gold and turquoise throne. Once she settled into place, the rest of the court gathered around us to witness the formal announcement. I'd not been kind to Nefertiti, and I'd not allowed anyone to prepare her for what was to come. I longed to hurt her as she'd hurt me. I wanted to see her writhe in her place before my royal court.

And now it began. As planned, Ipy came before us first and fell to her knees with her ceremonial bowl upraised above her head. This traditional birth announcement might not shock my wife, but it was only the first in a series of blows I was set to deliver. "Bless me, Daughter of Isis. I am with child," she purred to my wife in her childlike voice. To my utter disappointment, Nefertiti did not blink or hesitate in acknowledging Ipy. She accepted the pitcher of water from Saho's hand and walked down the stairs.

I could not see her face, as she had her back to me, but she did everything that was expected of her. She poured the water into the bowl and said in a pleasant voice, "I, Nefertiti, the Daughter of Isis, also called Neferneferuaten by my loving sovereign and husband Akhenaten, bless you, Ipy. May your child be born with beauty, health and wisdom as befitting the child of our sovereign, Akhenaten. Rise and be blessed." Nefertiti passed the pitcher to her servant Menmet and graciously helped Ipy to her feet. Ipy drank from the bowl, accepting the blessing of the Great Queen. Then to everyone's surprise, Nefertiti hugged the concubine as if she were greeting a long-lost relative. Applause thundered through the court at the unexpected show of affection.

Once decorum was restored, Nefertiti spoke in a commanding voice that was a beautiful mask. "Come now, Ipy. Take a seat of honor beside our Pharaoh. The goddess has blessed your womb with precious life. In you is the seed of our Pharaoh's greatness." The gathering clapped respectfully now as Ipy and Nefertiti ascended the steps together. I glared at them both, and Nefertiti calmly glided toward me and stood beside my throne as if to remind me of her place here. I could feel the tide of sentiment turning in Nefertiti's favor. Ipy's smile seemed silly compared to Nefertiti's serene expression. Ipy had no idea what had just happened. She glanced at me expectantly as she rubbed her stomach and smiled stupidly. I felt Nefertiti's hand on my shoulder, and it felt like flame on my skin. How could I still love her? How was it possible to feel the depth of hatred that I felt yet yearn for her so intensely that I would even now forgive her if she would only ask me? Aggravated by my own sentimentality, I waved to Saho to continue the order of events.

Somehow Nefertiti had known what I planned; she knew what to do. Someone had betrayed me and my wife, the Great Queen, outplayed me. Once again I could not give Ipy what she wanted most, to be named the wife of Pharaoh. Her expectant expression did nothing to persuade me. Instead, I waved my hand again, signaling for the service to move along quickly. Suddenly, the shiny gold doors of the court opened once more, glinting like flames in the midday sun.

"But…" Ipy whispered to her handmaiden. One look from me and she said nothing else. This at least I would do. I would not allow my wife to steal this moment from me. She would not have my son. If he wanted to marry, let him also learn how to rule. Today I would make my son co-regent. It would be a symbolic gesture but one that would surely capture his loyalty like a bird in a snare. Never again would he plot against me with his mother, as I knew he had earlier. He did not approve of my judgment, but he would soon learn who was the master here.

"Come forward, Smenkhkare. The throne recognizes you." I felt Nefertiti shift nervously beside me. *Ah, so she did not know this…*

That knowledge pleased me greatly. Smenkhkare's tall frame reminded me of someone I had not thought of in a long time. How much he looked like Thutmose! It was truly uncanny! The sight of him made me shiver, but I leaned forward and summoned the young man closer. He closed the distance quickly and knelt in humility. He also had no clue why he'd been summoned to the Court of the Aten. Birds chirped and a cloud flitted across the open pavilion, casting a small shadow over the affair. It did not stay long, and the murmuring it caused ceased with just one look from my prophet, Saho.

"Today, my son, Smenkhkare, first born of my sons and son of the Great Queen Nefertiti, I bestow upon you the honor of co-regent. Rise now and be crowned." The crowd gasped at the astonishing news. The effect gave me great pleasure.

Smenkhkare raised his eyes to me; they were wide and filled with surprise. I smiled at him, and the servant came quickly to my side. The boy journeyed up the steps and knelt again, this time at my feet. He whispered, "You honor me beyond my worthiness, Father."

"You are my son and indeed worthy. Rise now, Smenkhkare, co-regent of Upper and Lower Egypt. Let Egypt look upon you and all your splendor." The boy breathed hard once and rose with his chin held high. With a determined look, he faced the crowd and accepted their applause and cheers. Ipy removed herself from the throne beside me, with the help of Saho, and I led Smenkhkare to the vacant seat. "Forever as one we are, father and son, obedient to the Aten for eternity."

As he took his throne he said in response, "For eternity, my father and pharaoh. Obedient to the Aten." The crowd roared, tears on their faces, and even Nefertiti applauded joyfully. Did she not understand that she would never again sit upon the Great Throne of Egypt? I gripped the carved handgrips on my throne and glared at her. The mother of my children, the stealer of my heart. The cheers of my court did not gladden my soul. I rose and raised my hands in the sign of the Aten. I blessed the people as was my custom during these formal affairs. Let them cheer for my son. I was tired of them. All of them. All I wanted to do was disappear, perhaps lose myself in worship to the Aten. Yes, I would become one with the Aten. I needed none of these mortals; I would be one with my god.

Despite my desire to avoid her face, I was to be denied. "Please, Akhenaten. Wait. We must talk." Nefertiti shuffled behind me. She wore all gold today; the color always suited her, unlike Ipy.

"What now?" I waved my attendants away and faced the woman I had once loved with all my soul, all my being.

"Thank you for what you have done. Appointing Smenkhkare as co-regent is a wise move. He is worthy of your trust."

I smirked at her. "So you acknowledge that I outplayed you? You thought you would steal my son's love?"

"What? Never would I do such a thing. I want only the best for our children, all of them. And…I love you, Akhenaten. I have not stopped loving you, even though it has been many moons since you have come to see me. Or come to my bed. It's not too late, my husband. We can fix whatever is broken between us. We are young still."

"Not so young, I think. I hear you can no longer bear children."

She drew back, the hurt in her eyes plain. "Who would say such a thing? It is not true." Her eyes shimmered with tears, but they did not melt my heart. I'd seen tears before. "And why would you believe such lies? Why have you not come to me to ask me yourself? I know you blame me for the death of our daughter, but I too feel the loss. She was my child too, husband."

Ignoring the pain in her voice I said, "A wife who can no longer bear children is of no use to a Pharaoh—or a god."

Her carefully painted green eyes widened at my words. "What are you saying? Do you plan to declare yourself a god now? Why would you do such a thing? That goes against everything we've believed in—everything we've worked for! Would you abandon all that you've done? You remember what you said, Akhenaten. Freedom to choose, freedom to worship. Those were your words. By doing this you'd be no better than the priests of Amun." She touched my arm, and her hand felt cool. Her words stung, but I let her touch me. I missed her touch. Over the past months, my heart had traveled too far away from her, too far to go back now. "Please, speak to me, my love. I feel as if someone has poisoned your mind against me. We are one, are we not?" I could smell her scent, a blend of sweet cinnamon, white lotus and something else that was indefinable. Only she wore this scent, and it drove me mad.

"We were once."

Her jaw quivered as she whispered, "Where did we go wrong, Akhenaten? What happened? I must know."

I stepped closer to her, closed my eyes and breathed her in one last time. Yes, one last time. Then I would banish her from my sight and my heart forever. "The bastard child, Aperel and of course, your Red Lands lover, Alexio. How often you spoke his name while you slept in my bed."

"What?" She gasped in surprise.

I touched her face with my hand and stroked her jaw for a moment before I clenched her throat. She did not fight me. "You thought I didn't know, but I knew. I always knew. I forgave you because you were young and foolish. But then you took Aperel to your bed. I saw you two talking, your heads bent together, conspiring against me. You cannot deny it, Desert Queen."

"I do deny it!" she said in a hoarse whisper. Smacking my hand furiously, she took her life in her hands. My guards stepped closer, but I waved them away. "Aperel never betrayed you, and you murdered him. It's as if I do not know you at all! Since I've been your wife I have been true to you, husband. Yes! I was true while you took more wives and concubines. You have openly shamed me with your dalliances and liaisons, yet I've said nothing! I hoped you would come to your senses and remember who we are, what we hoped to do."

"How dare you speak to me about shame? You shame me by bringing the deceiver's child into my court, practically nursing him at your breast. Have *you* no shame?"

"Kames? Can't you even say his name?"

"You knew I didn't want him here, yet you claimed him, you made him our son. The bastard son of my disobedient general and his Meshwesh whore! It is because of him that Sitamen is dead! And you made him our son. What do you care about shaming our house?"

"He was a child! I didn't kill Sitamen—the priests did. And you let them!"

Fury rose in me like the River Nile, and I slapped her across her face. It immediately left a vicious palm print on her pale skin. Although she clapped a hand over it, she did not back down.

"Go ahead! You can kill me too! That would solve everything, wouldn't it? You could raise up a new queen, one who would simper and roll over like a dog whenever you spoke. I promise you this, husband. She does not have your best in mind."

"What do you know? If it's Ipy you speak of, you must know I have always loved her. I loved her long before I laid eyes on you," I lied through gritted teeth. "Long before my mother paraded you before me like a foreign prize. It is time to do what is right for Egypt, Nefertiti."

Swinging her robes behind her she said, "From this day forward, I am no longer Nefertiti. I am Nefret. Kill me now if you like or kill me later. It is no matter to me. I see now that my husband, the great Akhenaten, is dead."

I flinched at her declaration. It was a grievous sin to speak of death so loosely, especially in reference to a pharaoh. It was as if she had declared a death sentence over me. The others around us hissed their disapproval, but she did not seem to notice.

She spun on her heel and left me gaping after her. As she walked away I had the curious sensation that I'd witnessed this before. In a dream, perhaps. I couldn't explain it, but I knew one thing.

I would never see her again.

Chapter Eight

A Golden Son—Tadukhipa

A portly steward led me into my chambers, as if I'd forgotten where they were, and I frowned thinking of what I would tell the Hittite king about this newest turn of events. My father was dead, and my uncle now ruled, but that would not help me. Long ago I had been given a task, and I had failed. After all these years Akhenaten was no closer to elevating me than he had been at the beginning of our marriage.

They should have listened to me and killed the red-haired witch while they had the chance. I dismissed the steward and sat at the table while I watched my scribe set up his pens and papyrus. Of course, one of my husband's court was attending this meeting so I could not express my true heart in any of these matters. He would report whatever I wrote, as was the tradition, but venting my frustration would not help me. No one helped Tadukhipa. I always helped myself.

But at long last I would have some measure of revenge on this court. That I had decided. I could not leave this world or face an ousting by Ipy without exacting my revenge on the Old Queen. Even now my faithful servant was procuring my method of torture for use against my old rival. This would certainly close the lid on her sarcophagus. To my surprise, my husband Akhenaten came to see me. His scribe and I rose and bowed ourselves before him, and I waited until he spoke my name. It had been the longest of times since I'd had a visit from him. I was both delighted and terrified, for according to the recent reports his moods were very changeable as of late.

"Wife, forgive my intrusion," he said in his smooth, deep voice.

"Never say it. You are always welcome here, lord and pharaoh. Please allow me to pour wine for you." He nodded and took my vacant seat. "Go, scribe. You are not needed now," I said in a pleasant yet stern voice. With my own hands I poured the cup, sipped it and passed it to him. He also sipped the wine but then extended his arms to me.

Indeed, this is unusual.

He held me close to him and kissed my cheek before releasing me. "I was pleased to see you in court today."

"Your invitation to attend honors me. I would never refuse an invitation from you, my lord." I smiled sweetly and took a position next to him at the table. *And yet you hardly summon me and didn't blink when I asked to retire to the Royal Harem, away from you and your Desert Queen.*

"You could have refused, but you chose to honor my son Smenkhkare. It was a deed that did not go unnoticed. Is that hawk necklace worn in his honor?" As he smiled, the grooves around his mouth deepened. Yes, he was handsome still. Did I feel affection for him? Was it true? Did I actually love Akhenaten? No, that couldn't be possible. I would never allow my heart to behave so foolishly. I suddenly felt old and unattractive. Perhaps I was.

"Of course. What a handsome, intelligent young man! He will surely make an excellent regent. And I am sure his mother was pleased as well." I couldn't resist the dig, but Akhenaten did not take the bait. However, I saw a shadow pass over his handsome face. *So the rumors are true! The Desert Queen has lost her power over him. Perhaps now he will do as he has always promised. He will make me Great Queen!*

"Although it is always pleasant to visit with you, I have a purpose for my visit today."

"Yes?" I said with great anticipation.

"I have not forgotten my second son, Tutankhamen. I have been thinking of the future, Tadukhipa. He too is to be honored before Egypt. I have decided to make him the Hawk Prince, now that his brother is co-regent. He will serve as honorary regent during special events and when his older brother Smenkhkare is away from court. This is my desire."

"Then it shall be so." I smiled politely, my heart sinking. *So nothing for me, then?*

"I thought you would be pleased. He is a fine boy. A credit to my house. And he has your wit, although I say at times it is very sharp for one so young. I will announce this soon, but I wanted to tell you first so you could prepare the boy for his duties."

"He will no doubt be as deeply honored as I am by whatever honors you bestow upon him. Thank you for your kindness to our son, Akhenaten." With a gulp he finished his drink and walked out of the room, pausing at the doorway as I called to him. "Please, husband. Come see me soon. My arms are hungry for you," I said, feeling a rare measure of vulnerability. To my own surprise I meant those words. Without looking at me, he nodded once and left me alone.

I twisted the edge of my gown and ran to my bed, collapsing in a heap. I screamed into my pillow, the frustration and anger welling up inside me. I beat the pillows with my fists but refused to cry. I gasped for air and finally rolled on my back. *He honors my son but not me. Never me. I have nothing for all the emptiness. For all the loneliness. I have nothing. Even now when Nefertiti's star falls, I have nothing.*

How tired I was of hearing her name and seeing their weird statues. It was as if the artists were portraying them as one being. Others could not see it, but I did. But apparently that wasn't so anymore. Her image was no longer the object of every artist's rendering. For that at least I was thankful. I dreamed of taking a chisel to her face, a hammer to the stonework, pounding it into dust. I hadn't been alone in my shock and surprise. The entire court gasped when the new paintings appeared a few years ago. The portrayal of Akhenaten's strong, masculine figure as an effeminate, misshapen monster had offended everyone. Surely this had been her idea, they whispered, and I agreed. The Desert Queen wanted nothing more than to destroy Akhenaten. What better way than to present him as a monster to his people?

I slid my sandals on my feet, tidied my wig and went into the hall; a phalanx of servants fell in behind me. I'd chosen to wear pink this morning. Pink had been Tiye's favorite color, before she lost her mind. I hated the color, but I wore it to offend her as I knew it would. In a few hours, when the night fell on Pharaoh's city, Mure would fill the Old Queen's chamber with bats. Oh, how she hated those creatures! I smiled at the idea. I had long planned to present her with such a surprise, but I had to wait until Akhenaten no longer cared so much for his mother. And indeed, now he did not. I couldn't remember the last time he had visited her. That pleased me greatly.

I prayed I would hear the screams all the way in my chamber. That would be an excellent turn of events.

I strolled past the Great Queen's chambers, not bothering to offer my greetings, and continued on into the smaller, less impressive rooms. I hoped to find Ipy and to find her alone. I was not disappointed. She stood immediately when she saw me, bowed angrily and then crossed her arms like a spoiled child who'd missed her evening treat. Ipy had plump arms and full breasts. It had been a long time since she'd been pregnant. Her daughters were old enough to marry now, and yet here she was again, having another one of Pharaoh's children. It seemed so unfair.

I had three children; Tutankhamen and Anuksunamen lived, but my third child died in my womb. I thought I would die then, so great had been the pain in my heart and my body. But I had lived. Lived long enough to see Ipy raised from the harem into the queen's courts. Even though she was not yet a queen of Akhenaten, it was only a matter of time. Now I'd obviously caught her in the midst of a tantrum. She'd been throwing things about, having a fit. Without much interruption she continued.

"He promised! He promised me!" The clanging of brass cups and breaking dishes filled the open space. Confused servants lingered back, unwilling to stop their mistress from destroying Pharaoh's treasures.

"Here now! Is there a war I have not been told about?" I asked her loudly with some amusement.

"What are you doing here? Have you come to gloat?"

"Why should I gloat over your disappointment, Ipy? It is nothing to me."

She pulled her hair from her face and straightened her back. She stalked toward me, her fists clenched. I did not act afraid. What would I fear? She might strike me. I hoped she did so that I could have her killed. To strike a queen of Egypt would mean her death. She remembered in time to save herself. "I ask again," she said, baring her teeth at me, "why have you come?"

"I came to offer you my friendship, Ipy. It seems you are in need of friends these days."

"What do you know about me, Queen Kiya?"

My back prickled at hearing the old insult. "Call me what you will, but I have a crown on my head. What do you have, Ipy? Should I tell you the names they call you behind your back?"

"What names?"

Oh, how easy this is! She took the bait without being pushed!

"Let's see. I think I've heard 'Ipy the Squint-Eyed' most recently. It is true that you struggle to see, isn't it? You do squint quite a bit. It is most unattractive."

She kicked a tall brass brazier. Luckily for her there were no coals inside, or else she would have caught herself on fire.

"Shall I tell you what they call you, then? Sister?"

"You are no sister of mine, Ipy. You are not queen yet. But perhaps we can solve that problem. Perhaps I can speak to my husband for you."

That quieted her. "I don't believe you would do that. Why would you?"

"I don't know why you don't believe it. I do such things for my friends."

"I have heard about your friends, Tadukhipa. I have no need or desire for such friends." Her intimation was clear. She referred to my Inhapi and the few who followed her. Fine! Let her mock me. Let her see what love in this court was all about.

"Having me as an enemy would be a mistake, Ipy." I rubbed the head of a gold lion as I glanced up at her. "A very big mistake. Why don't we work together? You can have what you want; I can have what I want. It makes sense. That is how things work here. Those who advance must work with others. You must work with me, or else you will be left behind."

She snorted at me. "You mean *you'll* be left behind. I have no doubt that Akhenaten will make me queen, perhaps even Great Queen. I do not need your help, Tadukhipa. You see I have done well for myself, and you have never helped me before. Why start now?" She did not wait for an answer but continued, her voice dropped in a mocking tone, "I know why. Because it is you who cannot accomplish your task. How long have you been a lowly queen? You let the outsider take your place, and now I will take hers and yours. Make no mistake, Queen Tadukhipa. I am not your friend. I will never be your friend. Now get out."

My servants gasped behind me. What a low, common woman to speak to me in such a way. I felt at my hip, but my blade was not there. Instead I grabbed her arms and pulled her to me. We were nose to nose, eye to eye. She grunted and twisted, but I was taller and too strong for her, despite her plump arms. I pinched them hard and growled in her face. "And now you will be no more, Ipy! You will be nothing! No one! You will be fortunate to go back to the harem from whence you came!" With a deliberate thrust of my knee into her swollen belly I released her. She dropped to the ground, and I stormed out of the room, calling my servants to me as I left.

Now was the time for vengeance. Yes, let them all burn with my vengeance!

Chapter Nine

The Gift of the Bee-Eater—Nefertiti

"The Great Queen of Amenhotep is dead! The mother of our Pharaoh has passed! Weep and wail, Egypt!" The somber call rang in my ears before I fully woke. Then my young servant girls were around me, Menmet's face the picture of sadness although I could hardly believe she felt that way about Tiye's passing. I sat up in my bed and listened as she gave me the full report. The old woman had died last night; her room had been full of bats, so many that even now the palace servants were beating the animals out of the curtains and drapes where they liked to hide from the sun.

"This is Tadukhipa's work!" I whispered, drawing the blanket up around my face before I began weeping. As my own mother had died shortly after my birth, Tiye was the only mother I'd known. I wept with my ladies. Finally I wiped away the tears and said, "Oh, Akhenaten! I must go to him. His heart must be broken."

Menmet shooed the others away and raised her dainty hand in warning. "No, lady. Our Pharaoh does not wish to see anyone. He has hidden himself away in his mother's tomb. He oversees the preparations for her journey to the Otherworld."

"Surely he would want me by his side. I am the Great Queen!" I said defensively, knowing that I would never go against my husband's explicit instructions. "Did you truly hear this from Akhenaten's servant?"

"Yes, my queen. He has also refused Ipy and the other queens. Except Tadukhipa. She is mourning with him."

"I am sure she is," I said as I climbed out of the bed. "No gold today. I will wear colors of mourning, Menmet. As will you all. Put away anything that shines. We will not parade about in gold and silver while our mother, the Mother of Egypt, makes her passage to the Otherworld. Tell the others."

She bowed her head and scooted away to make my wishes known to my personal court. I began to weep again. Although it had been a long time since Tiye had been involved with her son's affairs, I felt alone now. I had no allies here. No one to help me navigate the increasing danger from the Amun priests and those who resented having a Desert Queen as Great Queen of Egypt. I had no time to wallow in sorrow and isolation. I was still Akhenaten's queen. I would go to the court, go to the people. I would comfort them in this hour of grief. My head itched, but I postponed shaving it again. Secretly, I mourned my hair. I trusted that Pah knew what she was doing, although for the life of me I could not understand the reason for it. But as she indicated, the stars of the royal family were beginning to fall. I could not allow Smenkhkare, Meritaten and Tasherit to disappear into the dark night! Although I rarely saw my daughters anymore, by order of my own husband, I longed for them with all my being. I would do whatever it took to protect them. I trusted Pah to help me protect them.

Pah must have heard the news. Not fifteen minutes later, her acolyte appeared at my door with a tiny wicker bird cage in her hands. Inside perched a familiar green bird with a hooked beak and nervous eyes. He eyed me suspiciously, as if I'd been the one to stuff him inside his tiny prison. Yes, this was the promised Bee-Eater.

"What does this mean, lady?" one of my maids whispered.

With a quick lie I replied, "It is a sign of sympathy often exchanged amongst my people. Let us set him here where he can view the courtyard." I walked to the open doors of my balcony and positioned the cage on an empty table. I would set him free before I left. Yes, this was the sign that I must move swiftly. I could no longer postpone my plans. I had to begin my escape in earnest, and I would need help. I dressed quickly in a somber black silk dress with a dull black belt. I paced the floor for a few minutes as I chewed on my nail, a bad habit that I had never been able to shake. To involve another would be to seal their doom if we were caught. It was one thing to put my own life in danger but quite another to place someone I loved in similar peril. It would have to be Menmet! Who else could I go to? Memre was dead, and even if she lived I doubted she would help me defy her mistress' son.

As I waited on Menmet's return the bird began to chirp. It was a strange sound to my ears, a sound from my past. How long had it been since I'd allowed myself to think of those days in Timia and

Zerzura? After a few more chirps the bird sang steadily, as if his song could set him free. The city around us wept and mourned for Queen Tiye, but the bird sang his persuasive song. A song of hope. A song of defiance. I listened to his message. Like the Bee-Eater I would have to keep my hope and avoid the many birds of prey that called Akhenaten's court home. I had to! For Smenkhkare, Tasherit and Meritaten!

"My queen, will you break your fast now?" Menmet arrived with a small plate of food. I rarely ate this early, but it was kind of her to ask.

"No, Menmet. I will not eat today. I have too much to do. Everyone, leave us." With a nervous eye, Menmet set the plate down and folded her hands in front of her in a poised position to show she was ready to serve me. "Sit, Menmet." She sat on the carpet before me. "No, here. Please." I patted the seat beside me. She sat down, her catlike eyes narrowing slightly.

"I need your help, Menmet. I have to know, can I trust you?" I searched her eyes as if I would see the truth swimming there in the dark depths.

"Always you have trusted Menmet, have you not? I have been your constant companion all these years, my queen. It hurts me to think you must ask this question. How may I serve you, lady queen?" Menmet's soft oriental accent betrayed her origins. It was an echo from her childhood when she lived with her mother far away from the dangerous courts of Thebes and Amarna. I hated her father, but I loved Menmet like a little sister. Sometimes I liked to pretend that she was Paimu, still alive and with me. And despite the fact she was a servant and I could not openly show favoritism, my heart was soft toward her. Would I really put her in this kind of danger? What would I do if she refused me? But she would not refuse. I knew that now.

"Menmet," I whispered, leaning closer to her, "I must leave the palace. I cannot tell you more than that except to say it will be soon."

"No, lady! This is our home. Where will you go?" She covered her open mouth with her hand, and her eyes widened in surprise. "Why must you leave? Has your husband sent you away?"

"No, although I am sure he would if he could. It is not that. You saw the stars fall, didn't you?"

"Yes, but the High One, Nephthys, told us that it was a fortuitous sign. That Pharaoh's glory would be shed upon the earth like the stars falling from on high. Is this not true?"

I shivered at her inclusion of my sister in this conversation. "I cannot speak to that; I only know that I am in danger. My children are in danger. There are shadows moving here in the court, Menmet, shadows that would kill us, kill my children. I must keep them safe. Will you help me?"

"I always help. You are my queen." She touched her fingers to her forehead, making the sign of respect, as she'd seen some do from my homeland. The gesture touched my heart, yet her expression was steady and stern. "What can I do? Where will you go?"

"Because I love you, Menmet, I cannot tell you where I am to go. It would put you in grave danger, and I would rather drown than do such a thing. You are like my own sister."

She looked down at her hands and pouted. "Yes, but you will leave me behind, won't you?"

"I cannot take you with me. It is too dangerous. But if we make the preparations carefully, you will not be harmed. Of that I am sure."

"I am your servant. I must go with you. No preparations can save me from Pharaoh's wrath, Great Queen."

"Trust me, Menmet. If I were to take you with me, I would place you in more danger than you can imagine."

Her lip trembled, but she said, "Tell me what I must do."

"Please try to understand, Menmet." Her disappointment was apparent, but I told her the truth. I could not risk additional harm to those I loved. For the next few minutes I whispered my wishes to her, and then she left me to begin her work. I would pray to the Shining Man later. I would pray and hope he listened. It had been so long since I'd seen him. I'd had no dreams, no visions. Surely Akhenaten and I had lost our way. Then I remembered that long-ago dream, the one I would not share with my husband.

He'd been on his throne. A crowd of leopard coats, a larger crowd than any I had seen, appeared before him and then around him. They began chanting and moaning dark phrases, all of which were directed at my husband. Akhenaten began to shout at them, but they would not cease and they would not listen. Soon, darkness wrapped around his glorious throne and I saw him stand, pushing against that blackness. It did not leave him. As he opened his mouth one last time, a black crow emerged and he fell down the steps in a heap as the leopard coats crowded around him.

The recollection of the dream filled me with dread. *Oh, my love! If only you would let me help you!* But it was too late now. Too late to fix any of this.

"Great Queen, you have a message." I wiped my eyes with a handkerchief and listened. "Adijah, the ambassador of Grecia, has come at your request. He is in the gallery. Would you like to see him now? Or should I ask him to step into your chambers?"

I thought about that for a moment. Where could we meet? I had to take care not to anger my husband, who already thought me an unfaithful woman. I could not meet with Adijah today, but when? Where? "Tell Adijah to meet me in the vault beneath the palace tomorrow when the sun goes down. I will meet him by the records room." The unknown servant bowed nervously, and I thought for the briefest moment that I saw the hint of a smirk on her face. I certainly wasn't going to call her back and ask her about it. I watched her disappear and heard the bird's sweet song again. No, this must not wait.

Carrying the cage to the balcony, I opened the door to allow the bird his freedom. He had completed his task. He watched me for a few seconds and then suddenly took flight, speeding away from my balcony and our palace. I watched him disappear into the sunshine, feeling nostalgic for home and for freedom. Was it possible that I would be free? And what of my daughters and my son? Would we all die under the weight of my husband's hand?

I did not know, but I refused to wait here to find out.

I'd been waiting too long already.

Chapter Ten

Womb of Spiders—Ipy

A wise woman once told me, "To live in the royal palace is to live in a womb of spiders." I did not understand those words when I first heard them, but the meaning had become very clear to me of late. In the womb of a spider, there is more than one biting mouth that can harm you, more than one spider to kill you. If you want to avoid becoming another casualty of the spider's hunger, you must become a more vicious spider yourself. This epiphany came to me one afternoon while I sat bored in Pharaoh's harem, staring out the window and dreaming of life beyond the palace walls, as we all did from time to time. I was no longer Pharaoh's favorite; he'd cast me off because of some sin my father committed. Even after my father's death I remained with the other women, a pitiful emblem of the conquests of Amenhotep—or as he preferred to be called now, Akhenaten. I'd once known a life outside this lovely prison, and the memory of that other world stabbed at my heart each day.

Until I began to watch the spider.

She spun, caught her meals without any help from anyone She mated and killed and cared for her sack of children. I envied her. On more than one occasion I saved my muse's life from the whisk of a broom. The other women believed me to be simpleminded when I shoved them away. Unlike them I did not care who wore purple. I cared not about the latest lovers' tricks, the scandals of faraway courts. None of these things intrigued me when I was a girl, yet the spider continued to inspire and amaze me. Even after I woke one morning and found her dead in a tight ball of black legs and torn webs she inspired me. She'd achieved her task. And I waited for the moment when I could achieve mine.

Eventually it came. And what a strange thing it was, too. I'd been invited to Akhenaten's court by his Great Queen, and I'd never left. She too thought me simpleminded, never realizing that inside me was a spider, waiting and watching and spinning. I could not tell what day it was that my web had caught my prey, so slowly had I woven it. At first Akhenaten barely looked at me, but as he saw that I forgave him and believed that I adored him still, the web tightened. All the while I hated him.

Now, in my womb, I carried my own spider. I would never allow my child to be weak. Never would my child be abandoned. I would teach her—for I was convinced it was a girl-child—that love was an illusion, a spell. It was not real.

I had not always thought so. My father had served the old pharaoh, but I never liked my father. He reeked of garlic and handled me more than I liked. Also called Ipy, my father had a way of using everything and everyone at his disposal, always for his betterment. I was not sad when he was executed for treason, although my mother mourned for him. No, indeed, I was not. Until I was banished from court, away from Akhenaten forever. Or at least until the arrival of the new Great Queen. When she summoned me I knew she was in trouble. Why else would she call upon me? I was no one. Amenhotep did not love me, as he had proved. Rarely did he come to see me, and even then only long enough to get me with child. Although it had been in his power to call me to him whenever he liked.

I did not dislike the new queen. I hated Tadukhipa much more than I hated Nefertiti. But I loved no one, except for the spider in my belly.

"Lady Ipy. May I come in?" Speaking of spiders, here was another. She stood in the shadows, but I recognized her pretty face. This was Menmet! *Aw, all the pretty spiders are at work today.*

"You may. I seem to be very popular with queens today. Tell me, is it true the old queen is dead? I have heard so, but I don't dare believe it." I sat primly on the couch and waited to see which way the wind would blow with this one. This was the Great Queen Nefertiti's servant. I'd seen her in the court and at other times, always at the queen's beck and call. She did not look me in the face; in fact, I thought she might run away, for she displayed an extraordinary amount of inner struggle. She set her chin and nodded.

"Yes, lady. It is true. We are all to mourn for the next forty days."

"Is that why you have come, Menmet? To express to me the Great Queen's wishes? I know enough to mourn when appropriate. I do not need a mother!" I barked at her. And where were my servants? I wondered absently. Oh yes, I'd ordered them out after Tadukhipa's visit. Now would be a good time to see them return. Did no one care for me here? I would speak to Amenhotep about this later. I mean, Akhenaten. How strange it was to say that name. As if changing a name would change the man. He would always be what he was, a philanderer. An incompetent leader.

"No, indeed it is not. The Great Queen does not know I have come here. In fact, she cannot know at all." I smiled at her answer and patted the cushion beside me. *Oh yes, here is another spider.*

"You are Heby's daughter, aren't you? Has he sent you here, then?"

She shook her head, her wig bobbing prettily. Finally she cast those angled eyes upon me, and they were full of tears. "I don't know what to do, Lady Ipy. I know something, something troubling, and the burden is too great. I must tell someone who has our Pharaoh's ear. He must know this or else I may perish!" I held her hands soothingly, reminding myself not to be too greedy with my response. "I would rather die than return to my father's house or fall under the weight of my Pharaoh Akhenaten's anger!"

"Come now, Menmet. Calm yourself, dear. I can see you have come to me with troubling news. I will surely speak to Pharaoh on your behalf. You have no need to worry. Tell me, what is on your heart?" I made my voice soft and sweet, just as I did with Amenhotep.

"I would never speak against my lady queen, but I know I will die if I do not. She doesn't know what she is doing. I think she is riddled with grief because of the queen mother's passing. That must be it. Yes, that is it." She wept now and sat in a blubbering heap beside me. *How long must I endure this? Oh yes, be patient, little spider.*

"So you have no wish to tell me what you came to tell me, then? You may leave if you like, Menmet. Without worry that I would betray your concerns. Please know that I am here whenever you need me." I hugged her even though I hated to do so. This kind of contact did not come naturally to me, but I knew it soothed others. And this woman was a fountain of information, and this spider would benefit from the information. I stroked her wig and patted her shoulder, ready for there to be more distance between us.

"No, I must tell you. I came to you because I know something of your past, lady. I too have a father who has fallen out of favor with Pharaoh. I am content to serve the Great Queen, but I cannot help but worry for my sister and myself if the Great Queen succeeds in her plan."

"Oh, Menmet. What a heavy burden for such slender shoulders! I cannot believe our Great Queen would put you in such a delicate position. It must be grief, yes, that must be it. And yes, you and I have much in common, but we need not be defined by our fathers. We are our own women, called into the service of our great Pharaoh Akhenaten. Let us serve him with all our hearts, even our bodies if we must."

She nodded and whispered, "The queen makes plans to leave, Lady Ipy. She will not tell me when and where, but she will leave us. How can this be? What do I do?"

I squeezed her hands and mimicked her sad face. "Serve the Great Queen. Be her friend, as you have always been. I will find out the truth. Rest assured all will be well, Menmet." I rose from the couch, anxious for this meeting to end. Menmet was ready to be rid of me, having done what she came to do. What a shameful thing! I wondered why she would betray her queen in such a way! She would never serve in my court. This was further proof that all women were spiders.

"And you will speak for me, Lady Ipy? You will not let me die in the flames?" Her shimmering black eyes searched mine, and I gave her a sympathetic, solemn look.

"You can trust me. I will not abandon you. Go now and do your mistress' bidding. Keep your face dry, and let no one know what you have told me. I will speak to my husband, I mean, Pharaoh."

No, I would never trust her, nor would I help her. In fact, as soon as she left me I planned to break Akhenaten's ban on solitude. He would want to know this, and I should be the one to tell him! With an awkward glance over her shoulder Menmet disappeared into the shadowy corridor and I turned to my mirror.

What does one wear when overthrowing a queen?

Chapter Eleven

The Broken Man—Pah

Walking at a steady pace, I moved through the Green Temple. I kept my eyes on the distant statue of Isis, the center of all this attention. Today was a day of mourning in the city. Queen Tiye's body had been removed this morning and taken to the priests for her preparations for her journey. Or so the Egyptians believed. Despite the overwhelming sadness that hovered over everything, rumors of my betrayal flitted about all of Akhenaten's city. As sheltered as they were, the priestesses were not immune to the gossip. Ignoring their stares, pretending that all was well, I carried an armful of sweet flowers to the image of Isis in honor of the late queen. These were rare yellow blooms—expensive and hard to find in the city. It was well known that I grew them with my own hands on my balcony from seeds. What most didn't know was that those seeds had been a present from Adijah a few years ago. When I pushed the seeds down into the soil I had visions of faraway Grecia, but I knew full well I would never see that fair land.

I liked Adijah, and that was not something I could say about most people. Perhaps that was why I excelled in my role as priestess. I had to do very little speaking, and when I did those who listened hung on my every word. Yes, I liked Adijah. He looked very much like a foreigner compared to those around us, but I supposed I did too. He had trustworthy eyes, and I did trust him. What other choice did we have now? Allies were few and far between in Akhenaten's court.

The whispers of the acolytes rose as I approached the towering image of Isis.

"This is strange indeed for the high priestess to arrive unannounced," I heard them say. "Something must be amiss! Can the rumors be true?"

With a wave of my hand I dismissed them. Arranging the flowers at Isis' feet, I knelt as the last of the attending priestesses left the room. The High One's worship was sacred and not to be witnessed by anyone. Only one priestess lingered—Maza was her name. Her dark skin looked otherworldly and bright compared to the soft yellow gown she wore. Yes, Maza would be the one who would rule this place after me. I stared at her unflinchingly as she slowly closed the door behind her. Like me, she had likely seen our entwined fates in the fire and the water, but she was not yet the ruler of this place. Not yet. But soon.

I did not waste time wallowing at the statue's feet. The old queen was dead, and it was the current queen and my sister who needed my help. What prayer could I offer for Tiye, the tiny Red Lands woman who ruled Egypt with an iron fist until she lost her mind—and her power over her son? I quickly set about my task, searching through the many baskets that lay at the goddess' feet. Inside one of them I would find what I was looking for. Surely he had not let me down. Not this time. After plundering through a dozen offerings of fruits, meats and breads, I found my prize. Yes, here it was!

It was a small piece of papyrus hidden under an orange. If I'd been paying closer attention I would have recognized the Grecian flowers, the same kind as the ones I'd offered, tucked in the corner. No matter now. I found it! Clutching it in my hand I fell before the statue and began to sing a song of mourning as I'd been taught.

Eyes watched me now. The awareness made my skin crawl, and I could feel those eyes, wondering, watching, observing my every move. I slid the small papyrus fragment into the bosom of my gown as I waved my arms about and bowed before the statue again and again. Yes, I heard the shuffling of sandals not far behind me. It could only be Maza, for no one else dared to enter this holy place unsummoned. I pretended that I did not notice her presence; I continued until my knees ached and my arms grew weary. Finally, I took some of the flowers and tossed them into the sacred fire. They burned quickly, leaving nothing but soot behind. Such a shame to burn such beauty. It had been my intention to gaze into the fire before I returned to my apartments to prepare, but I could not, not while my watcher hung nearby. Instead I burned another handful of the flowers and shut my eyes against whatever I might see.

That was a mistake, for Maza was close enough to see for herself what was in the fire. I heard her gasp, and I spun about to meet her face to face. But it was not Maza who looked into the fire. It was my servant and student Shepshet.

"Shepshet! What are you doing here? You know that you cannot be here."

Her eyes were wide and her mouth open in surprise still. She could not shake her gaze from the fire and instead sank to her knees and began to weep. "Oh, lady! What have I seen? What have I seen?"

I fell down beside her and cupped her face with my hands, forcing her to break her fiery vision. "You have seen nothing, Shepshet! Nothing!"

She shook her head slowly, miserably, as tears slid down her cheeks. What had she seen? "I did see. I saw you die, Nephthys."

"No, Shepshet. Listen to me. Look at me. Look into my eyes. Do not stare into the fire again." Finally she did as I asked, her body limp, her emotions clearly raw and ragged. At least one person would mourn my leaving this world. Better that than the thousands of Egyptians who only pretended to grieve for the loss of Queen Tiye. For the past twenty-four hours they had paraded in and out of our courtyards, making sure they were seen by anyone who cared to look. Each hoped that word would travel back to Pharaoh Amenhotep, as if he would be impressed by their devotion. These Egyptians thought of nothing but politics. They did not impress me with their displays of mourning—ashes on their bald heads, arms free of gold. "You have seen nothing but what must be. You cannot prevent this. And you must not."

"But…"

"No, Shepshet. I do not wish for you to share my fate. Do not tell anyone what you have seen. You must obey me in this. I cannot meet whatever lies before me knowing you are in danger. It would be too much to bear. And remember, we are all in her hands." I glanced up at the statue, and Shepshet's fearful eyes followed mine. Then she clung to me and sobbed. I allowed myself to feel self-pity for a few seconds but not for too long. I could not afford to lose faith now. I had to continue on if I wanted to make peace with Paimu and see Alexio once again. Oh, to step on the soft grass of Timia again, to see the ones I had loved all those years ago.

And when did you leave this world, my love? How is it that I didn't sense your passing?

"You must leave now, Shepshet. I must continue with my ministrations, but I will return to my apartments soon." We rose together, and I hugged her one last time. "Now, do not let anyone see your tears. Pull your veil down. And Shepshet..."

"Yes?"

"See that no one else comes in. I want to be alone for a while."

"Yes, lady." She did as I asked, pulling the veil over her face and quietly exiting the room. I watched the door close and quickly walked behind the statue. Now I was truly alone. I dug the papyrus out of my dress. Looking around one last time, I unrolled it with shaking fingers and stared at the painted emblems.

There were three. But that was all that was needed. I touched the script with my fingers as if I could make the emblems speak to me. The first was simple enough, the sign of the Meshwesh. The careful squiggles represented the falcon, the symbol of our people, only it was upside down. Next to it was an unusual image, the horns of a bull. I stared at the last picture—the broken man, his arms and legs detached from his body.

My uncle's message was clear. The falcon's day had ended. Horemheb left Egypt with Kames by his side, as I had instructed. Somehow, Ayn's son would be crucial for the survival of the Meshwesh. He was the bull, as his name suggested.

I stared at the broken man. It could only mean that Pharaoh's judgment was against me. Horemheb would know this. Until recent years he had been one of Amenhotep's favorites, and even now his tenuous connections kept him abreast of the ebb and flow of Pharaoh's mood. Apparently it now flowed against me. He had already purposed in his heart to tear me asunder. He was unable to deliver his rage upon Nefret, so it would fall upon me.

I would be the broken man.

Chapter Twelve

Hidden Places—Nefertiti

Sleep struggled with me, but eventually I grasped it and quiet darkness took me. But it didn't stay dark for long. A glow surrounded me, and my skin tingled with warmth. I was floating, and in that strange levitation there was peace and stillness. Yes, this was where I wanted to be. Let me stay here a little while. Away from my troubles and despair!

Now I was falling. Terror seized me as I stretched out my hands. I struggled to find something I could use to break my fall, but the fall continued, seemingly endless. I felt as if time stood still as I whipped around, head over feet again and again. The motion threatened to make me sick as I spun faster with each passing moment. I screamed for what felt like a lifetime, but no one heard me, nothing happened and eventually my voice failed me. Yet I continued to fall. I forced my eyes shut and hugged myself as I waited for the impending crash. Surely I would die.

Then I wasn't falling—I was standing in the Red Lands, the sand warm beneath my feet. I gasped in surprise because I was not alone. The Shining Man stood beside me; as always his face was obscured by the light that surrounded him—no, he was the source of the light. He watched me but said nothing at first, and I felt uneasy under his gaze.

What could I say? What could I do but wait to hear what he would say? Would he impart to me another dream? Another vision for the future? And why should he trust me with a new vision, seeing that my husband and I had failed so miserably with the dream he'd given me? No, I was not worthy to be here. Surely this was a mistake.

"What makes one man or woman worthier than another?"

I couldn't hide my surprise. He could read my mind!

"I do not know," I began hesitantly. "But I am sure you do, sir."

Although I could not see his face, I could *feel* him smile. It gave me confidence to continue standing in his presence, for without it I am sure I would have perished.

"Worthiness is a human measurement. Worthiness is man's attempt at reasoning with the workings of the divine." His words both comforted and disturbed me. *Why then do men try to please the gods?* I thought, forgetting that he could read my thoughts. I quickly repented of the question; before I could sort out my many emotions, he touched my shoulder with a firm grip, and in that moment everything became clear to me. Who he was, who I was, where we were and where I would go next. I knew that far from failing him, failing the vision, Amenhotep and I had *accomplished* his desires. And the knowledge of that brought me much peace. Peace of a kind I had not known in my waking life. No matter what happened, no matter what I lost or who I lost. All would be well. In fact, as I woke, I heard him speak those words to my heart.

All will be well...

As I opened my eyes and exited the dream world, the knowledge I had so richly enjoyed fluttered away from me. It flew away on invisible wings, vanishing on the rays of the approaching dawn. It seemed like I had been there only a moment, but apparently I'd slept soundly through the night. Morning was arriving. As I had when I fell, I grasped the air around me as if the knowledge were a tangible thing to be possessed. It was not. I could remember nothing except the Shining Man's words.

All will be well. And strangely it was enough. I rose from my bed quickly to dress myself. I had taken to sleeping alone now. I did not need to worry that Amenhotep would discover the change in my hairstyle; he had not come to my bed in nearly a season. But if I was to prevent my servants from knowing I had shaved my head, I must be alone. I had to admit I missed Menmet's nighttime chatter. She had always been so entertaining. I pulled on my morning wig and a loose robe and opened the outer door to my sleeping chamber. To my surprise there was no one about. This had never happened before, and it was a strange thing indeed.

With my heart pounding, I examined this new development. What could possibly have occurred? Reality struck me. Queen Tiye was dead, along with the last of her influence and presumably also mine. Or maybe this was a sign that Menmet had deceived me.

Soon the palace guards would set upon me and take me before my husband.

"Lady? I did not hear you rise. Are you hungry? Won't you take some food, my queen?"

"Where is Menmet?" I asked the girl.

She stammered, "I do not know. I woke to an empty room, lady." She stood at attention and glanced around nervously. Even this inexperienced girl knew all was not right here. Well, I wasn't one to cower because a few servants had left me for higher ground. *All the more reason to leave as soon as possible. Do not let her betray me! Let me have my daughters and my son, and I will ask for nothing more!*

"What is your name?"

"Yerye, Great Queen."

"Yerye, I am hungry. Please bring me a tray to the balcony. After my devotion to the Aten, I will take some food. Then you may help me dress."

"Oh, yes, lady!" She smiled with great delight, immediately forgetting the strange predicament we found ourselves in. I took some comfort in her obliviousness. She waited as I offered my worship to the Aten—I would need his favor if my plan was to succeed.

I took a few bites of food and said as absently as I could, "Yerye, after I dress I want you to send the steward to fetch my daughters for me. They are at the White Palace."

"Oh no, lady. They are not. They are here." She blinked as she set the blue pitcher down on the table beside me.

I gripped her wrist as quickly as a cobra striking his prey. "Tell me where you saw them! Have they been harmed?"

She winced in surprise and pain but did not pull away from me. Instead she fell on her knees and said, "They seemed healthy, lady queen. I did not speak with them, for I am just a servant." I released her wrist and waited to hear more. "I saw them playing in the Great Hallway with Lady Ipy and her dogs. I can fetch them now if you like." As she spoke, my anger rose. How dare Ipy reach for my daughters! Yes, I must go tonight! Adijah must help me as Pah promised he would.

"Yes, that will be fine. Only don't bring them here. I will go to my gardens. You can bring them to me there, Yerye."

"Very well, Great Queen." I heard the doors to my chambers, but I did not turn my head. I kept my eyes on the horizon while I reclined on my balcony. It would not do to quiver like a coward before my husband's guards, if indeed they were the ones who were barging in on me.

"Great Queen, I had hoped to return before you woke. Forgive Menmet for not being here to help you dress. As I have always done." Angrily I launched from my couch and swung my gown back as I stepped toward her. As petite as she was I towered over her, and as angry as I was I didn't mind reminding her of my advantage. I wanted to strike her in the face for her betrayal, for I was sure she had betrayed me, but before my hand could fulfill my wishes my daughters rushed onto the balcony and encircled my waist with their arms.

"Mother!" Meritaten kissed my cheek and hugged me close, closer than she had in a long time. I kissed her back and rubbed her chin as I did when I greeted her. When she was a babe, it was the only thing that kept her from crying. Pharaoh had wet nurses and servants aplenty for our children, but only I could care for my daughter, my own Meritaten. She would have no other until she got older and decided she no longer needed a mother. But perhaps I was being unkind. Like all the other women in her father's court, including me, she had little to say about where she went and who she saw. Meritaten had her father's sculpted mouth but my green eyes. She had my height, and I believed she'd grown since last I saw her but I did not say so. She was a sensitive girl who was prone to be upset about the slightest perceived offense. In that she reminded me of Pah and at times Sitamen, who preferred solitude over court life.

Tasherit came next. She was Tiye made over with her big dark eyes and flat feet. Would she ever grow? I could not tell, but I always told her that she had. I sat again so I could scoop her into my arms. Menmet beamed behind them, and I immediately felt sorry for my black thoughts toward her. "Thank you, Menmet. That will be all." She winked at me and stepped back, making the sign of respect as she did. I noticed that my chambers were now full of servants, but most of them I did not know. Something was mightily wrong here, but at least I saw my daughters.

"Mother, what a sad time. Our grandmother has died. Will you die also, my mother?" Tasherit's young voice broke my heart.

"Someday we all will leave this world for the next, but I promise you that the Otherworld is a wonderful place. Even now your grandmother, the Great Queen Tiye, is walking the shores with your grandfather Amenhotep." I noticed that Meritaten sighed a great deal as Tasherit and I spoke. She was obviously unhappy and wanted me to know it. Yes, I had been away from my daughters for too long. How foolish I'd been! This was real love.

"Why do you tell her these tales, mother? We both know that not all stories have a happy ending." *So that's it, then. Meritaten has heard the news. Smenkhkare will marry Ipy's daughter.* If only she understood the much greater danger that faced us all. And how could I tell her that we would leave her father's kingdom like bandits in the night? This I could not do.

"Tasherit? Go to Mother's ivory table, the one by my bed. Open the middle drawer. I think you will find a treasure there. It is something that flies."

She showed a gap-toothed smile. "If I find it and bring it back to you, will you tell me a story?" And she quickly added, "And can I keep my treasure?"

I laughed at her enthusiasm. Of all my children Tasherit loved my stories—and my treasures—best. "Why, yes! Now go, my smart girl!" She took off running, her bare feet slapping on the floor. She was truly a tiny little thing.

"What is on your heart, my daughter? You can speak freely to me."

"There is nowhere free here." Meritaten crossed her arms and stared out across the city to the sands beyond. After a minute she added, "I used to hate you, Mother. I don't now, but I used to."

"Why?" I asked, completely surprised by her admission. "Have I wronged you in some way?"

"No, it is not that." She sighed, turned her back to the railing and tapped her fingers on the carved wood. "I thought you did not love us. I remember those times when my father would wave you to his side and you would leave us. We cried for you, but you never came. Sometimes for weeks. I would think, how can any mother leave their child for such a long time? Even if her husband is the great Pharaoh? But that was before—before I knew what love was myself."

"Before you knew you loved Smenkhkare?"

"You know?"

"Of course I know. I am his mother too."

When I said nothing else she added, "And you don't approve?"

"I never had the opportunity to approve or disapprove. My son told me of his intentions after it was too late for me to intervene. I cannot go against the wishes of the Pharaoh. And sadly, even if Smenkhkare had consulted me earlier, I am not sure it would have availed much."

Suddenly Meritaten threw herself in my lap and wept loudly. The servants paused and whispered, but no one dared to invade our privacy. Except Menmet, who stood nearby. I waved her back and stroked Meritaten's arm.

"There now, sweet daughter. All will be well." *Ah, yes. Those words did bring comfort to us, didn't they?* "You have to trust fate. If it is meant to be, it will happen."

"How can that be? He is to marry that awful girl! He doesn't want to—can't you help us? Don't you understand how it feels?" She looked up at me, her pretty face filled with deep emotion.

"I wish it were that easy. You can't give up hope, Meritaten. You must keep hope."

She pushed me away and sobbed in the corner of the balcony. "And that is your advice? Keep hope? I will not stand idly by and watch him marry her!"

I rushed to her side. "Hush now, daughter. You cannot lose control like this. It will not do you any good. Believe me, I know."

She spun around, her eyes now streaked with makeup, her lip quivering. "How has that worked for you, Mother? Has silently waiting like a dutiful wife helped you at all? There is open talk that Pharaoh will make Ipy Great Queen. Do you know what that means? We will all be ruined! And you do nothing? By the gods! She wears your crown, Mother!"

She shouted at me now, but I gripped her hands and said in a low whisper, "There are spies here, Meritaten!" I stared her down to demonstrate the danger. When she stilled for a moment I continued, "No one here is my friend. Keep your voice down. I will help you as much as I can, but if you do not keep silent, I cannot help you at all. What now would you have me do? Throw a tantrum as you have done? And whose lap can I fall into? Let Ipy parade around in whatever crown she likes. I face more dangerous things than the loss of a crown or a few baubles."

She snatched her hands away and said in a vicious whisper, "Yes! Yes, you do."

Without waiting for my leave, Meritaten stormed out of my chambers, pushing past even Tasherit who had appeared with the promised treasure in her hands. My younger daughter's eyes were full of fear and worry. She glanced from me to Meritaten's vanishing figure. I held out my arms to her, but I could see the conflict on her face. She'd been with her sister all these months. Leaving the paper bird on a stick on my table, she left me and ran out.

"Meritaten! Wait for me!" she called as she vanished from my view. I nearly collapsed into my chair. Then I caught a glimpse of Menmet as she slipped behind the curtain. I saw a smile on her face.

Chapter Thirteen

The Bones of Ayn—Tadukhipa

From the comfort of my bed I watched the young man put on his clothes, fully appreciating his perfect physique. It was true that looking at him pleased me, but it was an empty pleasure, not like what I had felt in the arms of Inhapi. Men were not capable of love. I had never experienced that kind of love or witnessed it. All men were unfaithful. They were like animals, really, useful for only one thing—perhaps two, depending on the man. I spun the sweet-smelling rose over my nose as the young man returned to my bed to steal another kiss before leaving. But I did not give him one. "No more today, Seker. You must earn your next kiss."

He smiled at me and said, "Haven't I done that, my queen? What can I do now to please you? Just name your desire, for it pleases me to please you."

I had no doubt that he meant it, even though I was old enough to be his mother—or at least his much older sister. Such stupidity in those exquisite eyes, but I liked a stupid man. I had no worries that Seker plotted against me, and I knew he would he ever incite me to overthrow my husband.

The downside was he had no idea that I was on the verge of losing my claim to the high queenship, which would surely come available soon, as soon as Amenhotep mustered up the courage to execute the Desert Queen. That high place would go to Ipy. Once she became the next Great Queen, she would have complete control over us all. That could not be borne! How cruel to see my plan backfire on me so! After hearing of the Desert Queen's treasonous affair with Aperel, Amenhotep was supposed to put her away or burn her—not raise the fat Ipy to new heights. As always, Pharaoh was unpredictable. And weak when it came to Nefertiti.

"Go to the Great Queen and command her attend me. Tell her I wish to see her in my chambers in one hour." If I could not work with Ipy, I might be able to entice Nefertiti to help me rid us both of her nasty presence.

His smile vanished and he stammered stupidly, "I cannot command the Great Queen, but I'll be happy to relay your request to her."

I slapped his face with the rose, and a thorn left a long scratch across his cheek and cleft chin. "Get out and don't return," I shouted. Blood poured from the scratch, and he held his hand to his face. I rolled over on my back and ignored him as he stomped away to tend to his wound and obey my command. Yes, he brought me pleasure from time to time, but he had no courage. Feeling aggravated still with his insubordination, I rolled out of my bed and poured myself some water.

Hours later I was still mulling over my situation, and I began to regret my hastiness. Seker did not return—in this, he obeyed me—and I had too much pride to send for him so soon. But I regretted sending him away. He risked his life night after night crawling into my bed. That was proof of his courage, wasn't it? What else did I want? For him to throw himself into the Burning Bull? I shivered thinking of Ramose and Sitamen, burning and twisting together in death. It had been a horror to witness.

"Queen Tadukhipa, you have a visitor."

"Yes? Who is it?" Perhaps it was Seker returning to beg my forgiveness!

"It is the Great Queen, Neferneferuaten Nefertiti." My servant bowed her head and waited for me to command her. This was an interesting turn of events, wasn't it? I never thought I would see the day when the Desert Queen darkened my doorway. Sailing past the bowed servant, I entered my main chamber to find my sister-queen waiting for me. She'd not waited for me to invite her to sit. She sat already—and in my chair.

"Queen Nefertiti? To what do I owe this rare pleasure?"

"Leave us," she said to my retinue of slaves and servants. They did not hesitate to obey her, but they went only as far as the antechamber. Obediently they closed the door and left us alone. Had we ever been alone before? And where were her servants? Didn't they fear for her safety? How foolish to trust me!

"State your business, *Great Queen*," I said sarcastically. "Have you come for my help with Ipy? I can tell you from personal experience that she is an unpleasant sort of woman and not moved by common sense. I am afraid you are too late to overthrow her. You should have asked me before you invited her here."

She did not hesitate to speak, but she did not address my comments at all. "I know it was you who caused the death of Queen Tiye." I did not deny it, and she kept talking. "I know it was you who spread the rumors that the Master of Horse and I met privately. That I was involved with him in an illicit manner." I did not deny that either. A small smile crept across my face.

"And what of it?" Did she want me to deny it? I was happy that she recognized my handiwork, but I was in no mood to play games with a pouting queen—one who was destined for banishment or worse.

"Be sure your own sins will find you, Tadukhipa. Those who do evil always find their deeds revisited on them."

Unimpressed with her scolding, I sat at smaller chair at the square table between us. This table and the elegant chair the queen claimed for herself had been a gift from my father; they were a few of my wedding gifts. Each piece served as a reminder of who I was and the blood I came from. Royal blood. I used to love looking at it, running my fingers in the grooves, reading again and again the story of the Hittites that was scripted in the panels. So strong we were—absolutely ruthless when necessary. But even though those things were treasures to me, what rested in the box between us was the most interesting thing in the room. I was sure Queen Nefertiti would want to see it. I just had to wait for the right moment! I rubbed my finger over the top of the box. It was a plain thing but a fitting home for what lay inside it.

"Tell me, Great Queen. Did you come all this way to tell me a story about virtue and morality? I hear you are very good at telling stories, but I am no child and have no time to hear one. I have many things to do today."

She gave me a lovely smile, and immediately I sensed the danger. She said sweetly, "Indulge me, my sister. This will not take long. I think this story will interest you a great deal, probably more than any other you have heard lately. It is the story of an evil witch who cast a spell on her husband. While he was under her spell, he made many poor decisions. He did many things he regretted. But one day, a little bird came to him and whispered words in his ear. Those words were magic words, and they broke the spell of the witch; his evil wife had no more power over him. The husband realized his mistake and immediately corrected it. He cast out the witch into the darkness and called her wife no more."

I leaned forward and stared at her in disbelief. "Is this supposed to frighten me? It's no wonder that Ipy climbs so high. I despise game-playing. Tell me what is on your mind and be done with it." My skin crawled in anticipation of what she would tell me.

"Very well. Seker, your most recent lover, is now before the king. He is blubbering like an infant and has fully confessed to his crimes. He will die, just as innocent Aperel died. Except Aperel never accused me or confessed to the accusation, for it was only that. I have never taken another man to my bed. Seker says he has been your lover for some time."

Springing to my feet I beat the table with my fist. "You lie!"

She smiled even wider. "I have it on good authority, Tadukhipa. It is a shame, though; he was so young and inexperienced. I am sure there was much you could have taught him if given a chance."

I stared at her, hardly believing what she said. It couldn't be true! Having delivered her hateful words to my face, she acted as if she would leave me.

"No! Wait, Great Queen." It was my turn to smile now; my turn to give her a gift. "As you were kind enough to visit me today and deliver this news personally, it is only fair that I give you something." Nefertiti's back straightened, and she watched me as I opened the box. I pulled back the black cloth that covered my treasure. How long I had been waiting to show this to her! I revealed the bones and plucked out the necklace I'd stashed with them. She should recognize it. I tossed the thing in her lap and stepped back, waiting to see how she liked her present.

The leather and turquoise necklace was unique but obviously not as finely made as anything Egyptian. Just another desert treasure not worth the time it took to make. She gingerly picked it up from her lap. I noticed that she wore black today again—and like an undignified foreign queen, she wore no gold or jewels. Did she believe Tiye would have done the same for her? Still in mourning for the crazy old woman, I supposed, and how much more she would mourn now. She rubbed the pendant and looked at the bones. I picked up the skull and rolled it around in my hands before offering it to her. "Do you recognize her? She is quite a bit thinner now." I laughed at my own joke, but it yielded no response from her.

She slid the necklace around her neck and rose from my favorite chair. "Well? How do you like my gift?" I asked her. She did not accept the skull, and I tired of holding it. I bounced the gaping thing back in its box and smiled innocently, satisfied that my arrow had hit the mark. If she had not thought me evil before, she would certainly think me so now. "Answer me. I am not used to being ignored."

"You are an evil woman. And not just evil; you are mad. I have long made peace with Ayn's passing, but you must live with your lover's death today. That is enough."

I screamed with fury and shoved her as hard as I could. Nefertiti fell on her backside but did not stay down long. She raced across the room, I thought to escape me. But instead she charged for the long golden spear on the wall. With surprising strength she pulled it down and hefted it like a warrior. I firmly believed she would drill a hole in me if she could.

I picked up a small bust of Amenhotep and pitched it at her. It landed at her feet; the enamel coating cracked, but it did not break. A few more inches and it would have struck her. She poked at me with the spear as I searched for a weapon. I tossed a platter at her, which she quickly dodged, but soon I spotted what I'd been looking for. The long blade stood in the corner. It was a blade like those used by a queen's guard, left here for some reason just yesterday. Such a strange thing to see because I already possessed many ceremonial weapons, most of which had been given to me by my father and uncle. Perhaps my husband hoped I'd run myself through with the guard's sword so he could finally be rid of me. That I would never do. If he wanted me to die, he would have to see to it himself. And if Seker betrayed me, Amenhotep might very well do it after all.

I had no training with a sword, no skill with a blade, yet my black anger would not allow me to relent.

"You are making a mistake, Tadukhipa. Another mistake."

I sliced at her, but her spear kept me at a safe distance. She was toying with me now. "I hate you! I hate you!" I screamed at her.

"Stop this madness!" she screamed back, but I noticed she did not lower her own weapon. Suddenly the doors of the chamber opened and the servants rushed in. They cried out—at what I did not know. Perhaps they were warning us to stop; my mind was full of angry bees, and I could barely hear anything over their buzzing. Then the cries rose up, like a strange tide, from the surrounding palace and the city below. I lowered my sword and beheld Mure's face.

"What is it?"

"Pharaoh is dead, mistress! Our sovereign is dead!" She fell to her knees and began weeping, as did the others. They hardly seemed to notice that I held a sword and Nefertiti a spear.

"What will become of us? What will become of us?" another cried out in agony.

I dropped my sword and fell into my chair. I could not help but scream. I clawed at my arms and beat my chest with my fists. "No! This cannot be true! Amenhotep! Husband!" I said again, pushing my servants away. Through my tears I saw Nefertiti drop the spear, and it clanged against the marble floor. Without another word or a hint of emotion she departed quickly.

My mind screamed, "Now is the time! Kill her now!" but my heart would not allow me to act. It was broken. All my love had been squeezed from it. All my hope.

It was in that moment that I realized the agonizing truth. I had loved Amenhotep—from the first day I saw him to this day. I *had* loved him utterly and completely. And like Inhapi, he was gone.

I had nothing else to live for.

Chapter Fourteen

Love's Light—Meritaten

Tasherit cried herself to sleep after our brief visit with Mother. The poor girl cried so hard she made herself physically sick. My little sister begged me to go back and apologize to our mother for leaving so abruptly, but I would not. I told her to go back herself if she wanted to, that I would not hold it against her, but she would not leave me. That both comforted me and filled my heart with guilt. Eventually Tasherit stopped asking me to return to Mother and closed her eyes. Once her breathing settled she succumbed to sleep and I left her—for a little while. I would never leave her for too long; all we had was each other. But it was difficult to find time for myself, so I selfishly stole it whenever I could.

It was only a matter of time before my sister and I were shipped back to the White Palace, and I wanted to visit the stables again—these were far superior to ours. My father kept his finest breeds at his palace, and some were protected by armed guards as they were rare and very costly—I especially loved the black chariot horses, although they were smaller than the war horses. Smenkhkare loved his war horses. Not me. I would trade any of my treasures for a pair of these chariot horses. And these two were powerful animals and demonstrated great loyalty to one another. Loyalty. It was such a rare thing.

My servant, Sarai, whom I'd named Lurker because of her tall frame and saggy dark eyes, stayed in the palace after first defying my commands several times. It wasn't until I threatened to thrash her that she obeyed me. Sarai was so slow that it wasn't really difficult to leave her behind, but she was very persistent. She did not speak much, and that at least was something. Tasherit talked non-stop from the time she woke up until her head hit the pillow at night, so Sarai's quiet presence did not irritate me often. I craved quiet.

I found the horses quite easily in the closest set of stables. As if they remembered I always had treats in my pocket, they began to stamp and snort at the sight of me.

"Hail, Raja and Kamara. Yes, I have something for you."

Despite my current sadness and worry, the animals pulled a smile out of me. I held out some sugar cubes and let them take turns licking my palms. Once they had their snacks, I rubbed their noses lovingly. I wondered what it would be like to ride a chariot horse into battle. Last year during our visit here, Aperel let me sit atop one. Of course I was not allowed to ride freely, not without his hand holding the reins. He'd warned me that these were too powerful for a young girl to master. But that minor encounter with the horses did not satisfy me.

Aperel had been a nice man, and I found him to be intelligent. And he obviously held great affection for the animals in his care. I had been surprised to learn he was a traitor. Like everyone else, I'd heard the rumors about him and my mother, but unlike Smenkhkare I did not believe them to be true. Anyone with brains knew Mother had eyes for no one except our father. And what would have been so wrong if she had loved another? In the past few years Father had become a distant man, pushing away all those he once cherished, including his children. I could not explain this change in him, and it was easier to just blame Mother. She should have tried harder to keep his love intact. For if he had not fallen out of love with her, we would all be happy still.

Surely that was her fault.

"Yes, Raja. You are a greedy one, aren't you?" The dark horse nudged my pocket, and I gave him my last treat. Kamara snorted in offense, but I had nothing else to give. "Too bad, handsome. You should have been more persistent. Now your brother has taken it all." I smiled again as Raja's tongue searched my palm for his prize. He flicked his ears at me with pleasure as Kamara turned his head away for a moment. He did not trust me now, now that he knew I had favored his brother.

Ah, you'd better get used to that. Life is not fair, and neither are the gods and goddesses who so cruelly rule us all.

"I knew I would find you here, Meri-meri."

I didn't turn around. "Nobody calls me that anymore. That's a childhood name, a name I would like to leave behind." The truth was, our father had called me that, back when he loved me still. I couldn't bear to look at Smenkhkare. Not without crying like a baby. I reached for a brush from a nearby rack and began carefully stroking Raja's coat. He did not need it, but I needed something to do with my hands. I had never been allowed to perform this task myself, but I had watched the horse masters enough times to know how it was done. You started at the animal's back and swept the brush down in even strokes; it wasn't hard. And if I could brush Tasherit's hair, this would be an easy job. Raja seemed to enjoy the treatment, even if it was administered by inexperienced hands. He shivered in appreciation and nuzzled me repeatedly.

"I don't want to see you, brother. There is nothing else to say."

"Why call me brother? You know we are more than that. But I have something to say to you. Please, Meritaten, listen to me."

With tears stinging my eyes I answered him, "Then say what you have to if it helps you. I will not stop you—you are co-regent now, aren't you? It is your right to speak to whomever you choose. Tell me, have you visited our sister yet? Did she welcome you with a flower wreath and some pomegranates?"

"Why do you say such things? And you should not blame Ankhesenamun. This was not her idea. She is a child, Meritaten, and must obey. May I remind you this was a marriage I did not want?"

"I see you are broken up about it." I turned my back to him again and continued brushing Raja's silky coat.

"You misunderstand me, Meri-meri. I will not accept her. I intend to refuse the marriage; it is my right as co-regent."

His words made me stop in mid-brush. With a glance over my shoulder I asked, "How do you intend to defy our father? You know you can't do that. If Father said it, it is the law."

"I have a plan." He touched my shoulder, and it burned my skin. I could not help but feel hope rise in me just as Mother had predicted.

Hope, Meritaten. You must keep hope.

"What is your plan?" I whispered as I fought the urge to abandon all and fall into his arms.

"Kames. He will help us, I am sure of it. As the eldest brother, he must marry first."

"And what if he has no mind to marry? What then?"

"If he must be compelled to take our sister as wife, then I will compel him to do it. It is true—I have consulted my scribes, and they tell me this is how it is always done in Pharaoh's family. Pharaoh may choose whomever he likes for co-regent, but his sons must be afforded marriage according to their ages. Kames must marry first; at the very least we will have more time to find another way." Pulling himself up to his full height he added, "And if I must, I will die before I marry Ankhesenamun. You are my true love, Meritaten. It is only you I love. I want no other wives, and no other shall take your place, my love. You are everything."

I flung my arms around his neck and hugged him with the weight of my body. I sobbed in relief. "I love you too, Smenkhkare. You are my life and breath! If I had to choose from all the men in all the world, I would choose you. Always! There is no one but you for me." I laid my head upon his chest as he stroked my hair.

Let this moment be for always. Yes, let it be for always!

"Let them try to separate us!" he said in a savage whisper. "And no matter what, we will be together. Even if we must perish, like Ramose and Sitamen." I shivered to hear him say so, but I agreed with all my heart.

Then all the world erupted into screams—as if they had heard our words to one another. Screams and cries erupted from the palace and swept across the complex. People ran outside and tossed heaps of sand upon their heads.

"What is happening? Are we being invaded?" I asked fearfully.

"No, that's not the sound of an invasion. This is something else." He gripped my hand and gave me a grim look. "Stay with me, Meritaten—no matter what." I nodded my promise, my eyes wide with terror. As the sounds of fear rose around us, he repeated himself as if one promise wasn't enough. "No matter what—you stay close."

With my heart pounding and my hands sweating, I let Smenkhkare drag us to our fate.

Chapter Fifteen

Bloody Sheets—Nefertiti

As soon as I left Tadukhipa's rooms, I found myself surrounded by the medjay. Their fierce tattooed eyes let me know that I faced grave danger. Horus, my husband's most trusted medjay, spoke to me directly. It was a strange thing to hear the mostly silent man's voice. "Great Queen, come with us." I didn't immediately obey him. What if they were here at the behest of one of my enemies? I had too many to count now. If the reports were true, if my husband was dead, there would be no protection for me. But how could I know if they were true? Perhaps he himself had orchestrated all this just to have a reason to seize me?

Horus spoke calmly as if he read my mind. "It is true. Your husband, our Pharaoh, is dead. Please, Great Queen. Come with us. We must keep you safe."

I held back a thousand questions and a thousand tears—this was no time to release either of those torrents. I would have to go with them now, willingly or forcibly, and what would be would be. I nodded my permission, and immediately the medjay surrounded me. They moved in precise, synchronized lockstep, their left hands holding their spears and their right hands upon the hilts of their gleaming daggers. They banged their spear ends on the ground, and we began to walk toward whatever destination they had in mind.

If the blow is to come, let it come now!

I would not close my eyes to the danger but stared at the back of Horus' bald head as he barked orders to his men. No attack came, and I breathed a sigh of relief. I made my face a serene mask, a skill I'd learned from my time here at court, and kept their pace. We walked through the Grand Court, where many hundreds of people were already gathered. The people were looking for consolation from the royal family, some assurance that all was well. Things were most assuredly not well. Someone recognized me and began wailing, "Great Queen! Our Great Queen!"

My first instinct was to stop and comfort those who needed me, but Horus was having none of it. "No, lady. It is not safe. There is an assassin in our court. Please, there is no time."

"My children!" I exclaimed suddenly. "Bring them to me!"

"It shall be done, Great Queen." Four of the medjay broke off from the group as others surrounded me, and I watched as the dispatched men ran to various locations to find my three living children. *Please let them be alive!*

To my surprise, the medjay led me to my own chambers. Horus opened the outer door and looked nervously up and down, as if he expected an army to run down the Grand Hall. Perhaps he did. "What happened, Horus? I must know?"

"An assassin murdered Pharaoh as he worshiped. He—or she—left him bleeding in the Sun Room. By the time we found him he was dead."

"She? Has the assassin been found? Does my son know of this?"

"We are looking everywhere. We suspect Lady Ipy of involvement, as her servant discovered Pharaoh's body."

I could tell by his expression that he was not telling me everything. "Please, Horus. Do not hide anything from me. If I must protect our regent, I must know what you know."

He nodded in agreement. "The lady was distraught. Pharaoh was to send her away. I can only gather she was disappointed." Horus hesitated but continued, "At one time, he intended to make her his wife. I believe that was no longer the case. She is being held in her chambers. The priests have been summoned to rule in this matter."

"What priests? Do you mean the leopard coats? Surely not, Horus! You know they have no love for us! Would you deliver us into their hands?"

In his deep voice Horus said, "All things must be done according to the law, Great Queen. It is the priests who administer justice in such matters."

Defiance crept up my spine. "No! It is Pharaoh's regent, Smenkhkare, who must administer justice for his father! If you do as you say, you will doom us all. Is that what you want?"

"No, lady. I only seek to protect you."

"Then please, listen to me. Find Smenkhkare! Do not give the priests such authority until you have spoken to your prince. Swear it to me."

He looked unsure, but he agreed. Under no circumstance would I ever allow the priests of Amun to pass judgment on any in the royal family, not even Ipy. If she was truly guilty, she would be punished—if she had done as he suggested, I would kill her myself! But it would be a mistake to give the Amun priesthood the power of life and death over any of us. Pharaoh had taken that away from them, and now by law the medjay would give it back?

"When you find my son, please bring him to me. I must see him."

"Yes, Great Queen."

I hurried inside to change my clothing and prepare to flee the city. Despite what I told Horus, I would not stay here. Not for any reason! My children and I would never be safe! "Cara! Miane!" No one answered. I hurried through my living quarters and rushed into my bedchambers. Perhaps they were there. I heard the sounds of a woman crying, and it was a familiar voice—one that I knew as well as my own. As I flung the doors open, I was again surprised to find that all my servants were gone, except for Menmet, who was in a crumpled pile on my bed. She was sobbing as if I had died. Perhaps she believed that I had.

"Menmet! I am here. See? I am here."

She shot up in the bed, and then I noticed she was not alone. There was another woman in my bed—and Menmet was covered in blood!

"Menmet! What has happened? Is that the assassin?" I peered through the thin veil around my bed and stumbled back in horror. My own sister lay in the sheets, her face so like my own and wearing an expression of surprise.

Menmet turned and hissed at me. With a scream she said, "No! You are dead! I have killed you! You are dead!" She glanced from me to Pah, only now realizing that she had stabbed my sister.

My head spun with grief and shock. "Lady Nephthys? Pah?" I screamed at my sister. Her mouth was slightly open as if she had called out for help with her last breath. She was not moving, and I could see no signs of life. This could not be! She could not die like this, betrayed by my own maidservant. "Move, Menmet! What have you done?"

As I stared in horror, I saw the pale sheer fabrics of my bed turn crimson—it might not be too late! The blood still flowed! I could save Pah! Then my eyes fell upon the instrument of death in Menmet's hand; a curved golden blade with a bloody edge. She rose and held her arms stiffly at her sides. Her hands were hard fists of determination and hate. She did not relinquish her blade as I instructed. Her face was a mess of makeup and blood, and she was breathing hard. I could see her skin was pale even beneath my sister's blood. "Move, Menmet. There still may be time to save her." I put my hands in front of me to calm her. She screamed, and the sound of it chilled my bones.

"You were dead—I killed you! But you are here and I must kill you again! Why did you return? Why, lady? Must I kill you twice?"

"Menmet…grief has made you mad. Please, stop what you are doing. Stop now! It is not too late, Menmet. Let me tend to my sister. Let me see her."

"Sister? Then I did not kill you?" She stared from me to Pah. "Yes, I see now. She is Nephthys! But how could you know? Nobody knew I would come here. This is your trickery at work, Desert Queen. Let that be your final thought—you killed your own sister with your trickery and deceit!"

"How long have you hated me?" I asked as I moved backwards, away from the dangerous arc she made with the blade. "Why have you done this?"

"I do not hate you, Great Queen, but I will not die for you. Lady Ipy has promised me more than you ever offered. Have I not waited on you day and night, cared for you in sickness? Have I not given you everything? And you to deny me my freedom?"

"What are you talking about, Menmet? I have denied you nothing! What do you mean?"

"Lady Ipy told me what you did. How you sold me, how you intended to offer me to Pharaoh as amusement. But I won't let that happen! I won't!"

"I never did such a thing. You have let Ipy poison your mind, and she has used you to kill me. You were my friend!"

"Ha! Friends, were we? When was the Great Queen of Egypt ever my friend? My father is right—you are the poison in the ka of Egypt! We must purge our souls if we want to be reunited with Amun! Lady Ipy has done her part, and now I must do mine!"

I saw Pah move on the bed behind Menmet, her fingers only, but she moved! I had to draw the deranged girl's attention away and get help. "Move, Menmet. Move now! I will forgive you if you move. I will help you!"

She answered with a yelp and charged at me. As she came toward me, her knife raised high, she swung again and again. I dodged the first two attempts, but then I fell on my back and she struck my arm. It was only a glancing strike but she made her mark and left a gash on my forearm. Blood poured down my arm as we wrestled together. I continued to scream, "Menmet! No!" but it did little good. She gritted her teeth in anger and struggled with me as if she did mean to take my life—again!

"You should have died the first time, Great Queen!"

"Menmet!" Another voice echoed through the chamber—my son drew his blade and rushed toward me. Meritaten screamed in surprise as she entered the room, but Menmet didn't seem to hear them, so focused was she on her murderous deed.

"Menmet, stop!" I screamed at her as I saw that Smenkhkare had unsheathed his blade. He drove it through her tiny body, and she lurched beneath his blow. Blood surged from her mouth, and I felt her urinate on me as the curved blade fell out of her hand. She toppled over to the right, and her wig covered her face. I could not see if she was alive or dead. I did not care. I crawled to the bed and leaned over Pah.

"Pah! Pah! Quickly, Meritaten, call for the physician!" My daughter flew out of the room as Smenkhkare examined Menmet. "Please, sister, look at me!"

She had little life left in her. How could she live with all the blood she'd lost? I was not proficient in the healing arts, but even I knew this. "Pah, don't leave me."

Her brow furrowed slightly and her mouth moved, but no words came forth.

I leaned closer. "What is it? My sister, please don't leave me."

"Nef-ret…for-give…"

I sobbed and held her cool hand. I kissed it and nodded. "Yes, I forgive you. Forgive *me*, Pah. Please don't leave me."

"A life…for…"

And then she was gone. Pah's eyes closed, her breathing ceased, and her face went slack. It was peaceful, as if she knew that at last she would have peace.

Meritaten was not gone long. "Mother, the physician cannot be found. The palace is in turmoil…and the medjay. They are gone!" Meritaten touched my shoulder as I wept. Her words snatched me from my grief. I could not allow my treasures to perish under the blades of the priests. With clumsy fingers I took Pah's bracelet. I had to have something of hers.

"We must go! Where is Tasherit?"

"I know where she is. She is safe, in Princess Sitamen's aviary, but how will we get there without being seen? Will the priests kill us, Mother? Did the priests kill Father?"

"Never doubt their hand was in it, no matter who drew the blade, Meritaten. I have made arrangements for us to leave—I feared this day would come." I glanced at Pah one last time. "We must get Tasherit and leave, for the city is lost to us."

"No!" Smenkhkare shouted in anger. "I am the Pharaoh of Egypt. I will not flee like a child in the night. I will fight for what is mine."

"You might fight, but you will lose. Come with us, Smenkhkare. It is the only way. There will be another day for fighting."

He stepped back and shoved his sword back in his sheath. "No, you must go. I will take my throne. And when I do, I will send for you."

"No!" Meritaten yelled at him through her tears. "You promised we would always be together. You cannot leave me, brother. You cannot!"

He held her by the shoulders and spoke to her in low tones, "Please listen to me. You must take care of Mother and Tasherit, but I have many others I have to care for. Do you think I can leave Egypt, our Egypt, in the hands of the priests of Amun? I cannot do such a thing. Father has trusted me with this, and I will not fail him. Now go. I will send for you." As Smenkhkare kissed her, I ransacked my dresser, pulled out a few private treasures and stuck them in a bag. I hid the bag in my skirts and took Meritaten by the arm.

"Come, show me where your sister is," I said. Smenkhkare left us, and Meritaten called after him. He did not return. "Please, Meritaten," I continued. "Show me where. Where have you hidden her?"

"I told you—she is in Sitamen's aviary."

Without a word, I grasped her hand, and together we fled down the Great Hall. I feared greatly that someone would see us and seize us, but no one did. As we traveled through the corridors I saw heartrending displays of greed—the people were looting the court! But then the medjay appeared and with them a battalion of armed priests. "No! Meritaten! We must go through the tunnels."

We ran through the Bull Room, and I slapped the trigger wall to open the door. Then we slipped through the small entranceway. It was dark inside, so dark that I could barely see my hand in front of my face. Meritaten tripped over her own feet and whimpered in the dark, but still I pulled us on toward the aviary. At least I thought it was the aviary. Where was I? A light shone in the distance, and I didn't know whether to run toward it or away from it. I was thankful my sometimes-wise husband had built these tunnels into his palace; perhaps all along he knew this day would come. I never would have dreamed that one day all of Egypt would turn on us—especially not my dear Menmet!

"Mother, this way!" Smenkhkare! I ran toward him.

"I couldn't abandon you—the palace is too full of priests. I have hidden Tasherit there!" I saw the lid of a large clay pot lift, and my daughter's head poked out. She cried when she saw me.

"My treasure!" I lifted her from the jar and kissed her cheek.

"Quickly! They are coming now! I can see them in the distance. Where do we go, Mother?"

Please, Amenhotep! Help me!

I heard a scraping sound to my left. Someone had opened a nearby wall. There were many entrances into our secret tunnels, and unfortunately someone had discovered one very nearby.

Go to the right, to the wall that leads to the Crescent Pool. And then on to the Green Temple.

Adijah would meet us there—or so we had arranged. But what if he betrayed me as Menmet had? Then let me first die! I pushed ahead of them. "Take your sister's hand, Meritaten. Follow me!"

I raced down the narrow corridor. The voices of the intruders now bounced off the stone walls, and they were getting closer. I glanced back to see my son turn with his weapon drawn. "No! Run, Smenkhkare! Run!" Thankfully he listened and we surged forward, Tasherit crying while Meritaten prayed. I could hear the running of the water—the Crescent Pool was near here. "Wave your torch this way!" With one flick of his torch I could see the brass handle on the wall. I pulled it, and my children and I ran out of the hall. Smenkhkare attempted to push the door back, but I warned him, "It won't move. It is set on a sand timer. Come now!" We ran to the small gate; it was a minor entrance, one used by the gardeners who stocked the pool and cared for Pharaoh's private sanctuary. The guards must have overlooked or forgotten it. We ran through the shadowy arbors and out the open gate. *Thank you, Amenhotep!*

When we got to the streets there was chaos. Fires were burning, and the leopard coats moved quickly to rid the city of heretics— any Egyptians that were faithful to Amenhotep and Nefertiti were the first to be dispatched. I recognized some, but there was nothing I could do for them. There was no trial for these innocents; they were guilty of believing in Amenhotep's vision. Guilty of abandoning the Amun temples. They were delivered a speedy death on sight.

I wept against the wall but did not allow myself the luxury of grief for long. "We must go to the Green Temple. A friend waits there for us." Smenkhkare took in the sight of the murders, and I saw his jaw set, just as his father's had done when he was overcome with anger. I touched his arm, and together we journeyed to the Green Temple. Smenkhkare came across an abandoned wagon; he searched through it and tossed us all some clothing.

"Cover up. The closer we get to the Temple of Isis, the greater the chance that someone will recognize you. Leave your robes and wigs here, Mother. Here, put this on." Taking the bundle of rough fabric he handed me, I did as he asked. Smenkhkare also shed his headdress and put on a plain brown robe. He tossed his gold prince's cuffs in the wagon as payment for our robbery. His eyes widened to see my shaved head, but he said nothing. There was no time for such questions.

"Tasherit, Mother will carry you. Mother, Meritaten, keep your faces covered."

We scurried down the colonnade that led to the front gates of the temple. We were too late; the priests of Amun were here and were attempting to enter that holy place. I gasped at the sheer number of them.

As if she read my mind, Meritaten whispered, "There must be hundreds. They will kill us!"

"Nefertiti," a voice whispered. A hooded figure stood at the end of the nearby alleyway. He pushed back his hood, and I could plainly see Adijah's fair hair. He waved, and I began to run toward him.

Tasherit whimpered, and I shushed her. "Keep quiet, Tasherit. We will be safe soon. All will be well."

"Yes, Mother," she whispered into my clothing.

We made it to the Grecian warrior, and I struggled for breath. I had not run so far in so long. My lungs were burning, my feet ached, and my arms hurt, but I would not put my daughter down. "This way, there is a wagon that will lead us out of town. We must go to the hills for now. We will hide until the priests stop looking and then go across the sea. I have everything ready, as I promised your sister I would. Here, let me hold her." I handed Tasherit to Adijah and reached behind me for Meritaten. But she was gone. As I looked down the alley I could see Smenkhkare and Meritaten running hand in hand back to the city.

"No!" I screamed in anger. I tried to run after them, but Adijah prevented me.

"You cannot help them. If we go back into the city, you will die. They have made their choice, lady. We must go."

"I cannot leave my treasures," I said in tears. "What will become of them?"

Adijah's voice did not scold me. He simply asked, "And what about this one?" Tasherit was sobbing for her sister.

He was right; there was nothing to be done. I had to leave Meritaten and Smenkhkare to their own fate. What was done was done. Could I allow Pah's sacrifice to be in vain? She saved me—and she saved Tasherit.

"Very well. Let's go." With tears streaming down my face, I left Amarna behind. Never again would we see the glory of Egypt. Never again would I behold the face of my son, the face so like my husband's. Sweet, loving Meritaten would always be absent from my arms.

Farewell, Amenhotep. You will remain in my dreams.

Epilogue

New Treasures—Tasherit

"Come let me hold you, my own dear treasure." Mother's aged hands reached for me, and I did not hesitate to put my hands in hers. She was not prone to show affection, at least not as she once had—I learned to accept it when it was offered, for I loved her with all my being. I pretended I did not notice how twisted and old her hands looked. I winced at seeing the scars again, painful reminders of the sacrifice she'd made that last night in Amarna. I had similar burns on my legs, but they were not as severe as hers. The flames had licked me, but I had healed. Her skin had been forever changed by the conflagration. The once-proud queen had taken great pains in recent years to keep her hands covered in her robes when they weren't working hard at whatever task she was working on. Most days that was drying fish or selling ribbons to the visitors who came to our island for its healing waters.

Adijah had abandoned his sword long ago and traded it for a boat. That had been our life since our escape from Egypt. After months of grieving and mourning for my siblings, Mother had come around again; ready to face life and whatever challenges it might offer. And she was finally mine exclusively, except for her nights, which she spent with Adijah. But that was all coming to an end now. She would be gone soon.

I had seen myself grieve—but now I must live it. And with her passing would pass the last of my family.

"Oh, my Meritaten. I have missed you." I sighed as she enveloped me in her bony arms. It would do no good to correct her. She would be dead before the sun rose. Yes, I had seen it in the fire and the water many months ago. Until her sickness last moon, I had no reason to expect her death. From my first memory until that moment, my mother had always been a vital woman, full of energy and focused on whatever purpose she put her mind to.

Although the memories of the painted walls of Egypt had faded to muted scenes from another life, tonight they were all around us, at least in our spirits. I could almost see my favorite panel shimmering behind her, as it had when I visited her apartments in the Great Palace. There was no lack of colorful things to see in Amenhotep's city, but this particular scene had enchanted me to no end. Besides the broad swath of blue water, which represented the Nile, there were many boats and fishermen. But best of all there were hundreds of animals. I recognized the cruel crocodile and the spindly storks, but there were also strange fishes, half-fish and half-human creatures, and so many animals that I had never seen before. And that was saying something. As the children of Pharaoh, we were often gifted with queer little animals and playful birds and even fish in colorful bowls.

During those visits to Mother's apartments, I would quiz my sister until she grew bored and then Mother would invite me into her lap. She would repeat the names to me and tell me stories about them. And such stories she told! Mother had a way of making everything seem magical.

Perhaps it had been a silly goal, a child's dream, but how I wanted to see the river before I died! I could not understand why no one would take me. It wasn't that far. However, during every Sed and Sokar Festival and on every journey to the Island Temple, I was left behind with a promise that next year I would be permitted to attend.

But I never saw the blue waters of the Nile. I ached for the river. I longed for it as if it were a part of me. A part I would never know.

"Mother, tell me about the river." I leaned against her and let her stroke my hair. It was no matter that my hair was as white as hers. It was no matter that I had children of my own—no, I now had grandchildren. None of that mattered. For a few minutes she was the Great Queen Nefertiti still and I was her beloved daughter, Tasherit. I closed my eyes and waited to hear her tell me the story of the river and all the animals that called it home.

"What shall I tell you, Tasherit? Surely you recall all their names by now." My heart fluttered to hear her call me by my name, my true name! No one called me by my royal name anymore. Not even my husband, Herxes. Here, on the small island of Cythera, we were not to mention the past. Even now I could see Adijah's disapproving look at the mention of my former name. But what could it matter now? Egypt's evil priests did not search for us any longer, if they ever had. They had peaked in power. I prayed that somehow they would be called to account for the blood they had shed. No, Adijah did not frighten me—and I knew he would deny my mother nothing. He loved her more than she loved him, but he was not unhappy with that arrangement. To the once-mighty warrior, she was always the Great Queen of Egypt, even if he did not want anyone to know his wife's true identity. He always treated her with great deference and honor.

"Tell me, Great Queen, my mother. Tell me about them."

"Let us look, then, Dearest One. See there? There floats the mighty Zephonites—the strongest crocodile in the river. He is very old, so old that he takes very long naps, sometimes for months, before he reappears to fill his belly with fish—or whatever else he finds. And that in the corner there is the Hydrus! No animal can defeat Zephonites but Hydrus. Ah, he is clever. He allows himself to be eaten, and when the King of the Crocodiles thinks he's won, the Hydrus bursts out of his belly and kills the monster." I did not shiver as I once had when she told me such tales, but I loved hearing again the tale of the Eternal Battle. She was skipping many details, but she was tired. I knew she was tired. I would not correct her or ask her excited questions to dig for more information as I had when I was a child.

Thinking to redirect her mind from the monstrous creatures and thoughts of death and destruction I asked, "What of the Singers, Mother? Tell me about them." She did not answer me immediately but clutched me to her as she coughed and struggled to claim another gasp of air. Her breathing sounded shallow, and I could hear the rattling of her lungs, but I could not let her go. I would not. I wanted to keep her talking. If she was talking, she was living. It was selfish, but I couldn't let her leave me. Adijah offered her a cup of water, but she shook her head. I closed my eyes and clung to Mother as if I might go with her when she died, if I were quiet and still.

Yes, perhaps I could fool death. Maybe Osiris would take me too. He hung in the sky tonight...maybe he would!

"The Singers now appear as frogs, croakers large and small, but they were once beautiful women who gathered at the river and sang to Osiris every night. They hoped to seduce the god and have children by him, but Isis intervened and transformed the sisters into green frogs. Osiris had pity on them, and although he could not change them back, he did grant them their wish. He entered the water and cast his seed upon them. And now as frogs they continue to reproduce, and they sing there still."

I said suddenly, "Mother, do not leave me. How can I live without you?"

"Oh, my own daughter. You are stronger than you know. You are brave and have treasures of your own now. And I promise you, we will see one another again. All will be well."

A moan caught in my throat. "How can you know that, Mother? How can you possibly know that? And I am not strong, not at all."

She kissed my head and said quietly, "Hush now, Tasherit. I know because I have seen it in the fire—and the water. The same as you."

"But I have not seen that, Mother. How I want to see that! Show me, please."

She coughed and patted my shoulder. "Yes, I will show you. Stir up the fire, daughter. Stir it up and we will look together."

I didn't want to move from her arms, but how could I deny her? I had asked for this, hadn't I? I left her arms, tossed a twisted grass log onto the fire and watched it smoke. There were few trees here, but the grass logs burned long and hot. I tried not to spy on Adijah as he came to her, whispered in her ear, kissed her and quickly departed. Even after all these years, it seemed strange that Mother would kiss anyone but Father. She'd been so devoted to him; we all had, until he cast us off. Her love for Adijah was not white-hot and long-suffering as it had been with the Pharaoh of Egypt, but it seemed to make her happy. He glanced at me sadly as he left us alone. As always the warrior was uncomfortable with our magic. He did not believe in such things, but neither did he speak against it.

"What do you see, Tasherit?" She leaned back against her pillow and closed her eyes.

I squatted and poked at the fire pot. "Nothing yet, Mother. I look still." And I did. There was nothing in the flames, only color and sparks.

"Keep looking. You will see. Soon you will see."

I reached behind me and squeezed her hand briefly, but I kept my eyes on the fire. I wanted to see. I *had* to see. I needed to know! Would I see her again? And what about Smenkhkare and Meritaten? We knew about their horrible deaths—they had ruled for less than two years before they too were murdered. Smenkhkare never sent for us. They had traveled to the Otherworld together, and together they would always be, as they wanted. But what of my glorious father and my aunt Nephthys? I stared hard and began to see the shifting in the center of the flames.

"I see a figure, Mother! Something is moving in the flames!"

She coughed again, but I kept my focus. "Keep looking, Meritaten." *Oh no*, I thought. *Her mind is wandering again.* She would soon forget my name forever. *Please, let me see before she leaves me and forgets me.*

The flames shimmered, just as they always did when magic moved in them. I gasped as the image cleared—I could plainly see the painted wall! "Mother!" I exclaimed at the sight.

"Keep looking," she whispered assuredly. I saw my sister's round face, and my hand flew to my mouth in surprise. Never before had I seen the dead in the fire or the water. I laughed with joy. "Meritaten!" I pointed at her excitedly. Suddenly, standing beside her was our brother Smenkhkare. He looked handsome, his royal garments clean and white, as they always were in life. His arm went protectively around Meritaten's waist. I saw no horrific wounds, no bloody gashes—whatever they suffered through was no more. Death was not as I had imagined. No, here they were alive and together somehow.

Then there were other familiar faces. Some I knew by name; others I did not, but they knew me. I could see by their expressions that they knew I watched them through the flames. My eyes burned and my throat felt raw from the heat, but I would not relent. I called to them, but they did not speak to me. They spoke only to each other, but they were happy to see me. This I knew. Then they faded and my father appeared. His hands were on the shoulders of my brothers—and yes, there was my little sister. She had died when she was just a babe, but she was a babe no more. How did I know she was my sister? She looked so much like me—and my father.

"Mother, I see them. I see them all!" I cried with joy to see them, and then I felt the air shift and change. The warmth of the fire faded, although the flame continued to flutter about. The cold was so deep it hurt my bones, but it passed over me quickly and the warmth returned. I heard a sigh behind me, but I could not bear to look away from the scene before me.

And then I saw her in the flames.

There was Mother's face—young and beautiful. Long red hair flowing, green eyes playful and happy. She wore no makeup, no heavy eye paint as used to be her custom. Yes, she wore the prettiest smile I'd ever seen on her pink lips. It was as if she were young again. Father held his arms out to her, and she fell into them. They embraced one another as if all was forgotten, all was forgiven. I sobbed to see their reconciliation. Then I felt a great sadness because they had forgotten me. Or so I thought, until I remembered her words.

Tasherit…you will see…

Unexpectedly the flame died, and with it the images. Despite my desperate attempts to revive the fire, I could not call them back. I would never be able to see them like this again, for with her passing all my magic left me. I would learn this later.

I turned to see what I already knew. My mother, the Great Queen of Egypt, had left this world for the next. It had not been a vain seeing. I had seen her. There would be no fine funeral for her. No sacrifices made, no hidden tombs or mystical prayers. She was here, and now she was gone.

But I had peace now—heavy grief, but peace came too. I *would* see her again. I would see them all one day. Until then, I would tell everyone who would listen the story of the Desert Queen. She had been the Falcon of the Meshwesh, the mekhma of the Red Lands. The Beloved Queen of Amenhotep, Neferneferuaten.

Yes, I would be the one to make sure everyone knew the truth—despite what Adijah said. What was there to fear now? I arranged Mother's body on the pallet. I gently placed her arms at her sides and smoothed her long hair over her shoulders. I tidied her gown and covered her hands as she always liked.

Tonight all the people of Cythera and the surrounding islands would come to honor her. And after they said their words and cast gifts upon her, I would tell them a story. I knew what I would say.

Come closer, my Treasures...let me tell you the Tale of Nefret.

Read more from M.L. Bullock

The Seven Sisters Series

Seven Sisters
Moonlight Falls on Seven Sisters
Shadows Stir at Seven Sisters
The Stars that Fell
The Stars We Walked Upon
The Sun Rises Over Seven Sisters

The Idlewood Series

The Ghosts of Idlewood
Dreams of Idlewood
The Whispering Saint
The Haunted Child

Return to Seven Sisters
(A Sequel Series to Seven Sisters)

The Roses of Mobile
All the Summer Roses

The Gulf Coast Paranormal Series

The Ghosts of Kali Oka Road
The Ghosts of the Crescent Theater
A Haunting at Bloodgood Row
The Legend of the Ghost Queen
A Haunting at Dixie House
The Ghost Lights of Forrest Field

The Sugar Hill Series

Wife of the Left Hand
Fire on the Ramparts
Blood by Candlelight
The Starlight Ball

Lost Camelot Series

Guinevere Forever

The Sirens Gate Series

The Mermaid's Gift
The Blood Feud
The Wrath of Minerva

Standalone books

Ghosts on a Plane

To receive updates on her latest releases,
visit her website at MLBullock.com
and subscribe to her mailing list.

Printed in Great Britain
by Amazon

82131911R00322